LARGE
PRINT
EDITION

RANDOM
HOUSE

JANE SMILEY

The All-True Travels
and Adventures of
LIDIE NEWTON

A NOVEL

Published by Random House Large Print
in association with Alfred A. Knopf, Inc.
New York 1998

Library of Congress Cataloging-in-Publication Data
Smiley, Jane.
The all-true travels and adventures of Lidie Newton : a novel
Jane Smiley.
p.   cm.
ISBN 0-375-70223-7
1. United States—History—1815–1861—Fiction.
2. Large type books.   I. Title.
[PS3569.M39A79   1998]
813'.54—dc21   97-31895
CIP

Random House Web Address: http://www.randomhouse.com/
Printed in the United States of America
FIRST LARGE PRINT EDITION

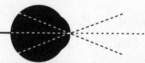

This Large Print Book carries the
Seal of Approval of N.A.V.H.

Acknowledgments

THE AUTHOR WOULD LIKE TO THANK Professor David Dary of the University of Oklahoma and Professor Theodore Nostwich of Iowa State University for their invaluable assistance with this project. Whatever mistakes have slipped into the text have done so in spite of Professor Dary and Professor Nostwich's best efforts, and are entirely the responsibility of the author.

BOOK ONE

BOOK One

CHAPTER 1

I Eavesdrop, and Hear Ill of Myself

Let every woman, then, bear in mind, that, just so long as her dress and position oppose any resistance to the motion of her chest, in just such proportion her blood is unpurified, and her vital organs are debilitated.
　　　　　— MISS CATHERINE E. BEECHER,
　　　　　　A Treatise on Domestic Economy,
　　　　　　for the Use of Young Ladies at
　　　　　　Home, p. 117

I HAVE MADE UP my mind to begin my account upon the first occasion when I truly knew where things stood with me, that is, that afternoon of the day my father, Arthur Harkness, was taken to the Quincy graveyard and buried between my mother, Cora Mary Harkness, and his first wife, Ella Harkness. My father's death was not unexpected, and perhaps not even unwelcome, for he was eighty-two years old and had for some years been lost in a second childhood.

I could easily sit beside the floor grate in my small former room above the front parlor of my father's house and hear what my sisters were saying below. The little bed I had slept in as a child was pushed back against the wall to make room for discarded sticks of furniture and some old cases. I sat on a rolled-up piece of carpet.

Ella Harkness's daughters numbered six. Of those, two had gone back to New York State with their husbands. Our three, Harriet, Alice, and Beatrice, were all considerably older than I, the only living child of the seven my mother had borne. Miriam, my favorite of the sisters, a schoolmistress in Ohio, had died, too, of a sudden fever just before Christmas. Some twenty years separated me from Harriet, and all the others were even older than she was. I had many nephews and nieces who were my own age or older and, it must be said (was often said), better tempered and better behaved. Some of my nephews and nieces had children of their own. I was what you might call an odd lot, not very salable and ready to be marked down.

"I don't want to be the first to say . . ." I could see Harriet from above. She squirmed in her seat and smoothed her black mourning dress for the hundredth time. She wore the same dress to every funeral, and the only way we'd gotten her into it this time was to lace her as tight as a sausage. The others let her be the first to say it. I leaned back, so my shadow wouldn't fall through the grating. "It don't repay what you feed her, since she don't do a lick of work."

"She an't been properly taught's the truth," said Beatrice, "but that's her misfortune." No doubt here she threw a look at Alice.

"I've had my own to worry about," complained Alice. Since Cora Mary's death, I'd been seven years with Alice. The easiest thing in the world for Alice was to lose things—her thimble, her flour dredger, her dog. If you wanted to stick by Alice, then it was up to you. She was a churchgoing woman, too, but whenever she forgot her prayers, she would say, "If the Lord wants me, he knows where to find me." That was Alice all over. Needless to say, I generally found myself elsewhere, and I would wager that was fine with her. Her own brood numbered six, mostly boys, so they were more often than not busy losing themselves, too. It was my niece Annie who kept the engine running at Alice's. Right then, in fact, Annie was out in the kitchen, getting our tea. It wouldn't have occurred to Harriet, Beatrice, or Alice to lift a finger to help her. It occurred to me, of course, but that hole of kitchen work was one I didn't care to fall into, because it was easy to see how those women would pull up the ladder, and there you'd be, hauling wood and water, making fires and tea, for the rest of your life.

"We could have sent her on the cars to Miriam. Young people her age seem to go on the cars without a speck of fear. Or Miriam could have come got her." This was Harriet.

They pondered my sister Miriam, a spinster who'd taught reading to little Negro children in Yellow Springs. Harriet's tone revealed some sense of injury that Miriam was no longer capable of being of use in this way. But Miriam had been a strict woman, the sweetest but the strictest of them all. Her fondness for me had been mostly the result of the distance between us and our lively correspondence. I knew that even if Miriam were still living and I had gone to her on the cars and tried to stay with her, the sweetness would bit by bit have gone out and the strictness bit by bit come in. But I missed her.

"Miriam was genuinely fond of her." Beatrice expressed this as a great marvel.

"Where *is* Lydia?" The sofa emitted a heavy groan. Harriet must have leaned forward and looked around for me.

"Outdoors," said Alice, and I would have been, too, but my heavy mourning dress, wool serge and buttoned to the throat, gave the sunny summer hillside that was my usual resort all the attractions of the Great Sahara Desert. I had crept upstairs and undressed down to my shift. The black armor I would soon need to don again seemed to hold my shape where it lay over the back of a chair. I lifted the hem of my shift and fanned myself with it. "Out in the barn, most likely." Alice amplified her speculation with all the assurance of someone who never knew what she was talking about.

"Oh, the poor orphaned child," exclaimed Beatrice, and for a moment I didn't realize she was speaking of me. "Alone in the world!"

"She's twenty years old, sister." Harriet's tone was decidedly cool. "I was safely married at twenty, I must say. If she's without suitors, who's to blame for that?"

"And she has us," said Alice.

Oh, the poor orphaned child, I thought.

It was true as they said that I was useless, that I had perversely cultivated uselessness over the years and had reached, as I then thought, a pitch of uselessness that was truly rare, or even unique, among the women of Quincy, Illinois. I could neither ply a needle nor play an instrument. I knew nothing of baking or cookery, could not be relied upon to wash the clothes on washing day nor lay a fire in the kitchen stove. My predilections ran in other directions, but they were useless, too. I could ride a horse astride, saddle or no saddle. I could walk for miles without tiring. I could swim and had swum the width of the river. I could bait a hook and catch a fish. I could write a good letter in a clear hand. I had been able to carry on a lively dispute with my sister Miriam, who'd been especially fond of a lively dispute.

Worse, I was plain. Worse than that, I had refused the three elderly widowers who had made me offers and expected that I would be happy to raise their packs of motherless children. Worst of all, I had refused them without any show of gratitude or regret. So, I freely concede, there was nothing to be done with me. My sisters were entirely correct and thoroughly justified in their concern for me. It was likely that I would end up on their hands forever, useless and ungrateful.

I stood up and moved away from the vent, suddenly weary of the certain outcome of their speculations. Back to Alice, back to the strange languor of that life. It vexed me, too, that though their afternoon of complaint and self-justification would result in nothing new, they would make their way through it, anyway, like cows following the same old meandering track through their all too familiar pasture and coming upon the same old over-grazed corner as if it were fresh and unexpected.

I looked out my window upon the slope in front of my father's house. There had been no funeral supper, none but the quietest and most subdued gathering of the few around town who'd known my father. Each of my sisters' husbands had returned to his business or farm directly from the graveyard. All of us, I knew, would find a way to put off our mourning clothes as soon as possible. Even before my father lost himself, he was a silent and vain man. Just the sort of man who would approach a plain woman like my mother without the least pretense or compunction and invite her to leave her own parents and come over to him, to care for his six daughters and bear him a son. He had been fine to look at, with glossy curling hair and full whiskers. Perhaps she was gratified at being chosen at last for the very usefulness she had cultivated so long.

My hair, as usual, was falling about my face. I unpinned it, set the pins in a row beside my small looking glass, and picked up my brush. My hair was long and thick. As I lifted it off my neck and pulled the brush up underneath it, I couldn't help feeling that in spite of every iota of evidence to the contrary, something was about to happen.

My sister Beatrice's husband, Mr. Horace Silk, sold dry goods on Maine, at Lorton and Silk. Mr. Jonas Silk, the old man and Horace's father, held the reins of the business in a tight grip. Lorton was long dead. As a result, Horace was as little consumed by his interest in calico and muslin as he was much consumed by his interest in western land. Iowa, Nebraska, Kansas—the walls of L and S Co. were papered with bills that offered, for a fair and reasonable sum, city lots in lovely, tree-shaded towns, country farms watered by sweet flowing streams, gristmills, sawmills, ironworks, every sort of business. Brother Horace and his cronies pored over the bills, comparing and contrasting the virtues of every region, every town, every named river and stream. They were forever putting together their investments, forever outlining schemes, forever scouring their relatives for funds, but in truth Mr. Jonas Silk was as niggardly as he was jealous, and my sister Beatrice had as much interest in Kansas as she did in the czar of all the Russias, and so my brother Mr. Horace Silk worked out his plans in a white heat of frustrated eagerness.

Of all the women, it was only I who listened to the men, though I made no show of doing so. The towns I favored numbered three: One was Salley Fork, Nebraska, where the grid of streets ran down a gentle southern slope to the sandy, oak-shaded banks of the cool, meandering Salley River and where the ladies' aid society had already received numerous subscriptions for the town library, which was to be built that very summer. Town the second was Morrison's Landing, Iowa, on the Missouri, where the soil was of such legendary fertility and so easy to plow that the farmers were already reaping untold wealth from their very first plantings. The third was Walnut Grove, Kansas, where the sawmill, the gristmill, and the largest dry goods emporium west of Indepen-

dence, Missouri, were already in full operation.
Horace himself had a fancy for a farm on the Marais
des Cygnes River in Kansas, which was the finest
farming land in the world and, according to the bill,
located in the best, most healthful climate—just
warm enough in the summer to ripen crops, always
refreshed by a cool breeze, and never colder in the
winter than a salubrious forty degrees. Fruit and nut
trees of all varieties, bramble fruits, and even
peaches were guaranteed to grow there.

For many months, one of my main pleasures in
life had been to linger in L and S, prolonging my
errands there for Alice and gazing upon the delightful bills, with their neat street maps and architectural
drawings. Quincy, which had been a mere handful of
buildings when my father arrived, seemed old and
run-down by comparison. Even so, my chances of
getting to any of these places seemed at least as
remote as Horace Silk's, and as often as I gazed upon
my favorite bills, I also vowed to put away the
thoughts that agitated me. My sisters were as fixed in
their various homes as stones, and as difficult to lift. I
had no money of my own and no companion. Even
my father's old horse had died some three years
before, never to be replaced, since my father had no
use for a horse. That horse was the last familiar creature that he remembered the name of. As recently as
six months before his death, sister Beatrice found
him in the barn, looking at the horse's empty stall
and muttering, "Wellington." That was the horse's
name, after the duke himself.

I turned from the glare of the window and crept

back to the carpet roll. There I squatted and peered down. Harriet was fanning herself. Her face was bright red. Beatrice was saying, ". . . a nice chicken business."

"And where," said Alice, "would we set her up with this nice chicken business? And . . ." She paused and caught her breath indignantly. "If Horace is going to set anyone up in a nice chicken business, then in my opinion Annie is far more deserving and would certainly do well at it. Annie gets very little consideration, I must say. You have more room on your farm, Harriet, for any sort of nice chicken business than we have on our town lot, a double one though it may be and as big as any."

"I know the end of that," complained Harriet. "More work for me when she lets her chickens run wild. I have my own chickens, as many as I can handle."

I wanted to shout down through the grating that every woman in Quincy had a nice chicken business, that the chicken trade was over-subscribed, but I held my tongue.

"I still think," continued Harriet, "Beatrice . . ." There was a portentous pause while Harriet made sure to stake her claim to Beatrice's full attention. "Bonnets! She can trim bonnets for Horace and Jonas. She's all thumbs with a needle, but—"

"Lydia is all thumbs!"

"Annie, on the other hand, has a tremendous gift for trimming bonnets! She—"

I let out a single stifled bark of merriment. Harriet looked around, startled, but didn't guess where the noise was coming from. I have to say, though, that my sisters' ventures into the question of what was to become of me had taken an unexpectedly creative and comic turn. It was clear that I would have to make an effort, or I would soon find myself gainfully employed.

Below me I saw the top of Annie's head glide into view, neatly juxtaposed to a large round tray covered with tea things. The severe white parting that ran from the front of that crown to the back was so fine and straight it might have been done with a knife point.

"Shh," said Harriet. "Thank, you my dear. Lovely."

It was a principle of the family that no business was discussed in front of Annie, who was generally considered too innocent to withstand the shock of most topics, though of course not too fragile to be worked to death. They did not invite her to take tea with them, so she set down the things and once again removed herself.

"This whole question," said Alice, "is too much for such a day as this. We've just buried our dear pa, after all."

"He was a fine-looking man," said Harriet. "The very picture of a patriarch."

"Mrs. Rowan said he was the fairest creature of either sex she ever saw. She told me that yesterday when she was in buying sugar," said Beatrice. " 'He cut a wonderful figure.' Those were her very words."

They all sighed.

CHAPTER 2

I Become Acquainted with
Mr. Thomas Newton

*Wash the fine clothes in one tub of suds; and throw
them, when wrung, into another. Then wash them,
in the second suds, turning them wrong side out.
Put them in the boiling-bag, and boil them in
strong suds, for half an hour, and not much more.
Move them, while boiling, with the clothes-stick.
Take them out of the boiling-bag, and put them into
a tub of water, and rub the dirtiest places, again, if
need be. Throw them into the rinsing-water, and
then wring them out, and put them into the blueing-
water. Put the articles to be stiffened, into a
clothes-basket, by themselves, and, just before
hanging out, dip them in starch, clapping it in, so
as to have them equally stiff, in all parts. Hang
white clothes in the sun, and colored ones, (wrong
side out,) in the shade. Fasten them with clothes-
pins. Then wash the coarser white articles, in the
same manner.*

—p. 286

THOMAS NEWTON WAS WHAT Harriet's husband,
Roland Brereton, called a "d—— abolitionist." So
was our sister Miriam. Roland Brereton called her
"your d—— abolitionist sister Miriam." Roland was
forever d——ing everything, even those things he
was fond of, like his dogs and his horses. Roland was
from Kentucky; he and his three brothers had moved
across the Ohio River into Illinois when Roland was
a small boy. Roland's family had gotten entangled in

an Illinois legend almost as soon as they set foot in the state, and all the old settlers knew who the Breretons were.

The story runs as follows. There once was a family of killers who lived down near the Ohio: an old man, his four sons, and the women who might have been their "wives." They lived in the woods in a primitive fashion, making camps at night and taking shelter as best they could. It was said by reliable authorities that the women took the babies away from the camp every night to sleep, because they knew that if a baby cried, the old man would kill it. To meet up with these men was almost certain death. Many men of that day were lost and never heard of again until their bodies were found. One man was caught and tied to his horse. The horse and the man were blindfolded, and then the horse was driven over a high bluff. Another time, a group of pioneers got separated from two of their children, as it was easy to do in those days, and when they found the children, a day later, it was only to discover that they had been run down and brutally murdered for the sake of stealing what little clothing they were wearing. This father and sons were said to have killed over a hundred men, women, and children in two years or so, and heaven knows how many before they came to Illinois.

Roland Brereton's father, Lyman, came into Illinois from Kentucky right at the time when all of these killings were taking place, and sure enough, one evening, when they were pushing their way along a woodland track down in Edwards County, three men, one old and two young, jumped up in front of them, far gone in drink but deadly. Lyman was walking along at the horse's head, Roland and his two brothers were in the wagon. The mother was behind the wagon, and their dog, some sort of Kentucky hound dog, was walking next to her. As soon as the three men approached, the dog slunk away.

The brutes were greedy, and they paused to rummage through the Breretons' belongings, though they didn't pause long. Any object was good enough for them to kill for. But the dog had made good use of this moment to seek out Burton Brereton, Lyman's brother, who was some yards ahead of the group. Burton was one of those Kentuckians who seemed to take after red Indians rather than his white ancestors, and he was there before they even heard him coming. The only one of all of them who saw him was the mother, and what she saw was Burton setting the muzzle of his long rifle against the back of one of the sons' heads and pulling the trigger. At the very moment of the shot, she called out, "Praise the Lord!" at the top of her lungs. The old man and the other son got away and lived to kill other pioneers, but the Breretons got famous all the same for at least reducing their number.

For all that, Lyman and Burton Brereton didn't make much of a success in Illinois. According to Roland, they didn't have any use for good prairie soil and stuck to little patches here and there in the woods. Like most Kentuckians, they were satisfied to shoot something for supper and have some greens with it. But Roland had made himself a nice prairie farm out east of Quincy, and the only Kentucky left in him was the everlasting d——ing of this and that, and the dogs that over-ran the place, all said to be descendants of the famous hound that saved the family. Roland wouldn't have a slave, not even in the kitchen, but he'd die for the right of all his second and third cousins that he'd never met to own as many slaves as they wanted. I doubted he'd be called upon to offer his life, unless he died as a result of an apoplectic fit after a dispute with some d—— abolitionist. But abolitionists weren't all that common in Quincy, though there were some who sympathized with "poor Dr. Eels," as Beatrice called him, who'd tried to rescue an escaped slave who'd swum from the Missouri side, back when I was a little girl, and had been convicted on account of the wet clothes that were discovered in his buggy. Most people in Quincy didn't go out of their way to help the swimmers from Missouri, but they didn't go out of their way to return them across the river, either. My brother-in-law Horace once said, "My opinion is, it's a pretty short swim over but a pretty long row back, and I just don't want to make the effort." That was Quincy all over.

I found Thomas Newton much milder and quieter than you'd think a "d—— abolitionist" would be. He was so mild and quiet, in fact, that the first time I met him, when he came over to Harriet's in the company of the neighbor Howell, who was also a d—— abolitionist, I didn't find out a thing about him. I was out at Harriet's helping her boil bed linens about two weeks after my father's funeral. I was trying to be as little use as I could be, but I could hardly fail to stir the boiling clothes, my assigned labor. It was a hot day, and I had tied up my skirts to keep them out of the fire and rolled up my sleeves to keep them out of my way. My hair was so heavy with damp from the work that it hung around my shoulders. Harriet's boy Frank was tending the fire. Howell drove up in his wagon, and he and a tall fellow with pale hair and fair skin got out and went into the house. I can't say that I made much of him. There was a creek down behind Roland Brereton's farm, and I was thinking mostly about taking a swim back there if I could slip away from Harriet after the clothes were washed.

But Harriet was thinking about something else, and not three minutes after Howell and this pale fellow went into the house, they came out again, with Harriet right behind them, and she had a tray in her hand and on that a jug of cold spring water. Pretty soon, she set them up on a cloth in the shade of a big hickory tree, went back in for glasses and a plate of cakes, and then she sang out to me, "Lidie! Surely those linens are clean by now. You better fix yourself up and come over here and have a glass of water in this heat! Isn't it sweltering!" And the two men made themselves comfortable, all smiles.

This neighbor, Roger Howell, hadn't owned his farm long. He'd come down from Wisconsin, along the bluffs of the Mississippi, and was said to be consumptive, which was why he found the winters up there too much to bear. He had gingery whiskers and a bald head with a gingery fringe around the sides, and he was always taking his hat off and putting it on. Harriet told me that every night he smeared on his pate a mixture of hartshorn and oil, which Jonas Silk swore would grow hair on a stone, but no new shoots were as yet in evidence. The only thing I'd ever heard him talk about was his mare, which he was very proud of—he'd won her in a poker game from a Missouri man, and she was a long-legged, haughty-looking thing with a white circle around her left eye and a wide blaze.

"Well, Tom," he was saying as I came up, "you were impressed. I saw you holding your hat, but that mare wasn't even stretching out. On the one piece, that straightaway before you get to the gate here, she whipped Solomon Johnson's colt, hardly even breathing. Broke that colt's heart—"

Thomas Newton started to stand up, but I sat down so quickly on the cloth that he didn't have a chance. Harriet pushed a glass of water over to me and beamed on me as if I were her dearest child, while at the same time shooing away Frank, who was twelve at the time. "Yes, Mr. Newton, here is my sister, my baby sister Lydia, the last of us girls. Do you know, my father had thirteen daughters altogether?" She motioned to me to straighten my bodice and otherwise surreptitiously rearrange myself, but it was too hot for that. I sat down as I was. "Good land," Harriet went on. "It's miserable weather for boiling clothes, but Lidie simply would do it. There was nothing I could do to stop her."

Howell remarked, "My mare don't notice the heat. She hardly turns a hair in this heat. Tom Newton, you ever seen a mare like this one? I swear!"

Frank stood opposite us, under the hickory tree, with his thumbs notched in his braces.

Now Thomas Newton spoke for the first time. His voice was low and agreeable. "You know I'm not a horseman, Howell. And you weren't, either, the last time I saw you. You've been transformed by this Missouri mare!"

Howell grinned at this as if it were praise. Harriet grinned to be agreeable. Howell said, "Now look at her just stand there. She—"

"Miss Harkness, are you fond of horses?"

"When there's one to be fond of I am."

"Lidie's just a miracle worker with dumb creatures," said Harriet. "More of our delicious spring water, Mr. Newton? Will you be with us long?"

Very slowly and with much aplomb, Frank pulled the stub of a seegar from his pocket and put it between his lips. A moment later, he pulled out a lucifer and lit it. He sucked through it and then let the smoke pillow out of his mouth. Harriet, I could see, was trying to ignore him. Mr. Howell seemed to be ignoring him, too, except that he turned suddenly and spat a thin brown stream toward the woods. Thomas Newton, it appeared, neither smoked nor chewed.

I came to realize that this is what my sisters had decided on, marrying me off to the first stranger to pass through Quincy, or the second, or the third.

He said, "Only as long as I can help it . . ."

"Tom Newton's on his way to Kansas," said Howell. "He's with the Massachusetts Emigrant Aid Company. Roland around?" Now Howell grinned again. "I do want to make sure that Roland meets Tom. I know he'll want to."

"My goodness me," said Harriet. "You mean you want to give him a fit! Are you an argumentative man, Mr. Newton?"

"He's from Boston, an't he?" said Howell, laughing aloud.

"Let me suggest, sir," said Harriet soberly, "that you refrain from engaging Mr. Brereton in discussion if you find him armed."

"He's always armed," said Howell.

Harriet nodded at this, as if to say, There, you see.

Howell roared, "He's itching to kill some d——— abolitionist!"

Thomas Newton paled and quickly took a sip of his water. Howell shouted, "Here he comes now!" and Harriet started and looked around, and Thomas Newton kind of hunched into himself, but Howell was laughing to beat the band, pleased to have made fools of us. I finished my glass and stood up, ready enough to get back to stirring the clothes, but Harriet said immediately, "Lidie, pass Mr. Newton one of these cakes you made yesterday," and what could I do? I passed the cakes, which I had never seen before, and they began to slide off the plate, and he didn't have the sense to catch them, so they all fell in his lap. A hapless young man, that much was clear.

Frank fell over laughing.

Harriet seemed to place the blame on me. She exclaimed, "Oh, Lidie, for goodness' sake!" Howell was laughing, too, but I got up without glancing at Mr. Newton and went back to stirring my clothes, which heaved and billowed in the steaming waters. It seemed the most harmless thing I could do.

Soon enough the bald-pated older man and the pale young man got into the gig and went off, and not long after that, Harriet, with a distinct air of disappointment married to long-suffering resignation, declared that she was going to her room—"because, Frank, you have given me a headache with that infernal cheroot"—and after we were finished with the rinsing, would we leave the clothes to sit in the bluing tub, and so we did, Frank pausing twice to relight his seegar, because, taken all in all, he wasn't nearly as experienced with it as he liked us to think.

The stream below Roland Brereton's farm cut down its banks in muddy steps, and in spots you could stand in the middle of the stream and see only the sky and tufts of thick grass edging the banks high above your head. By late afternoon, there were two shady spots, cool under the giant cottonwoods, and at one of these Frank had dammed a little pool that in mid-August ran about a foot deep, deep enough for bullheads, sunfish, a crappie or two, and, of course, numerous scuttling crawdads. The small terraces that defined the height of the waters in earlier periods of the year were dried and cracked into angular shapes. Frank liked to pluck the little squares out of the mud and spin them into the pool, or follow the crawdads with a stick and poke after them into their hiding places. A few late rays of sunshine through the cottonwood leaves fell on the muddy water and sparkled, but without disturbing the sense of cool shade and privacy that I always felt in this spot. I could hear Roland's cows lowing in the pasture above us, but the banks of the creek were too steep for them until some quarter of a mile downstream. Often, we saw turtles in the water, snakes, which held no fear for me, and the tracks of coons and skunks in the mud. The banks had a number of otter holes, and a ways upstream the otters had made a slide, but we didn't often see the otters themselves, unless it was the flash of a rounded little head accompanied by the sense of being looked at with sharp, black little eyes, and then, as soon as you turned toward them, they were gone. The creek had a different, more solitary and less appalling, feeling than the big river, which I also frequented. The high banks and tall trees gave it the almost domestic air of a dwelling place. Of course, I resorted to it far more often than Harriet thought proper for a young woman of my station.

But in fact, my station was clearly low and dipping lower.

Though he died owning a house, my father hadn't made much of himself either in Ohio, where he'd gone after marrying Ella and where he'd met my mother, or in Quincy, where he had brought his many daughters to marry them off around the time I was born. He had no knack for farming—preferred a more convivial life than that, with theatricals and clubs and levees and daily social intercourse. Some years, he would broker some grain down the river or some cotton up; other years, he would have an interest in some dry goods or some horses to sell. The lot where he built his house came to him through a trade—a German man owned the lot but needed a quantity of barley to make beer, and my father happened to have an interest in a quantity of barley. The house itself got built in the same way, and it was a house with a pleasant air about it, because my father liked to make a good appearance above all things. But he was sixty-two when I was born, and the novelty of daughters had worn away long before.

My mother doted upon me—perhaps not so much at first, but more as I lived longer and longer and proved myself healthier and less likely to follow my mother's other babies to the grave week by week and month by month. By the time I was four and had outlived them all, I could do no wrong in her eyes, nor could she do any wrong in mine. I was a good-tempered child, for I had my own way in everything, and she poured out on me all the love and attention she had stopped up over the years. I knew my letters at two, could read a newspaper and do sums at four, tell stories from the family Bible at five. She found me other books, with no discrimination of judgment or taste. It so pleased her to hear me read that she would listen to me read anything, thinking, perhaps, that the matter of the reading simply ran through me like water through a spigot. She sewed for me and tatted for me and cooked me special dishes, persuaded my father to procure me a pony, and altogether we lived like a potentate and her adoring

servant, and it was a fine life for me, my delight and
my due. But she was a shy woman and had few
friends. Perhaps we were such friends to each other
that she felt she needed no one else. And then there
were Miriam, Beatrice, Alice, and Harriet, making
their usual noise. That might have been enough for
her. When I was thirteen, the cholera came up the
river, and of all of us, only my mother took ill. She
died within three days. She was forty-seven.

This time, my father, who was seventy-six, didn't
look around for a new wife, only for some place to
put me, and that is how I went to Alice's, where I was
hardly a potentate but only one of many, and there I
discovered my taste for that sort of freedom, the freedom of not being attended to. To my old bad habits of
indiscriminate reading and stating my opinion whenever I desired to, I added new ones of wandering
about, spending time at the river, avoiding house-
work, and improving my fishing and hunting skills
with the help of Alice's many sons. But I cannot say
that Alice or her husband, Frederick, who had a small
lumbering mill, or any of their sons was blessed with
connections, either, so Harriet's notion of my station
was largely a fiction.

Frank said, "I got some money."

This was hardly unusual, as Frank was an enterprising young man, who, moreover, was as much
master of his own time as any boy twice his age. I
said, "How much do you have?"

"Four dollars."

Four dollars, on the other hand, was a considerable sum, suspicious in a boy.

"How'd you get that?"

"I only get to keep four bits. But I got it here in my pocket."

"How'd you get it, I asked you."

"Mr. Thomas Newton gave it to me. He told me to take it. You want to come with me?"

I didn't answer anything, but he started walking down the creek, keeping in the middle and careful, I quickly saw, to refrain from stepping in any muddy spots. Frank pulled out the last of his seegar and stuck it between his lips, but he didn't light it. We didn't say anything. We passed the lower banks of the cow pasture, but the cows couldn't be seen from the creek. Everything was quiet. We kept going until we came to a small cave, a spot that I knew Frank had explored extensively. We stopped, and Frank looked eagerly in. I did not. I could hear well enough: movements of some large body, audible only when they suddenly were stilled. I knew there would be a dark face in there. I didn't have to see it. Frank picked up some stones by the creekside and heaved them idly into the water, the way a boy would do, aiming at this snag or that one. Then we walked on until we got to the next cow pasture, where we came up out of the creek and paused to pick mulberries. I said, "Well?"

And he said, "I left it under a rock."

"Did anyone see you?"

"Only the one that was supposed to see me."

We carried the mulberries home in Frank's cap. Mulberries are funny. Most of the time they don't taste like a thing, but these were sweet as could be.

Harriet didn't know whether to be pleased with the mulberries or angry at the stains all over our faces and hands. It was my responsibility to admonish him, she declared. But the fact was, I always seemed to let Frank do just what he pleased.

CHAPTER 3

I Improve My Friendship with Mr. Newton

The early training of New-England boys, in which they turn their hand to almost every thing, is one great reason of the quick perceptions, versatility of mind, and mechanical skill, for which that portion of our Countrymen is distinguished.

—p. 165

NOW THE TIME CAME for the sale of my father's house, of which I was to be a principal beneficiary. The house was on Seventeenth Street, a block down from Broadway, and luckily for all of us, a large piece of property very nearby happened to have been sold early in the year for a lot of money. Considerable building was going on in that section, and Horace had managed to interest someone associated with one of the lumber mills in my father's house. My sisters, including Hannah and Ella Rose by letter from New York State, now began subtly to vie with each other to be the one whose husband was so prosperous that she, but she alone, could assign her share to me. Each sister was generous. Ella Rose wrote, "My darling Beatrice, I find it so sad to think of poor Papa and his little house on its little town lot, that I leave it to you to do as you please with my portion. It will hardly make a difference to Mr. Logan and me." Hannah followed some days later with, "Dear Harriet, This communication is only for you, my dearest and best sister, but I must tell someone in the family that Ella Rose can certainly not do without any small infusion of funds that might result from the sale of Papa's very eccentric property. She wants only, of course, to do something for her beloved younger sisters, but as always she is sacrificing herself. I am pleased to say that my husband has had an exceptionally good year with his barrel workshop, and our sons, too, are prospering. Our youngest sister should be aided out of our portion. Knowing how anyone outside of the family must feel about the unusual nature of Papa's architectural choices, I can only presume that the sum realized in the sale will be small to begin with."

Alice said, "Frederick's business is fully capable of taking care of Annie, though I notice no one has even asked."

Harriet said, "It brings on a headache for me even to speak of it. I will happily resign my portion just to have the matter over and done with."

Beatrice's opinion was a bit different: "I am happy, positively glad, without reservation, to add my portion to the poor girl's, if that is what it takes to help her into some useful place and occupation. I am at my wit's end with her."

Harriet added, "Ella Rose and Hannah may talk all they please about prosperous this and prosperous that, but some people aren't so young as they once were and might be thinking of the future, if you ask me."

All considered it a favor of Providence that

because of Miriam's death no portion would go to "educating those little darky children, after Papa was a lifelong Democrat." They agreed that there'd been something unnatural about that whole business, but Miriam had never listened to reason and didn't have sense enough to come in out of the rain, which meant that instead of pouring the fruits of her life of labors into the useless teaching of those who couldn't benefit from it, she should have established herself in a lucrative chicken and egg business. But thankfully, in spite of the tragedy of her early death, things had turned out well in the matter of my father's political principles.

Taken all in all, they felt that this discussion was a credit to the family and further evidence that as a group, the sisters were superior to the more typical squabbling over estates that you saw everywhere around you. "Our mother taught us better than that," asserted Beatrice complacently, and the others agreed. They were referring to their own mother, not mine. "And you," said Harriet to me, "stand to profit. You should be mindful of how fortunate you are." I did, and I was.

Roland Brereton resolved the tangle, though of course with much d——ing to h—— of the whole prolonged negotiation. He counted out the sum of money, picked up a handful of notes and gave them to me, then divided the rest into six equivalent portions. In my hand, I found that I held $472. Harriet said that she had to admire the way Roland always went to the heart of things, and that was the end of

our father's house. Even after Father had gone to live
with Beatrice, for as long as he could he had walked
to the house on fine days with his silver-handled stick
and stood and regarded it from every angle, like a
man wondering whether to purchase it.

The next time I saw Thomas Newton was at a
dramatic exhibition at Danake Hall. My brother-in-
law Horace had a fondness for every sort of singing
or theatrical performance, but my sister Beatrice disapproved of the man who put them on, George
Adams, who was called "Crazy Adams" by some.
Even so, she let Horace escort Annie and me to the
performance, because she had heard there was to be a
demonstration of elocution edifying to young ladies,
comprising in part a reading of the last scenes of Mr.
Dickens's *Dombey and Son,* wherein young Florence
Dombey is reconciled with her father, and some
other pieces of the same sort. A Mrs. Duff, all the
way from New York, a woman proficient in portray-
ing virtuous young ladies, was to act the part of Florence.

Since the episode with the money at the creek,
my feelings about Mr. Newton had changed somewhat. I could not figure out how he had communicated with Frank, or given him the money, or even
how he knew that Frank would know where the cave
was. Obviously, Mr. Newton and Roger Howell had
conspired together ahead of time, but Mr. Newton's
subtlety in these operations made me sense that there
was more to him than met the eye. And then there
was the generosity of the gift. Quincy was full of

people who left out some biscuits or an old shirt or a worn pair of shoes, and knew when these objects had disappeared that some fugitive had been helped along the way. But the difference between giving away something easily done without and a not inconsiderable sum of money impressed me. And it was true as well that Miriam's death had piqued my interest in her principles in a way that her example had never done. This time, when I espied Mr. Thomas Newton in the hall before the performance, I looked at him a little more closely, and I saw that he had two sorts of manners. When he thought he was unobserved, his glance was alert, his demeanor brisk and attentive. But when his friends drew him into conversation and introduced him to their acquaintance, he seemed to go almost dull, almost slack. He smiled enough, produced the expected responses, but his qualities seemed almost to disappear. This made me want some conversation with him, just to see whether I would have a similar effect on him, especially as I didn't know whether he knew that I knew of Frank's errand. And now that I thought of it, I did have some curiosity as to the outcome of that errand. It had been more than a week since we'd left the money beside the cave. It was so universally true that every fugitive emerged briefly from a mysterious realm, only to disappear again into the same mysterious realm, that people simply got out of the habit of wondering what became of them. And the fate of Dr. Eels was a lesson to all that the best way to leave something unsaid was to have it be unknown, as well.

I can't say that Mr. Newton made his way toward me, or that I made my way toward him, attached as I was to Annie and to Horace Silk, but nevertheless, not long after I noticed him, I was introducing him to my companions. He asked Annie if she was fond of theatricals.

"Yes, indeed, sir! This is only my third outing, but I like it better than anything!" I could see my own astonishment at this reflected in Horace's face. I had thought Annie preferred hemming handkerchiefs to every human endeavor.

"Then I will arouse your envy by telling you that before I left Boston, I saw Rachel as Adrienne LeCouvreur."

He pronounced the French words in a French way, it sounded like. But Annie, though she kept grinning, didn't know who those people were. She said, "Sir, I am frankly envious of everyone you might have seen, especially in Boston." Her face was flushed as I had never known it before, and I doubt she even realized what she was saying, as she could not resist craning her neck to look toward the proscenium. Horace, too, was eager for the exhibition to begin, but Thomas Newton seemed almost indifferent to the activities at the front of the room. To me, he said, "The weather has cooled since last week."

"Still no rain, though. The creeks around my brother's farm are very low, even for this time of year." This wasn't actually true.

"Quincy has a noble prospect above the river. The Missouri shore by contrast seems quite low and flat."

"People here think we are uniquely favored and destined for greatness."

"Every town in the west believes the same thing."

"And Boston, your home?"

"Boston doesn't believe such a thing. Belief implies the possibility of doubt. The greatness of Boston is a known fact, among Bostonians." He smiled. "My kin are from Medford. We resist the greatness of Boston with all our might."

The crowd was moved to begin to find seats, and Mr. Newton left us to rejoin his friends. He seemed to have reacted in no discernible way to the hint I had dropped, but I gave up thinking about it soon enough, after the curtain went up and Mrs. Duff came out onto the stage. She was a tiny woman, who soon entranced us all with her warm, melodious voice and her maidenly gestures. She was Florence Dombey to the life—unfailingly devoted, never as happy as when she was most useful, beautifully transfigured by the desire to give her filial love entirely to her father. I entertained myriad poignant regrets at my own useless selfishness and felt much chastened and revivified by the whole experience when the interval came. Annie was in tears. Horace was in tears. I wasn't in tears, but beneath many layers of what I knew to be passing sentiment induced by the art of Mrs. Duff, I did feel a hard nub of fear. No one I knew knew what was to become of me, and I didn't know, either.

At the end of the interval, Horace came inside with Thomas Newton, and they were talking about

Kansas. The first thing I heard Horace say was, ". . .
only another week, then?"

"The rest of my boxes should be arriving next
Tuesday on the *Amanda Lee*. I've been waiting for
them these two weeks."

I made myself very quiet.

"Now, Kansas," said Horace. "That's wonderful
country."

"You've been out there, then?"

"They say the land around the Marais des Cygnes
is a blooming paradise."

"I'm eager to get there. My companions have
been there almost a month now, and I haven't heard
from them. We bought land below the Kaw, or some
call it the Kansas River, between Lawrence and
Topeka. But they think I'm on my way, so they
haven't known where to—"

"If I were a younger man, or my wife were a
younger woman—"

"They're so occupied with building and getting
things in order for the winter. As mild as it is there,
you have to—"

"Quincy is no place for someone with real enterprise. A few men have everything firmly in their grip.
It's all very well for some to sit and wait, but—"

"The main thing is to ignore rumors and just wait
and see what's what when you get there. It certainly
can't be as bad as some say—"

"I wasn't really cut out for a storekeeper. I was
meant for a more active life than that, but—"

They paused, then glanced at each other and said
in unison, "Well, Kansas is a fine country!"

"Yes, indeed," said Horace, and Thomas Newton beamed.

They parted, to all appearances much satisfied with their conversation. I said to Annie, "Wouldn't you like to go to Kansas? I would."

"Why?"

"I suppose because it's dry and warm and open."

"People are always getting killed in the west."

"That's not true—"

"Don't you think Mrs. Duff is the most elegant lady you ever saw? And Mr. Duff makes me shiver."

"People are not always getting killed in Kansas more than anywhere else."

"I said, in the west. Mrs. Duff is from England."

"Annie, Horace said Mrs. Duff was born in Philadelphia."

"Then she's been in England for a very long time. I'm certain of it. You should stop thinking about Kansas. You would be better off taking your money and going to England. Then when you came back, you would be so elegant that people would never stop looking at you."

"What money?"

"I know perfectly well that you have money from the sale of Grandpa's house, and since you have it, I don't know what you are waiting for. If I had it, I would board the next steamboat, and I would tell everyone on it that I was a famous actress, Mrs. Helen DuMont, fresh from an engagement in Saint Louis!"

"I'm tempted to give you some just to see you do it." I laughed.

"Please do, because I am ready to take it." She turned with a flounce that belied the neat smoothness of her hair and the soft youthfulness of her round face.

A few moments later, Horace returned to his seat, and we suspended our conversation.

Now events began to move very quickly. One thing I've noticed is that when a particular notion enters your head, then its very particularity makes everything tend toward it, and the tending goes faster and faster. One day you will have barely thought of something, and that little thought inspires such excitement and fear that you don't want to think of it again, but some few days later, maybe three or four, the thing you could hardly think of is now done, and you are embarked upon a new life.

I happened to see Thomas Newton again the very next day, this time on Maine Street. I was taking a pair of Alice's shoes to be repaired. Maine Street was crowded, as usual, but just after I saw Mr. Newton coming toward me, the sidewalk grew strangely deserted. I saw him glance around just as he smiled at me. He said, "Well, Miss Harkness, you are out early this morning after a long evening."

"It's a fine morning. I wanted to get my errands done before the heat of the day—"

He touched my elbow and turned me to walk along with him, then said, "Mrs. Duff gave an excellent performance last night, but I thought Mr. Adams rather stormed and ranted a bit." George Adams and Mrs. Duff had given us a scene from *Macbeth,* the climax of the evening and entirely lit by two burning torches, one of which Mr. Adams held above his head. Much of the audience had been distracted from the impresario's eloquence by the proximity of the flaming torch to the curtain above the stage, but Mrs. Duff, required by her role to look upward at that very moment, had managed to sustain her concentration, only stepping gracefully across the stage and clinging briefly to Mr. Adams's upraised arm.

"Mrs. Duff showed considerable presence of mind. I admired that very much."

"I've heard something about you, Miss Harkness."

"That's not a very kind thing to say, sir."

"You have swum across the river."

"My nephew Frank told you that."

"He did."

"You and Frank seem to be on terms of great intimacy."

"We are."

"I have to admit that he wasn't lying, but it's been over a year since I did that, and the river was lower then and not so fast. I wouldn't try it this year."

"Few girls can have done the same."

"None that I know of, but my sisters would say that the fact hardly speaks in my favor. Quite the contrary."

"And you ride your brother Roland's horses bareback and have beaten Frank in every race."

"You shouldn't be quizzing Frank about me."

"I would if I had to, but I don't. He's terrifically proud of you. He considers you hardly a female at all."

This I would have taken as an insult, if Mr. Thomas Newton hadn't said it in such a merry way. As it was, his tone made me laugh out loud, and then he looked at me most candidly, and I found myself having to look down to my shoes. This reminded me of Alice's shoes, and I saw that we had long since passed the bootmaker. I exclaimed, "Oh!" and turned around, and Mr. Newton caught me tightly by the elbow. I said, "I've forgotten my sister's shoes!"

And then we walked back there in silence, and I am sure that we were both thinking hard. I certainly was.

After the bootmaker's, he walked me back to Seventh Street. We hardly spoke, but I was aware of his presence every step of the way, as if something about him had grown excessively large and was pushing at me. This was new in my experience, and I didn't know what to think. I glanced at him a couple of times and noticed that I found his looks much more pleasant than I had only a few days before. Where I had seen only pale fecklessness, I now saw a subtle play of expression, evidence of considerable intelligence, and a certain grace of figure that was set off by plain, everyday clothing. I saw evidence of cogitation and choice where I had seen only a dull surface before.

When I took him in to Alice, who was hemming shirts by a window in the parlor, it was clear that she as yet saw only the dull surface. She hardly looked up, said, "You'll be Mr. Newton," and promptly stuck three or four pins between her lips.

I said, "I can pick up your shoes Monday, Alice,"

and she exclaimed, the pins falling into her lap, "Can you believe it, those boys had a squirrel in here! It was running all over the house! I would have fainted dead away, except that I had to help them catch it!"

"A wild squirrel?" said Thomas Newton.

"They snared it on the roof! They've been climbing out on the roof and setting snares all summer! Can you imagine? It ran right over the dining room table; I will never eat there again!" She took three or four angry stitches. "And last week, they caught a crow and brought it into their bedroom and kept it there all night in a box!"

I laughed.

"This is most assuredly not funny! I am not amused in the slightest. Why the good Lord should have sent me five boys, and the last two hooligans, and I am nearly in my dotage, I shall never in my life understand. Ahh!" She threw down the shirt. "And now you'll be wanting tea, though what wild animals have been nesting in the teacups I cannot tell you. You will have to take your chances!" She said this in a tone of doom and steamed into the kitchen.

The silence fell around myself and Mr. Newton with muffing thickness. Any words I might then have uttered seemed destined to fall unheard to the floor. Thomas Newton said, "You live here with your sister?"

"Yes; seven years it's been. Lawrence was one then and Frederick three, and I was meant to be useful in all ways and to lighten Alice's maternal load with an ever eager helping hand."

With regard to that largeness I felt in Mr. Newton, I thought it was best to be candid about who I was. Mr. Newton allowed his admittedly pale but, even so, well-shaped eyebrows to lift inquiringly.

"I found that I preferred to read. It's not hard to hide from Alice. And I fear I've allowed my niece Annie to do more than her share of the household chores."

"She was with you the other night, at the performance."

"Yes. It turns out that she would like to board a steamship under an assumed name and pass herself off as a brazen actress, but nevertheless, she is a remarkably useful girl, and in my opinion, it's only a matter of months before some widower with a dozen or more small children offers to make her the happiest girl in the world."

I had never talked this way before. The voice coming out of my mouth was strange to my ears and yet strangely my own. I tempted myself to go on and on. "It was the fate of my poor mother to devote her life to a man of exceptional vanity who already had six daughters. That's his likeness on the wall beside the door, there."

Thomas Newton stood and stepped over to the daguerreotype. My father had been in the horse business then, so he was carrying a whip and wearing a top hat. Mr. Newton said, "A handsome man."

"That was the first daguerreotype ever made in Quincy. A man came through, and he and my father found each other as if by predestination."

When he turned to look at me, Mr. Newton seemed very merry, though eager to hide his merriment. Alice entered with a tray and set it down on the tea table with emphasis. She said, "I found some cakes, and I've checked them over for animal hair, so you may eat them with assurance." She sat down and poured the tea, immediately commencing to draw out Mr. Newton. "And so, I am told you are off to Kansas, sir."

"Yes, I—"

"Your antecedents are in Boston, are they not?"

"Medford, ma'am."

"Near enough."

"You have parents, brothers and sisters?"

"My father and brothers have a sailmaking factory."

"You don't work with them, then?"

"I did for a while. And I was a minister of religion just out of college."

"And which sect would that have been?"

"We practice Unitarianism, ma'am."

"That's hardly a sect of religion, sir."

Thomas Newton kept smiling but said, "Many would say that any practice performed by New Englanders soon amounts to a religion."

Alice handed him a cup of tea without changing her expression. She set mine on the table, and I reached for it. I expected her to inquire further into Mr. Newton's history, but she grew a bit defensive.

"We are Methodists, and we do not condemn our brethren in our church for beliefs and domestic arrangements that are not like our own. Dr. Hawkins just gave a sermon on that very topic this Sunday past."

"No, ma'am."

"And you have funds of your own that your father gave you for this Kansas adventure?"

"I worked for him in his sailmaking factory, yes. I also have associated myself with the Massachusetts Emigrant Aid Company."

"I see."

Now Alice fell silent, drinking her tea. It was as if the words "Massachusetts Emigrant Aid Company" startled or discomposed her, and she couldn't think of what to say.

I said, "Mr. Newton is an abolitionist, Alice. Just like Miriam was."

All she said was, "I should have known." By this she meant that an abolitionist was just the sort of person with whom I would crown my life with her by bringing home.

"Yes, sister, you should have known, because Harriet knew the day we met Mr. Newton."

Alice cleared her throat.

Now we sat quietly for some ten minutes, sipping our tea and eating the cakes. Alice sat in her rocking chair, rocking furiously. From time to time, Thomas Newton glanced at the likeness of my father on the wall. He still seemed amused, which I found pleasant as well as curious. Nothing Alice said touched me, because, without naming it to myself, I knew that I would soon be on my way to Kansas.

CHAPTER 4

I Embark on the Ida Marie

In packing household furniture, for moving, have each box numbered, and then have a book, in which, as each box is packed, note down the number of the box, and the order in which its contents are packed, as this will save much labor and perplexity when unpacking. In packing china and glass, wrap each article, separately, in paper, and put soft hay or straw at bottom and all around each. Put the heaviest articles at the bottom, and on the top of the box, write, "This side up."

—pp. 316–17

I MAY NOT HAVE MENTIONED earlier in this account that when I was fifteen, I attended the Quincy Female Seminary, which opened on Sixth Street and Maine. Miss Doty was our principal, and Miss Catharine Beecher herself, the very woman who wrote *A Treatise on Domestic Economy,* came to Quincy to supervise all aspects of the school. I must say that the good opinion that the citizens of Quincy perennially maintained of themselves was always bolstered by the number of prominent Americans who lived in, passed through, or involved themselves in the town's affairs. Of course there were always Senator Douglas and Mr. Browning, but there was also Miss Beecher, and Miss Beecher's rumored views on the slavery question hardly dented her fame in Quincy. When our school closed its doors after a few months, every pupil was given an inscribed copy of Miss Beecher's volume. After Mr. Thomas Newton went away that afternoon, I went up to my room and pulled Miss Beecher off my shelf for the first time ever. I opened it, and this was the first thing I read: "The number of young women whose health is crushed, ere the first years of married life are past, would seem incredible to one who has not investigated this subject, and it would be vain to attempt to depict the sorrow, discouragement, and distress experienced in most families where the wife and mother is a perpetual invalid." I must say that this observation did not surprise me at all, but even so I did not consider that it applied to me, or, for that matter, to life in Kansas, where the climate was known to be supremely healthful—just mild enough, of course, but just brisk enough, too. I cannot say that I knew exactly what Miss Beecher was talking about. I presumed that she was referring to the deleterious effects of cooking, cleaning, making fires, washing, ironing, and dusting, not to mention shirtmaking, knitting, embroidery, and all other forms of coarse and fine needlework. I pitied poor Annie. When I pictured myself in Kansas, I saw myself plucking apples and peaches off heavy branches, strolling by the side of one of those refreshing streams, or taking a brisk walk through tall grasses, perhaps in pursuit of a pretty little cow who would have come into my possession somehow. I would lead her back to our (weathertight and cozy) cabin and later enjoy having churned her milk into cool and delicious butter.

At Miss Beecher's I had excelled in the area of daily exercise, and my health had never been threatened from that time to this. Miss Beecher had been emphatic on the subject of "calisthenic exercises," which we girls were obliged to perform daily, to the accompaniment of Miss Ivins playing the piano, in a large room in the school fitted with giant windows, which were open in the coldest weather. Miss Beecher was a great believer in ventilation. Every month that we were there, Miss Beecher herself checked our spines for distortions. We wore loose clothing and undergarments, and I have to say the whole experience gave me exactly that enjoyment of free bodily movement that was such a matter of despair for my sisters. Reading Miss Beecher's book was much like watching her stride down the hallway, feeling her brisk fingers on one's shoulders and back, listening to her speak. She did what she pleased and wasted no time.

It was dusk when I stood up and stretched my arms above my head. I had read about the girl who comes home from her boarding school, whose mother is laid in the grave, and who has to take over her duties. I read about the girl who visits her sister in a distant city and assumes her sister's role. I read about the woman removed to the west, *whose health failed.* I thought, Mary Simmons, Eliza Carson, Bella Morton. But of course, I did not think, Lydia Harkness, not once. I had looked at the pictures of my bones and muscles and brain and sacrum and nerves and spine and heart and lungs. I wondered if Thomas Newton had ever seen such pictures or knew that "the throbbing of the heart is caused by its alternate expansion and contraction, as it receives and expels the blood." I wondered if he knew that one's skin was continuously "exhaling waste matter in a form which is called *insensible perspiration.*" I looked at the back of my hand and smelled its skin. I wondered if he knew, as I now did, that frequent changes of garments worn next to the skin prevented the reabsorption of those very noxious products earlier thrown off by the skin and the decay that resulted therefrom. I wondered for a moment about the organ of touch. "This office," Miss Beecher wrote, "is performed through the instrumentality of the nerves of feeling, which are spread over *all parts* of the skin." Miss Beecher seemed to know a great deal more than I or my friends in school had ever given her credit for.

Excitement suffused me. It felt like dread, but a sort of eager dread, which moves toward its object rather than away. I knew that I should not have kept reading Miss Beecher's manual, because now, in addition to looking forward to a strange future in a strange place with a strange man (and all men were strange enough to me), I, with my *cerebellum* and my *left ventricle* and my *lacteals* and my *follicles,* was strange as well. I remembered one thing Harriet had said to me years before in exasperation when I threw down the sampler I was attempting to stitch and declared that I hated sewing most of all. She said, "If you don't furnish your brain with what everyone knows, then it will furnish itself with what no one else knows! And a female's brain is too weak to hold those sorts of things!"

Our courtship, of necessity, proceeded apace, as

it was foreshortened by the arrival of Mr. Newton's boxes and the knowledge that September was at hand and therefore those who were departing for Kansas must make haste and do so, so as to make as much use of the mild fall weather as possible. Mr. Newton was, in general, a reserved suitor, though kind, always kind. We sat in silence much of the time, which he seemed comfortable in breaking only by raising two subjects, my virtues and Kansas. Both subjects were delicious to me. Mr. Newton had never met anyone quite like me, so strong and vigorous, so freely spoken, manifesting so few traits of false modesty and fearfulness, in which, he led me to believe, I was unique among females of his experience. I could ride a horse! I could shoot a gun! (Frank's character reference.) I could swim! I was fond of reading! I could walk many miles in an afternoon! All of a sudden, my uselessness had been turned upside down. These qualities, he assured me, prepared me wonderfully well for Kansas, and I had every reason to believe him. One night, in particular, I remember quite well. The August heat had mitigated somewhat, and we were sitting by a window in Alice's parlor just at dusk, with our heads together, enjoying the cool breeze. Mr. Newton was talking enthusiastically about Kansas, and I was soaking up every word. This was, possibly, the only time in my experience of Mr. Newton up to that time that he spoke with such enthusiasm.

"You can't imagine such a fine and intelligent man as Dr. Robinson!" His eyes glittered with admiration. "Of course he maintains the highest princi-

ples, or Mr. Thayer—he's our benefactor—would
never have associated himself with the man, but
added to that, well, he's been everywhere, to California, even, and made a great profit, and he's said to be
a wonderful doctor, compassionate and knowledge-
able far beyond the general run! He has matters at
Lawrence—that's where we are going—entirely in
hand. We had assurances of that before we left the
east. We couldn't have chosen a superior leader to
Dr. Robinson, and his wife is just the thing for the
west—you'll admire her, I know. I've seen her twice.
There's utterly no nonsense about Mrs. Robinson.
She's the very type of a mother!" He sighed with
pleasure and grasped my hands. "You need have no
fears, my dear! Our Emigrant Aid Company has
everything so well organized! When the Missourians
see what New Englanders can do in the west, they'll
come around, that's assured! I fully expect that these
few conflicts I hear reports of will be as short-lived
as they are exaggerated. We have nothing to worry
about."

I couldn't help tweaking him just a bit, saying,
"Are you reading aloud to me from some bill?
Because this is a great advertisement for Dr. Robinson," but then, when his face fell, I offered, "You
know, my sister Miriam ran a school for the children
of escaped slaves in Ohio. I might have gone to teach
there."

His answering smile was delighted and delightful.

As far as we knew, we had no place of our own
waiting for us, but Mr. Newton was ever sanguine

about how quickly things would fall into place once we got there. Our wedding was small and quickly planned, and that very day we saw our boxes, his and mine together, loaded onto the Galena packet for transport to Saint Louis and west. We went on board ourselves, my first time on a steamboat, and we stood at the rail, I in a new bonnet, my only bit of wedding finery, and waved off my sisters and brothers-in-law and nieces and nephews: young Frank, who was smoking his seegar openly, even though Harriet kept trying to snatch it out of his mouth; dear Annie, who I believe was counting the days until a much larger steamboat would be taking her away; Roland Brereton, who was d——ing the stevedores every minute but giving them tips for each box of ours they picked up and carried on board; Horace Silk, who was nearly in tears at not being able to go with us; and Harriet, Beatrice, and Alice, who looked amazed and relieved that I had been gotten rid of so suddenly and smoothly, after all.

The Galena packet, the *Ida Marie,* was a rather small, older boat with only a handful of staterooms, which carried the mail between Saint Louis and Galena, alternating with its sister ship, the *Mary Ida,* which ran the opposite direction. We boarded in the late morning and toward noon cast off. It was August 27, and the captain himself was the first person ever to address me as "Mrs. Newton."

It was a fine, warm day, bright and breezy. We mounted the stairs to the passenger deck, but not before I had a glimpse of the open machinery at the interior of the lower deck—the boiler and the gears—

and the boatmen and steerage passengers standing
around, watching the whole works. We walked deliberately aft, and for all their age, the white railings of
the boat dazzled in the noonday sun. Mr. Newton
stood beside me as the high Quincy bluff and my
family disappeared behind us. The great wheel
churned and splashed into the turbulent brown water,
and after a brief time Mr. Newton led me to the
ladies' saloon, which occupied a portion of the lower
deck just in front of the wheelhouse. Inside, three
other ladies had made themselves at home, but the
air was stuffy and close, and the windows were
begrimed with soot from the firing of the boiler. On
the other hand, the floor of the ladies' saloon was
more or less free of the brown stains of tobacco juice
that decorated the sunny decking. Men, even married
men, weren't allowed, except to sleep with their
wives in one of the few staterooms at night. By the
same token, women, even married women, were not
welcome on the deck, except under the unusual circumstances of an accident or a sight of special importance, and there were none of those until just above
Saint Louis, when the boat would cross the mouth of
the Missouri.

As I stepped over the threshold, all three ladies
looked up, first at me, then at Mr. Newton—until he
backed away and closed the door—then at me again.
Two were gray-haired, already at their needlework,
and one, dressed in black, was about my sisters' age.
Seated next to her was a little girl, also in a black
dress. When the door closed behind me, everyone
smiled. I found myself a seat beside one of the small

windows and carried my bag over to it. I felt the largeness of Mr. Newton's presence, which was only the more pressing now that we were man and wife, move off a bit. I fancied that I could feel his weight shifting the boat as he moved here and there. I wasn't sure about this; it was a characteristic of marriage that neither Alice nor Beatrice, who for some nights had been preparing me for my new duties, had mentioned. Underneath my chair and through my feet, resting on the floor, I could feel the rumble of the boat's engines and its swaying passage through the water.

The water, which I knew was below me, seemed distant and unreachable, as unreachable as the girl who, a year ago, had stepped into the brown river about a mile above Palmyra and emerged an hour later about a mile below Quincy. Frank had conspired with me to row a boat we borrowed from friends of his, to carry my shoes and stockings and petticoats and dress, to watch out for and serve as a screen against passing steamers and other craft. The water had been brown, of course, though it looks blue from above, on top of the bluff, and it was full of debris—branches and logs, pieces of broken-up boats and other planks and boards. There were shoes and a pair of pantaloons, a shirtsleeve and two hats and an old cap, caught upon rocks and snags. Half sunk in the mud were bottles and bits of metal, pieces of rope and a bent barrel hoop or two, bits of leather straps, broken fragments of tin and brass and iron. There was a raccoon carcass and the skull of a horse, the hind limb of a deer. The true grandson of my

father, Frank picked up what looked useful or salable, until I stopped that and got him to row with me
to the tiny cove where I sent him off and undressed
down to my shift. When I had pushed into the water,
he rowed himself to a group of rocks and retrieved
the things I'd left there.

The first time I stepped into the river, I was just
about the age of the girl across the cabin from me,
twelve. I had taught myself to swim that summer, by
spying on the boys and mimicking their actions. My
mother thought I was visiting Beatrice, who thought
I was visiting Alice, who thought I was at home. That
first time I stepped into the river, I was royally self-
assured, until I took two strokes and felt the continental power of the brown water seize me and drag
me from shore. Two strokes turned into a spluttering
ten by the time my feet found the bottom again. But
seven years later, when I was nineteen, I knew parts
of the river very well, and I knew how to use and relish the six-miles-per-hour push of the water, to go
down and over, down and over, how to not be afraid,
and to not even attempt a swim unless the river was
low and its tributaries more or less dried up. I knew
how to hold my breath and dive, how to keep an eye
out for logs and debris. I knew that some of the boys
swam the river all summer. I knew that there was a
drowning when I was fourteen and a drowning the
summer I was seventeen. I knew that every man on
the river chased the boys back from the big water but
that the boys flocked there even so, building rafts,
stealing boats, catching catfish and suckers. You
couldn't stay away from the river; at least I couldn't.

The notion to swim across it came over me suddenly, mostly because that August the river was lower than it had been in years. All sorts of sandbars and islands were dry ground that no one had ever seen before. Even so, the Quincy bluff always made the river faster and deeper than it was farther downstream or upstream. The choice was narrow but fast, or wide and not as fast. But I can't say I really made a choice. It was like going off with Mr. Newton. One day I knew I was going to do it, and two days later, when Frank got a boat, I did it. The whole time we were rowing across, I was feeling the push of the river against the boat, feeling it try to turn us around or turn us over. Every time we took a boat it was that way, and you could lose a boat in the Mississippi in a second. I knew that. But you always learn things a new way when you've got a reason to pay attention. That's what I told Frank.

By the time I got to the cove, I was ready to forget the whole thing, but Frank was concentrated on it, and I had the feeling that I was going along with him, even though this was my idea. And then I didn't want him to see me in my shift—I could just hear Harriet on that subject—and so I got in the water, and then I had to take a few strokes just to stay above water, and then Frank was rowing alongside me, and laughing and cursing. He didn't smoke seegars then, but he had some twig or something he was chewing on, and I concentrated on that. He rowed upstream of me and used his oars to push snags and trash out of my way. I went slowly, knowing my waterlogged shift was dragging me down. The river kept piling up, too, and pouring over my head, but I was a good enough swimmer so that I saw it coming and didn't take any in. It stank of fish and other, rotten things, but that was just river smell. It was water, a lot of water, warm, and I was drawn to that. I can't say anything happened. Frank later said there were a couple of logs heading my way that he pushed off, but I had no sense of danger, only the water all around me—its sound and smell and wetness. It seemed to last a long time, and when my feet set down in the Quincy mud, I seemed to wake up. I'd swum the three-quarter-mile-wide river in about a mile and a half—you can't swim right across it—and I walked out in my shift with the water streaming down and I forgot completely about where I was or what I was doing. Frank had to pull the boat up and then wrap a sheet around me. I think I staggered around, but then, a few minutes later, I felt the heat of the sun. That made me come back to who I was and where I was. I dried off and put my clothes back on, but I smelled of the river. The strongest soap couldn't get that out of my hair in less than a week.

Roland Brereton thought it was a d—— good joke. My sisters, of course, were flabbergasted, but they didn't start in with me. I later decided that it was such a strange thing for me to do that they made up their minds that I hadn't done it. I didn't try it again. I wanted to savor the one time, and the summer was coming to an end, anyway. This year, the steamboatmen were all happy, because the river started high and stayed high, and only a young boy or a fool would brave it.

The two gray-haired dames now put away their needles. One of them had out her pocket watch, a man's gold one, with a cover. She nodded to the other and said, "They'll be serving in five minutes, Annabelle. We'd best get ready."

At this, the younger woman nudged her little girl, and all four went to the door of the ladies' cabin, opened it, and peered out onto the deck. The one named Annabelle turned to me and spoke. "Now, have you ever been on one of these packets before, my dear?"

"No, ma'am. This is my first trip away from Quincy."

"Well, if you expect to have your dinner, then you'd better get ready for when the doors open, or the menfolk will push you right out of the way. The ladies are supposed to go to the head of the line, but you can't be sure what will happen."

"I'm sure my husband . . ." I said the word as if I were used to it.

"Oh, dear," said the other one. "You can't rely on him. We five will all go out in a body and into the dining room, and they'll make way for us. That's the best way."

"They don't mean to," said Annabelle, "but there's just such a rush for the vittles that a lone woman don't stand much of a chance. Wouldn't you say so, Dorothea?"

Dorothea nodded, and the little girl pressed into her mother's skirts. Annabelle said, "What's your name, dear?" to me, and I said, "Lidie. Lidie Newton now."

"Here we go," said Dorothea. "Take each other's arms, ladies, that's the best. If your skirts drag a little, so be it." We took each other's arms, with the little girl clinging to her mother's waist, and we pressed as a group out onto the deck, just as the door to the dining room opened. All around us, male figures in black coats and hats and boots jumped up, but Dorothea and Annabelle smiled, stared straight ahead, and strode forward at a brisk clip. We others stuck to them, and the men fell back around us. We nearly gained the door. Only then was there a little pushing and shoving, but we kept smiling, and Annabelle lifted her voice in firm command: "Mind the ladies! Mind the ladies!" In a moment we were through. Annabelle and Dorothea shepherded us to a place at the long table, somewhat back from the entry, where I noticed that the dishes were quite plentiful. I looked around for Mr. Newton, but he hadn't made it in yet. I was wondering whether to wait for him, when Dorothea said, "Sit down, Mrs. Newton. Sit down and eat, or you'll not get a thing!" And it was true; all around us, men were jerking out the chairs, throwing themselves down, and ladling all manner of comestibles onto their plates, one thing on top of another. I sat down.

Near me was some bread, some salt pork, some pickles, another meat dish of some kind, some boiled potatoes, a dish of applesauce, and some johnnycake. I did as the others did and piled it all on my plate, taking as much as I was likely to want, because already the dishes and bowls were beginning to empty. Down the table I saw a dish of sliced cucumber in vinegar, which I liked very much, but there was no one to pass it, and even as I watched, wondering how to get some, a boy about Frank's age served himself almost every slice on the plate. I started to eat what I had. What noise there was in the room was entirely made up of the clatter of china and utensils, the scraping of chairs, the moist sound of mastication, the rustle of wool and calico. There were some twenty people in the room, and at last I espied Mr. Newton, at the far end of the table, looking around for me. He had a slice of ham on his plate, and that was it. As he was reaching for some bread, the man next to him took the last piece right out from under his fingertips. "Eat! Eat!" exclaimed Annabelle. "The porters will take your plate away!"

I did as I was told and found myself doing what all the others were doing: shoveling my victuals in by the forkful, hardly chewing, and certainly not enjoying myself. Before I was half done, the men around us began to wipe their plates with their corn bread, push back their chairs, and leave the table. Mr. Newton caught sight of me and raised his hand with a smile, and I thought that it was a fine thing after all to see him from a distance. He had a grace and a reserve that the men around him had none of. At Saint Louis, our plan was to stay one night at a hotel near the landing, called the Vandeventer House. As I looked at my new husband, my spirits lifted in anticipation. Five minutes later, all the food was gone, and all the men had left the room. Dorothea and Annabelle breathed a common sigh. Annabelle said, "Now, ladies, I think we may leave the dining room with a bit more decorum, but be careful of the spittoons that have been pushed about." Indeed, the one against the wall behind my chair was more than half full of dark, odorous liquid.

We got back to the ladies' cabin without mishap.

Our common battle had broken down the strangeness between us, so for the rest of the journey we sat in an intimate circle, just as if we were friends, and told one another bits about ourselves. The two gray-haired ladies introduced themselves as the Misses Tonkin. "Now, my dear," said Dorothea, the older one, "I know that sounds just as if we were Chinese, but we come from Cornwall, in England. Tonkin there is like Tompkins somewhere else."

"But we don't come from there any longer, Dorothea. We come from Wisconsin, not far from Galena. Every year, we take the Galena packet to Saint Louis and shop for winter things. It's a nice trip for us, don't you see. We get to see the river, which is so lovely, and all the best French things are in Saint Louis. You can see this lace, here." She held up her sleeve, and it was true: the black lace that edged it was delicate and handsome. "If Mr. Tonkin, our brother, only knew how we were spending our money!" The two of them laughed.

"But he does know, sister," rejoined Dorothea. "That's part of the pleasure!"

"Our brother Nicky has been dead these ten years," said Annabelle. "He was a most serious man, and we took care of him all our lives. On his deathbed, he promised to look upon us from on high and continue to guide us, but thankfully we have never noticed anything of the sort since then. We are quite at our own disposal."

"None of the three of us ever married."

Annabelle leaned toward me. "He was unusually exacting, my dear. He would have been quite a trial to an unsuspecting young girl." The two sisters exchanged a cheerful look.

I said, "I just got married this morning, and Mr. Newton and I are on our way to Kansas."

"My goodness, Dorothea," said Annabelle. "What a lovely thing to say! There is all the hope and happiness in the world in that one sentence. 'I just got married this morning, and we are on our way to Kansas!' You are the envy of everyone in the United States, my dear, if not the world!"

"The climate is supposed to be mild and healthful—"

"I hope you married for love, my dear," said Dorothea. "If you are going to marry at all, that is the best way."

At first I only smiled, not liking to reveal myself to strangers, even friendly ones, but then the other woman in the saloon looked at me with very serious eyes, and then her daughter did, as well, and with their dark eyes staring so sadly out from under their black bonnets, I said, "I did. Yes, I did." I thought of Mr. Newton, his pale skin and his pale hair and his long fingers, his intelligent look, and his amusement, and my sense of how large he was, larger every minute, it seemed, and how much, deep down, I was looking forward to seeing him again at the end of this journey, and I thought that that made up "love" as

much as I knew it. The woman and her daughter took
each other's hands and squeezed. Dorothea said,
"This is Mrs. Evelyn and her daughter, Mary. They
have suffered a bereavement."

Dorothea addressed her, said, "Now, Mrs. Evelyn, if you don't mind my saying so, I hope you have
some money of your own, and won't be at the mercy
of your brother. He may be very dear to you and you
to him, but . . ." She shook her head.

Annabelle filled the silence that ensued. "Our
father was a Cornishman to his very heels, and when
he died, he left the whole property to our Nicky, even
though in this country a man need not do that."

"Our Nicky was a tight-fisted gentleman." They
took up their work and sewed industriously. The
steam engine hummed and the boat churned. I
thought again of the water below us.

Mrs. Evelyn said, "Mr. Evelyn trusted in the
Lord to provide for us."

"Perhaps He will, my dear," said Dorothea. "But
until then, here is a bit to tide you over." And she
pressed a small black silk purse into Mrs. Evelyn's
hand. No matter what that lady then did, Miss
Dorothea Tonkin would not take the purse back
again. Finally, Mrs. Evelyn put the black purse in her
pocket. Mary, who possibly had some private worries about these very matters, smiled a quick, secret
smile, and her mother said, "You ladies are too generous! I don't even know you! I'll remember this as
long as I live!"

"What we say to ourselves, dear, is that we cannot make it up to all of those who needed something

of our Nicky while he was alive and were turned away, and so when we have the opportunity, we do for him what he should have done for himself. He was a religious man, but I fear he was mistaken in his beliefs, because he substituted many very austere doctrinal restrictions for charity. What Dorothea and I suspect is that he was much disappointed when he came to receive his reward."

"What you might say is that we are buying him off." The two chuckled together. "At any rate, my dear," continued Dorothea, "we have no family, so we are always tempted to spend too much on our own amusement, so say no more!"

Mrs. Evelyn said no more but did pat her pocket in a wondering fashion. Not long after that, Mr. Newton appeared at the door of the ladies' cabin and declared that we were passing the mouth of the great Missouri River and that I should come to the railing and see what those waters had brought from the west. We all hastily put away our work and went to the door. I saw Miss Annabelle look Mr. Newton up and down. He helped her over the threshold, then held out his hand for Miss Dorothea. She thanked him. I was pleased to observe that the two Misses Tonkin seemed favorably impressed with my new husband.

It was close to dusk, but I could see that my familiar Mississippi had changed considerably and now ran much faster and browner. Had I imagined some sort of turbulent rush, a wall of water pouring over our river as over a floor, I was mistaken. The river only widened into a broader sheet, rimmed by a low fringe of trees. Mr. Newton stared as if he had never seen such a thing, and finally said, "My dear, I've read many an account of these rivers, and I've talked to many men who've made this journey, but I confess I am unprepared for the somberness of it. I expected to feel gratified and enlarged by the knowledge of the distance these waters have come. I find it oppressive." The dull red glare off the flat expanse had the same effect on me, and I realized only with difficulty that the glare was just the reflection of the setting sun. It passed in moments, but then the darkness seemed to filter up from the water into the trees. The lights of our boat, including the better-to-be-forgotten lurid reflection of the firing of the boiler, lay dimly over the opaque water. We weren't alone in being subdued by the sights. Only a couple of drunk men continued to laugh and shout. Finally, they flung their empty bottle in a wide arc over the railing and cursed the fact that they had drunk everything they had with them. Mr. Newton walked all of the ladies back to the door of the ladies' cabin. It was disturbing to hear the two lonely voices of those men cursing and braying against the noise of the boat and the splash of the water.

Back in the ladies' cabin, the lamps had been lit, and they cast a dim but pleasant glow over the papered wall and the few curtained cubicles that functioned as staterooms on this small packet. It was too dim for me to work, but the two sisters needed little light, as they didn't watch their knitting anyway, only counted the stitches and turned their work. Mrs. Evelyn seemed subdued by the gloom. Her daughter leaned against her. Sometime later, we heard a great shouting, and the clamor of feet upon the deck told us that we had arrived in Saint Louis.

Miss Annabelle put her hand on my wrist as I moved to rise from my chair. She said, "If you'll pardon me for making a personal observation, my dear, I must say that you seem a young woman of uncommon self-possession and fortitude. So many of these young wives we see, well . . ." Her voice faded as if ruefully. "The adventure is for the men, my dear; that's the way of it here in the west."

I said that this was surely true. But I didn't mean it.

CHAPTER 5

I Am Much Daunted by New Experiences

But, as society gradually shakes off the remnants of barbarism, and the intellectual and moral interests of man rise, in estimation, above the merely sensual, a truer estimate is formed of woman's duties, and of the measure of intellect requisite for the proper discharge of them.

—*p. 156*

THE TUMULT OF THE LEVEE at Saint Louis burst upon my sight, unlike anything I had ever seen before. Our boat was undeniably moving toward the land, but the water was so dark and so crowded with other boats that it seemed to be magically pressing itself through a tangle of decks and railings and chimneys and freight. Above the waterline, all was alight with great lamps on poles and torches and fires, and there were as many people about as if it were broad day. We made our way through a thick field of boats, large and small, glorious and humble, empty and full, busy and quiet, among them the most famous Saint Louis–Pittsburgh packet, the *Allegheny Queen,* which just that summer had won a race from Cincinnati to New Orleans, jostling with the most famous Saint Louis–New Orleans packet, the *Paul Revere,* whose railings on the passenger deck gleamed with gold in the flickering light. Their names were clearly painted in ornate script on the wheel housings, and I told Mr. Newton what I had heard of each one in Horace Silk's store, where talk of the best steamboats and their pilots and captains and owners came second only to talk of Kansas. We passed two steam-wreck salvage boats that lay side by side among the others, giant flat platforms on two hulls with a great complex framework like a metal forest that rose into the dark night. Mr. Newton stared at them in perplexity. I said, "That's what they use to raise exploded hulks from the bottom. Otherwise, the river would fill up end to end and bank to bank with wrecks." One of these, or a vessel just like it, had raised a wreck upstream from Quincy earlier in the summer. My cousin Frank had been the first boy at the scene, pushing himself forward to see, he said, what crinolines and combs and corpses he might be able to catch a glimpse of.

Where the river ended and the land began, the boats gave way to horses and drays and piles of freight, but there was as little room amongst all of these as there was between the boats. Everywhere, every human, animal, and machine was making as much noise as possible—the blowing of horns and ringing of bells and belching of steam formed the background to the shouts of the mates and the draymen to stand aside, or hand it over, or move it this way, or coming through, or watch the lines, or careful of the horses! The horses stamped and jingled their harness and whinnied and snorted; their carts and wagons and carriages and drays creaked under the thumps of the boxes and bales and people loaded onto them. Always there was shouting. Boys

younger than Frank, black and white, looked as full
of business as the white-haired men: "Planter's
House! Baggage wagon here!" (The Misses Tonkin
solicited the attention of that well-dressed porter, and
he recognized them with a happy smile.) "The
George M. Hardy! Leaving at first light for the Falls
of Saint Anthony! One of the foremost sights of the
known world! Embark tonight for a convenience!"
"New Orleans in five short days! The *Arkansas
Hopeful* is the fastest boat in the west! Sixteen dollars!" "Newspaper! The *Missouri Democrat*! Tomorrow's news tonight!"

We were hardly out of our cabin and had only
begun pushing our way through the mob trying to get
onto the *Mary Ida,* when I saw that they had begun
unloading the freight. Seeing this, too, Mr. Newton
began urging me through the crowd with some insistence, his one hand grasping my elbow tightly and
his other arm outstretched. A few men scowled at us
as they gave way, and one muttered, "Boat must be
about to explode! Save yourself, brother!" as I was
hurried past, but then all we did on the levee was
stand there as the boxes came off the boat. Almost
the very last was the one Mr. Newton was waiting
for, and when he saw it, he relaxed.

This box, with our two small bags, he directed to
accompany us to the Vandeventer House. The others
were to be loaded onto the *Independence* for passage
to Kansas. I must say that what had seemed a vast
pile of baggage when we left Quincy now seemed
but a paltry collection of trinkets easily dragged
away by the (no doubt) sneering draymen. Kansas!

Kansas! If busy Saint Louis was so vast and frightening, how much more so the solitudes of *Kansas*!

I will pass over our ride through the busy streets and my impression of the Vandeventer House. If I were to linger over everything new, I would prolong my story far past the reader's patience. Suffice it to say that all things were fresh to me, and the moments, which passed slowly, were full of shock, interest, and some fear. I sensed that Mr. Newton, too, felt more strange than he expected to, and more tempted by dread and low spirits. From time to time, we exchanged a glance. I could hardly see his face in the darkness, yet I knew he was full of wonder at how little we had foreseen, he had foreseen, the consequences of our impulses. I said to him in a low voice, "We are true Americans now, husband. We don't know where we are going or what for, nor do we know anyone we're traveling with. But we're perfectly certain it will all turn out best in the end."

He took my fingers in his and spread them apart, staring at my hand as at a strange and wonderful object. At last, he said, "Better than Quincy?"

"Already better than Quincy."

The conviction of my reply perked him up, and I saw for the first time that I wasn't merely to follow him to Kansas but was sometimes to lead him. My husband was less sure of himself than my suitor had been.

In our room at the Vandeventer House, he set our little carpet bags by the door and the large, heavy box, which he'd carried up the stairs with the heaving and groaning help of the porter, between the bed and the window.

There were two chairs beside the window, and after I took off my bonnet, Mr. Newton led me to one of them and sat himself in the other. We rocked back and forth without speaking. We had the bridal room, which meant that no one else was sleeping in our room with us, though should our departure be delayed, we would have to move the next day. The bridal rooms in Saint Louis were in such demand that you could have one to yourself only for one night, or so they told us at the Vandeventer House.

After some minutes, Mr. Newton said, "Did your sisters speak to you about marriage?"

"They told me what they knew."

"What was that?"

"Harriet said if at all possible not to allow you to fire guns in the house, but if I had to give way on this point, to draw the line at pistols, but absolutely not to allow horses into the better rooms, because sometimes they panic and damage your good furniture. She learned her lesson the hard way with a two-year-old colt Roland had—"

Mr. Newton began laughing.

"Well, he did kick to pieces a very nice lowboy she had, with a shell design on the drawer fronts . . ." I cleared my throat. "And Alice told me that my husband would figure very significantly in the conception of children, but she couldn't bring herself to describe exactly how. She just said that I would be better off if I kept a table between us at all times, especially early on in the marriage. Another tactic was to always have a cup of hot tea in my hands, day and night. Those were her words exactly. Day and night."

I laughed, too.

"And Beatrice said that every town in America had lots of clubs and public betterment organizations, so that if you played your cards right, you could spend an evening with your husband maybe once or twice a year and have the rest of your time to yourself. . . ."

"You're making these things up!"

"Do you have anything to add, Mr. Newton?"

"My dear, I am as ignorant as you."

"Then," I said, "I suppose we'd better not worry about it."

"Miss Dorothea Tonkin gave me some advice."

"What was that?"

"To always let you do as you please and to never require you to ask for money."

"I didn't see you two speaking."

"I vowed to do as she suggested."

Now I fell silent, a bit startled.

"She said, 'Your wife is the sort of young woman who will always be thoughtful and prudent, and so you need not prove your authority over her by means of undesirable constraints.' "

"I hope that she knows me better with our short acquaintance than my sisters do after twenty years, because they would hardly agree." I didn't know that I agreed with this kind assessment, either, but I held my tongue. Of course, later events tested my prudence considerably.

He shrugged his shoulders, as if to say that my
sisters were so long gone as to be of very little
import. And it was true. In all the time from that day
to this, my sisters have never seemed so far behind
me as they did that night in the Vandeventer House.

I found Mr. Newton a remarkably pleasant and
agreeable man, more so with every passing hour.

The next morning, after we had dressed and
taken our first marital breakfast and been informed
by the porter that we would have to vacate our room
before ten, Mr. Newton led me by the hand over to
the heavy box, and as I stood there, he pried off the
lid. I can't say that I understood at first what I was
seeing, so unexpected was it. I looked at Thomas,
then back into the box. They were still there, gleaming as darkly as before in the rays of morning sunlight. Impulsively, I stepped to the window and drew
the shade. I said, "Have you had these with you all
these weeks? Since before we met?"

"I have."

"Does anyone know about them?"

"My friends in Kansas have been waiting for
them these four weeks."

"How many are there?"

"Twelve."

I looked at them again. They of course didn't
move, but they seemed alive. He said, "Sharps rifles.
Twelve Sharps rifles."

I said, "Their barrels are very short."

"They're carbines." Then: "Can you really
shoot? Frank said you can."

"Will I be required to?"

He didn't answer that. "I haven't heard from my friends, but the newspapers I've seen around here today run pretty hot. Of course, you never know what they're putting in just to work people up."

"I can shoot a bottle or a pumpkin. Frank and I did that."

We were silent for a moment, looking at the short black barrels of the weapons, then he slipped his arm about my waist. He said, "When I set out from Massachusetts, I knew these might put me in danger once I got near Kansas. The danger isn't going to be any less just because I found a wife on the way."

"Oh, it might be," I said, "if I look sufficiently girlish and you seem sufficiently callow. My goodness me, just what are those ugly things? How *did* they get mixed up with my quilts and feather beds? I thought we'd ordered a stove!"

"I calculated in the night that we can still go back up the river and cross through Iowa and Nebraska and then turn south."

"I thought we were in a tremendous hurry. September first is in three days."

"It's a dilemma. In Quincy, I estimated the danger as rather small, but here in slave country, with what the Missouri papers are saying—"

"You're too used to looking and acting like an abolitionist. Do what Roland Brereton does: smile at the Negro children and frown severely at the men and women, as if you are ruminating over some soon-to-be-deserved punishment, and you'll fit in perfectly. You mustn't be eager to befriend the porters and the draymen and the serving maids, or to

make it up to them that they live in bondage. It's one
thing to be an abolitionist passing through Missouri,
and it's quite another to be an abolitionist passing
through Missouri with twelve Sharps rifles."

He nodded, then pulled me more tightly against
him. My tone of course was light, but I wasn't happy
by any means about our baggage.

He nailed the lid back on the box. An hour later, I
watched it being carried aboard the *Independence*
with as much apparent indifference as if it contained
the "harness" that was written on the side.

Travel up the Missouri was slower and more
distressing than travel down the Mississippi. I had
plenty of time to ponder the rifles Thomas was trans-
porting to his friends in Kansas, people I had not met
but whom I'd imagined as a small group of aspiring
farmers whose ambitions ran to a few head of cattle
and horses, a few acres of corn and flax. That they
shared his abolitionist feelings I'd taken as evidence
of benignity and charitableness—my sister Miriam,
after all, though peppery and uncommonly plainspo-
ken, was the kindest person I'd ever met, the only
truly kind person in our family, if kindness could be
defined as eagerness to do good in things large and
small whether that goodness accrued to one's own
benefit or not. When Roland Brereton made of abolitionists great demons of aggression whose first
delights were stealing Negroes and killing their owners, and, if that wasn't possible, forcing the Congress
and the states to pass laws that would do the same
thing with less fun about it, I thought of Miriam and
of Roger Howell or of "poor Dr. Eels," who suffered

so for his beliefs. I'd thought Roland saw the dark shadow of his own self in those supposed abolitionists. It was Roland, after all, who said from time to time that folks were going to bring slavery back to Illinois, mark his words, and everybody would be the better for it, not only the poor niggers. After one of these speeches, Harriet would roll her eyes and whisper, "He doesn't mean that! He's harmless as a baby!"

But now I'd seen those rifles, rifles I had heard of, that were made in New England and coveted by everyone for their pinhole accuracy. It's a fact that no bride knows what layers are in her groom, that every wedding is a lottery, too. All weddings are alike in that. But it was also true that with my money from the sale of my father's house in my pocket, I'd seen what I wanted to see in Mr. Thomas Newton. Those rifles that I didn't like to think of were part of my bridal portion, and I dared not speak about it, even to Thomas.

Thomas, himself, continued agreeable and affectionate. We shared a tiny stateroom off the ladies' cabin, and each evening he came to me about ten o'clock. We also made it a point to take our meals together, but the customs of travel made it diffcult for us to begin experiencing any prolonged marital intimacy. I did see that apart from me, Thomas seemed not to be establishing much acquaintance on the boat. When I asked him about it, he smiled and said that at one end of the men's saloon, the gamblers were fleecing the emigrants, and at the other end, there was much praying going on, and it was interest-

ing to observe, he said, which of the prospective settlers regularly made their way between the two enterprises. But apart from these observations, he had
some books to read, and spending his daylight hours
sitting beside the aft rail of the hurricane deck
improving his time in this quiet fashion would prepare him best for the weeks and months of hard work
to come.

There were a dozen or so ladies taking passage in
the ladies' cabin, and many more taking deck passage
below. We were a widely assorted bunch, and there
were a few I might have spoken to more readily if I
hadn't been so mindful of those rifles. Four of the
women were going to Kansas, and two of these had
small children. Each of the four was from a different
place: One woman and her husband and two sons
were coming from Pennsylvania; another was traveling from Louisville, Kentucky. A very small young
woman, whose baby looked sickly, had come all the
way from Nova Scotia, in Canada, to meet her husband, who was an American and waiting for her in
Leavenworth. A girl of about my age had lived four
years in Saint Louis with cousins but had come origi-
nally from Bavaria. She had more cousins in Kansas,
including one young man whom it was expected that
she would marry. She tatted without ceasing, the lace
rolling out from between her fingers as if from a
machine. She smiled all the time, too, the way foreigners do, but when she spoke, it was almost without
accent. Under different circumstances, I thought, I
could have made a friend of her.

It was readily apparent to me that I wasn't the

same person on the steamboat that I had been in Quincy. Certain fixed elements of my character that my sisters and I had always taken for granted seemed to have disappeared. For example, I'd always gone my own way, without making close friends of any girls my age, even my schoolmates, when I'd had them. Those girls seemed foolish to me, too interested in dress patterns and bonnets and pretty things, and I drew back from them. But really, they were smaller and daintier than I was, and pretty things looked flattering on them. I looked best in plain. And of course, there was the problem of my father and sisters. The fathers of my acquaintances were young, healthy, and mostly prosperous. My father's friends, what few he had, had all died years before, and anyway, he had been a man who made deals, not strong ties or even alliances. He was interested only in men who had something to buy or sell, and each one of them was his potential antagonist. His dearest relationship had been to his horse, or possibly to his house. My sisters, too, had few friends, because always, and over everything else, they had each other, and none of them was really interested in anyone outside the family. An ax ground away from the family whetstone couldn't even take an edge for them. And so for various reasons, mostly my own, I'd been friendless and liked it that way, been quiet and proud of it. Now, on the *Independence,* all the women and girls had some feature of note that made me long to speak in a friendly way, but the rifles shut my mouth.

And then there was the question of usefulness.

There was plenty of time, as the days passed in the ladies' cabin, to observe the other women and their children and, as well, to dip into Miss Beecher's book. One moment I would watch a mother's agile fingers as she brushed and plaited her three daughters' silky hair, never losing patience with the flyaway wisps that made me, from across the room, desire to yank them out of the child's head in frustration; the next moment I would read: "At least twice in the twenty-four hours, the patient should be well covered, and fresh air freely admitted from out of doors. After this, if need be, the room should be restored to a proper temperature, by the aid of a fire. Bedding and clothing should be well aired, and frequently changed; as the exhalations from the body, in sickness, are peculiarly deleterious. Frequent ablutions of the whole body, are very useful. . . ." I looked up. Here was the German girl, finishing off the sleeve of a child's knitted jacket that she had begun just an hour before. I read: "In selecting carpets, for rooms much used, it is poor economy to buy cheap ones. *Ingrain* carpets, of close texture, and the *three-ply* carpets, are best for common use." My eyes drifted down the page. ". . . cannot be turned . . . ," ". . . black threads . . . rotten . . . ," ". . . begin to cut *in the middle* of a figure. . . . ," ". . . ball-stitch . . ." Beside me, a mother sat with her little boy, reading from an alphabet book. Every second or two, she said in a low voice, "Robbie, pay attention to what I'm telling you, now. Don't kick the chair runner. What is this letter? Well, then, what is this picture? Robbie, look at the book with Mama." Robbie said, "I'm hungry,

Mama! Don't you have a bit of something to eat? When will they have dinner?" My book fell closed, and when I opened it again, I read: "It is wise, therefore, for all persons to devise a general plan, which they will at least keep in view, and aim to accomplish, and by which, a proper proportion of time shall be secured, for all the duties of life." I was surrounded by all the useful things that I was unable to do, had until now never desired to do, but would soon be required to do. It was all very well to tell myself that Thomas had been apprised of my uselessness. He had seen what he wanted to see in me, just as I had in him.

And I who could run and swim and ride a horse and write a letter and walk any distance now languished half asleep in my chair, lulled, or perhaps numbed, by the book in my hand and the quiet activities all around me. Indoors! Indoors! Even in Kansas, no doubt, most of my life would be spent *indoors,* doing what Annie and Alice and Harriet and Beatrice had been doing all my life while I was outside. Here, indoors in this cabin, the curtains were mostly drawn, and I felt as though I were stifling. All around me, the others were getting on with their useful business, unaffected, while I was suffocating.

And then the bell rang for dinner, and everyone ran for the door.

It was hard traveling so late in the year, with the river so low. It seemed that the boat grounded on a sandbar every hour, day and night. There would be a jolt and a shudder, then yelling and running, then she was up and over, or they'd floated her back. Twice the passengers all unloaded—according to some, for fear of explosion, and according to others, simply to lighten the load. Stories of this wreck and that explosion and the other accidents that resulted in so many deaths and injuries abounded, but in spite of the horror and the dread, daily activities went on quite smoothly, as if only a real explosion could prove to passengers and crew that there *could* be an explosion. Only our actual slow progress up the river seemed the possible thing. The scenic bluffs were impressive; the drinking water cleared a little as it sat in the glass on the table. Those who were used to it attested to its tangy flavor and healthful properties, but some said it made them ill.

Thomas and I improved our acquaintance at night, in our tiny stateroom. The only barrier between us and the cabin at large was a green curtain, under which, often enough, you would see one or two thrusting male stocking feet, as they allowed the single men to sleep on the floor of the ladies' cabin after the ladies had gone to bed, which was at about eleven. If a lady had an emergency in the middle of the night, she had to step over a score or more of long bodies wrapped in cloaks or blankets, and by morning the air was insufferably close.

Thomas and I whispered to each other from our respective berths, I on the top shelf, he on the bottom. All around us, people were snoring, coughing, expectorating, sneezing, groaning, rustling, muttering, talking, laughing, and even crying. The whimpering of the sick baby went on and on, even though the poor mother talked to it and walked it and nursed it and tended to it, it seemed, twenty-four hours a day. Only the bustle of a grounding drowned out the somber noise of this child's suffering and the low patter of its mother, saying, "He's always such a good, happy baby. I don't know what can be wrong with him. Forgive me the disturbance. . . ." The help of the other women, who offered to hold or to walk the baby, so the mother could get an hour's rest, only made her more apologetic. I would lie in my berth after Thomas and I had finished whispering back and forth and I was sure he had fallen asleep, and listen to that sad baby and its sadder mother and feel as low as I had ever felt in my life. It was all I could do to keep in my mind a picture of the orderly grid of streets on the bill advertising Salley Fork, Nebraska, or my image of Lawrence, Kansas, with its gristmill and library and lumber mill and evening lecture society and salubrious climate.

At the first light, we woke up and fled for the fresh air of the deck, along with almost everyone else in the cabin.

We never mentioned the rifles, and Thomas never looked at the Negro waiters who served the food nor at the five slaves who were traveling on the boat, three women and two men who were kept perennially busy tending to the wants of their owners. All had come on in Saint Louis. A man and a woman got off the first day, and the rest got off the third day. I believe they were Thomas's first actual slaves, since he had never traveled in the south. I had been to

Palmyra, Missouri, of course, and Hannibal, too.
Slaves and their masters were common enough passing through the streets of Quincy, to tell the truth.
Even so, I could not help seeing them as if with
Thomas's eyes. In the general hustle and bustle of
everyone on the boat doing for themselves and their
kin, these white women who waited to be served
stood out boldly different. Once, when the boat
grounded and we all had to get out and step through
shallow water to a low spot on the shore some fifty
feet away, a woman stood on the deck long after
everyone else had gotten off, waiting for her slave
girl of about fifteen to fetch her other shoes. It later
turned out that the crew wouldn't let the girl get the
shoes but put her off on the other side, and so the
slave owner just stood there grasping at her ebbing
dignity with two hands. It didn't help the girl fifteen
minutes later when she was crying and explaining in
front of everyone what had happened. Her mistress's
shoes were ruined with the wet, and she slapped the
girl, in spite of her tears or for her tears, or both.
Thomas whistled to himself and walked up and down
on the shore, away from the others. I kept thinking
that it was those rifles that were weighing down the
boat and that soon they would be thrown off with
everything else, the box would break open, and
something terrible would happen, far worse than a
slap. After we got back to our saloon, there was an
argument between the slave-owner woman and
another woman, in the presence of the slave girl. "Of
all of us on this long, tedious journey," said the one
woman, who spoke in New York State accents, "you

are the only one who has dealt a blow. This child is entirely in your power—"

"You know nothing about it," snapped the slave's mistress.

"I know what we all see, that for the sake of a pair of shoes—"

"A new and expensive pair! Believe me, if I could free myself of the girl, I would. You have a smart traveling outfit on, and you and I are about the same size. I'll tell you what. I'll trade you the girl for your dress and the hat I saw you wearing with it. Then you can give her her freedom or not, as you please."

The New York woman was much taken aback and soon realized that the rest of us had all fallen silent and were watching her. The young slave woman was watching her, too.

Finally, her face went red, and she turned her back and walked away to her stateroom. The slave owner said, "You see? She didn't buy you. Go back down to the lower deck with Pearl; I can't stand the sight of you anymore."

The northern woman came off at a considerable disadvantage from this, with many in the ladies' cabin saying, "They are plenty happy to be telling us what to do, but that's all they really care about" and "They are perfectly happy for us to be with the niggers on an equal footing, but you know, they won't touch them" and "All you really have to do is stand up to them, just like any other bully." There was much nodding and consenting to all of this.

I didn't say anything, but I thought that the slave-owning woman had shown considerable wit, and I only wished that the northern woman had matched her. I know what I would have done. I would have said, in a very dignified manner, "I have no desire to own slaves, but I will give you my shoes if you will set her free." You could always take off your shoes right then and there, and that would be a seizing of the advantage.

That night, when I related the incident to Thomas in the privacy of our stateroom, he was much interested, but he didn't think as ill of the northern woman as most of the women had. "You see," he whispered, "she couldn't even put a girl and a dress in the same category."

"The girl herself could. She was ready enough to be traded for a dress."

The thing that always struck me about these disputes was that most things most people said seemed right enough for you to agree with, but the more sentiments you agreed with, the more confused you became. I asked Thomas if he was ever confused about this issue. He said he was not.

The next morning, the slave-owning woman and her party disembarked at Lexington.

From there it was only another day's journey to Kansas City, hardly a city, or a town, or a village, but only a high bluff above the river and a little track running along it, nothing like Saint Louis. There were bigger towns farther up the river, which some of the other passengers were going to—Leavenworth was the name of one and Weston another—but as our preliminary plan was to go to the town of Lawrence and find Thomas's friends, we disembarked at Kansas City. There had sometimes been discussion of Kansas City as a thriving western metropolis at Horace Silk's store, but this village was not the Kansas City they were referring to there. Nor did I see how Kansas City could ever become the populous city that Saint Louis was, for great tree-clad declivities towered above the levee, and all goods had to be hauled up them on narrow paths. They were diffcult to scale, even unburdened with goods.

There were plenty of folks around, though, and here in Kansas City we saw yet another new sort of person. The place was full of men I would soon come to know and fear as Border Ruffians. These men were Missourians, and to tell the truth, they reminded me forcibly of Roland Brereton, everlastingly G—— d——ing everything, everlastingly working at a plug of tobacco and spitting every minute or so. Their hair hung down, long and dirty. They went armed, even walking down the "street," a big pistol or a Kentucky long rifle or some kind of knife to hand at all times. And these men were everlastingly loud and always talking about themselves: "No man ever throwed *me*! I'd like to see the one who'd try! I'll whip two if I have to! Haw—if I *get* to! Ask me! I like to give a good whipping, I do!" I said to Thomas that "I" seemed to be their favorite word. Thomas stood out among them like a church steeple among chimneys, with his neat black trousers and his well-trimmed red beard and his shirt collar.

They looked at him, too. At the time, I thought the contrast between them and him was all to our advantage. I must say, also, that their respect for me was exaggerated. Someone was always stepping into the mud so that I could pass, or touching his hat, or nodding at me, or offering to show me the hotel or some fine wagons or a good mule. These men would look at Thomas, then talk to me. I thought that this was just a quirk of the Missouri men, but later I realized that it attested to the depth of hostilities. Conflicts between strangers weren't open yet, but the Border Ruffians were ready for them to be.

It was under the eyes of these men that the black stevedores unloaded our "harness" and the rest of our belongings, and it was these men who shouted out, "There's a heavy box, an't there? Can't hardly lift that one, Joe, now can you? Got some books in there, don't he?" The beating of my heart actually quivered the tucks in the bodice of my dress. "There *are* books in there," said Thomas, as if impressed by the talkers' perspicacity. "There's a very fine set of leather-bound sermons in there." Thomas never even removed his hat or his coat, though it was as hot a day as I had ever endured.

We asked around for a hotel and were directed to the Humphry House. It was nearly dusk, maybe just about time for our supper, but by the time we had walked from the landing to the door of the Humphry House and had climbed the plank ramp that served for steps, we could see no sign of anything like supper. The proprietor, his wife, some children, and two or three others were sitting between the doorway and an open window. "There's a bit of a breeze," said the woman as we walked in. "I felt it."

"I felt it," said the proprietor. "A good breeze."

"Yes, ma'am," said one of the others.

"Yes, ma'am," said another, with such conviction that I expected someone to roundly disagree. If anyone had done so, it might have been me, for I felt no breeze at all.

"You're too late for supper," said the wife, looking at us. "If you're hungry, you can go on up to bed and sleep on it. That's the best way." Her tone was friendly, as if full of good advice and entirely disinterested.

"Hot up there, though," said the proprietor.

Thomas said, "Perhaps you could show us the accommodations."

"Well, I could," said the proprietor, leaning back in his chair until it screeched, "but you can see them for yourself, up that staircase."

As we climbed the steep, railless steps, the wife called out, "Them beds is for the ones who's down with the shakes. If you're okay, you got to sleep on the floor!"

The sleeping room did for everyone and ran the whole length and width of the building, maybe twenty feet by thirty. They had laid out blankets on the floor. The beds were taken already by a full complement of sick people, and a small, dark-haired woman who didn't look all that well herself was turning from one bed to another bed, a couple of spoons and a large cup in her hand. She glanced at us as we came up the stairs but looked too exhausted to say anything.

There were four beds, three holding one person each and the largest holding two men. The woman leaned over one of these and gave him a sip of water. He groaned, a deep, manly, and agonized groan.

"He's bad," she said, as if to no one. "He an't going to make it." The man was struggling mightily with his fever, throwing himself about and kicking out at his bed companion, but that one was so thoroughly asleep that he lay there moveless and inert under the blows.

I said, "You're good to nurse him."

"He's my husband, you know," she said, again as if to herself. "But he an't going to be for long." She gave the struggling man a long, unreadable look, then turned and carried some water to one of the other beds. Thomas said, "Are these other members of your family, then?"

"Never seen any of the others before." She shook her head, then half fell into a chair, seemingly beyond exhaustion.

I said, "May I get you something to eat?" before I realized that I had no idea where to get anything to eat, but she said, "No. Can't eat. Can't eat yet. Maybe tomorrow." She closed her eyes, and for a moment all of the patients were quiet, as well. Mr. Newton led me down the stairs. "How they doing up there?" said the proprietor's wife. And before I had even opened my mouth to speak, she was shaking her head ruefully.

Out in the street, I said to Thomas, "We might find another place to stay."

But there was no other place to stay, and when we came back later, the floor of the sleeping room at the Humphry House was covered with bodies wrapped in blankets. The stars and the moon were clearly visible through chinks in the wall, and there was a breeze. It came in at every crack and was warm and thick. The provisions made for the ladies on the steamboat were nowhere to be found in the Humphry House. The best the half dozen of us could do for ourselves was to cluster at one end of the room behind a curtain that one of the ladies made from an old piano cover she had brought along with her from Tennessee. Did she also have the piano? she was asked. "Why, no," she said. "Never did have a piano, but I thought this was a nice first step." The floor was cottony, and it was easy to hear what was going on below through the chinks between the boards.

"You hear what some boys did up in Atchison?" I couldn't see the speaker, who pronounced the name of the town "Atchinson." He laughed. "They got this black abolitionist who was trying to sneak out of the territory, back to that Boston hellhole he come from, and he was going around town saying some things, you know, black abolitionist buncombe, and they lashed him to a couple of cottonwood poles and pushed him out into the river and told him if he lived he'd be sorry, and if he lived and come back there, they'd kill him some other way!" A lot of laughter greeted this tale.

"Kill every one o' them treasonous scoundrels,

you ask me. What are they doing coming out here? They got no business out here!"

"Well, one more of 'em knows that now. Just shoot 'em as they get off the boat, I say. Bam bam bam, like ducks on a pond. We'd be better off, and them too!"

"Kill 'em for their own good!" This was followed by considerable hilarity, as every man in the lower story appreciated the witticism. Thomas's optimism had not prepared me to hear the expression of such sentiments, and I was much dismayed by them. I turned my face into the pillow I had made of my petticoat. After a moment, the woman next to me, who I'd thought was asleep, said in a whisper, "The only real danger is if they get drunk and start shooting through the floor and all, but Laster, that's the owner, he can generally push 'em out before they get that far." She spoke with a decided Kentucky or Arkansas pronunciation, so I didn't answer her for fear of identifying myself with my first word. She smiled. I smiled. I thought I would never go to sleep, but the next thing I knew was a mighty rustling and stamping, as everyone got up with the sun pouring through the walls and started pulling on boots. There was a small basin for washing, and beside it a large pitcher with a little brown water in the bottom. Above these, a mirror hung on the wall and beside it a single comb and a single cloth. Long dirty hairs hung from the comb. I went downstairs and outside. Thomas, whom I hadn't seen anywhere in the sleeping area, was talking to a man in a large slouch hat at the foot of the ramp. When I came up to them, he said to me, "David Graves, here, has a wagon and has agreed to carry our boxes as far as Lawrence."

"If you're going to Lawrence," said Mr. Graves, "you'll be wanting to go on to Big Spring I'll bet."

"Why is that?" said Thomas.

"Well, they got doings up there in a day or two. Now, I may be one hundred percent sound on the goose question, but I been around, and I know that not everyone can be like me. You know, there's two types of folks around here. One wants to have things go their way, and the other just wants to see what happens. My guess is that you are a man of the first type, while I am a man of the second type. I can get along with you." Mr. Graves gave a huge laugh, a huge expectoration, and a huge belch, then he walked off to find his mules and his wagon.

Thomas took my arm as we walked a little ways down the "street."

"In Lawrence, we'll find where my friends have gone and what sort of claim they've got for me."

"What are the doings in Big Spring? Where's that?"

"I suppose it's farther up the territory. I heard a lot of talk last night."

"I did, too, about lashing some abolitionist to a log and—"

"Tarring and feathering, too. And killings."

We thought simultaneously of the "harness."

He said, "I've checked our boxes at the steamboat landing. Untouched."

"The harness stays in Lawrence, then?"

I could have sworn that Thomas nodded frankly in answer to this question, because it was my fixed impression that soon, very soon, we would be relieved of its burden and confirmed in our simple identity as a newly married couple intending to settle in Kansas, drawn by the salubrious climate and the numerous improvements to towns and homesteads already achieved by the hard work and enterprise of settlers whose only goal in life was to welcome the rest of us and smooth our paths. But perhaps my impression was wrong, because as we turned back to the Humphry House to find our breakfast, I was shocked by the sight of some men coming out of the door carrying a long plank covered with a blanket, under which I could easily make out the form of a man, and whatever feelings of mystery I felt were at once dispelled by the sight of the dark-haired woman I had seen the day before, picking her way down the ramp behind the bearers. She looked as pale and exhausted as she had at her nursing, but more resolute and less confused. We stepped aside, and they passed us. I heard her say to the bearer nearest her, "I heard that the *Independence* goes downriver tomorrow, and I mean to be on her. In a week I mean to be in New York State, and a few days after that in Connecticut, where we started out when we got married five years ago and more. I've been in five states and I've buried one of my babies in every one of them, and after I bury him over in Kansas, that will be six, and I can be done with it."

"You can find a husband around here, no trouble."

"Any husband around here is already looking west, no matter what he says. One husband looking west is enough for a lifetime."

"Well, you're right," said her interlocutor.

I put my hand through Thomas's arm a little more firmly, and we made our way up the ramp. I had been hungry, as we'd had nothing to eat since before disembarking from the *Independence* the day before, but as we sat down, I found that my appetite had vanished, or, perhaps, had been displaced by the starkest terror. I looked at the food before me—a dish of pork, a dish of corn bread, a dish of pickles, and other dishes, too—and I looked at the strange faces around me, Thomas's being not the least strange, but perhaps the most. I looked at the flimsy walls of the Humphry House and the soft floor filmed with cottony grit. I looked at the Negro boy who was bringing in more dishes and listened to the sound of the proprietor's wife yelling at him to get back there, into the kitchen. The very brightness of the sunlight streaming in the door and the warmth of the breezes eddying about the room and the casual indifference of the men spitting and yelling and gobbling their food caused a wave of dread to run down me like a swell in the current of the river, and then another and another. These sensations seemed to fix me in my seat, to fix my stare upon the table and my hands in my lap. It was as if all the impressions of the last day, or perhaps the last week, since leaving Quincy, had finally convinced me that my life literally could not be lived, at least by me.

And then the Negro boy set a small dish of hot corncakes near my plate, and the fragrance that rose off them reminded me that I was hungry, and so I took a couple and began to eat one, and the food in my mouth started me up again. After that, I ate and smiled and spoke to Thomas, and went on as if nothing had happened. By noon, we were jolting along in Mr. Graves's wagon, our boxes tied behind us.

CHAPTER 6

I Enter Kansas Territory

The popular maxim, that "dirt is healthy," has probably arisen from the fact, that playing in the open air is very beneficial to the health of children, who thus get dirt on their persons and clothes. But it is the fresh air and exercise, and not the dirt, which promotes the health.

—*p. 118*

I DID NOT SPEAK TO Thomas of my moment of fear, for surely that was what it was—the effects of a moment so short that it lasted only so long as it took for the patrons at the table to see the dishes of food and then reach for them, and yet it leaked into and colored every subsequent moment. Even now, as I recall our ride to Lawrence, the rolling golden prairie with its lines of distant trees and its distant dome of blue seem infused with shadows. The road, for the most part, was hard enough, and Mr. Graves knew where all the mirey spots were and avoided them. Nor was there solitude to oppress us—we met men, women, and children, wagons and walkers and riders, and everyone shouted out in the friendly way that westerners have on the road. The landscape was just as we expected it to be and displayed the expected open sort of beauty. Even so, the very sunshine looked dark to me, and the heat of the day, which was waxing moment by moment, seemed cold. I could not imagine any cabin, any town, any society, that would relieve my spirits.

Thomas, on the other hand, admired the country and was pleased as he could be to have arrived, and he spoke to Mr. Graves with thorough animation and lack of reserve. Eavesdropping, I added to my knowledge of my husband.

"I knowed you was a preacher," said Mr. Graves.

"I was for a few months only," said Thomas. "After leaving Harvard College. But the work didn't suit me. When members of my flock sought my counsel, it struck me dumb."

"That an't bad," said Mr. Graves. "Most folks like to talk themselves into whatever it is that they want to do, anyway. I did some work in the preaching line myself, but it didn't pay. Folks expect the word of God to be free for the asking."

"Then I did some schoolteaching around and about Medford—"

"Well, that don't pay, neither. I done plenty of that, though I only know my tables up to six, but you know, six is half a dozen, and as soon as you know a dozen, you can sell what you got to sell. That's what I told my boys."

"Then I went onto a merchant ship with my brother for a year, carrying loads of rosewood from the Amazon, and then I made sails in my father's factory."

"You may say what you please about the sea," said Mr. Graves. "I an't never seen it, I don't know what's there. I an't never been to New Orleans, even." With this, though I was eager to hear of my husband's maritime adventures, Mr. Graves declared the subject of seafaring a closed one. We jolted along in silence. The ears of the mules flicked forward and back and the wagon squeaked and creaked. Mr. Graves began to hum a tune but broke off abruptly and said, "Got me some warts. You got any warts?"

Thomas allowed that he didn't have any warts at the moment.

"Well, I tried one cure. Worked for me years ago, but it didn't work at all here in K.T. What you got to do is give 'em away to two men riding on one gray horse. Saw a couple of men like that in the spring, so I wrapped up some one-cent pieces in a packet, as many as there are of the warts, and I had those men carry them one-cent pieces to Shawnee, but them warts didn't follow them a-tall. I was disgusted! I looked for those two men on that one gray horse for six months or more, then it didn't work! But now I found another cure, and we got to stop here and put it into effect. Whoa, back, boys!" he shouted to the mules, then jumped down off the wagon and went around to the rear, where he pulled out a neatly wrapped parcel. Thomas gave me a smile. "Here you are," said Mr. Graves. "You know what this is? This is twenty-six grains of barley. That's one grain for each wart." He grinned and set the package by the side of the road. "See them warts?" He flourished his hand in my face. "As soon as some unsuspecting abolitionist comes along and picks up that package, well, them warts will start fading away." He thrust his warty palm under Thomas's nose. "Abolitionist can't resist picking things up. Might be worth four bits! That's what an abolitionist thinks, 'cause they're all Yankees, you know. So when that abolitionist picks up my pretty little package here, he'll be picking up my warts. But he's got to do it on his own. You can't give it to him. He's got to steal it for himself. That's the only way it works."

He arranged the package on a clump of grass and climbed back into the wagon. "I know plenty of charms and cures. Most people here in K.T., they call me Mr. Graves, because I'm so respected for my healing powers, but I don't make much of it, because it's a gift, you see, from the Lord, and I can't take the credit."

After we'd gone forward a few yards and Mr. Graves had looked back at the package three or four times, he said, "I'm sure sorry for you that you can't watch the healing, but it could take a day or so, and I know you want to be finding your place and setting yourselves up before then, but it would do you good to see it."

"Perhaps it will happen more quickly than that," said Thomas.

"You can't tell," replied Mr. Graves. "No, one thing about this life is true, and that is that you can't tell."

Mr. Graves's flow of conversation remained strong throughout the day and only petered out after we'd settled on the prairie for the night. We settled on the prairie for the night because Mr. Graves said that it was a quiet night, warm and clear, and taken all in all, the open prairie would surely be more congenial to us than the nearby cabin of Paschal Fish, "because I am an observant man, Mrs. Newton, and I have noticed that you have something of a distaste for expectorating, and between us, ma'am, Paschal Fish's clientele have a genius for expectorating, and since the man himself makes a practice of never looking down or taking off his boots, he don't know quite how it affects others."

The sunlight seemed to evaporate off the prairie like steam off a vat of boiling water, leaving behind darkness that had already been there; on the other hand, the pale prairie flowers all around us shone against the grasses with a prolonged, dusky brilliance until the darkness simply extinguished them suddenly and at last. Night on the prairie was not like any other night I had ever seen: the blackness was below us and the light above, field upon field of stars stretched over our heads, rolling in every direction until your eyes lost the ability to see them. The bright pale road of the Milky Way beckoned toward Santa Fe in one direction and Iowa in the other, wide and smooth. After a bit of this, Mr. Graves pulled some sticks of wood from the wagon and built a fire. "No use," he said, "in taking chances. Better all around that folks know we're here. I been thinking about it, and this is what we'll do. If anyone rides up, we'll put on that we're sleeping, and then when they shout out and rouse us, we'll try to discern their views on the goose question by the way they talk. Now, if they talk like they're of your party, you can speak up, and if they seem to be of my party, why, then, I'll vouch for you."

I said, "Mr. Graves, what is this question about geese?"

"The goose question is slavery, ma'am. If you are

a proslavery man, then out here we say that you are sound on the goose." He was smoking a pipe, and he tamped it down and put some more tobacco in it, then said, "I'll tell you something. Anyone out here who is one hundred percent sound on the goose question wants to talk about it. You folks don't, so you see that give me the first inkling that you an't sound on the goose question. But I don't ask. And I only tell you this for your own good. And Lawrence is a den of black abolitionists, so it won't matter when you get there, but when you are away from there, then you got to talk like you're sound on the goose, or susss-pisssshhhhuns *will* be aroused."

Thomas asked, "Why do they call it the goose question?" but Mr. Graves shook his head. "No one knows. Anyway, I don't."

I glanced at Thomas, wondering if he had noticed, as I had, that Mr. Graves's mode of speech had changed. He now spoke more roundly and fluently, as if his former "Ruffan" expressions had been a trick. This gave him an air of mystery to me and made me wonder about him, but I only had a minute or two to ponder this, for as soon as he fell asleep, we unrolled ourselves from our blankets and sat close beside one another, unable to sleep. The night before, I had been afraid of shots through the floor, and the night before that, of a boiler explosion on the *Independence*. Each scene seemed to have passed in an earlier lifetime, as distant from these stars and this fire as the Roman Empire. The prairie was full of sounds—the wind through the grasses, but also the yipping of what I later learned were coyotes;

the whine of mosquitoes, but also the liquid call of night birds. Nor did every traveler stop with the darkness—I heard the clip-clop of horses' hooves, the calls of one man to another. They didn't molest us, though.

Thomas held my hand between his. I did not have the tiny hand you read about in books—it did not disappear between the two of his—but I was just as ready to have it held. The requirements of traveling had given us little leisure, and arrangements on the steamboats and in the hotel after Saint Louis had conspired to keep us apart. Always in the past I had accepted without much thought the flocking of men with men and women with women. It was no surprise to me that Mr. Graves presumed that my husband's conversation would be with him. Once he had made me a comfortable place to sit and helped me into it, it was clear that Mr. Graves considered me well taken care of. Once in a while, he would address some informative remark to me, as a courtesy to Thomas's manhood, as if not wishing to imply ignorance on Thomas's part. Perhaps this was the key to his differing modes of expression, too: he lowered his style to a manly roughness for Thomas, elevated it for me. And if Thomas attempted to have any private conversation with me, Mr. Graves would eavesdrop and hem and haw, waiting to stick in his two cents' worth. He wasn't the first to distinguish between us; this was the way men and women behaved, were supposed to behave. I was perfectly familiar with it, but now Thomas and I seemed to be like two souls in separate lifeboats (speaking of maritime adventures—and I had never seen the sea, either; when I read about a governor of Illinois who had recently been much laughed at when he went to Baltimore and asked in all innocence, looking at the tide, if the place flooded like that twice a day every day, I hadn't gotten the joke), who could never quite reach each other, never quite get close enough to converse. Except that now that we were that close, I could not begin to think what we would say to one another. He said, "Every time I set out on what seems very much like an adventure and imagine myself lost in some vast solitude, I discover when I get there that there are plenty of men before me, and that they are all great talkers."

"That is certainly true of Mr. Graves," I said. "But I must say that I didn't mean to find vast, solitary places here in Kansas. I meant to find pleasant new towns with all manner of services that had sprouted out of the prairie like mushrooms. That's what all the bills in Horace's store promised. Space enough for all mankind, but no inconvenience."

Thomas laughed.

"I've been reading Miss Beecher. I understand that my duties as a wife will include making ball fringe for our carpets and regular dishes of light egg custard."

"Are you afraid, Mrs. Newton?"

"Of egg custard?"

But he didn't laugh this time. I dropped my eyes. I wanted to be precise, and he rubbed his thumb over mine and then looked at me soberly.

I pondered, wanting to answer truthfully, at all costs, but suddenly not knowing exactly what that meant: Are you afraid? Just at that moment, in fact, I was quite serene, possibly because Mr. Graves was so comfortably asleep that he cast a radiance of assurance that covered us, too. On the other hand, I had been afraid the night before and just that morning, with a fear so new and overpowering that it was as if I had never felt fear before. That feeling seemed to be right beside me; I could find myself slipping into it if I didn't pay attention. I said, "I should be, but I'm not. Just like on the steamboat. You know it could blow up any minute, but it just seems like it won't. This is wild country, though. The woman sleeping by me last night said she just prayed they didn't get liquored up and shoot through the floor."

"I thought of that. Compared to Boston, or, in fact, any place I've ever been, everyone you meet is armed to the teeth."

I coughed, but Thomas seemed oblivious to the fact that we ourselves carried an arsenal. It occurred to me that Kansas and his own activities there must have until very recently presented themselves in a rather abstract way to Thomas. I said, "How many slaves are there in Kansas Territory?"

"I don't know."

Mr. Graves turned over in his sleep, as if any discussion at all of the goose question concerned him. I said, "Are *you* afraid? You've been on the sea. You've been to the Amazon."

"And to the Indies. And to Cuba. And also to Haiti. And parts of New York City aren't so friendly, either. But in those places the reasons men have to kill you are simple—they want your money, most of the time, or something else you have. And the reason they have to kill each other is simpler still—family enmity. Here it seems like anything is a reason to kill you—disagreement on the slavery question is one thing, but just how you talk or how you look is another, or, maybe, just how the killer feels at that moment. Killing you might just be boasting by other means."

The night air was undeniably soft and fragrant with some exotic but comforting scent. I said, "My sisters would have it that my father was a handsome gentleman, and he certainly turned himself out that way, to the very last. But he had a great affnity for rough river characters who had something to sell or could be made to buy. Once, when my mother told him how much they frightened her, coming to the house, I heard him say, 'Any man who says he's killed somebody, or claims he's going to on the smallest provocation, certainly has not and absolutely will not. I'm safer with a boaster than I am with a silent man who doesn't drain off his resentment a few words at a time.' "

"I've been thinking of that. But Kansas, here, seems like a new place entirely. We can't tell if anything we already know is true."

I said, as if my first day in Kansas Territory hadn't been the strangest of my life, "How bad could it be?"

Now we pulled our blankets to us and spread them as best we could on the long grass and made what seemed to be a comfortable bed, but when we lay down in them, it turned out that our heads were below our feet, a most uncomfortable position. And simply turning in the other direction somehow transformed grass that had been soft and welcoming into tufty bumps. We shifted again, this way and that. I was sleepy, now, and sure Mr. Graves would be up and discoursing at the first light or before. I drifted off, felt a hump under my hip, turned, moved an inch or two, eased onto my back. Suddenly, the prairie made me a perfect bed, formed just for my shape and ease. I opened my eyes to better appreciate the miracle. There was the moon, rising late, and there, against it, was the box of "harness." I turned back to Thomas, intending to solicit a promise that he would dispose of it tomorrow in Lawrence, or the next day at the latest, but he was peacefully asleep.

The embers of our fire faded and died, the moon rose higher and diminished to the size of a small coin. Mr. Graves and Thomas slept on, Mr. Graves, it appeared, in perfect comfort, as his loud, moist snores were uninterrupted and nearly mechanical in their regularity. My husband had a worse time, often turning and jerking against the hard ground, or sighing, or groaning. But I thought he was sleeping, at least lightly, while I seemed to myself wide awake, though in retrospect, I would say, my anxious resolve to keep my eye on that box indicated that I, too, was partly dreaming. Nevertheless, I did hear the very first approach of men on horses, the only ones since early in the evening. After some minutes of only the clopping sound of shod hooves, one of them said in a low voice, "Now what do we have here?" The tones were distinctly Tennessee, and I, who had always expected to be bold and enterprising, closed my eyes at once and played possum. The men were not drunk, or if they were, they were very quietly drunk, because another man answered as softly, "Found us some Yankees, huh?"

"Could be."

Then a third horse came up, and this man *was* drunk, because he started shouting, "Git up, you G—— d—— Yankees! Sun's up early this morning! Git up! Haw haw haw! Time to greet the G—— d—— day!"

Thomas was on his feet in half a second, no playing possum for him, but Mr. Graves took a moment, and then only sat up in his blankets. I opened my eyes. It was nowhere near dawn. Even though I hadn't been asleep, I felt shocked and groggy—my flesh seemed to be ringing with the suddenness of the intrusion. Then I felt a hard edge like the end of a pole poking into my side. It was the barrel of a long rifle. One of the men had dismounted. He said, "You, too. You git up, too." I stood, and my hair fell down my back to my waist.

"G—— d—— if it an't a woman. A big, ugly one, but—"

"Dick, shut up! You're drunk and I'm tired of you and I might have to shoot you one of these days if you don't quit spouting off your mouth."

Mr. Graves, still sitting in his blanket, said, "How are you boys tonight? Is there something we can do for you?"

"Where ya headed?"

"California road," asserted Mr. Graves.

"You an't taking this wagon to any California, haw!"

"Well, sir," said Mr. Graves, "I can fully comprehend your skepticism, though folks have made it all the way to Utah Territory on foot and with handcarts, but no, this vehicle don't look like a California-bound vessel—no covering, for one thing, and the sun gets high and hot out there—but I myself am not going to California, nosirree. I myself am going back to Missoura as soon as I join these folks with their party out past Lecompton. They got their mas and pas waiting, and nearly a regiment of sisters and brothers and all. We've been hurrying to meet up with them." I noticed that Mr. Graves's mode of speech had shaded perceptibly toward "Tennessee."

"Late in the year to be going to California."

"That's what I said," declared Mr. Graves. "That's exactly what I myself told them."

I could still feel the mark where the rifle barrel had touched me, and even in the dark I could see that one of the men was looking through the wagon, pushing boxes around and lifting up lids. Thomas saw it, too. Though he kept his eyes on the two men talking to us, he kept his arm tightly round my waist, and every time I stared in the direction of the wagon, he pinched me gently.

"They said, 'All the better opportunity to trust in the Lord.' Can you believe that? These folks are from a sect out Indiana way. They don't believe in marriage nor having children, nor anything like that. Go ahead and talk to them, but all you'll get out of 'em is the children of Israel and the blood of Isaiah and suchlike. This trip an't been nothing for me in the conversation line."

"Shut up," said the leader of the three men.

Thomas cleared his throat. I felt mine close up. He said, "That's not quite right. We do believe in marriage, but we remain celibate even inside marriage as a discipline and a form of reverence."

"G—— d——!" exclaimed the drunk man. "Henry, you oughtta hear this!"

"What?" said the man at the wagon.

"My bet is you're headed for Lawrence," said the leader.

"Haw!" shouted the man at the wagon, triumphantly. I watched him lift out the terrible box, not without difficulty, though obviously he was a strong man. Thomas pinched me, and I turned to look at our interlocutors.

"You got Free State written all over you," said the leader.

"Look et this!" said the man at the wagon. "Some luck!" I closed my eyes.

"What?" said the drunk man.

"Highly rectified whiskey! Half a barrel! Full to the top!"

The drunk man ran to the wagon to see the miracle. Out of the corner of my eye, I could see the harness box sitting on the ground, untouched and disregarded.

"Folks in sects don't carry whiskey," said the leader.

"Well, that's my whiskey," said Mr. Graves, his

voice hollow with regret. "I do a bit in the trading line, you see," he offered. "Sometimes a little milk or vegetables or flour. I had a stove once. Bought her for five dollars and carried her out to Big Spring and sold her for twenty. That was a good—"

"Shut up. You think we're thieves?"

Mr. Graves coughed, not quite knowing how to answer this question.

Dick said, "Haw! We're just citizens looking for some of them Free State traitors they bring in to vote for them black abolitionist laws and steal our niggers! We got farms! Just out patrolling the countryside, makin' sure of the peace!"

"Put the whiskey back, Henry!" said the leader, whom no one had named.

"Would you boys like to tap that barrel and have a taste?" suggested Mr. Graves. "To kind of break your fast?"

"Haw!" said Henry, still standing by the wagon, his foot nearly on the harness box. "Dick, here, an't fasted from whiskey in ten year! Not for a day, not for a hour!" Now he began to laugh, and Dick joined him, as if drunkenness were the funniest thing in the world. Dick pointed his rifle toward the sky and must have pulled the trigger. The sudden report was so startling and frightening that a red fog or veil seemed to jump up in front of my eyes. I only distantly heard the leader say, "Dick, you're a stupid man. If you weren't married to my sister, I'd shoot you right now."

"She don't like him, anyway," said Henry.

Out on the prairie, a surge of yipping and howl-ing. Coyotes, no doubt. And I saw that the mules, though hobbled, had disappeared.

Thomas stood up straight and quiet, unarmed but gazing calmly at the man still sitting on his horse. Somehow, the clownishness of Dick and Henry had shifted the tone of the situation, and the man on the horse soon dropped his gaze, as if embarrassed. But he said, "I know what you look like, Free Stater, and I hope not to have to see you in these parts again." He turned his horse and galloped away, leaving the other two, but they mounted not long after that, as if they could do nothing without him. Dick did shout, as he was galloping off, "You are ugly, ma'am! I know you can't help it, but you are!"

The first gray strip of dawn paled our faces as we sat down again in our blankets. We all looked at one another for a moment, but to be honest, there didn't seem to be much to say except, as Roland Brereton's mother had said so many years ago, "Praise the Lord!"

By the time the men had caught the mules and I had found some biscuits and other comestibles in Mr. Graves's traveling kit, it was full day and promising to be a hot one. I had put my hair up, but I could feel perspiration trickling down my back, so that I had to roll up my sleeves and unbutton the collar of my bodice. Thomas gave me a quizzical look—he didn't seem, and hadn't yet seemed, to even feel the warmth. I put on a white poke bonnet that I had pur-chased in Kansas City. No one had ever seen the like of it in Quincy, but it worked wonders. When we set out, I walked alongside the wagon. Lawrence, Mr. Graves said, was but ten miles or so from where we were standing.

It took about five of those miles for Mr. Graves to resume his former volubility, and another mile after that for him to put the three intruders in their place. "I was never impressed by those three," he said. "They was just talkin' through their hats. I seen the one, the quiet-spoken one, though I an't ever heard his name. Now, the point of these encounters is just to put a little fear into those who an't quite sound on the goose question. It's harmless, really, just a little fun. I'll admit we're a rough sort of folk out here in K.T., but we an't badly disposed, taken all in all. You just got to know how to take us."

He rattled on, but Thomas, who had at least held up his end of the conversation the day before, remained silent. I kept walking, a few feet from the wagon, happy to be on my own. I knew perfectly well how to take Henry and Dick and their leader, whoever he was. I hated them.

CHAPTER 7

I Am Taken in by Some Citizens of Lawrence

There is no point of domestic economy, which more seriously involves the health and daily comfort of American women, than the proper construction of houses. There are five particulars, to which attention should be given, in building a house; namely, economy of labor, economy of money, economy of health, economy of comfort, and good taste.

—p. 258

I'LL ADMIT THAT after our night in Kansas City, I had lost a portion of my faith in the bills I'd seen back in Quincy advertising lovely towns with their wide streets and gracious buildings. Lawrence was, even then, a famous town, though it has become so famous since that I can hardly remember how famous it was before I saw it. I do know that as I was walking along, I imagined our destination as a pleasant, neat, whitewashed New England village, replete with steeples and mercantile establishments, a library and a school, set neatly in the midst of a smiling, tablelike prairie. I foresaw that when I got there, a glass of clean drinking water, a clean, private bed, and perhaps even a bath might be waiting for me. I was eager to see Lawrence.

But first we came to Franklin. The road had taken us through a stream called the Wakarusa—a trickle of water at the bottom of a steep hill was what it seemed to me—and then, a bit after that, some cabins, sun-bedazzled and humble. It did not look as if anyone had made an effort to build anything here that wasn't absolutely essential to survival, nor, in fact, did it look as if there was a reason for this town to be here at all—the river was thin and forbidding of access, and there was no other advantage to the spot. We passed Franklin.

It was clear long before we got there that Lawrence was a town where a great deal of business was conducted. We met up with wagons of all descriptions—open like ours, or covered with white canopies; pulled by mules, horses, or oxen; full of goods and full of men, women, and children. Once, we got in among a group of four wagons from Ohio carrying seven families heading for the town of Manhattan, K.T.—some thirty people in all, including (and I looked closely at these two) a woman who had given birth to her baby two days before and was now sitting up on the seat of the wagon, laughing and talking as easy as you please. She had the baby in her arms, but she was shading its little head from the sun with her shawl, so I couldn't see it. Her six-year-old walked along beside the wagon, and two others peeped out from inside, their faces round and cheerful. The lady herself was a rebuke to Miss Beecher—she looked blooming and none the worse for her confinement. I thought about her all the way along the river road that runs into Lawrence.

Franklin was a good preparation for Lawrence, in that after Franklin, no town could disappoint. And as soon as you got into Lawrence, you saw that whatever the town might then lack, such things would not be lacking for long, because everyone in Lawrence was as eager as could be. I have to say that my sisters and their husbands were used to laughing a bit at New Englanders. Harriet said that you could keep a neat house without puffng yourself up so much about it as New Englanders did, and Roland Brereton d——d all New Englanders as interfering and sanctimonious do-gooder abolitionists that needed to be shot (though he was abashed enough around Thomas, possibly the first New Englander he'd ever been related to, and anyway, the satisfaction of marrying me off overwhelmed all other considerations), but it was wonderful to see, in Lawrence, what a set of New Englanders could do in the way of setting up a town in new country and making it run.

All the streets were named for states, and the best street was Massachusetts Street. There were buildings of all kinds and in all states of construction— stone walls rose beside frame buildings, which sat next to lean-tos built of hay. Some residences were dug right into the ground, and their owners were busy building over them. Other houses had come in pieces, or so we were told, from the States; one hotel, where we wanted to stay but decided not to, because of contagion, was called the Cincinnati House, because it had been floated somehow from Cincinnati and put back together in Lawrence. The streets were dusty paths, but they looked very much as if they wanted to be streets and soon would fulfill their ambitions. Almost as soon as we got to Lawrence, Mr. Graves took us into a new store, run by a man named Stearns, that was well stocked with not only local produce, like butter, eggs, apples, and melons, but also stoves and chairs and tools and buckets and plates and cups and yard goods and even books. Mr. Graves swelled its stock of highly rectified whiskey and seemed pleased with the price he got. He also sold the man some spoons, a black coat, three boots, a wooden leg with the fourth boot glued onto it, a bushel of unripe pears from Missouri, and a saddle. Then Mr. Graves was happy and carried us, as a favor, to the top of Mount Oread, the great Lawrence landmark, which looked out of town toward the prairies to the south. By this time, it was nearly dusk, and Mr. Graves invited us to gaze upon and enjoy the prairie sunset as if he himself had arranged it for our benefit.

Thomas had asked at the Cincinnati House after his friends from Massachusetts, but no one there knew any of them, or rather, everyone at the Cincinnati House who had been in Lawrence for any time at all was ill, and everyone still on his or, mostly, her feet was almost as new to the country as we were. Mr. Graves himself, afraid of infection, only called in at the window—he wouldn't by any means enter the door. At the Stearns establishment, we were told that almost everyone was at Big Spring for the day, making up a government for the Free Staters to war against the illegitimate government that the Missourians had forced upon the state. I have to say that I heard all this, sometimes sitting in Mr. Graves's wagon and sometimes leaning against it, but I didn't pay much attention. I was too busy staring at the building here, the business there, the animals and people walking to and fro from here to there. There was a kind of New England righteousness about it, about the way that the town looked and the way that the people carried themselves. Thomas, who had been a bit of an odd but intriguing duck in Quincy, looked right at home here.

Thomas did not let either the undesirability of the Cincinnati House or the absence of his friends perturb him now that he was in Kansas, and I found myself taking on some of his equanimity. As we rode down from the top of Mount Oread with Mr. Graves, a man passed us on horseback, and Thomas said, in a voice entirely unsurprised, "There's Bisket now. Hello, Bisket!"

Mr. Bisket was an exceedingly tall and thin young man, certainly no older than I. His long arms and legs seemed to gangle around the compact dimensions of his pony. He drew to a halt. "Newton! We stopped looking for you and thought sure you were dead! But you an't! Halleluia!"

Mr. Bisket turned his horse and walked alongside our wagon in the deepening evening gloom. Thomas turned to me. "Well, Bisket," he said, "I was delayed in Quincy with Howell, and so I found myself getting married! Lydia, my dear, this is Bisket, Charles Bisket! He's a member of our company! Bisket, my wife, Lydia Newton!"

Mr. Bisket leaned over and extended one of his wandlike hands in my direction. I could see that Mr. Graves was waiting to be introduced, as well, just as if he were one of the family. I said, "We've been taken under the wing of Mr. David Graves, here."

"David B. Graves, David B. Graves." Mr. Graves grinned and took the wand into his own paw. Even though Mr. Bisket had generally adopted the garb of the west—blue jean trousers, a blue shirt, a red neckerchief, and a hat with a large brim—the two men looked as if they belonged to different kingdoms—one animal and one plant, perhaps. Mr. Bisket declared that we had missed it this time.

"What's that?" said my husband.

"Well, now. The new governor's come in the last few days, and they love him up in Westport, and he loves them, too. He's all for the bogus legislature, and he told those fellows up there that it would be well for Kansas and Missouri institutions to *harmonize*! He's proslave all the way!" Mr. Bisket glanced suddenly at David B. Graves, who adopted a look of bland impenetrability.

Thomas said, "What about our claims?"

"Aw, that'll be okay. That'll work out fine in the end. But I wish I would have gone up to Big Spring for the convention. I bet that was something!" I rather thought that the presence of Mr. Graves, though, modified his enthusiasm.

"Bisket, here's my wife! Do we have a place to live?"

"Well, I'm staying at the Jenkinses' house in town tonight, and you can stay there with me, and then we'll see about tomorrow when the others come back. It an't far—just a little ways up here on Vermont Street."

He led us off the road we were traveling, and in a few minutes we found ourselves in front of one of those leaning buildings. He said, "It an't bad here in this weather. Hot and dry makes the hay smell kind of sweet. It's something in one of them Kansas storms, though. There was one just after we got here that wasn't like anything I ever saw before in my life for thunder and lightning. Two houses got struck—it come right down the roof beam—and two children got stunned practically to death. They were just sitting there for the longest time, then they got up and started staggering around, and one of them thought she was back in Massachusetts for two days. Lucky they weren't killed, everybody said. Here's Mrs. Bush. You remember Mrs. Bush, Newton."

He dismounted as a handsome, full-figured woman with a youthful face but pure-white hair came through a piece of cloth—a tablecloth, maybe—that had been hung for a door. "Mrs. Bush! Look who turned up! Tom Newton an't dead, after all! And he's got himself a wife from Illinois, to boot!"

Then some other women and another man came out of the building with lamps and candles, and pretty soon we were unloading everything, including the box of "harness," and not long after that I saw Thomas give Mr. Graves four dollars for carrying all of our things, and then he was gone, and I wondered for just a moment if we would see him again—but that was a lesson I learned about K.T.: for all the thousands of folks who came in and passed through and went back to the States, for all the strangers that you looked on every day, there were plenty you thought you would never see again who turned up time after time.

Mrs. Bush and two of the other women, Mrs. Jenkins and her daughter, Susannah, made much of Thomas, for it appeared that everyone really did think that he had been killed by the Missourians, because no evil deed seemed to be beyond those devils. "Why, there's a free Negro in town," said Mrs. Bush as she stirred together some corncake batter, "a young man who's got a claim not far from ours, and they've been threatening to go out there and take him back to his master, but they don't know who his master is! He doesn't have a master, but you can be sure they'll find him one! They hate the sight of a free Negro!"

It was a warm night after an exceedingly warm day, though a hearty breeze blew through the leaning house and set all the doors and windows to rattling. The house possessed a stove, but the stovepipe stopped a few feet above our heads, and the smoke was meant to issue out of one of the openings at either end of the ceiling. Perhaps because of this unorthodox arrangement, or the wind, or both, the stove was difficult to light, and it took some time for the corncakes to be cooked. The three ladies were friendly and eager for conversation. They asked all about me, and Mrs. Jenkins whispered to me at one point, "Oh, my dear, everyone is so fond of Thomas Newton! He is a good, sober man!"

Mr. Bush and Mr. Jenkins, it turned out, were out at Big Spring, at the convention, and the women didn't know whether to expect them that night or the next day. "But whenever they come," declared Mrs. Bush, "I guarantee you they'll have done some business, because they were fit to be tied when they left. You know about the gag law?"

I did not. I didn't know anything about Kansas politics to speak of, but I quickly learned, because that was all anyone talked about. When Thomas and I arrived, even though K.T. had been open to settlement only a few months, events had very much begun.

Mrs. Bush pushed up her sleeves and opened the throat of her bodice another button, then hitched up her skirt. When she saw me staring, she laughed and said, "Lydia, Kansas is no place for gowns and petticoats! I an't going to burn up, is what the women from Missouri say when they cut off their skirts, and for once they're right! And you're always having to raise your skirts anyway, owing to the tobacco spittle! Anyway, there's a law coming in one of these days—"

"In nine days, on the fifteenth," interjected Susannah, who had finally gotten the fire going and was now giving the corncakes another stir.

"—that says that if you even talk about freeing slaves, or write about it, or bring a paper like *The Liberator* into the territory, you can be put to death for it!"

"Oh, Helen," said Mrs. Jenkins. "Surely not for just subscribing to *The Liberator.*"

"Yes, indeed! Doesn't Garrison advocate freeing the slaves? Doesn't he advocate conspiring together to do so? There you are. Ten days from now, if they see that paper in your hands, they could arrest you and put you to death."

We contemplated this. I wondered if Thomas, who I knew was carrying some eastern papers in his bag, was aware of this law.

"And," said Mrs. Bush, "if you so much as give a fugitive a drink of water, that's hard labor for ten years!"

She flipped the cakes, which were now smoking on the griddle. "But listen to this! This is the worst! You get two years of hard labor just for saying that someone in K.T. doesn't have a right to hold slaves! I swear!"

"Helen," said Mrs. Jenkins. "Don't swear."

"And if someone gets convicted of one of these offenses, not even the governor can pardon him."

"That shows they an't sure of the governor."

"Well, they weren't sure of Reeder, but they're sure of this Shannon." She turned to me. "He's the new governor. He's one of them."

"That Stringfellow is the worst," said Susannah. "He will print anything in that paper of his. It scares me."

"It don't scare me," said Mrs. Bush. "It just makes me mad. That cup and saucer are mismatched, Lydia, dear. All my cups and saucers from England that I got for my wedding, all but three cups and two saucers from two different sets, were smashed on the way here. I'm sure I'd like this place better if that hadn't happened."

She handed me a cup of tea and a plate of corn-

cakes. I set them on a tiny table at my elbow, which
looked to be made of two boxes set one on top of the
other. It was dark, because the candles had blown out
in the interior breeze, but my eyes had adjusted. Mr.
Bisket, Thomas, and the third man, or boy, came in
and sat down. Mrs. Bush handed Thomas a plate of
corncakes, too.

I said that they were delicious.

"Well," said Mr. Bisket, "you need a big hunger
for corncakes if you're going to live in K.T. Though I
saw that Mr. Stearns has butter and eggs and apples
and plums in his new store."

"If they'd stick to that store and give over speculating, they might have a business someday," said
Mrs. Jenkins. "But half the time both of them are out.
Here's what I think: They say claims are the making
of this country, but to me they're the breaking of it.
Nobody wants to settle down to business, because
everybody's distracted by some venture or scheme.
And you can't build this or you can't plant that,
because it might end up that what you think is your
claim an't it at all, and you've got to give up what
you built or planted to someone you've never seen
before!"

Everyone present clucked sympathetically, and
later Susannah confided to me that her father had
built a nice twelve-by-twelve cabin on their claim
outside of town, only to be sued by another claimant
for the same bit of property. "We ended up losing the
cabin and twenty rods of fencing, and that did set my
father back, you know. Kind of took the wind out of
his sails."

"How could you lose your claim?" I asked. "I thought if you claimed it, it was yours. And who is Reeder?"

"Oh, my dear," caroled Mrs. Bush. "Here you are just arrived, and we talk to you as if you know everything there is to know! We've been here a little over a month ourselves, and we feel like old settlers! Reeder was the territorial governor, but they drove him out. You must get to know Dr. Robinson. He is our Winthrop, you know. He seems to have come out here a hundred years ago, but really, he only claimed Lawrence a year ago July. Isn't that something? Look how far along we are after only a year and a month!"

Indeed, events moved with considerably more swiftness in K.T. than ever they did in Quincy. Already the territory had finished up one governor (Reeder, the one the Missourians apparently didn't like) and had just received the second (Shannon, the one the Missourians apparently did like). Already an election had been held (the previous March), and already a scandal had ensued from it. Most of the voters had come over, or been brought over, from Missouri, and they had elected their own slate of nonresident officials, who had, already, made a mess of things, according to Mrs. Bush and the Jenkins ladies. "Those who *can* read," claimed Mrs. Bush, "are generally too drunk to do so, and they made a terrible botch of the territorial constitution—"

"It's not a botch, Helen, it's a crime!" said Mrs. Jenkins. She turned to me. "My dear, it is a constitution written in the H—— of slavery for the imposition of that H—— upon others! A sane person cannot read it, simply cannot! Mr. Jenkins tried four times to get through it. It gave him a fever, and he was down for three days. My true feeling is that if he had not tried to read that constitution when he did, we wouldn't have lost our claim!"

Mrs. Bush gave me a skeptical glance, but said, "Perhaps not, my dear."

But the Free-Soil party, to which all my new acquaintances belonged, and which had been surprised and overwhelmed in the spring, was stronger now. "Look at us!" said Mrs. Bush. "We swell the ranks. My own opinion is that Dr. Robinson is far too kind a man, and far too good. He was unprepared by his own virtues for the sheer malice of the other side. And Eli Thayer! Well, he is a cousin of Mr. Jenkins's mother's cousin, and I've met him, and say what you will about this money and that money, and how much he has and how he got it, he is an innocent babe!"

I said, "Thomas mentioned Mr. Thayer."

"He's our benefactor!" said Susannah. "He founded the Massachusetts Emigrant Aid Company. He's a terrific abolitionist!"

"Such an inspiration," added Mrs. Bush.

I didn't know what to think. These people were all so friendly and warm and welcoming, and the leaning house was breezy and quaint, and the corn-cakes were hot and delicious, but every word that they spoke amazed me. It wasn't just what they reported—I didn't doubt for a minute that the men who had challenged us the night before were full of menace and hatred, and that wherever they came from, there were plenty more like them. I didn't know why the three Missourians had threatened us and then ridden away. But the strangest thing was how differently I saw things in K.T., even after but one or two days, than I had seen them in Illinois. Every river town is full of braggarts and ruffians; Illinois was full of wild-talking Roland Breretons, whose fathers and uncles were from Kentucky and Tennessee. But what I had known about such types— that they would go so far into violence and no farther, that the talk was all—I no longer knew. Rather, it seemed just the reverse—that these new men, or the same men in this new place, preferred hurting us to not hurting us. That was amazing enough, but what was even more amazing was the way my new friends spoke of these events. They deplored them, of course, but in addition to that, if the tones of their voices were to be believed, they were a little thrilled by them. They sounded inured to such things but also fascinated by them, even drawn to them.

"Who is Stringfellow?" asked Thomas.

"Ha!" exclaimed Mr. Bisket. "You don't know Stringfellow? I thought he was famous all over the States. Not so long ago, he made a speech telling his hearers to mark every scoundrel they knew who was in the least bit contaminated with Free-Soilism and exterminate them. He's always calling for tarring and feathering or lynching or hanging or exterminating or shooting or cutting up or driving out. They love him in Missouri. And his brother's the speaker of the bogus legislature."

"That's not the worst," said Mrs. Bush, and the others nodded, all apparently knowing what the worst was but not daring to say.

"Remember Park?" said Mrs. Jenkins. "He had a paper over in Missouri, and after the elections he ran an editorial. All it said was that the people in K.T. ought to be allowed to run their own affairs."

"They attacked his office and threw his presses in the river, and they were about to lynch Patterson, the editor."

"They had the rope around his neck," said Mrs. Jenkins. "Would have scalped him, too. They do that."

"But his wife just hung on him and begged for his life."

"That's all that saved him," said Mr. Bisket.

"And he was proslave all the way," asserted Mrs. Bush. "But if you an't for everything—slavery, stealing elections, driving out northern settlers and burning down their houses, and, most of all, extending slavery everywhere—then they hate you as bad as anyone else."

"There an't but a handful of slaves over there, anyway, and those are all house slaves. I'm telling you," said Mr. Bisket, "a citizen from South Carolina or Louisiana wouldn't know Missouri was a slave state. And nobody who comes over here to lynch us or burn us out ever actually owns a slave."

"Well, you know . . . ," said Mrs. Bush.

"It's true," said Mrs. Jenkins.

Susannah blushed, and Mr. Bisket looked at his shoes. Thomas and I exchanged a quizzical glance. After a moment, Mrs. Jenkins said, "Mercy me, you must be tired! I do so wish I could show you a nice chamber with windows and a soft bed! My mother's house in Ipswich has five bedchambers! Goodness, I dream about that house as if it were heaven itself! There's a fireplace in every room." She shook her head. "My mother has such neat ways. It's almost a failing with her. I don't know what she'd think of K.T."

The only possible arrangement, it turned out, was to put up a curtain across the one room of the leaning house and to have the men on one side and the ladies on the other.

The next day, all the men returned from Big Spring. In addition to Mr. Bush—a little man, smaller than his wife, but with bright, terrier eyes and a cheerful manner—and Mr. Jenkins, who had white hair and a white beard and, beneath his irate manner, an air of resignation, there were four other men, all single: Mr. Smithson, his son, his brother, and Mr. Bush's nephew, Roger Lacey, who, Susannah told me, had a wife and three children back in Massachusetts, waiting to come out. "But," she whispered, for she was a great whisperer and confider, "he won't bring her and won't bring her and keeps saying he's not ready. Papa says he's not really all for Kansas, but Mama says he's not really all for *her*!" She laughed. We had been sent to the river for water. There were wells, but the leaning house was closer to the river than to the nearest well, and the water was only for washing. We each carried two heavy buckets. "Just wait," said Susannah cheerfully, "till you get out to your claim. You can spend the whole day going after water until you get the well dug."

She asked me about myself, then said, "Oh, we're the same age, then. But you seem older, because you're so tall, maybe. You have beautiful hair. My hair is the bane of my existence, which Mama says is a good thing, because it is a daily rebuke to my vanity. But I don't see why my vanity needs to be rebuked on a daily basis."

I paused and set the buckets down, then shifted them. They were lopsided and hard to carry. She said, "If I had nicer hair, perhaps Thomas would have thought to marry me." I stared at her, looking for some evidence of rancor or disappointment, but she said it just the way you might say that you should have bought one pair of shoes rather than another. And then she skipped to another topic. She said, "I saw you looking at Mr. Newton last night when we were talking about Stringfellow."

"You were very mysterious."

"*I* wasn't. I'm not supposed to know what he said, and of course Mr. Bisket wouldn't say it in front of the ladies, but everyone knows what he said."

"What did he say?"

"He said that men will of course do low and cursed things with women, that's their nature, and in a slavocracy, it's a protection for the white women that the slave women are there for the men. He said that's the best thing about slavery. But don't tell Mr. Newton, or I shall die of embarrassment, and don't let on to Mama that I told you. She already thinks that this life in K.T. is making me coarse and wild."

"But none of the lynchers are slaveholders, they said."

"Do you expect the Border Ruffians to make sense? I don't."

We walked on.

After a moment, she said, "And it *is* making me coarse and wild here. We're all loosening up. The congregation in Medford that gave us some money to come out here would be shocked. For one thing, we went to services back there every Sunday, sometimes twice, but here, with one thing and another, we're lucky to go once every three weeks. But you're from the west yourself, so it probably isn't much of a change for you."

I said, "I don't know. Ask me in a month."

There had been big doings in Big Spring, and the next thing would be a constitutional convention a few weeks later, where the Free Staters would write the laws that they intended to live under. By the time we got back to the leaning house with the water, Thomas was up to his neck in all the issues. And I saw that the box of "harness" was not where we had left it but pulled out into the middle of the floor, by the stove. The men were lifting out the carbines and admiring them. Later, in the evening, they divided them up. That was how long it took us to become Free Staters all the way.

It turned out that it was waiting for the carbines that had delayed Thomas in his first departure from Massachusetts: accompanying them had been his assigned task, though all had joined in purchasing them. And so it turned out that it was to the box of Sharps rifles that I owed my marriage.

Mr. Bush and Mr. Jenkins knew just where our claim was, right between theirs on the river about three miles north of town. It was good land, they said, with a gentle slope to the river, but it had no timber. They were both prepared to cede us a timber lot in exchange for access to the river. Bush, in particular, had to have a way to get his cattle—his future cattle, which he didn't yet own—down to the water. At the moment, he had a cow and a calf out there. They were grazing our place. Now that Mr. Jenkins had been squeezed on the other side by a claim jumper whose rights had been provisionally upheld just three days before, he was still deciding what to do. He had two town lots, and maybe he would give up the farming idea and go into business in town. All the men agreed that it would take a few days, at the most, to put up a livable cabin for us and that I could stay here, at the Jenkinses' place in town, while Thomas and the other men attended to this matter. They also agreed that they had better get started with it, because they wanted to get it up before the constitutional convention in Topeka, which would take place in less than two weeks and last several days. They were already talking as if it were understood that Thomas would be at Topeka, wherever that was, with them. I wondered what it would be like, three miles out, in my new cabin, all by myself.

CHAPTER 8

I Make an Unexpected Purchase, and Suffer an Expected Illness

A sick-room should always be kept very neat, and in perfect order; and all haste, noise, and bustle, should be avoided. In order to secure neatness, order, and quiet, in case of long illness, the following arrangements should be made. Keep a large box for fuel, which will need to be filled only twice in twenty-four hours. Provide, also, and keep in the room, or an adjacent closet, a small teakettle, a saucepan, a pail of water, for drinks and ablutions, a pitcher, a covered porringer, two pint bowls, two tumblers, two cups and saucers, two wine glasses, two large and two small spoons; also, a dish in which to wash these articles; a good bucket, near by, to receive the wash of the room. Procuring all these articles at once, will save much noise and confusion.

—p. 238

I STAYED IN Lawrence for nine days. The weather was hot enough to cook meat, and no one, man or woman, ever went without a large-brimmed hat. Modesty had nothing to do with it, and survival all. I thought, from living in Quincy, that I knew heat. The first day or two, in fact, I inwardly preened myself that this heat all these New Englanders kept exclaiming about was routine for us westerners. But in fact, this was K.T., and K.T. wasn't Illinois. In Illinois, the heat rose around you, thick and damp, and hung there, unmoving, day and night. You got used to it. In

K.T., the heat bore down on you during the day like a bright blue lid and then swept through you all night, a bullying, heavy wind that took your breath away rather than refreshing you. All but the severest, thinnest, most enervated ladies wore their garments turned up and folded back, their buttons unbuttoned. Petticoats stayed at home, corsets loosened and disappeared. The layers of clothes we were used to back in the States simply vanished, and no eyebrows went up, no remarks were made. For all the talk there was in Lawrence—and Lawrence was all talk—no one ever mentioned this. The men, too, put off their jackets and rolled up their sleeves. Quite a few went clean-shaven, and barbers in Lawrence did excellent business.

On the third day, I bought a horse and his saddle and bridle. I had given Thomas a hundred of the dollars from the sale of my father's house, and I had spent thirty-seven dollars on provisions in Quincy before our departure. The rest I had sewn into my traveling dress. Perhaps Thomas knew it was there and perhaps not—one of my sister Harriet's pieces of marital advice had been to keep my financial affairs in my own hands as far as I could, and I was predisposed to take this advice, anyway, as Thomas and I were all but strangers on the day of our wedding. How it happened with the horse was this: I was walking along Massachusetts Street, carrying my buckets to the river. Susannah was at home with the shakes—she shook every third day, and today was her shaking day. On her shaking day she was useless, so I had offered to carry her share of the water. This was my second trip, my first time out alone, so I was looking eagerly about. Thomas had left for the claim the day before, and we had agreed that I would continue to buy provisions, though of course nothing had been said about a horse. Thomas had never actually owned a horse, which showed, to my mind, that he really was from Massachusetts.

I was passing the Stearns establishment and looking through the door, thinking, no doubt, that for variety and wealth of goods, the Stearns establishment suffered by comparison to Horace's place in Quincy, when a man on a black horse trotted by, with three other horses on a string, two bays and a gray. There were plenty of horses in Lawrence, and it was second nature to me to look at them—Roland Brereton had taught me what was good in a horse and what wasn't—so I looked at this string and I was immediately taken with them. All three were healthy and shiny, well fed and clearly not overworked. They looked spirited but well broke, and the gray, especially, had a look of intelligence, in that he paid attention to his surroundings even while trotting along with the others. At that point, my only intention was to admire. I walked along with my buckets, and the man led his string of horses around a corner and disappeared.

Later in the day, though, I saw them again. I had just been looking at stoves, imagining that I would soon have a house and would need a stove to put in it. The proprietor of the store had two models, and I had pretended that I needed to think about my choice and that I would return. I had pretended to a judicious-ness that I didn't feel. Actually, the more I looked at the two stoves, the less inclined I felt to buy one. The fact that someday soon I would have to buy one, and then install it and use it and make it my daily companion, made my choice between the two seem more like a punishment than a purchase. I decided to go home and read Miss Beecher for a bit to fortify my resolve. When I came out of the store, I saw the back of a livery stable, and there, enclosed with some other horses in a corral, were the two bays and the gray. I went up to the bars. The horses were milling about some piles of prairie hay that had been thrown on the ground, and the gray was right beside the fence. I bent down and saw through the bars that his legs were clean and tight. He turned his head and looked at me, his ears pricked and the muscles in his neck arching compactly. He had a lovely throat, which meant he would be easy to ride, and his eyes were large and mild, dark in his almost white face. The owner of the livery stable, the man I had seen leading the horses, came out into the street and spit, then bit off another chaw, looked around, and spit again. When I approached him, he smiled.

"Good afternoon, young lady," he said.

"I'm Mrs. Newton."

"Good afternoon, Mrs. Newton. I'm Reverend Moss." He took off his hat, then put it right back on again. The sun was brutal.

"I like that gray horse."

"Where is Mr. Newton?"

"He's out at our claim. May I look at him?"

"He's a six-year-old. Young and healthy, but not

foolish. Well broke to ride, well broke to harness. Fine animal."

"May I look at him?"

"You sound like a Kentucky girl! That's a good horse." He didn't move. His reluctance gave me second thoughts. I had meant to be buying a stove right then, and my conscience began to awaken. The money for the stove was in the pocket of my dress. I touched it, suddenly knowing that the larger of the two stoves was no doubt the right one. I turned.

"Well, sure," said Reverend Moss. "Have a look at him. You won't be disappointed."

He went inside for a rope, then opened the gate and led the gray horse out. It turned out that I wasn't judicious at all. Rather than looking the horse over, checking his teeth, feeling for heat in his legs, pressing his back, I just took the rope and handed the reverend the money in my pocket, thirty-five dollars. He unfolded it and laughed. I began scratching the horse on the face, between the eyes. His presence was large and sweet-smelling. I'd forgotten how good it felt to stand close to a horse. Reverend Moss said, "You expect to give me thirty-five dollars for a fine horse like this?"

I pulled out my pocket to show that it was empty. Of course I said nothing about the rest of the money, sewn into my skirt. The reverend could not stop laughing as he handed me back the bills. I stood with the horse a minute, then turned and began to walk away. "Hey, ma'am!" called the reverend. "Hey! Mrs. Newton!"

I stopped and looked at him.

Still laughing, he said, "Now, ma'am, you'll be needing a saddle and bridle for this animal, and I do believe I have just the thing for you."

Ten minutes later, I led the horse away by his bridle, on his back an ancient military saddle, but one very like the one my father had used on old Wellington, the one I had taught myself to ride in.

Mrs. Bush, Mrs. Jenkins, and Susannah, who rose from her bed and came out to look at the horse, were full of consternation at my foolishness. "A mule," said Mrs. Bush, "would have been a far wiser choice, my dear. Or a pair of oxen." She shook her head. We corralled the horse down the street, and I paid the man who owned the lot a dollar for hay. It was clear to everyone, even me, that if Thomas had not been out at the claim with the other men, building our cabin, there would have been no horse, and of course I regretted buying the animal. Mrs. Bush said, "Maybe you can sell it, dear. How much did you pay?"

I told her. From the expression on her face, I surmised that that was a lot to pay. The next morning, another hot one, I rose before dawn and had already fetched the water for the day by the time the others were up. I had also laid the fire in the stove and set a pan of water at the back to heat up. As soon as our breakfast of corncakes and bacon was over—the only hot food we would have all day, because the leaning house became simply too intolerable if we kept a fire in the stove—I leapt up and washed the dishes; then, even before Mrs. Bush had a chance to say anything, I rolled the blanket beds and swept out the dirt floor and straightened the few chairs and the two little tables that served as furniture. I chased away the mice, who were more of a problem at night, anyway, and made sure all of our food was tightly sealed. Mrs. Jenkins and Mrs. Bush were astounded at my industry, until I solved their perplexity by saying, "I am going to ride my horse now."

"Oh, my dear, I hate to see you going out on the streets by yourself unless it is absolutely essential. Those Missourians are always starting such brawls—" Mrs. Jenkins began, but I was already out the door. When I looked back, a moment later, I saw Susannah, no longer shaking, standing with the tablecloth door in her hand, staring after me. I waved to her, and she smiled.

The horse came over to the fence when I approached. The day before, I had given him some prairie hay three or four times and spoken to him, and now I intended to ride him, but I realized that all the assurance I had been feeling the previous day was based on what the reverend had said, that he was well broke to ride and drive. Well, from the dealer's point of view, every horse in the United States and its territories is well broke to ride and drive. All I really knew was that when he threw the saddle over the horse's back, the horse didn't seem to mind. I looked at the horse and said, "Jeremiah. That's your new name. You're Jeremiah." His ears swiveled back and forth. There was a kind of shed, very tiny and made of cottonwood, that sat beside the corral, and there I went to find Jeremiah's saddle and bridle. The bridle was old enough, but all in one piece. The saddle,

though, was perfectly dilapidated—rough and discolored, with a couple of little rips. He took to them
well enough, standing steady while I cinched up. It
was early yet, and even the owner of the corral was
still in his house, two lots away. That was fine with
me. I stepped up on the fence and climbed aboard,
spreading my skirt underneath me and pulling it
behind, over the cantle of the saddle, the way I had
always done in Quincy. I settled my weight. Jeremiah's ears flicked forward and backward, and he
gave a little grunt, shifting his weight to his back legs
and coming up a little in the front. This, I knew, was
a bad sign; he might still be hesitant, but he was
thinking about bucking. The flesh over his haunches
shivered, as if my skirt was bothering him, and I
quickly swept my hand over it, bunching it toward
the saddle. Still no movement, but now it felt as
though he wasn't just standing still, rather as if he
was getting ready to explode. I lifted the reins
slightly. We stood there. My throat felt blocked with
fear. The horse's ears now stopped swiveling and
turned backward. He suddenly dropped his head. At
last, finding my voice, I said, "Jeremiah! Don't buck
me off! You're a good horse, and I'll take good care
of you! Just walk, please." His head came up, and he
walked forward.

Now, I must say that although I had ridden my
father's horse and some of Roland Brereton's animals and had been fond of one or two of them the
way you are of a pet, I would never have attributed to
any of those horses an understanding of the English
language. From that first moment with Jeremiah,

though, I believed viscerally that he listened to what I said and understood both the wishes I expressed and the fear in my voice. He chose not to hurt me. He walked forward mildly. It thus became impossible to sell him, either before Thomas returned or subsequently. We strolled around Lawrence, perhaps the only horse and rider with no business in hand. And I was certainly the only woman I saw who was riding like a man. Most were walking, some were seated in wagons; all glanced at me. I said to Jeremiah, "My goodness, they do admire you, Jeremiah." Perhaps they did, perhaps they didn't, but here in K.T., where petticoats and buttons and manners were all loose and loosening further, I decided that I would ride my horse as I pleased, the Missourians and their brawls notwithstanding. That would be the compensation for everything else.

And I did buy a stove. I unstitched the money sewn up in my skirt and bought the larger, more expensive model. I also bargained Mr. Stearns down from thirty-five dollars to twenty-nine. I must say that he considered me very critical of his wares and hard to please. He didn't call himself a reverend, either.

After three or four days, I was quite used to Lawrence; in particular, its combination of money and politics was always curious and stimulating. The stories they told of the last year, since Lawrence's very founding, stood your hair up but also made you laugh. One friend of Mrs. Bush's had been there from the beginning and was there the day that the Border

Ruffians decided to come over and drive the settlers out. "The first thing they did, you know, before we even came out to K.T.," said Mr. Johnson to me, "was pass some resolutions. As soon as they ever heard of the Emigrant Aid Company, they resolved that they would remove us and that they would promote other societies, dedicated to our removal. Oh, when we came, they were ready for us!" We were alone in the leaning house—the Jenkinses had gone to visit friends of theirs, newly arrived at the Cincinnati House, and everyone else was still out at our claim.

"It isn't slavery, in my opinion, that's the problem," said Mrs. Bush. "It's that they want the whole territory to be settled by slovenly, coon-hunting squatters like themselves. They are such a shocking class of people, taken all in all—"

"Certainly, ma'am." Mr. Johnson smiled, and Mrs. Bush fell silent.

"Of course, the pretext for our removal was to be that there were prior claims, but Dr. Robinson and his associates were perfectly legal in their assertion of the claims. They bought out Stearns, who wasn't even here but was back at his real farm in Missouri, for five hundred dollars, and they let the other fella be, since his claim was outside the town. Then it was like turning over a rock. This Missourian showed up with a claim, then that one, then the other one. They expected claims to be honored that had been staked illegally, before the Indians vacated. Well, half of them cared about the slavery issue, maybe, and were set to drive us away, but the other half just wanted to get some money out of us if there was money to be got."

"You know," said Mrs. Bush, "that's what makes me mad! They shout and rant about our aid company and all the money we've got to finance our malicious invasion of their rightful territory, but they can't get enough of our money themselves. If they don't have their hats off and their hands out, then they've put a gun to your head. It's just like everything else they say—they need to do it, they have a right to do it, and anyway, they're going to do it. Take your money or drive you out or kill you. It's all the same!"

Mr. Johnson smiled again. "We soon showed them we weren't leaving! Well, they sent a war party over. And I can tell you, we weren't especially well armed then. All of them, we thought, had pistols in every pocket and a traveling armory of Kentucky rifles."

"Not to mention," exclaimed Mrs. Bush, "a bowie knife to scalp you with!"

"Well, they came over in a train of wagons and set up on the north side of the ravine there, and you could hear them from everywhere in town, shooting and shouting and cursing and threatening how they were going to 'exterminate all the d—— Yankee abolitionists that dared come into K.T.' We listened to them all day, and then some more came late in the afternoon. Our tents were within range for them. Must have been a hundred or more. Whether they were going to shoot us out of drunkenness or out of intention, it would all amount to the same thing, and I tell you Dr. Robinson was deadly concerned. The carousing went on all evening. We sent over some representatives, to ask the meaning of their display, and they said that we all had to leave or we'd be cleared out and all that. . . . They got quiet about midnight—"

"When the whiskey ran out," asserted Mrs. Bush.

"Then some more showed up about dawn, just screaming and yelling, so then there were about a hundred and fifty. Not long after that, they sent over what they called a formal notification that we were to take down our tents and pack up our things and get out of K.T. for good, and we had till ten a.m. to do it. At ten a.m., they would cross the ravine and do the job. So we drilled with what we had—sixty men or so, and some rifles. Well, ten a.m. came and went, and along about ten-thirty, we had another formal notification that they would give us another half hour and no more to pack up our tents. Of course, this one was more threatening—they would not hold themselves responsible for what might happen should we exhibit further resistance!"

"Pah!" Mrs. Bush almost spit, except that she held spitting in the extremest contempt. "They don't hold themselves responsible for anything; that's the whole trouble with them!"

Mr. Johnson allowed his little smile to grow larger. "You know, that hour went by, and then they formed up in military style and just *stared* at us across the ravine, and then one of them came along and said, 'Ten more minutes, or the direst consequences will follow!' We were laughing! Dr. Robinson was laughing hardest of all, and you bet they could hear us over there, because they were cursing and yelling and shouting oaths, and screaming that we didn't know the danger we were in!" He paused, and now Mrs. Bush smiled, knowing the last of it. "Toward dusk they just loaded up their wagons and moved off. Once night came on, they weren't slow about it, either. You almost had to think that they were a little scared we would chase after them and do a little damage ourselves!" He finished with a shout of laughter, and Mrs. Bush and I joined in, especially Mrs. Bush, but then she got serious and said, "You can't count on them all being cowards. If a party of them gets you alone out somewhere, on the California road or something, well." She shook her head. Yes, the Ruffians had been routed once, but it could go differently the next time. Mr. Johnson and Mrs. Bush fully agreed that there would be a next time. I agreed, too.

For I was all for Lawrence. None of my antecedents had come from New England—New York and New Jersey and I think Pennsylvania, places where life was slacker than it was in New England, were the states they all hailed from, and before that England itself and Halifax. They were not the sort to make a stand but the sort to go along. My sister Miriam had been considered very strange, and offensive, too, for purporting to live by her conscience. She stood accused of putting herself above the rest of us, adopting moral airs, even though she didn't press any of my sisters on the subject and never even spoke of it unless she was asked. Merely doing what she did was flaunting enough for Harriet, Beatrice, and Alice, not to mention their husbands. I had often heard Harriet exclaim, "I don't know why she brings these *ideas* into the family! You sit down to supper, and there's *ideas* there; and then you get up in the morning and make the tea, and there's *ideas* again. It makes you feel all outside of yourself, looking out the door of your own house, that you look out of a hundred times a day, but there's *ideas* making it look all different. There's no comfort in it, I'll tell you that!" All the sisters agreed. What they disagreed about was whether she did it on purpose to annoy them, or whether she had simply been strange since childhood. Another thing all the sisters and all their husbands agreed upon was that even though Miriam might have considered herself better than the rest of them, this certainly wasn't so. I had always liked Miriam the best, but not because of her *ideas*. I had always thought her livelier and sharper. And to tell the truth, she had always liked me. That was enough.

Alice would have the last word: "Miriam is an uncomfortable woman and was an uncomfortable little girl, and that's just what she likes, taking your own hearth and home, that you've worked hard for, and making it just as uncomfortable for you as she can."

Following Miriam's yearly visits to Quincy, a feature of every June, such conversations would go on for days. Then all of the sisters found a way to end the yearly visits. "She only does it out of obligation to Father," said Alice. "But Father doesn't know her anymore, so . . ."

"So she might easily save herself the expense."

"Each year, one of us should go visit her, instead. We can easily afford it. We can be better sisters and better friends one at a time, anyway," said Beatrice, but although Miriam stopped coming, no one ever went to Yellow Springs to visit her. I suppose that her visits stopped when I was about twelve, and so when she died, I hadn't seen her for eight years. I have to say of my sisters that they were sorry enough when they heard of her death. After that, all the discussion was pitying rather than vexed: if only poor Miriam had been prettier, she wouldn't have wasted herself on such muddleheaded ideas but would have gotten a husband and some children to occupy her.

These thoughts reminded me to write my sisters.

September 11, 1855

Dear Sisters:

I am writing to let you know that Mr. Newton and I arrived safely in Lawrence, Kansas Territory, about five nights ago, after eight days traveling. We are now staying at the home of some friends of Mr. Newton's from New England

There was nothing I could tell my sisters about the architecture of the leaning house that would not excite and appall them, so I paused, then passed over that subject.

named Jenkins. His name is Mr. John Jenkins, Vermont Street, Lawrence, K.T., and you may send me letters in his care for now. Mr. Newton and the other men in the company (well, not all of them, for there are some I haven't met) are out at our claim putting up a cabin for the winter. I am in town, making purchases of provisions. I have bought two chairs, two pans, two buckets, some forks and spoons and tin plates, and additionally a stove and a horse. The stove is of the newest type. I will say that although not everything to be had in Quincy is to be had in K.T., what is here from the States is all of the newest sort, though sometimes a little worse for wear from the travel, and always, always very expensive. Horace would be amazed at what he could ask in price for the simplest piece of merchandise if he had a store in Lawrence. You may tell brother Roland that I have bought myself a horse that he would be proud of, who is "as smart as I am and twice as useful," as he used to say about Dolly. The weather is hot, and everything is fine. We made the trip in excellent health, though there were many, even most, who were not so lucky. The saddest story I have heard is about a man who came out here with his wife and five-month-old baby, whose wagon broke down and whose baby died, and he had to carry the baby on foot to three Missouri towns, wrapped in a shawl, before he could find a coffinmaker to make a baby coffin, or a preacher to say a service. The wife didn't see the husband for three weeks after the baby died, and stayed with strangers, waiting for him to return and grieving for her child. This happened to a woman who has been pointed out to me in the street. Of course, one wishes to say a word of comfort, but then that would reveal that she is the subject of gossip; even though it is gossip of the most sympathetic variety, it would be painful. I've heard many sad stories that people in the States simply would not believe. Everyone in Lawrence has a story.

But everyone in Lawrence is full of energy and enterprise, and I like it here very much. Soon I shall be writing you from our very own claim, on the river. Mr. Newton's friends speak very highly of it.

Your affectionate sister,
LYDIA

Postscript: Please give my best to Frank, and say that I wish he were here with me to stroll down the streets of Lawrence and marvel at the sights.

And I did wish that, I really did.

After writing my letter, I rode Jeremiah through the streets of Lawrence and then up to the top of Mount Oread. The vista over the prairies from there was large and delightful. From a distance, I saw the much-discussed Mrs. Robinson. Many people said that for sheer singleness of purpose, Mrs. Robinson had her husband all beat. Later, both he and she became famous—he for being the governor of Kansas, and she for her writings. Although we didn't speak, Mrs. Robinson gave me a friendly smile, and I watched her after she walked on. This encounter stuck in my mind, I must say, because very shortly—

by the time I had gotten back to the corral and the leaning house—my confident notions about my health in Kansas became false. As I walked toward the tall, triangular end where the doorcloth hung, the whole thing seemed to swell to vastness, then shrink to glittering smallness. When I pulled aside the door-cloth, the interior seemed pitch black. I could see nothing, and I felt a vapor of perspiration start from every part of my body at once. Then I fell down.

Many settlers in Kansas fell into such fevers and, if they returned to themselves ever again, did not do so for many weeks. My fancy, however, throughout my fever, was that Mrs. Robinson was walking toward me, and that it was she who was the doctor, not her husband. It was my fixed belief that when she got to me, she would say something, and I would be cured of my fever. She came closer and closer, always with that friendly, self-assured smile, the "Kansas smile," I called it in my dream. And then she did approach the bed, and then she did speak, though I couldn't decipher the words, and then I woke up, feeling weak but lucid. The woman beside the bed was Mrs. Jenkins, holding a basin of broth and a spoon. I said, "What did you say?" and she said, "Mr. Newton should be back today," and by that I knew that I had been in my fever for only two days. There was much speculation as to what it might be— typhoid? bilious fever? a case of the ague? Mrs. Jenkins said, "Well, my dear, it's passed off so quickly that we didn't have a good chance to look at it."

I was a real pioneer now, for in those days it

seemed that everyone was sick with the fever or the ague more often than not. Susannah Jenkins could have stood for a portrait of the typical settler of Kansas Territory. Her face was pale and sallow-looking from the ague, even though her shaking days were only one in three and she wasn't as bad as some on those days. People said it was the land itself—it was so rich that when a man first plowed it up, it sent off a miasma that made everyone ill. Sickness was just the price settlers had to pay for the good things that would come later. There was much nursing back and forth. Every woman got plenty of practice nursing strange men who were sometimes so sick that they couldn't say who they were or who their friends and relatives were. All of the women I knew had cared for at least one man who died unknown and whose fate friends back in the States would forever wonder about. Some of these men were boys, really, younger than I was by three or four years. Mrs. Bush, who was a great believer in Spiritualism, always tried to persuade us that they would come to their mothers somehow, but even so, it was wrenching to see them dying, to hear them cry out, and, worst of all, to be thanked and loved and called "Mama," when those who really loved them were a thousand miles away. Mrs. Bush said that surely the Missouri-ans had no hearts at all if they could look on such suffering, "the true face of Death," and then go to lynching, shooting, hanging, scalping, and clearing out. "There's enough suffering in this country already," she exclaimed, "and they want to make more!" I told her I thought it was deplorable. We were getting to be good friends.

I was still weak from my fever when Thomas returned. That, I think, is why I didn't actually recognize him at first. Also, he was wearing K.T. clothes now—blue trousers, a blue shirt, a red neckerchief, and a large-brimmed soft hat. I, of course, looked different, too, no longer quite the tall, strong girl that I had been when he left. I saw that we looked at each other, for just a moment, in the speculative way that strangers do, and that that moment was followed, for each of us, by a moment of shock: *She* my choice? *He* my choice? I realized just then that for all our plans and travels, I had somehow expected Thomas to bring Boston to me, not to lose Boston in the west. I closed my eyes and pretended to sleep for a few moments. When I opened them, he was sitting beside me, his hat off, holding the basin of broth that Mrs. Jenkins insisted was to be the sole element of my convalescent diet. I could smell the fresh corncakes cooking across the room.

Thomas said, "My dear, our cabin is rather humble. There was no window glass to be had, and the floor is only partially planked, but I like the claim, for both convenience and fertility."

I said, "Did they tell you I bought you a horse?"

He nodded. "An extremely fine horse. A horse from Missouri."

I sat up. "Who told you that? I don't know where he's from. The man had a string of horses, all for sale."

"I saw the horse. We may be sure that he's a horse from Missouri and that he's used to elegant work." He looked at me steadily. "But at any rate, he's ours, and we need a horse. Jenkins was generous with his mule when we were building the cabin, but that can't last."

"I should have bought a mule."

Thomas cocked his head, and for the first time I saw that amused look I remembered from before. He said, "Mrs. Newton, you were not moved to buy a mule."

"His name is Jeremiah."

I told him about the stove, the buckets, the forks, the pans, the plates, and the chairs. He told me about the river, the soil, the planking, and the cow a neighbor of ours planned to give him when, one of these days, he gave up and went back to Indiana. At the end of all this discussion, I had taken the broth. A bit later, my husband slipped me a hot corncake.

Later that evening, I listened to them talking about the *Kansas Weekly Tribune*. While I was down, the editor, Mr. Speer, had published a defiance of the gag laws, on page three, all in large black type, with words like "Now we DO ASSERT and we declare that PERSONS HAVE NOT THE RIGHT TO HOLD SLAVES IN THIS TERRITORY," and coming out for freedom of speech and freedom of the press. Everyone in the room, all our friends, were warm in their praise of Mr. Speer, and all had bought copies, for keeping and using to paper the walls of our dwellings.

My fever meant that we put off our departure from the Jenkinses' house for two extra days. On the second night, another family from the east—a man named Holmes, his wife, who was Mrs. Jenkins's cousin, and their small children—came to stay with us. We now had a crowd of fifteen or more, but that was K.T. for you, as Mrs. Bush would say. In the emigrating season—that is, spring and early summer—you might find fifty in one house.

The great topic of conversation was that just the night before, the new governor of the territory, Shannon, the very man who had been feted and celebrated by the Missourians in Westport around the time of our arrival in K.T., had passed through Lawrence and gone on, after only just looking in at the Cincinnati House, where the contagion had passed. Two or three citizens went to him and urged him to stay for the night and meet some of the people of Lawrence, but he had declined them in no uncertain terms, for the sake of traveling convenience! He elected to spend the night in Franklin or thereabout, rather than in the largest town, the only real town, in K.T. Everyone said that he had no time for Lawrence but that he proposed to spend his Sunday, the next day, with a slave-holder who lived at the Shawnee mission school.

The indignation of our friends knew no bounds. Shannon's sentiments were clear and his want of manly qualities, according to the few who had caught sight of him, evident in his person. "Shambling Shannon" was what Mr. Bush named him. He was a tall, rough, undistinguished man, red-faced, red-nosed, clearly a man both sound on the goose question and equally sound on the highly rectified whiskey question. Mr. Bush and Mr. Jenkins were

horrified but not surprised, for it was their firm belief
that the stealing of the Kansas elections by the slave
power in Missouri and everything that had happened
since, including the departure of Governor Reeder,
who had been inclined toward the Free Staters,
expressed a policy that had been colluded in, and
even devised by, the Pierce administration, which
was, Mr. Bush said, in the thrall of Jefferson Davis
and all the rest of them. No one knew what hold these
southern men had over the President and his advis-
ers, but, said Mr. Bush, whatever it was, it was a
powerful one. "The lawlessness," declared Mr. Jenkins on our last evening in the leaning house, "runs
right to the top."

Mr. Holmes, fresh from Boston and the same age
as myself, though with two children already, said the
same conviction was rampant in New England.
"Every man of sense says so. They made up their
grand plan in '48, when they couldn't get Texas in as
six states but only one."

Mr. Bush responded, "First there was the Fugitive Slave Act, then they repealed the Missouri Compromise. Then they stole the elections here, made up
a government as quickly as they could, and recognized themselves. Here we are. Our sentiments are
against the law now, and our officials are preparing
to subdue us. We may wonder if Shambling Shannon
ignored us out of enmity or shame or policy, but it all
amounts to the same thing. It doesn't take a genius to
know what they're doing."

"And there're more of them than us in every
office in Washington, D.C.," said Thomas.

There was a long pause while everyone considered this.

"We'll have our own territorial government in a day or two," said Mr. Bisket, who planned to attend the convention in Topeka that was to take place three days later.

"Evil people must spread their evil everywhere," said Mrs. Holmes, who was considerably older than her husband. "Scripture is absolutely clear on that. That *is* the nature of Satan. I've seen it already, and I've been in the west only a few days. Evil is all around us."

Mr. Jenkins said, "All I say is that it's a plan concocted by men. I won't say what motivates them to do it. Pure greed, most likely."

Susannah Jenkins looked at me and lifted her eyebrows slightly. I knew she was thinking of Mr. Stringfellow's remarks about the real purpose of slavery, but I ventured to say, "My brother-in-law Roland back in Quincy always says, 'No man's going to roll over on his back and let eight hundred dollars' worth of property walk off, or eight thousand, or eighty thousand.' "

Mrs. Holmes glared at me. "They have trafficked in human souls!"

I said, "Well, he said it, only. He didn't own any slaves himself." I defended him, but really, to these citizens of Lawrence, Roland Brereton looked, walked, and talked just like the Missourians. I knew he was a kindly man himself, covering generosity with bluster, but nevertheless, two things happened at one time—I defended him in front of the Holmeses, but I felt my affection for him shrink and harden.

Thomas cleared his throat. "My wife's brother-in-law is a down-to-earth and practical man." He made this remark without giving away his own sentiments. At least to me. Mrs. Holmes sniffed.

I felt that the Holmeses brought tension into what had previously been a congenial and welcoming group. When Mrs. Holmes then turned away from me, I sensed that I had been found morally wanting. I felt torn between trying to please her with some conciliatory remark and trying to return the insult. Mrs. Jenkins served tea, and Mr. Jenkins returned to his favorite theme of the slave power's step-by-step plan for making slavery legal everywhere in the United States, but our pleasant group felt chilled and uncongenial, and when Thomas and Mr. Bisket and I left in the morning, Jeremiah and Mr. Bisket's horse together pulling Mr. Bisket's wagon, I was happy enough to go.

Mr. Bisket was to spend the night with us on our new homestead, then ride his horse to Topeka, returning after the convention to work around his own claim, which was about half a mile from ours. As he was to be riding his horse, I didn't understand how he would be able to take along the box of "harness" that I saw had been loaded into the wagon. When Thomas went with me to get water for the horses, I said, "We're not leaving all of the 'harness' in Lawrence, then? I thought they were divided up."

He shook his head, and I waited for more, but nothing was forthcoming. My husband's intentions continued to be a mystery to me that I dared not plumb. I would have said then that I loved him as a wife should do, that he was kind to me, and that I felt no desire to be secretive myself. Indeed, whenever I felt that I was revealing something about myself to him that others, for example my sisters, might have disapproved of, it was clear to me that he did not disapprove at all but was, in fact, approving, pleased, and even amused. But he afforded me no answering self-revelation. In Illinois, this had seemed to be simply his nature—not secretive but laconic. In K.T., it seemed to be his design—not merely laconic but conspiratorial. I estimated that of the twelve Sharps rifles, we still had six with us.

CHAPTER 9

I Begin Life on Our Claim

Unless a parlor is in constant use, it is best to sweep it only once a week, and at other times use a whisk-broom and dust-pan. When a parlor with handsome furniture is to be swept, cover the sofas, centre table, piano, books, and mantelpiece, with old cottons, kept for the purpose. Remove the rugs, and shake them, and clean the jambs, hearth, and fire-furniture. Then sweep the room, moving every article. Dust the furniture, with a dust-brush and a piece of old silk. A painter's brush should be kept, to remove dust from ledges and crevices. The dust-cloths should be often shaken and washed, or else they will soil the walls and furniture when they are used. Dust ornaments, and fine books, with feather brushes, kept for the purpose.

—p. 306

WHAT NEEDS TO BE SAID about our cabin? Thomas and his friends were neither builders nor joiners. It was a western cabin, neither so primitive as some nor so comfortable as others, twelve by twelve, built of green logs, chinked with twigs and mud that it would be my job to maintain, no window glass yet, not much floor, but a good chimney, a large hearth, an actual door in the doorway. The roof was not quite finished—the ridgepoles were laid and about a third of the shakes were laid across it. Over the rest was, Thomas explained to me, a sail, or rather, a large piece of sailcloth from Thomas's father's factory in Massachusetts. As we approached from the south, we saw the sail roof shining like a white pearl on the sunlit prairie. And inside the cabin, the sun through the sail lit everything up.

Since we had left the Jenkinses' house before dawn, we arrived at our claim well before noon. After unloading the wagon, Thomas and Mr. Bisket set about splitting shakes for the roof. Mr. Bisket said that we couldn't count on this weather for long, as weather in Kansas was both changeable and dramatic. The sail would have to be replaced as soon as possible. One of my best memories of K.T. is of those few early days in our cabin, with the high prairie sun shining through the white sail roof as I arranged our belongings and set up our household.

The two men split shakes until deep twilight. The plan was that Thomas would climb upon the roof the next day and begin setting them between the ridgepoles and the weight poles that were presently holding the sailcloth in place. I spent the afternoon getting water from the river, which was low and sluggish but not actually green as yet, and fetching firewood from Mr. Jenkins's woodlot, which was about a quarter mile distant. I used Mr. Bisket's wagon for this, hitching up Jeremiah by himself and then walking alongside him so that he wouldn't have to pull my weight in addition to the weight of the wagon and the firewood. I stopped frequently to sit down or to at least lean my head against Jeremiah's neck . . . I was still weak from my fever, but of course, illness was the normal condition of many people in K.T., and those who had lived there four or six months were strong on the theme that weaklings may complain that they have no silver forks or silken coverlets, but real settlers "make do, do without, and do it anyway."

For supper, we ate a pile of cold corncakes that Mrs. Bush had sent along with us, some cold bacon, and apples and peaches from Stearns's store that Mrs. Jenkins had purchased as a special gift for us. We also had tea, which was well boiled over the first fire I built in our new hearth, and the flavor of the tea nearly masked the flavor of the river water. We were too tired to talk, and as Mr. Bisket would be leaving before dawn, we lay down early on the blankets and quilts we had spread over the floor. Mr. Bisket offered to sleep outside in his wagon, as it was a clear night, but Thomas wouldn't hear of such a thing. The two men fell asleep at once—I could hear them snoring. Above me, the white sail was blue with moonlight and rippling and snapping in the perennial Kansas breeze, as a sail should do. Our cabin smelled new, both woodsy and earthy. There were plenty of chinks where the mud and twigs had fallen away, and the moonlight was visible between the logs, but on a mild night like this one, such a thing was more pleasant than not. Here I was, weak and possibly a little feverish from the day's work, lying on a rough floor, my quilt wrapped tightly about me to fend off the mice and other vermin that would be abroad as soon as I fell asleep. And my enemies were out there, men who would like to "clear out" my cabin and its Massachusetts sail. Had my sisters known that this would be my destination when they sent me off, they might have had a second thought or two (maybe not). But as I fell asleep, I thought that my home was good enough for me.

We now entered upon a period of relative solitude, the first of our month-old marriage. I say relative, because there was no real solitude in K.T. So many families were coming into the territory, or leaving, or setting up house, or building, or doing business, or trying to make a small trade or a large one, or developing a claim, or challenging a claim, or, for that matter, making and breaking political alliances, that someone was at your door every day, or even spending the night. Even so, we ate many meals by ourselves and spent many nights alone. There was, of course, no planting to be done so late in the season, but once we had completed the roof, then Thomas commenced splitting rails for a fence and building Jeremiah a pen. The cow, if it came, would graze the prairie at will, and one of my jobs would be to pen her in with Jeremiah at night and let her out in the morning. After that, we began digging a well. In all of these endeavors, once I had more or less recovered from my fever, I worked as well as my husband. The other thing I did was to hunt game with one of the Sharps carbines from the box in the cabin. It was a breech loader—I had always used an old muzzle loader of Roland's. I have to say that there was nothing in Miss Beecher about hunting game over the prairie. Nor had I ever shot anything myself except a jar or a large vegetable propped on the fence behind Roland Brereton's cow pasture. And the Sharps carbine was rather different from my brother-in-law's long hunting rifles. It was soon apparent to me, for example, that the rapid-loading feature of the rifle had no use in bird hunting—one shot had to kill the feathered creature, or it was gone. A slower or more numerous quarry was what the Sharps carbine was intended for. But I got a few turkeys. What I would do was scout about during the day, looking for the spots in the trees where the turkeys were roosting, then I would come back at night, if there was a little moonlight, and find the turkeys and shoot one. Prairie chickens, which were hard to shoot and easy to snare, formed the main meat in our diet. We soon learned from our neighbors to eat the legs and wings and dry the breasts for winter. I would say to my own credit that we ate meat almost every day, and to the credit of Miss Beecher that it was cooked in a palatable fashion most of the time. Of course there were corncakes and mush and corn pudding and corn on the cob and then more mush and corncakes and corn pudding and corn on the cob. But I also found walnuts in Mr. Jenkins's woodlot, and hickory nuts and hazelnuts, along with some sour grapes and wild plums. A man on his way west paid for a night with us with two pumpkins. We dried the flesh and saved the seeds.

We chopped wood "just to be safe," though we were confident the winter ahead would be mild and sunny, with only enough snow for a picturesque effect.

We built ourselves a bed, strung with ropes. Once the roof was up and the sail came down, I used part of it to make a bed tick stuffed with prairie grass that I gathered. I stuffed pillows with the feathers of the birds I killed and plucked. I wouldn't say that any of these efforts were easy for a woman of my limited skills, but throughout the end of September and into October, the one thing that we seemed to have a supply of was time. There were no errands, no engagements. Our tasks were right at hand, and we did them. Many times it seemed that just when I was perplexed about how to do something, a knock would come, and someone making his way over the prairie, or eager to talk or trade, would be standing there, and that person would know just what to do to spit a chicken or keep off the ants or preserve wild plums or paste newspapers over the walls. And of course, Miss Beecher's book was always at my elbow. Thomas knew someone who knew a cousin of the Beechers. We marveled at the coincidence. I congratulated myself on my choice of a husband.

The only other male I had been alone with for any time at all in the course of my life was my cousin Frank, who was twelve years old and whom I had known since his babyhood. Once in a while, my father or one of my sisters' husbands and I found ourselves in a room together for a few moments, but in general, in Quincy and, as far as I knew, everywhere else in the world, men and women avoided one another's company except in groups. It was thus a novelty and a surprising pleasure to find myself alone with Thomas morning, noon, and night. I could not help covertly watching him, trying to discover his ways and attitudes. I drew a few conclusions. One was that he was not like most men I knew—he never put his feet up or tipped backwards in his chair.

He neither wore his hat in the house nor threw it down when he came in, but always hung it neatly beside the door; nor did he smoke or chew tobacco and expectorate. He enjoyed reading. When I asked to look at his books, I saw volumes by Charles Dickens and William Thackeray and Anthony Trollope, as well as new books he'd brought from the east—a book by Mr. Thoreau, a book called *Ten Nights in a Barroom and What I Saw There,* Mrs. Stowe's book (which many people owned and I had read parts of), and a poem by Mr. Longfellow called "The Song of Hiawatha." Some evenings, when no one was visiting, we would read parts of these and other books aloud. Thomas had a flat New England voice. I never read any of those authors later without hearing his voice in the telling of the story. Something I at first found disconcerting in Thomas was that he never offered an opinion until asked, and then his opinion flowed forth quickly and fluently, as if, I thought, he had been waiting for me to ask and that I had even been tardy in my asking. This sense that a life was being lived in my presence that was partly, or largely, unrevealed to me seemed eerie—the very hallmark of marriage. My sisters seemed to have learned to live with this other life by either ignoring it or dismissing it, which I attributed to their common lack of imagination. My aim was different—not a place to live with some children and a man you ignored as much as you could, but some sort of apprehension of him, out of which the other things would grow. That was what I called love. The mysteries of Thomas, who was awkward with tools but strong and persistent, who seemed never out of temper, who was less at ease with a rifle than I was and yet had brought along a large case of them, seemed like a treasure that it was my God-given task to explore. I watched for signs and clues. I wasn't sure what my reward would be, but I was sure that it would be a delightful one.

Of course, we were eager to hear the news when Mr. Bisket returned from the Topeka convention, where the Free Staters were to frame a proper constitution that would stand as a model against the "abomination," as Mrs. Bush and Mrs. Jenkins had called it, of the proslave constitution. Much of interest had occurred, and one thing in particular that interested Thomas very much. I began to notice the name of a man called James, or Jim, Lane. Folks in Lawrence had talked about him, though not in the same way that they talked about Dr. Robinson, with respect and care. Mr. Lane later became a power in Kansas and, it was said, in the United States, for he was, or reported himself to be, a great friend of Mr. Lincoln. At any rate, people always talked about Jim Lane in the same way, from beginning to end: with some approval, some deploring, plenty of amazement, and a good deal of fascination. The fact was that he was born to be famous and was eager to assume his birthright. I had heard Mrs. Bush mention him in Lawrence. She didn't like him and said that he had only gone Free State because he saw that that was where the future of Kansas was.

"But he saw that when few others did," said Mr. Jenkins. "Either it speaks well of him that he had the perspicacity, or it speaks well of us that we look like the coming party."

"Well," Mrs. Bush had said, "I won't speak well of him no matter what."

This Mr. Lane figured in two interesting incidents at the Topeka convention. One was that he offered to fight a duel with Mr. Lowry when Mr. Lowry told some gossip about Mr. Lane and Mrs. Lindsay that had been going all around town already, anyway. The other was that Mr. Lane pressed and finally won the inclusion of a Black Law in the convention, for the purpose of excluding all Negroes, free or slave, from Kansas.

Thomas was astonished, but Mr. Bisket was not. He said, "You know, Tom, most folks think that if you look at it one way, well, they bring all sorts of problems with them, even when they don't mean to. The problems just flock along after them, like Missourians. And then, well, a lot of folks were making one pretty good argument, I thought, and that was that you can't make a party of abolitionists. Most people in the United States, at least outside of Massachusetts and New York, they hate abolitionists. You see, they can't call us abolitionists now, can they? Everybody was for it, for just that reason. Whatever we may think ourselves, we got to appeal to ones who don't care all that much about slaves and slavery."

I thought this was a good, or at least a practical, argument myself. I said, "And who's to keep them out? There are all kinds of laws in Illinois that try to do this and that, amounting to the same thing. But no one enforces them. They just reassure people that they aren't turning into New Englanders." I gave Thomas a sidelong glance and a smile. He smiled back at me, getting the joke in spite of himself.

"Anyway, Tom, when you hear Lane speak, he'll draw you in just the same as everybody. Jenkins said he talked like the very devil, and it's true, he does. Folks just stand there with their mouths hanging open."

Thomas didn't smile at this, though, nor was he very friendly to Mr. Bisket for the rest of the evening, which meant, in consequence, that Mr. Bisket followed him around, trying to get him to laugh at his sketches of the men he met in Topeka, but finally he fell back on saying, "Well, you should have been there. I wanted you to go. There weren't enough there who spoke out against this Black Law. You haven't seen Jim Lane go like we did. When he goes, he goes like thunder." Finally, Mr. Bisket offered to sleep in his wagon, and Thomas, this time, didn't stop him.

I realized when we lay down for our rest that he wasn't extremely pleased with me, either, though he was, as always, kind and courteous. He said, mildly, "Mrs. Newton, you always speak up for these western men who have no principles."

"You mistake them if you think they have *no* principles—"

"Principles that are cruel and evil, then, and against Christian charity as well as righteousness."

"You sound like Mrs. Holmes seeing the work of Satan all around her."

We settled into our bed tick and pulled up the quilts, for though the days were still warm, the nights were getting cooler. He said, soberly, "I try not to see it that way, but I'm tempted. In what way is the system of slavery not evil incarnate? In what way do the slaveholders not argue like Satan himself, talking themselves and others into seeing good where none exists? They've been lying about it for so long that they believe their own lies."

"But it's their concern. Slavery is their institution and—"

"In Kansas, it's *our* concern. And anyway, I knew free Negroes in Boston and Medford and on the ship. They were not men that deserved to be excluded."

"People like to be with their own kind. It's more comfortable that way for everyone."

"There's nowhere I've ever been where people may be with their own kind exclusively. And should I consider the Missourians to be my own kind? In what sense? A moral sense? A religious sense? Do they have the same habits as I do? Do they feel a regard for me? Or I for them?"

"Mr. Graves wasn't so bad."

"Mr. Graves was willing enough to do a job for us, and entertaining in his way, but he himself said that when the fighting comes, he intends to stand back and watch. We may count on our friends only." He paused and glanced toward the door, then said, bitterly for him, "Some more than others, it appears."

My husband nestled down into the bed and pulled the quilts up to his face, as we always did.

Even though our bed was on legs and off the ground, there was no telling about the vermin who would come in as soon as we slept.

But I did not want to let the subject drop. I sat up. "Are you saying that we must associate only with those who think like us in every particular? I don't know if the Black Law is good in itself or bad. I haven't thought about it. But perhaps it's a wise step for the very reason Mr. Bisket stated."

"So that the other side won't call us black abolitionists? I *am* an abolitionist. I don't mind being called what I am and am proud to be."

"Husband, you are in the west now, not in Boston. Don't you realize that westerners hate abolitionists? Abolitionists are people who . . . who . . . who keep turning over rocks and making everyone else look at what's under there or, worse, smell it and touch it. Abolitionists won't let anyone alone. Westerners hate that."

"Men and women and children are being sold for profit. They are being beaten and killed, wrenched from their families. Women are being used for breeding, like horses, and their babies are sold away from them. Children are being raised with no sense of God or of their own humanity. People are being treated like animals every day. Every hour of every day!"

"Since I know you've never been in the south, I know that you are getting most of your information from books, and I saw Mrs. Stowe's book in your case."

"Is the book wrong?"

"Surely not entirely wrong, but it's a story—"

"If you doubt these things, then, my dear, I am surprised at your ignorance."

He said this mildly, signaling, I knew at once, that we had arrived at a significant moment in our young marriage, and perhaps in his estimation of me. I had been speaking with fervor but, let's say, also with good humor, as if all the ground we were on was safe, solid, and well explored. It was not. I knew at once that all his kindness to me, and care of me, and interest in me, which I had come so quickly to rely upon and enjoy, would shift—not in quantity, because he was a kind man, but in quality, because he would see me in a new way and be disappointed. There was a proper answer here, and I had to give it. That I was glad to give it, I immediately realized, told me that I did love my husband, though I hardly knew him. I said, "I don't doubt them. But I've never seen them."

He nodded his head slightly, acknowledging my reply.

"You should have asked my sisters. They would have told you I am disputatious."

"Disputatiousness, even in a woman, even in a wife, is not so unpleasing to me at all. Besides, every woman in Kansas is disputatious."

"Then I will continue and say what I detest about those Missourians is what they say of us, how they would restrict and injure us. What they do among themselves doesn't . . . doesn't inflame me in the same way."

We were silent for a few moments. I could tell that he was ready to distinguish between me and Mr. Bisket. I got down into the quilts and laid my head upon his shoulder. Soon after that, I understood that we had agreed to disagree.

CHAPTER 10

I Broaden My Acquaintance

Another branch of good-manners, relates to the duties of hospitality. Politeness requires us to welcome visiters with cordiality; to offer them the best accommodations; to address conversation to them; and to express, by tone and manner, kindness and respect. Offering the hand to all visiters, at one's own house, is a courteous and hospitable custom; and a cordial shake of the hand, when friends meet, would abate much of the coldness of manner ascribed to Americans.

—p. 144

AFTER THE TOPEKA CONVENTION, our area began to fill up, mostly with folks we knew, or Thomas knew, from back in New England. Many of them, like the Jenkinses and the Bushes, had town lots with some sort of building upon them. Others were in a situation similar to ours—they needed to put up shelter either in town or on their claims before winter. We were one of the few claimers who had built so substantial a cabin; most of our party had been both busy and divided about what to do and where to live, so many of them had simply driven a stake in the middle of what they judged to be a hundred and sixty acres. Since we were all friends, the plan was to adjust things in the spring, at the commencement of planting. Should there be planting. It seemed to me that most of the New Englanders, who had come out to K.T. from towns, weren't all that eager to get into the country and take up the farming life. Should some mercantile or speculative venture over the winter preserve them from the necessity, I thought most would be relieved.

Nevertheless, what happened was quite a shock. Mr. Jenkins's lost claim had been a nice one, along the river. The winner of the dispute was a man of no party except, perhaps, the party of pure self-interest, from Ohio. This man, Mr. James, mostly went his own way, except, of course, he did not want overt conflict with his neighbors, and so we got to know him a bit, and also his wife and child, who was a boy of some four years old. There was no doubt that Mr. James was a hard man and that his wife and child were not built for the country. She was down with the shakes for much of the fall, and the boy was quiet and subdued, seemingly already concerned that he was a disappointment to his father. Mr. James was a very handsome man, with long curling mustaches and thick golden hair, and the wife, whose name was Ivy, looked as though she had been a beauty. I am sure they went to the altar much celebrated and envied. I began to visit Mrs. James every few days, taking along some game each time I went, or wild plums, or honey. Whenever our friends came out from town, they brought us some delicacy or other, because they all liked Thomas so well. Mr. James was such a hard man that most folks bypassed their cabin altogether. Sometimes Mrs. James was strong enough to come to me and drink some tea.

The track between our cabin and the James cabin meandered through the woodlot and along the river flat. One day, after she had sat down and received her cup of tea, and little Eddie, as well, was seen to, Ivy said, "I see Mr. Jenkins is putting up his cabin at last."

"If so, then I'm hurt that he hasn't come by, because I would like to repay him some of the hospitality the Jenkinses showed us in Lawrence."

"It's at least sixteen by sixteen. And I saw a window propped up against a tree. I suppose they're going to have a glass window."

"Well, their house in town is only a lean-to built of hay. I'm surprised they have the money for something like a window."

Mr. Jenkins's new claim, a piece all the members of our party had contributed to, was almost in the middle of the group of claims, and also a piece that all of us knew the location of, including Mrs. James, who was somewhat abashed that her husband had already, or perhaps once again, caused conflict in the community. She wanted only to have friends in a place where he wanted only that others not underestimate him.

Two days later, I saw the cabin myself, and I also saw that none of those working on it was familiar to me. They were working fast, and the window, indeed a glass one, was already set in place. I was hunting, and soon got onto the track of a turkey, and so forgot the cabin until that evening, when Mr. Bush, Mr. Jenkins, and Mr. Bisket came knocking at the door and declared, as soon as they got inside and took off their hats, that some Border Ruffians had jumped the

Jenkins claim and were raising a building on it, and furthermore swore that they had three hundred and twenty acres, twice the customary and legal number. Such a large acreage swallowed up everything of the Jenkinses' and something of everyone else's as well.

"They had a Negro woman there working," said Mr. Bisket. "I saw her."

"You didn't see anything of the kind," said Mr. Jenkins. "But they're Missourians for sure."

"At all events," said Mr. Bush, "they aren't anyone with our company or anyone we know. It doesn't matter whether they've got ten slaves there or whether they've got ten Congregational ministers. They took Jenkins's claim and some of mine, and some of yours, too, Newton, that bit of a corner there between those two big oaks we marked. I won't stand for it."

"We've got to make up a party and go over there and see how far the building has gone, and we've got to do it first thing tomorrow, before they start moving women and children in," said Mr. Jenkins resolutely.

"The only woman I saw was that Negro woman," said Mr. Bisket.

Mr. Jenkins dismissed him with a wave of the hand.

Thomas said, "Has anyone been over to see them yet?"

Mr. Jenkins shook his head. "We looked on from the woodlot. I counted five men and a half-grown boy. If there's going to be an argument, I want to have at least that many men." He paused and looked at his feet for a second. "Though I'll say this: I don't think we should go armed for the first talk, or at least well armed. It might be just a misunderstanding."

"A twenty-by-twenty-foot cabin changes whatever was a misunderstanding into something else, in my opinion," said Mr. Bush, who seemed more exercised by the event than Mr. Jenkins.

"Mrs. James said she thought it was sixteen by sixteen," I put in.

"Now, Daniel James might go in with us," said Mr. Bisket.

"Why would he?" said Mr. Jenkins.

No one could answer this, so they sat for a moment. Mr. Bisket and Mr. Jenkins pulled out their pipes, and Mr. Bush pulled out his chewing tobacco, then looked at me and put it away. The others lit up.

"Holmes. Lacey. The Smithsons. We don't need more than that," said Thomas. "At least for now."

"One step at a time," said Mr. Jenkins, as if the property weren't even his. "Maybe I'm better off in town, anyway."

"Well, I am not going to give away my piece," said Mr. Bush.

"And," declared Thomas, "if they are Missourians bringing slaves, then we don't want them in our midst. I care about that more than the property."

"Then you and I make a good team"—Mr. Bush laughed —"because when it comes right down to it, I care about the property. If they are claiming three hundred twenty acres, well . . ." He shook his head in disgust, and everyone else smoked in silence. I served tea that Mrs. Jenkins had sent out to me the previous week, steeped in water from our well. I made it weak, so you could see all the way to the bottoms of the cups.

After everyone had had some tea, Thomas raised the question that interested me. He said, "How could someone start building on your land, Jenkins, and you don't know it until the cabin's mostly done?"

Mr. Jenkins shrugged. "I've been in town. Fact is, I lost that other claim and all those improvements, and it took the stuffing right out of me. I don't have the fire right now to be a farmer. I thought I would plant a crop in the spring and see how it came up, then make up my mind."

"His land, our land, it doesn't matter," said Mr. Bush. "Our party's got all this land spoken for, and the fact is, these folks from Missouri could see that plain as day. The stakes are out there. Your cabin and the Jameses' cabin are up, and Bisket's, here, too, and the Holmeses have felled a lot of trees for theirs. This is just Missouri aggression, pure and simple. Pretty soon this'll be a voting precinct, and it'll turn out that all five thousand of us have voted for Stringfellow, you mark my words."

Everyone nodded, including me. This seemed like the truest thing said all evening.

The others soon left, to go about to the cabins of our other friends. None of the women had come out from Lawrence, and Mr. Bush and Mr. Jenkins were staying the night with Mr. Bisket, whose cabin was now entirely enclosed. At dawn, the plan was, the men would get up and gather at Mr. Bisket's claim. When they judged that enough of a party had gathered, they would investigate the newcomers in a body.

I remember getting ready for bed and feeling some surprise that this had come up so suddenly. It didn't speak well of Mr. Jenkins's ability to look after his own interests that total strangers had seized his land and established themselves upon it, and he only noticing when everything was more or less complete. I thought of something brother Roland Brereton had sometimes said about why he wasn't particularly neighborly: "Why should I look after those who can't look after themselves? When the time comes, they'll be too behindhand to look after me." But that was Illinois, and this was Kansas, where, as Thomas and I in our separate ways were both coming to know, you had to choose whom there was to choose. Even so, I went to bed in a stimulated but contented state of mind: we'd had company; something interesting was going on; things would work out well enough in the end. And here was Thomas, too. That made things seem fine enough to me.

Not long after dawn, Thomas rode away on Jeremiah. Not long after that, I got up and began idling about the cabin—smoothing the quilts, driving off the mice and other vermin, sweeping the floors, adding some sticks of wood to the fire we'd kept damped down in the stove all night long. We were well into October, and the nights were, it seemed then, pleasantly cool after the heat of September. The mornings were crisp. I put on an extra shawl and did some chinking of the joints between the logs with a paste of mud, grass, and twigs that I'd mixed together the afternoon before. Then, where the chinking I had done several days earlier had cured, I began carefully to paste up, with flour-and-water paste, leaves of *The Liberator* and some other papers that Thomas had brought with him from the United States. This, he said, would serve the threefold purpose of advertising our views to our visitors, reminding ourselves of the arguments to be made in the cause, and keeping out the wind. Every leaf, according to the new laws of Kansas Territory, was treasonable.

Thomas came trotting into the yard late in the afternoon, and he didn't look happy. I helped him curry Jeremiah and put him in his pen for the night, then we went inside. The fire was still going, so I stoked it up and beat together some corncakes.

"Holmeses are down with the shakes," he said, as we came into the cabin and he hung up his hat. "Mrs. Holmes is shaking every day. Can hardly get up to feed the children in the morning."

"I'll go over there." Neither of us had been eager to improve our acquaintance with the Holmeses, and their claim was far away, though, of course, Jeremiah made any trip short and pleasurable.

"The Smithsons have put up a mile of fence, but they're still drinking out of the river." He took off his heavy jacket and hung it below his hat, then he set his rifle beside the door, and took the ammunition out of his pocket and looked at it for a second, then put it back into his pocket.

I waited. He looked at me. He said, "I'm not proud of what went on this morning."

"No one's been shot, I hope."

"Not yet."

The griddle was hot, and I spooned a bit of grease over it, then some corncake batter. It was lumpy, I knew. I batted at the lumps for a moment. He said, "Well, the fact was, Jenkins was drinking. Bisket said they were up all night after they left here, so there weren't many cool heads when we gathered this morning, and there was some talk about waiting until tomorrow, but Jenkins wanted to do something by then—"

"He'd worked himself up to it."

"Yes, and he wouldn't talk to Daniel James, claimed this was all his fault, and then James got a little threatening, but he knows he can't go it alone, and Jenkins knows that he himself is old and James is young and strong. But all the squabbling didn't cool us off, I must say. And then Bisket fell off his horse. Don't ask me why—he was behind me—but I think he was that drunk, which wouldn't take much, since he never had a drop before coming out to K.T."

We both suddenly smiled, but Thomas sobered in a hurry. "I wish it were funny, but it isn't. Those Missourians were waiting for us. Been waiting for us, if you ask me."

I served up the corncakes with some wild plums I'd cut up in honey.

"They picked up their rifles as soon as they saw us, and carried them out to meet us, then they drew up side by side in a long line. Well, I don't mind telling you they looked like they wanted a fight right there, but I was in the lead, and I kept my head down and just smiled a little like I was making a friendly visit. One man, a short little plug, spoke up and said, 'Lookin' fur me? This is my claim.'

"Bisket piped up from the rear, 'Well, it an't!'

" 'Who says it an't?' This fellow was very belligerent and red in the face. So there was a long silence, and then Jenkins says, 'Well, now, I guess it's me who says it an't; it's not, that is, because you see my stake's in the ground here and this is about the middle of my claim, and we all have land around here—'

" 'You boys git off my land right now, or I'll have ta kill ya.' That's what the little guy said, and lo and behold if the window behind him didn't suddenly explode, and I turned around, and there was the Smithson boy, just grinning. Well, everyone started running around then, and that Negro woman Bisket had seen came running out of the house screaming, and she said that a bullet had gone right past her ear, and of course the Smithson boy wasn't grinning after that! But the Missourians didn't shoot. I thought they would, but they actually fell back a bit, like they were startled. Then the little man started yelling, 'You went and shot my winder! I brought that winder all the way from Lousiana! That winder's been up the Mississippi and up the Missouri, and the d——steamboat exploded and the winder survived, and now you gone and shot it!' And he leveled his gun at the Smithson boy, and then old Smithson kind of interposed his horse between them and pulled out some money and offered to pay for the window, and behind him, you could hear the boy saying, 'I'm sorry! I'm sorry! I didn't mean to shoot it,' but we all knew he did.

"Then Jenkins seemed to feel bolder, and he said, 'This is my claim, and you got to leave. I an't going to have my claim jumped for the second time in a year, and I'm telling you you got to leave!'

"And then we all stood there. Because, you know, nobody was ready to start shooting, not even the Missourians, or Louisianans, or whatever they were. The hard part was to turn tail and leave. We couldn't do it. We just milled around for a bit, and then Bush called out, 'We're not done with this matter!' and we filed off, but then, well, you know how it is—everybody felt a little ashamed, as if we'd been driven off."

Thomas dived into his corncakes, and we were silent for a bit. The door was open for air, since the evening had stayed warm, and I could hear some yipping far out on the prairie. We had had a frost, and the nightly sawing and buzzing of insects had stilled. My senses were not yet attuned to the prairie sounds, so the world seemed largely silent to me, and uninhabited, and, perhaps, desolate. The fact is that in those days, our little cabin floated like a raft in a populous sea. We were certainly observed by Indians, by foxes, by buzzards, hawks, deer, skunks, jackrabbits, badgers, magpies, and meadowlarks. But even in the midst of this story my husband was telling me, I couldn't rid myself of the impression that we were far away from everything and everyone, safe in a wilderness of space and nuptial contentment. I felt calm and only distantly interested in these events. All they did for me was render him all the more mysterious and appealing.

"Before long, of course, everyone began to regret how peaceful we'd been. 'They think they've got it now,' said Bush, and Jenkins got angry. He kept exclaiming, 'I'll not let it happen again! I'm an old man, but I'm still a man for all that!' Then Holmes piped up. 'Satan is working among them! Through them, he comes into our company and begins casting his glance around at us!' I'll say this, that man intones every word as if he's addressing a prayer meeting, and he's hardly more than a boy, to boot."

"What can you do? The house is up. They sound like they've got guns and the will to use them."

"Bush says they'll move off like Missourians always do if you stand up to them." He sounded doubtful.

I said, "But—"

Thomas pushed his plate away and looked at me. "Our party claimed the land, it's true, but Jenkins didn't build anything. The law says you've got to put up a cabin and start living there."

"But—"

"We can't have slaves in our midst, and men who want to kill us and drive us away."

It was a conundrum, the K.T. conundrum, the sort of moral dilemma that men I respected, like

Thomas, had to ponder and work over in their minds. I said, "You better not lose the advantage, if you've still got it."

After that, Thomas lit a candle and read some bits of "The Song of Hiawatha" out to me, and after that we went to our rest.

CHAPTER 11

I Am Surprised and Then Surprised Again

Next to the want of all government, the two most fruitful sources of evil to children, are, unsteadiness in government, and over-government. Most of the cases, in which the children of sensible and conscientious parents turn out badly, result from one or the other of these causes. In cases of unsteady government, either one parent is very strict, severe, and unbending, and the other excessively indulgent, or else the parents are sometimes very strict and decided, and at other times allow disobedience to go unpunished. In such cases, children, never knowing exactly when they can escape with impunity, are constantly tempted to make the trial.

—p. 228

THE NEXT DAY WAS Sunday. For some weeks, all of our party had been planning to meet at the Smithsons' cabin for a service and then, should the weather be favorable, an outdoor supper. Mrs. Bush and Mrs. Jenkins and Susannah had planned to come out from town, and there was some hope among the women that Mrs. Lacey and her three children would have arrived by that time. Otherwise, we all acknowledged, she might as well stay in the east. But when, as we were standing there watching Mr. Bisket's wagon approach us from the south, bumping and humping over the prairie grasses and throwing its passengers into all sorts of wild postures, we saw a strange figure, it was no grown woman with three children. It was rather a very slight man or a boy, alternately leaning over the side so far he was nearly falling out and jumping around like a monkey. From a distance, also, someone could clearly be heard to whoop, probably this small figure, since Mrs. Jenkins and Mrs. Bush were notable for their staid dignity in almost all circumstances. As they came closer, I could make out something like a seegar protruding from the lower parts of the new visitor's face, but that didn't render me any the less astonished when I beheld my nephew Frank leap from the wagon and run toward me a few moments later.

"An't ya surprised to see me, Lidie? An't ya?" Frank was grinning but otherwise suddenly very cool, and instead of throwing his arms around me or allowing me to do the same to him, he stopped suddenly and stuck out his hand, and shook first mine and then Thomas's, and said, "I told Ma you'd about fall down when you saw me, but she thought you'd get her letter before that. But you didn't. Here it is. She should have known not to send me to mail it to you, because I just kept it in my pocket."

He presented me with the letter, folded over and neatly sealed, balanced on the palm of his hand. While I read it, Thomas took him off to meet our new friends. I even astounded myself with the fullness of my pleasure in seeing Frank again. I'd steamed away from my family in something of a cold fever to leave all that behind and try something new, and with the novelty of marriage and new scenes, I hadn't knowingly missed anyone, but I might as well have been pining for Frank day after day, because that was how glad I was to see his sassy face and his jaunty demeanor.

"Dear Lydia," read the letter, only a note, really,

Frank pesters me day and night until I think I am going to scream. All he can talk about is you and going to Kansas. Roland and Horace see no harm in it, though, to tell you the honest truth, I am sure they see no harm in it because they would just as soon be doing it themselves! Roland thinks if the boy is well armed he should have no trouble on the way! I ask you! But I throw up my hands, as a mother's tears are of no avail with any of the three of them. I am sending you this letter to inform you that my Frank will be leaving here on the *Mary Ida* on October one and should come to you a week after that, as the agent of the steamship has assured us that every effort will be made to oversee his passage every mile of the way. If he should not arrive by October ninth at the outside, then you must—oh, my dear, I can't go on with that. I just can't bear to think about it. Mr. Newton and his friends will know what to do should the worst happen, may God preserve my boy. Mr. Brereton maintains that the boy can take care of himself and that it's high time that he put his energies to something useful, and he has no interest in his schooling.

I close with my heart in my mouth.

Your loving sister,
HARRIET

It was now October 16, a week past the outer date of Frank's passage, and though it gave me something of a turn to think of what he had been doing in the previous two weeks, well, here he was, safe, sound, and full of life, and I was sure that he would fill me in on his adventures soon enough.

We had our Sunday service, preached by Mr. Smithson, and then we set our dishes out on a trestle table the Smithsons had put together from boards they had milled in Lawrence, which were meant for their roof later on in the week. All the talk that wasn't of Frank was of Mr. Jenkins's claim.

Mrs. Bush was full of Frank. "My dear Mrs. Newton, I must tell you, I didn't know what to think when I saw this little man come swaggering up Vermont Street, easy as you please, taking bites out of an apple and asking everyone in a loud voice where this 'hay house' of those Bushes and Jenkinses was! And then he tossed the core over his shoulder and pulled out this seegar stub and stuck it between his lips, and then when he got to our place and saw me standing in the doorway, he pushed his hat back on his head and thrust his hands in his pockets and gave me the once-over! I could barely keep myself from laughing! He'd lost his cap in the Missouri River, he said, and bought some old black slouch hat off a man in Missouri for a nickel! Well, he came right up to the door and said, 'You'd be Mrs. Bush, maybe, and I'm looking for my cousin Lydia Harkness, Newton now. She's not expecting me, because I am set on giving her her death of a shock! She here?' And then he swaggered in and looked around. You know, he sold that hat the next day for a quarter, and he had a whole case of junk with him, and he sold all of that, too. I bet he has forty or fifty dollars on him now. I said did he want one of the men to ride him out here day before yesterday, when he just arrived, but he said he'd wait, because he had some business to attend to! How old is that boy?"

"He'll be thirteen in the winter."

"And then when he'd come in and looked all around, he began pulling out knives and guns and piling them on the table! I nearly fainted. He looked at me and said, 'Well, I didn't have any trouble on the road, so I suppose I won't be needing all of these here in K.T.' "

We looked over at him where he was standing with the men, his thumbs hitched into his braces, his left foot resting on his right. Mr. Holmes spoke and then Mr. Jenkins, and the whole time Frank nodded thoughtfully, just as if he were deep in their councils.

I looked wonderingly at my cousin from time to time, when I could do so tactfully, because it was clear that he didn't want me to make much of his sudden appearance. He was in high spirits, but so was everyone else. It was a pleasant day. A ribbon of smoke or two from distant prairie fires drifted on the blue horizon, and nearby the river went its slow and silent way. It was deep enough for a swim, but I was a married woman surrounded by folks from Massachusetts. I didn't even take off my shoes and stockings, though I longed to do so.

We got home late—well after dark, though there was enough of a moon to light our way. There was no bed for Frank, and I was busy laying out some quilts on the portion of the floor that we had finished, when he stopped me. "Lidie, you an't going to make me sleep in this little box with the two of you, are ya?"

"It's twelve by twelve. That's big for K.T. People have ten by ten or—"

"I got my heart set on sleeping outdoors. I tried to tell that to Mrs. Bush, but she wouldn't hear of it, and we was squashed all together. That boy they had there, I don't know his name, one time in the night he rolled over on me and pinned my arms against the floor, and I couldn't move to save my life. That fella had me, and if he hadn't been asleep, I would of given him the Jesse for that, but I didn't want to wake him. Don't make me sleep inside!"

"The nights are getting cold, Frank. Inside, we keep a little fire in the stove—"

"That's worse. I can't sleep when I'm hot."

"I don't know what your mother would—"

"It would be all right with Pa. Pa would be all for it!"

I knew that was true.

"All right."

And that was how Frank began living with us and went on in the same fashion. He was no boy but a self-reliant man. He came and went as he pleased—I stopped even looking out for him or worrying about him. His vocation was finding, or it was trading, or it was both, because he was never so happy as when he had found something and traded it for something else, even if it was only some chokecherries that he traded for some salt or tea.

But I'm getting ahead of my story. On the very next day after the Sunday Frank got there, affairs with the Missourians got a little hot.

About midmorning, Thomas looked up, to see all our friends coming to get him, and when he left, he took his gun as well as his hat. He did not take Jeremiah but got up behind the Smithson boy, who had a big, rawboned mule. That Jeremiah was still grazing peacefully in his pen must have been what set off Frank, because he would not let me be until I agreed that we would follow and see what might happen. I didn't need much persuading, I must say, but it was Frank who suggested that I put on some of Thomas's clothes and pin my hair up under a hat.

We got on bareback, me in front and Frank behind. Jeremiah, who was working every day, now accepted almost anything, since over the weeks he had been hitched to a wagon single and double, had been ridden with saddle and without, single and double, and had had all sorts of things, from newly slaughtered turkeys and strings of prairie chickens to bundles of wood, thrown over his back. He still looked elegant and interested, and I had found out that a more realistic price for a horse of his quality was a hundred dollars or more. Frank had a knife in his boot and was carrying one of our Sharps carbines, which he had seen first thing in the morning and appropriated at once.

We circled around and approached the cabin through the woods, trying to keep as quiet as we could and to reconnoiter before revealing our presence.

The Missourians had been busy in the five days since I'd walked past. The walls were well chinked, and the window was still in place, one pane shattered and blocked off with sheets of oiled paper but the other panes glinting in the sunshine. A door was hung, a real door, too, with a hole where the latch would be installed and where a loop of string now hung. There was a stoop, too, with two steps going up to it. The builders had brought more than the usual knowledge to their building. It was a desirable dwelling, in K.T. terms. They had also split quite a few rails for fence, and these lay in a stack. The men of the place—I counted five, with the boy—stood behind the stack, and each of them held a long rifle of the Missouri or Kentucky sort. All of our men, numbering eight (Mr. Bush and Mr. Jenkins, my husband, Mr. Smithson and the Smithson boy, Mr. Holmes, Mr. James, and Mr. Bisket), faced them, five mounted and three dismounted.

The man who seemed to be the owner of the cabin was short and red-faced, with long dark hair that hung below his shoulders, a full beard going gray, and bushy, almost white eyebrows. He was glaring at our men, who had their backs to Frank and me. I halted Jeremiah and held him quiet, and Frank, eager for a better look, slipped down and edged forward before I could stop him. I didn't dare call out to him—I was even less anxious to attract my husband's attention than that of the strangers. Frank knelt down behind the crotch of a tree. His rifle was well within his reach. As far as I knew, Frank's expertise in shooting was the same as mine—jars and squashes, squirrels, and a variety of feathered quarry—but he cozied up to that tree with his rifle nearby as if he'd been in a lifetime of armed confrontations. The angry man—my enemy, I knew without reflection—was saying, "Well, I an't gonna move. The legalities are on my side. I got a cabin built, I staked my claim. And I an't gonna be bought out, either."

"You've got a slave woman," said Mr. Holmes.

"I do, and I got more comin', so you better git used to it. This is gonna be a slave state, or it an't gonna be a state a-tall. You Yankees are goin' against the law and tryin' to tell us out here what to do with our own belongings, and we an't gonna stand for it. I maybe only have two slaves, but if you tell me I can't have none, then I'll git me two more. You try to tell me what to do and I'll do the opposite just to be ornery, and fight you for the privilege!"

"This is our land!" exclaimed one of what seemed to be the man's sons.

"My friend Jenkins was here first—" began Mr. Bush.

"This whole country!" shouted the young man. "We been lookin' at this whole country for years, watchin' the government hold it for them d—— Indians, and then they open it to us one day and you Yankees come and git it the next."

Another one called out, "We know they pay you a hundred dollars a head to come out here and vote the black abolitionist ticket! Should of stayed in your own d—— part of the country! You never cared about this country till you found out there was gonna be slaves here. What I think is, you don't want this country—you jest don't want us to have it!"

Now Thomas spoke up. "If you live here, you'll be surrounded on every side by people who hold views that are opposed to yours. How can you expect us to be neighborly after you stole our friend's land? And what will it be like for you if you have no neighbors you can befriend?"

"Sir," shouted the old man, "look on these four boys! These are all the friends I need, and they are all the friends they themselves need!" He now fell silent, as if attributing to them the desire for neighborly relations was the reddest insult of all.

"I repeat," said Mr. Bush, "we are willing to buy you out, with as much over as we can afford to repay your labor and your trouble—"

"There are settlements not far from here that you would find more congen—"

The old man shot his rifle into the air. Frank reached around and picked up his. The other horses spooked, but not Jeremiah, and everyone stood absolutely still in anticipation of the shooting to come. The old man said, "We're talkin' too much here. When I say no, it makes me mad to keep talkin'. You men keep talkin', and now I am mad."

There was a long silence. Once again, it appeared, all parties were finally reluctant to level at one another the weapons they all had with them. The leaves on the trees, which were still green but had begun to dry, rattled suggestively in the breeze. Finally Mr. Jenkins said, bravely, I thought, "Well, we aren't finished talking. I've got more to say, but perhaps it is best said another day."

I was being quiet, but I was not being quiet enough, because the next moment, two of the Missourians looked in our direction, and then our men turned around to look, too. Not wishing to seem furtive, I urged Jeremiah out of the copse he was standing in and walked him toward the others. I was conscious that I was strangely dressed, and surely Thomas and all the others recognized me, but no one laughed or even betrayed amusement. Jeremiah's hooves made the only sound, of snapping underbrush. Frank stayed where he was. I noticed that the Missouri boy was whispering to his brother, and then he suddenly called out, "Whooie! Lazarus!" Jeremiah's ears swiveled forward inquisitively. Then the boy said, "That's Lazarus! I know that gray horse!" I came up to our men and reined Jeremiah in. I tried to act as if I had heard nothing.

The old man said, "Henry White had some horses stolen a month ago, that's true, and one was a gray horse with a white tail." They peered at Jeremiah suspiciously, and I made up my mind to back away if they tried to come any closer. Jeremiah betrayed no knowledge of them, but then he wasn't a dog, and they weren't claiming to be his owners, either. The old man called, "Son, you better get down from there and bring that horse over here so we can have a better look at him!"

It took me a moment to realize that they were talking to me. Thomas now spoke up and said, "I

don't believe that our two parties are on such terms
as would permit my friend here"—he slightly
emphasized the word "friend," and I felt that thing
we shared, an enjoyment of oddities, pass between
us—"to believe that you really do recognize this animal, especially since he has no particular distin-
guishing marks. Let's allow that issue to rest for
now."

"Those are fine words for a horse thief, is what I
think," said the old man.

"Lazarus!" shouted the boy again. Once again,
Jeremiah's ears swiveled toward the sound. But Jeremiah was a remarkably alert horse in every way. His
ears always swiveled toward interesting sounds.

"Now," said the old man, "you got nine men here
and a boy lying in wait back there." He gestured
toward Frank. Thomas glanced in that direction and
rolled his eyes heavenward. "We got the five of us.
You may drive us off if you dare, but we an't gonna
go quick and we an't gonna go easy."

"We'd prefer to buy you out," said Mr. Bush,
evenly. In answer, the boy who had shouted stooped
down suddenly and picked up a stone, which he flung
at Mr. Bush, knocking off his hat. With all the quick
movements of our men in response to this, our horses
jumped and snorted. Thomas bent down and picked
up Mr. Bush's hat and handed it to him. I was afraid
of what might happen, but then Mr. James said in a
loud, compelling voice, "We'll be back," and he
turned and rode off. Momentarily, we all followed
him. Reaching Frank, I pulled him up behind me,
then followed the others. When we came to the spot

where we were to turn off to our claim, Thomas slipped down from the Smithsons' mule and I slipped off Jeremiah. We walked along at his head, and Frank sat on his back. There was so much now to be said that I kept my mouth shut and waited to see what Thomas would want to say.

We struck out over the prairie grasses, following a pale track. The grass, like the leaves, was green but dry, and it rustled with our steps. Buzzards and hawks floated in the blue sky above us. Thomas was wearing a bleached muslin shirt, and it glowed in the early-afternoon sunlight. He said nothing. Behind us, Frank called out, "There're some prairie chickens over there—you want me to shoot 'em?" He didn't care much; when we didn't answer, he started to whistle. My trousers, or rather, Thomas's trousers that I was wearing, were easier to ride in than to walk in, but I found myself getting used to them. They didn't need to be held up, and they didn't snag on upthrusting weeds and burrs.

The Missourians had seemed obdurate and threatening. I didn't see how we could either accommodate them in our midst or remove them. Their evident sentiment that they were tougher and manlier than we were seemed true—our men made a picture of frustration and ineffectuality. The southerners' bragging and posing had had an effect on me, and it looked to me as though it had had an effect on the men, too. I wondered why they didn't simply shoot us. Clearly they were tempted. Of course, we had our Sharps rifles, designed for something other than killing game. It was as if a veil hung between the two

parties that prevented calculated attack. Just then, the
veil seemed to me wispy and easily rent, as if shooting would be as easy as not shooting, but really, I
didn't know what the veil was made of or what passions it could resist.

Thomas said, "I don't want to have to shoot
them." His voice was calm.

"I don't want them to have to shoot us."

"It's better all around if there is no shooting at
all."

"Our men look so . . . helpless!"

"Do they?"

"Yes. I—"

"Then you needn't watch, my dear, because spectators always increase the possibility that someone
will shoot just to raise himself in the spectators' estimation. I assure you that those men took one look at
our weapons and revised any notions they might
have had about our helplessness." He smiled. "Even
before reinforcements arrived."

Frank called out, "It was my idea, Tom Newton. I
got her to wear them clothes and take me over there.
Next time, I'll just go along with you."

"Are you angry that we came?"

"Well, now, I don't know. Your coming into danger, our coming into danger, Frank's coming into
danger—the causes of all this are so compounded
together that I don't know who to blame and I don't
know who should be restricted or why. I don't want
my wife to get hurt, but I think your firsthand knowledge of the course of events will benefit us in the end.
And you shoot better than I."

"No doubt Frank shoots better than the both of us, but that doesn't mean we want to train him as a murderer."

Thomas lowered his voice and leaned his head toward me. "He should go back."

Frank sang out, "I an't going back. I might go on to California."

We walked on in silence, until Thomas said, "We have to discuss the Jeremiah problem."

"I bought him in good faith! I won't give him up to them just on their say-so!"

"Nor would I, but we have to recognize that he might be a stolen horse."

"They were just saying that to get at us. How would they prove it?" My voice rose with challenge, as if he were trying to take the horse away from me right there.

"We'll find out, I suppose."

Now we came into our own yard. All was quiet at our cabin. The plank door was closed and tied with a string, just as I had left it. Thomas and Frank put away the horse, while I went inside and changed into my own clothes. On the whole, I was not pleased with my adventure. I felt as Pandora must have: there was an undeniable thrill to opening the box—the thrill of action, perhaps, which was much opposed to the customary routines of a woman's life—but the consequent evil was plentifully mixed with chagrin. I was not sure there would be any benefit to my knowing the course of events firsthand, especially if the course of events took an ugly turn.

It was midafternoon; the episode at the cabin had

taken surprisingly little time. Thomas, Frank, and I
settled back to what we had been doing in the morning, which was splitting supports for a lean-to room
for Frank off the end of the cabin. In the evening,
after our supper, I sat beside the stove sewing a bed
tick for him, while Thomas read aloud an essay or
two by Mr. Emerson. Frank, apparently, did not find
this to his liking, as he fell asleep in our bed nearly as
soon as Thomas began to read. After a while, the candle Thomas was reading by got too low to burn
steadily and began to flicker in its holder, but when I
opened the candle box for another, he said, "We'll
save that for another night." He moved Frank to
some quilts on the floor and wrapped him against the
vermin. I went out to check on Jeremiah and saw that
his saddle was hanging over the fence, and the bridle,
too. When I came back inside, Thomas was cleaning
his Sharps carbine in the unsteady light of the piece
of candle, and he still had his boots on. I sat down
across from him. He had grown more handsome to
me, but no less enigmatic. He consistently showed a
pleasant strength of character and mildness of temper that won me and intrigued me at the same time.
Something, perhaps the presence of his friends or
settling onto our claim, had driven off whatever evidence I had once seen of fear or weakness. He
seemed to draw strength from his very capacity for
amusement. On the other hand, he was hardly one of
those handy New Englanders you heard so much
about, who could build a schoolhouse with one hand
and a ship with the other, while running a loom with
his foot. Our cabin was full of the deformed results

of our attempts to do for ourselves. Were we to prove better farmers than house builders, my first plan was to procure more manufactured goods. And there were any number of things I could do better than he could, starting with riding a horse and shooting a turkey and running right through splitting firewood and building a fire. Come spring, I suspected, I would be doing my share and more of the plowing, which was, indeed, more to my taste than nursing, making ball fringe, or tatting. I knew he had a skill that I didn't—New England sailors often knew how to knit, and Thomas did have a garment in his boxes that he had knitted for himself. I wondered if all the other men in our party were as interesting to their wives as Thomas was to me. For the most part, it didn't seem so, though at our Sunday service I had discovered all the Smithsons to be possessed of lovely voices, many skills on the instruments they had brought along with them to K.T. (in preference to pots and pans), and a deep knowledge of songs, both religious and secular. I pondered Thomas.

He said, "Would you care to go along tonight?"

This surprised me. "Do you wish me to?"

"Remember the Misses Tonkin? They said never to restrict you or tell you what to do."

"I think they were talking about finances, not violence."

"I don't know that I'm talking about violence."

But I knew that he was. Having lived all his life among New Englanders, he thought that the talking could go on forever and arrive finally at reason. Having lived all my life along the river, I knew the more likely outcome. It scared me, and I shook my head. A bit later, he got up, took his hat and jacket and gun, and went out the door. Shortly after that, I heard Jeremiah trot away.

Now, of course, there was no sleeping. I didn't bother to change into my nightdress but merely rolled up in my favorite quilt and lay down on the bed. Over the weeks, I had chinked the cabin, not well, but well enough. The chill air crept in, rattling the newspapers pasted to the logs, but the pale light of the moon and stars was excluded; the inside of the cabin was as dark as a cistern. Already our peace of a few weeks before, when the weather was warm and the moon shone upon us through our sail, seemed long past and much to be yearned for. I feared for my husband. His quiet resolve could easily, I thought, press him toward a fight. On this slavery question, he didn't know or understand how to take a realistic position. Southerners were well known to argue and bluster about slavery, but they would fight to the death about one thing only, and that was what they called honor and what my sister Miriam had called prickly pride. They didn't like to be injured, but they hated to be insulted. And you couldn't always guess in advance which was which—partly that depended on the level of whiskey intake that had been achieved. I remembered an incident from long before, sometime when I was a child. I was at Horace's store with my mother. It was deep winter, and Horace was putting on his boots to go out into the snow, when a man pushed through the door, his pistols drawn, shouting, "Horace Silk, you will cheat me no more! Those mules I sold you for a hundred dollars you turned around and sold to Jed Bindle for two fifty, and you an't given me none of the profits!"

Horace took a moment to stamp his feet into his boots and then shouted, "Kite, you are lying to blacken my reputation in front of my family!" And then Kite leveled the pistols at him and said, "I wasn't going to shoot you before, Horace, I just wanted my share of the profits, but now you have insulted my honor, and if I don't shoot you, then I will never speak to you again!" He was serious, too, but then Horace's father, Jonas, interposed and explained to the man Kite the role of the middleman in every mercantile transaction, and my mother stepped forward and persuaded him to come farther into the store and get warm, knowing that he was less likely to shoot Horace right in front of her. We had always told this as a funny story, but now it seemed only frightening.

A northerner, insensitive in some ways and full of self-righteousness, could gravely offend a southerner in a second. The northerner would be giving his general opinion, more than likely unasked for, and all unknowingly challenging the southerner's every deeply held belief, not to mention, with sundry looks and expressions, suggesting that the southerner was possessed of numerous flaws of character and person. The southerner was bound to see offense in every suggestion, insult in every difference of opinion, and to act upon his stung pride. Better a man were dead than that he thought ill of you. The northerner, the Yankee, didn't seem to care about differences of opinion. He had the blithe and unsociable conviction, which poured out with every utterance, that he was so completely in the right that what other men thought didn't bother him. I thought these Missourians, or Louisianans, whatever they were, would get fed up at last and shoot everyone of our party, and then—

And then they would come over to this cabin, and they would see what we had plastered on our walls, and they would burn it to the ground. And if my husband hadn't been shot but was just their prisoner, they would shoot him for treason to the Territory of Kansas, under the new laws, and possibly me, too (I didn't know how the laws applied to women). And perhaps Frank would get himself in trouble, though it was obvious that he was only a boy, but what did they care about that?

I began to shiver in the chill night air, convinced I was already a widow. Below me, on the floor, Frank stirred. I shivered harder and pondered the thought of my burying my husband in Kansas. It was unbearable. . . .

Then I heard Jeremiah trot into the yard again. Thomas dismounted. The horse trotted into his pen. A few minutes later, the door opened and closed, and I knew Thomas was in the room.

Suddenly ashamed of my fears, I tried to make my voice sound sleepy. "Are you—"

"We threw them into the river," whispered Thomas. "We tied them to a couple of logs and sent them down the river."

"All five of them?"

"There were only two, the old man and one of the sons. The others had gone for reinforcements, because they didn't think we'd come back till tomorrow. Daniel James thought that would happen. That's why we went back tonight."

"Where are they now?"

"James and Holmes fished them out of the river about a mile down. They're keeping them in the woods for the rest of the night, then marching them back to Missouri in the morning. Bisket and I are to stay here and watch out if anyone else comes. Jenkins decided to sell the hay house and his town lots and move out here for the winter, just to be on the scene." I couldn't help shivering inside my quilt. It was a cold night. Thomas, when he came into the cabin and subsequently got into our bed, carried an extra dimension of cold with him, and I didn't envy the men who'd gone into the river. But I was elated to see my husband and to know that our side had suffered no losses. And the Missourians with their slave woman had been run off. Some festering that had promised to disturb us was now averted. Thomas, himself elated and chilled with his adventure, matched my gladness at his return with his own.

CHAPTER 12

I Am Swept Up by Events

A third method, is, for a woman deliberately to cal-
culate on having her best-arranged plans inter-
fered with, very often; and to be in such a state of
preparation, that the evil will not come unawares.

—*p. 151*

IN THE FEW DAYS AFTER the Missourians were driven
off, there was plenty of talk about what should be
done with their property. What had been done with
one item of it was a mystery, though—no one knew
what had become of the bondwoman who'd run out
of the cabin when the Smithson boy fired through the
window. Thomas said that she had not been in evidence; though he had privately planned as they rode
through the darkness to offer her her freedom, events
had driven the thought out of his mind, and he'd not
sought after her in the night. Each of the men had a
theory—either she'd already been taken back to Missouri before they arrived, or she sensed what was in
the wind after they came, and she went off on her
own account, or she'd hidden out in the woods and
was possibly still there. Whether they should have
liberated her had they found her was a matter of
rather hot debate—more tempers flared over this
question than over any other element of the
encounter. Thomas, Mr. Holmes, and Mr. Smithson
were all for giving her her freedom and doing so
openly—"challenging Satan," said Mr. Holmes;

"acting according to principle," said Thomas; "showing the bunch of them," said Mr. Smithson. Mr. Bisket came down much on the other side and got quite exercised over it, saying, "Freeing that woman would be adding in something extra to the whole business! We an't disputing them having a slave woman right this minute. Right this minute we're disputing their claim. My view is, you follow out your disputes one at a time—"

Mr. Smithson exclaimed, "You sound just like a lawyer, Bisket, drumming up business. If you got 'em on the run, then you make 'em run as fast as they can. You don't make 'em trot for one thing and run for the other!"

Everyone laughed. Mr. Bisket got red in the face. "They can't live with us if they think we're going to steal their slaves every time they turn their backs."

"They can't live with us," said Mr. Holmes. "We can't live with them. We can't look upon them holding bondmen without going blind to the will of the Lord, nor can we live beside them undirtied by their filth. We have our souls to think of as well as theirs and the souls of their slaves."

"There an't one person in ten here in K.T.," said Mr. Bisket, "who thinks like you do, Holmes, and eight of the nine who don't would like to kill you for that sort of talk. I think if we keep our mouths shut, those slaves'll disappear from here soon enough. Can't do anything with them in K.T. They don't grow cotton here."

"But," said Thomas, "they grow hemp right over in Missouri, and tobacco, too. Slaves do that work."

Mr. Bush said, "I give way to no man in my aversion to slavery and the slave power. Eli Thayer is a
personal friend of mine, and I feel no less strongly
than he does about it. But even so, I hesitate to free a
bondman I've never met from an owner I don't
know, and send him or her off to a life she may not
understand or want. Do we come upon a woman in
the night, wrench her from sleep, tell her she's free,
and send her packing? Where does she go? Who are
her friends? What funds does she have? I ask myself
if I'm prepared to guarantee her for a week or two, to
send her to friends. If I'm not, then I'd better not
meddle."

I said, "You might have asked the woman what
she wanted to do."

All the men turned and looked at me. This
remark put a stop to the conversation. All in all, I
thought, it was no doubt better that the woman had
been gone. Northerners, even abolitionists, knew
more about how and why to chop down the slavery
tree than they ever knew about what to do with its
sour fruit.

There was less discussion, let me say none, about
what should be done with the Missourians' cabin.
The Jenkinses moved into it within a few days and
did just as we had, though with a degree more satisfaction—they papered over the log-and-mud walls
with sheets of the treasonous *Liberator.* I was
pleased to have Mrs. Jenkins and Susannah in the
neighborhood, and they immediately became friends
with Mrs. James, who was a sweet lady and, Susannah said, not at all like her husband. That the Jenk-

inses' new cabin was a considerable improvement over their old one seemed to render them extremely forgiving. Now there was a woman or two every half mile, or even closer. It made the country seem settled and gave our windy cabins a cozy feel.

I think we all thought we were settled now, that we had passed through a few trials, done some unpleasant but necessary deeds, and established ourselves. Certainly, Thomas and Frank and I felt that way. In the course of our labors, there was much visiting back and forth, sharing tasks, and discussing every little thing.

Susannah, who now went four or five days between shaking, told me that she liked to come to our cabin above all, and tried to do so every day or two, always bringing along her own bit of tea and a few corncakes, and her own cup and spoon. "You know," she said, "I do like being out here with Mama and Papa, and the cabin is ever so much nicer than the hay house is, but I wonder how my husband is to find me out here. Mama and Papa discussed it the whole night before we came, standing outside the hay house and trying to keep me from hearing." It was true that their place was a little more out of the way than ours, and they had fewer passing visitors.

I said, "The whole night?"

"Well, long enough for the subject to become tedious even to me. But they never disagree, you know. When they talk about something, first Papa says one thing, then Mama says another, then Papa says what Mama just said, and Mama says what Papa just said. In this case, Papa said that we couldn't very well leave the cabin empty, and Mama said that a young, well-grown girl had to be in the way of traffic, not out on the prairie, and then they each said what the other said, and then Papa said, 'Well, what about Mr. Bisket?' and Mama told him the story about Mr. Bisket."

"What is the story about Mr. Bisket?"

"Mr. Bisket courted me for two days some weeks ago."

"He did?"

"I suppose so, or maybe he thought so. He came to the hay house and sat beside me, and he asked if I would like to hear a song, and I said that I would, and so he sang 'Camptown Races,' and then he asked if I would like to hear another, and I said I would, and he sang one I didn't know, and then some men came in and wanted to talk about Jim Lane, and I suppose that it wasn't very nice talk, because Papa said they should take their talk elsewhere, and so they did, and Mr. Bisket went with them. But he came back the next day and he sang three more songs—one of them was 'Camptown Races' again. But you know, I didn't have a thing to say to him. I've just known Mr. Bisket for such a long time, since I was ten and he was fourteen, and I thought it very hard that I should come all this way and after all settle for Charles Bisket, when Mama says there must be four men for every woman in K.T. Mr. Bisket wasn't considered very enterprising back in Massachusetts. Not nearly so respectable as Mr. Newton."

Just then, Thomas and Frank came in for their own tea, and our conversation turned to other topics, namely the Jameses. Susannah had stopped there the day before and discovered that Mrs. James's cow had disappeared. "And you know," she said, "she couldn't go after it as she might have, because she is in such a condition, and she would have had to carry the boy, and even though he's not very large, well, he is four, and she isn't very large herself. I told her she might have left the boy off with us, but of course she feels uncomfortable, and so they lost their little cow. She was utterly dejected, and nothing I could do would cheer her up."

"Cow ken git to Missouri from here," put in Frank, "if it keeps runnin'." This was true. I heard of two or three lost cows being found in Missouri, or so it was said. After Frank and Thomas went out, and Susannah and I were clearing up the cups, she said, "I didn't want to say this in front of the others, but Mr. James was fit to be tied when he found out the cow was gone. It made me want to leave right there, but I didn't dare look like I was running away. He has the devil of a temper."

"Did he abuse her in front of you?"

"Why, no, and she's so pretty that you wonder how he ever could, but when he came in, the boy exclaimed, 'Don't tell Papa about our little cow, don't tell him!' and ran and hid in the bed! And then Mrs. James did tell, and he flew out of the house in a rage and didn't come back while I was there, but she said to me in a low voice, 'He would never hurt us. He has terrible passions, but he would never hurt us. Don't think that he would!' Well, after that I left."

I shook my head, not knowing what to say, then

changed the subject. I was torn, for while I didn't care to be seen as gossiping about my own husband, I knew that Susannah had known him longer than I had, perhaps considerably longer. I hazarded, "Well, if you've known Charles Bisket since you were ten, when did you meet Thomas?"

"Oh, well. Mr. Newton." She glanced out the open door, then looked into my face, then settled her hands on her hips. "He's not an old friend of ours, like Mr. Bisket. Papa and old Mr. Bisket were schoolboys together, you know. But old Mr. Newton has tremendous means. He makes sails for all the ships, and his father did it before him. They are just the sort of people who would consider someone like Mr. Newton a disappointment to them."

"They do?"

"Well, I shouldn't speak so openly to his own wife, but they are deathly proud, those Newtons. And the brothers are worse than the father, Mama says, but I don't know about that. The oldest brother is as old as Papa, and the father has run that factory since 1800, if that's possible." She gave me a look, half sheepish and half impish. "Mrs. Bush said, before we left Massachusetts, 'Thomas Newton is only going with us because he knows his papa will never pass on.' Though they are great abolitionists, too. Old Mr. Newton is very tall, you know. A head taller than your Mr. Newton."

And Thomas was a bit taller than I, so his father was possibly the tallest man I had ever heard of. I said, "A head taller?"

"At least. He's well known for it. Mama always

said it was a blessing they had no sisters—" But then she looked at me and blushed.

I said, "Thomas hardly ever speaks of his relations. It makes me wonder if there's ill feeling."

"I don't think so. You could ask Mama. But everyone is always wondering what Mr. Newton thinks. It's quite a feature of our group. They chose him to bring over those rifles because they thought he was the least likely to divulge the information. Or any information of any kind."

We couldn't gossip away the afternoon, because Susannah had duties at home. I saw, though, that there was much to be learned, and I was eager to learn it.

Thomas, Frank, and I made pleasant companions, and I didn't at all mind Frank's presence—for you had to call it that, even though the boy was perennially off doing something. Once he and Thomas had built him a lean-to on the side of the cabin and a little bed to put in it, we weren't always sure where he was. He thought nothing of running off to Lawrence, for example. Literally running. Thomas and I could walk to Lawrence, if the ground was hard, in half a morning. On Jeremiah it was an easy hour. Some days, Frank would go off to Lawrence before breakfast and come back before supper, his pockets full of bits of things he had found and was keeping to trade, or of pennies and dimes he had gotten through his trades. One night, he said, "I an't never seen such a place for folks dropping stuff."

"Haven't ever seen," said Thomas.

"I'll be goin' along, an't nobody around anywhere, and here I see a saucer buried in the grass. I
picked one up yesterday, all painted with violets and
all, gold rim, and it said 'Hampton' on the bottom.
Not a single chip, but no cup, neither. And this morning I got me a perfectly good boot, almost new,
hardly even broken in yet. Just sittin' there. Folks in
town is just as bad."

"Are just as bad," I said.

"You just got to keep your eyes on the ground. I
got me a dollar between today and yesterday. Mr.
Stearns give me two bits for that boot, 'cause he said,
'Someday a one-legged fella's gonna walk into this
store looking for a boot, and if it's the left leg he's
lost, well, then, I'll fix him right up.' "

But for Thomas and me, Lawrence seemed a long
way off. We didn't leave the claim twice in a week,
except to go to a neighbor cabin. And it wasn't only
that our work at home filled our days; it was also that
we were disinclined to be swept up in the talk and
upsets of town. It was easier to deepen our well with
a shovel and a bucket and a rope and a pulley, wet
and shivering, than it was to know what to think with
every new bit about the depredations of the Missourians. Frankly, we considered the Missourians
less important to our future well-being than the well.
Now that our little area was more thickly settled by
our friends, I had to go farther afield for game, and I
had to bring more home, too, because I knew that
what we weren't sharing now (and we were sharing
some) we would be sharing later. It was a source of
wonder to the New Englanders that Frank and I were

such successful meat gatherers, and they put this down to our western nature. Mrs. Holmes, for example, asked me if Quincy was in Kentucky, and when I said no, it was in Illinois, she guessed that such places were all the same in the end, weren't they, and did we have animal skins stretched over the outer walls of our house in Quincy, and did my brother-in-law the farmer have to carry his rifle into the fields with him to frighten off the red Indians? But she thanked me anyway for the meat and told me I would be repaid in heaven, as if she had a personal account there. Well, I didn't like her, I admit it.

Every night, Thomas read us something from his store of books. Before Frank, we had been having Mr. Emerson every night, but Frank yawned and sighed and fidgeted so much under Mr. Emerson that Thomas had to try something else. It wasn't much better with Mr. Thoreau, nor even with Mr. Lowell, but when we got onto Mrs. Stowe, Frank sat quietly with his chin in his hand. I did, too. Those were our best evenings, and even though candles were an expense, we would have given up tea or maybe even corncakes before giving up candles.

Some nights, we visited others, and the talk wasn't always of politics and the hardships of our present lives. Now that we were settled, it seemed, for a while, as if we might talk about home a bit. K.T. may have exerted a leveling influence on my friends, but back in Massachusetts, it appeared, they hailed from many different strata of society and knew each other mostly because of the Emigrant Aid Company and their common beliefs in the abolition of the institution of slavery. Mr. Bush, who knew Mr. Thayer and was on an equal footing with many of the rest of them back in the east, had sold his prosperous ship-outfitting business to come to K.T. "You know," he claimed, "I was tired of it. It was all bookkeeping and close work and noting this and writing that, and I barely got off my seat of a morning to look out at the water. My bones were aching for something to do."

I don't think Mrs. Bush's bones had felt the same ache, but Mr. Thayer himself worked on her, for she was the more fiery of the two on the subject of Negro bondage. "After living in comfort all my life," she told me, "it seemed the least I could do. And it is. When I think of all the years that Isaac toiled in the wilderness, I do not consider Lawrence, K.T., a hardship."

Mr. Jenkins, on the other hand, was one of those being aided by the company, as his farm had failed some years before and he had tried his hand at two or three enterprises, such as buying and selling cattle, picking apples, and teaching school, before coming to K.T. Mr. Holmes had just begun his life as a preacher, and as there were few enough churches to be had in New England, there being an abundance of preachers there, Mrs. Holmes's father, himself a preacher, had financed their journey to K.T., with some help from his members and some help from Mr. Thayer, who liked there to be one minister of good New England stock for every twenty emigrant families (or so Mrs. Holmes said, but I never heard anyone else say this of Mr. Thayer, who was the subject of a good deal of talk).

The Smithsons had printed books and intended to get into the book-printing trade once again, but upon arrival in K.T., they had lost the money they'd saved for presses and type through being cheated by a gambler. In a year, they thought, they would have replaced their funds through trading town lots or something of the sort, and the older Mr. Smithson said, "Printing is a dangerous business out here, anyway, more so than I care for. My thought was a ladies' book, with receipts and lace patterns and a few stories. I don't yet see a spot for that out here, but no doubt the time will come." They intended to while away the time farming or speculating. I thought their interests were peculiar, as there were no Smithson ladies, but Susannah said yes, it was true: Mr. Smithson had told them all the way out from Massachusetts that there was a fortune to be made from reading ladies. He'd kept counting the ladies on every boat and in every town between there and here, alternately pleased and downcast, depending upon how many there were. He even had a stack of bills, which he now used to paper up the walls of his cabin, that advertised *"The Western Ladies' Journal,* A Monthly, Published in Lawrence, K.T., for the Entertainment and Edification of All." Another time, Mr. Smithson confided to me that he was disappointed in the Missouri ladies he had seen, many of them barefoot and clearly ignorant. He said, "Lawrence is all very well, but Missouri isn't Lawrence, and Lawrence is hardly a pockmark on the face of the prairie. I didn't think it would be that way, from the bills we saw." He was thinking, of course, of his project, but I subsequently found this observation appropriate to every feature of our situation. And once, when Susannah was going on again about whom she might marry and when he might appear, I mentioned the Smithsons, as there were three of them. She stared at me as if I were out of my mind. Finally she said, "In the end, I do think it's ill advised to know your affianced very well before the wedding." But it was hard to see what she was looking for in the men we saw outside of our group.

At any rate, we visited and gossiped among ourselves as if we would be friends for the rest of our lives. That was K.T. all over. You had to be acting every day as if your life would go on from that moment, full tilt, because if you held back, you would settle on nothing—make no claim, dig no well, have no friends. All the same, you could embrace something with all your might and have it turn to empty air only so many times. But I wasn't thinking about that then.

At the end of October, the weather turned a bit brisk. On the other hand, Thomas, Frank, and I were well equipped with sturdy clothing and boots we'd brought along, and plenty of quilts and blankets. We had a woodpile stacked as large as the cabin, and the cabin was thoroughly papered and chinked. Jeremiah had a bushy, full coat, with furry ears and fetlocks. The prairie hay was snowless and nourishing, and he trotted around in fine fettle, keeping himself warm and fit. He was a good lookout—a lone horse always is, especially for the approach of any other horse.

All in all, I could stand at my door and feel satisfied enough with my situation, or I could glance about my little cabin and feel satisfied enough with my situation. Along about then, I received a letter from Harriet, acknowledging the tidings I had sent her of Frank's safe arrival, which had slightly elided its actual date. She wrote:

My Dear Sister, and Frank, too:

I write to assure you that my fears are largely set at rest by yours rec'd today. To be perfectly candid, I will say that on the very day after Frank's departure, we had news of the Kansas rebels and their so-called constitutional convention at Tomara or someplace like that, Roland knows the name, and I had tremendous fears of the battles that might ensue, because I am here to tell you that the southerners are not going to give anything up without a fight, for you know they are Scotch-Irish, and you know how they are, they invented the terrier dog, Roland says, and it wasn't without a reason. Now that Frank is gone, Alice's boys are all clamoring to go as well, and I might as well take to my bed. Alice has had animals in the house for four months, as the two boys found an injured crow, and now they have taught it to talk. It is an ugly black thing and hops all around and even though she leaves the door open as often as you can stand with this cold, it WILL NOT fly away, and Roland says why should it, it has found a home. It is a great storer of provisions, and Alice and Annie are always coming across its caches of trashy things. But that won't interest you. Lydia, I insist that you protect my child from danger and do not lead him astray as you have so often in the past. I can't feature what persuaded me to allow this. But now you are a married woman, and you must come to your senses, and keep out of trouble, especially as, though you have not said anything about it, you are no doubt in a condition. I will say that it makes considerable changes in your state of mind, which you yourself will find in no time. Well, just that thought makes me miss you a bit, and so write again right away and let me know how everyone is. We miss you, though I will say that our life is quieter here, esp. as we do not have a crow in the house, that is Alice.

Your loving sister,
HARRIET

Well, I was not in a condition, but I thought that was just as well, with the winter to look forward to. Mrs. James, who was in a condition, looked as though she sorely missed her little cow, and so did the boy.

I wish I could say that I savored and appreciated each of those quiet days in the fall, but I cannot. When the wind ripped my papers and the cold air crept into the cabin, when the stove went out and refused to light again, when my hunting was poor or my husband preoccupied, I felt prickles of dissatisfaction. My own ineptitude annoyed me: our bed tick was misshapen; when I sewed Thomas a shirt, I had to rip out and refashion the second left sleeve I set in;

I was vexed with the mice and moles and other vermin who found their way into the house and against which we had to be ever vigilant.

But in the midst of it all, I did have some valuable moments with my husband. One rainy afternoon, our conversation turned to the Missourians who had been driven off, whom we hadn't mentioned in the intervening weeks. I had been over with the Jenkinses that morning, making soap, and I commented upon what a comfortable cabin I found it, and Thomas said, "I didn't think we should have sent those men down the river. It was a miserable thing for them."

"I'm sure it was."

"We couldn't find one of them for a bit. The rope tied to the log came loose, and he drifted off in the dark."

"What did you mean to do—"

"I thought sure the log had turned over and drowned the fellow, but it just drifted into some snags and hung there. He was deadly quiet, but Bisket saw him when the moon came out."

"But what—"

"We had the guns. Bush was all for shooting them and getting it over with, and maybe they deserved it, because they shot at us when we rode up, but I said I hadn't brought all those Sharps rifles out here for that—"

"Well, what did you bring them out here for?"

"Defending our claims. But we were all hot to do something to them, and a dose of the river didn't seem so bad in prospect. Afterward, I saw that we didn't know what we were doing, and those men were just fortunate."

"But you wanted to run them off, didn't you?"

"Yes, Lidie, I did." He sighed, then smiled a bit and said, "I generally want to do things, but often I don't want to have done them."

He must have seen alarm in my face, for I had been wondering that very day whether his quiet manner hid regrets about his choice of a wife, but he put his arm around my waist and drew me to him, then he murmured, "Small things only," and kissed me.

A day or two later, we were alone again. Frank had gone to the Holmeses', carrying a pot he had bought for them in Lawrence and brought home—he got a penny for running these errands. That evening, Thomas was in a more jovial mood, and he said, "Well, wife, we've been married three months now. Has your experience borne out your sisters' advice?"

"I think that must be United States advice, not K.T. advice."

"That you'll have to write up yourself."

"Perhaps I can have an article in *The Western Ladies' Journal,* or even make a regular appearance: 'How to keep your skirts from rustling when you are shooting turkeys.' "

"How do you?"

"I tie them up about my waist. It's a scandal."

"What else?"

" 'Prairie Mud: Would you be better off on stilts?' "

He laughed.

I said, "The ladies' boots have not been invented that can handle prairie mud, that is for sure."

"You seem content enough. I've been watching you."

"Have you? I've been watching you, too, and I hadn't noticed."

"Do *I* seem content enough?"

"On balance, yes." I felt myself flush.

"And you? Are you amazed and displeased to find yourself here?"

"Amazed, yes. Displeased, no."

"You've been watching me?" he said, softly.

"Of course. Everyone does."

"What do you see?"

"Oh, well. I suppose I see the promise of a prolonged investigation."

"Lifelong?"

"Lifelong, indeed."

"You are a mysterious woman, Lidie."

I considered this high praise.

I was always astonished at the speed with which news traveled in K.T. The solitudes of the prairies came later than my time—while I was there, the place was alive with travelers, messengers, and plain old gossips, galloping here and there to keep us all abreast of the latest events. So it was that on the very day it happened—*it* being the murder of a Free State man by a Missourian—we knew about it in our little cabin: Thomas had been over building fence at the Jenkinses', and Mr. Bisket rode in from Lawrence and told them. Mr. Bisket being a single man, and not

all that certain about his vocation, whether specula-
tor, farmer, or merchant, he spent a lot of time riding
from place to place and pursuing his avocation,
which was talking politics. It didn't hurt that he was
helpful; he had never built much on his own claim,
only split a few logs, but his friends' places were full
of his contrivances. While he worked, he talked.
Over the subsequent days, he was like our own private newspaper.

The story was that a Free State man named Dow
had been shot "forty times" in the back by a Missourian, his neighbor, named Coleman. In the morning, Dow and a friend of his, named Branson, had
driven Coleman off the land they were disputing
about, and then in the afternoon, some friends of
Dow's found his body by the side of a road down near
Hickory Point, some ten or twelve miles south of
Lawrence, and so about fifteen south of us. It looked
as though Coleman had pursued Dow and shot him
down. This murder provided the perfect occasion for
the officials of the state government to demonstrate
that holding office rendered them responsible to all
the citizens of the territory. But of course, no one
expected such an outcome.

Free Staters thought nothing of the so-called
sheriff, just as they thought nothing of all the other
"state officials." These "duly constituted" authorities, from the governor on down, were creatures of
the slave power that had stolen the original elections, instituted the gag law, and rammed through a
proslave constitution modeled on Missouri's. There
were no laws in Kansas that didn't contaminate the

very word "law," and no officials that weren't parti-
sans. The sheriff was a proslave partisan who used
such authority as he had to harass and oppress Free
Staters. As a southerner, his philosophy was that he
wanted to do it, he ought to do it, and therefore he
was going to do it—and what couldn't be done by
persuasion could more easily and amusingly be done
by force. Coleman was a rich man from Missouri,
and Dow and Branson were typical Free Staters—
men of moderate means and independent habits. The
sheriff knew what side his bread was buttered on
without even thinking about it. No one knew Dow—
he was new in the country—but he was a Free Stater,
and his death quickly became an example of what
they would do to all of us, under the guise of authority, if we didn't stop them.

The Bushes and the Jenkinses considered all the
men of the southern party, top to bottom, to be liars
and proud of it, either owing to the fact that their
slave system was based on the lie that Negroes
weren't human, meaning that southerners couldn't
tell the difference between a truth and a lie, or owing
to their determination to force the system upon others, which meant that they knew the difference and
dissembled by design. Free Staters believed nothing
that the other party said about Dow or his murder,
assumed their every word and action was intentional
deception. Was this true back in the States? I didn't
know. I'd come to think that before I came to K.T.
I'd known nothing at all and that everyone still back
there continued in that same state of ignorance.

The night of Dow's murder, the sheriff, an infa-

mous little tyrant named Jones, stayed up in Leavenworth and did nothing. Folks in Lawrence were
appalled but not shocked. That the southerners who
styled themselves "state officials" would let one of
their own go scot-free after killing one of ours was
something all my friends declared they'd expected
all along. Even so, it rankled. By Saturday night, a lot
of people in Lawrence had decided they weren't
going to stand for it anymore. Some men went down
to Hickory Point—Mr. Bisket and one of the Smithsons among them. Thomas, whose fund of pugnacity
had been used up by the incident at the Jenkins
claim, stayed home but prowled our cabin and yard
the whole evening. Of course, we heard all about it
the next day.

"Those boys said Coleman shot poor Dow in
self-defense," said Mr. Bisket. "They just looked us
in the eye and swore they would lie about it. Dow
wasn't even armed, and Coleman shot him forty
times in the back! Yes, that's self-defense in K.T.!
Well, they're gone back to Missouri now."

"How's that?" said Thomas.

"All of 'em up and left. We got our Sharps rifles,
you know. Every time they turn tail and run, they say,
'Them d—— abolitionists got their d—— Sharps
rifles, so we better get outta here!' " We laughed, but
then, of course, it turned out that three of the Missourians' cabins were burned down. This, the Bushes
and the Jenkinses felt, they had done themselves, to
cast blame on the Free Staters, who would never
have done such a thing. The Holmeses felt the burning was so appropriately Satanic that forces not of

our world could well be at work. The story was that some men, two Free Staters, had wanted to set the cabins afire, but the others had stopped them. Maybe they'd gone back later, but if they had, they were keeping mum.

The tyrant Jones didn't want his people threatened, so after the murderer Coleman took refuge with the governor, Shannon, he took Coleman and went to arrest Dow's friend, Branson, because Coleman said Branson had threatened him—the sheriff went with the murderer to arrest a friend of the victim! As Mrs. Bush would say, and did say, that was K.T. for you all over—everything was turned upside down. I said, "Well, you know, to a southern man, his honor is always worth another man's death."

"They don't think like we do, that's the certain truth," said Mr. Jenkins, and everyone nodded. If there was any sentiment truer than that, I don't know what it could have been. So Jones turned up with Coleman at Branson's cabin and arrested him. They put Branson bareback on an old mule and rode him off, but they didn't get far before a group of Free Staters intercepted them, freed Branson, and drove Jones and his ilk off, with, of course, plenty of blustering threats from Jones. Mr. Bisket knew all about it, but by the time *we* heard, of course, no one who'd been in on the freeing of Branson was talking about it. Even the names of the members of the party got to be a secret. Dr. Robinson called a meeting and said that the time had come to keep to ourselves and wait. There was no talk that he had been involved in the raid, but you got the feeling that plenty more about every little thing was known than was acknowledged.

Now the Free Staters were in trouble, and we shivered with it all the way up to our place. To hear the southerners tell it, we were a band of illegitimate rebels in open defiance of the authorities—their fraudulently elected government was legal, their pernicious laws were valid, their method of using the system of laws to press forward personal feuds was the order of the day and the shape of days to come. We had laughed at them all fall, but suddenly it was much more frightening.

Jones, like all Missourians and southerners, immediately began to shout that he was going to arrest and jail every abolitionist ——— and treasonous son of a ——— up in Lawrence. He had the guns and the men, and as with all their threats, it was hard to distinguish the bluster from the intent, and a wise precaution to act as if he *did* mean it and *would* do it.

In our little cabin, Thomas and I felt each of these bits of news as a blow. We knew right off how to think of them but not precisely how to feel about them. A danger, yes, that galvanized us, yes, but also an intrusion, it seemed to me, like an unwelcome trickle of water that looked, at first, as though it might be stanched easily enough. Mr. Bisket and others came and went. We gave them tea and corncakes or whatever we had. We listened, exclaimed, deplored. They left, and we exclaimed and deplored some more. Thomas got restless. He had taken no part in the rescue, had been to no meetings, got the news rather than made it. He repeated, "I didn't much like driving off those Missourians."

I said, "But it's better for everyone that they went. You yourself told me that they couldn't live with us."

"I know."

Then, a bit later: "Driving off those Missourians wasn't what I expected when I came out here."

"Didn't you think you'd have some fun?" asked Frank. "I did."

"But," went on Thomas, "you have to expect that things aren't going to be what you expect. You have to expect that your convictions will be tested."

I said, "Maybe Branson's rescuers made a mistake. Maybe they acted too hastily."

That evening, Thomas picked up Mrs. Stowe again, but he didn't even open the book. He said, "I suppose I'm of a reluctant turn of mind. I like to think I'm evenhanded and judicious, but perhaps I'm just reluctant. Perhaps I'm just one of those who hang back and then make up a good reason to do so. Perhaps I can't see the moment when it comes."

"What moment?" My tone was a bit sharp. I knew he was talking himself into something, and I didn't know myself how I felt about what he was trying to talk himself into. What I knew was that we hadn't had quite enough of those richly married evenings yet, and even as I tried to hold on to them, they were getting away from me. This sensibility made me suddenly breathless and ill. He didn't answer my question, only looked over at me, surprised at my sharpness and, I could tell, somewhat put off.

I suppose the people of Lawrence, or whoever were responsible, thought they had done a small thing in rescuing Branson. After the killing of Dow, no one knew what would happen to Branson once Coleman and his friends got hold of the man, and the Free Stater was reputed to be hotheaded, to boot, so likely as not he would have gotten himself killed. Therefore the people of Lawrence now did another small thing—they refused to turn Branson over to the "authorities" and also refused to say who had perpetrated the rescue. In retaliation, the Missourians poured over the border and joined the ranks of the territorial militia, which Governor Shannon, apparently in thrall to the tyrant sheriff Jones, ordered out. In other words, they did what they had been itching to do all along, which was to make war on Lawrence!

Here was the end to all the talk of killing, hanging, shooting, and clearing out—they were going to do it.

In the midst of this murder, it got to be December, and we had to admit that it was truly winter. Perhaps because we had had such faith in the advertisements that had brought us to K.T., or perhaps because, as well prepared as we thought we were, we knew we weren't really prepared enough, we found this hard to believe. Each morning would seem colder than the previous one, and we would get up surprised, but something about the murder made us believe in the cold, too. The two seemed linked.

At any rate, with no preamble, we began discussing whether to stay on the claim or move into town. Frank, who had been home for a few days, complaining that he couldn't get to Lawrence because the wind was going to blow him away, was all for moving, but Thomas and I were undecided, even though the Bushes and the Jenkinses had decamped a week before and, the last we'd heard, the Holmeses and the Smithsons had been talking about it. We'd heard nothing of the Jameses.

At first, I took the pro position and Thomas the con. I said, "Whatever the chances there for fighting, the only chances here are for freezing."

Thomas's rejoinder: "The weather is just as likely to moderate as not. Everyone says Kansas has a salubrious and mild climate, but every place has spells of bad weather."

"The weather isn't bad yet. This is good weather. There's no snow, the river isn't frozen, but we still can't withstand it."

"I think we can get used to it. It's no use moving to Lawrence; the weather's no different there, and the Missourians might attack anytime."

The next morning, we switched positions. Thomas said, "I ought to be there. Bisket and the Smithsons are there, and the Bushes and Lacey, too."

I said, "I think it's warmer today. And the sun is shining. If we go there, where do we live? It's one thing for us all to pile into one house in the summer, when we can spend a lot of time outdoors, and quite another now, all thrown together. And all our things are here."

"At any rate, I have to get these carbines over

there. We don't know what Jones will do, or Governor Shannon."

"If you and Frank leave here and take Jeremiah,
anything could happen. We're cold here, but all in
all, we're better off staying out of it, I think."

But after I'd surveyed our stores again, I said,
"Whatever happens, Thayer will make sure that
Lawrence is provisioned. There's safety in numbers.
And we need to show what side we're on. . . ."

"There's so much work to do around here. If we
leave now, no matter what we find, we might not be
able to come back during the winter. If we let everything go, there's no telling whether . . ."

I dreaded any step we made out of the cabin and
away from our claim. I felt we'd hardly begun to live
our life. And yet it was windy cold and discouraging.

It was said that meanwhile the Border Ruffians
were massing for a fight at Franklin. The carbines
were needed in town, and Thomas was, too. All the
men in Lawrence were busy drilling and building
earthworks and talking of strategies for defense, but
Lawrence was all too vulnerable—approachable
from almost any direction, and especially open from
the bluff. Against a real attack, with artillery and
cavalry charges, the people of Lawrence could not
defend themselves. All they had were their Sharps
rifles and the moral high ground.

There were thousands of Missourians massed to
attack Lawrence, and the first thing they did was sit
and wait, allowing their numbers to swell and the
people of Lawrence to ponder their fate. Nevertheless, we both sensed that even with many of our

friends around, the pondering we did out on our claim was lonelier and more fearful than what they were doing in town. What if Lawrence *was* sacked, burned to the ground, cleared out, our friends hanged, shot, tarred and feathered? It was not a prospect to contemplate by yourself. Had we been in Lawrence, I thought, we'd be drilling and building, digging and talking, making preparations for our own defense. It would at least be lively and invigorating. Late in the afternoon—that would have been Friday—we did what people with dilemmas always do—we tried to have it both ways. Thomas got on Jeremiah and rode into town, leaving Frank, over loud protests, with me, and carrying the last of the Sharps rifles, except for my own, in saddlebags over Jeremiah's rump. He intended to reconnoiter the "war" and return in the morning. If he didn't return (but of course, he would), he would send someone else, either to get me or to stay with me.

The transparency of this plan didn't escape any of the three of us, but it allowed us to act. After he left, Frank and I busied ourselves for our evening and night as if it were the last—a project that we wouldn't have to repeat. We allowed ourselves a good supper—corncakes and dried apples and some honey and a stew of prairie chicken and wild onions. We built a good fire in the stove—not eking out our wood supply but pouring it on. Every time we thought of what might be happening in Lawrence, we put on another piece of wood. Without mentioning it, we both sneaked glances around to the southeast, toward Lawrence, to see if the sky was alight.

But the night stayed dark and crisply chill; no fires on
the horizon. I lit a candle and brought down "The
Song of Hiawatha" from Thomas's shelf of books
and tried to read it aloud to Frank as Thomas would
have, slowly, savoring the words, letting their
rhythms form a little music in the cold air. I let
myself think about him already being dead, as a way
of preparing for that. All over Kansas, no doubt,
women were praying, and men, too. That was the
way with most folks in K.T., and in the States, but
Frank and I didn't pray. It didn't occur to us. We had
swum in the ocean of religion all our lives and not
gotten wet. After our reading, we went to bed, again
as if for the last time, bundling into the quilts and
blankets and embracing sleep as if we'd never sleep
again.

In the morning, I woke up early, just after dawn,
and already knew that Thomas had not returned.
Whatever elevation of spirits we'd achieved the
night before was utterly gone now, in the teeth of the
wind and the flat gray sky and the white frost over
everything, inside the cabin and out. The stove was
barely warm and would gulp down much of our
wood just to get hot enough to cook breakfast. My
pitcher of water had a thick film of ice. Nothing, it
seemed, could be touched without pain. We lay in
bed, disconsolate. I asked Frank if he regretted his
journey to Kansas now.

"Nah," he said. "Something might happen. Nothing's gonna happen at home. Everything's fixed
there. Here everything's loose."

"Loose and sliding downhill," I said.

"I'll tell you one thing, though. Thomas an't no farmer."

"Isn't."

"He's got schoolteacher or something written all over him. My pa says that's how you tell an abolitionist. They're all goldurned schoolteachers, and I have to say that I gave that aspect of things plenty of thought before I come here."

"Came here."

"But he's left me alone about it and hasn't made me write anything. He's about as handy as a brick. It makes me nervous when he gets out there with that ax."

"He goes slow. He's not practiced."

"It's like he wasn't ever a boy."

"Well," I said defensively, "he wasn't a western boy, a rude boy who gets to do everything he wants to all the time."

Frank shrugged. To myself, I acknowledged this was true. It was very much as if Thomas had never been a boy but had always been a man. This was what set him apart from the other men I knew.

We lay in bed chatting all morning, as though we hadn't a thing to do in the world, and then, toward midday, Mr. Bisket arrived with his wagon, hitched up to his little horse and Jeremiah, and we ran out of the cabin to greet him. In no time at all, we had all our things packed that we would need for a prolonged stay in Lawrence—clothing, bedclothes, weapons and ammunition, books, candles, a skillet, all of our provisions. There was no question, no remonstration. The very wagon and horses carried

about them the air of bustle and great events that
were not to be missed. We rolled away from the
claim, over the crispy hard and frozen prairie, without a backward glance.

There was plenty of news. Sheriff Jones was hot
to invade Lawrence and kept sending for Branson,
the fugitive. No one was saying where he was, but
Bisket speculated that he was well on his way to
Iowa by now. Jones planned to use the search for
Branson as a pretext to roust out folks he particularly
hated, and most people in Lawrence expected at least
a few of their homes to be burned down, in retaliation for the burning of the Missourians' homes.

Mr. Bisket had been drilling all day the day
before. He said, "They're afraid of our rifles, deathly
afraid. And you know why? They know you an't got
to be much of a shot to hit something; you just got to
have plenty of firing caps and balls and black powder. They all pride themselves on being able to pick
the eyeball out of a squirrel at a hundred yards, but
they know we an't got to do that. We got these rifles;
all we got to do is keep loading and firing. An't got to
load anything down the muzzle one time. I wish we
had us some artillery. Robinson's been talking about
it. He wrote off to Thayer, they say, asking for some
fieldpieces. I'd like to see that!" He laughed.

I asked if Thomas was drilling.

"Nah. They got him digging at the fortifications.
Anybody who an't exhausted has to do that. That's
hard work. Tomorrow's the attack."

"Why tomorrow?"

"I don't know. That's what everyone says. Depends on when they run out of whiskey. When they run out of whiskey, first they get mad, then they sober up and get smart. They got to attack while they're mad but before they sober up. Jones has the whiskey coming in to them by the barrel. Some folks are all for us attacking them, since we could take 'em easy, but Robinson says we got to sit tight and let them make the first move, or the U.S. Army'll be down on us like a blanket."

"I thought there were thousands of them."

Mr. Bisket shrugged.

A bit later, he handed me the reins and slipped down off the wagon seat. He motioned to Frank to join me in the front and then whispered, "I'm gonna look around. You an't carrying anything suspect, so just ride on into town and go to the hay house." Then he walked away.

Darkness was coming on; I hustled the two horses up to a trot and shortly came to some Border Ruffians huddled around a fire. I kept on without speeding up, or looking toward them when they shouted. They let me by, but another set stopped the wagon, held Jeremiah by the bridle, and peered at us.

"What's your name?" There were three of them, wearing soft hats, their faces lost in their whiskers. They had on layers and layers of humble clothing against the cold and carried long Kentucky rifles that looked awkward and outmoded by the standards of the Sharps carbine but were nevertheless deadly. I opened my mouth to speak but hesitated just a moment, unsure of what to say. In that moment, Frank said, "She can't talk. She can't hear nor talk. I go along with her everywhere."

"Where are you going, then?"

"We're going into town."

"There's a war in town."

"Nah!" said Frank, dumbfounded. "Who's fighting?"

"We're gonna clear out them d—— black abolitionist traitors!"

"Well, good," said Frank.

"What's yer name, boy?"

I shook the reins, and the horses tried to step out, but the Ruffian tightened his grip on the horse's bridle. He said, "Tell her she can't go nowhere till we get to the bottom of a couple of things." Frank tapped me on the shoulder, and I looked at him alertly. He made some enthusiastic motions with his hands and face, at which I nodded. Then Frank said, "I'm Frank Brereton. Who are you?"

One of the others spoke up. "He's an abolitionist's worst nightmare! Haw!" He spit on the wheel of the wagon.

"We're gonna burn them out down in that hole of abolitionists. We're just waitin' for some stuff! What's her name?"

"She's my cousin Lydia Brereton. We're visiting from—"

"Illinois!" exclaimed one of the men. "Haw!"

Frank didn't even look nonplussed. He said, "That's about right."

"You know Burton Brereton, then?" said the man.

"He was my paw's uncle. He *was* a killer," said Frank. I sat stock-still, a blank look on my face, as I struggled to pretend that I couldn't hear this very interesting exchange. "I never met him," said Frank, conversationally. "He died before I was born. But we had them dogs."

"What dogs?"

"Them dogs that were descended from the bitch that warned Uncle Burton about the killers."

"I never heard about no dog."

"Well," said Frank with some animation, "that's what happened. The dog snuck away and went to get Uncle Burton, and the killers didn't realize it, and then Uncle Burton, who was raised among the Indians, snuck up and killed those men. He slit their throats."

This was not the story I'd heard, but I remained impassive.

"Hunh," said our interlocutor. "Well, my paw lived in Edwards County for five year before he come to Missouri, and he always said that a man named Burton Brereton was the death of the meanest and worst criminal who ever lived. So here you are."

"Here I am," said Frank, taking credit for the whole thing.

"And she's your cousin." He pointed to me.

"Yes, she is, but she don't know the story," said Frank.

"She's a big one," said one of the men, in an unkind tone of voice. One of the others laughed.

Frank said, "You don't have to insult her."

"I thought you said she can't hear nothing."

Frank didn't quite know how to answer this and fell silent. "And ugly," said one of the other men, speculatively, smiling at me. I smiled back at him. "Ma'am," he said, still smiling, "you are about as plain as an old sow."

I nodded and grinned.

He grinned back at me. "I bet you are an old maid!" I laughed and tossed my head flirtatiously. All the men guffawed.

"Deaf as dirt from the day she was born," said Frank.

"I'm cold," said the man who was holding Jeremiah. "What are we doing here?"

The man who had known about Burton Brereton said, "If they want to go to Lawrence, I say let 'em."

"We gonna check the wagon?"

"Nah. Nah. It's too cold for that." The men stepped back, I waited, and then Frank nudged me. I shook the reins until the horses were trotting briskly through the dark. In a moment, my teeth were chattering, and there were a hundred things I wanted to say to Frank, but I kept as silent as I would have if those men were perched on the back of our wagon, waiting to hear me speak.

Lawrence was busy with warlike preparations. When we came along Massachusetts Street, we could see groups of men lit by long wood fires. Some had shovels and were digging and mounding up fortifications, while others had guns and were watching over the guns of those who were digging. As I noticed this, Frank crawled into the back of the wagon and brought out our guns, my Sharps rifle and the rifle his father had given him. I tried to discern the figure of Thomas, but there were so many men and they were so busy and ill lit that I couldn't make him out. I wondered, with a pang, when I might see him. When we were driving along with Mr. Bisket, it seemed a matter of course that I would see my husband practically as soon as I arrived in Lawrence, but now I saw the real state of things, and I had misgivings about leaving our claim—at least if I were there he would know where to find me. The horses were tired, but I urged them more quickly to the hay house, eager though I was to see my husband. This was the first thing I learned about war—that it makes the briefest parting almost too painful to bear.

The hay house was considerably deteriorated. The thatching that had looked so neat in the summer was now partially fallen out and patchily replaced with hay, sticks, cloths. One end of the house had slumped. My misgivings about leaving our claim swelled, and then swelled again with the revelation that in fact, in K.T., there was no place of refuge now. And then I called out, and Mrs. Bush came bustling out of the house with a light, and she looked excited and happy!

"My dear!" she said. "I've been looking for you all evening! Thomas was here for his supper, and he was most anxious for your arrival—we hear Ruffians from Lecompton were all along the road to the north, and I so feared you'd be turned back, or worse! And Frank—"

Frank jumped down. "I told them she was deaf and dumb, and then I lied about everything else, too. Is supper over?"

I said, "He talked their ears off, till they were too cold to listen and let us go on. But we lost Mr. Bisket. . . ."

Frank took the horses and wagon down the street, where Mrs. Bush said Thomas had found a place for the horses to be fed and the wagon goods to be stowed for the time being.

Inside, sitting around the stove with Mrs. Bush, were some new people—the hay house was never too ramshackle to hold a good set of visitors, and these were the famous Laceys from Massachusetts. Mrs. Lacey was a round, fresh-faced woman of maybe thirty-five, I guessed, from the size of her sons, who were fourteen, twelve, and eleven, and all big, stocky boys, still dressed in their New England clothes. Consciousness of our women's gossip about the Laceys had rendered me both disapproving of Mr. Lacey and a little ashamed of how we discussed him. I said, "You've waited so long to come, and now there's a war—"

"But I wouldn't have missed it!"

"Oh, my land of mercy," said Mrs. Bush. "I am happy to miss any war going, but now that they've carried it to us, well, then, we must see it through! But I am all for Dr. Robinson. Tonight, at the Free State Hotel, he said to the men that if the Ruffians attack us, then all of the north will rise up in a rage;

and if they go off without attacking, then they'll be simply a laughingstock; and so we can't lose, if you ask me, but of course the poor men are out there in the cold, drilling and digging—"

"And we have to sleep with our rifles on our pillows!" said Mrs. Lacey, apparently invigorated by it all.

I said, "Do you really think all of the north would rise up in a rage? They seem so far away and intent on their own business."

"You may mark my words, my dear," said Mrs. Bush happily, "the slave power is driving them into our arms one by one, every day. If you lived in Lawrence, you would see it. People come here from those soft, careless places like Indiana or Ohio, and they don't care one way or the other about slavery or about the Negro, and then they feel the resolve of the slave power, and they can't help but resist. Mr. Bush and I are far more sanguine than we were even a few months ago. Look at General Lane. He didn't care one way or the other about slavery till he came here, and now he is with us all the way."

I was surprised. "I thought you hated General Lane!"

"He is a dissipated man, and every month there's talk about him and some new woman. Mrs. Quinn has three small children, one of them a babe in arms, and she went to his house in front of his very family and wept and cried for him until her own husband had to take pity on her and drag her away!"

"Thomas thinks it would be better to have General Lane as an enemy than a friend—"

"I've known your husband for a long time, my dear, and he is a very particular man, which I admire, but sometimes a man can be too particular." She shook her head. "And you know, Mrs. Quinn hasn't been entirely right in her head since."

"Well," put in Mrs. Lacey, "doesn't that make you wonder exactly where the fault between them lies? General Lane is a compelling figure of a man, mo-o-ost assuredly." She spoke brightly, and Mrs. Bush gave her quite a look, as if she had appropriated all K.T. privileges first thing, without even earning them.

Frank, who had been eyeing the other boys and, as it were, circling them, asserted that he slept with a rifle on his pillow and had every night of his life. I laughed, thinking of my sister, but the other boys looked at him with visible amazement. All of them were bigger, but not even the eldest carried himself with quite the same self-reliant demeanor. Frank turned to me. "I'm going out," he said. "I got some things in the wagon to sell, and everybody's up, it looks like. I heard that when there's a war, you can get pretty good prices." He disappeared through the door of the hay house (no longer cloth, but now real wood) faster than I could remonstrate with him.

Mrs. Lacey and her boys all looked after him, startled. She said, "How old is that boy?"

"Twelve, almost thirteen."

Her elder two boys' faces took on expressions of wondrous anticipation—the K.T. effect on boys.

Thomas came in sometime after midnight. The Bushes now had bedsteads, but the rest of us arranged ourselves in the usual fashion, dividing the room with a cloth between the men and the women. I'd stationed myself nearest the door and was wrapped in my dressing gown and a shawl. I was wide awake, and I'd intended to jump up and greet him with all sorts of effusions, but in the event, I lay there as if asleep, covertly watching him. Mr. Bush had left a candle burning, and there was also light from the fires outside in the street. First he pushed the door open slowly and peeped in, then he took off his hat and set his carbine down just inside the door. Then there was a pause, as he must have been engaged in removing his boots, because he entered carrying them, in stockinged feet.

These little movements, bespeaking both exhaustion and thoughtfulness of others, struck me with a pointed tenderness. He yawned two or three times and rotated his shoulders, first the left and then the right, then he put down his boots and reached around to the back of his neck with his right hand, and rubbed and pressed there. I sat up and said, "Would you like me to do that?"

At the sound of my voice and the sight of me sitting up in my quilts, Thomas smiled with ready and evident warmth. I didn't know that I had been watching for his smile, but I had been, for the remarks of the Border Ruffians that cast aspersions on my person had not gone as unnoticed as I'd let on. All he said was, "You're safe, then, my dear wife. I'm very glad. I was torn about your coming, and worried, too." He sat down on the quilts, and we clung to each other. I said, "Frank preserved us."

"What happened to Bisket?"

"He melted away in the darkness, and we haven't seen him since. Mrs. Bush said that we wouldn't worry about him until the morning."

"Did you meet up with any of the Ruffians, then?"

"They did us no harm. Frank talked us through." But I didn't want him to know the degree of danger, so I forbore to tell him the story, even though I suspected it would amuse him. He pulled the end of a quilt up over his stockinged feet. The hay house was cold, though the night was more moderate than recent ones out on our claim. I put my arm through his and smelled the nose-tingling mix of cold air, wood fire, earth, sweat, and wool in his clothes. I commenced rubbing his shoulders with my fingers, rotating them and pressing them into the flesh of his neck. We sat like that for a few minutes, listening to the snores and rustlings of the sleepers around us. He said quietly, "There are two hundred down by Franklin."

"How many do we have?"

"That many or more. Some men came in from Ottoman Creek and from Palmyra, too. Remember that fellow Paschal Fish, that Mr. Graves talked about? He's come in, and offered to bring in some Wyandots. The Indians prefer us, at least."

"Mr. Bisket said the attack would come tomorrow."

"Some say that. I don't think they'll attack, myself. Our fault is that we like to underestimate the intelligence of their leaders. They have everything to lose by attacking, if you ask me. Every day we're more strongly fortified, we have more men. They waited and lost the momentum. Of course, they declare themselves eager to attack, burn, kill, hang, and all."

I relinquished my grasp of his neck, and he lay down beside me, breathing out a sigh of relieved fatigue. "Still," I said, "the citizens of Quincy would be mighty surprised if the citizens of Alton attacked them, or even the citizens of Hannibal, on the Missouri side. The citizens of Hartford, in the state of Connecticut, would hardly attack those of Springfield, Massachusetts. And yet here we are, building fortifications against Franklin!"

But he was half asleep and hadn't the energy for astonishment.

There was no attack on Sunday. We were up before dawn, eating our griddle cakes, and then the men went out to drill and work on the fortifications. The plan was that we would gather in the four forts when the attack began, but until then we were free to go about as we chose. As the sun was coming up, Mrs. Bush hurried myself and Mrs. Lacey along toward the Free State Hotel.

"This is what we do all day," she said, "make cartridges. And talk, of course. Before this, they were piecing a quilt. Lidie, my dear, I don't think you know Mrs. Wood." I did not, but soon she would be quite famous.

The cartridge-making factory was the roomy Wood cabin, right beside the Free State Hotel, and three or four women were already at it, two of them still in their dressing gowns, with their hair hanging down their backs. As we came in, one of the women was saying, ". . . finished counting. There are but thirteen cartridges apiece for two hundred twenty men."

"Most will have their own, surely," said another woman.

Another—Mrs. Wood herself—looked doubtful. "We mustn't depend on that. Folks have enough shot and powder for a day or two of hunting game. War isn't the same thing."

"How long do you think thirteen balls would last?"

"Not a day. They might sustain their attack for three days, my husband says. They've intercepted all the goods that are coming to Lawrence and stolen all the guns and ammunition. They'll use what our merchants have coming against us."

You could load and fire a Sharps carbine in ten or fifteen seconds—that's why the southerners thought they were repeaters. Thirteen cartridges was two or three minutes. The point of the Sharps was to be careless of ammunition, not careful of it. I said, "What about firing caps?"

"There seem to be plenty of those," said Mrs. Wood.

"You're certain all the balls and all the powder in town are here?" said Mrs. Brown, whom I had met in the summer but who, I thought, probably didn't recognize me. She was a slender and sharp-featured older lady, whose manner made you eager to please her.

Mrs. Wood sniffed. "That fellow Eaton gave up his powder yesterday morning when we three ladies impressed upon him the possible consequences of civic irresponsibility. I haven't heard any tales of another hoard."

"I've been wondering about General Lane," said one of the younger women.

The others laughed.

"General Lane," said Mrs. Brown, "talks like he has twenty kegs of powder in his cellar, but he's the same in everything. When the time comes, he'll borrow freely of the men closest at hand."

"And abuse them into the bargain," said one of the women who hadn't yet dressed. We all laughed, but our laugh reminded us of the fix we were in.

"Someone must tell Governor Robinson how low supplies are," said Mrs. Wood. So now he had become Governor Robinson.

"Tell Mrs. Robinson. She can tell him."

We all agreed that this was a good plan, but it didn't solve the problem.

"You know," said Mrs. Bush, "there's powder and lead, both, out on the Santa Fe Trail, if someone could go get it. Does anyone know Mr. Graves?"

"I do." I spoke up, not having said anything before.

"He's settled now, in a cabin out by that little crick out there—Patterson Crick they call it."

"And there's two other caches," said Mrs. Brown. "My cousin's brother has at least a twenty-five-pound keg. He had two in the summer."

"But who'll go get them!" exclaimed the woman

who'd been counting the cartridges, despair in her voice.

"I will," said Mrs. Brown and I in unison.

I said, "My nephew Frank and I got through just last night. But we need more than money to trade with Mr. Graves. He knows we aren't sound on the goose." We talked for a moment about this. Of course, there were doubters—Mrs. Bush felt responsible for me and said to me in a low voice, "What will I tell Thomas when he comes in for his supper?"

"We'll be back by then."

"Who is 'we'?"

"Frank won't let me go without him!"

Mrs. Wood—who was, along with her husband, always eager to make the Missourians uncomfortable—Mrs. Brown, and I huddled together. The two of them would take Mrs. Wood's buggy and her fast mare. Frank and I would take Jeremiah and borrow a light buggy from another of the ladies. Mr. Graves, it was said, had his place some five miles out, along the Santa Fe road. I explained to the women that I needed to be supplied with a certain liquid commodity over and above the money I would be taking with me. The women hesitated, but then one of them went away. She came back half an hour later, muttering, "It's on the seat of the buggy, wrapped in a quilt."

Mrs. Brown's cousin was not quite as far as Mr. Graves, and her other friend was near to him but off the road a ways. With two buggies, we all agreed, there was more of a chance that one or the other would get through.

"Getting back will be the trick," said Mrs. Wood. "A keg of powder looks like a keg of powder."

"We'll think of something," said Mrs. Brown. "Don't we always?" They were very self-assured, these New England dames.

I met Frank lounging along Vermont Street, watching the drilling. He told me that one of our men, Pomeroy, had been taken and another man shot, named Barbour, who was riding his horse south to his claim to see his family after days in Lawrence. He was unarmed.

"We'll take that as our lesson," I said.

Frank perked up.

We had Jeremiah hitched to the buggy in a few minutes and then went back to the Wood cabin to get the money they had gathered. Mr. Graves, of course, was known, at least by repute, to everyone, and my mission was considered less probable of success than that of Mrs. Brown and Mrs. Wood. As we drove south along Massachusetts Street, Frank practiced gesturing to me as if I couldn't hear a word. But though there were roving bands of Missourians all along the way, and though I knew we would be relieved of our keg of highly rectified whiskey should any of them stop us, we saw only two or three, from a distance, and no one obstructed us in any way. This was, perhaps, more disconcerting. I couldn't shake the conviction that they were there, hidden in the brush, behind trees, down in the bottoms of the Wakarusa River, which ran south of Lawrence. That they didn't come out gave them mystery and power, and made them all the more deadly. Of course, I upheld the masquerade of deafness, but I listened to Frank's talking and singing with a heart that beat as rapidly with excitement as with fear. Jeremiah moved through the cold air at a steady fast trot, his ears forward and his look as alert as a watchdog's might be, but after a few miles of seeing and hearing nothing, I felt a little oppressed.

"Now, Mrs. Newton—for you see, I recognize you perfectly—" said Mr. Graves when we called him out, "I take the arrival of you two young persons as a sign that my southern friends have shown their usual forbearance in refraining from burning out and looting the noble city on the hill, or rather, under the hill." I saw that Mr. Graves had altered, or developed, his mode of speaking yet again. He was a mysterious man, possibly more dangerous than he allowed himself to appear.

"Still might," said Frank cheerfully. "They got some fieldpieces over there."

"Do they, indeed," said Mr. Graves, doubtfully. He showed no signs of asking us in, bitter cold though it was, and now that I was here, I realized that I had not developed a plan for gaining his supplies, should he have any. I said, "How are your warts, Mr. Graves?"

He lit up. "Now, ma'am, I'd forgotten that you were a party to, or at least a witness of, that most successful medical strategy. Yes, indeed, not one week after I left that package beside the road, I woke up miraculously—and I say miraculously, but indeed, the remedy was pure science—relieved of that dermatistical burden. I may say that the Indians of Kansas Territory look upon me as nearly a god."

"Are you running a store, Mr. Graves?"

"A store, a school, a church, a surgical dispensary, of sorts. I have four cows to be milked, and I sell the milk. It's a quiet life, somewhat remote from the concerns of society—"

"But I thought you enjoyed—"

"I go among them, they come to me. It's all much the same. You, for example, have come to me. Bringing with you a most prepossessing young man."

"You a trader?" said Frank.

"I am."

"Look at this, then." Frank pulled a large kerchief from his pocket and opened it on the footboard of the wagon. Mr. Graves stepped over to look. Along with a paper of needles, a tarnished spoon, half a dozen square nails, a small bit for a pony, and the head of a hammer, I was amazed to find myself perusing a pair of woman's earbobs, elaborately fashioned of what seemed to be gold, small diamonds, and large, tear-shaped pearls. Mr. Graves said, "How much you want for that hammerhead, boy?"

"You got money?"

"I do."

"K.T. money? Or U.S. money?"

"Silver money."

Frank whispered to me, "I got that for an old bucket I found. How much should I ask?"

"Fifty cents."

"Four bits," said Frank to Mr. Graves.

"Pah!" said Mr. Graves. "An't got a shaft. I can get a new hammer with a shaft made in Cincinnati, Ohio, for four bits."

"If," said Frank, "you intend to wait to do your hammering, but if you want to hammer now, this is the hammerhead I got."

Mr. Graves laughed and put his hand in his pocket. He handed Frank two quarter dollars and pulled his ear for him. Frank handed him the hammerhead.

"Mr. Graves," I said, "how are you supplied for, uh, powder and lead?"

"My needs are taken care of. Powder and lead have come under heavy demand lately, I will say."

"Other things, too, I'm sure," I said, cocking my head toward the wrapped-up keg of whiskey.

Mr. Graves now looked directly at that and, I think, realized for the first time what it was. He grew very smooth, saying, "When the first two are in requisition by my compatriots, the last is highly likely to be wanted, as well."

"Yankee owned, Mr. Graves, but Kentucky made, I'm told."

Mr. Graves walked around the buggy. The keg of whiskey seemed to take on a rather queenly bearing, wrapped as it was in a crazy quilt made of silks and satins. He looked again, then walked forward to Jeremiah's head and gave his ears a tickle. Jeremiah flicked them back and forth.

"Sir," said Frank.

"Yes, son?" said Mr. Graves.

"Them earbobs are the real thing. They come

from New Orleans, and when they were new, they cost three hundred dollars."

I said, "Frank Brereton, how did you get hold of such a thing? Who in the world would give those to you? If you picked them up on the street, you have to return them to their rightful owner!"

"I didn't pick them up on the street. I an't a thief."

"I am not a thief."

"I know you an't. I an't, either."

I pursed my lips in frustration, while Mr. Graves said, "Let me see those again, boy. I need to get a feel of them."

Frank pulled out the kerchief and untied it. Now all three of us looked shamelessly at the earbobs. All I could tell was that the gold had a clean look. Mr. Graves took them up and cradled them in his hand. After a moment, he put them back, his expression sober, and said, "You young people have taken a great risk coming here. There were Missourians here all night last night."

"Then," said Frank, "you must be clear out of whiskey."

Mr. Graves turned on his heel and walked into his cabin, closing the door behind him.

We sat there for a long time, but the door didn't open. At first we were quiet, but then Frank plucked my sleeve and said, "Mrs. Lacey gave 'em to me. She said they were nothing to her. If Mr. Lacey was to get killed for having no ammunition, she could never wear 'em, anyway."

Jeremiah shook his head, rattling his harness, and

I was impatient, too. Though we were standing in the lee of the cabin-store, the wind whistled around it and seemed to swirl into the buggy and drive out all possible warmth. I said, "Well, we can't wait all day for nothing. It's past noon already."

I threw off the quilt I was wrapped in and got down from my seat. I was going to turn Jeremiah around, but too many items—cases, barrels, and kegs—were stacked in the way, so I led him forward and saw that the easiest way was around the cabin. I pulled my shawl more tightly around my face and ducked my head. Jeremiah rattled his bit at having to go into the wind, and we stepped forward.

Behind the cabin, sitting on some stacks of hay, were three kegs of powder. I murmured, "Hey, Frank," and pointed. He jumped off the buggy seat and ran over to the kegs. I was amazed they stood there in full view. Mr. Graves could have hidden them behind a stove he had also stored there, or covered them with pieces of sailcloth and wagon wheels. Those, too, were near at hand. On the one hand, Mr. Graves's store was five miles from Lawrence. On the other, the "war" had been going on for almost a week. "This one's mostly empty," called Frank. And then: "But this one's full." It weighed some twenty-five pounds, probably a quarter of Frank's weight. He hefted it out of the hay and carried it over to the buggy. After a moment, I helped him lift it onto the seat. Then we unwrapped the keg of whiskey and, together, carried that over to the spot where the powder had been. I looked around carefully, but I didn't see any evidence of balls. I even peered through a chink between the logs of the cabin wall, but there was nothing to be seen—the space had been well mudded and papered over on the inside. There was no sign of Mr. Graves.

Now that we had made our trade, we quickly wrapped the keg of powder in the quilt. The day was far gone past noon. I led Jeremiah the rest of the way around the cabin and out into the prairie track. I'd forgotten about bands of Missourians, but now I remembered them and thought that I saw some men and horses some distance away. We jumped into the buggy, and I whipped Jeremiah into a gallop. The cold wind made our eyes tear up so that we could see nothing and had to trust to Jeremiah's sense of direction. Nor could I see whether people were following us, but I acted as if they were. I never looked back to see if Mr. Graves came out of his cabin, but I knew I had given him two boons, and they were a barrel of highly rectified whiskey and the right to say that we black abolitionists had stolen his powder—he hadn't aided us of his own volition. Jeremiah was all the horse we thought him to be: he flew with the buggy back toward Lawrence, only breaking to a fast trot when we were nearly there. Perhaps there were stories behind us—of men who almost caught us, or saw us, or shot at us, but we didn't know them.

There was only one story ahead of us. Two men, bearded and wrapped up in hats and coats, stood their horses broadside in our path as we neared Lawrence. We could see the light of the fires up ahead and even smell them faintly. I simply drove Jeremiah at these men, thinking to push through, but at the last moment, one of them grabbed Jeremiah's bridle and hauled us to a halt. The other man trotted over to the buggy. He trotted to the wrong side, to Frank's side rather than to the side that the keg was on. I was sure they were Border Ruffians, since that was how they were dressed, but I never heard them speak, because as soon as the one man put his hand on Frank's arm, Frank held out his other hand and said, "Here's something for you, sir!" When the man opened his hand, Frank dropped the earbobs into it, and I shouted, "Get on, Jeremiah!" and I have to say that my whip flicked the man who was holding Jeremiah's bridle. He let go, I drove on, and Frank looked back in the gathering gloom. After a moment, he sat up in the buggy seat, grinning. "They're looking at them. The one man just whooped, and now it looks like they're about to have a fight over them."

"Frank Brereton! We might very well have got through without you giving those Ruffians Mrs. Lacey's earbobs!"

"Might of, but then she would of been awfully disappointed, I think."

Back at the Woods' cabin, Mrs. Wood and Mrs. Brown had themselves just returned. They'd been more successful than we had, having gotten both powder and lead, and they had also had more adventures evading the enemy. They made quite a picture, for they had torn the wadding out of their dresses and petticoats and inserted the powder and lead. They had gone out thin and come back fat, and the Missourians had smiled, tipped their hats at the ladies, and waved them on! We spent the whole evening making more cartridges, or rather, the women did. Frank was much happier prowling around the town. That night, Thomas and I slept downstairs at the Free State Hotel. In spite of the death of Barbour, whom everyone considered to be the unarmed victim of the Missouri Ruffians, and who later was buried with a soldier's funeral, the "war" seemed to wind inexorably down. Our readiness to defend ourselves was not met by equivalent eagerness on the other side to attack us, and so when Governor Shannon served as peacemaker, the proslave faction was happy enough to go home. Of course, there was also a blizzard, and they were living out in tents. Mrs. Bush said that the real reason the Missourians went home was that they ran out of whiskey and it grew too cold to play cards. It was true that Mr. Bisket, who had been captured and held by the Missourians after leaving Frank and me on the road, was required each of his five nights as a prisoner to help hold up a blanket against the wind so that his captors could play euchre beside the fire.

CHAPTER 13

I Discover Something About Advertising

Every mistress of a family should see, not only that all sleeping-rooms in her house can be well ventilated at night, but that they actually are so. Where there is no open fireplace to admit the pure air from the exterior, a door should be left open into an entry, or room where fresh air is admitted; or else a small opening should be made in a window, taking care not to allow a draught of air to cross the bed. The debility of childhood, the lassitude of domestics, and the ill-health of families, are often caused by neglecting to provide a supply of pure air.

—p. 311

AFTER THE WAKARUSA WAR (as it came to be known) was over, Thomas and I were once again faced with the question of where to live and what to do. Our joy at the war's end was soon driven out by what ended it—the snow and the cold. Each night seemed colder, and in fact, each night was colder. The stove at the hay house soon failed to warm that interior at all, and a mug of water placed next to it froze as quickly as though it were standing out of doors. We all retired to our quilts early in the evening, shortly after sunset, and it was the rankest cruelty to be called out of them for any reason. As the nights progressed, however, it quickly became apparent that the largest stack of quilts wasn't insulation enough for sleeping on the ground, outdoors or in, and Thomas and I began

looking around for another place to stay. We discussed returning to our claim, but as the snow continued to fall, that got farther and farther away. Soon
there was no question of such a thing; it was cold in
Lawrence, but there was plenty of food to be had: not
only pork and beef and venison, prairie chicken,
turkey, rabbits, and squirrels, but apples of two or
three different varieties, both green and red, pumpkins, other squashes, and sweet potatoes. Mr. Stearns
had stacks of sealed cans of oysters from far away,
and there was, of course, corn flour and meal, wheat
flour, lard, salt, sugar, honey, and maple sugar,
almost everything, for a price, except eggs, which
froze in the cold, and butter. But in Lawrence we
really didn't need eggs—the water was so full of
lime that it leavened any cakes and made them light
and delicious.

We moved for a time into the Free State Hotel,
right beside the Woods' cabin, where we ladies had
made cartridges. The Free State Hotel was famous,
and meant to be so. Not only did it stand four stories
of stone, but it had round, fortress-like windows in
the fourth story, which the Missourians viewed as
designed for defense, if not, indeed, for aggression.
Governor Robinson, General Lane, and the others
had made the Free State Hotel their headquarters
during the "war." It was a large, imposing building,
and the Missourians considered it just another way
that the people of Lawrence were attempting to lord
it over everyone else. In spite of its importance,
though, and the money that had been spent on its
building, winter had obstructed the completion of its

interior—one reached all four stories by way of a staircase made of rickety boards, through which you could see all the way to the cellar, if you dared to look down. I did not, but climbed as close to the wall as I could, holding on to the carved banister that had been installed before the stairs and planning how I would catch myself if the steps gave way. But they never did so, even under the burden of the sickly and feverish men and women who were carried up and down on pallets.

While we were installed at the hotel, the constitution that had been written at the Topeka convention came up for a vote. What with the "war" and the weather, I don't suppose that as many people in K.T. had a chance to read it as the Free Staters had hoped, but the voting in Lawrence was heavy, and all our friends cast their ballots. Elsewhere, the Missourians got up to their usual tricks. One man told us, and he a reporter for some eastern newspaper, that at Leavenworth he had witnessed the Missourians coming in boatloads to our Kansas election. Kansas elections had been overrun by Missourians every time before, and so, I suppose, this was what the elections officials expected, but the Missourians had other ideas: once enough of them got there, they stole the ballot box! One man tried to hide the box under a table and then run away; he was caught outside the store where they were voting and beaten with clubs! A Missourian with an ax raised it over his head to strike, and only was prevented by being unable to get in a clear blow! After that, the Missourians got the ballot box and took it away, and the Free Staters, who weren't as well armed as we are in Lawrence, didn't dare to go after it. There was tremendous gloating on the part of the Missourians, especially as the evening progressed and they got deeper into whatever barrels of highly rectified whiskey they could find to warm themselves up. They also threatened, loudly and clearly, to destroy the presses and the office of the Free State paper there, the *Register,* but these threats apparently were met with promises of reprisals against the slave-power paper, called the *Herald,* the one that so savagely and so frequently called for the death of all abolitionists.

It wasn't much different in any river town, and in Lawrence we fumed, our hatred, and I might also say our fear, of the Missourians sharply renewed. But the weather and the season cooled us rather quickly. According to the election, Governor Robinson now became the governor, and after it, we all were careful to call him that.

What drove us away from the hotel was the illness. There was fever everywhere, and as the weather got colder, more and more of the sick were brought to the only really sturdy building, which was the Free State Hotel. At least the thick stone walls, thicker by far than the thickness of an ax-hewn shake, kept the wind out. But there came to be feverish and delirious men and women in every room, and anyone who was healthy was obliged by charity to help care for them, especially in the nights, when the cold grew to be more than any man-made thing—be that trousers or shirts, socks or boots, quilt or cloak or shawl or hot drink or fire—could stave off. The more you craved to be huddling in your quilts with your head muffled by pillows, the more you were obliged, it seemed, to stir up fires, hunt for wood, boil some ice into water. After two weeks, Thomas and I were both hollow-eyed and exhausted, more or less resigned to succumbing to the fever ourselves, as most of the nurses did sooner or later.

Just then, though, Mr. Bisket found us a place to stay, through himself getting suddenly married to a widow that he met at the beginning of the war, a few days before he was captured. Mrs. Bisket was not so tall as Mr. Bisket but twice as big around, and Thomas and I thought he must have married her for the warmth: her cheeks were always red, and she never wore more than a light shawl over her shoulders in the coldest weather. She and her first husband had brought a great carved rosewood bedstead all the way from Connecticut at huge expense, and a second bedstead as well, though a humbler one, of maple. She kept all her feather beds and quilts fluffed up and inviting. Her name was Louisa. Her property amounted to a brick storefront with two rooms above on Massachusetts Street, two blocks down from the Free State Hotel. Louisa had a stove in each room and checkered oilcloths on the floors. She showed us around with pride. "I said to my first husband, Mr. Wheelwright—isn't it funny that Mr. Wheelwright was a wheelwright?—that I would not be traveling to Kansas Territory as a wretch, but as a woman of property. We shipped our goods from Boston to New Orleans, then up the river. We brought three wagons from Independence. We sold the extra two and the

mules, at a tidy profit, I must say." She smiled beatif-
ically, as so many New Englanders did when pro-
claiming similar sentiments. Thomas and I moved in
that same day. Since Mr. Bisket now had two wagons, three mules, and a horse, as well as a ready-
made home to live in and a ready-made inclination
toward prowling around and contriving this and that,
he set himself up in a sort of business. Hauling was
what he called it, but hauling was only its excuse. He
might haul a barrel of apples and, say, a load of
wooden shakes to a man on Pinckney Street, and stay
there awhile to help nail up some shakes, then be
offered the job of clearing some brush or chopping
some wood or, as December progressed, clearing
snow. Sometimes both wagons would be required,
and on those occasions, Thomas would drive the second. So it was that we supplemented our diminishing
funds after we moved into Lawrence. And then
Thomas's father sent him a quantity of sailcloth, and
this we sold by the piece from the old wheelwright
shop below. Needless to say, this life suited my
nephew Frank right down to the ground; he slept in
the shop below and came and went as he pleased.

We and our friends weren't the only ones to come
in from the prairie. Every house had two or more
families living there, and each of the hotels had half a
dozen strangers living cheek by jowl in each room.
The streets were full of Delawares, too, and Indians
of other tribes, all of whom declared that even the
oldest of their number hadn't seen such cold in their
lifetimes.

It had to be as cold in Missouri, which of course

was only a few dozen miles distant, but it seemed to many of us that the cold was an especial mockery of our ambitions, for of course, many had come on the promise of the sunny, warm, dry prairie winter. Since only September 1, Thomas Newton and I had found blistering heat, relentless winds, cracking tempests, cold wet misery, and cold frozen misery. And during the month of October, we'd seen fires everywhere, snaking over the prairie and dimming the blue sky with smoke. The fires, like much of the weather, had a grand and powerful beauty of their own, if you could lift your mind out of fear and discomfort long enough to appreciate it, but anyone who had hoped that Kansas Territory would gently embrace men and their civilization was quickly and repeatedly dis-abused of these notions. In Lawrence, there was con-siderable talk of California, more as the winter deepened. The New England women—Mrs. Bush, Mrs. Jenkins, Mrs. Lacey, Mrs. Bisket—began to talk more frequently of the neat villages and towns that they'd left behind. These Yankees weren't the impoverished emigrants that most westerners were or derived from. They had emigrated on principle rather than out of need, and many had left houses and farms and thriving businesses behind, though, as Mrs. Bush reminded us, and perhaps herself, "Pros-pering in New England takes plenty of contrivance, too. I won't hide from you that I was looking for things to be a bit easier here than there."

I didn't say what I had been looking for in K.T.—something I myself didn't know, something alien and unexpected, perhaps. If that had been it, then I had certainly found it.

On the day before Christmas, it was said by those who knew that it was seventeen degrees below zero. On Christmas morning, it was thirty below. I reckoned that we were colder by fifty or more degrees than we'd been on our last days on our claim, when we'd felt ourselves so unbearably cold. But cold as it was, the people of Lawrence, and we with them, kept up the flow of commercial and political activity. It went the same as with everything else: The first time your fingers or nose or toes got a touch of the frostbite, you were shocked and terrified. The fourth time, or the fifth, you were hardly impressed at all.

Louisa Bisket, ensconced in our stone building, kept the stoves burning hot with big chunks of black walnut that Mr. Bisket hauled in from the banks of the Kaw, as behooved a woman of property. She was a good cook, too, especially at concocting soups and stews. Her appetite for conversation was a grand one, and she couldn't hear enough, or say enough, about Mr. Bisket.

"I love the way he talks," she said. "He's delightfully expressive. Now, Thomas is a quiet sort—he barely says a word, though he reads beautifully and has such a deep, powerful voice, but Mr. Bisket! Well, *he* has a way with words, and a flow of talk! When I first met Mr. Bisket, well, my head turned right around. I knew . . ." She lowered her voice. "Everyone is quite aware that it's been a mere six weeks since Mr. Wheelwright suffered his unfortunate accident, and I was heartsick, as you can imagine. . . ."

"I thought," I said, "that Mr. Wheelwright died of a fever. . . ."

"Well, he did, but you know, it came on as a result of . . . well, he was trying to get our wagon across the river, and he fell in, and he couldn't swim! He just about drowned then, and he never recovered. When he went down with a fever three days later, I said right then to myself that he wasn't to live."

She looked genuinely stricken. She was ironing tiny pleats into one of her petticoats, while I sewed a shirt of a sort for Frank, who had grown in K.T. by an inch or two. She had the ironing board pulled as close as possible to the stove, but even so, it was so cold that the iron chilled in the air as soon as she lifted it, and the work went slowly. My sewing was twice as awkward as usual, and every five stitches or so I nearly had to put my fingers right on the stove to thaw them.

"But I must say, though it sounds hard, that it's for the best that Mr. Wheelwright and I had no children. Mr. Wheelwright was not sympathetic to imperfection. A very learned doctor in Massachusetts, who was familiar with all the latest systems, said that it was clear to him that this daily working with circles, this daily seeking after what you might call rolling perfection, well, it made the man a bit inflexible." She lowered her voice. "I made myself clear to Mr. Wheelwright. I was not going to be brought to compromising my own standards. I was an older bride, twenty-five, you know, and we, as a rule, are a stiff-necked bunch. And so Mr. Wheel-wright and I had made our peace."

"Mr. Bisket is younger than Mr. Wheelwright, then?"

"Oh, yes. Mr. Wheelwright was nearly sixty. I may be wrong, but it seems to me that Mr. Bisket looks to me for guidance. That is not the ideal most people hold, the husband looking to the wife for guidance, but I can't see why it shouldn't work, can you?"

I thought of my sisters and my mother, and their husbands. It had been a long time since any of them had looked to her spouse for guidance. I said, "I don't feel I know much about marriage. I've only been married since the summer."

"My dear," she said, "as far as I'm concerned, you can be married for twenty or thirty years in our day and not know a single thing about marriage if you don't strive to learn. We live in fallen times. My learned doctor friend in Massachusetts felt that relations between men and women were certainly different in former times, to the benefit of all. Woman should not be subject to male whim, as we are, but should live in full exercise of her capacities. I, for example, was never ill another day in my life after I made my position clear to Mr. Wheelwright."

It was more difficult to live as two couples than as one. Since there were two rooms, the question always arose of where we would sit in the evenings. Thomas and I didn't feel comfortable sitting in our room, which we might have preferred once in a while, because to do so seemed unsociable. And yet

Louisa and Charles, as I now began addressing Mr. Bisket, must have craved some time alone, too. If Louisa had been thrifty and warmed only their room, the larger of the two, we wouldn't have felt the waste of leaving our room empty while we sat with them, but she was prodigal in all things, one of her significant attractions in a world where frugality was the norm and the frugality of others always worthy of remark. It seemed as though to live smoothly, we needed one room or three. Two was just the wrong number. But I dared not complain, even to Thomas, or, indeed, to myself. Every day, I saw others who were sick and shivering.

Louisa had strong opinions about slavery, too, which she did not hesitate to detail. She was more radical than her husband and more outspoken by nature than Thomas, so she often held the floor on the subject when we sat about the stove in the evenings. In her mind, and according to her learned doctor friend and many of the best people, she said, back in Boston, the lives of women and those of slaves were not so much different. When Charles and my husband smiled or squirmed at this (and glanced about at Louisa's grand furnishings), she caught them up short. "Now," she said, "you are looking at my things and judging the general estate of woman by a very particular, and I might even say peculiar, gauge. A slave may wear beautiful clothes, read and write, and do his master's business with perspicacity and care, and he may even have some appreciation of and gratitude for his lot in life, and he may certainly be attached to his master, but his circumstances do not therefore reflect or mitigate the circumstances of millions of others who live under the thumb of someone else, who have no freedom and no money and no say in their own fate. Just because one person has made a separate peace with one other person, the whole institution is not thereby redeemed. . . . How do you regard your corset, Lydia?"

I have to say that this was a question I had never before been asked. I didn't know quite how to reply.

"I regard my corset as a saddle." She went on, "We've all heard of slave gangs where they bridle the troublesome slaves so as to both assert and proclaim control. Well, we women are similarly tacked up, though with corsets rather than bridles. They stifle our breath and cut us in two and shape us to the liking of our masters."

I would have to say that Thomas did not care for Louisa. He was careful to inform me that while he didn't object to her sentiments, he could not quite like her manner, but I found it arrestingly daring and nothing if not genuine. Charles was hog happy, as Roland Brereton would say. He was fed, warmed, loved, and told what to do, and his sentiments about every matter quickly came to mirror his wife's. K.T., he said, was the making of him, and it was true that in after years he prospered as well as any of our friends, died the father of eight and the grandfather of thirty-six, and spent sixteen years in the Kansas state legislature. And General Lane (later Senator Lane) always claimed that he admired Louisa Bisket and was admired by her in return, which was, of course, a recommendation to some and not to others.

We spent our holidays cozily enough, and in the
new year, Lawrence looked about as up-and-coming
as a frozen town could look. There were sleighs and
drags everywhere in the streets, and building continued in spite of the weather and the sickness. Not long
after New Year's Day, regular mail was established
between Leavenworth and Lawrence, and there were
plenty of goods everywhere, not only food. As Mrs.
Bush would say, "Some days the Ruffians want to
shoot us, and some days they don't, but they never
stop wanting our money."

Charles was one of the carriers for mail and
goods from Leavenworth, and in typical K.T. fashion, a few days after the route was established, he
and Thomas made up their minds to combine a little
trade with a little politics.

The situation was this: Our Topeka convention,
which we Free Staters had held in October, called for
elections to state offices on January 15 (they'd been
imagining a different January 15 than the one we
got—a mild, sunny day and not a bitter, blustery
one). The men of Lawrence voted properly, on the
fifteenth, but the next day everyone heard that as a
result of the fracas in Leavenworth the month before,
the Free Staters there had been afraid to vote. The
result was that they planned to gather at a certain
farmhouse in a village eight miles from town on the
next day, the seventeenth, and cast their ballots.
Some men from Lawrence, including the mail car-
rier, Charles, and his assistant, Thomas, wished to be
present and well armed, just to insure that the voting
was carried out in good order.

The men got up long before dawn and headed for Leavenworth, with Charles's hot little gelding and Jeremiah in the traces. We resolved the question of Frank's going along by the men's sneaking out without him, which obliged him to sulk about the wheelwright's shop all day. But for all Frank's enthusiasm for the excitements of our life, on the one hand, and Thomas's growing belief that events in Kansas must be brought to a climax in order for the slavery issue to be resolved once and for all, on the other, I often feared what Frank had gotten into with us, and I caught myself wondering how I would phrase the news of some disaster in a letter to my sister. Not all disasters, it now appeared, might come through the general bearing of arms by parties who hated one another; these days I also wondered how I might tell her that her boy had frozen to death.

Louisa and I were anxious throughout that day and into the next. We stayed up all night and kept sending Frank out into the street, as if there might be something to hear all the way from Leavenworth. As it turned out, we were worried with good reason, for the Missourians had indeed discovered the voting. The night before, they had attacked the farm where it was to take place, and in the morning, before our husbands got there, they'd attacked a party of voters heading out to the farm. There were so many Missourians that the Free Staters ran off for fear of their lives and never got to vote at all. Shortly after Thomas and Charles got to the farm, the Missourians came around for the second time that day and shot off their guns into the air and vowed to break up the

ballot boxes "and a lot of heads into the bargain" and
to "hang some black abolitionists" or "throw 'em out
onto the ice," but the Free Staters gathered inside
shot off their Sharps carbines and drove them away.
No one knew how many Free Staters were prevented
from voting or chased away, but all those who got
through swore they'd done so at peril of their lives.
Our husbands decided to stay the night—everyone
was sure that members of a group who styled themselves the "Kickapoo Rangers" would attack the
farmhouse—but after a while, a man, his son, and his
nephew decided to hazard a dash for home. These
three did get chased, and trapped in a fence corner.
The man and one of the boys had to try and hold off
the "Rangers," while the other boy ran back to the
farmhouse for help. Thomas and Charles were in the
house, and they happened to be the only two with
Sharps rifles, as all the other Lawrence men had left.
Charles, who was a better shot than Thomas, agreed
to go out with the party of rescuers, who were in the
charge of a Captain Brown, still another Brown, a
man of thirty-five or so, well liked by all the Leavenworth people, who was a committed Free Stater.

Not long after that, the two parties converged.
The Free Staters were on the verge of driving off the
proslave party, when a larger party of these Kickapoo
Rangers arrived. Now there was what I suppose
would qualify in Kansas as a bona fide battle. Brown
on his side drew up his men in a line, and the others
did, too. The firing commenced, and Charles said
that he had never been so scared in his life, even
when he was taken prisoner by the Missourians dur-

ing the "war" and threatened with hanging. After a while, the Missourians got into some houses nearby and fired at the Free Staters, who were in the open. Captain Brown made Charles lie down behind a snowbank and keep firing with his Sharps carbine, while the others went more slowly, muzzle-loading after each shot. Pretty soon, though, the Free Staters themselves retreated to some of the nearby buildings, and then the battle petered out, as no one's rifle had enough range to do much damage in these circumstances. Brown had the men retreat to the cabin where the election had taken place and where Thomas still was, with some other men and the ballot box. Two of the Free Staters were hit and slightly wounded. About the Missourians, they were soon to find out.

The cabin was crowded, and after a while men began to agitate to leave, both to get back to the safety of their own homes and to remove the ballot box to a safer place. Finally, Captain Brown decided to take a buggy and a wagon and seven men and try to get back to Leavenworth. Thomas and Charles resolved to wait until morning and come on to Lawrence, as they had the mail with them and no need to go back to Leavenworth.

As they were making their way down the road, Captain Brown and his men passed another wagon but ignored it. Then, coming around a curve in the road, they saw two more wagons and were surrounded and taken. These, again, were the Kickapoo Rangers—there is a town up by Leavenworth called Kickapoo, and it is full of the lowest sort of characters—and they took away the weapons of all our men and dragged them off to a local store where the owner sympathized with the slave power, all for the sake of working to death a little Negro boy of some ten years.

Now was when the real horror commenced, for the Kickapoo Rangers were drunk as they could be, and instead of destroying the ballots and paroling the men, which is what they said they were going to do, the southerners got a length of rope from the owner of the store (gratis, I presume) and threatened all the prisoners with hanging. It turned out that one of their number had been killed, a man named Cook, and they were howling for revenge. There was a proslave man who was more reasonable, some sort of army man named Captain Martin, and he argued for the release of all the prisoners. Eventually, he managed to engineer the escape of all of them except Captain Brown, who was being held in a separate room. Another man went off to Leavenworth to try and bring some men to help, but no one would come.

When the news came back to Lawrence of what they did to Captain Brown, we were convinced at last and permanently that the Ruffians were animals—worse than animals, merciless fiends who had no thoughts in their heads except of the most brutal sort. They killed him with hatchet blows and kicks, then got drunker, then threw him in the wagon and drove him home to his wife, where they threw him in the yard and shouted, "Here's Brown!" and drove off, laughing. Some people said that he was still alive and died in her arms, but others said that he was dead. It was shocking enough either way.

Charles and Thomas knew the beginning of this story by the time they got home, but not the end. They had met Captain Brown and liked him; he was not an old man by any means, but someone like us. After everything was known, they were speechless in the way you get when some vile thing has brushed past you. All of Lawrence was talking of nothing else, but they didn't want to talk of it at all.

We sat silent around our fire the next few evenings. Louisa knitted busily and I attempted to sew, but Thomas and Charles said nothing and did nothing. When I suggested that Thomas might read from one of his books, he said, "I can't think which one," and Louisa didn't dare suggest that Charles sing, one of his favorite amusements. Louisa and I traded glances over and over. I was not sure what she was thinking, as she was of an especially, you might say uniquely, sanguine temperament, and K.T. seemed to suit her very well; but I was thinking fearful and bitter thoughts, all mixed in together. I was of course glad that my husband had escaped without injury, but that gladness gave way to horror every time I thought of Mrs. Brown, who seemed, in my mind, to be myself in a different dress. I hated the Missourians for these deeds with a fresh hatred—as fresh as if my friends and I hadn't known for months how the Missourians were. But I also resented our men, even Thomas and Charles, for going off and getting into it. I could both imagine and not imagine what they had seen, and I couldn't throw off the feeling that they hadn't needed to witness it and therefore to bring it home; and so, while I knew they weren't at fault, I seemed to feel, some moments, as if they were. And yet, Thomas's dejection aroused my pity, too. No authorities on marriage that I had encountered had ever discussed this welter of uncomfortable emotions that seemed to go with the condition. I feared that K.T. was going to bear me down in the end. I suppose we all did so.

On the other hand, the speed of events didn't give us much leisure to ponder them, and it was hard to tell whether that would, in the end, contribute to our salvation or our destruction.

CHAPTER 14

I Do Yet Another Thing I Have Never Done Before

Those persons, who keep their bodies in a state of health, by sufficient exercise, can always be guided by the calls of hunger. They can eat when they feel hungry, and stop when hunger ceases; and then they will calculate exactly right.

—p. 98

AFTER THE DEATH OF Captain Brown, the Missourians who were prepared to hang, shoot, dismember, kill, and otherwise clear us out of K.T. began to gather in the border towns and prepare their springtime strategy. Some of their papers came into town, and in one, the very voice of the Kickapoo Rangers, the editor reflected our own sentiments back to us in a way that seemed astounding, given the horror of Captain Brown's death. Declaring that "forbearance has now ceased to be a virtue," the editor called for the proslave faction to "strike your piercing rifle-balls and your glittering steel to their black and poisonous hearts!" Their strategy seemed to be like that of a man who attacks another in a barroom and then, when he has his victim at the point of death, starts screaming that he is being terribly injured and must kill his victim in order to save himself. For the most part, these papers and the reports of what the proslave faction said of us were almost more inflaming than their actions, because they seemed calculated to insult us and deny the truth of what was all around us. Many in Lawrence, I have to say, were nicely warmed by resentment of these insults.

But for others, myself among them, the prolonged frigid weather made even the prospect of being hanged, shot, dismembered, killed, or otherwise cleared out rather an abstract one. The possibility of being frozen to death was distinctly more likely. Every day at the end of January and the beginning of February, gangs of men went out on the ice of the river dressed in every item of clothing that they could find, plus buffalo skins and blankets, like the Indians, to chop wood and carry it into town on every form of sledge or sleigh. The horses and mules wore blankets, too, though they were as furry as they could be. Most days, Charles and Thomas went with these parties, though some evenings the two of them were detailed to guard the town. No one knew when the Missourians would cross the border and make their attack. On the one hand, we feared it would be soon, and given Lawrence's position, we would be unable to defend ourselves, but on the other hand, we feared it would be later, when there would be many more of them.

Some days, Charles and Thomas went to Leavenworth to get the mail, only to find once they got there that the mail had been stolen or destroyed in Missouri. Of course, the postmaster at Leavenworth didn't say that the absent mail was stolen or destroyed, but all of Lawrence knew that it had been—enough got through to indicate what had not gotten through: all sorts of people were expecting bank drafts, letters, and goods that their relatives and friends in the east proposed to send or had sent, but they disappeared in Missouri.

Louisa kept her fires going and put on another light shawl, and when the men were out, she marched back and forth between our two rooms, knitting as she went. Unlike me, she was an excellent needlewoman, and it took her only a short time to knit up a cap or some mittens from her stock of wool. Most of these she knitted in children's sizes and gave away to anyone she heard of who was poor or cold. I sat beside the fire, doing my best to get through our sewing. Louisa was alive to the rights and wrongs of our cause, and it was at this time that she somehow got to be acquainted with General Lane, an acquaintanceship that, as I have said, soon extended to Charles and lasted as long as General Lane was alive. And yet, even though General Lane and Louisa quickly became intimates, there was never the least gossip that their friendship was of the wrong sort. Considering General Lane's well-deserved reputation, this was a great testament to Louisa's strength of character.

I doubt that General Lane remembered from one time to the next that he had ever met me, but I certainly noticed him, for he was very noticeable and liked to be noticed. Perhaps knowing that he would never pass for a figure of elegance, he adopted quite the opposite standard and dressed very roughly, even for a Kansan. But he was a compelling-looking gentleman, as Louisa would say (often did say), with thick dark hair, pleasing, regular features, and a surpassingly intense gaze. His great rival then and for the rest of his life was Dr., then Governor, Robinson. Of the two, Robinson had lived the wilder and more exciting life, with stints in California and the war in Mexico, but he had the looks and demeanor of a steady man of middle age, while General Lane, who was ambitious, certainly, but had simply come to K.T. from Indiana, had the looks and demeanor of a great romantic adventurer.

General Lane, Louisa told me, was utterly convinced that the Missourians were poised to attack, and a few days after the incident in Leavenworth, he wrote two letters to President Pierce himself. Though they were over the signatures of both General Lane and Governor Robinson, they sounded much more like Lane, the hotheaded one, than Robinson, who was always advising patience. At any rate, I was alarmed: one letter said that we had authentic information that an attack was imminent, and the other that the Missourians had artillery to use against us (and both said that they planned to "butcher" the Free Staters of Kansas). Copies of the letters, or papers people said were copies, got passed around all over Lawrence, and I won't say that everyone thought the Missourians were either massed or poised to attack. Owing to his recent experience, my husband thought they were ready to do anything but only "poised" to take advantage of any situation that might offer itself for the many to waylay the few. Thomas and Louisa, in fact, had a small debate about this very subject a few days after the letters were carried off to Washington.

"If we think in military terms," said Thomas, "we'll get it all wrong. However much they call themselves captains and lieutenants, they are but bullies, and they think as bullies think. We've the arms and the men to handle them."

"The Missourians are but a portion of the forces arraying themselves at the border, and rapidly getting to be the smaller portion. Real military men from all over the south are ready to stir this pot and see what bubbles to the surface, if you ask me," said Louisa, with a sip of her tea (tea was plentiful and hot every night). "General Lane hears from his sources that slave-power newspapers are filled with advertisements for regiments of soldiers."

"Bands of emigrants—"

"Bands of armed emigrants, with no women, no children, no plows or sickles or seed."

Thomas ostentatiously pulled his shawl more closely about his shoulders and chuckled. "I hope they get here soon, because they will surely get a surprise if they do."

Charles interposed. "Anyway, we've elected our officials. Jim Lane says they have to comport themselves like elected officials now, or we an't got a chance. I think calling for troops to protect us is an excellent strategy. Puts us in the right but shows them we know our way around these things."

"We are already in the wrong, according to them. I don't know if there is any strategy that will put us in the right," said Thomas. "And another thing here is that we're talking up these Ruffians as if they know what they're doing. Didn't we just finish a war, so called? Weren't you a prisoner, so called? And what did you do? Why, you held up a blanket so the fire wouldn't go out, while they drank themselves silly and gambled themselves poor. When we write to the President in these terms like 'butcher' and 'artillery,' we're convincing ourselves to be scared off, and we forget what we already know."

"It could have easily been worse," said Charles.

"I do not believe that," said Thomas.

"However it was," said Louisa, "they may learn their lesson like anyone else. If we count on them remaining ignoramuses, then we are the fools. According to General Lane—and he told me these things himself—we are sitting here in the cold thinking all of these matters are far away, but the United States is getting ready to settle them and settle them quickly."

I said, "Frankly, speaking of the cold, how can they have slaves here? Cold like this would be death to slaves. It's practically death to us, and the Indians can hardly abide it, either."

"I'd like to see them bring a few slaves into this cold," said Louisa. "You don't give a child a little open-necked shirt and send him barefoot into this weather. They'd soon have to dress those slaves like men and feed them properly, and then they might learn something!"

In general, this is a fair example of how the talk went in the weeks following the letters to President Pierce. Folks disagreed about the extent of our danger and how to deal with it, but no one doubted that the government in Washington would act to save us once alerted to it.

Unfortunately, one thing that Louisa did not have in her rooms above the wheelwright's shop was a door, or rather, there was one door, but it was used at the top of the stairs. There was no door between the two rooms. For two newly married couples, this constituted something of an inconvenience. I felt my husband, the husband I had known out on our claim when we were all alone together, slipping away from me. I discussed this, obliquely, with both Thomas and Louisa, saying that I spent more time with Louisa and Thomas with Charles Bisket than ever we spent with our spouses. Each replied characteristically. Thomas gave me a slow, knowing smile, acknowledging in his way the justice of my concern, but then said, "My friends on the ship see their wives perhaps once every two years or so, and my father and brothers spend twelve hours out of every twenty-four in the factory, then three or four more associating with other sailmakers, or other townsmen, or other members of their party. On Sundays, when there are no other activities, the whole family troops off to services, morning and afternoon." Now his smile grew warmer, and he put his arm around my waist. "My mother and father call each other Mr. and Mrs. Newton. Perhaps they've forgotten each other's Christian names." And he gave me a kiss. Louisa was more blunt. "Marriage," she said, "mustn't be too sweet, my dear, or it would start to cloy. Domestic delights are like Turkish delight, best taken in small bites after a larger meal of Christian endeavor. I do not actually care to come to know Charles Bisket quite as well as I came to know Ruben Wheelwright. Marriage needs a little distance as a preservative." And in addition, I gave myself to understand that not only would our circumstances pass, but I ought to be thoroughly grateful for them. Every shivering, pale, and suffering countenance that I met on the street smote my conscience each time I questioned our situation. Surely what my sisters had always said, that I was spoiled to the core and thought only of myself, was true.

Nevertheless, I couldn't help regretting that our favorite amusement of former times, reading aloud, went by the board, as Louisa preferred to converse and Charles preferred to sing. With much encouragement from Louisa, Charles sang every evening for a period. He had a high, fluting tenor voice, and he liked any kind of song. In the spring, the two were planning to purchase some sort of piano or melodeon, or even a little concertina, for him to accompany himself on. Some nights, others came in and sang parts, and these evenings went late. I am sure many of the singers were singing, not for their supper, but for their warmth.

On the coldest nights, my nephew Frank slept near the fire in our room, fully clothed and wrapped in blankets. Otherwise, he stayed down in the shop. If there were other boys there from time to time, some of the boys who had come out to K.T. without families or money, just hoping to see what was doing and make something of it, neither Louisa nor any

other of the adults cared. And they were a hardy
bunch, as we could not keep a fire in the stove in the
shop all night. One of Frank's associates was the oldest Lacey boy, whose name was Roger. He was perhaps a year older than Frank, and considerably taller
and brawnier. At fourteen, he had almost the size and
strength of a man, and he had quite a head of hair—it
stood straight up, so strongly that he could hardly
press it down with a hat. On mornings when he came
by, we saw that he would have combed it down with
some sort of grease, or water, but as the day went on,
it persisted in rising, so that by evening it was standing again. Roger had permission of his parents to go
out with the men cutting wood on the riverbanks, and
Frank sought the same permission of me. All I could
think of was Missourians hiding in the trees and
picking off the woodcutters one by one—had I had
the murderous intent that we allowed in the Missourians, that's what I would have done—but there
had been no incidents, and so I let Frank go. In general, I had let Frank fall away from all civilizing
influences, I had to admit. He could have gone to
school—a man in Lawrence, I heard, ran a school
whenever he had the wood to keep his schoolhouse
warm—but Frank never even saw the place. He
could have more frequently gone to church, but what
with the war and the cold and sickness and the over-
all alarms and difficulties of K.T. life, there weren't
all that many services for any of us to go to. He could
have kept company with Louisa and me, and we
might have improved him as the company of women
is widely said to improve men and boys, but with all

the friendliness in the world, he managed to slip away. K.T. was a boy's adventure, that was for sure.

By the end of January, I had now written two letters to my sisters since Frank's arrival, in which I was careful to portray my care of him as responsible. My conscience smote me a bit. Only Frank and I considered my handling of him remotely responsible. Thomas thought he should be in school, and Louisa thought he should be gainfully employed. That he made a few dollars each week with his trades didn't impress her. She said, "My dear, it's a fact that merchants are a cancer upon the honest labor of those who actually produce a beautiful or useful object by the skill of their hands. We must vow between ourselves whenever possible to honor men's or women's labor by meeting them face-to-face and giving them our money ourselves, or better still, offering them the fruits of our own labor in barter. K.T. will be a true paradise when none of these goods in the stores that come from the east are available and all have been replaced by objects of Kansas manufacture, objects that we may thank their creators for personally!" She was vociferous in her urging that I steer Frank toward smithing or milling of some sort, "before his course is set." But Frank's was a boat not easily steered, small though it was, and I had just begun my third letter to my sisters, and to Roland, with news of Frank:

My dearest sisters,
    I write to inform you that all here are surviving the cold weather as well as might be

expected. My husband got the frostbite twice, and I have gotten it only once in a toe and once in my nose, but we are fully recovered. My nephew Frank has avoided the frostbite altogether, though he is outdoors and active all the day long. You may be sure that he is a good boy—he is supporting himself and bringing home some money to me, and is respectful at all times. He told me to tell you, brother Roland, that he has traded his old rifle for a Sharps carbine and he likes it very much. He advises you to get one for yourself as soon as possible, and asks me to tell you particularly that they are manufactured in Connecticut, in case you want to know that. Let me say here that the school has stopped running because of the cold,

I had no actual personal knowledge of the school or the schoolmaster.

but I fully intend to send him there as soon as it resumes. You have perhaps read in the papers about our troubles here. I won't say that things have been easy

and here I left off for a day or two.

It was just that day, a Sunday, that Frank showed us that he had gotten further out of hand than I imagined. The night had not been one of the very coldest ones, and so Frank had slept downstairs. Sometimes in the mornings when he got up early and had some money, he went over to the Cincinnati House or the Free State Hotel for something to eat. When he

didn't show up for breakfast, I thought little of it.
Thomas ate his corncakes and drank his tea and went
off himself, to ride with Charles to Leavenworth.
Though they didn't expect the mail to be there, they
were obliged to go for it, as every man and woman in
Lawrence was obliged to stay as far as possible out
of the wrong. But soon after leaving, Thomas
returned. For once, he banged open the door and
shouted my name. As soon as he did so, I could hear
Louisa in the next room jumping out of bed and
throwing on her wrapper, alarmed as I was at the tone
of his voice. Jeremiah was gone.

We did not think of Frank, of course, we thought
of the Missourians, especially those Missourians,
never mentioned but always in the backs of our
minds, who had possibly once owned Jeremiah.

I exclaimed, "I put him in that corral with the
others last night myself! Were any of the others . . . ?"

"Gate's closed and locked, all the other horses
are there. Jed Smith's man hasn't seen him all morning. He thought we'd gotten him out early and didn't
think to mention it, until I showed up!"

"There's men everywhere, all night long. They
come over here to sell things and buy whiskey," said
Louisa, pinning up her hair. "I've often thought we in
Lawrence are too trusting."

"What now?" I said.

If we had been entirely confident of our claim on
Jeremiah, we would have reported his loss all over
town.

Thomas said, "Bisket's taking his horse to look
around the other corrals. I should take the mule—"

"You can't ride that mule!" said Louisa. "He's a terrible bucker under saddle."

"I can," I said. "I want to, anyway. I've got to find Jeremiah!"

I can't say that when I got out into the morning air I didn't feel a moment's recoil. Normally, Louisa and I tried to find things to do indoors until midday or after. But Jeremiah! My own horse, who nickered to me every time he saw me, who was as easy to ride and willing and pert and sound and neat as a horse could be! I caught Louisa's mule, threw on my saddle and bridle, and mounted him from a rail of the corral fence. Jed Smith was talking to me the whole time. "I an't ever lost a hoss before, Mrs. Newton. I got good fence here, and nobody comes around. Two men watch all night, and then Nowl and I are here all day. Unless some of them Indians spirited him away. I don't know what to say, but it seems so impossible he's gone that I know he's here somewhere. I'm still looking." He switched his plug of tobacco from one cheek to the other and spit into the frozen muck of the corral.

"You didn't see anyone around all morning, or over the night? Not Lawrence people, but strangers?"

"Naw. Dead quiet all night. I tell ya, ma'am, he's gonna turn up, and we'll say, Now, how did he git there? and maybe it's something we'll never know. Indians got medicine for everything. . . ."

I coiled a length of rope around my waist. My fingers, though I was wearing gloves and mittens, were already stinging with the cold.

"Good luck to ya, ma'am!" Mr. Smith spit again, this time at the mule's feet. "While you're gone, I'll think this one through."

Mr. Smith was from Michigan. While not of the brightest intelligence, he was kind with the horses and fed them well.

As I rode down Massachusetts Street, looking in every corner and crevice for a wandering gray horse, I was trying to remember, if I ever knew it, the name of that family we'd run off Mr. Jenkins's claim in the fall. I was just thinking that I could hardly remember what anyone had looked like, so hirsute and tangled had they been, the father and his sons, when I saw a group of men and horses gathered in a field, and then I saw Roger Lacey, who wore a distinctive green coat, and then I saw Jeremiah, and then I saw Frank, and then I realized that the men were having some races. A pair of horses and riders took off as I watched, causing the mule to buck and kick. I slapped him with the end of the reins and urged him forward. His big ears arrowed toward the running horses, and he nearly pulled me out of the saddle. "Harlan!" I cried, trying to hold him. "Are you a racing mule?" They had those in Missouri and Arkansas, I knew.

Frank ducked behind Jeremiah when he saw me, but I didn't say anything except, "Hello, Jeremiah." Roger Lacey backed away and vanished completely.

I waited. The mule curvetted and kicked out, but then settled down. The two runners finished their race and headed back to the group, led by three or four men who had manned the finish line. Lots of men were milling around, and I was the only woman. There was money in every hand, laughter and license in every face, and brown saliva flying everywhere. One of the men, with black whiskers up to his eyebrows, it seemed, and wearing red fingerless gloves and black instead of the usual blue denim trousers, took hold of the mule's bridle. He said, "This is rough business, ma'am, and there's unmannerly behaving going on. I don't advise—"

"That gray is mine. And the boy hiding behind him is mine, too. And I don't want my horse racing in the snow, if at all."

"Already raced, ma'am. Won, too. This snow an't bad. Too dry to be slick. Hosses can really dig into it and git some speed. That gray's a fine hoss. Beat Ben Matthews's black over there all to—all to—all to pieces, ma'am."

I coughed to refrain from smiling and tried to marshal my most disapproving face. I said, "If he already raced, why is he standing around in this cold?"

From behind Jeremiah, Frank's voice shouted, "I cooled him all out, Lidie! And his legs are tight as can be and cool, too!"

"He's got another heat, ma'am. I mean, if you'll let him, of course." He moved closer and lowered his voice. "The boys'll be disappointed if he an't gonna run, as they've got a load of money on the animal."

I didn't answer immediately but instead kept quiet, looking at the man and at the horse, who looked at me, his gray, furry ears alert and his dark eyes in his white face intelligent and interested.

Though he looked happy enough, I did not think that Jeremiah himself *wanted* to race. Frank peeked under Jeremiah's neck, then eased around between me and the horse.

"He won by four lengths," said Frank. "And he wasn't even trying."

"Did you gamble, Frank?" The man who was holding the mule's bridle had by this time let go. Now he looked at the far horizon.

"Well, of course I did," said Frank, indignantly. "You think I'm a fool? I won six dollars."

"Frank! If your mother knew I let you—"

"On a dollar bet! That's good investing, Cousin Lydia. And you know Pa don't hold betting on horses against anybody. Betting on horses is a natural human act! Pa says you *got* to do it."

I was sure that Roland did say so, but I was equally sure that Thomas Newton did not say so. I hated Thomas's disapproval. "Ma'am?" Another man came up behind me, and as I turned, he said, "Do you remember me? I am the Reverend Moss."

He was, indeed, the man who had sold me Jeremiah, and he was dressed in his Sunday preaching clothes, perhaps—a black suit, with a heavy Indian blanket over his shoulders.

"I recognize you, Reverend."

"Horse looks very good."

"He's been satisfactory. Now, I think, I had better take him home. Frank, you find Roger, then you have to ride this mule. You've ridden Jeremiah enough today."

"Ma'am, my doctrinal view is that no harm and

considerable good might be done for all these boys here if they were to see that horse run again. That horse is a beautiful example of God's work, an inspiring example. Perhaps you know the Book of Job? He saith among the trumpets, Ha ha, and he smelleth the battle far off. That passage could easily describe this horse."

I regarded Jeremiah, who regarded me in turn. He was calm and relaxed. The reverend remarked, idly, "The price I'd put on that horse now? Two hundred U.S. dollars. New York dollars. Philadephia dollars. In Lexington, Missouri, where they are indeed fond of horseflesh, I could get three hundred for this horse."

"My nephew took the horse without permission. My husband is out even now, beating the bushes, trying to find him. We were extremely concerned."

"I myself asked the boy, as soon as I recognized the horse, whether he had permission to bring him out, ma'am. And he said he did."

"Frank," I exclaimed, "lying, stealing, and gambling are enough sins for one Sunday! You get up on this mule and start home. Where is Roger? I will follow you smartly." I dismounted and hoisted him onto the mule, then slapped the animal's rump so that he trotted quickly away. Jeremiah was wearing a saddle I didn't recognize. I undid the girth and handed it to the reverend, then led the horse over to a tree stump and got on bareback. His flanks were warm against me. As I followed after Frank, I saw Roger separate himself from the group and begin to walk toward me, head hanging. Then I heard a shot, then saw two more horses, a brown and a chestnut, gallop away from the starting line. All along their course, men called out, "Go, Lizzie!" or "Run, Hawkeye!" And Roland was at least partly right—it was a natural human act to watch them and to favor one over the other, even not knowing either. I favored the mare, the chestnut, as it turned out. Pinning her ears, she stretched out in a long, flat gallop, looking exactly like she was resolved not to lose. The other horse closed to just a neck behind her, but she pinned her ears even flatter to her head and increased her speed. He seemed to slow down, and she opened daylight between them. I looked down at Jeremiah. He was watching everything with interest, and when they passed their closest to us, he gave a little crow hop.

Frank, on the mule, hadn't gotten very far toward town. Roger had stopped dead, gaping.

It was a beautiful sight, the sight of that gleaming mare stretched out at a full run against the white snow, and all the men, rough characters that they were, waving their hats and sticks and seegars and jugs and hands, and shouting, all senseless of themselves and abandoned to the moment. As soon as the mare won, of course, some of the items that had been thrown into the air were flung upon the ground and stomped on, and then the scene changed, and men began paying off their bets, cursing, grinning, pushing each other, slapping each other, taking pulls from their jugs, and blowing into their cold fingers. It took her rider five minutes or so to slow down the mare

after they crossed the finish line, while the brown
horse was ready to give it up within a few strides.
The riders jumped off, and they led the horses past
me. A few men glanced in my direction, sobered
themselves, smiled, tipped their hats, but the others
didn't notice—possibly were not quite sure what to
do with a woman at a race meet, even in K.T., where
women went almost everywhere.

Frank and the mule got even farther from town—
they were right beside me. I flicked the reins and
turned my face resolutely toward the buildings in the
distance.

"That filly an't nothing compared to Jeremiah.
He could eat her up. She just looked good because of
that nag they put with her."

"I'm displeased with you, Frank."

"I was just saying. I wasn't suggesting."

"We were very worried. You deliberately hid
your intentions from us. Thomas is still worried, and
I have to find him and tell him that Jeremiah hasn't
been stolen."

"Jeremiah runs like silk, or like some weasel or
something. Like water. You an't never seen nothing
like it."

"Haven't ever seen anything like it."

"Well, then, you an't."

"I thought you rode him."

"Naw. One of the boys rode him. I an't that good
a rider. I paid him a dollar."

"You let a stranger ride Jeremiah?"

"You can't race your own horse, Lidie. Only

fools do that. It's very poor economy, sort of like being your own lawyer."

"What do you know about being your own lawyer?"

"I got my eyes open, don't I? Horace was his own lawyer once. He lost the money, too." This last Frank spit out as if he could barely let such words lie on his tongue. And it was true that Frank generally made a profit. He said, "Some folks think paying someone to do what they know how to do better than you is a waste of money, but I an't of that opinion. You can't do everything yourself."

"Frank, you are trying to pull a veil over my eyes."

"Naw, I an't. I know you won't punish me any, and Thomas will look at me sadly and sternly, and I'll feel bad, but then I'll remember how Jeremiah looked like something not of this earth when he was running along, and I won't feel so bad anymore." He gave me a sideways look. "But you don't even know how bad you should feel, if you never see what I saw. They was gonna give him a go against that sorrel mare, if you let him. That would of been some race."

"I can't let you race Jeremiah. It isn't seemly, and Thomas and Charles are looking for you. And I shouldn't be here among these people. You don't know who's here. These aren't your usual Unitarians and Congregationalists from Massachusetts. They talk and look like Missourians, if you ask me. And what about Roger? I'm sure his mother is worried about him, too."

He ignored this last.

"Well, there's all kinds of folks in Lawrence, and when the races are going, I don't ask questions. But if you trade with me and go over there to that clump of trees, nobody's there and you can see good. I hate this mule, anyway. He trots like he's falling to pieces."

"I'm determined not to reward you, Frank."

"Come on, cousin. You an't never seen nothing like it. And you haven't ever seen anything like it, either. I went along with you when you wanted to swim the river."

"The footing is snowy. What if Jeremiah hurts himself?"

"Jeremiah is a cat, Lidie. He an't going to hurt himself."

My misgivings as I watched Frank ride Jeremiah back to the group of men and horses smoking and steaming in the cold air were agonizing. My mind raced to all sorts of tragic endings, but most often to the image of Jeremiah slipping in the snow and breaking a leg, the rider falling off and being killed, and myself having to relate all of these events to Thomas, who should have been after the mail by now but couldn't be, because I had both the mule and Jeremiah with me, and Charles and Louisa's one horse wouldn't pull the wagon with the other mules. So to top it all off, I was letting my husband, the most responsible and judicious of men, fall more deeply into the wrong with every passing minute. I stationed myself under the rattling branches of a clump of trees as Frank and Jeremiah came up to the group of men—or rather, were joined by men who saw him approach. The race was arranged in a trice. The chestnut mare had by this time cooled out and rested—she was walking around with a blanket and someone's coat over her back and neck. These they pulled off, while Frank jumped down and approached one of the men, who promptly took the reins and mounted Jeremiah. Jeremiah stood up alertly now, and I could see him, even from a distance, lift his head and snort. After that, he side-stepped under the new rider and arched over his bit. I might have said he did know what he was about to do.

The air was crystal clear—K.T. clear, we always said, the sort of air that lets you see all the way to the curve of the horizon in the distance. I saw men lead the horses to the starting line. I saw the breath of the horses plume out of their nostrils in the cold. I heard the laughter of the bettors, and shouts—"This'll be a good one!" "Go, mare!"—then the report of the starter's pistol. The mare stood between me and Jeremiah for a moment, then Jeremiah leapt out from behind her, already stretched and flying. The mare was no laggard, though. She ran as if her nose were glued to his haunches, for many strides matching him leap for leap, bound for bound. Her ears were pinned to her head. Jeremiah, on the other hand, ran with his ears pricked forward. They came around the wide curve, and his body seemed to elongate and lower a bit, as if he had made up his mind to buckle down to his work.

Seconds later, they swept past me, her nose still

beside his haunch, her ears still pinned, but because I was now on his side, I could see his tail streaming out like smoke against the snow. He did run as if made for it, his back legs stepping well ahead of his front legs, and yet everything effortless and graceful as a breeze riffling through prairie grasses. They came to the finish line and crossed it. From my angle, it looked as if the mare had gained a foot or two. It was a close race. My heart was throbbing in my head and throat, and I was as warm as I'd been since summer. I threw off my shawl and laid it across the mule's withers.

As with the earlier race, I could see the men shouting, exclaiming, exchanging money. Once again, the mare was unruly and hard to handle, tired as she must have been. Jeremiah broke to a smart trot, then settled. Frank ran to him with some other men, and when they reached him, the rider jumped off. I could see his grin from where I stood. All the men clapped him on the back. Frank reached out for the horse's reins, and the rider handed them to him. I decided to get a little closer, so I kicked the mule. I was still in a state of pleased excitement just at the sight of it, as Frank had predicted. The mule trotted toward the group of men, and I saw someone, the Reverend Moss, I realized, throw the blanket he was wearing over Jeremiah. But then the Reverend Moss looked up and around, and when he saw me, he began hurrying the horse, hurrying him a bit carefully and cautiously in my direction. Momentarily he stopped to throw Frank up onto his back, then Roger, who was grinning. They came up to me a few moments later. The reverend was smiling, but he wasn't grinning.

"Well, ma'am, I'd say that was exceptional, and I thank you. Best take the horse on home now. He's bushed—that filly gave him a run. I don't expect"— he glanced over his shoulder—"he thought he would have to try so hard, but she's a tough one and experienced. Hiram's raced her all over. He makes money on her, as a rule." He reached up the reins to me. "You're a fine lady, ma'am, and words of praise for your name will be on the tongues of many this Sabbath evening. Now you'd best be getting off home, ma'am." He thrust the reins into my hand, though I was happy to take them, and then he gave the mule a little slap, and off we went. Jeremiah came along willingly enough, only a little tired from his exertions. Frank and Roger were more than pleased, until I made them dismount and walk.

Frank exclaimed, "They gave a prize, you know. The bettors who won passed the hat and gave me fourteen dollars."

"No!"

"I gave the rider two fifty. He said he'd ride the horse anytime."

"Frank!"

He glanced at me. "You never know, Lidie! Jeremiah is a gold mine!"

"Thomas will never allow it! I don't know what to tell him now!"

"It's true he don't understand horses. It's like farming with him. . . ." He shook his head.

"Please don't. You are in sufficient difficulties already."

We continued toward home without speaking further, but I felt the warmth of what I'd seen all the way there.

My misgivings with regard to my husband proved well founded, and he was seriously displeased with Frank's activities and with mine. He and Charles had looked for the horse until finally giving him up for lost or stolen. They were now a day late for the mail, and at any rate, they would have to hire another horse for that trip, since it would be far too much for Jeremiah now. Frank handed over his winnings—sixteen dollars and fifty cents—and Thomas ordered Frank to stay with the horse, making sure he was kept moving and warm. A dollar would go to Mr. Smith for extra prairie hay. All in all, horse racing certainly qualified in my husband's eyes as a frivolous and dangerous and inconvenient enterprise that sixteen dollars and fifty cents didn't begin to pay for.

I agreed with him, but that didn't make me any less culpable in his eyes. I wasn't favored with any conversation at all. When Charles and Louisa tried to rally me about the incident, Thomas remarked that he would prefer not to hear about it.

That I knew I was culpable, and had known the entire time that I'd allowed Frank to persuade me to race the horse that I was culpable, did not go far toward resigning me to my husband's coldness. Try as I might, I could not help a few resentful thoughts, a swell of resistant feelings. Frank, I knew, was unrepentant. I wondered what that felt like. In everything, Frank endured his punishment without taking it personally and then went his own way. I had, I thought, once been the same—with my father, with my sisters, with those whose punishments were arbitrary and, you might say, selfish. I had cultivated my own selfishness, I thought, to protect myself against theirs. But now I had been selfish, and my husband was both hurt and angry, and all with good reason. Or so the argument within went. But then a new argument began, this one not so much between what I had done and what I ought to have done as between the two halves of what I was. As it happened, I now believed, I had devoted almost every thought and every action since August to Thomas Newton. Everything about my situation in K.T. was bound up with our marriage and his desires. This had happened without my being especially aware of it and constituted what I knew of as being married. All the advice my sisters had given me about controlling or evading one's husband I'd laughed at and dismissed as nonsensical. This day, though, all unbeknownst at the time, I had set a little space between us when I watched the race and thrilled to it and came home half pleased with myself and wholly pleased with Jeremiah. I resented my husband for not allowing me to communicate what I saw—that was the root of my resentment—but then I knew also that I could not have communicated what I saw to him, however eloquent I might be, because he hadn't the interest or capacity or phrenological bump to be thrilled by such a thing. And part of me found him wanting for this. Thus I sat across from my husband in Louisa's pleasant room, listening to Charles sing, watching Louisa smile at him, and glancing at my own husband, wondering whether he was the closed, dull, stiffly upright, and self-righteous person part of me seemed to see, or the pained, lonely, and worried person another part of me seemed to see. This was a breach. In the past, I had rather favored breaches between myself and others, but this breach confused and frightened me. It was a side of marriage I had forgotten I might need to endure.

Well, these feelings passed off, but Thomas was not one to discuss Frank's and my bad conduct. He left our consciences to deal with us, and they did, in their own ways. But the loneliness of his disapproval passed off more slowly than the disapproval itself. And I wasn't sure if I had learned my lesson.

I have to say that the next day, Jeremiah was none the worse for his adventure.

I put aside my letter to my sisters, not quite knowing what to write about Frank's behavior. There seemed to be less and less news from K.T. that a person could tell in a way that would make it understandable.

Some days later, we in Lawrence received a reply to the letters General Lane and Governor Robinson had sent to President Pierce. It was in the form of a proclamation. Of course most people said that they weren't a bit surprised, but of course people were, otherwise they wouldn't have stopped to discuss and deplore so often and at such length what the President had to say. The gist of it was this: *We* were in the wrong and had set ourselves in defiance of the territorial laws (for example, incurring the death penalty for aiding a slave to escape, incurring ten years of hard labor for subscribing to *The Liberator*) and of the territorial government (the tyrant Jones and his friends the Kickapoo Rangers). It was true that the President spoke against armed incursions from outside, but true also that he spoke against insurrections within the state and promised to protect only law-abiding citizens. It was as hard, Mrs. Bush said, to know what a law-abiding citizen was as it was to be one.

The language of the President's proclamation was general and high-minded, saying one thing as if saying another. But it could be read by those who had the eyes to read it.

And then there was another piece of news. We heard that the Slavocrat, as Pierce got to be called, had sent along a message to the other slavocrats in the Senate describing the Free State government we'd just formed as "treason" and asking Congress to authorize the formation of a state government by the slavocrats in K.T. The President, it appeared, was resolved that Kansas would be a slave state no matter what. To think about it gave you a hot and cold and stiff feeling, all at the same time. Now everyone echoed Mrs. Bush—what happened in K.T. only revealed the larger plan of the slavocrats, to bring slavery to every state and territory, every town and street, every family. That's what slavery was, said Mrs. Holmes, and others, too: an uncontainable contagion. It wasn't some marbles or stones you kept in a jar, but a miasma that would get in everywhere, tainting and destroying everything. All us ladies nodded over our sewing. We agreed that the low sort of life people followed in Missouri—ignorant, dirty, bloody, and slothful—would follow slavery everywhere, like a fever in the wake of a cough, part and parcel of the same disease. "I will die first," said each of the New England ladies, one right after the other, and I said so, too, though I'd lived next to slavery all my life in Illinois. We were all different now, weren't we?

Now an interesting thing happened. The course that our party followed was one Louisa presented to us late one night. "We should act," she said, "as though we haven't even seen such a proclamation, have never heard of such a letter. This is what you do with these sorts of men we have in the Washington slavocracy—you keep smiling and going forward and requiring them to show themselves, and when they show themselves sufficiently, others of proper Christian principles eventually recoil from them."

"What do you mean?" said Charles.

"Simply this. General Lane is going to Washington with the constitution for the state of Kansas in April."

"We haven't enough people for statehood," said Thomas.

Louisa shrugged, her face set in a complacent smile.

"And we haven't a state constitution," said Charles.

"We will in a few weeks," said Louisa. "As a piece of strategy, this is an act of genius. General Lane was here today, and he told me all about it."

CHAPTER 15

I Warm Up

The number of young women whose health is crushed, ere the first few years of married life are past, would seem incredible to one who has not investigated the subject, and it would be vain to attempt to depict the sorrow, discouragement, and distress experienced in most families where the wife and mother is a perpetual invalid.

—p. 5

PRESIDENT PIERCE'S BETRAYAL of everything he was for the sake of southern friendships and southern votes (those few in Lawrence who were themselves from his home state of New Hampshire were the loudest in their indignation toward him) was the primary topic of discussion at the party we went to on Washington's Birthday, given by Company A of the Kansas Militia. The weather, I must say, was terrible—snow, snow, more snow, and then ice—but Louisa would not be denied. Since it would be cruel to pull the horses out, we walked, wearing our heaviest boots and swathed in shawls and blankets. Thomas and Charles complained the whole way, but once we got there, we saw another of the joys of town life—light and company and food and drink and good fellowship, all together in one room. It looked to me as though most of Lawrence was there, but perhaps that was only because I saw Governor and Mrs. Robinson in the midst of a merry group, and wherever they were, they seemed to outnumber themselves. Louisa kept looking for General Lane, but later we heard two stories—either he liked to avoid gatherings where the Robinsons held sway, or else he was visiting the wife of one of the officers of the company, who was too ill at home to go out in such weather. No doubt both of these stories were true. In K.T., it was often the case that every version of every story was equally true and equally false, owing to the complexity of every set of circumstances. At any rate, in the rivalry that was quickly developing between the two generals—now, since our Free State elections, widely called the "governor" (Robinson) and the "senator" (Lane), to uphold the view that our government was the legitimate one—the Robinsons were much favored by family men and their wives, for they were a pleasing couple and sought to move K.T. forward judiciously, in a manner that would preserve as much as possible of what we all had already. She was, if anything, more talkative and opinionated than he was, a quality Louisa disapproved of. ("She is so public," exclaimed Louisa. "A woman's influence should be a private one!") I liked her, though, and was pleased when she came up to me and introduced herself. She said, "And so you must be Lydia Newton, the wife of the man who risks himself every week going among the Border Ruffians and attempting to wrest our mail from them."

"He and Charles do their best, but they aren't always successful."

"And where are you from, my dear? You are far

more blooming than many of these young ladies I see around here."

"I came from Illinois. Quincy."

"You're used to the west, then. So many aren't." She shook her head. "I'm of course glad to see that spring is at hand, but when the ice breaks up, I fear the fevers will set in. Yet it's lovely country all the same."

I nodded. That was our whole conversation, but she had a lively manner and a pleasing smile. I wanted to tell her how the image of her face had carried me through my own fever, but I was too shy to do so.

She moved on to another group, and I found Susannah Jenkins, who was so thin from the privations of the winter that I was shocked, though I didn't say anything. She told me her parents were thinking of returning to Massachusetts. Winter in the hay house had been dauntingly arduous. All their relatives back there were urging them in every letter. "But we can't go now," said Susannah. "The rivers are frozen, and the Missouri roads would simply kill Papa. Something is going to. We aren't so pleased with K.T. as we were." She gave me a rueful smile. Had I heard about Mrs. James? Her little boy had died in the cold weather, and now she had a new baby that didn't look very ready for K.T., either. "Mama says grief will carry her off if this one dies, too. That man made her stay out there by herself all winter, even after everyone else had come into town."

"All the cruel ones aren't on the other side, are they?"

"Well, Papa says he's a spy. At any rate, he seems just the sort of man who does everything he pleases. But he's such a fine-looking man. It makes you wonder."

"What does it make you wonder?"

"Oh, my dear, don't you always give fine-looking men all the credit in the world? I do. It's a weakness of character, I suppose."

"I would say it's only a weakness of judgment. But sometimes those are worse, aren't they?"

"I wonder what Mrs. James would say if she were here. No doubt she still loves him." Susannah looked around the room. "At least you can tell why she chose him. I do so wonder sometimes why this one goes with that one. And then, after you're married, you always have to make it look satisfactory, don't you?"

I regarded Susannah with some interest, not sure how general, or personal, she meant these remarks to be. Gossip was Lawrence's main recreation, so I wondered how carefully I should reply. And then I thought, what difference would it make? I said, "Each marriage works in its own way, is what I think. No one looking in ever knows how those looking out are feeling."

"Well, poor Mrs. James."

"We're going out to our claim in a day or so. I'll take her some tea and some other things."

Poor Mrs. James, indeed. The very thought of her troubles made me feel low. And she was so pretty, or

had been. I was as bad as Susannah in my way—
even though Mr. James's good looks didn't move
me, Mrs. James's good looks did.

Some of the singers of Company A now got
together and put on a program of songs, including
one that had all the New Englanders nodding but
made me laugh. It was to the tune of "Old Hundred"
and went:

> We ask not that the slave should lie
> As lies his master at his ease
> Beneath a silken canopy
> Or in the shade of blooming trees.
>
> We ask not eye for eye that all
> Who forge the chain and ply the whip
> Should feel their torture, while the thrall
> Should wield the scourge of mastership.
>
> We mourn not that the man should toil:
> 'Tis nature's need, 'tis God's decree;
> But let the hand that tills the soil
> Be, like the wind that fans it, free.

As Roland Brereton would have said, this song
was those New Englanders all over. And they all
knew the words, even Thomas, though I had never
heard it. They joined in lustily, as if actually singing
a hymn. Did they really not pray that the slavocrats
be punished for their sins? Why not? I did.

A few days later, with the weather calm but the
party still fresh in our memories, Thomas and I took
the mule and Jeremiah out to our claim to plan our

return there, as we couldn't live with Charles and Louisa forever. The weather had moderated but was still freezing—the ice on the river was solid, and the prairie was covered with snow. Even so, we rode hatless; Thomas had his coat thrown open, and I laid my shawl across the mule's withers. We thought it must be in the twenties—a bona fide heat wave.

Perhaps because we remembered our contented moments of the fall, we were happy and eager on the way out there. Thomas grinned at every sign of the coming spring, and I did, too. Soon it would be my birthday. I would turn twenty-one in K.T., and it seemed like a fine thing, and who knew what my twenty-second year would bring? With luck, a child, the end of the war, and everything else that was good, as well. At any rate, all the signs looked hopeful to us—the black shapes of crows and hawks wheeling in the blue sky, the moisture on the dark branches of the trees along the river, the tracks of animals in the snow, revealing the lives that were starting up again all over the prairie. There were even hoofprints and the tracks of sleigh runners, suggesting the eagerness of settlers who refused to wait for the spring to make their entrance into K.T.

Thomas thought the war would end. "I'm telling you, Lidie," he said, "this winter goes to prove that slaves can't live here, and that news will get back to South Carolina by the time the snow melts here. There's a man they talk about, over to the west somewhere, who had his six slaves with him, and they were so cold they couldn't work, so he had to take care of them all winter, and his wife had to cook for them! They're leaving as soon as the thaw sets in."

We had a laugh over that.

"No," he said, "people eventually see the truth of their situation. Right now, the slave power is mad because they think someone is trying to tell them what to do. They hate that more than anything. But that's the reaction of a hothead. I think cooler heads will learn from our experiences here. This was surely a winter for New Englanders!"

I didn't disagree; I was ready to go him one better. "What about the Missourians? They've felt this winter, too, so they must see the writing on the wall. Once folks in K.T. show them what can be done in such a place, well, maybe they'll stop and think."

Nor did we hesitate to speculate on more personal matters. We planned for them to go all our way, as well. For a girl, I had always liked the name Emma, and for a boy, Thomas favored the name of his father, Abel. Why not twins? I thought, though it seemed like tempting fate to say such a thing aloud. But I gave that mule a good kick, just for the joy of the thought, and we trotted out over the prairie snow, laughing and calling out to one another.

I should say that because Thomas was ten years older than I, I always assumed that he knew more than I did. His experience was wider, and he had seen parts of the world I could barely imagine, not least of these Boston itself. A wider experience, I have found, generally gives one a larger expectation of evil. No one can foresee the future, but those who

have lived longer can foresee a little bit of it a little
better than others. Nevertheless, when we came to
our cabin and saw what had become of it in the winter weather, it seemed to me that Thomas was more
surprised and more shaken than I was. For both of us,
though, all giddiness evaporated. The place looked
demolished, dreary, and desolate.

First of all, the fence was broken down almost
completely, the fence posts knocked over and the
rails scattered and broken. Animals had come along
and gnawed at them, too, attesting to the scarcity of
forage for the prairie beasts. All the outdoor arrangements we had made were scattered and destroyed—
foxes, deer, wolves perhaps, raccoons, skunks, all
had passed through and rooted among our things in
their separate ways, leaving our kegs and boxes, few
as they were, broken and tossed about. You could say
there was even evidence of frustrated anger in the
way the work of human hands had been smashed and
destroyed by animal feet and mouths.

As for the cabin, the roof had caved in from the
snow, and all the chinking had fallen out from
between the logs. The door, which had come unse-
cured, had been taken by the wind and was somewhere else now. Inside, our treasonous sheets from
The Liberator were ripped to shreds and faded to
unreadability. Animals had gotten in here, too, and
searched for food everywhere, gnawing holes in the
sailcloth bed tick to get to the prairie hay that I had
stuffed into it. The bed tick was nearly flat—mice
and rats and other animals had carried almost every
stalk away. I had left a flocked wool quilt on the bed;

something had eaten away great patches of the wool. The bedstead itself was broken down, our two chairs were tipped over, the candle holder had been opened and the tallow candles removed, my kitchen utensils had rolled everywhere. Shakes from the roof lay everywhere in the cabin, and sunlight shone in, revealing rather than cheering the devastation. Everything was covered with wet snow, and creeping moisture darkened every stick. It was a most inhospitable place.

Thomas came in with the news that the well had collapsed and would need to be dug again. He looked around the cabin.

I said, "I forgot it was so small."

"Twelve by twelve."

Indeed, more than the destruction, the true sight of what we had had was the discouraging thing. I had remembered lying in my bed on those early warm nights, looking up at the blue shine of the moonlight through the sailcloth and feeling satisfied with my kingdom. My bed had seemed spacious, my hearth had seemed roomy, my little house had seemed an abundance of privacy. Over the winter, I'd remembered thinking of the passersby—be they Indians or animals or settlers heading west under the moon, and imagining them envious of our dark and snug little dwelling, so neatly set beside the trees, between the openness of the prairie and the convenience of the river. But really, I saw, it was as tight as a shoe, as lonely as a star, as ramshackle as a pile of leaves, hardly a dwelling for humans. Thomas's face mirrored my thoughts, and our exhilaration of what seemed like just a few minutes before might as well have never happened.

We had discussed our finances a few days earlier, and I knew that the winter had been expensive. Even though Louisa let us live with her without paying rent, we had paid out more over the winter than we had taken in, especially during the weeks we'd stayed at the Free State Hotel. Charles and Thomas had not made much, and because we were not paying rent, almost all of what they'd made had gone to Charles. The bolts of sailcloth Thomas's father had sent I had sold for a total of thirty-two fifty. We had two bolts left. Sewn into my dress was three hundred dollars. Thomas had about eighty of what he had brought with him. That was our fortune. And we were looking right now at the remains of about two hundred and seventy-five, or so we estimated we had spent on our claim before the winter.

I must say that it came as a shock. I thought to remark that Jeremiah had won about sixteen dollars in his two races (and for that matter, there was no telling what Frank had in his pocket), but I kept my lips tightly closed. I saw that in his mind, my husband was compounding bad luck and personal failure. He looked again toward the broken bedstead, and his eyebrows lowered. He said, "We should have stayed out here."

"We might have died."

I was given to know through his lack of response that such an outcome seemed, momentarily at least, appealing.

"The James boy died of the cold. Mr. James

forced them all to stay out here by themselves. Now Susannah says the woman and the baby are very poorly, as well."

He turned and walked out of the cabin, down the little step we had placed, which still defined our stoop.

What we had longed for so—the coming of spring, sunshine and relative warmth, survival, friends, and, in fact, each other, now seemed like nothing. Soon I would be twenty-one, but the future seemed like a block of stone a mile high, a mile wide, a mile deep, that I had to but could not get into.

Now we sat together on the stoop, gazing out over our snowy field, where we hoped to plant flax or oats. We sat together until I shivered, at which point Thomas circled my waist with his arm. "I saved my books, at least."

"And we have our clothes and most of our cooking things."

"The tools will be wet and maybe a little rusted, but they'll be fine."

"I'm sure it looks worse than it is, with all this snow."

We sighed, hardly hearing our own hopeful words. I thought what an ugly place Kansas was. Folks in Lawrence generally took another line—that Kansas was not only fertile and clement but beautiful. I thought that perhaps I had never really seen a beautiful place. At the moment, I couldn't think of one.

Thomas said, "This is how you feel after a shipwreck."

I looked at him. "Have you been shipwrecked?"

"No hands were lost. But yes, our ship broke up in a freak storm off Martha's Vineyard, and we lost the cargo. That's when I decided that maybe the sailor's life wasn't for me. The seas were twenty foot, they said, not so high. Men have lived through forty footers, but I didn't want to."

When my brother-in-law Roland got discouraged, he would load his gun and go shoot something. That's what I wanted to do right then. I suddenly hungered for the fresh meat—Louisa could roast it in town and serve it up, sizzling and delicious. That would be good. But mostly I just wanted to shoot something. I smiled. I said, "I think I'm turning into a wild Indian."

"I wonder what I've made of my life. My brothers do a good business with my father. Their wives and children are well taken care of. They all live in brick houses. If any of them are restless, I've never heard them say so. I always considered them dull. None of my three brothers opens a book from one year's end to the next, and neither does my father, except for the Bible, and then he only looks at the bits he already knows. They make up sails for all sorts of ships from all over the world, but they never ask the owners or the captains what they've seen or done, and they never long to see or do it. They do their duty and are pleased with that. But me, I don't know what life I'm fitted for. K.T. has sorted me out, my dear."

I said, "Thomas, you ride Jeremiah and I'll ride the mule. We've got to go to the Jameses'—I promised Susannah—and it's getting late."

We let the dread of what we might find at the Jameses' enliven us a bit by removing our thoughts from our own situation.

And then Mrs. James was so glad to see us, though she couldn't rise from her bed and had to call out to us to come in, that we rode upward a little bit on that, too.

They had fashioned a latch of the sort that came through the door, so I lifted that and walked in, while Thomas looked about the place for Mr. James. Mrs. James, Ivy, was as tiny as could be, hardly making any shape at all under her quilts. Her cheeks were pinched and yellow, but her eyes were huge and formed the bright centers of two dark hollows in her face. She had been very pretty once; now she was wondrous-looking, her beauty enhanced but rendered frightening by her illness. Beside her lay an extremely tiny, quiet baby, who looked, even to my unaccustomed eye, very close to his own end. Only his little face showed. His eyes were open. He, too, had regular, lovely features, but not of this world. She said, "Well, I'm waiting for him. Thanks for waiting with me."

"Waiting for whom, Ivy, dear?"

"Waiting for my boy, here, to pass on. Then I'll go with him." Her voice was striking, neither weak nor strong, but penetrating. She ran her hand over the child's face in a tender gesture.

"Are you alone? Where's Mr. James?"

"He went out on his trapline for a bit. He thought there might be some meat this morning. I told him to. He's very distraught."

"My dear, you should have come into town for the cold weather. There was room! Folks were all jumbled together, but it was warmer that way!"

"Daniel said the cabin would fall down and we would lose everything. It was me who wanted to stick it out. It really was. And then, when, uh, my older boy went on, well, I didn't want to leave him out here by himself. Daniel is exceedingly angry at me for being so stubborn, but I just couldn't do it."

"Oh, Ivy! I wish I'd been a better friend to you!" It hurt me to think of my days passed so easily with Louisa, when I had hardly given a thought to the Jameses. None of us had, what with the war and the cold and the murder in Leavenworth and this and that. Well, there was always an excuse, wasn't there?

She said, "Is the war still on?"

"The war?"

"From before Christmas. Isn't it almost spring?"

"Yes, it is, and the Missourians are quiet for the time being. Thomas thinks they're going to go their way now and give in to reason. But it's much warmer today. Can't you feel that? If you hold on for a week, you'll be warm as toast."

She shook her head. "He can't suck. He's too weak. He came before his time, weeks and weeks. Daniel tried giving him some pap, and I squeeze out the milk when I can and put it in his mouth, but it isn't enough. K.T. isn't for him, I'm afraid. But that's okay. Daniel can take care of himself, and the rest of us need each other. I'm happy to go after my boy. He never thrived in K.T., either. I would hate to be one of those women who leave all their children behind."

She smiled, and I have to say that she did look at peace.

"Are you hungry? Can I make you some corn-cakes? There's a bit of a fire." I wondered where Thomas was, but I didn't necessarily want him to come in.

She said, "Oh, my, it's been so long since I had corncakes! That sounds heavenly."

"Corncakes are not heavenly, Ivy; they are of this earth and meant to keep you here."

She shook her head, smiling. I went away from the bedstead and began rummaging about for the griddle and a pot. The kitchen area was neat and orderly. Daniel, I suspected, could indeed take care of himself.

Still the baby made no sound. Sometimes he had his eyes open and sometimes he had them closed. That was the only way I knew he was alive. While I mixed up the cakes, Ivy fell into a doze, rousing from time to time to stroke the baby's face and give him a kiss. I stoked the fire and added some wood. When the cakes were done, nice and light from the limey water and fragrant, too, she managed to sit up. I forked pieces between her lips. She chewed slowly and with concentration. Finally, she said, "When I woke up this morning, I told Daniel it was going to be a good day. Maybe today we shall be released."

"Maybe."

"My boy will get me into heaven, I know. Even though I've been vain and giddy and selfish, and thought too much over the years about dresses and shoes and petticoats. Lidie, I was so spoiled! It aston-

ishes me now to think of it! I fancied myself altogether too much!" She laughed, and it had a merry
sound. "But I had my boy with me for four years and
two months, and he was such a good boy, and he
taught me to think of someone other than myself."

I gave her some more corncake, and she chewed
it deliberately, then swallowed.

"May I talk of a womanly thing, even though you
haven't a child yet?"

"You may talk of anything you please."

"When my boy was born, and they brought him
to suck, I was so sore that I wanted to scream. I shudder to think it, but I hated the sight of him! That's
how frivolous I was, and shallow. He would cry and
cry, and it didn't matter what they said to try and help
me; I was mean and sour inside, and I turned away
from him for weeks. Daniel didn't say a word to me,
but I was very bad and asked him to find me a wet
nurse. But my mama finally talked to me one day.
She had never said a cross word to me in all my life,
no matter how many cross words I said to her, but
she came to me, and she said, 'Ivy, I am ashamed of
you and of myself, for I have made you the way you
are, and now my heart is sick, because I can see you
turn away from your own child, who is the sweetest
child in the world!' "

She took some water from a cup.

"That day, I made up my mind to be his mama,
and things got easier after a bit. But mostly I was
sorry I'd lost all those years thinking of myself."
Now her voice fell into a whisper. "You don't think
that I know what they say about Daniel, that he's

cruel and hard. He's not so cruel and hard, but he is scared of K.T., more scared than Thomas seems, or some of the others. When Daniel is scared he bares his teeth and attacks, just like a wolf or some wild animal. He would like to attack death itself now." She sighed. "But all of this is very far away, too."

I offered her a bit more corncake, but she shook her head. The baby's eyes were open. I said, "I hate to leave you like this. Maybe Thomas should go back to Lawrence, and I should stay with you."

"When Daniel returns, we'll be fine. This is a good day."

Now Thomas came in, and Ivy held out her hand to him and let him give it a squeeze, but she didn't talk anymore. After a moment, Thomas said, "I found James. He's had some luck. He should be back before long." He sat down in the other chair, and we stayed there quietly, me holding one of Ivy's hands, until Daniel James opened the door sometime later and came into the cabin. He was, in my estimation, in a towering rage, but he was polite to us and kind to his wife. She opened her eyes and said, "Daniel, Lidie made us some corncakes. There's plenty left." Then she closed her eyes again. He nodded his thanks, and shortly after that we left.

We'd mounted and ridden a good distance, when Thomas said, "When I found him, he was beating his head against a tree. He said over and over that he had a good farm in Ohio, and now he'd killed his children and his wife, and he would never forgive himself, and his wife's parents would never forgive him, as they'd begged him not to take her west."

"Oh, Thomas."

"We are all fools, Lydia, every man in K.T."

"You leave the women out?"

"We men—"

"Don't leave the women out. We have lessons to learn of our own."

We rode back to Lawrence, much subdued. We heard that Ivy James's baby died two days later and herself a day after that. And then Mr. Jenkins died, too, and he wasn't the only one. Some had had the will to make it through the cold, cold weather, it seemed, but when the pressure let up, the will to live abandoned them, too. In fact, in many ways it seemed as though fate or luck was separating all of our acquaintances into layers. Here were Mrs. James and Mr. Jenkins, dead, and the other Jenkinses, and many besides them, ready to backtrack as soon as the weather would permit, their Kansas adventures failures and worse. Then, here was Louisa with her shop and her two rooms, seemingly set on a course for comfort and prosperity; and beyond that, here were the Robinsons, we heard. Their house on Mount Oread was going up fast, a wooden house, all of black walnut, it was said, with oilcloths and papered walls and furniture in every room, a regular house that would be rich, folks said, even for the States. This house was the subject of a great deal of talk. Some, of course, said, Why not, he has the money, and K.T. needs this sort of thing to show the way, or to make us look respectable enough for statehood, or just for the good of the work (you can't bring good workmen into the territory and expect them to split logs for the rest of their lives); but others said, Where'd he get the money? Who does he think he is? He an't got to be governor yet, according to Washington, D.C., and she an't, either. The joke about it was that once the house was built, Jim Lane would be moving right in. But I thought, Well, Americans always sort themselves out one way or another into rich and poor, and then everybody gets blamed for however he ends up. Lawrence was the biggest town for gossip I ever saw, and it was only during a war that what folks said about each other was either respectful or kind.

K.T.'s march toward statehood, and free statehood, went forward. Charles and Thomas went over to Topeka, some fifty or so miles away, in early March. Thomas went to see what was doing, but Charles went as an avowed supporter of Jim Lane. They all drafted a memorial to the U.S. Congress and signed it. Thomas signed it, too, and Charles. They said so, and we knew it. That got to be important later on, after what happened. When they'd written up the memorial, Jim Lane and some others went off to Washington, D.C., to find someone to present it to Congress. Louisa was sure that would show the Missourians a thing or two.

Underneath her sympathy about the devastation we'd found on our claim, I could see that Louisa was both annoyed and anxious. For the first time all winter, she seemed ready to be rid of us, and I couldn't blame her. Thomas and I had two bolts of sailcloth and not much money—and we agreed not to apply to his father for more, since any forthcoming funds would be accompanied by urgings to return to Boston and go back to work in the sailcloth factory. We continued to live at Louisa's for a time, but now we two couples kept to our respective rooms and hung a quilt in the doorway for privacy. I went out each day and got the wood for the fire in our room, and I did most of our cooking. From time to time, visitors traipsed through our room, which was next to the stairs, to get to theirs, for evening gatherings that we weren't always invited to. It was an arrangement that looked a bit like an estrangement but wasn't, really. It was just some people finding their true levels with one another. It seemed as though it could not go on, but it did, day after day. While the men were gone to Topeka, Louisa and I resumed our old friendship and even slept together in her rosewood bed a couple of nights, so I saw that the problem was only our two families drawing into themselves, the way families do. One of these nights, Louisa said that she was pregnant. That was her word, right out, as if she were a cow or a dog. And she said she intended to be out and about all the way to the end—the most advanced authorities were very much against restricting women to their beds and their houses in such a condition, and she herself was very much against pretending to be ill when she wasn't ill at all. And so forth. I was envious.

In the meantime, the Missourians continued to gather at the border, preparing their assault. It was the same rumor every day, and we ceased paying any attention to it. People who talked about it got to be known as newcomers or panickers. We all knew what the Missourians were really capable of, with all their big talk, and it was only an occasional brutal act, nothing concerted. Even so, I began to think that every circumstance was pushing us back toward our claim—the warming weather, the situation with Louisa, the dangers of living in Lawrence. Things would look different out there when the sun was shining and the ground was dry and ready to be planted. Frank was so alarmed by these signs that he began trying to soften me up to the idea of his staying in town.

Building in Lawrence and round about was like a pot that is boiling, its lid held down. The winter put the lid on it, but at the very first signs of spring, the lid popped off. New houses made new streets, new settlers had new money, everyone with anything to sell was busy selling it. Charles and Thomas raised their hauling prices, then raised them again. I was glad I'd saved my two bolts of sailcloth—I could get the same for two lengths, enough to sew up one bed tick, as I had gotten in the winter for a whole bolt. Frank brought in nails he found in the streets, hammered them out straight, and sold them for a penny apiece. The dullest man in the world could make some money if he was willing to split shakes. Anytime we worried about Missourians massing on the border, we looked around us at all the activity, all the new faces. They could mass all they wanted, but they could never put a stop to this, could they?

March turned into April much faster than December had ever turned into January or January into February. Thomas and I got behind in our plans to return to our claim, but we told ourselves that there was so much business to do every day—when things slackened, we would get out there.

Now I will tell in proper sequence what happened to the congressional memorial for statehood, even though it took a while longer for us to hear about it. And it was very Jim Lane, very Jim Lane, indeed.

When he first got to Washington, "Senator" Lane had a hard time finding someone to present the memorial to Congress, but he managed to find General Cass. The oldest man still working, General Cass must have been quite dim of sight, because after he presented the memorial, the other members of Congress told him that it was full of crossings-out and interlineations. And all the signatures were in one person's handwriting! General Cass was embarrassed, of course, but Jim Lane wasn't. He told them in an affidavit that he'd been given the authority by the Topeka convention to revise some of the phraseology, and then, well, he had lost the signatures, so he and his assistant had put their heads together and tried to remember who had signed and just appended those names.

The southern congressmen were incensed, of course. On the one hand, they declared the whole thing a forgery, and on the other, they said that the names appended were all names of "fugitives from justice."

"Senator" Lane continued unembarrassed. He now turned in another document, and this time he got the attention of Senator Douglas himself, who saw that he had crossed out some bits about the exclusion of free Negroes from the state, something Thomas, of course, was glad he crossed out, even if he had done so just to win some northern senators' votes and not out of principle. But Senator Douglas's views were different from Thomas's, and he pronounced the whole procedure a fraud and roundly chastised "Senator" Lane, and the whole effort made the Free State party in K.T. look both wrong and foolish. The Robinsons and their friends were said to be royally upset, but there was nothing for it. Jim Lane was Jim Lane, as Louisa and Charles and everyone else said. If the Robinsons wanted it done their way, they should have left off building their house and gone to Washington, D.C., themselves.

Jim Lane would never admit that he'd done a thing wrong. He did what he had to do, he told everyone, and in the end, he did get Congress to vote for admission, because the northern states were more populous and had more congressmen than the southern states. "But," he said when he came back, "no one can get around the 'Little Giant,' or, as I prefer to call him, the 'Little Tyrant,' or the weight of the slave power in the Senate and in the cabinet." Everyone knew this was true, even the Robinsons and their supporters. We all ended up agreeing that no doubt we looked somewhat foolish, after all, but "Senator" Lane had gotten as far with his memorial as anyone else would have, given what he was trying to do and where. The result was that Jim Lane went on as before, and so did everyone else. You couldn't get rid of Jim Lane. What some senators and congressmen said of us began to trickle back, through newspapers, letters, and talk. More than one thought the Free Staters were moving toward treason, were acting outside the law, were criminals, but this was so patently untrue that we looked to the source—always a voice from the southern side—and laughed. Mr. Thayer, in Boston, and the other men back in Massachusetts thought sentiment was flowing, even surging, our way in the north, especially the northeast. We just had to sit tight and wait, they said. Do this, don't do that. And there was a lot of discussion in Lawrence, especially once the Free State Hotel was completed and everyone had a place to gather.

Could things have gone another way? I've often wondered that since. What if Jim Lane had not been a factor, or if he'd been a quieter, less flamboyant man, never carried into bungling by his own rhetoric? What if instead of Lane and Robinson there had been two like Robinson—two conservative, thoughtful, and cautious men, content to wait, build, and do business? But then, when I think this, I realize that there could never be two like Robinson; there always has to be a Lane, because there's a position open for a Lane in any controversy. As for doing this and not doing that, not everyone is equally well instructed in what they should do, or equally willing to do or not do. I have since thought that five Robinsons could not have directed the people of Lawrence in a course of action wise in every particular, because the people of Lawrence could not be directed. That was why most of them had come to K.T. in the first place, because they expected less direction here than elsewhere. And anyway, some people just wanted a fight. Some people always want a fight, and they aren't always the men. There were times when I just wanted a fight myself. Thomas, though, Thomas never just wanted a fight. What he wanted most was time to think things through.

CHAPTER 16

I Am Hopeful, and Receive a Surprise

Women, European contempt for, 30. American esteem for, 30. Influence of, on individuals and nations, 37. Exercise taken by English, 45. Responsibleness of, 53. Eating without being hungry, 98. Responsibility of, as to intemperance, 106. Precedence given to, in America, 141. Importance and difficulty of their duties, 155. General principles for, 158; frequent inversion of them, 160. Men engaged in their work, 164, 165. On their keeping accounts of expenditures, 173, 174. Imagining themselves domestics, 205. See American women.
　　　　　　　　　　　　　　　　　—Index

IN APRIL, Thomas got into the habit of taking Jeremiah out to the claim every so often and thinking things through out there. He cleared away the destruction bit by bit, put things away, assessed what was left and what it would take to put it back together. He built some more fence and cleared a few acres of prairie. We talked about what we might plant there: some flax? some vegetables for local consumption? oats? rye? buckwheat? Different men had different advice, and we listened to it all. The fact was, we were doing so much business in town that the claim seemed as remote as California. I took my profits from my two bolts of sailcloth and sent them back to Thomas's brothers, who sent me eight more bolts as well as a lot of good rope. Even though we knew lots of things were being confiscated in Missouri, these managed to get through—there was no rhyme or reason to what got through and what didn't, though there were always rumors of Sharps rifles not getting through. I found it amazing how many uses men could find for good rope, and my rope was in high demand. Charles bought another wagon and another team of mules and let Frank drive them. On the days when Charles and Thomas were out of town, Frank went around from job to job in his wagon, with his mules, shouting things like, "Watch the mules, there! Careful, now! Wagon coming through!" He continued to sleep in the shop downstairs, but with the mild weather and the sunshine, I couldn't say how much he was actually there. The school started up again, over on Vermont Street, but Frank wasn't in attendance.

One thing that happened was that three congressmen came to town to look into things. There was a man from the north, Howard, of Michigan, another man from the north, Sherman, of Ohio, and this man Oliver, from Missouri, who was said to be one of the worst of them. They set up in the Free State Hotel, and all kinds of people went over to testify, and even more went over just to have a look. It seemed like while they were there, they surely would end up seeing our side. Even Oliver was friendly enough in his official capacity, and none of them ever turned down one iota of Lawrence hospitality.

And so everything in Lawrence was business and making money, until Sam Wood came back to town. Sam Wood was the husband of Mrs. Wood, who had made the celebrated dash for powder and balls, and he had been away most of the winter after the killing of Dow and the freeing of Branson, which started the Wakarusa War. Mrs. Wood and I maintained a cordial acquaintance, as I always admired her enterprise in substituting that shot and powder for the wadding of her dress, and she always admired my willingness to outrun any and all pursuers in the same endeavor. She was much older than I was and spent a lot of time in her sewing circle, so our paths didn't often cross, but I knew, as did everyone, that Sam was coming back, and why shouldn't he?

Except that in the eyes of the tyrant Jones, the so-called sheriff, Sam Wood was a fugitive.

Frank happened to be on the scene with his wagon, as some furniture was being moved from the house across the street to a house at the other end of town. But Frank had a knack for being on any scene, so I was hardly surprised to hear all about it only an hour or so after it occurred.

Jones hadn't been around much, and whatever official functions he performed away from Lawrence were performed by our own authorities in and around Lawrence. Mostly this would have amounted to keeping the peace and limiting the brawls and fights that accompanied arms and drink wherever you were (though the New Englanders, of course, always maintained that brawls and fights were something visited upon them by settlers from other parts of the country, never their own folks). Anyway, Jones and some men he had with him came up to Sam Wood on the street and laid hold of him, saying, "I'm taking you prisoner."

Wood shrank back and asked by what authority that was, and Jones called out, "I'm the sheriff of Douglas County, by G——!" (This is what Frank said, though all of it was reported later in much soberer terms.)

Wood threw off Jones's hand and exclaimed right back, "Well, by G——, I don't recognize that authority," and turned on his heel and walked away. He was very cool, said some, and very hot, said others. The tyrant Jones grabbed him again, and then some of the Free Staters who'd been standing around jumped in. One man—Mr. Speer, Frank thought—grabbed Jones by the collar, and another took away his pistol, and then there was a general melee, with men getting knocked down and hit and even throttled, but no shots were fired. Some of the other bystanders started shouting things. Frank said that he shouted, "Put 'em in the river!" as a joke, but they didn't do that. Jones said he'd be back to arrest them all for "resisting the duly constituted authorities," and the Lawrence men shouted, "Try it!" "Come back anytime!" and other, ruder imprecations. The whole thing was quick, lasting maybe ten minutes. After the Missourians rode away, Frank and everyone else went back to their business, as if nothing had happened, but by later that afternoon and evening, people began to believe that something had happened, partly through talking it over and partly because a party of traders who'd met Jones on the road (one of them, I was interested to hear, was our old friend David Graves) declared that he was hopping mad and only going out to find more men before returning.

"You know," said Charles that night, "everyone knows he's got a list of all the members of the Branson rescue party. That's why he went after Wood. Once he's got him, then he's going to go after all the others, too."

"So tell us at last," I said, "were you one of the rescue party that night?"

"Yes, he was," said Louisa. "That's how we met." She smiled at him. "The first place they hid Branson was right here in this shop, while some men went out to look for a better spot. Charles stayed with him, and—who was it?—Sam Tappan and I brought them all tea for an hour or two, and then the next afternoon, Charles came by to thank me."

"I don't care two straws about being on the tyrant Jones's list, that's for sure. If he's got the right list, then it's got quite some names on it, I'll say," exclaimed Charles. But then, a while later, he and Thomas went out to a meeting at the Free State Hotel, and they didn't get back until we'd all gone to bed.

The next day, being Sunday, was a natural day to hold services, though of course services were held rather intermittently in Lawrence. This service was an interesting one, because they held it right in the middle of town, at the church closest to Sam Wood's house and therefore closest to the Free State Hotel, where plenty of others who didn't manage to get a

seat for the services were loitering. All of the atten-
dees at the services happened to be men, and all,
including Thomas, Charles, and Frank, happened to
be carrying their weapons with them. So did the Reverend Lum, who was doing the preaching. The service lasted quite a while beyond the customary time,
and the congregation sang many hymns, which they
later said did their souls good, and presently the
tyrant Jones appeared with his henchmen. The band
of Missourians rode down the street and drew up in
front of the Woods' residence. According to Thomas,
it was pretty clear that the whole party was drunk—
"in their official capacity as Border Ruffians," said
Louisa.

Sam Tappan came sauntering down the street, as
planned, and the tyrant jumped on him himself. Sam
gave a holler, and all the men came pouring out of
the church, the Reverend Lum in the lead. Tappan
turned on Jones and knocked him flat to the ground.
Jones just looked up at him and smiled. Then he got
up and dusted off his pants and got back on his horse.
The Missourians rode off.

Now, our men had expected a little more of a
fight, and yes, this behavior was as suspicious as
it looked, because Jones, we later found out, ran
straight to Lecompton and reported to the governor
that he'd been attacked while discharging his duty,
that Lawrence was therefore in revolt against the
state and federal governments, and that the governor
had better call out the federal troops! And the governor agreed to do it!

This was how the slave power sorted themselves

out: The senators and cabinet members, for example Jeff Davis, told the President what to do, and then the President told men like Shannon and Jones that they could do what they wanted, using his men. This was how they made the illegal and immoral look decent and necessary. But in Lawrence that Sunday, we didn't know yet what was up. The men who were there thought a fight had been averted, and some were relieved and some were disappointed. Thomas and I were to go have our supper at the Bushes' new house on Sixth Street, and we walked out easy as you please, talking again about going to the claim for good on Wednesday. I was reluctant; it still seemed a bit as if I could avoid some evil fate if I stayed in town, but the roof was mostly repaired, the weather was good, something had to be planted, everything was for it, and I partly wanted to go—the Smithsons, the Holmeses, the Laceys, and Mr. James were all out there. We missed Mrs. Jenkins and Susannah, who had gone home to Massachusetts, and of our friends, besides Louisa, only the Bushes remained in town. I'd been out there myself twice and cleaned the stove and set the kitchen in order. Thomas and I agreed that trading was good business but not reliable, nothing to build a life around, and so on. We chatted as we walked down Massachusetts Street, making plans and feeling generally sanguine. As usual, Massachusetts Street was popping with activity, which was always enlivening. I was not yet in the same condition as Louisa, but I thought I might be soon.

By the next day, Monday, most people knew something was up, and by Tuesday, everyone was talking about something being up. And one thing I learned in K.T. was that four out of five rumors are true, even those as unbelievable as the one we learned then, that the governor was calling out the troops against the citizens of Lawrence.

The troops numbered ten dragoons, and they showed up with the tyrant Jones on Wednesday, just about daybreak, which is not to say that the Free Staters weren't ready for them.

It was a gloomy, chill, and overcast day, portending rain but holding off from the time we got up. Charles was out already, Louisa not saying where. The dragoons came pounding at the door to the shop just as we were sitting down for our breakfast. Thomas and Frank went down the stairs. Louisa got up from the table and went back to her bed, drawing the curtain to her room behind her. I followed Thomas in time to hear the captain of the dragoons say, firmly but politely, "I have a warrant for the arrest of Charles Bisket here. Are you Mr. Bisket?"

And Jones said, "G—— d—— it, he an't Bisket! Bisket's a skinny fellow!"

"Are you Mr. Bisket?" repeated the captain.

"No, sir. Mr. Bisket is away," said Thomas.

"Is he aware Sheriff Jones and the United States Army are looking for him?"

"Well," said Thomas, "this is the first we've seen of you, and I haven't seen Mr. Bisket all—"

Frank interrupted, "What are you arresting him for, then? He an't done nothing."

"He has not done anything," said Thomas, correctively.

The captain said, quietly, "Is Mr. Bisket attempting to evade capture—"

"Well, d—— ya, an't they all? You sound like you're on their side! The governor sent you to help me!" brayed Jones.

They stepped back from the door, which Thomas closed. Then he and Frank put their ears to the door and soon were smiling. After a moment, Thomas looked at me. "They haven't managed to find anyone. Jones is mad as Tucker." We all laughed. There was another knock. Thomas opened the door. The captain of the dragoons, backed by two of his men, cleared his throat and said, rather fiercely, "You are required hereby to inform Mr. Bisket when he returns that he is subject to arrest and that any further evasive action on his part will result in prosecution for resisting arrest and a sentence in the county jail."

"What is he being arrested for?" asked Thomas, mildly.

"Aiding in the escape of a prisoner. This is a felony under the laws of the Territory of Kansas." He cleared his throat again.

Frank said, "You must be joking," but Thomas pushed him back and began to close the door. He said, "I'll tell him. Thank you, sir."

We turned and ran up the stairs to watch them out the windows. We were just in time to see Jones throw down his hat and stamp on it. The dragoons ignored him and got back on their horses. Their uniforms were clean, their sabers shiny, and their horses good ones. They looked uncomfortable in the company of Jones and his men, who were dirty, hairy, and unkempt.

They kept at it all day, returning to us again (Thomas was extraordinarily polite and thanked them for being so assiduous in their duty "as they saw it"). The men on the list, those who knew who they were, anyway, skipped from house to house, sometimes only just sitting down for a cup of tea or a bite to eat when the knocking came. They looked for Sam Wood everywhere, because he was the one the tyrant Jones was angriest at. Up and down the street, up and down the street, up and down the street, all day long. And I have to say, most people's business, no matter what it was, took them outside, just to watch. But that doesn't mean any of us saw any of the fugitives fleeing out back doors and running off here and there.

By the time it started raining, which was just before supper, they'd arrested maybe a half dozen or fewer, all men of no importance, who were rather flattered to have been on the list. As for looking for the ones they wanted outside of Lawrence, on this claim or that one, well, they didn't have the men, or the imagination, or the energy, or the will, or maybe the interest. And they did keep Jones from doing things the way he would have liked to, barging in and knocking people about, or breaking something up or in some other way venting his anger. Thomas said, "I expect the troops haven't been quite the help

Jones thought they would be." Later, we heard that some Lawrence folks were quite a bit ruder than we were—John Speer's wife threw water into someone's face, and one or two fired off shots. It all seemed more like a game than anything else, that is, until someone killed Jones.

The Missourians and the troops had set up camp in some trees by the river, and the sun went down. It was a wet night, but the rain cleared off a bit after supper, and some Lawrence men decided to go down by the camp, to keep an eye on it. And, said Louisa, who was beginning to worry a bit about Charles, "to invite trouble." Thomas was asked along but for once agreed with Louisa and declined. Little did we know that Frank did go, with the Lacey boys. We thought Frank was still working somewhere, since his little wagon was in great demand, and he'd been making a considerable sum each week. The fact is, I should have noticed that his rifle was gone, but I didn't.

Thomas and I spent the evening in our room, making ready for our departure to our claim, which we had put off one day. We had packed all of Thomas's books, so when we were finished, we asked Louisa if she would like to wait for Charles with us. She seemed worried and down in the mouth, as she and Charles hadn't actually made much of a plan, so she didn't know where he was or when he might be back. She knitted, Thomas sat quietly, no doubt pondering our soon-to-commence life as farmers, and I attempted to sew a little bit on the cuff of a shirt I was making for Frank. In fact, I expected Frank to come in, and had just said, "I told him for the last three nights that he had to put his things together, and when I look down there, it looks like he hasn't done a thing."

Louisa sighed. "You don't have to leave. I've been thinking about it. You're going to be very lonely out there, is my opinion."

"Lots of folks have moved out there already," I said.

"But they aren't necessarily your close friends. They don't necessarily know how to promote your interests. Charles will miss you exceedingly, Thomas. In the business and otherwise." She sighed again and laid her hand over her middle. Her condition was not yet in evidence, but it was very much on her mind.

Thomas didn't say anything, no doubt feeling that even to discuss the issue was to allow an opening that he wanted to avoid. We had spent a large sum on seed—barley and flax. Having it meant we had to plant it, didn't it? But town still seemed bright, lively, and open to me, while our claim seemed small, dark, and silent, a rock on the prairie, a home too small in a world too vast. Try as I might, I couldn't seem to make myself into one of those I saw all around me, who, no matter what their present circumstances, were already living in their futures—bright white clapboard houses with real United States windows looking out on broad, richly cultivated fields, but I thought if I willed myself to improve my character, I would get along well enough.

"Won't you at least stay until Charles returns? If something unfortunate should befall him . . ." She put her hand across her eyes. "I'm a strong woman, and I never flinched, all through Mr. Wheelwright's painful end, but such a blow at this time, well . . .'"

Thomas looked at me, not sure of what to say, and just then there was another knocking at the lower door. Louisa cried, "Oh, my land! What is that!"

Thomas went down. I stepped over to Louisa's chair and put my arm around her shoulders. She laid her head against me. Thomas was back up the stairs in a moment. His face was flushed, and he was more upset than I'd ever seen him. He said, "That was Lacey and some others. Jones has been shot!"

"Hurt?" exclaimed Louisa.

"Killed," said Thomas, in a deep, horror-struck voice.

We jumped up in alarm. The danger to all of us in Lawrence as a result of this was only too apparent, and perhaps the danger to Charles was vastly increased. Thomas put on his coat and grabbed his hat. Then he seized his Sharps carbine and some rounds. I looked to the corner by the door where my carbine and one of Charles's also stood. Thomas and I didn't say aloud that we expected an attack before morning by the Missourians who had been threatening such an action for months, but we both thought it—we were both certain sure of it. Thomas said, "I have to find out what's going on, and I have to find Frank, and I'll try to find out something about Charles, too. But I have to go out. I can't sit here."

"We'll be fine, but you do have to find Frank," I said, "and then you have to give him a hiding, because he is scaring me to death."

And he was gone.

"Well!" said Louisa as the door closed after him. "We need to get ready!" She was no longer sighing, at least. She ran down the stairs to the shop, her wrapper flying behind her, and locked the door, then I helped her draw some heavy boxes in front of it. The shop had two small windows, and in front of these we tacked up blankets. Then we dragged all of the goods that might have any value to a back room and locked that door. After that, we ran up the stairs and closed that door behind us, and pushed the bedstead Thomas and I had been using in front of it, then we retreated to Louisa's room and climbed into her giant rosewood bedstead together and hid down under the quilts. Louisa couldn't shoot, but I had the two carbines near at hand.

We took somewhat different positions on the shooting of Jones. We both agreed that it had to be done, on the analogy of removing a burr under a saddle or easing an unbearable goad. "Now he's gone," I said, "things will actually calm down, because he's been the moving force behind Shannon and the rest of them, even President Pierce, I'll bet. None of them cares about Lawrence as much as Jones did."

"But now they will," said Louisa. "Now, by killing him, we've proved our very lawlessness. They'll view him as a martyr, if you ask me. This will galvanize them!"

"But everyone, everyone in his right mind, knew what Jones really was!"

"Who is in their right mind? When the K.T. question comes up in certain quarters, it drives people right out of their right mind."

I must say that though we were worried about our husbands and Frank, at the same time our own coziness gave us a deep-down faith in their safety. Louisa, who had followed some of the more advanced thinkers in Boston and the east, even said that should something happen to any of them, we would feel it, a sort of unearthly vibration, communicated to us from the spiritual realm. That sounded reassuring to me.

Mostly what we thought about the killing of Jones was that now things would go one way or the other, that our uncertain spring, all fraught with speculation, would turn into a summer where at least all the parties knew where they stood. We blew out the candle, and then we drifted off, or I did. The next thing I knew, Louisa had let Thomas in, and he had Frank and Roger Lacey with him. Two candles were lit. I sat up in bed. I said, "Is there a war?"

"Everything is quiet," said Thomas. "And I know where Charles is." Louisa nodded. Across the room, the two boys were silent. I thought they were tired. I said, "My goodness, Frank! What do you mean by getting Thomas out at all hours to be looking for you? I am going to have to send you back to your mother if I can't handle you! You are as wild as an Indian and twice as self-sufficient!"

Thomas said, "Frank was out by the Missourians' camp."

"What in the world were you doing out there, boy? I thought you were getting some supper."

"We went out there," said Frank.

"Well, we know that."

"Everybody was out there. Governor Robinson was, and Senator Lane. The whole town was out there."

I looked at Thomas. He cocked his eyebrow and shrugged, as if to say he didn't think so, and then said, "They had their guns with them."

I was shocked. "Whatever for! You are boys! You do not need to go armed about your business!"

The boys didn't say anything.

I said, "Frank, I'm going to take your gun away from you before it gets you in trouble, I swear! Or I'm going to send you back to Illinois, because another night like this, well . . ."

But the fact was, Frank was already out of hand, had been out of hand even back in Quincy. As a last insult, I said, "I don't know what is going to become of you, Frank. You have no schooling to speak of, you run around on your own all the time, I don't know what you eat or when you sleep. You do not live a well-regulated life!" But whose fault was that?

"I got a hundred dollars, though," he offered.

"Oh, my goodness! Go to bed!"

It was three a.m. We bedded the boys down on some quilts in the shop and forbade them to leave before morning. Later, when Thomas and I went to bed, he said to me in a low voice, "He knows who shot Jones."

"How does he know?"

"He knows. I heard him and Roger whispering

about it when I was bringing them home, but when I challenged them, they clammed up."

"If Roland were here, he would beat it out of him."

"We'll see," said Thomas. "We'll see if it comes to that."

The next morning, everyone got into position with regard to the shooting. Jones had been taken to the Free State Hotel, and his wife and the editor Stringfellow, who was also a doctor, had been sent for. As soon as they came, things got very secretive, though Governor Robinson, also a doctor, and Mrs. Robinson tried to be very attentive. The Missourians took Jones and left the next day. Everyone who saw the tyrant Jones said that he didn't look deathly at all, but he was plenty mad. The people of Lawrence were, of course, shocked, appalled, and astounded. Thomas went to a meeting, where they passed a resolution that went something like: "This was the isolated act of one vicious citizen, in no way sustained by the community," though I do remember there was a phrase in there that referred to Jones as the "so-called" sheriff, or the one who "claimed" to be sheriff. The newspapers in the Missouri River towns, Leavenworth, and Kickapoo were beside themselves. Stringfellow vowed to sacrifice every abolitionist in the territory in revenge, to level Lawrence, and to destroy the Union, if need be.

Of course, the tyrant Jones was not dead, we all knew that; it turned out there had been two shots, according to the colonel of the dragoons, one through his trouser leg and one more telling, though I never understood rightly if he got hit in the leg, the hip, the shoulder, or the jaw. Alive though he was, the Missouri papers were full of memorials to him and vows to avenge his death with a war, if at all possible. These newpaper reports circulated all around Lawrence, and mostly we had a laugh at them, but it did give you cause to wonder at either the egregious lying or the egregious stupidity. Maybe that was the thing about the Missourians that made the people of Lawrence so angry in the end—they were either too stupid to credit or too outrageous in their lies. As the days went by, most people in Lawrence decided that the shooting had actually been committed by a southern sympathizer. Why not? In the first place, no Lawrence man, no New Englander, would do so rash a thing, and in the second place, Jones was unloved by even his own men—what better for them than the small sacrifice of a tyrant for the sake of blackening the character of the citizens of Lawrence? The Missourians would do anything; we already knew that about them. Or what about this—the whole shooting was a hoax arranged among Jones and Stringfellow and Jones's wife? As the time passed, it was easy to forget that Lawrence people had been there, too, tending to the wounded tyrant.

Thomas and I never quizzed Frank on what he knew. But there was a segment of the town that held the opinion that a boy had done it, one of the group of boys who had been out near the camp. Almost no one agreed with this group—they could never come up with the boy, or said they couldn't. After long thought, I decided that Frank was not the boy. But I believed Thomas when he said that Frank knew who the boy was.

A day or so after the shooting, Governor Robinson offered a five-hundred-dollar reward for the capture of the perpetrator. The captain of the dragoons thought he had something to say about the whole affair, too—he sent Governor Robinson a letter, which said that Jones's shooting had been reported in Washington, D.C. (no doubt, said some jokers, by the ghost of Jones himself, who appeared to the President in his worst nightmare), and that it was being taken most seriously there, etc.

The congressional committee departed in haste, which seemed ominous.

And then there was further fuel for outrage: one of the men who'd testified to the committee was followed home and attacked by some very vocal southern sympathizers and left for dead. He lived, fortunately, but there was nary a peep out of any federal body about the attack on him.

Now the relative calm of the spring, made up of moneymaking and business and planning for the future, gave way to one upset after the other. Sheriff Jones's deputy, an illiterate who was nevertheless fully armed and eager for any pretext, persisted in trying to arrest everyone involved in the Branson rescue. Sometimes he had the dragoons with him, in which case he would stop people but then let them go if he found nothing against them. Most times he didn't have the dragoons with him but had other men, men who spoke in the accents of the deep south and looked like roughs, but not entirely like our Ruffians. We all knew they were bringing men in from the south, especially from the hot-blooded places like South Carolina. Thomas and Frank got stopped every day or so. Frank finally got a little pass from the deputy that read: "Let this man pass I no him two be a Law and abidin Sittisin." Well, these were our duly constituted officials. As New Englanders, and generally well educated, the citizens of Lawrence were especially galled to be insulted and arrested by fools and ignoramuses who couldn't contain their glee (spitting and staggering from tobacco and drink) at getting over New Englanders.

What was the most outrageous insult? One followed right after another. Some days after the shooting, one of their judges, Lecompte, called a grand jury in Lecompton, the town they'd named after him, and Lecompte instructed the jury about exactly who would be found and indicted as a traitor. Of course, all of our leaders were to be indicted—everyone, from former Governor Reeder to Governor Robinson to Senator Lane, who was in any way responsible for keeping Lawrence moving safely forward. They all escaped, decamped, pursued our interests elsewhere. Reeder hid out in Kansas City for two weeks, then managed to find a steamer that would take him down the Missouri; Governor Robinson got detained at Lexington, Missouri, and was held under arrest. Mrs. Robinson went to plead his case in the east. Jim Lane got off to Iowa, a hotbed of abolitionist sentiment, especially among the Quakers there. All the leaders

who weren't arrested were looking for money or support outside of Kansas—that seemed now to be our
only hope.

And there was more—the Missourians kept
stealing our horses and mules. Charles's mules and
one of his horses got taken, and he and Thomas and
two other men had to go find them. It took two days,
and in the end they found only the horse and one of
the mules. I was terrified that Jeremiah would be
taken, but we kept him in town as much as possible—it was more usual for horses to be taken on the
roads outside of town, or from claims. This was one
of the reasons we ended up staying in Lawrence past
our departure date, then way past our departure date.
Jeremiah was so appealing and so obviously of value
that he would certainly call attention to himself and
to us. Better, in spite of our best plans, to take refuge
in the populous melee of town. Three days, Thomas
and Frank and I walked out to the claim early in the
morning and back in the evening, to plant our seed.
But there was no tending it. If it must come up, it
would; if we were to get anything from it, we would.
That was our only plan at that point.

Well, a lot of things happened, I can't list them
all, and at any rate, all of them were swallowed up by
what happened next. Sometime in mid-May, on the
eleventh or twelfth, I think, the grand jury, so called,
announced its findings. The next day, the federal
marshal issued a proclamation, all toward Missouri,
of course. The news proclaimed was that the marshal
needed a "posse of law-abiding citizens." What they
were going to do was buried in some sort of legal rig-

marole, but we knew what they wanted to do—band together, get their weapons, and clear us out: hang us, shoot us, burn us, knife us, get rid of us. The only question, for Thomas and me, was where we would endure the attack—alone on our claim, with one horse, one man, one woman, and one boy, not to mention four carbines and a hundred rounds, or in Lawrence with our allies.

May can be a lovely time in Kansas, or so I was told. I only lived one May there, and it was a wet one. Heavy storms marched out of the west nearly every day, great gray curtains of water that moved across the horizon, preceded by thick wet winds. The prairies and the prairie tracks were deep in mire. The native vegetation seemed to thrive well enough, but what people planted was drowned or washed away. The rivers were full and difficult to cross, and that was what saved us for a while.

Thomas and I were concerned about our seed. Every stormy day seemed yet another burden. In the mornings, we went out of the downstairs door and gazed as well as we could toward the west, trying to spot breaks in the clouds. Every noon, when Thomas came home for dinner, we stared at the rain streaming down Louisa's little windows and brooded over what was surely happening out on our claim, more money wasted; and every evening, we gazed up at the few stars that seemed to appear here and there through the cloud cover. Thomas wasn't saying much. He divided his time between wondering what our future in Kansas could possibly hold and hauling goods with Charles, who remained unarrested, so

simpleminded were the officials trying to arrest him.
We got a letter from Susannah Jenkins. She wrote:

> I feel as though I am writing to the figures of a
> dream, so distant and impossible does K.T. seem
> to me now. Even though our life is sadly
> changed by the death of Papa, both Mama and I
> feel that we have made an escape and that life
> here in Northampton is all the more to be
> savored. My looks are of course ruined, and I
> doubt that I shall find a husband, all in all, unless
> it is some old man with lots of children, but
> things that we often complained of before we
> ever left here, we now hardly remark upon, so
> pleased are we to still have life and to be living
> that life in the civilized world. I have two new
> books from the library today, isn't that a mira-
> cle? This is how I think, now. I think of all of
> you every day, and Mother and I both pray for
> you and your safety. The papers are full of K.T.,
> and two editors have already called upon me to
> ask whether I would like to write a small article
> for them about our experiences. To any of you
> who would like to, I say, write me a good letter
> about events there, and I will see that it is pub-
> lished.

I also got a letter from my sister Harriet, who
wrote:

> Since you have been a lifelong troublemaker,
> Lydia, and never in one place for more than two
> seconds from the time you could walk, I am sure

you are in the thick of all these unnecessary ABOLITIONIST troubles. I heartily regret sending my child Frank to you, and if I could have controlled him for one minute, I would not have done so, but that's in the past now, and his Father considers that the experience of the prairies will be good for him, I don't know why, but it is not my way to say anything, as he IS the Father. I sincerely sympathize with the Missourians in this, as they never asked for anyone to come to Kansas Territory and tell everyone what to do there, just as we never asked sister Miriam to come sit at our tables and tell us what to do, or rather, what to think, since owning slaves is illegal in Illinois, though I'm not sure why, since nobody in Illinois cares one way or the other, any more than folks do in Kentuck or Missouri. But that is the way things turn out. I suppose if people do care, they could simply stay in the towns they were born in, like MEDFORD, MASSACHUSETTS, though far be it from me to condemn the activities and chosen life of a member of our family. But these discussions of slavery are getting way out of hand, and everyone wants to talk about it now, when they didn't want to even last year, much less when I was a child, and it was considered beneath anyone's polite notice. In my opinion, it all comes down to the age-old servant problem, and if we all lived like Quakers and had vast quantities of children to work for us, then that would be one thing, but of course not everyone wants to live like that, on a small neat little farm always and everlastingly doing your own work day after day. But you can't get a servant girl in America. As soon as they get here from wherever, Ireland or Germany, even, well, they want to work for themselves, not you, and so what are you going to do? Will there never be any relief, though running a plantation full of niggers is hard work, I'm told, of a sort. But anyway, and this is just between you and me, I sometimes wake up in the morning, and I think about the day ahead, and I think I would be happy enough to know that some old reliable slave-women were down in the kitchen making my breakfast, but in these days, I suppose they would be sharpening the knife for my throat, like as not. Well, these ABO-LITIONISTS have stirred things up, no doubt about it, and I wonder how you are, out there in ABOLITIONIST territory and for goodness sake, don't get hurt or send young Frank back in a coffin, I would be beside myself. We miss Frank very much, and you, too.

Love,

Your sister HARRIET

In Lawrence, of course, we all knew that something was going to happen and what it was. The question for us seemed to be how we would best defend ourselves, and then it turned out to be whether we would defend ourselves at all. Committees of safety met—one was disbanded and another formed. Most of the citizens wanted there to be drilling and provisioning and manning the forts, as there had been during the Wakarusa War, but for one thing, the committees of safety were reluctant to call upon the merchants for more provisions, as they had hardly been paid a thing for what they'd given in December, and for another, the committees were reluctant to call in the farmers from around the town. Everyone knew how important it was for the fall crop to be a good one. But really, the fact was that the President's proclamations and the congressional contretemps and the sight of Jones in the company of the captain of the dragoons, and then the findings of the grand jury, all put us so far in the wrong that everyone was of two minds what to do. We knew we were in the right, but there was moral ground that had been taken away from us. We wanted to be in the right, but also to be *seen* to be in the right. The ranks of the Missourians were rapidly filling up with southerners full of conviction, but our ranks weren't filling so rapidly. For whatever reason, the north, even New England, didn't seem to care all that much about us. Those in charge, now that Robinson and Lane were out of the picture, did what people always do when they don't know what else to do, they decided to wait and see what would happen.

Now the twenty-first of May came around, and it was a sunny, beautiful day. The prairie ran away in every direction, lively and bright with flowers. We all woke up to the sight of men massed on the top of Mount Oread, not far from Governor Robinson's new house, looking down on what amounted to a town without defenses. They had plenty of weapons and ammunition, and as we found out later, they even had cannon. They also had a red flag, which read "Southern Rights," and right next to that they carried a Stars and Stripes, and there were other flags, too. From this band, a group of ten "duly constituted authorities" rode into town and started arresting people. Charles was one of the first—they came to the house and arrested him about eight o'clock, and then he rode around with them as they arrested some of the others. Charles made no resistance. It had been decided that no one would make any resistance. And the arresting party, which didn't include Jones or any of his men, was somewhat more polite than Jones would have been. After Charles left, and Louisa and Frank followed after him, to see what might happen, I said, "Our claim probably looks lovely today."

Thomas replied, "We should be there. We should have Frank there. I wonder that we find ourselves in a town that has no wish to defend itself." And then he, too, went out—the hunger to watch, and to know what was happening, was an almost irresistible one. I was left alone to clear up the breakfast dishes. The sun poured through the small front windows, lighting up our rooms. I was careful to clean the dishes well and put them away neatly. I didn't feel any of the fear I had felt before—on coming to K.T., on the commencement of the Wakarusa War, or any other time. Rather, I felt that cheerful peace you always seem to feel when a long dreaded event begins to happen. It is as if something about you is suspended, and while you are waiting for the worst, you get a few moments of actual joy—your room looks pleasing and comfortable, your tasks seem light and delicious, the pre-

sent life, which you know is about to go away from
you, seems the best possible life, and you are grateful
for it. When I finished, I went out. Not much business was being done, only the business of arrests.
The citizens of Lawrence looked out their windows
or stood in the streets or congregated in shops. The
day wore on and got a little warm, but it was a pleasant change from the recent damp, chilly weather. We
each expected different things. Women and children
had been told to leave town in the morning, and some
did, crying and carrying off what things they could
manage, not having been allowed to take horses or
mules with them (the Missourians wanted all of
those). I suppose those people expected the worst,
burning and shooting and clearing out. But most of
us wanted to stay; Thomas didn't even ask me to
leave, knowing that I would leave only when he did.
I suppose we expected to see something we had
never seen before in our lives.

I strolled down Massachusetts Street, then up
some other streets. I should have felt in danger, but I
didn't. Instead, I marveled at how much Lawrence
had changed since September—how many more permanent buildings there were, how the streets had
straightened and widened themselves, how much the
place looked like a town instead of a congeries of
structures. There were even flower boxes and
patches of garden here and there, fenced off carefully
from pigs and other marauding herbivores. It was a
wonder, really.

The arresting party, or at least the leaders, went
over to the Free State Hotel and enjoyed their mid-

day dinner. Some even went into shops and came out with goods, though whether they paid for them was a point of some dispute later. Mr. Eldridge, the manager of the hotel, said for years afterward that none of the "duly constituted authorities" had so much as offered to pay for his dinner. But people went along with them, whatever they cared to do.

Another example of that was the way General Pomeroy, who had come back from the east, where he'd gone after the Wakarusa War to raise money and support for the Free-Soil cause, let the southerners have our cannon. These artillery pieces, which were smuggled into K.T. by means of various ruses in the winter, had been buried under the foundation of someone's house—Mr. Roberts's house, Louisa said—in early May. General Pomeroy had some men go out and dig them up, and then he handed them over as a gesture of good faith. More women and children were leaving town now, not carrying even what they could. They were all crying. Perhaps they expected to be shot and never to need anything. There was no logic to what folks did—each did what he or she thought best, and so each one might do just about anything. There was no logic to my own alternating waves of fear and curiosity, but they came one after the other.

It got to be afternoon. Thomas, Louisa, Frank, and I had done only one thing, which was to move the mules, horses, and wagons out of the center of town. We were threatened only once, and not very seriously, by two very young men. We just pushed past them and went on. Because of this, we were away from Massachusetts Street when the arresting party under their marshal decided to disband themselves and join the men on the hill. We did see Senator Atchison (Louisa knew what he looked like) ride toward town with some men. Senator Atchison had acted as our enemy throughout the spring, agitating his constituents and promoting our conquest. I remember thinking that it wasn't good to be seeing him right there on a downtown street. And he looked drunk, too.

Once the arrests had been made in the morning, the huge posse of Missourians that had gathered on Mount Oread began streaming into town, and who was at its head but the miraculously resurrected tyrant Jones, proclaimed as dead and memorialized by all of Missouri not two weeks before!

The first thing they did was go over to the offices of the *Herald of Freedom,* one of the Lawrence newspapers, which was on the second story above a shop. They threw out all the type, smashed the press with a couple of sledgehammers, and carried as much as they could in the way of supplies and equipment down to the river and threw it in. Another band was doing the same thing over at the office of the *Kansas Free State,* the other newspaper.

Late in the afternoon, they bombarded the Free State Hotel. They told the residents to get out, then they drew five cannon up across the street from it and started firing. We all ran from wherever we happened to be and watched as best we could, though there was a fair amount of smoke. The noise was fearsome if you'd never heard cannon before, a loud cracking roar followed by the whistle of the ball leaving the barrel of the cannon, then a great whump as the ball hit the stone wall of the hotel, a noise that was also a feeling of the hotel shaking the ground, shaking the world, shaking you, standing there. Had the hotel been built as a fortress? It withstood the cannon with hardly any sign of damage. "Got to build for the ages," Mr. Eldridge was heard to say. "If something's worth doing, then it's worth doing properly." Women and children were crying for a while, but as the hotel continued to stand, that seemed a little beside the point.

When the cannon had little effect, the attackers carried in kegs of powder, intending to blow the place up. After they had taken them in, they made time to carry out whatever they could find, like bits and pieces of furniture and draperies and clothing, not to give to the owners but to keep for themselves. Then they found the liquor, and they came out with bottles and kegs and cases. They opened them right there and got into it. As for the powder kegs, when they got around to lighting them, the onlookers backed away, imagining the four-story stone walls blowing outward in a great hellish boom and light, but Eldridge kept smiling a little, and shortly we knew why. Some windows that had withstood the cannon fire shattered, but the hotel stood. Now the southerners were drunk, and angry. They started screaming, "Fire it! Fire it! D——n, it will burn!" I'd hardly been in the hotel since the winter. I remembered the rickety wooden stairs, four floors of them, and you could see all the way to the cellar if you cared to look. The roof was wood; the interior was all wood, with wooden furniture. I knew it would go up, and it did. Soon enough, flames were shooting from every window and from the roof, and smoke was driving us back toward the river. When I saw him, Mr. Eldridge still had a little smile on his face, fixed there and forgotten, perhaps. Certainly, the sight of our beautiful hotel going up in flames was a great shock to me, but I couldn't tell what it did to him. At last, the walls began to fall. I heard later that one of the southerners was killed by a piece of falling rock, because he was too drunk to move away from the conflagration. Behold the moral stature of our conquerors!

When we were driven as far back as Louisa's place, we ran up and checked our things. The booming and crashing had broken her windows, so we swept up the glass and gave thanks that we had put quilts over them and had wrapped the dishes and cups and set them away. Then the smoke drove us out of there. We grabbed our shawls and a few necessary belongings and ran out again, intending to take refuge with the Bushes, who were at the other end of town from the hotel, in a newer section of buildings that were built just that spring. We covered our mouths and noses and made our way around to the west—Thomas, Frank, Louisa, and myself. It was very late, almost dusk, which meant it must have been seven-thirty or eight o'clock. I was running along with my head down and my hand to my face when Thomas plucked my sleeve. "Look over there." He gestured upward, toward Mount Oread. We stopped and gaped at the sight of the Robinsons' new house, all black walnut, full of books and old writings and furniture and family treasures, we'd heard, going up in a great bonfire on the brow of the hill. And even from where we were, we could see the Ruffians dancing around the place, black figures against the yellow brightness of the fire, and we could hear them shouting and screaming drunkenly, jubilant at the destruction. Later, we heard that they hardly bothered to steal anything but burned it all, just to show Governor Robinson a thing or two. "Look at the devils," said Louisa, "howling with glee!" It was fascinating, but darkness was falling fast, the smoke was thick, and there were little bands of drunken Ruffians everywhere, so Thomas pushed us onward; we had to practically drag Frank by the ear.

The Bushes had seen nothing, as they had huddled inside all day, expecting the worst, so they were appalled and shocked by the news we had for them— all the more appalled and shocked for, of course, being totally unsurprised, according to Mrs. Bush. "Nothing you tell me can turn a hair on my head," she said, her face white as the moon. "I don't put anything past those animals. And mark my words, they won't stop there! They'll burn us all out before morning! There are twenty-four thousand of them, haven't you heard? Three thousand Missourians and twenty-one thousand real southerners, with slaves saddling their horses and making up their food in camp. I heard all about it! Five thousand from South Carolina alone, and every one of them came to K.T.

with a thousand dollars in his pocket, from the sale of slaves down the river—don't you know? A cabal of planters got together, and each of them sold ten slaves for a thousand dollars apiece, and that's five hundred slaves! I swear you don't know which is worse, sending that trash to burn us out and kill us, or selling those poor slaves away from their wives and husbands and children in order to send them. Oh," she said, "their souls are black indeed! Blacker than the blackest skin on the darkest African!"

Mr. and Mrs. Lacey and their boys came, saying that the Ruffians had come knocking and then thrown them out into the street and told them to go back to Massachusetts and let them all know back there what a Kansas tea party was like! Then, as they ran off, they heard the drunkards smashing things and even saw them running out of the house. "Two low types were carrying some chairs, and the captain, or so he had styled himself, had my dishes in his hands!" exclaimed Mrs. Lacey.

Then we all got into a discussion of whether the southerners would be punished by the Lord for their iniquities, and all except Thomas agreed that they would, with only Louisa disputing the grounds of the discussion, saying that "the Lord" was actually a diffuse higher presence in the universe that manifested itself as positive or negative energy, and that of course the Missourians might find themselves afflicted by an excess of negative energy in years to come but they wouldn't have the wit or the spiritual education to understand what was happening to them. Everyone fell silent for a bit, pondering these remarks, and I knew that Louisa felt that she had put the capstone to the discussion; but everyone else rather felt that these ideas were too embarrassing to go on with, especially as we were all worried about Charles, whom Louisa had last seen in the late morning, with the arresting party, when they took him up to their camp.

We prepared for attack. Or rather, the house was as prepared as it could be, which wasn't much—the door was locked and the window was covered and there were pails and pots of water for dousing flames, and once these measures had been taken, we sat about a single candle and drank tea and deplored the Missourians. There were four Sharps carbines and forty rounds among us. We agreed that the Laceys, unsure of what the Ruffians wanted, had been hesitant to fire, but we wouldn't make the same mistake. In the event, our resolution wasn't tried, for we sat up all night, and at dawn, which came before five, we realized that the Missourians had in part decamped and in part keeled over where they stood, but at any rate, they were satisfied with what they had done, and there would be no more destruction for the time being.

We should have been fatigued but were not, at all, so eager was everyone of our party to view the aftermath. We drank our tea and went out, Thomas and Mr. Bush, each armed, in the lead, and the rest in the middle, with Frank and me, also both armed, bringing up the rear. But the Missourians were gone. The only people in the streets were ones we recognized, either because we knew them or by their grieving and incredulous countenances.

The citizens of Lawrence hadn't, in the end, been hung, shot, knifed, dismembered, or cleared out, but our houses had been robbed and damaged (the Missourians loved more than anything to shoot out a pane of glass or leave bullet holes in a wall), our furnishings had been left in the street, smashed, ripped, and broken, our crockery and dishes lay in fragments, our bedclothes and hangings and blankets and sheets, even our nightgowns and commodes, had been tossed in the street; our flowers were trampled and pulled up by the roots. Here's something—the streets were full of papers blowing everywhere: these were not only "contraband" sheets of newspapers from the north or old copies of our local sheets, but also family letters and legal papers, diaries and cookery books and novels and schoolbooks, scattered and torn by angry hands, precious photographs sundered in two or three pieces. I saw a wreath woven of some beloved person's hair, cut and destroyed in a way that only those who desired above all things to hurt you in your heart would think of. That was what was shocking—you could stoop down and pick up some papers out of the dirt and see that they were just letters from someone's sister or father, and yet some stranger had taken the time and effort to tear them up and toss them. They had put real thought and real effort into their hatred.

There were those who started looking on the bright side of things at once—Thomas was one of them. No Free Stater killed or wounded, the Robinsons thankfully absent, all damage to buildings other than the hotel and the Robinsons' house superficial. Better than that, as far as we knew (and this turned out to be true), no Free Stater had perpetrated anything that might be construed as an offense. The attack on Lawrence could not be called a war but had to be called a sacking, a depredation, a crime. "You wait," said Thomas. "The men from the eastern newspapers will be here by balloon if they have to. Remember that fellow from New York, Brewerton? And there are plenty of others. They'll turn Lawrence, K.T., into a woman in a white dress, lifting her pale arms and pleading for mercy! It looks worse than it is."

At Louisa's place, the lower shop had been wrecked and my last length of rope stolen. Someone had taken our ax to the stairs and hacked three of them out, so it wasn't easy getting to the upper story. And a fire had been set, though, lacking fuel, it had gone out—we could still smell the smoke. Upstairs, the rosewood bedstead had been shorn of its clothes and jerked about; it had one ax cut in the footboard. The bedstead we'd used was intact, but the ticking was torn, and good New England feathers lay in white bunches here and there. Our things that we had packed for going to the claim were rifled and spread around, but the only things missing were Thomas's red flannel shirt and his shaving brush. A dress of mine had a big rent in the skirt. Louisa's clothes, being richer, had suffered more—two of her dresses were gone, and a shawl and a pair of shoes. Her jewelry—two necklaces and two sets of earbobs—was missing, too. And odd things were gone—a candleholder, a worked pillow, one of Charles's boots. But they hadn't touched the books or the little guitar, and my sister's last letter lay open on the floor, as if someone had read it and then not bothered to tear it up. We looked, but we didn't even begin to clean things up, as it was imperative to look for Charles.

Louisa, having sensed on the spiritual waves no disruption in her connection to Charles, was not especially worried. Nevertheless, Thomas and Mr. Bush went over to the site of the burned-out hotel to see if there was news of the arrested men. Frank and I set out to find our animals. The first thing we saw was Senator Atchison, much changed from the day before. He rode at the head of his men, sober now, or possibly not, his coat buttoned up to the chin and his hat pulled down over his eyes. Did he look ashamed? I wanted to think so. His band looked dirty and rather sick, and they dragged one of their cannon with them.

"I could shoot him," said Frank.

"You left your gun at the Bushes'."

"Don't need my own gun. Any gun would do. I could borrow one and follow along behind them and shoot him when he crosses the river."

"You are not going to shoot a man."

"I know, but I'm just saying I *could*. Saying I could feels better than just letting him go by."

Well, that was true. All around us, the people of Lawrence stared frankly at the Missourian. Everyone knew who he was, since he was tall and striking, and his picture had been in the papers when he was Vice President. I'm sure we weren't the only ones talking in such strains. But the senator and his weary group trudged past unmolested, got to the river, crossed it, and vanished into the trees.

I dreaded what we would find when we came to the corral where we'd left the animals, thinking it was out of the way and safer. Clearly, from the destruction, there had been enough of the Ruffians so that they had sought out most corners of Lawrence and done damage everywhere. We knew a lot of horses and mules had been stolen, not to mention the cattle they had "pressed" into the service of their stomachs, because people we met complained of missing animals. When we got there, in fact, there was no corral, only broken rails and knocked-down posts, evidence of many trampling hooves in the dirt, and no animals to be seen. This, after everything else, caused me to burst into tears. Some men were standing nearby, and when they saw us looking at it all, they came over.

"Well, they drove 'em off, don't you know?" said one of them. "I guess there was twenty hosses and mules here for a bit, but they rode in and drove 'em off in the middle of the night. There was screamin' and yellin', let me tell you."

Another man said, "Laban, here, and myself, we come out and shot a few times into the air, but it was just for show. We couldn't do a thing. There was ten men, anyway, and they was far gone into their cups."

Laban sighed. "I had me the best team of mules I ever had here. Just bought 'em a couple of weeks ago. They shone! Cost me a hundred dollars apiece. Gone now."

I walked away. It just seemed like Jeremiah had to be somewhere, that if I looked I could find him. It had to turn out with Jeremiah as it had with our other things—a bit of damage, but nothing serious. For a few minutes, I wandered around, looking among the houses and buildings in this part of town. There was the same destruction here as elsewhere—interiors of homes broken up and turned over on the street, men, women, and children picking through things, looking for things, talking and crying. I was like one of them. I saw a woman pick up a cup and grin, then call to her husband, "Here's one that's not broken!" and I expected to turn a corner and find Jeremiah looking at me, his dark, large eyes in his pale face intelligently recognizing me, his ears swiveled forward. Never once had Jeremiah failed to approach me when I came for him, never once had he ducked my grasp or tried to get away or run off. But of course they would have been yelling and hooting, shooting in the air to panic the horses and mules. The animals in the pen would have been rolling their eyes and snorting, tossing their heads in that terrified equine way, and Jeremiah, who was an intelligent and responsive horse, but still a horse, would have been one of them, as terrified as the others. It hurt me to think of it, all the whinnying and bumping up against one another, the flailing of hooves and the danger, and then they would have been running, and I didn't know how to think of that, where or how they had gone, so my imagination went dark.

Well, sentiment was a cruel joke in K.T.

And practically, of course, now we had no horse, and Louisa and Charles had no animals, either, and so how would we get our things out to our claim, and how would Charles, should he return from his imprisonment, make an income, and how would we all, in Lawrence, go on from this and recover even what we had had two days before, which was little enough in any case, if you thought of Susannah Jenkins's letter, and how she counted up the losses she'd incurred in K.T. and settled happily for any sort of life at all, if only it wasn't in K.T.?

Everyone we knew was worse off than a year before: Mr. James had lost his wife and children; the Jenkinses had lost their husband and father and, it appeared, most of their means. The Bushes lived in a tiny fragment of a house, far humbler than what they'd left in Massachusetts, and were grateful for it. Louisa, for all the good face she put on it, had lost a husband and now, perhaps, another one. The Laceys? After she came, he was absent more and more, and now the rumor was that he was staying with a woman at the other end of town most of the time, but of course no one spoke of it, and all pretended that he was just very taken up with business. The Holmeses? They had barely made it through the winter on the charity of their friends, and any hopes he had had of forming a congregation had been dashed—no one in K.T. seemed to cotton to his fiery brand of Christianity. The Smithsons? They were farther from their publishing project than they'd been in the fall, and old Mr. Smithson had broken his arm, to boot.

Thomas and myself? We had little money, few hopes, and now had lost our most valuable possession. And who had not seen the waves of men and women who were worse off than ourselves and our friends, who'd died of fevers and other illnesses far from all friends and far from their homes, at the end of their funds and without their names being known to those caring for them? Even the Robinsons. There was the model for us all. They had risen the highest and had now fallen the lowest—he taken by the authorities, their house burned to the ground. The Kansas prairie was full of graves where people had buried everything they loved, everything they knew.

Frank, who was walking beside me, said, "I don't know when I been this mad before."

I gave a little bark of bitter laughter.

"It an't a laughing matter."

"Isn't a laughing matter."

"Well, you are laughing. That just makes me madder."

I looked at him. His eyebrows were low over his eyes, and he was frowning mightily. He didn't look especially boyish. He said, "My feeling is, they shouldn't have done it."

"Well, of course not. Look at the suffering. . . ."

He caught my gaze, as if the suffering were beside the point. Transgression was the point for Frank.

"Men do what they think they need to do. I hate to say it, but the Missourians think they have right on their side, also. They think—"

"I an't going to try and know what they think. I

am going to fix my thoughts on what they did." He walked a little ahead of me, and I caught up.

"Frank—" But I didn't have anything to say. You could look at it both ways. We were fools to have come to K.T. in the first place, or they were knaves to have destroyed us (hastened our destruction, perhaps a realist would say). Or both were true. As I've said elsewhere in this narrative, in K.T. most things were both true and false, and it depended on your circumstances how you chose among them.

Finally, I said, "Well, now we can say that maybe we shouldn't have come here. When I look back to how I felt in Quincy, it seems like some kind of idle whim, the fruit of thoughtless ignorance. But back then, it seemed like everyone wanted to come to Kansas."

"It don't matter how we got here or whether we regret that, and I don't. I would have got here without you as well as with you, Lidie. But what matters is whether they should have done this, and they shouldn't have, and I an't going to think any more about it than that." He turned off abruptly as we came to Fourth Street, and I watched him go for a moment before I recollected myself and called out to him, but he waved me off without turning around, and I thought right then that I would never get him into school again in his life, and here was another loss, Frank's future, for he was making himself a K.T. man, a ruffian of a sort, no matter what side he was on in this controversy, and I didn't have a word of influence over him.

CHAPTER 17

I See the Bottom of the Well

*If an artery be cut, it must be immediately tied up,
or the person will bleed to death. The blood from
an artery is of a bright red color, and spirts out, in
regular jets, at each beat of the heart.*

—*p. 240*

THE BEST BIT OF NEWS WAS THIS, that when I got
back to Louisa's place, there was Charles, smiling,
dirty, and tired. When his captors had fallen into the
stupor that was the natural end of their revelry, he
had simply walked away, pausing only to select two
of their better rifles and some hundred rounds of
ammunition. He showed us the weapons and was
much pleased with his escape. But he had bruises,
one on his cheek and one on his neck, and a cut
above the eye. When he afterward went out for a
moment, I asked Louisa about them. "Well," she
said, "they had their usual fun with him, knocked
him down and kicked him once or twice, and of
course some offered to hang him right there, but others restrained them. That's the sort of people we have
to deal with."

I said, "I suppose they know that when they start
anything they'll be too drunk later to finish it." We
exchanged a sour laugh. It was galling to be at the
mercy of such low characters.

Now everyone in Lawrence commenced to do as
he or she thought best. There were those, hard to

understand, who decided to ignore the sacking of the town and get on with their business of farming or keeping a shop or milling or whatever, and, it's true, there are always these sorts of cold stones who look like men and have wisdom on their side. Others, perhaps those who hadn't liked K.T. much in the first place, hastened their plans to backtrack and shortly left for Ohio and New York State, or decided that Nebraska was, perhaps, a colder Kansas, but one without conflict. Hotter-blooded ones were even harder to understand. We all agreed that stay we must, simply because the Missourians wanted us out, but there agreement stopped. Charles was all for carrying the war to the Missourians, somehow, or at least to their fellows in Franklin and in Leavenworth and in Kickapoo. What they had done to us should be done to them, summarily and with even greater force, and not only because such were the measures men like that could understand, but also because now that they had done it once, with success, they would be all the more likely to try again, with even less restraint, and for even more slender reasons. Hadn't they vowed to hang, shoot, knife, dismember, and clear us out? If we expected them to stop now, we were sadly mistaken, Charles thought. Louisa was, by contrast, all for defending the town. We should conserve our weapons and our provisions, rebuild the fortresses and earthworks, commence the drilling. If another attack was to come, and it was, according to both Charles and Louisa, then those with weapons should be at home, using them to protect, rather than running around the countryside, where they were likely to get in trouble, for one thing, and likely to do no good, for another. Thomas declared that in all the fighting, sight of the main goal had been lost, and that was making Kansas a free state, as a first step to abolishing slavery everywhere, which Thomas thought would take a generation or two but was inevitable *if* K.T. could be won. "This is the summit of the mountain," he said. "The water will fall one way or the other. If it falls to the south, then in a generation or two there will be slaves in Massachusetts, and free labor will be everywhere driven out. If it falls to the north, then, the south will be free in the same period of time. But it all depends on Kansas." Thomas, who was not a fighting man, wanted to renew our applications to Congress and work for the election of a good Republican, and free any slave that he should happen across on the side.

As for me, I held many incompatible views in a kind of seething soup or stew, and I wondered at the consistency of the others. I thought that in a place like K.T., you could easily act one way one minute and another way the next minute, and smile or laugh or cry all in the same minute. I wanted to kill something, preferably a Missourian, preferably the man who had driven off Jeremiah, preferably more than one. Before they died, I wanted them to give back Jeremiah, apologize to me, and know what brutes and liars they were. At the same time, I wanted no more violence of any kind, no disturbances to my system, to the town, or to the spring that was shaping up before us. I wanted no more burnings or screaming, no more of those revelations of loss such as I had

had when I saw the broken and empty corral, which made you feel suddenly drenched with grief. I wanted no more fear such as we all felt right then, fear of the Missourians, yes, but a greater fear of something else, which hadn't yet happened but had certainly been set in motion.

I wanted Frank to stick right with me and show me at every moment that he was safely himself, a thirteen-year-old boy interested in money and business; but he wasn't, and I simultaneously wanted him out there, where I knew he was, banding together with other boys who had their weapons with them and righteousness on their minds. My brain held many contradictory thoughts, but I knew Frank's didn't. Frank's brain held a simple thought, and I wished for his sake that he knew the many complexities, but also I wished for my sake that I believed in the simple.

Ah, well, I was agitated. All over Lawrence, citizens were praying for various things—revenge, peace, war, fortitude, wisdom, safety, the death of enemies, the elevation of the bondman. Had I been the praying sort, I would have prayed only for a quiet mind.

We went to bed that night, Thursday, and the next. By Saturday, the cold ones were getting on with business, and Lawrence seemed calmer. Charles had bought a new mule of a backtracker, and Thomas and I had agreed to borrow the mule on Sunday to take our things out to the claim.

There was an old man in K.T. who afterward became famous, by the name of Old Brown, old John Brown. He came from Ohio or New York somewhere, and wasn't related to any of the other Browns—there were lots of Browns in K.T. I can't say that I ever saw him, though Louisa said that she did. Perhaps we saw some of his sons or associates, as there were quite a few of them, riding through the town or buying something here or there. They had a place south of town, down on the Marais des Cygnes, where my brother-in-law Horace always talked about settling. Free Staters and proslavery people were all mixed up down there—it wasn't pure enclaves, as it was in the north. Later Mr. Holmes said that he saw Old Brown with his famous weapon, some kind of thing like an adze or a pike, odd-looking. But afterward, as with everything else, all sorts of people wanted to get next to it, and that is why I want to stress that I never saw Old Brown or his sons or friends, nor did I know at the time that what Old Brown did would become the most famous thing about K.T. in some quarters and utterly unknown in others. The fact was, what Old Brown did, and to whom, and why, was a common story around the time that it happened, and it showed us all the new world we had gotten into and what that meant, and so most people didn't say much about it, because that was a world that most people in their right mind didn't enter willingly.

We went to bed Saturday night. Sunday morning, we got up and Thomas went to hitch the mule to Charles's smaller wagon. I made breakfast for Louisa, Charles, and myself. Frank was out early. I had let our insistence that he come with us to the claim slip by. Charles said he could use him, and so,

officially, he was to stay with Charles and Louisa and
be a help to them. Louisa was still up and around
most days, but she was a bit ill that morning. I gave
her dry wheaten cakes, which settled her. All we
were thinking of was that now the parting had come
and that we all would miss our intimacies. I liked
Charles Bisket enormously now—he was so cheerful
and agreeable and tall and languid-looking and ready
to help anyone at any time. Charles made you think
about good luck, which he always seemed to have.
Was there such a thing as luck, really, or was it just
Charles's good nature reflecting back onto himself?
As for Louisa, for all her faults and pretensions (and
I felt that I could catalogue these with perfect clar-
ity), there was a solidity in the bond we shared that
seemed unshakable by things as trivial as annoyance,
let's say, or foolishness, or vanity, on one side or the
other.

I wrapped up a stack of cakes in a cloth for later
in the day, and Louisa rose from her bed to present
me with some other things—tea and honey and the
last of her dried apples. Then, through the broken
window, we heard the wagon and the mule pull up
outside, and Charles trotted down the stairs. I
embraced Louisa and gave her a kiss and drew her
wrapper more closely around her shoulders. I saw
Thomas and Charles and a man I didn't recognize in
confabulation where Thomas was holding the mule. I
didn't see their faces until I got down there, though.
Their faces, when I saw them, were pale in the spring
sunshine, and I said, thinking nothing, "What's the
news?"

"It's a terrible thing," said Thomas. He opened his mouth and closed it, then said, "I can't say it."

"Some men were killed," said Charles. "Some proslavery men down south about thirty miles."

I saw by their looks that there was more to it than this, but I restrained my curiosity. The stranger shook his head and walked off. Charles and Thomas continued to load the wagon, though we hadn't very many things, and they were shortly done. As we drove north out of Lawrence, we saw knots of citizens gathered in the streets. I looked deeply into Thomas's face, but he was looking steadily at the mule's haunches, and everything about his demeanor warned me off. We went along in silence. The ride to the claim normally took about an hour on horseback, somewhat longer in a wagon. This time, the prairies were wet from the spring rains and we had to pick our way rather carefully and circuitously. After about an hour, we were still but halfway there. I didn't mind. This drive, I thought, was our last respite before the beginning of seriously hard work and heavy solitude. Finally, Thomas cleared his throat and spit off to the side, which was odd for him, as he didn't chew tobacco. But he was spitting out what he had to say.

"A man and his two sons, and two other men, also, were killed last night down around the Pottawatomie area. They were killed by Free Staters in sight of their wives, who were begging that their lives be spared."

"Who were they?"

"Do you know that fellow Allen Wilkinson, who's a delegate to the bogus legislature?"

I nodded. This Wilkinson was something of a loudmouth.

"He was one. The man and his sons were named Doyle, and then there was another man, whose name I don't know. He was visiting, and they called him out in the sight of three other men."

"Who did the shooting?"

"It wasn't just shooting."

"What was it?"

"I don't want to tell you."

"Don't, then."

"It was hacking."

"You mean like up in Leavenworth? With axes?"

"Something of the sort."

We pondered this in silence.

I said, "Tell me who did it," fearing that it would be someone we knew. Daniel James was angry enough for that.

"Brown."

"Brown the newspaper editor?"

"Another Brown. They call him Old Brown. I think I've seen him. He's one of those that make you want to cross the street with one look. He had his sons and some others with him."

That was Sunday, the day we borrowed Charles's new mule and went to our claim. I remember it clearly, and so that's how I know what folks knew about that, and how quickly. My first reaction was a hardhearted one, I admit. I said, "If the southerners kept their mouths shut a little more, they might fare a little better."

"These were unarmed men, whose wives were begging for their lives."

"How many times do they vow to hang us or shoot us or clear us out? How many times do they call for our destruction in the bloodiest terms? It seems to me that if people talk all about these sorts of things long enough, they can't be surprised when these things happen."

Well, Thomas was not pleased with my less than womanly response, but he didn't condemn me. We rode along. The mule went easily enough. The plan was that we would unpack our cases and belongings, and then Thomas would drive the wagon into town and walk out again. He didn't expect to be back with me until after dark. I estimated that that was enough time for us to digest each other's views on the subject of the killings, or, as it later came to be called by some, the massacre. Of course, in Lawrence, folks always referred to it as "those killings." As for a mule or another horse, well, it was possible that something would turn up, but our funds were exceedingly low, and we were pondering what we had that we might sell. What with the "sacking" and our poverty, our future seemed to have gotten rather short, and we didn't try to look far into it. Over the years, I've noticed that about impoverishment and danger—both make the present moment seem full and almost agreeable, but with the sense that you must keep your head down and your eyes on your feet, for fear.

We came to our cabin and drew up the mule in

front of the door. It didn't look too bad—it looked familiar, easy to claim as our own. In spite of the wet weather, the stands of wheat and barley looked good enough, to our untutored eyes. They were green and tallish. Thomas had broadcast the seed more thickly than thinly, and the wet earth was hidden in the green. These green bits were only patches in the larger sweep of the flowery prairie, and there was just a light breeze—none of that heavy K.T. wind. In one of his previous trips, Thomas had set the door on its leather hinges again, and that did wonders for the look of the place. We carried in our belongings. The spaces between the logs that I would soon be chinking with mud let in some light, and things seemed cheerful enough. By noon, we had eaten some of our wheat cakes from the morning, and Thomas and the mule had rattled away again. I watched them go for a long time, until they had disappeared over the rim of the prairie. My husband's back pleased me, for how straight it was, how strange and yet how characteristic of him. I still couldn't say that I felt about him as other women seemed to feel about their husbands, that they were essentially familiar and without mystery. But I wasn't thinking these thoughts at the time; I was just watching the prairie fill up with loneliness around his receding figure and persuading myself that his return would effect the opposite.

The first thing I did was build a fire in the stove— a good stove, and worth the money I had paid for it, since it went through the winter unused and emerged as if still new—with some of the wood we had chopped and set inside the cabin to dry on earlier visits. Then I poured off some river water I'd set out on my last visit and put the kettle on the stove to heat. After that, I swept out bits of dirt and debris that had sifted through the walls. My plan was to start digging out the well again as soon as we could. The river was pretty high now. That reassured me that you could drink a bit of it, anyway. I had to carry river water up to the cabin for the endless mudding that had to be done, but I was putting that off, as the slope to the river might be a bit slippery, there might be snakes at this time of year, and at any rate, the walk back with the heavy pails was not a pleasant one. But soon I had done all the little tasks I could in good conscience do, and I picked up two other pails we had and settled them on the yoke I laid across my shoulders. It was easy when they were empty, and I rather skipped down the slope, not thinking of much and taking no care to be quiet.

Sure enough, I heard rustling and cracking in the woods ahead of me, no violent sounds, but neither the sounds of scurrying prairie rodents. I startled, and the yoke fell off my shoulders, and the pails went rolling down the slope, making something of a clatter. Now the other creature startled, too, and cracking and rustling turned into crashing and then snorting. I stood where I was and wished for my rifle. No man would make such noises, and yet weren't the Missourians everywhere? I thought at once of Old Brown and the men who had been killed, and my observations about them, and revenge. Then there was a flash of paleness, and Jeremiah burst into the clearing next to the river, his ears swiveling and his nostrils wide. He snorted at me, and then we stared at each other, and then he bent his head to snort at one of the pails, which was not far from him, and then we stared at one another again.

Even so, I thought that he had expected to see me far more than I had expected to see him. I said, "Hello, Jeremiah," in a low and soothing voice. A horse isn't like a dog, who likes to be greeted enthusiastically. A horse, especially a spirited animal like Jeremiah, is always weighing the option of flight. I laid down the yoke and held out my hands, low and wide. Jeremiah continued to snort. I took a step or two toward him, still murmuring his name and any reassurances that came to my lips. My skirt caught on some brush, but I stopped and smoothly released it, then stepped forward again. I had no bridle, no piece of rope to throw around his neck, and, of course, no guarantee that I could get him the three hundred yards or so back to the cabin without them. Jeremiah stood still, looking at me, and then, at last, put his head down and moved toward me, pausing only to shy a bit at the other fallen pail. When he came to me, first he nuzzled at my hands, looking, I suppose, for a bit of dried apple, then he put his velvety, whiskery lips against my neck and blew out. I put my arm around his neck from below and said, "I have some bits of apples and sugar back at the cabin. Want some?" Then I turned and walked away, leaving the yoke and the pails where they lay. Jeremiah waited a moment, then walked after me, not steadily—I had to stop and let him make up his mind over and over—but willingly enough. When we got back to the cabin, I rewarded him at once with the promised treats. After that, I found a rope and tied him to the railing of his corral, which Thomas had repaired during the spring. He was sufficiently fat—there was plenty of prairie forage in the spring—but he was covered with scratches and had a large cut on his left haunch, crusted over with dark blood and bits of vegetable matter. The area around it was hot to the touch, and he switched his tail and stamped his hoof when my hand got near it. I felt his legs; they were cool and tight. His eyes were clear, and he walked with a steady step. I got some of our well water and washed his wound with a rag, then found some comfrey leaves and made a poultice, which I held on the wound for a few minutes to cool it, then I untied him and gave him the freedom of his corral, which was rich with prairie grasses.

Only then did I allow myself to marvel and to swell with delight. Jeremiah, who I had thought was certainly lost, certainly in Missouri somewhere, certainly as far from me as the moon! Jeremiah! Here he was! Our diminished future expanded again! And in addition to that, well, he had come of his own accord. He had followed the road between Lawrence and our claim, a road he knew well, of course; he had acted on some intention, some expectation, had he not? Was this possible for a horse? Perhaps, if only because every old horseman had some such story, and yet to see it happen, to be the object of his intention, was intensely gratifying. I stood by the rail and stared at him where he grazed, until the shadows were long and the evening wind had picked up strongly. Then I recollected my pails and more or less ran to the river. By the time I got back with the heavy water (as Miss Beecher always said, "A pint's a pound, the world around"), it was nearly dark, but I could still see Jeremiah's luminous shape in the blue light. Only after darkness had enveloped him did I go in and light a candle.

Thomas, who had had second thoughts about a trek over the prairie when there was no moon, waited to leave Lawrence until daybreak. He could not believe his eyes at the sight of Jeremiah standing by the fence, and me poulticing his cut again, and our good fortune right there, big as life. After I put down the poultice and untied the horse, Thomas grabbed me about the waist and kissed me and spun me around. He kept saying, "I can't tell you how sure I was we'd have to backtrack! I didn't see any future here, I was as low as I've ever been, but now . . . !"

Well, how were we to know? At any rate, it was a splendid thing to feel my husband's arms and hands press against me and to lean into his chest and to hear his joyful voice in my ear, and to look into his face and have him put his fingers into my hair and take all the pins out, one by one, and then pause to put them carefully in the pocket of his shirt. Then I shook my hair out, and it fell to almost the middle of my skirt, and we went inside the cabin.

I caught a catfish in the river and fried that up with some corncakes for supper, and over supper it came out that we still were not in agreement over Old Brown. Those killings had taken place Saturday

night, and it was now Monday. As always in Lawrence, Sunday had seen no lack of talk. Some were
saying that the five men were having a meeting when
they were surprised by a group that may have
included Brown and may not have. The killings were
intended to preempt plans the men were making to
attack Free Staters in their beds that very night. The
men had been armed and had returned fire, had even
begun firing. Another story was that Old Brown, or
someone, had indeed killed four of the men, just shot
them fair and square, the way you shoot people in
K.T.—a shooting was a shooting, which was different by far from a hacking—but that the fifth man had
died on a hunting expedition that strayed among the
Indians, and the Indians had done the hacking. The
proslave forces had only made it look like Old
Brown, or someone, had hacked him up in order to
reflect against the Free Staters. Others said that it was
the same with these five as it had been with Jones—
their own sympathizers, some men from South Carolina, in fact, had done the killings in a drunken fight
and then decided to make it look as though Free
Staters had done the deed. Old Brown was a bona
fide character and hated by many because he invoked
the Lord on his side all the time, so he was ripe to be
slandered. And still others said it was just like Jones
in another way, too: No one was dead, all were alive
and only slightly injured. The whole "massacre" was
trumped up by the Missouri papers to incite another
attack on Lawrence, this time with "justified" execu-
tions. Old Brown and his sons hadn't been anywhere

near the spot. I liked this last story myself—it fit in
so neatly with what we had experienced from the
Missourians before—but Thomas shook his head.

"I think the story we heard Sunday, the first one,
has the ring of truth to it. When they told it, people
were horrified and didn't want to utter such words.
Now they're all talking fast, with eager looks.
They're making up stories, and all the stories are
going to bury the truth of what really happened."

"I think the stories show that nobody knows what
really happened. What's Old Brown himself say?"

"Nowhere to be found."

"Well, K.T. is a big country. That doesn't mean
anything." What I really wanted to say was that the
killings didn't seem like our business, as we hadn't
known about them or done them, of course. But they
agitated Thomas, and he was eager to tell me all the
news, so I kept quiet. He said, "In my opinion, this
has broken new ground, ground we shouldn't be on."

"There were killings before."

"But they were more incidental. Folks weren't
going out to look for people to kill, with lists in their
hands."

"He had a list?"

"They say he did. The ones who say he did it, at
any rate."

Here was the question, to me: In a place where
everything was true, could it be true that Old Brown
and his men had done the killings and that they had
been five miles away from the killings, both at the
same time? In the United States, these things

couldn't be true at the same time, but in K.T. it seemed as if they could.

We were alone for the next two days, and we didn't have any visitors or news, but Thomas couldn't leave the subject of Old Brown alone. I would say, "Don't you think Jeremiah seems to have less heat around that cut now?" and he would say, "That man Wilkinson was one of the worst of them, but . . ." Or I would say, "We need to find some papers for the walls," and he would say, "If they would just come forward and tell the story, then maybe we'd know it wasn't so bad. But this running off and disappearing, well, that doesn't look good. Of course, in K.T., just traveling to and fro can look like running off. . . ."

On Wednesday, a week after the sacking of Lawrence, we had another great rain, and though we set ourselves things to do inside, it was monotonous and uncomfortable to hear the rain on the roof and to have it coming in everywhere—we hadn't enough pots and pans and dishes and receptacles to catch any but the worst streams. The mudding I had done was still wet, and I could see it crumble and trickle away. We had dry wood and made a fire in the stove and boiled up some tea, but the tea reminded me of Louisa and her two bedsteads and four chairs and little guitar and cups and saucers and warm, dry apartment, and I felt sick with longing all the time that I tried to make myself happy by renewing my gratitude at Jeremiah's return. We had been sitting silently for a long time, the afternoon so dark with rain that we had a candle lit, and I was sewing up holes in our bed tick and Thomas was cleaning the guns, and he broke the silence by saying, "Why couldn't they leave well enough alone? This is another mistake. Rash acts are always mistakes, because from a distance they look more than rash, they look evil, and that drives—"

I flared up. "I'm glad they did it! Well, I'm not glad they did it, because I'm sorry for their wives and children, but for land's sake, Thomas, don't you understand the need for action? Even if it's just one's own need? Things build up! You can only take so much after a while! A person can't be cautious, cautious, cautious every minute of every day. I don't condone what they did, but I understand it, don't you?"

"No, I don't."

"Then how in the world can you call yourself an abolitionist? You know, I'd hardly ever met an abolitionist before you, but I feel I'm more passionate about it all than you are. Your plan is to wait and wait until slavery goes away. Well, generations could die before then, including our own generation, here in K.T. Time as you live it is much longer than time as you look forward to it. It's all very easy to say, Well, in fifty years this and in fifty years that, but they could kill us tomorrow. Don't you ever want to say, Well, bring it on, let's have it out?"

"That's the way *they* think. Fighting it out."

"Well, perhaps I'm one of them. We aren't from New England where I come from, and I don't always understand New Englanders! You seem ready to talk all about it and tell everyone what to do, but then when they talk back to you, you just keep talking! A westerner doesn't understand that. Talking has to come to fighting, one way or another, and if it comes to fighting on their side and not on ours, then we suffer."

"You make no sense."

Well, that stung, because perhaps it was true. I said, "It seems perfectly clear to me!"

"I don't see how you can doubt my commitment to abolition! My opinions are open; I haven't hidden them."

"Opinions are common as salt!"

But you know, I can't say I meant all of this. I knew he was sincere and true in his opinions and that given the chance to make a telling gesture in favor of freeing a slave or two, he would do it. We westerners have always been willing to make a dare and take a dare; I don't know why that is. That's what I felt like then, with that dispute. I was daring him, just for effect, because I was in an ill humor and tired of hearing about Old Brown.

Thomas looked struck, or stricken. He stared at me for a moment, then lowered his eyes. I didn't know what to think about this look, so nakedly surprised and doubtful was it. It interested me as a failure, one of the few, of his natural reserve, and I felt that by it I had lost something as a wife but also, in a way, gained something. When one's husband is a man of such self-control as Thomas usually was, then any failure of that is interesting, at least.

I knew right then that I should have confessed

my insincerity in this argument. I wanted not for him
to go out and fight someone but for the rain to stop
and the cabin to be dry and tight. But my blood was
up, and I made no confession. I continued making
my repairs as if I were utterly serious, and after a bit,
Thomas put the guns carefully away and went outside. That was Wednesday. We didn't talk anymore
about Old Brown. I sourly told myself that that, at
least, was a relief.

In that first week, we saw a few of our neighbors.
Daniel James came by, hunting, but stayed outside
and talked only to Thomas. Mrs. Holmes walked
over for tea, bringing some corncakes. We drank our
tea, but I couldn't like her, as the half of her conversation that wasn't bitter and critical was all about the
vengeance of the Lord. I induced her to talk about
her life in the east, which usually softened up women
in K.T. with fond memories of warmth and a mod-
icum of comfort, but Mrs. Holmes could only recall
those members of her father's congregation who had
done her family ill turns, or, as she said, returned evil
for good. I had been pleased to see her, but I was
even more pleased to see her go. With the Jenkinses
gone and the Bushes still in town, our little group
seemed to have no center. One day, out hunting, I
passed the Jenkins claim, which our men had
defended against the Missourians. One wall of the
house had broken in, and the roof was gone, but the
window still glinted there, intact except for the hole
the shot had made. I pondered the ironies of this for
the rest of the afternoon, and it wasn't until I was
home again, plucking my two prairie chickens, that I

thought perhaps we could have that window. When I proposed it to Thomas in the evening, we looked right at each other for a long moment, and then he said, "Well, let's go over there first thing and have a look around."

There were a few things there—a store-made chair and a stool, a half-dozen milled boards, a stack of flowered plates, five of them, but no other crockery or utensils, a hammer, a half keg of black powder, a newspaper from Saint Louis, which would have belonged not to the Jenkinses but to the old man who built the cabin. Nor would the Jenkinses have gotten rid of it—whatever its sentiments, it was valuable for insulation against the wind, and I took it without hesitation, for my walls. Other than that, we didn't at first touch anything but went outside again and sat down on the stoop in front of the closed door. We could, I knew, take the door, too.

Thomas said, "We can write the Jenkinses, but I don't honestly think these are their things. I think they themselves left them behind, because they had no associations with them."

"They surely would have taken those plates with them."

In front of the cabin was the same rail fence that had divided our men from the Missourians. The rails, for the most part, were unbroken. Jeremiah was tied to one. I watched him for a moment. He was a young, vital animal. It had taken him little time to heal. After a bit, and with no further discussion, we gathered up what we could carry, including the plates, which were nicer than anything I had, though too small to be really useful, and we took it home. The next day, we went back and made a travois by lashing together some of the rails from the fence, and we dragged home as many of those as we could. The day after that, Thomas brought home the door and the window. I was so happy to have that window! I stuffed the bullet hole with a piece of cloth. That was one chink the wind would not get through. At first, of course, we pondered the ironies of the situation: Were we prospering from someone else's loss, either the Jenkinses' or those Missourians'? But shortly we stopped cutting it so fine, and not only did we make good use of what there was; we half hoped to come upon another such cache. I thought of Susannah Jenkins's own observation that K.T. had coarsened her. But that made it seem as though how K.T. changed you was all bad. In my opinion, K.T. made you see the world as it was. Your actions followed that.

We lived quietly until mid-June. The rains tapered off, and our crop seemed to be doing well enough. The hunting was good, though not so good as the autumn before, and we ate well. I got used to the loneliness, even started to like it. Sometimes Thomas and I went a whole day without saying much and then didn't read in the evening, either, but sat on our step and stared out over the prairie at the lengthening shadows and the golden sunshine and the wide, busy sky. We didn't share what we were fancying, but I wondered about Louisa's condition, and how it would be if I should find myself in the same condition, and what our claim would be like a year

thence if there was a child upon it. I made up rules—
I would go into town for the winter again, so as to
avoid Mrs. James's fate; I would keep hunting all
summer and fall, to have good meat every day; I
would forage for some plants I knew were good in
such times; I would go into Lawrence and stay for a
few days, so that Louisa could teach me to knit; I
would get Charles to build me a real cradle, a rocking
one, so that I wouldn't have to run the danger of having the child in the bed with us. I knew all about how
I would do it, down to the last detail. But I didn't tell
Thomas a word.

Now the eighteenth of June rolled around,
exactly four weeks after the sacking of Lawrence.
We had borrowed a little wagon from Mr. James—
four wheels and a platform was what it was, really, a
handmade, K.T.-type wagon, and our plan was to go
into Lawrence. We had some business, I forget what
it was, but really, I think, we felt that we both desired
and deserved to go into town, see our friends, and
find out the news. I also had conceived a terrible
apprehension about Frank, who had been out to see
us but twice since our departure from Lawrence.
When I'd left him in Louisa's charge, it seemed a
good solution to his reluctance to go out to the claim
(a reluctance I sympathized with), and I hadn't
thought about it much for the first week or two. But
then I'd awakened one night with the certain knowledge that Louisa was simply letting the boy run wild
and Charles, his nominal employer, would have better intentions but fewer opportunities for overseeing
him, as he was still traveling to Leavenworth, now

twice a week, to carry the mail. And so we hitched up the little wagon and left the claim without a backward glance. It was already a heavy, windy day, even early in the morning, and there wasn't much freshness anywhere.

When we got to Lawrence, there was talk of Old Brown, indeed, but not of "those killings"; rather of a battle that had taken place ten days after them in the Black Jack ravine, down south and east somewhere. It appeared that a few southerners had set out from Lecompton to look for Old Brown, "thinking," said Mrs. Bush, "that those events down near Pottawatomie might be traceable to him or his sons. And they captured two of his sons, and burned the one boy's house down, and made him and his brother march in chains under the hot sun back to Lecompton, and he went mad! It was a crime! Well, Brown found them, and they had taken a couple of prisoners, can you imagine, just men who were standing around in the street! They had a pitched battle, and Brown drove them off, and of course there were casualties!" The dragoons had then entered in, somehow, and made the peace, and there was much sympathy for Brown because of what happened to his sons—it was said that the oldest would never be the same and that a third one had been shot and killed. I leaned toward Mrs. Bush and said in a low voice (for that was what seemed appropriate), "What did he ever say about the Pottawatomie business?"

"Oh, nothing. No one knows what really happened down there. The Missouri press says massacre, of course, but you can't believe them—they lie routinely. My own feeling is that it was a local dispute, and whiskey and Indians got into it somehow. You can't pay attention to every act of violence that happens among the southerners, as they are prone to that sort of thing."

Louisa didn't even think it was interesting enough to talk about anymore, and it was true, we had other things that were more pressing than what the Pottawatomie affair had become, a bit of unpleasant gossip that folks preferred to keep mum about. Frank, it turned out, had bought himself a horse. He was keeping it in the yard where Charles kept his animals. "He had the money," said Louisa. "It must have been fifty dollars. Anyway, I must say, he's been around hardly at all since then."

"Can't you keep him around? I worry about him."

"Lidie, dear, you couldn't keep him around when he was on foot! I certainly can't keep track of a young man who owns his own horse and has his own money, especially in my condition. I hardly get out of our rooms."

She said this to me as we were walking briskly down Massachusetts Street, but I took it as it was meant, an acknowledgment not that she couldn't watch over Frank but that she wouldn't. I said nothing, as I did not feel I was in a position to press her. Perhaps, indeed, she could not. I said, "I'll have to send him back to Quincy, then."

"How foolish of you to think so! Open your eyes, Lydia! The boy is grown up and out of your control. He was the same last fall, and you were making the same noises you're making now. No doubt he's running about with one of those little bands that are raiding the Missourians from time to time. It's all boys that are doing that."

"What bands?"

"Well, you know. Since the attack, the boys have been wild! You can't control them at all. They all have horses and guns, Sharps carbines if they can get them. They live in camps and ride around here and there. I'm sure it's ninety percent a game, but if they come into something good, then they take advantage of it." Her tone was light, and I let myself be lulled by that. It was summer. I imagined a kind of elaborate freedom—hunting, camping, doing a bit of mischief. When I thought about it, I decided that Frank could probably take care of himself—he was a good shot. But I decided I wouldn't write to Harriet about it just yet. Anyway, Frank had turned up at Louisa's just two nights before, in the company of Roger Lacey. The boys had bedded down in the shop, slept for a long time, and woken up hungry. They looked healthy and happy. Louisa said, "He knows where to come if he gets in trouble—he's got friends all over town, and he can go to your claim, too. He's far better off than some of these boys, not a year or two older than he is, who come here as strangers and have to make their way. He's an enterprising boy, and he helps Charles, too."

Well, I was uneasy, but I put that away. Louisa gave me some wool and a knitting lesson, but I didn't say why I sought one. She looked blooming and pink of cheek. We drank tea and knitted all afternoon, while Thomas went around with Charles and saw the rebuilding and repairs.

Of course, there was other news. Governor Robinson was still detained, and his life had been threatened more than once; we Kansas rebels were still in bad odor with the proslave administration in Washington; but on the other hand, more eastern newpapers than ever had sent their correspondents to Lawrence—there was even a man from the *London Times,* in England. Because of these men, it was now generally felt in Lawrence that the sacking had been a good thing—a way that the southerners had revealed themselves to the world. Sentiment was shifting to our side, or at least it would soon. Any number of these eastern correspondents were writing *books* about our trials in K.T., and some of these books, it was said, would be out as early as the fall, in time for the election. And at the election, there would be a Republican candidate, too, black as black, of course, the proslave faction said. "But," said Louisa, "Senator Lane is wonderfully hopeful. They may condemn what comes from Free State Kansas all they like, but if it grows all around them, like daisies in the grass, then that's another story. The other states are watching now. They have to ask themselves whether they will allow the southern plot to succeed."

This seemed to be true.

As it was almost midsummer, the days were long, and we stayed through the late afternoon. There was still plenty of light for driving home, and the night would undoubtedly be light, too, should we be delayed. We were happy going home. The wagon bumped along, and we elected to walk beside it for the first mile. We had got a few things, only some flour and some corn meal and some salt, but it seemed rich to have those, and rich to know that when we tired of walking, if we did, we could bump along on the wagon. It seemed certain that another wagon would turn up that we might be able to purchase.

As we walked along, Thomas said, "You know, they don't feel in any danger at all in that town. I thought somehow that everyone would huddle in their houses with their weapons by the door, but—"

"But they just laugh at the southerners and go out with their weapons in their hands!" I shook my head in disbelief and just then noticed Jeremiah's ears flick forward and his head come up. With the rustling of my skirt through the grass, and the creaking of the wagon, which rattled like it was going to come apart any minute, I didn't hear anything, but a horse has sharper senses than a person. Thomas was saying, "And there looks to have been hardly a pause in the building—" when three men, or rather, a boy of sixteen or so and two men, rode up out of a copse of trees that was just ahead of us. Jeremiah stopped dead in his tracks, and the sack of cornmeal fell off the wagon. Thomas went around to pick it up, and one man, without greeting us, as was usual in K.T., called out, "Don't bother to do that!" in almost incomprehensible southern tones. I went rigid at once, but Thomas only smiled and turned to look at the men, putting his hand on the Sharps carbine we had brought along with us and saying, "Is there something you men would like?"

And the other man grinned and shouted, "Sure! We'd like to shoot us a G—— d—— abolitionist!" and he raised his pistol and let off two shots. Then Thomas fell on the other side of the wagon, out of my sight, and at the same time Jeremiah reared between the shafts, and the boy raised his weapon, a long rifle, and shot the horse in the neck. Jeremiah gave out a deep groan and went down on his side. I climbed over the wagon to Thomas, and I heard the three horses gallop away.

Thomas was lying chest-down, with his face turned away from me. I was certain as a rock that he was dead, but when I went around and knelt down, I saw that his eyes were open and that he blinked them. I was kneeling in his blood. Jeremiah wasn't far away, and his blood, a surge of it, bright red in the late sunlight, flowed toward us in a way that seemed to stun and paralyze me. The horse continued to grunt, but Thomas didn't make a sound. I put my face close to his and felt his breath, then I sat up. I remember that I could still hear galloping, and then, after a bit, that sound was gone, and there were no sounds at all.

I did not begin to know what to do, but I did something, anyway. I turned my husband over on his back to have a look. I didn't know what I was seeing, and then I did, I was seeing his black coat, and so I unbuttoned that and opened it, and against his blue shirt the red blood coming from his stomach and shoulder stood out more tellingly. It was warm, so I opened his shirt, and after that I saw the wounds. I looked at them for a moment, then stood up and stepped out of my petticoat, the cleanest thing I had about me, and started ripping it into bandages. Here's what I did—I rolled up some strips into two thick wads, then bound them tightly against the wounds, not actually thinking that would stop their bleeding but more because I couldn't stand to look at them any longer, they were so frightening. Then I closed Thomas's shirt over his chest and covered him with my shawl. I thought I might get him onto the wagon, somehow, but I was afraid of the pain that would give him, and anyway, then what? I crawled over to Jeremiah. The horse was just then still barely alive. His visible eye was open, and I am sure he looked at me. I put my hand on his ear and stroked it, then bent down and blew gently into his nostril, something my brother-in-law Roland had always told me horses did to greet one another. After that, Jeremiah passed on. I crawled back to Thomas, who at last gave a groan, his first sound since they shot him. Now, all of a sudden, I started talking and couldn't stop. I said, "Someone will come along. They always do. Remember last year? The prairie was a regular highway. Folks came by every day. Remember, we saw those people early this morning. Someone will come along. It's a warm night, we'll be fine." I didn't tell him about Jeremiah. Then he started swinging his head back and forth, and after that he opened his eyes and whispered, "Go get someone. Go get Charles."

"I can't. They shot Jeremiah. I want to stay with you."

"Go get Charles."

"I want—"

"Go get Charles." Then he let out an exhausted and painful groan and closed his eyes again.

Now, of course, I couldn't sit there with any conviction but must be thinking that I should go for Charles, or someone, especially as dusk was at last beginning to fall. And yet leave my husband stretched out on the prairie, with only a shawl to cover him? And yet sit there helplessly with him, not even trying to find aid? I stared at him, but his eyes were closed. I put my hand on his forehead, but no wisdom came into me. At last, I made up my mind, and this was what I thought—that if he was dying, the right thing would be to stay, but if he was to live, then the right thing was to get help; and that if I had resolution, the resolution that he would live, then I should act on it by finding someone who would know how to save him. Now staying seemed a way of accepting defeat, so I prepared to leave, but then leaving seemed impossible, so I sat down again and made up my mind to stay, but then I saw that night was really upon us, and so I kissed Thomas on his lips and eyes, and said, "I'm going to Charles," and then he nodded slightly, and so I stood up, and yet actually walking away was almost more than my strength would allow. The upshot of that was that instead of walking, I ran. I ran toward Lawrence as fast as I could.

My skirt kept tripping me up, getting caught on burrs and bushes, until I stooped and tore the bottom tier with my teeth and ripped it off. Then I heard noises, and realized that I had left the carbine on the wagon bed, and had nothing with me in case those men were around, or other men, or animals, or just in case I wanted to shoot something, to do what had been done to me, which seemed an attractive possibility right then. I ran, and it got darker. The prairie wasn't as trackless as people said it was, at least around Lawrence, but I did sense at one point that I was getting lost and veering to the left of Lawrence, wherever that was. So I veered back to the right and slowed down, but then I couldn't bear to be slow, and I started running again, but then I couldn't breathe, so I slowed down again. I knelt on the prairie grass and put my face in my lap to try and keep from fainting and to catch my breath, then I got up again and saw a small cabin, but when I ran to it, it was empty and deserted, the fences were broken down, the door was out of its frame. I thought for a second, in fact, that it was my own cabin, but I was able to remember that we had fixed our cabin. Was it the Jenkinses' cabin? I made myself think and observe, even in the near darkness, because that would mean that I knew where I was, even though where I would be was farther from Lawrence than where I had started, but no, it wasn't the Jenkinses' cabin. There was no blank spot where our window had been. I ran on, thinking all of a sudden that if I didn't know where I was then, I certainly wouldn't know how to get back to Thomas, even if I found something, and then, at that thought, I started moaning and wailing, because every step I took was leading me deeper and deeper into confusion. I stopped running and stood still, with my hands in my hair, trying to think where I was, where Thomas was, where Lawrence was, but all I could think was of blood ebbing away, of the men who raised their guns, who had hated us enough, just by the sound of Thomas's voice, to kill him, had hated Jeremiah enough to not even bother to steal him but to kill him, too. The wailing must have increased. It seemed to increase all around me, and then I heard the creak of harness and of wheels and wood, and then a voice said, "Now, ma'am, you are in a powerful state. You need a drink of highly rectified whiskey to bring you around."

I spun in my tracks. A horse and a wagon loomed out of the darkness, and then a lantern was lit, and a figure that I could only dimly make out climbed down from the wagon and walked toward me. I stood there dumbly and then saw the face of David Graves. And he saw my face. He said, "Why, Mrs. Newton, I am astonished to find you here!" Then he handed me the southern cure, and following instruction, I took a drink. It was such a shock that I was able to talk again, which I suppose was the point.

"They shot my husband, and I don't know where he is, and they shot our horse, too! I've been running, but I can't find Lawrence, and I'm sure he's lost. We have to get there before morning."

"They shot Thomas Newton?"

"He said one word! He asked what they wanted! They shot him!"

He bundled me into the wagon on top of the goods, then he made me sit quietly and gather my thoughts, and then he started asking questions, one by one, and I'll always be grateful to Mr. Graves because he did so. He said, "Is Mr. Newton still alive?"

"Yes, in the road."

"What road?"

"We were traveling from Lawrence to our claim."

And so on and so forth, all the while driving slowly here and there over the moonless prairie in a fashion that seemed random until I saw Mr. James's little flat wagon, and Jeremiah a dark mass in front of it. I leapt out of Mr. Graves's wagon and ran to Thomas. He was awake, and looking up, and when I knelt beside him and he saw me, he smiled.

Mr. Graves drove his wagon in a big circle around Jeremiah, but his mule snorted and shied, anyway. Meanwhile, I was talking to Thomas and wrapping the shawl more closely around him. "Mr. Graves came along. I was at my wit's end, but he found you. Oh, your cheeks are cold."

And then I lifted his head and Mr. Graves put the cup of whiskey between his lips, and Thomas groaned and winced and smiled again, and I was as happy as if the shooting had never happened or as if by dawn we would all be the same as we had been.

Mr. Graves had some milled boards with him, and we held two of these together and got Thomas onto them, and then we half heaved and half slid him onto the top of Mr. Graves's goods. I sat on a keg and held my husband's hand in my two hands and tried to judge by how cold he was how much blood he had lost; as for that blood, I hated leaving it out there on the prairie, uselessly soaking into the ground, lost forever. And Jeremiah, too. He who had not abandoned me, I had now abandoned. But that was K.T. Sentiment was a deadly thing in K.T. Folks back in the U.S. didn't know that about K.T., did they?

And the whole time, Mr. Graves continued to croon at us. "Now, I know all about what to do with a gunshot. All we need is some light on the subject. First thing, after you stop the blood coming out, is you take a magnet, and you hold it over the wound, and it draws out the shot. Why, my brother had such a strong magnet when we were boys that once he shot himself in the foot by mistake and that shot just popped out of there, flew to the magnet, though he held it a couple of inches from the wound. It didn't hurt him any, so we tried a few things out, like how far from the wound could you hold it so it would pop the shot out, and would the magnet stick to his foot through the skin and flesh and bone, from the other side, you see, if the shot was in there? Well, he said it did, but I myself didn't see that, but I thought if he had left the shot in there and tried that magnet from the other side before he took any out, it might have, but we didn't think of that first thing. I always wished we had."

Wasn't shot made of lead? But his talk was like a lullaby, or a work song, and I focused on it to ease my passage to Lawrence.

"I knew another man who got shot, some years ago, and if you'll pardon my language, ma'am, he said that the thing to do was to make water on the wound, to clean it out without touching it, and so me

and some other men, two of them, we stood there and
made water on the wound—it was in his hip—and
then he left it open to the air. And after four hours, he
had us make water on it again, and so on, for two
days. Well, I mean to tell you, this was in Arkansas,
and you can never tell why they do some things in
Arkansas, and no doctor would approve of such a
procedure, I am sure, but after two days, the man got
up and walked, naked from the hip down on one side,
of course, walked right into town like that, easy as
you please, but he did get over that wound in no time
at all. Said the Indians told him about that. But that's
what everyone says. If the Indians always said what
they are supposed to have said, then they would be
talking all the time, but as you know, Indians are by
and large a taciturn folk. . . ."

And then we were in Lawrence, and then we
were at Louisa's, and then it was dawn, and then
Thomas was back in our old bedstead and me next to
him, holding his hand, and somehow I dozed off
while Louisa was tending to the wounds.

A doctor Charles knew came. I woke up to find
him bending over me, and then I sat up and realized
that he was bending over Thomas. He glanced
toward me and said, "Hello, my dear," and I eased as
quickly as I could out of bed and straightened my
clothes. I looked at his face before I looked at
Thomas, and his face was grave. Then I dared to look
at Thomas. The doctor had bared his wounds and
was probing the one in his shoulder with his
penknife. Thomas's skin was impossibly white and
his face nearly blue. He winced one time, but other

than that, he was unresponsive. I put my hands in front of my face, and Louisa put her arm around me and walked me over to one of her chairs and sat me down. She said, "I hope you are prepared for the worst, my dear."

I nodded to say that I was, and perhaps I was: he had already been alive twelve hours or so longer than I had expected him to be; but perhaps I wasn't, because at the same time that I sat there among the sober faces and the low tones of voice and the shaking heads, I also did not trust for one moment that these were actual scenes. I knew better: this would fade away, and something more familiar would come in its place. The doctor said, "Well, he's full of lead, that's for sure," and I thought, Then they won't be able to get anything out with a magnet, will they? I said, "Has he spoken at all?"

"He asked after you right at first, but he hasn't spoken since."

"That isn't good, is it, Louisa?"

She shook her head, then said, "Lidie, dear, the fever's set in."

I nodded, to show that I understood what that meant, but I didn't, really. I didn't know why the fever had set in.

"I can pick at it," said the doctor, "but I hate to. I hate to do that. I'd rather put on a plaster that'll draw the foreign matter out and let the young man's system take care of itself. Myself, I don't like surgery. I always say that surgery does more harm than good in the end. To tell you the truth, a body can incorporate considerable foreign matter if it will, and if it won't, you can't make it." Everyone nodded, but this seemed nonsensical to me. If there was something that the southerners had put into my husband, I wanted it out. Then the doctor spoke in a low voice to Charles, who was standing right beside him. Charles nodded.

I said, "What was that?" and the doctor looked at me sharply, then said, "To tell the truth, ma'am, I don't truly believe that your husband could tolerate any surgery. I think it would be too much of a shock to him, myself. He's pretty far gone, ma'am."

We stared at each other, then he broke away, put his penknife in his pocket, and turned to don his coat, a blue coat, K.T. all over. I didn't believe he was a doctor at all. Perhaps he was a governor pretending to be a doctor, just as Governor Robinson was a doctor pretending to be a governor.

"Now, Lidie," said Louisa, as if I had spoken aloud, but of course I hadn't.

After the doctor went down the stairs, I said, "You've got to find another doctor, a real doctor."

"Now, Lidie."

I turned to Charles. "Please? Please, Charles, you must know someone else, or some woman who knows . . ."

Later, a woman did come by. She was the wife of one of the legislators, and she had some emetic with her and the makings of a poultice for each wound. She told us what to do—to give a dram of the emetic every hour, and to change the poultices twice a day. Louisa felt that we should also get some broth into Thomas when we could, and a bit of whiskey now and then. We listened to our instructions and set up our sickroom as if we would be there for weeks—as we would be if Thomas should recover. Louisa and Charles bustled about, Mrs. Bush and Mr. Bush came in, and also Mrs. Lacey and one of the boys; the woman with the poultices had a friend, too, so in general there was a crowd and much talk, some of it about Thomas and his injuries, much of it about who had shot him. I told the story over and over. The only telling detail I could come up with was the sound of the one man's voice—very southern—and the look on the boy's face when he shot Jeremiah: he looked pleased. Perhaps I would know them to see them, but perhaps not—I couldn't remember them, exactly. My only hope was that the looks of one of them would strike me should he appear before me again. Everyone speculated about who they had been, even bringing up names and looking toward me, as if I could say yes or no and that would be the one. I tried to explain how quickly it all had happened, and then everyone was sympathetic and declared that I should be bothered no more. And then, after a moment or two, they resumed speculating. When I asked what had happened to Mr. Graves, no one knew.

In the evening, I fell asleep again, and after I woke up, everyone was gone except Louisa, who was sitting beside Thomas, gazing at him. When I opened my eyes, she said, "Feel better?"

"Yes and no."

She smiled. "He spoke again. He asked where his carbine was."

"What time is it?"

"After midnight."

"You must be exhausted yourself."

"Well . . ." She nodded.

"I'm fine to sit up. I'm not tired at all." Really, what I suddenly wanted was to be alone with my husband. Here we had been married all of ten months, had known each other for less than a year, and we had hardly been alone together, if you thought about it.

"I am tired," she said, "but I hate to . . ." Moments later, she went off to bed, and my conscience smote me at my feelings of ingratitude. I took my place in the chair she had been sitting in and looked down at my husband. Frankly, I was amazed, still amazed. It seemed that there was no way I could get past this amazement into something more appropriate, more like what Louisa and the others seemed to be feeling. They had gone right into anger, sadness, and fear, just like that, but I was stuck in amazement. More even than the inner picture of Thomas falling behind the little wagon, I kept seeing the picture of Jeremiah rising on his back legs and then crumpling between the shafts. And of course, we hadn't returned Mr. James's little wagon or the harness. Everything—our flour and cornmeal and salt and the horse's body and the wagon and harness—had been out there on the prairie all day, as if we had simply walked away from it, careless. It was very hard to keep everything sorted properly in my mind. I knew that Thomas, right here before me, should drive out all other thoughts as unimportant, but I was simply too amazed for that still.

And yet it seemed as though the sight of him should work upon me in some other way, bring me into the present and set my grief before me. His face didn't look like any Thomas that I had ever seen before, even Thomas sleeping. His face looked as if Thomas was absent and the absence was filled with something new, which I speculated must be pain. I thought that if the Thomas I knew were present, then he would draw me out of my amazement, but then if the Thomas I knew were present, I wouldn't be so amazed in the first place. I put my hands to my head and felt it. I thought it must be feeling feverish from the thoughts that beset me, but it felt cool enough. He turned his head slowly this way and then that way, and gave out a noise. I did what Louisa had told me, which was to wring out a cloth in an infusion of witch hazel and place it over his forehead. He continue to turn this way and that, and strange thoughts continued to beset me. I said, "Thomas! Thomas!" but he made no answer, and my voice seemed loud in the room, and so I fell silent again.

I sat there for a long time, deep enough into the night for the candle to gutter and expire. I regarded my husband without, I thought, taking him in. I did lie down on the bed, but then Thomas began turning his head back and forth again, as if in discomfort and pain, and so I got off the bed, for fear of making him worse. After that, I paced about the room for a while, looking out the little window to the dark street. Louisa had gotten a pane of glass somewhere. All of that—the troubles with the Missourians, the sacking of Lawrence, the Old Brown question—all of that had led to this, but this seemed such an astonishing thing for that to have led to! Thomas stopped turning his head back and forth and lay still. I couldn't see him very well in the dim light, so I took one of his hands in both of mine, and filled with the conviction that he was about to pass on, I said, "Don't be afraid, Thomas." I thought, A sojourn in K.T. ought to prepare the soul for any other journey whatsoever. Sometime after that, he did pass on, and sometime after that—I don't know how long—I realized it. I thought that if I had known him better, perhaps, or found a way to be more married to him in the past ten months, I would have known the very moment. I was sorry I had failed in that.

I kissed his lips, cheeks, eyes, and forehead, and drew his hands out from under the covers, and placed them in the proper position. His eyes were closed. There was little to do except adjust his bed so that he made a neat picture, then sit down and wait for Louisa to wake up. Now I was a new person, one I had never desired or expected to be.

BOOK TWO

CHAPTER 18

I Reconnoiter

But children can be very early taught, that their happiness, both now and hereafter, depends on the formation of habits of submission, self-denial, and benevolence.

—*p. 224*

IN THE TWO DAYS BETWEEN Thomas's death and his funeral, the news of the attack upon us rolled around Lawrence like ball lightning, setting the country aflame with indignation, or so I was told. Those around me seemed not so much indignant as stunned, and wondered why. I was stunned myself and wondered why. Hadn't we talked of something like this for months? Didn't we know something like this was always a possibility? Hadn't others been killed—Barbour, Dow, Captain Brown? I felt that we should not be stunned, and yet we were. It was a conundrum. Mostly, too, I wanted Frank to come back, or be found and brought home. If the news brought him, then that would be one good thing, the only good thing. I have noticed over the years that every tragedy has about it some good thing: At least it didn't happen in the winter, when it was so cold; at least we had ten months together; at least, at least. I thought, At least Frank may show up. But Frank did not show up, and then, thinking that he was staying away out of caprice or thoughtlessness, I got vexed with him and decided to put him out of my mind.

When I confided these thoughts to Louisa, she told me, soothingly, not to be so hasty, but I was hasty, and I was angry with him.

Thomas's funeral reminded me of my father's funeral only by contrast. Where the one had been obscure and even just, the other was wildly unjust and the occasion of much public clamor. Charles and Louisa and some other citizens of Lawrence urged me to go all the way and have a military ceremony, as they had done for Barbour, who was killed in the Wakarusa War in December. Were we not in battle, were we not engaged in an undeclared war with the Missourians, of which Thomas was a casualty? But that didn't suit Thomas, I thought, whose approach to every event in K.T. had been cautious and peace-loving. He was most comfortable and happy in his black New England clothes, reading a book of poetry by the light of our evening candle. And so it wasn't a military funeral, but it was a martial one, and a martyr's one, and highly arousing to the swarms who attended. The procession that followed his coffin to the grave was a half mile long, and everyone carried arms. It didn't matter at all that I couldn't supply enough information about our assailants to even begin to know who they were; the funeral was all about vows of revenge, repayment, and retribution for a crime that should never have been committed, a vile act of bestial cruelty that was simultaneously beyond the human pale and perfectly typical of the Missourians. Mrs. Bush walked along with me at the front of the procession and held my arm to comfort me. "Oh, my dear," she said in her kindest voice, "I knew that something like this would certainly happen. I knew it a year ago when we first set out for K.T. Those people—well, you hardly want to call them people—were fulminating and cheating at elections and vowing revenge for ills they had not suffered, and of course it had to lead to something like this, but I always wonder, why this one? Why does the Lord pick this one rather than that one? Why Thomas and not Mr. Bush? Just last night, Mr. Bush declared that it should have been him if it had to be someone, as he's lived a long life and done many things, and you and Thomas are just starting, were just starting. We've been along that road time and time again. I don't know, my dear, we never know, but I am just so heartily sorry."

The consensus of the group around the grave, most of whom were of a religious turn of mind, as most people are, was that the Lord would provide for Thomas, and handsomely, but that they would take care of the Missourians and assure them their just deserts.

The troubling question was, who would provide for me? For the second time in a year, I found myself the subject of this discussion: What would I do, how would I support myself? At least I had no children, as some of the other K.T. widows had. I will hasten to say that I did not know the answers to these questions myself. What we had had was our crop, our stove, our claim, our youth, energy, and hard work. None of these had much value, especially the claim. Claims had stopped rising in price in the winter and had even begun to decline. The wonders of 1855, where a man bought a bit of land for a hundred dollars and sold it for five hundred, had ceased. In 1856, he was lucky to get seventy-five for it, or fifty. Immigrants from the east weren't so desperate any longer, were choosy. And they were leery of Lawrence. It was as if the southerners and we ourselves had conspired to frighten the easterners away. You had to have convictions to live in Lawrence. The folks in Lawrence declared this with pride, but to most Americans, this was more of an accusation than a compliment.

Mr. James and two other men went and got the wagon and disposed of Jeremiah's remains. In fact, the prairie was dotted with the bones of oxen, mules, and horses that fell by the wayside. Jeremiah, so fast and so beautiful, had become one of these. Charles took Louisa and me out to the claim in one of his wagons. We passed the spot where the killings had happened, or must have, but though I watched for it, I couldn't recognize it for sure. It was just a stretch of prairie, after all. We gathered my things and Thomas's things. I gave most of Thomas's clothes to Charles, and we brought the stove back, too. I sold that to Mrs. Lacey for ten dollars. Mr. Bush said that if the crop came in in August, then he would give me fifty dollars for that.

My sisters wrote their condolences but didn't suggest, right then, that I return to Quincy (I suppose they weren't ready for that so suddenly). Harriet urged me to send Frank back, "since thinking of the two of you alone out there in that God-forsaken place simply gives me a such a turn I can't think about it." Thomas's father also wrote me by return post after receiving my letter detailing the murder. He lamented the news, which had prostrated Thomas's mother. He and his other sons had never quite understood Thomas's desire to travel, and they had felt that the Massachusetts Emigrant Aid Company would surely take better care of these boys than it seemed they had done. While the elder Mr. Newton shared most of Thomas's beliefs, and adhered to them still, he had felt a year before that the emigrants were on a fools' errand, which opinion this event had now shown to be true, perhaps, though Mr. Newton also felt that there were events afoot in the United States that were unprecedented. At any rate, as their daughter-in-law—though they had never yet met me, they felt they knew me through my notes to them (Thomas had written six letters and I had appended messages on five of these)—I was welcome in their home, and they knew a place would happily be made for me in their town. Mrs. Bush was partial to this plan, as the idea of living in Medford, civilized and orderly Medford, was akin to the idea of living in paradise to her.

"You just don't know what it's like there!" she urged. "The town is so clean and neat, and the ladies are so good to one another! Sometimes I think that I would gladly pass on if I could just take afternoon tea one more time in my old home! It would be a winter afternoon, and Mr. Bush would have hitched our pony to the sleigh, and I would drive over there myself and sit by the fire with my friends Elizabeth and Katherine Keys and my cousin Lucy, who is very dear to me, and we would eat Elizabeth's little cakes as the darkness closed in, and then Mr. Bush would appear, all snowy from his walk, and we would drive home in the darkness to a nice chowder by the fire. . . . Oh, my dear, you can't imagine, such bliss! You never mind the wind in Massachusetts, even in the winter. It stays outside, for goodness' sake, where it belongs! Oh, it hurts me to think about it, a little. You surely must take them up on this!"

Louisa wanted me to stay in K.T. She didn't say so, but I knew she was assessing which of the many single men who were about might be the likeliest prospect. She didn't have to say much—we both knew that many of the niceties of mourning for folks in the States disappeared fairly quickly in K.T. If it was hard for a man to be without a wife, it was all the harder for a woman to be without a husband, especially as most folks were so far from their families. And there were fewer women than men. A twenty-one-year-old with a claim of her own and no children was, well, not quite so attractive as the twenty-seven-year-old woman of property and experience Louisa herself had been only six months before, but the answer to my dilemma was there for all to see, and, as I had reflected so many times before, sentiment was deadly in K.T. When I said to Louisa, "But I don't know Thomas well enough yet for that," she could not grasp my meaning.

Thomas remained the great enigma, all the more now that he offered no additional clues. To discover who he was, why I married him, what that meant, I had to sift through the clues I already had, teasing out others that might be lurking there. As always—even more than always—other people interfered. I had never had enough time alone with him, and now had even less alone with my thoughts of him, since everyone wanted to do me the kindness of keeping me company, especially the kindness of talking about him and his virtues: He was such a thoughtful, calm man, very judicious and educated. Everyone looked up to Thomas, and so forth. More than one girl in the Emigrant Aid Company had set her cap for him. And a good husband, thoughtful and solicitous. Not every man in the world had to be the most enterprising. There was plenty of room for more deliberative types, like Thomas. And reserve was certainly a virtue, too. I listened to these remarks, but all they did was confuse me. They made a construction around the figure of Thomas that I was trying to get at, and I found myself very irritated but having to smile, anyway, and express appreciation of such kind thoughts.

And it was all the more frustrating that I didn't know what I wanted, what I had wanted all the time we knew each other, before and after we were married. Whatever it was, no other women around me seemed to want it. Charles came and went, working and traveling many hours every day; Louisa was taken up with her own affairs. Mr. and Mrs. Bush were comfortable with one another, and she talked freely about him, but on the other hand, she seemed to have all the pepper in her, leaving him bland and agreeable. Even his political opinions were paler versions of hers. And he was more often than not out at their claim while she was in town. What about the others? The Holmeses seemed not to see each other at all, in their focus on Satan, the Lord, and the missing congregation. The Robinsons? Though they were now in Lecompton, where he had been incarcerated, what was their home now? A tent or a cabin, or some such thing? Everything about K.T. seemed to conspire to keep couples apart: him in a man's world of riding here and there, going to meetings and conventions, taking up arms and drilling, working with other men at building or hauling or farming or clearing land or hunting; her in a woman's world of knitting and sewing, talking and cooking, cleaning and mending, making cartridges. But what had I wanted instead, while Thomas was alive? I had never been able to express it, had hardly tried to express it in a way that he would understand, and now I had to get it on my own or forget it. But in spite of the prudence of what Louisa silently urged upon me, it seemed far too early to begin with another what I seemed hardly to have begun with Thomas.

Of course, there were plenty of mourners in K.T. It was a school for mourning, in some ways. In the manner that you do, I began noticing all the other bereft souls, as I hadn't noticed them before my own bereavement. There was Mr. James, of course, who, it was said, had taken greatly to drink, but he differed from me in the fact that his grief was for his sons as well as his wife, and additionally compounded by remorse. He was an angry man, and most folks stayed away from him. There were plenty of others, whose wives or husbands or children had died of illness in the winter. I would see people on the street: There was a Mrs. Harrison; all three of her children had gone down with a fever and died, one right after another, and they'd had to wait three months to bury them, owing to the frozen ground. Mrs. Harrison was upright but languid and white, and seemed hardly able to lift her head. Here was Mrs. McChesney, whose husband had been hit by a falling tree and died with a corncake in his mouth. She was cool and businesslike, with plenty of energy (she had four daughters), but hard, they said. Some were languishing: a Mrs. Dalton hadn't left her bed since March, when her husband's horse fell on him one night and he died of exposure before the morning. Others had lost brothers, fathers, sisters; one man, hardly my age, had had a letter from neighbors in Indiana informing him that his parents and two sisters had died in a house fire three weeks after he came to K.T. to look for a claim for them. I came to see K.T. as a gathering of present and future survivors, differing only in when they came into survivorship.

As I was looking at others, so others were looking at me. Each bereaved person had a story; some of the stories were exquisitely strange and the subject of much fascinated and regretful gossip. My story, too, had a couple of features of interest—the suddenness, the ruthlessness of the southern-rights killers, my search for help, the briefness of our marriage. I knew I was the subject of gossip and speculation, that folks gauged my manner, that I was a martyr to the cause almost as much as Thomas was. But I had

lost all interest in the cause for the time being. I
didn't even want to cast my laments in political
terms. I tried to stay quiet and hide out a little bit
from my new fame.

And then there was Frank. Without any effort on
my part, my anger at Frank grew, for Frank, too, had
become famous, even though no one had seen him
since days before Thomas was killed—he didn't
come to Louisa's, he didn't come to the funeral, there
was no evidence at the claim that he had been there.
By July, though we hadn't heard from him, we had
heard of him. He was a guerrilla, and he and his
friends were known to have raided at least three
farms of southern-rights families and stolen a horse,
four cows, two oxen, a ham, and a chair. It was
thought that Roger Lacey was with them, too, as his
mother and father hadn't seen him, but as far as they
knew, he didn't have a horse or any money. Much
about these boys and their activities was unknown. A
rumor would spread through town, and then there
would be nothing for a week. One rumor was that
Frank had come to see me on the night of Thomas's
funeral and that I had charged him with revenge. He
was rumored to be eighteen, sixteen, fourteen, and
eight years old (by then he was thirteen, young
enough). He was said to be riding Jeremiah, the
horse he had raced over the snow. He was said to be
himself from Kentucky and to have turned against
his first friends because coming to K.T. taught him
the iniquities of slavery. All these rumors enraged
me, as they portrayed a boy so callous and careless of
my grief that I hardly knew how he had become that

way. Louisa tried to reason with me—clearly few or none of these stories was true. Charles would find Frank; others were on the lookout for him, too. Then we would know why he hadn't appeared. Was he, too, dead or injured somewhere? Tentatively, and then more firmly, Louisa made me ponder that possibility. But I preferred to feel misused by him. I just kept it to myself more. I kept many things to myself more. In my new state of supreme discomfort, I felt just a jot more comfortable that way.

Some political news pressed itself upon me in the midst of everything else. In the first place, money was rolling in, just as everyone had predicted. The New Englanders had raised thousands and, it was said, intended to raise more thousands. There were groups in Chicago, Buffalo, New York, Boston, and I don't know where else, all of which sent cash for Kansas relief. "We'll never know how much might be coming," said Louisa, "the way they are holding our things on the river and raiding our mail." But most of the money came through Iowa and Nebraska, carried by men known to be both loyal to the Free State cause and capable of protecting themselves. Once the cash got to Lawrence, the committee of safety oversaw it. I don't know what was done with it, except that some merchants who had provisioned the town for the Wakarusa War laid claim to payments, while others simply forgave those earlier debts in exchange for cash on the barrelhead in the town's present drive to provision itself for another such war. In many ways, it didn't matter, for the moment, how they disposed of the cash. It was more than anything a symbol of the support we had gained through the sacking of Lawrence and, in my opinion, a vindication of Thomas's view that the sacking had been all for the best. I told him that when I took my morning walk out to his grave. I was sorry he couldn't be there to see it. And then the slave of the slavocrats, President Pierce, issued another of his proclamations—that the Free State legislators were not to meet on the Fourth of July in Topeka, as planned.

On July 3, Lawrence emptied out.

On the Fourth, and a hot day, a hundred K.T. degrees, which means sunny and windy, parades commenced in Topeka right after breakfast and went on till noon, with a band and a banner and fireworks and all the usual speeches. Right at noon, a man came in who'd been posted on the road, and said that the troops were on their way, and then the legislature went into the "hall" and took their seats. Pretty soon the dragoons, some three squadrons (including cannon!), came up to the "hall" and arrayed themselves. They even set up and loaded the cannon, and had the cannoneers light their lucifers! The surgeon laid out his medical kit, which the Free State citizens didn't fail to notice, and then Colonel Sumner went into the hall.

There was some confusion with the roll; or, as Louisa said—she was there with Charles in spite of her condition and reported all this to me, saying that Thomas's death would be meaningless if I didn't begin to rededicate myself to the cause—"Many of the men were confused about whether they wanted to declare themselves present or not, in the teeth of the enemy, but of course, Charles spoke right up!"

Then Colonel Sumner stood up and announced, "Gentlemen, I am called upon this day to perform the most painful duty of my whole life. Under the authority of the President's proclamation, I am here to disperse this legislature and inform you that you cannot meet. I therefore order you to disperse."

"He's really on our side," said Louisa. "It was painful to watch a man so torn between duty and right sentiment."

And then he vowed to do anything to disperse the group.

"We knew," said Louisa, "that that meant everything up to and including firing on women and children with those cannon."

But Colonel Sumner got a cheer, anyway. His heart was in the right place.

"I tell you, Lidie," said Louisa, when she came home that night, "the tide is turning in our direction. It's a shame and a crime that your dear husband is not with us to see it."

I agreed with that.

I had become convinced that the boy who shot Jeremiah was the same boy we had driven off from the Jenkins claim in the fall, which meant that his companions were those men, or two of those men. This conviction had come over me bit by bit. The boy's face was the only one I'd seen, and I thought I remembered it looking familiar. I surmised that that was the reason the Missourians hadn't bothered to steal such an excellent horse as Jeremiah—that boy had recognized him, and therefore us, and decided to exact his revenge. My secret, all the time that my future was being discussed by my friends and relations, was that I was going to kill that boy. I didn't even think of him as a boy. He would have been sixteen, old enough to take mercy on a horse. He was a young man, only a few years younger than myself and perfectly capable of paying the full penalty for his actions.

A few days after she returned from the meeting of the legislature, and some three or four weeks after Thomas's killing, Louisa sat down with me in my room. I sat in a chair and she sat on the bed, which was more comfortable for her in her condition. She had her bodice unbuttoned and her sleeves rolled up, and her face was red from the heat. We fanned ourselves and drank tea, which Louisa said was known to be cooling—the British in India drank tea all through the hottest part of the day. What you couldn't do in such weather was drink intoxicating liquors: every sane person knew that, which was just further evidence that the Missourians, who drank intoxicating liquors day and night, all the year round, were both venal and stupid.

We knitted.

After we talked about the weather and the British and the Missourians, she said, "Please don't misunderstand me, Lydia, but I would like to know how much money you have. I want to know as one who will always be your friend and only wants the best for you."

As it happened, I had just been counting my money that afternoon, and so I came right out with it. "I have fifteen dollars."

She shook her head. This was clearly worse than she had thought. She said, "Oh, my dear. And K.T. is such a costly place."

"Mr. Bush said he would pay me for my crop in August."

She nodded and turned her work, then said, "You know, Lydia, although I am only a few years older than you, very few, I do feel that I must take you in hand just now. How well I know what is the customary duty of the wife to the memory of her husband back in the States, and it was certainly a source of grievous pain to me that I could not give Mr. Wheelwright his due upon his unfortunate passing. Everything taken all in all, Mr. Wheelwright was a good man and as kind to me in every way as a man of his temperament was capable of being. If he was a little curt, at times, and invariably taciturn, and remarkably unsociable, then these things were not of his own making, and it was up to me as his wife to accept them, which I did, and Charles and I have agreed to give our son his name as a second name, to honor him."

"You have?"

"Why, yes. Isaac Ruben Bisket." She smiled fondly. "Elizabeth Rubena Bisket, if a girl. But I'm wandering off the track. You should keep me to the subject, my dear, which is you, not me."

"I don't want to talk about me, Louisa."

"Now, that is very feckless of you, Lydia. You simply cannot be feckless in K.T. and expect even to live! K.T. demands boldness and energy. We have chosen an unforgiving home."

"Well, Louisa, I don't know what to do, and I don't have the money to do it."

"Charles owed Thomas some money when he— when he was murdered by those criminal slavocrats."

"He did?"

"Yes. A hundred and twenty-five dollars."

I stared at her, then said, "Louisa, I just do not believe you. Thomas hadn't worked for Charles in a month by then, and he never said a word about it to me, all the time we were worrying about the summer."

"Well, it's true."

"It's not true. Look at me."

She looked at me. It wasn't true. My heart sank, and I hadn't even felt it lift. After a moment, she turned her work again (she had been knitting quickly this whole time) and said, "Lydia, my dear, I have the money. It's no loss to me to loan it to you, or give it to you, or buy your claim with it."

"Then what? I can't stay in K.T."

"Oh, my dear, you can't backtrack! You won't be able to live back there after here! In my estimation, even with the dangers, K.T. is the only place for a woman, especially a woman of verve and imagination."

"Louisa, I don't think I am a woman of verve and

imagination. Thomas had the verve and imagination. I was just curious."

"Now, my dear, we all become disconsolate; you'd have a heart the size of a walnut if you didn't feel these sorts of things—"

"I want to go back."

But I didn't, really. There was nothing in the States for me. I did feel, though, that if I could get over to Missouri, to Westport or Lexington, I could find that boy who had shot my horse, whose friends had shot my husband. All the same, I wasn't being entirely deceptive with Louisa. I was simply believing two contradictory things to be true at the same time, a fine K.T. tradition.

"To Quincy?"

"Maybe, or even to Medford."

"I know Helen Bush has been talking to you, Lydia, but you mustn't listen to her. Once you've been to K.T., my dear, then you are simply the wrong size for the Bay State box. I lived there all my life; I know what I am talking about. You would feel things very tight there, and very small. We're western women now."

"But I've never been there at all, Louisa." I turned to my own knitting, and an inspiration came to me. "I owe it to Thomas to visit his mother. I told you what his father reported of her. And he was her favorite of the boys."

"I'm sure he was, Lidie. He was a favorite with everyone." She sighed. Finally, she said, "Well, I suppose there's no hope for it."

"What do you mean?"

"Well, I see that you should go back there, but I'm selfish. I fear if you go back there, you'll never return to K.T."

I didn't reply, because I feared, or hoped, the same thing.

What transpired was that Louisa loaned me forty dollars, which I added to my fifteen, on the understanding that Mr. Bush would pay her for my crop in August. She had offered to buy my claim, but she took that offer back; my claim, she was sure, would bring me back to K.T., but if I broke that tie, she would never see me again. Now she became quite sanguine about travel back and forth to the east. Look at Sam Wood, look at Mrs. Robinson, look at Jim Lane. These folks were running to Washington and Boston all the time. It seemed like you were halfway to California once you crossed the Missouri River, but that wasn't true, in fact. K.T. was practically the east, anymore, with railroads and steamboats. I would have no trouble at all. Charles could take me to Leavenworth with the mail and buy my ticket on a boat going downstream. . . .

She rattled on, but I had a slightly different plan, and it didn't include being chaperoned by Charles until I was able to get on the steamship. It included asking around for Mr. Graves, until one morning I found him at the Stearns store, bringing in some whiskey and some cherries from Missouri. As soon as he saw me, he pulled off his hat and became most solicitous.

"I have often animadverted to that tragic day,

ma'am, and rued the evil motives that fired up those boys. Your husband was a peaceable man, though unsound on the goose question."

I dipped my head, thinking he had changed his mode of talking again. I suppose I always thought of Mr. Graves as my friend, but this element of his character perplexed me and put me off.

"It's a tangled skein of loyalties and aversions that we in K.T. find ourselves caught in. Men such as myself, whose instincts are purely commercial, sometimes don't know which way to turn."

"Yes, sir," I said.

"But you seem to be holding up well, ma'am."

"I didn't get to thank you. I want to thank you. I feel that you are my true friend, Mr. Graves."

"I am, ma'am, and no thanks needed. When a fellow human being is in such distress as your late lamented husband, ma'am, the greatest heroism is but the simplest decency, as the Bard himself once said."

"I need to go to Westport and then on to Saint Louis. I am taking Thomas's last words to his dear mother."

What I really needed was to get Mr. Graves to talk about Thomas's killers. There would certainly have been much bragging about the killing, and the names of the killers would be known among the Missourians. Mr. Graves might even know those names now, as he was talking to me and looking at me. But I needed some time to draw him out. Fifty or sixty miles over the prairie, a day and a half, might well be enough.

"I consider that a lovely gesture, ma'am, and I and my animals are at your service."

I ascertained that he would be driving east in two days, and he agreed to come to Louisa's early that morning to pick up my things—my box containing my dresses and boots and shawl, a few garments of Thomas's for remembrance and perhaps to send to his mother. The carbine wouldn't fit in my bag, and so I wondered what I should do with it. When I mentioned this to Louisa, she knew right away. She said, "Charles has just the thing for you," and brought out a pistol, a revolver in a leather holster. "This is a black dragoon." She held it up. It was more a dark gray, shiny and heavy, with a smooth wooden stock and dull brass around the trigger. At some point there had been figures worked into the cylinder, but years of use had smoothed them away. "Put this in your bag," she said. "We can use your carbine here in Lawrence." She gave me the revolver and the holster, then pushed some money into my pocket. Later, I saw that it was twenty dollars, about the price of a Sharps carbine in New England. She also gave me the powder and the .44-caliber balls I would need, and a tin of firing caps. Compared to those for a Sharps, they were tiny indeed.

The reader may here express some skepticism at my judgment and my state of mind as I made these plans. I can only attempt to delineate both as clearly as I remember them. I seemed to myself to be thinking very clearly—as clearly and with as much focus as I had ever done. The connection between that boy in the fall and that boy in the spring seemed ironclad to me. And, I also felt, I had waited around for the citizens of Lawrence, who had been full of vengeance at the funeral, long enough. Nothing was being done. Indeed, I quickly saw that there was no one to do it: our leaders were still scattered or imprisoned, and Thomas had not been so important to our cause that avenging his death was an immediate necessity. The federal authorities, in the persons of Colonel Sumner's dragoons, were invariably slow to press Free State claims, invariably quick to press claims against Free Staters. There was no other machinery of a policing sort in K.T. Thomas's blood on the prairie was surely crying out for justice, but as far as I could see, it was crying out in vain. All the same, I didn't hold these things against my friends and fellow citizens. Thomas's death was my business. I was a good shot and a good horsewoman, a strong girl with no children and no ties that held me to my proper place. Taking care of these Missourians was my business, and I welcomed it. Frank, I thought, would have helped me, but I was eager to leave, and he couldn't be found. I held that against him.

As for my friends, they thought I was bearing up very well and accepting my loss with becoming strength and resolution. Those who heard about my plan to visit Thomas's mother applauded it. But, to be sure, K.T. was not the States in many ways, and in this way above all others: a woman's activities and conversations were not overseen as carefully as they were in the States; folks didn't take such an interest in one—they had too much to think of of their own, so there was a lot of room for even a woman to make her private way.

And so I visited Thomas's grave one last time. I expected, somehow, to make contact with him, perhaps in one of Louisa's disembodied realms, but looking down upon his grave, I felt only a simple and flat sadness, tedious and exhausting and endless. I could not say so, but I didn't mind leaving his grave behind. I couldn't be with him there any more than I could be with him anywhere else.

To my dismay, Mr. Graves had other passengers with him when he came to get my things—a man and a girl of about twelve. The man was sitting on the wagon seat, smoking a seegar, and the girl had found a seat on a pile of empty sacks in the rear. The man watched me get in, and made neither any conversation nor any attempt to relinquish the wagon seat to me. Mr. Graves gave me a sheepish glance, then said, "This here, ma'am, is my cousin, also David B. Graves. And this is his daughter, Davida, or Vida. You ought to give the lady your seat, David B."

"I seen too much of that," was all the cousin said. He was a fat man, and I would not say he was much under Mr. Graves's influence.

Louisa, Charles, and Mrs. Bush, who had turned out to see me off, exchanged a glance. Louisa said, "Charles would be happy to take you, Lydia."

"I want to," said Charles. "I'll take you right to the wharf, and stay with you there until you find a passage, and load on your things for you! You won't have to lift a finger!"

"I have perfect faith in Mr. Graves, Charles. We have a lot to discuss."

"Oh, darling!" exclaimed Louisa, putting her hands first to her belly, then to her face. "I thought it was going to be different!" She reached out for my hand and squeezed it. Mrs. Bush was shaking her head. "Perhaps when you return, my dear, these—" But she didn't go on, for fear of offending the two David Graveses. Mr. Graves clicked to his mules, said, "We'll be off, now!" and that was my parting from Lawrence. I didn't think a thing of it, to tell the truth, because my plans seemed to have driven everything else out of my head. My only concern was whether I would manage to speak with Mr. Graves, my Mr. Graves, or not.

We drove southeast, and soon we were out of Lawrence, farther than I had been southeast since September, as our claim happened to be north of town. The day quickly grew hot, and I tried as best I could to withdraw into the brim of my bonnet. The two Mr. Graveses sat hunched over, their hats pulled down. The girl looked at me for a while, then out over the prairie. The wagon lurched along well enough; the rains had stopped weeks before, and the ground was hard. In places, the grasses were tall and bent over, and the prairie presented the aspect of a meadow, but either because I saw things differently now, or because they were different, the prairie looked not at all wild to me anymore. A group of three wagons on the horizon, approaching us, was merely the most visible emblem of what K.T. was now—not an empty spot under the sky but a seething human landscape that had lost every vestige of freshness and the hope that went with it. The grass and flowers were oppressed by what lay scattered about—here was a wagon wheel, broken, here a broken keg that had held whiskey, here were some bones and the skull of an ox, here was the shaft of an ax or another tool, here some rails, split, broken, left, here a piece of milled lumber, or half a one. The busyness and building that had amazed and thrilled me from time to time in Lawrence had its cost, as I well knew. Everything carried there, made there, bought and sold there, moved across the prairie; some part of it was lost or broken or destroyed and left behind, evidence of the intentions of men. And I knew from my life there that those intentions were generally far from honorable, the main intention being always to make money, as much of it in as little time as possible. Should we pass the wagons ahead of us, should I look into the faces of their owners and passengers, the primary things I would see would be greed and fear—greed for the wealth every bill promised in K.T., fear of being too late. The New Englanders, as much as they liked always to display their moral preeminence, were as greedy and fearful as folks from anywhere else. And their fears were justified. If there had been a month or two in 1855 when a man could get rich on the dreams of those coming along behind, well, that month was gone now, and there was only jostling for survival left.

K.T. was already old with conflicts—that was the sharpest lesson. No sooner were the Indians removed (and who ever thought of them? a few missionaries here and there) than the newness of the place was used up through disputes that were as old as the United States. It was as if a bride and groom turned to one another at the altar, each expecting the other to be new and young and strong and beautiful, and found instead old age, old acquaintance, old battles, old hatreds. Where else in the whole United States had there been no honeymoon at all, no short space of good feelings? Nowhere else but K.T., as far as I had heard. The residents hadn't even taken the time to work up their own hatreds but had instead brought along what they already had plenty of. I thought of those few nights in the fall when Thomas and I had been alone in our little cabin with the sailcloth over the hole in the roof. The prairie had seemed so wide and pathless then, its emptiness as old as it was broad. That had lasted how many nights? Fifteen? Twenty? That was the length of our honeymoon, the total accumulation of our innocence, K.T.'s innocence. After that, we'd been caught up in the conflict, too.

The wagon jolted along, and the sun rose higher. Mr. Graves passed me a jar of water, and I took a drink, then passed it to the girl. We got closer to the wagons ahead of us, which were moving slowly, and I heard the two Mr. Graveses speculate that they were heading for the California road.

In fact, when I paid attention, which I hadn't been doing heretofore, I could make out what the two men were saying quite well, even over the humming of the girl. I set myself to listen, full of conviction that the information I needed would be forthcoming if I just listened long enough.

"It's a whole load," said the new Mr. Graves.

"Men's or women's?"

"Both. Mostly men's, I think. But they an't gonna cost you nothing. Their owners is all dead!"

"But I got to go all the way to Saint Louis to get 'em."

"Bailey might bring 'em up as far as Lexington."

"And I an't heard anyone talk about shoes. I an't sure there's much of a market for old shoes in K.T."

"Lots of 'em are boots. Anyways, you got to make your own market sometimes."

"In my opinion, David B., dead men's shoes are a risky venture."

"In my opinion, cousin, nothing ventured, nothing gained."

"I'll ponder over it."

We went along for a ways. Other horsemen and people in wagons were about, and sometimes the two men hailed them.

I dozed off.

A loud and merry laugh woke me up. "They did?" exclaimed the new Mr. Graves. "Sent 'em back down the river without their rifles? Haw haw! I like that one!"

"Jim Lane was in a state, let me tell you," said the old Mr. Graves. "When he recruited those boys in Chicago, he had to sober them up one by one, then teach the difference between east and west, so they'd know how to get to K.T.!"

"Paddy don't know the way, haw haw!" exclaimed the new Mr. Graves.

"And our boys, they said, 'Now, we'll give you two bucks apiece for your rifles, boys, but only if you don't fuss. If you fuss, we'll give you a kick apiece in the hind end!' "

"That's what they got, haw haw!"

By this time I was wide awake, perceiving that their conversation had turned to the political situation. I tried to be quiet, but I must have let on somehow, because they moved closer together and lowered their voices, so that I could catch only a word here and there. Two of the words I caught were "Lane's army" and another word was "Nebraska." I had heard about this before—Jim Lane had recruited another army in Iowa, in addition to the Chicago group the men had just been discussing, and was bringing it to Lawrence through Nebraska. It was supposed to be a well-equipped northern fighting band, plenty of guns and ammunition and officers trained in military colleges in Indiana and Ohio who were disaffected by the fact that the regular U.S. Army, like every other branch of the government, was in the power of the slavocrats. Louisa and Charles had talked about the plan a few days before. It was mixed up somehow with the idea of Kansas becoming an independent republic, as Texas had been for a while. An independent Free-Soil republic with its own army and the capital at Topeka. Well, people would talk about anything.

And suddenly Thomas was with me. Rolling

over that stretch of prairie that we had rolled over in such a state of innocence only a few months before brought him to me. I remembered how I used to feel his presence as a kind of largeness pressing against me, and then I would look over, and he would just be sitting there, mild and alert, taking everything in and thinking about it. That was the distinctive thing about Thomas: he was always thinking about it. You didn't have that feeling with most people; rather, you had a feeling that nothing was going on with them at all. Even Louisa, who was certainly an intelligent woman: if she wasn't talking about something, you didn't have the feeling that she was thinking about it. I remembered something I hadn't thought of since it happened—the time we'd camped on the prairie, our first night on the prairie ever, and Thomas had taken my hand between his and rubbed my thumb and asked me if I was afraid. Hadn't I said no? Hadn't the very grasp of his hand driven out the fear that I had felt earlier in the day? How strange that was, all things considered. And shouldn't I learn a lesson from that, to be afraid right now? And yet I wasn't afraid at all, even of the second Mr. Graves and all he represented. Having Thomas with me did that.

We went along all day. We didn't stop in Franklin, but we did stop at the store of Paschal Fish, and I got out while the two Mr. Graveses carried some kegs and chests in. In the afternoon, we stopped again, at another store. I understood without being told that these were rough places and that my best course of action was to stay with the girl in the wagon. I tried to engage her in conversation, in fact, but she was taciturn. When I pressed her, she said, "I an't gotta talk to abolitionists like you. Abolitionists think I'm no better than a nigger."

"Who told you that?"

"I figured it out on my own."

"It isn't that, exactly. . . ." I was ready to go into explanations, but suddenly they seemed worthless, and fruitless. And her evident aversion to me was disheartening.

After another moment, she said, "I know what happened to you. My pa told me."

"Most people do know what happened to me."

"You shouldn't have come to K.T. What happened to you was your own fault."

"You are a hard little girl."

"I an't a little girl." And it was true; she was the same age as Frank, who was not a little boy.

Mr. Graves was as kind to me as he could be. When we camped again on the prairie that night, he gave me the best bits of the prairie chicken that he caught and roasted, then he made me my bed in the wagon. I knew that he and I would have had a lot to say to one another, but his conversation with his cousin had died, and he didn't seem to wish any conversation with me in the hearing of his cousin. After nightfall, both men, and the girl, for all I knew, fell immediately asleep. I lay awake in the relative comfort of the wagon, looking at the sliver of moon and listening to the hobbled mules crop the prairie grass. The perennial K.T. breeze blew over me. I knew this was the last of these scenes for me, that once I had left, my horror of the place would grow and nothing would bring me back. That morning, I had looked on my friends with coolness, and impatience to be on my way, but right then I felt the attachment strongly, and it smote me that I wouldn't be there to see Louisa and Charles's child, to lift him into my arms and hold him up to my cheek. If there was any reward for living in K.T., perhaps that would be it. And I was sorry I had acted so coldly at our parting. I felt that if I were to tot up my regrets about my life in K.T., then that would be right at the top of a long list.

CHAPTER 19

I Go Among the Enemy

A person of strong constitution, who takes much exercise, needs less clothing than one of delicate and sedentary habits. According to this rule, women need much thicker and warmer clothing, when they go out, than men. But how different are our customs, from what sound wisdom dictates! Women go out with thin stockings, thin shoes, and open necks, when men are protected by thick woollen hose and boots, and their whole body encased in many folds of flannel and broadcloth.

—*p. 115*

IF LAWRENCE WAS BUSY with new money and new men, then Kansas City was a-boil. Just as each time I came into Lawrence from our claim, the experience of all that noise and all those people with their business was a shock and a revelation no matter how much I expected and longed for it, so the even greater level of activity and noise in Kansas City was an even greater shock. It was hardly the same town as it had been when we passed through in September. Every road or path leading from the town was jammed with wagons and men on horseback, and once you were well into town, there were no quiet sections. Everywhere, someone was building or tearing down or loading or unloading or yelling out instructions, admonishments, oaths, imprecations. And shortly I noticed that the town was all men and, as with Lawrence, all the men were armed, only they didn't carry just a carbine or a pistol; they carried a rifle and wore a pair of pistols, and you could see the handles of knives sticking out of their boottops and their pockets.

Mr. Graves turned to me now and said, "I know the captain of a steamboat, the *Missouri Rose,* and I think the boat is leaving for Saint Louis in the next day. I'm going to buy you a ticket right now and put you on there, ma'am. She's a safe boat with a shallow draft and an't gonna get hung up like some of them others."

"We got hung up on the way upriver. A woman on that boat beat her slave girl because she got her shoes wet." I glanced at the second Mr. Graves and saw the back of his neck twitch, but he didn't turn to look at me.

"Now, ma'am, I have to remind you that, as you are unsound on the goose question, you would be wise to maintain a womanly silence and gentleness of demeanor at all times, because though all Missourians and southerners honor the fair sex, by habit and from their earliest childhoods, no one can answer for the general irritability that I see all around me here. I am feeling that you should take your cabin on the *Rose* and stick to it and not say too much about your troubles in K.T."

The other Mr. Graves shifted on the wagon seat. My Mr. Graves said, "Now here is a lesson in point." He gestured to the large print of a newspaper that had been pasted on a wall we were passing. It read: "Abolitionists' Nest to Be Razed, Vows Atchison," then, in smaller but still blaring type: "No One Can't Stop Us!"

"Though I have an establishment of my own, where you yourself have visited me, I've been here half a dozen times this summer, ma'am, and I felt you had to see it for yourself to believe me. You can get out of this country safely, and I hope with all my heart you do, but you got to do it quick and you got to do it now, because there's a war coming and a conflagration that is going to roll over Lawrence, K.T., like a burning log, smashing everyone in its path. We been taking their weapons and turning them back, at the same time as our allies from the southern states have been pouring in to us, with fresh horses, fresh weapons, and fresh spirits ready for a fight as only southerners can be. I have an interest in you, ma'am, and I think you've seen enough and suffered enough. I would hate to see what is coming to them come to you."

Well, I admit that these sights and sounds, and Mr. Graves's words, too, were startling. I saw that his plan was just what Charles's had been—to bundle me out of harm's way. My plan, of eliciting from him the names of Thomas's killers, had been entirely unsuccessful, and I didn't see another way, just yet, but even as he was speaking, I was trying to think of one. I looked toward my bag, which contained my pistol and my rounds of ammunition, for inspiration. Mr. Graves's mules ambled through the crowds, slowly making our way for us to the boats I could see down on the river. Frankly, I had not imagined so

many people. Even if that boy were here, I would
certainly miss him in this crowd, unless some ema-
nation from him, such as Louisa maintained she was
sensitive to, was carried to me across the spiritual
realm. It was enough to discourage someone not
quite as single-minded as myself. But there they
were, as close as the inside of my own head—
Thomas turning to speak and falling out of my sight
behind Mr. James's little wagon, Jeremiah rearing up
in the traces, that boy's face as he shot him dead. You
couldn't rest with such a picture in your head, even
in the teeth of such scenes as I now beheld.

The girl spoke up. "We an't had nothin' good to
eat since two days ago, and I'm hungry." The two
men looked at each other. I said, "I'm hungry, too."

The second Mr. Graves barked, "We got stuff to
unload!" and the girl looked abashed, but then the
first Mr. Graves, a man who I could see was always
kindly in spite of himself, said, "We're going to Morton's warehouse. It seems to me there's a place down
around there that an't too bad, if we set by the door
and keep our eyes peeled."

"I can pay for myself," I said, as if the men's
reluctance grew out of stinginess, but I knew it grew
out of something else, perhaps only caution at the
general rowdiness.

There was a place—the Alabama Hotel, a building still under construction but already a going business—and after unloading, we went there. Vida and I
sat in the wagon for a moment, while the two men
checked on the activities inside. All was quiet

enough, and so we got out, tied up the mules, and went in.

The ground floor of the Alabama Hotel was cavernous, lit by six glass windows that ran along the back wall, facing the river over the bluff. It contained a vast number of tables, no two alike—some round, some rectangular, some finely finished, and others just rough boards. And pulled up to the tables were chairs, stools, benches, and kegs of all sorts, too. Clearly the Alabama Hotel was a business built on the failures of other businesses. While we stood in the corner beside the door, a half-dozen Negro men came running in from the back and started setting the tables, with a clatter of crockery and utensils. They then brought in big bowls of food and placed them in the center of the tables, also at a run. I saw that this was to be a meal on the steamboat model, and indeed, all around the walls of the room, men were gathering, waiting near the tables for the signal to be seated. The Negroes ran faster and worked harder as the top of the hour approached. The men around the walls were armed and rough-looking characters, and not likely to entertain any delay to the gratification of their appetites. There were shouts of "Hurry, boys! I'm hungry as a dragon!" and "Step it up, boy! Set down the food, then get out of the way!" There was even a shot, which made everyone jump, but then the rumor went around that the shooter had just let off his pistol exuberantly, out the window toward the river. The waiters didn't even react that I could see. I suppose they were happy enough that there was only

one shot. I noticed that a very rough-looking character, bearded from his eyebrows to his chest and with
hands like loaves of bread, was going around taking
money. He came to us, and the first Mr. Graves gave
him a dollar and some change. "That's one plate full
per person," admonished the man. "This is an honor
system here, but I'm watching you, anyway." Then
he went on to the man beside me, who paid him a dollar, and he said, "That's all you can eat, Morgan,
same as always, but you got to sit at that table." He
pointed. Morgan nodded and moved closer to the des-
ignated table. This man, the one who was taking the
money, had his pistols holstered at his waist, clearly
visible to all the rowdies. When he had gotten around
the room, and the Negroes had gotten out of the way,
he came to a gong and rang it, and the men poured off
the walls and into the chairs. After that, it was the
same wolfing of food that I'd seen on the steamboat,
with this difference, that there was passing of bowls
back and forth between some of the tables, until all
the food was gone and all the bowls were as clean as
if they'd been washed. I remember sitting with the
Misses Tonkin on the steamboat and watching
Thomas across the dining room, reaching for a piece
of something and having it snatched from between
his fingers. The thought made my throat tighten. Men
licked their knives, their spoons, even their plates. We
had some pork, some cucumbers, some corncakes,
some wheat bread, and some corn pudding. After a bit,
there was another sounding of the gong, and when I
turned to glance at the first Mr. Graves, he said,

"They're serving up a drink of whiskey to each man, out on the porch. That gets 'em outta here pretty brisk. We can finish up at our leisure."

"You can," said his cousin. "I'm gettin' what I paid for."

"I paid for it," said Mr. Graves. And I saw the cousin smile for the first time. "You set," the second Mr. Graves ordered Vida, though she hadn't moved, and then he pushed off.

"My cousin has high ambitions for Vida," said Mr. Graves. "She's a precocious young lady with considerable accomplishments already. Vida, sing your song!"

Vida was happy to oblige, and as all around us men were pushing back their chairs and rushing to the door, Vida sang four verses of "The Last Rose of Summer" in a high but tuneful voice. Mr. Graves clapped for her, and she nodded and simpered at him. Then he said, "My cousin keeps her by him, so that he can guard her precious talents. That side of the family was always musical. I don't share their talents myself."

"And I play the piccolo and dance," said Vida, proudly. "Pa says that I am going to go on the stage in a year or so."

"There's a great call for entertainment in the west," said Mr. Graves. "My cousin himself once did a lecture circuit, but since discovering Vida's promise, he's been devoting himself to nurturing it."

I couldn't help gaping just a little bit.

Once the patrons had cleared out, the Negroes

returned and began by sweeping up the broken crockery. After that, we went out.

We were joined by the second Mr. Graves. Vida said, "I sang my song for the lady. She liked it."

"Yes, I did—"

"Did she pay you?"

"Here," said my Mr. Graves. "Here's a dime." He handed his cousin a coin, and the second Mr. Graves pocketed it.

Now we made our way down to the river and began looking for the *Missouri Rose.* I had hoped that the cousin and the girl would find other business and I would be able to either elicit information from Mr. Graves or else elude him, but the two stuck to us like cockleburs. The girl was sharp-sighted, shouting, "There she is!" not two seconds after I'd spotted the boat and attempted to turn the two men. Mr. Graves was carrying my bag, and he marched us right down there and handed it to a *Missouri Rose* deckhand. The deckhand walked away with it, and I saw that I was sunk.

We went on board, up what I suppose you would call the gangplank, to the passenger deck, and there, to my dismay, we immediately encountered the captain, who was a small, rotund man with side-whiskers and a pince-nez. This man greeted Mr. Graves heartily, haw-hawing and throwing his arm around Mr. Graves's shoulder.

"When will you be getting under way?" said Mr. Graves.

"No later than tomorrow, crack of dawn, haw haw," shouted Captain Smith.

"What's the passage for this young lady here, down to Saint Louis, you old crook?" shouted Mr. Graves in return.

"Twelve dollars if she's paying, twelve silver dollars if you're paying, haw haw," shouted the captain.

"I'm paying," said Mr. Graves, "if you're really going off tomorrow, but if you an't, I'll find someone else who is. Got to get her out of this country, and that's a fact."

"She a G—— d—— abolitionist, haw haw?" shouted the captain.

"She's a widow woman, and made so at a young age, and her husband was a fine man, and that's all you need to know. Now, are you leaving when you say, or is it just a trick?"

I hated that word "widow."

"Tomorrow noon. Two o'clock at the latest."

"I'll keep looking. If I don't find nothing better, I'll be back."

He marched me down to the shore, where I stopped dead. "In the first place," I exclaimed, "I have the money to pay my passage. In the second place, I consider your treatment of me very high-handed! I am accustomed to making my own decisions, and I haven't made up my mind what I intend to do."

"Ma'am, I told you before—"

"I know what you told me, and I understand that you are motivated by kindness, but—" But I bit my tongue before speaking. I knew that my plan, such as it was, was so much in my mind that almost any word would reveal it, possibly without my knowing. I eyed Mr. Graves. Wasn't the key thing, after all, to be rid of him? I bent my head, then sought his gaze and said, more submissively, "I know what you want to do is all for the best, Mr. Graves, and you've always been a friend to me, so whatever you think is best, that's the course I will follow."

"Good girl," said Mr. Graves.

For the next hour, we visited each boat, one by one—there were four altogether—and at each we got a similar reply: perhaps tomorrow; but if you wanted to get right down to it, the next day or the day after that was more likely. Finally, we got back to the *Missouri Rose*. The captain showed me my little cabin and the ladies' saloon, which was neatly fitted out in red brocade with gold trim—"Just had this done down in New Orleans; looks like it, don't it, haw haw?"—and I watched while Mr. Graves counted out twelve silver dollars. Then I said, "But I need my bag. The boy took away my bag."

"You'll find it in your cabin."

"Which is?"

"Number seven."

And now, now at last, I came to bidding farewell to Mr. Graves. We stood on the deck, and he worked himself up to his highest state of oratory. He took my hand. "Ma'am, Mrs. Newton, I say this openly, with no thought to my own preservation or the opinions of my fellowman: You and your late husband were fine folk, who came here with the purest of motives, no matter what our scribblers of the presses aver. I consider myself privileged to have known you, and especially privileged to have had such a lengthy and enlightening conversation with your husband, that time we passed between this town, Kansas City, though hardly a city then, and your destination, which, in consideration to the feelings of passersby, I shall not name right now. We talked, as I remember, about the broad breast of the ocean, whereon Mr. Newton had made his fortune, such as it was, and about certain medical and educational matters. These medical matters, I recall, had a favorable outcome, which I then attributed and now attribute to the pleasant circumstances of our journey. And I say this, too: that I was struck at the time by the contrast between a threesome of our local citizenry and your husband—the one set was low in their appetites and belligerent in their actions, while your husband was a man of enterprise and wit. The contrast struck me sharply, though I didn't mention it at the time, and I said to myself, 'Well, these New Englanders aren't all bad,' and I date my period of enlightenment from that evening. Let me say this, that in my travels back and forth between that nameless town and this so-called city, my eyes have been opened to the worthy men of both sides of this tragic conflict. What will happen I of course cannot predict, but every day the contrast between what men might be and what they are grows greater. I wish you the best of luck far from these scenes of thievery and mayhem. I count the evening when I found you on the prairie and aided you in my humble way as one of the most significant of my life, and I will never forget it, or you, or your departed husband, and so good-bye." Here Mr.

Graves kissed my hand and then let go of it, and I saw that there were tears in his eyes. In front of all the world, I stepped over and kissed him on the cheek, and I said, "You are certainly a dear man, Mr. Graves, and I will always think of you as a friend."

I stood by the railing as he departed down the plank, and I watched him until he was well out of sight. Then I ran back to my cabin to get my bag, thinking I would make my own departure. My forty dollars was intact, thanks to Mr. Graves's friendship; I was full of food; I could carry my bag off and find a hotel, then make inquiries here and there. When all was said and done, freedom was everything wasn't it?

I went into the red-and-gold saloon, then made my way down to cabin number seven. My heart, strange to say, was lighter than it had been in weeks, as if my plan were to meet Thomas, not to avenge him. I pushed back the curtain of my cabin and saw at once the back of another woman, a small woman with a cap on her white hair. She turned right around and said, "Ah! You're Mrs. Newton! I am Miss Emily Carter, schoolteacher. The captain sent me over to chaperone you to Saint Louis. I'm sure we will have a lovely journey. I am well known on the *Missouri Rose*. I go back and forth from Kansas City to Saint Louis four times a year, and I always take the *Rose*. Isn't the new ladies' saloon inviting?"

I was so shocked that I could barely keep a friendly countenance. It took significant effort to transform my gape into a smile, to hold out my hand,

and to say to Miss Carter, "Oh, how lovely. I knew Mr. Graves would take care of me."

"Oh, Mr. David B. Graves and I are old friends."

"It's hard to distinguish them, isn't it?"

"You mean the cousin? I don't think of him as Mr. David B. Graves at all. He has a much more troubled reputation, don't you know? No, whenever you hear the name Mr. David B. Graves, most folks know who you're talking about. The one and not the other. Isn't that funny?"

"Yes, it is." I had regained a bit of my composure, but I was panting just a little. Miss Carter said, "Oh, my dear. You seem hot. I have just the thing. You recline a bit here, and I will fix you right up."

I did what she said, at the same time furiously attempting to come up with a plan.

"Now close your eyes, dear."

When I did, she laid a folded handkerchief dipped in witch hazel across my forehead.

"I will tell you right out, Mrs. Newton, that Mr. Graves told me a bit of your story, because he felt he could confide in me, though he did not tell the captain a word. Captain Smith is a very partisan man, I am sorry to say, and we all know the sort of things he's done in what I call the goose cause. It's a shame!" She clucked disapprovingly. "But I'm sure we will get down to Saint Louis with no problem. The lovely thing about the *Missouri Rose* is that it's a safe and well-run boat, perfect for the Missouri River, just a first-rate craft. And Captain Smith has enough backing, my dear, so that he doesn't run in an unsafe way—you know, trying always to get up more steam, or risking the sandbars. Oh! My land o' mercy! You may not know it, but the Missouri River was not designed by the Lord for steamboat travel, but men *will* defy Him! The key thing is always to find a boat with more than enough boiler capacity, so that going along does not in any way *test* the boiler, because a boiler is just the sort of thing to fail the test!" She laughed, then felt my cheeks. "There we go, dear. You're much cooler now, and your cheeks aren't nearly so red." She removed the handkerchief. "Well, I am sorry to laugh, because the tragedy when a boiler fails is beyond thinking about! But my own brother is an engineer, and he said to me, 'Emily, dear, I have gone over the *Missouri Rose* from stem to stern, and looked over the boiler, too, and I declare she's as safe as a boat can be, which isn't all that safe, but the alternative is Missouri roads!' "

I sat up and declared that I felt better. Then I said, "Do we stay all night on the boat, then? I'm new at these things."

"Well, *I* do, Mrs. Newton. I didn't use to, when I was teaching in Lexington, because Lexington is a fine old town, as civilized as Lexington, Kentucky, where I was brought up. But these western towns, especially since those abolitionists got in here! In these circumstances, staying on the boat is a lady's best course of action. The captain has agreed to give us our supper—he really is a good man underneath, you know—and I think we can make ourselves quite comfortable here! The saloon is lovely, and our cabin is very roomy for a steamboat cabin."

I forced myself to cool my impatience by making up alternative plans in my head: I could sneak off the boat at Westport or Lexington and make my way back if I had to. Wasn't revenge a dish best eaten cold, even in K.T., where most tempers were hot? But I couldn't raise much of an interest in Miss Carter, and so I didn't respond in a very lively fashion to her conversation, and after a bit she fell silent and took out her work, which was some tatting. I watched her out of the corner of my eye—her thread was impossibly fine, and the lace she made was intricate and filmy. Watching her put me into a sort of dream, which passed the time until supper.

We went on in this fashion for the rest of the day and into the evening. Our supper of steak and pickles and cherries and corn bread was brought to us in the ladies' saloon by a Negro boy, and it was accompanied by the usual glass of river water—cloudy on top, thick at the bottom. Miss Carter drank hers right up, saying, "I'm told that in the baths of Europe, only the wealthiest can afford such a glass. We in America are more democratic!" I couldn't be so enthusiastic—I sipped the top inch or so and then set mine aside.

It would have been the end of July, and so dusk was late and prolonged, but finally I saw that Miss Carter was making her preparations for rest. In all of this time, since our first meeting, she had not left me for even a few minutes. I hoped she was a heavy sleeper. I made my preparations for rest, too, though when I opened my bag, I was careful to hide it with my body from her sight and then to leave it open, with my shawl draped over it, so that I wouldn't have to risk the sound of the hasp later on. At last we were ready. I eased myself into the lower berth, which, fortunately, I had been lying in before. I said, "Good night, Miss Carter. I hope you sleep well."

"Oh, my land o' mercy. I will!" she exclaimed. "Have you seen these drops? I got them from a wonderful man, three-quarters pure Indian, knows all the Indian secrets! Everyone here in Kansas City swears by him. His name is John Red Dog. I can't do without these drops!" And she put a bit on her tongue, then climbed into the upper berth. Sure enough, by the time it was fully dark, she was snoring, long, deep, ruffling snores, as regular as the ticking of a clock.

I sat up and removed my shawl from my bag, at the same time making sure that the curtain of our cabin was completely closed. Then I stood up and looked, smiling in case she awakened, at Miss Carter. She was far gone in slumber, undoubtedly thanks to the drops. Her workbasket sat at the foot of her bed, and I opened it and took out her scissors, which were of only moderate size but large enough. Then I laid out my shawl and, kneeling, bent my head over it and cut off my hair. It fell in dark hanks, rather surprising me with its length and weight. But I felt no grief at cutting off my only beauty, merely a lightness and relief. Somehow, my hair had become Thomas's, and now he was requiring me to cut it. It would grow back. I wrapped it in my shawl and laid the shawl aside.

The next part was more difficult. What I was

engaged in now I had not planned, though I had brought along a few of Thomas's things for remembrance—two or three books, a pair of trousers, and a coat, but, of course, no hat, no shoes. I think that I had vaguely thought that if I should end up in Boston, I would give these articles to Thomas's mother, or father, or a brother. The trousers and the coat would now come in handy, but I had given his hat to Charles, and I had given his boots and other effects to a dealer in secondhand clothing, not three days after the killing. This man had offered me some money, but at the time I was simply horrified at taking money for them, and so I'd turned it down. Well, there was nothing for it, then, but to make the best of what I had. I cut the skirt off my cream-colored dress, below the waist, so there would be a tail, then I put Thomas's trousers on over the bodice as if it were a shirt, with his braces holding them up as best as I could fix it. Finally, I shrugged into the jacket, which fit much more loosely than the trousers. One thing I had saved and used, which now came in very handy, was his pocket watch. I opened the crystal and felt the hands in the darkness—ten-thirty—and slipped it into the pocket of his coat. I pushed my rolled-up shawl out of the way and slipped into my berth to wait for a favorable hour.

There was no going to sleep. I neither wanted to nor could afford to. I had no idea, for one thing, of how long Miss Carter's drops would remain effective. And I judged midnight or shortly thereafter to be the best time for departing the *Missouri Rose.* I knew that if I fell asleep, I would sleep through until morning and lose my chance. Lying in my berth in Thomas's clothes made me very sad. They had been folded tightly away for many weeks—they were not what he'd been wearing upon being shot, but I had retrieved them from the cabin—and beneath their woolly, musty scent was another, fleeting and almost undetectable, which I recognized as familiar. I was eager to think that it was Thomas's scent, that something of him still lingered around me, but when I focused my attention on it, it seemed to disappear, so that I could not say that it was really there. When I thought of Thomas, though, the pictures and the memories were striking: Thomas reading aloud by candlelight, his expressive voice bodying forth each story so that the characters seemed to be in the room, just outside the circle of the candlelight. Thomas coming in from working at the end of the day, his shoulders filling the doorway, his affectionate greeting, even though we might have seen each other only twenty minutes before. Thomas and Charles at the breakfast table, when we were living in town, laughing and regaling Louisa and me with stories of their journeys to Leavenworth to get the mail. Thomas, my husband, after the candle was blown out at night, so large a presence that I seemed to disappear into it; not something that memoirists customarily write about but, in truth, the very thing that I could not stop thinking of as I lay curled in my berth that night on the *Missouri Rose*.

The anguish of these thoughts eventually propelled me out of the berth at eleven forty-five or so. Miss Carter was still heavily asleep. I closed the hasp of my bag as softly as I could and peeked around the curtain into the ladies' saloon. If the *Missouri Rose* was anything like the boat that had brought us upstream, male passengers would be allowed to sleep on the floor of the saloon after all the ladies had gone to their cabins, but now, before the journey, the big room was empty. I crept around the curtain and across the floor to the big double doors, which were locked. Trying not to be disappointed or daunted, I then carried my bag along the row of ladies' cabins, looking for another way out. I didn't find one, but I found something better, a pair of men's boots, the toes sticking out underneath the curtain, and, when I listened, hearty snores behind it. I knelt, set down my bag, and slowly extracted the boots. They were unattached to their owner's feet and came easily. They were not new and did not smell sweet, but I hurriedly pulled off my own shoes and put the boots on, anyway. Though a trifle too large, they were certainly good enough.

This acquisition whetted my appetite for more, especially for a hat or a cap, and I grew bolder. I began to peek behind curtains, but only if I heard evidence of sleep, such as groans or snores. Behind the third curtain, hung on a nail, was the perfect hat— soft-brimmed and slouchy, good for hiding within. I took it. It was a good hat, of a southern style rather than a northern—no doubt made in Kentucky or somewhere like that. It fit, too. I walked my bag down the length of the saloon and found a window, which I opened and climbed out of, onto the deck. I didn't see anyone around. I closed the window

behind me and adopted a nonchalant demeanor, leaning my elbows on the rail, cocking one foot across
the other, and pulling down my hat, as I had seen so
many men do in my twenty-one years. And it was
well that I did, because just then someone rounded
the end of the deck and touched the brim of his own
hat politely in my direction. I cleared my throat and
nodded, but didn't alter my position. He said, "Pleasant evening," and walked on.

I stood still as he passed.

I saw at once that as long as I was a man, I would
be able to do whatever I wanted, and that I would
have a taste of freedom such as no woman I had
known, even Louisa, had ever had. I stood up and
strolled—ambled, really—down the length of the
deck, looking for the gangplank, not quite sure where
I was on the boat but thrusting one hand in my pocket
and carrying my bag with the other, kicking out my
feet as I walked, and altogether impersonating, I realized, my nephew Frank. The trousers hung around
me, and their inseams rubbed together as I walked.
But there was a lovely feeling to it of big strides and
nothing in your way, that I remembered from the last
time I'd worn trousers, the day our party had tried to
parley with the Missourians at the Jenkins claim.

Some Negroes were pulling up the gangplank as
I got to it.

"Hey, boys, wait for me," I said, as if I'd been
saying such things all my life, and the two men
looked at each other, then tipped their caps, and one
of them said, "All right, boss," and down it went. I
strolled off the boat, idling, to all appearances (I

knew I would have to get a seegar somewhere very soon). Down on the dock, I turned, watched them pull up the gangplank as if I didn't have anything better to do, then waved. One of them waved back.

Of course, I had no idea where I was going or what I was going to do for the rest of the night, but it seemed as though all I had to do was remain in character as a man, or rather as a boy of, say, sixteen, old enough but still plausibly beardless, and every opportunity would present itself to me. My name would be Lyman. Mr. Lyman Arquette, close enough to my maiden name, Harkness, so that when men— other men, that is—addressed me by my last name, which was the custom in the west, the name would ring a bell. I would at least look up, giving myself a single precious moment to remember who I was.

My state of mind, which was both exhilarated and fearful of discovery, belied my real condition, which was more in danger of eventual starvation than of anything else. Even though, having eaten well during the day, I reckoned I wouldn't have to eat again until suppertime the next evening (eighteen hours thence, but I didn't let myself think of that), what then? I had but forty dollars, and everything in Kansas City was dear. Signs outside of hotels I had seen as we were riding through town read "Rooms, three dollars," or even "five dollars," and that was only for one night! My limited funds put a time limit on my vengeance; my masquerade, as good as I could make it by aping the ways of men I knew, would stand up to neither doing manual work nor engaging in another common western practice—

sleeping two or three to a bed to save on lodging costs. Lyman Arquette would have to be a rather solitary, self-effacing fellow, always ready with a laugh, and ready to take a drink, too—Missourians required both—but keeping himself as much in the background as possible. I strolled away from the riverside and into manhood, trying to look alert and be alert. Every woman knew that men were rough and violent among themselves, and that anything could happen.

CHAPTER 20

Lyman Arquette Investigates

It may be set down as the unchangeable rule of physiology, that stimulating drinks (except in cases of disease) deduct from the powers of the constitution, in exactly the proportion in which they operate to produce temporary invigoration.

—p. 107

As SOON AS the sun was up, I roused myself from behind the wagon where I had taken refuge and began looking for a newspaper office. It had come to me in the night, as I was almost drowsing, that that was where gossip on every subject was to be discovered. As I walked about, I made up my own story—a boy from Palmyra, Missouri, a town across the river from Quincy that I had visited several times, my father a man like Horace Silk, but as for myself, no taste for retailing. Mother dead. My ambition was to learn print setting and newspaper writing, so that I could go west, out to California, say, and start up my own newspaper. I was a good Democrat, a follower of Senator Douglas and Senator Atchison, though of course too young to vote, and a believer in popular sovereignty. I practiced saying "them G—— d—— black abolitionists" to myself. But I planned on taking a great deal of refuge in silence and shyness.

Kansas City was both more and less than Lawrence—more in the sense that there were more people, animals, vehicles, buildings a-building, activity, and business; less in the sense that as quick as everything went in Lawrence, it had gone all the quicker in Kansas City and was therefore all the more ramshackle and make-do. In Lawrence there were women, which meant families, homes, farms, gardens, teacups, and a lending library (or plans for one). In Kansas City it didn't look like there were women, which meant a lack of all these same things. Kansas City was half business, half politics, all money. Kansas City was in Missouri, and so there were slaves, too, doing a considerable amount of the work and none of the idling. As an idler interested in politics, I was unremarkable among the other citizens.

I found a newspaper, the *Missouri Freeman,* shortly after seven—I know the time because I made a practice of ostentatiously pulling "my" watch from my pocket and looking at it, so as to get in the habit—and men were already going up and down the stairs of that office as if great things were stirring. One group of three men ran up the stairs, and I joined them. The door to the pressroom (the only room) was wide open. As we burst in, one of our number exclaimed, "Jack Morton! Wake up!" A man stooping over a table at the other end of the room turned around, as did all the other men in the room, who numbered six or eight. "Shannon's called in General Smith and ordered him to go and attack Lane's army before they get out of Nebraska, and Smith's refused to do it!" Now there were cries of "Traitor!" "Treachery!" and "Where's Sumner?" from all about the room, and the man Morton, who must have been the editor of the paper, stepped forward and said, "Now, Joe, where'd you get this story?"

"These boys," he said. "They're just in from Lecompton, and they had it from one of Shannon's own men!"

"They're going over! The soldiers are going over to the northern side, d—— 'em! I could of told you they would," exclaimed one man as he pushed his way to the front of the group.

"We got to do everything ourselves," said another.

"That's right!" exclaimed a third. "It's all very well what they say about keeping order and makin' them G—— d—— abolitionists obey the laws of the territory, but when it comes right down to it, them black abolitionists do what they want without so much as a by-your-leave, and the army jest sets there!"

"Okay, boys," said Morton. "Let's write this up. You come over here and sit down, and you talk and I'll write."

I was tempted to ooze along with them. No one had yet looked at me with much scrutiny, so excited were they by this news, but the editor's desk was far back in the room, and I decided it would be more prudent to stay by the door. I set my bag down next to the wall and stood looking at some papers from the previous week ("Paupers and Thieves Pouring into Lawrence; Backers in Mass. Say Prisons Will Be Emptied! Investigations by our correspondents have turned up a plot on the part of Amos Lawrence and his cronies to transport the thieves and criminals of the northeast wholesale to Kansas Territory. Prison officials are overjoyed at the prospect; most of the money for the transportation has already been raised from the usual backers. One man, who refused to be identified for our readers, declared, 'Everyone knows this will solve two problems at one time. Kansas will be populated by men who owe us something, at least a vote, and we will be freed of these misfits and foreigners. The backers have agreed to buy every man a claim, free and clear. I hope the claims run all the way to the western mountains!' ") or out the window at the wagons, horses, oxen, and men rushing up and down the street below.

I rehearsed my name, Lyman Arquette, and my story. By the light of day, I wasn't quite sure what sort of figure I cut. Thomas's jacket flapped around me, and of course my dress bodice had to be hidden, so I was buttoned up to the collar, with my hat pulled far down on my head. I seemed to have put on the braces holding up my trousers improperly, as they kept slipping uncomfortably off my shoulders, and I had to surreptitiously adjust them every few minutes. The trousers themselves and the shoes worked well enough, though, as my stockings were quite thin, I couldn't help wondering about the grooming habits of the man whose boots I'd stolen. All in all, I was both comfortable and uncomfortable in my new clothes, which made it rather difficult to attain the sort of slouching nonchalance that I hoped would keep me unnoticed and unremarked upon. I definitely needed a shirt. How much would that cost? The men I knew, including Thomas, had had their shirts made by their wives or daughters. In fact, I had made Thomas two shirts over the winter, but dissatisfied with my own workmanship, I had given them away with the other things. I glanced down again at the article I'd been reading ("Of course, the Free Staters, as they call themselves, will present their new citizens as bona fide homesteaders and family men, which makes us ask ourselves, 'Why is it they don't know the difference between criminals and homesteaders?' Our readers may hazard a guess. But the real outcome of these transportations may redound to our side in the end—law-abiding Missouri citizens and their sympathizers in Kansas Territory will be all the more justified in acting on our own behalf in clearing out the nests of malefactors"). The article, which would have had me and all my friends in K.T. spitting with rage, left me strangely unaffected, no doubt because I could hardly risk being or acting affected, but also because I couldn't quite take in such a ridiculous set of ideas. Best, however, not to read any further.

Morton now appeared beside me, startling me. He wore a friendly smile; his face was smudged with black, as were his fingers, and he had a pencil over his ear. He said, "Well, now, son, you're a stranger here. Are you lookin' for something?"

Without my even planning it, a low, breaking, breathy voice came out of me, almost a whisper. I said, "I'm looking for a job."

"Speak up, son."

"Well, sir, I can't, sir. As a child, I was the victim of an accident. This is the best I can do." Morton

looked instantly sympathetic, so I embroidered a bit
by putting my hand on my throat. "Drank something
caustic, sir. I was two. Back in Palmyra."

"What are you doing in Kansas City, son?"

"Making my way, sir," I whispered. "Got to do
the best I can, you know."

"What's your name, son?"

"Lyman Arquette, sir."

"Well, why don't you sit yourself down over
there, out of the way, and I'll talk to you later, after
the place clears out a bit."

I picked up my bag and strolled over to the desig-
nated chair, which was next to a cold stove. There I
sat down, leaned back, and put my feet up on the
stove, as I'd seen western men do all my life. It was a
remarkably comfortable posture.

It was also a good spot for eavesdropping, and
my hearing was all the keener for the danger I felt
myself to be in. It was more exciting than anything
else, and one thing I discovered about myself was
that as a man, or boy, I was bolder and more reckless
than I'd been as a woman. What might have para-
lyzed me in the past now stimulated me. Not three
feet away, one armed man (rifle, two pistols, two
long knives) was saying to another armed man (two
rifles, no pistols, one knife), "An't begun to do this
right, and that's a fact. You got to treat these G——
d—— abolitionists the way they done them Chero-
kee Indians down where I come from. One day, you
just go in and rout 'em out of there, and you make
'em move on, and you kill the ones that lag behind. It
an't purty, but lots o' necessary doin's an't purty at

all. What truly an't purty is the way all this stuff lingers until you lose in the end."

"Shoulda struck when the strikin' was good, you ask me. We had 'em out here, far from everywhere, before all them scribblers got out here, and we coulda done what we wanted to 'em, but of course them cooler heads prevailed. Now lookit us!"

"You never spoke a truer word, Loomis."

They shook their heads in anguish.

Some of the talk was of making money. One man (two pistols, no knives) declared, "It may not look like it to you, Jacks, but this area is finished. California is finished. Texas is finished. Mark me, 'cause I'm telling you something you need to know. If you see wagons, then that area is just finished. It just is. If there are wagons, then you're too late."

Jacks (one pistol, one rifle, one knife) shook his head. "You an't payin' attention to the two stages, Dixon. I told you before, there's two separate stages, and you can make a bundle in each. Just because the first stage, what I call the speculatin' stage, is over don't mean you can't make a pile. During the growth stage, as I call it, you got to have the imagination to refine your appeal. You got to be sellin' somethin' someone wants. It an't like durin' the speculatin' stage when everybody wants the same thing, which is land. Durin' the growth stage, folks all want different things. It's a better man who makes his money then, and to my mind, he makes better money, both more of it and more righteous money, I think. But an't too many share my opinion on that."

"Kansas is done, Nebraska is done."

"Well, where an't done, then, d—— it?" exclaimed Jacks.

"When I know that, you won't see me round here no more. You ask where I've gone, and then you come on behind me with your growth stage, haw haw!"

Neither man looked as though he had made any money in either stage.

Not every conversation was philosophical, like these. I heard that a Mrs. Cook had borne twins, that a Bill had fallen into the river overnight and drowned not ten feet from shore (drunk), that the price of hemp was falling, that I could get a pair of Arkansas mules for sixty dollars and a pair of Missouri mules for eighty, that the steamboat *Harvey Mack* had blown up downriver, near Hermann, and ten lives had been lost, that according to the Indians, every day in August was going to be a hundred degrees or over, and that a two-headed lamb had been born near Blue Springs and had lived a week, long enough for the farmer in question to find an artist, who had done an engraving of the animal and the farmer, and the farmer now wanted five dollars from Mr. Morton to run the picture in the paper.

I heard Mr. Morton say, "Just did a two-headed lamb in November. Can't do one of them more than once a year, that's my editorial policy."

"But this lamb lived four days longer than that one!" exclaimed the farmer.

"And my sister got married to a man who had a wagon and a pair of mules, and then another man came along who had two wagons and two pairs of mules, but she didn't get to change her mind, did she?"

The farmer went away disappointed.

I thought if I sat there long enough, I would hear mention of those who had killed Thomas.

Of course, the office wasn't only a place of gossip; it was also a place of work—Mr. Morton and his assistants setting type, doing things with the presses, bringing in paper and doing something with that; but they were more or less hidden from me by my hat and a corner in the wall. Almost no one spoke to me. When someone did greet me, I nodded and whispered, "Good day," in return. In the early afternoon, I slipped away for a bit. I saw that maintaining my masquerade put me on the stretch in more ways than one, and I needed to find a quiet spot and take a break. I came back in the late afternoon. It was almost suppertime, and I was trying not to pay any attention to the fact that I was intensely hungry. In my wanderings and explorations, I'd ascertained that breakfast was, in general, cheaper than dinner or supper, and I thought that if I got myself on a breakfast regimen, my money would go farther.

When I came back, the office had pretty much cleared out. Only Mr. Morton and two of his employees were present, and Mr. Morton saw me before I could back out the door and get down the stairs. "Arquette!" he called.

I stopped dead.

"Now, son." He looked at me quizzically.

I whispered, "Yes?"

"You say you're an educated boy, you can read and write and all that?"

"Yessir."

"Write me something."

He drew me into the office and brought me over to a desk, where he handed me a chair, a piece of paper, and a pen. I thought for a moment, then wrote a page about my long-ago swim of the Mississippi River, only changing my direction. "The grand and heavy weight of the continental waters pressed against me, almost bearing me under. But I did not pause to think of my death, knowing that such thoughts could only bring on such an undesirable result. I fought the brown force with all the strength of my limbs and sinews. . . ."

"A mite flowery," declared Mr. Morton, "but all the words are spelled right." He pushed his spectacles up on his head and scrutinized me so long that I thought the game was up, but then he just said, "Can you ride a horse, son?"

I nodded.

He leaned forward. "How long you been in these parts? Not long? Good. Here's what I'm interested in, Lyman. I want to know what it's like to be one of them boys out there in them bands that are marauding here and there. Are these just gangs of boys up to mischief, or are these soldiers for the southern cause in the making? You look to be about sixteen."

I nodded.

"That's the age of some of these boys. Now." He sat back and glared at me. "Are you one hundred percent sound on the goose question? Because you an't goin' nowhere in these parts if you an't."

I had stolen boots and a hat; I had stolen, in a sense, Mr. Graves's money that he'd paid for my passage; I had deceived Miss Carter; I had deceived all my friends; I had become a man—a boy, rather—and so it was no effort to me to nod. One hundred percent sound on the goose question. I did wonder, though, what Thomas would think about that.

"Good," said Mr. Morton. "There's a horse in the livery stable over a block, Colman's Livery. Brown horse named Athens. You get on him, and you find one of them bands, and you write about that, and if you do a good job, I'll give you regular employment. I'll tell you something: I don't know a thing about you, Lyman Arquette, but you strike me, somehow. Maybe it's your affliction, but I am moved to give you a chance, son."

I whispered, "Thank you, sir."

"Now," he said, "here's an advance on your pay." He put a dollar in my hand. "Go get yourself some supper at the hotel across the street, and I'll see you bright and early in the morning. You got a place to stay?"

"Yessir," I whispered.

Five minutes later, I was strolling away, as astonished as I had ever been in my life.

My supper, which I took in a nearby hotel, made what you might call an avalanche of sleepiness cascade over me, but I wanted to see the horse, so I walked around to the "livery stable," not an establishment the kind reader should confuse with a large building containing stalls and horses and equipment, but rather something quite similar to what I was used to in Lawrence—a large corral and a smaller building beside it, almost a shed, really, though this one was fairly large and contained prairie hay piled up in reserve for the horses, as well as tack and equipment hanging from the walls. There were eight horses and four mules in the corral; of the eight horses, two were chestnut, one was a dun, two were bays, and three were brown. Of these, two were mares, and so I figured Athens to be the round and somewhat sway-backed fellow scouting for wisps of hay in the dirt. He had a wide blaze from his foretop to his nose and looked well on in years. The contrast between him and Jeremiah made my throat tickle. On the other hand, the hay in the shed looked tremendously inviting, and I made straight for it and lay down upon it and nestled into it with a boldness born of irresistible desire. Not long after, an elderly Negro man was looking down on me. I could barely keep my eyes open, even in the midst of this confrontation, but I managed to say in my harsh whisper, "Please may I sleep here? I an't got money for a room."

"Cain't sleep here," said the man, in an accent that I found hard to understand. "This here's Massa Harry's place. Ain' no hotel."

"I work for the newspaper." I gestured toward Athens. And then I simply fell asleep, as if dropping over the side of a cliff. There was nothing he could do about it, or I could do about it, though I think that he jostled me. It was no use. I was without will, and no doubt immovable. I remained unmoved, and woke, right there, just about at sunup. I remembered the elderly man instantly and scrambled to my feet, but he wasn't around. No one was around except the horses and mules, who must have been hungry, as they were looking at me with interest. I picked the bits of hay off my jacket, reminded myself that I was a man named Lyman Arquette, that I had been hired at the newspaper and already owed my employer a dollar.

In the bright light of a good night's sleep, my new situation seemed impossible, and I saw that my successes the day before were surely attributable to good luck more than anything else. If my masquerade had the day before been something like sliding down a snowy hill on a child's sled, it seemed that today it would be like scrabbling back up that slippery hill. Such are the effects of mood, and my mood today, clearheaded and fully aware, was far more daunted by my project than it had been in weeks. But I had to go on with it, if only to gain access to the seething gossip of the newspaper office and the benefits of a horse to ride. I also knew, with utter conviction, that I was doing just the sort of thing now that Thomas would disapprove of. Thomas was a conservative man, thoughtful about the proprieties, loath to offend, eager, even in his abolitionist convictions, that righteousness and justice be made palatable to all, including those who were to be force-fed. Square and aboveboard was his habit and his ideal. And inside his clothes I was planning a tangle of deceptions that, I fervently hoped, would end in a killing or two.

But it was painful to think of Thomas and best not to be daunted by paradoxes, and so I made my way back to the newspaper office and managed fairly quickly to get an audience with Mr. Morton, who looked as if he'd been up for hours. He was brisk. Had I seen the horse? Was I ready to take on this assignment? Was I armed? I needed to be if I was going out into the countryside. (To this I nodded, telling the truth with the sense of telling a lie.) Well, then . . .

I whispered, "How do I find one of these bands?"

"Well, let me see, now. Two days ago, some boys rode up to the Welch place, three or so miles out on the Westport road, and asked for something to eat. You could start there. That's what got me thinking about this."

I nodded.

"Now, here's five dollars. You don't have to be livin' off the country the way these boys are. You identify yourself as one of my reporters, and you pay for what you get." I nodded, taking the money. "But," he said with a laugh, "that don't mean you shouldn't drive a hard bargain!"

I nodded, and Mr. Morton turned away. There was nothing else for me to do but return to the stable and get on my way. An hour later, I was astride old Athens, clopping through the bustle of Kansas City, looking for the Westport road. The southerners had stolen so many New England weapons from waylaid shipments that about one in five of the rifles I saw on the streets around me was similar to my old carbine. I was able to reflect on this with a surprising want of rage. I had envisioned my passage through the world of my enemies to be a wrathful one, with every evidence of the southerners' stupidity and evil driving me to an even sharper pitch of fury, but things weren't turning out that way. What seemed to be happening was that Lawrence and everything Lawrence meant was turning into a dream of a sort compared to the pressing reality of my new life as a man. Or perhaps it was that now that I was wearing Thomas's clothing, I was becoming more judicious, like him.

After a bit, I left the town behind, though the road was busy enough, and it was nearly a full-time job to touch the brim of my slouchy hat to every passerby, especially, I tried to remember, to the few ladies in wagons and buggies. All the same, it was pleasurable to be riding Athens. He hadn't much go, but his ears were forward, and he seemed content to amble along, taking in the passing scene. I saw a farmer fixing his fence, and I said, in a croaky voice, "This the Welch farm?"

"Nah. A half mile up that way." He shaded his eyes against the sun to look at me, then went right back to his work. It was eternally surprising to me the way no one questioned my masculinity.

There were two farms a half mile up, a prosperous one on the right, with a two-story house, one of those funny western houses you used to see, with a passage right through the bottom that was enclosed across the top, called a "trotway." This farm had plenty of outbuildings, was well fenced, and I could see the wife feeding chickens, the husband going into the shop, and some little girls jumping rope. Across the road was a less prepossessing place, with a small cabin for a house, and a shed for a barn, and no one around. I did what I would have done in a band of marauding boys: I turned in where it was most likely I would find abundance. The farmer came out of the shop to greet me, and all the females stopped what they were doing to look. Everyone seemed immediately suspicious—further evidence that the band of marauders had passed this way. I touched my hat but didn't take it off. I whispered, "Good morning to you," and the farmer stepped closer. "What was that, boy?" he said.

I dared to croak a little louder. "Morning, sir! Name's Lyman Ar-Arquette. I work for Mr. Morton, who has the paper. We were wanting to find out if some boys came by here a day or so ago. I'm looking for them."

The husband and the wife glanced at one another across the yard, but the girls went back to their game.

"Maybe," said the husband.

"You Mr. Welch?" I croaked.

He nodded.

"Well, we heard a bunch of boys came through here and asked you for a meal."

"Maybe."

"They did," piped up the wife. "Spent the night in the barn, too." She looked defiantly at the husband, who scowled.

"Believe me, Mr. Welch, I an't going to do nothing to them boys or to you. I'm just from the paper. I'm looking for them boys to see about them. It's just that the last report of them was that they were here-about."

"Still are," said the wife.

Now this struck fear into me. My plan had been to talk to the Welches. I hadn't let myself think much beyond that, because I didn't think my disguise would hold up under the scrutiny of boys, in a group, already suspicious, and without much to do except to inspect me. I tried to sound eager. "They are?"

The man gestured across the road. "Holed up in that old claim. Them people moved away to Texas. An't nobody took it over, so them boys went in there."

"I saw 'em last night at sunset," said the oldest little girl. "They was chasing something."

"Hog, no doubt," said Mr. Welch. "Them folks didn't catch all their hogs before they left, and now the hogs had some shoats. There's hogs all around here."

I cleared my throat. "How many boys are there?"

"Half a dozen, maybe; maybe not quite."

"Good eaters, too," said the wife, ruefully.

"Did they, uh, did they threaten you with weapons?"

"They surely had 'em along. We could see that plain as day," said Mr. Welch. "They asked where our niggers were, and when we said we didn't have none, they didn't like that. But they didn't actually threaten us, and they an't crossed the road since."

"I wish they'd move on," said the woman. "Over supper, they said they was gonna go out to K.T., but they an't yet."

Now the both of them turned away. They were finished talking to me, and I remembered that I hadn't taken any notes of this conversation, as had been my plan, just to flourish my profession a bit. The wife went into the house and the husband into the shop again. The four little girls were now playing "statues," a game I had played endlessly as a child. I turned Athens and went out to the road, then turned back toward Kansas City, rode a few yards, and stopped to look at the cabin across the road. No sign of life. Of course, these were boys, so I pulled out my pocket watch. It wasn't even eight-thirty in the morning, so it could be they were sleeping. I put "my" watch carefully back in "my" pocket—I was suddenly painfully aware that I wasn't who I looked to be—and then I gave old Athens a kick in the ribs and rode across the road and into the yard, the way you do when you think, Why not? and then don't let yourself answer that question. A horse whinnied from behind the cabin, putting to flight my last little hope that the cabin was empty, but no shots rang out, no shouting, no descent of boys upon my helpless self.

Athens went of himself around the corner of the cabin, and I saw that four horses were confined to a corral in the back. Its fence was intact, but it looked like the rest of the fences had been cannibalized to repair that one. This wasn't much of a farm—underbrush had already encroached on the fields, and sure enough, a couple of half-grown hogs were rooting around out there, along with some crows and a few buzzards. I dismounted Athens, thinking I would look in a window, but the only opening was covered with oiled paper, not affording much of a view, so I finally made an end to my hesitation and went up the stoop and banged on the door. The good thing was that I had the sun at my back. I banged again. Athens, and my pistol, were right behind me. He practically had his foot on the step with mine. The door opened suddenly, and Athens threw up his head.

A young man with no clothes on except his drawers stood blinking in the doorway. He looked as surprised as I did, I'm sure, as he said, "G—— d——, that an't you, Clark! I thought—"

"Who the h——," shouted a voice from inside. "That Clark? I'm starvin'!"

"An't Clark!"

Now there were three young men in the door, in different states of undress, and the third one to come up had a pistol, which he cocked. I dropped Athens's reins, pushed the door open with my left hand, and stepped into the room, saying in my croak, "Boys! I'm here to make you famous! We heard about you in—in Saint Louis, and I come from the *Missouri Democrat* to find out your story! From there, who knows—maybe it'll go all around the country." I figured even these boys would be impressed by the most famous paper in the state.

"Saint Louis?" said one boy.

"Where's Clark?" said another.

But the boy with the pistol didn't say a thing. I continued, "We got an artist all ready to take your likeness and then make an etching of you, three heads"—I saw another one sitting up in his blankets on the floor—"four heads in one picture, and Clark, too, that's five." It was hard to talk fast in my croak and still be understood, and the boys were sleepy and didn't look like they were quite following me.

"Who're you?" said Pistol.

Well, I didn't quite remember just at that very minute. "Don't matter," I croaked. "You boys are the ones who matter. I'm just a reporter—"

"What's your name?" insisted Pistol.

It came to me. "Lyman. Lyman Arquette. I'm from Palmyra!"

"Haw!" said one of the boys. "I'm from Hanni-bal! You know the Smart family up there in Palmyra?"

I smiled, readying an evasion, but the boy in the bedclothes got up, saying, "Shut up, Lewis." To me, he said, "You get in here and shut the G—— d—— door!"

I did as I was told. Once the door was closed, two things were apparent to me: I was a little distant from my weapon and, depending on Athens, getting more so, and it was plenty dark inside the cabin, with only the sunlight coming through cracks in the chinking to see by. Even so, as my eyes adjusted, I could see that the boys weren't all boys. The last to get up, who seemed to be the leader, was my age (as a woman) or older, as was one of the others—they had thick beards. The one who'd opened the door was younger, maybe fourteen, and the one with the pistol was a lit-tle older than that, maybe sixteen. They were all unwashed, hirsute, and in poor flesh, and the air of the cabin was overpowering. This group didn't look either happy or healthy. I croaked, "You boys killed any abolitionists?"

"Almost had us one," said Lewis. "We laid in wait for him, and he come right along, jest the way we thought he would—"

"He'd been out nigger-stealin' that very night, I'll bet," exclaimed the youngest boy as he pulled on a pair of trousers.

"But he musta heard us, because when we come out into the road to stop him, he had his pistols out already, and he shot Mabee's horse, here! Can you believe that? He shot his horse right out from under him and run off. I call that lily-livered."

"Didn't even stand to fight!" said the youngest.

"That's the only one we've found," said Lewis, "but the next time, we'll be ready, because we know they an't real men you ken expect a good fight from, but you got to shoot 'em down like a dog!"

This time, I had my notebook out and was scribbling at it. The older men hadn't said anything, but they hadn't stopped the boys, either. I said, "Who's the captain here?" There was a long pause, and then Lewis said, "Mabee is." We all looked at Mabee, who nodded. I whispered, "Perhaps you can tell me a bit about your background, sir." He smiled at this and softened, and I saw that I had a natural talent for this newspaper business.

"I come up from Louisiana about a year ago. If you want to know, I was working a steamboat, but she run aground and wrecked, so I thought enough a that, I'm a horseman, anyway, not a riverman. And I was sorry to lose that mare. She was a Kentucky mare. You could turn her on a dime, and she could go like sixty. If I ever see that G—— d—— abolitionist again, I'll kill him for sure!"

Once Mabee was chattering, then the last holdout started chattering, too, and I got busy scribbling notes as fast as I could, mostly for show, though, as I was sure I wouldn't be able to read anything I'd written down in such dim light. But they had more to them than one little article, and I knew I wouldn't have much trouble with my composition. A good half hour or so went by, and then I said, "What's your plan, boys?"

A silence fell over the room, then Mabee said, "Cain't tell you that! Can we? We live a secret life!"

Now the volubility went out of them, and they glanced back and forth at one another, and then at me. It must have just been occurring to them that I intended to publish their story and reveal them to the world. After a minute, Lewis, who had struck me as the sharpest of the lot, said, "If we get famous and have our pictures in the paper, how are we gonna get the jump on abolitionists?"

They all thought for a moment. I said, "Abolitionists don't read our paper. Abolitionists can't abide our paper."

Mabee said, "What would happen, we'd have to leave this area and conduct our operations in K.T. I been thinkin' we should push off that way, anyhow, because right here we're livin' off our friends. We want to live off our enemies."

I whispered, "This would be a kind of farewell piece, then."

They all thought for a minute, then nodded. Lewis said, "You tell 'em we're gonna go raise h—— in K.T., haw haw!" I laughed at this joke, then moved toward the door. Mabee said, "Where ya goin' now?"

"Got to write my article and turn it in before three o'clock, or it can't be in this week's paper."

"What about the picture?"

Oh, that artist I had waiting. I said, "I got to bring him out here tomorrow. He didn't want to come along today because I didn't know if I'd find you."

Mabee stood up and opened the door a crack, then looked out carefully, then opened it the rest of the way. He said, "An't nobody out there. Okay. Now, you bring that fellow right here tomorrow, but not too early. We want to be dressed and in all our gear when he comes. We don't want to be greetin' no artist in our drawers, haw haw!"

We went out on the step, and he stared at me. I saw that Athens was grazing in the yard, maybe fifty feet from the door. Jeremiah, of course, would have looked up and walked over to me, but Athens just continued to graze. Mabee (Joseph, his given name was) said, "You talk funny, and you look funny, too."

I nodded.

"But you're all right, anyway." He looked at Athens, then at me. He said, "You got any money?"

Only then, for the first time, really, did I think of Frank among just such a crowd (though, of course, of a somewhat higher tone, being New Englanders and reading men). I had been terribly angry with him, angrier than I realized. Really, there was no telling what he was doing, was there? Or what he had heard; what he knew about Thomas, what he knew about me. I had expected Thomas's death to simply call him back, like some sort of resonance vibrating all over eastern K.T. I pulled the five dollars out of my pocket and handed it to him. A little guilt about Frank began to seep through my anger and color it.

Mabee said, "Thanks," almost graciously.

He turned and went back inside, closing the door behind himself, and I ran down across the yard and just about vaulted onto Athens, all my fears rushing up just then, as if they'd been held down by a lid before. Once we got out on the road, I made Athens trot as fast as he would go (he wouldn't gallop) for at least a mile, until I got among other folks and felt my fears subside a little. I pulled out my pocket watch. It was only a little after ten yet, and really, I didn't have to give Mr. Morton my article for a day or so; I saw that now was the time to try a bit of investigating on my own project. I had Athens for the rest of the day if I didn't go back to the newspaper right away, and I thought saloons, where Missourians drank all day every day, and boasted the whole time, would probably be the place to start. After that, I thought, I might go back to the paper and sit at a desk and write my article, my ears pricked the whole time. I don't have to tell the reader that I had never been in a saloon before, but then I was no longer much daunted by doing things that I had never done before. They all said that K.T. coarsened a woman, but there was nothing for coarsening a woman quite like having her become a man!

I'd been warned all my life about low company. My father, for example, of necessity kept low company of the buying-and-selling, river-character sort, and by the time I was a child in our house in Quincy, I was aware that there were numbers of times when my mother and I would keep to her room while my father entertained low company downstairs. As I got older, though, and my father got a bit more prosperous, he found ways to keep the low company elsewhere. As my sisters grew older, they, too, were alert as terriers on the subject of low company. Each of their husbands' positions in life were a degree or two above my father's, and they were eager to make the most of the difference, especially Harriet, who was, and who saw herself as, the wife of a landowner (farmer if you absolutely had to look at it that way). Harriet sometimes acted as if the threshold of low company began with anything commercial (including Beatrice's husband, Horace, and his father), as if she had never bought or sold anything in her life. When I got to K.T., low company was everywhere in evidence—the Missourians were the very type of low company—and Mrs. Bush, and to a lesser extent, Mrs. Jenkins, and even Louisa, were conscious of their elevation as New Englanders. In short, low company was a sort of poison ivy that could infect a lady any number of ways, and if it did, the effects were both painful and evident to all. Without having a very clear picture of the pastimes of low company, or how they could hurt me, I felt a decided moral dread when I had ridden back into Kansas City and saw a saloon, and knew I must go into it and then linger there, and even ask questions. The closest thing in my experience that my feeling of reluctance came to was the moment of entering the Mississippi River that time I swam across it—the skin, the sinews, the brain, the heart, all recoiled against any such immersion. I opened the door and went in, my hand in my pocket, holding Thomas's watch for courage.

The low company numbered about eight men, including a profoundly bearded man behind a long table to one side. The room was grand in size but dimly lit, and furnished, like all of Kansas City, with an assortment of castoffs from other entrepreneurs and citizens who had gone out of business, moved on to other parts, backtracked, or died. A few of the men were sitting around a table playing cards, one of the principal occupations of low company. One man was sitting alone at another table, a pair of glasses in front of him, one full, the other empty, and two others were standing in front of the long table, chatting with the bearded man, who was dispensing whiskey, no doubt so highly rectified as to put his customers at risk for spontaneous combustion. Every single one looked up when I came in. This was another feature of low company—it was always inquisitive and unable to mind its own business.

"Hello, son," said the man behind the long table, who was, of course, the bartender, though I didn't know this term at the time.

I remembered to whisper my hello, and to touch my throat, then appear to try to whisper a bit more loudly: "Hello!"

Another man said, "Oscar, give the boy a drink. He sounds a little dry!" Everyone in the room laughed.

"Come 'ere, boy," said the bartender. "I'll give you a glass of water."

"Now, Oscar, water an't gonna kill the frog in that boy's throat. You give him a dose of that mule sweat you call whiskey, and that'll set 'im up right!"

"Hanson, I an't gonna give no boy whiskey, and you know it, especially a boy like this one, who looks like he should be home with his mama. How old are you, boy?"

"Sixteen," I croaked.

"Well, you're tall, but you an't sixteen. Fourteen more'n likely." He set a glass of water, of the usual kind, thick on the bottom and thin on the top, in front of me. I drank off the top and set it down again.

"Now, see," said Hanson. "You talk about your water, but drinking whiskey in this territory is just self-preservation, pure and simple. You see, whiskey's been distilled. That means there an't nothin' in it but whiskey. There an't no mud in it!" He held up his glass appreciatively. "You ken see all the way through it! G—— d——, but I hate the taste of mud!"

"What do you need, son?" said the bartender.

"Well, I just come into the city, and I'm looking for my pa, my uncle, and my cousin, and here's the fix I'm in. I know they changed their name, and I don't know what the new name is!"

"What was the old name, son?"

"Well, it was Miller." I leaned over the table and

whispered in the bartender's ear. "But my ma heard from some folks that they killed them a G—— d—— abolitionist and had to change the name, but you see, now my ma is sick, she had a baby that died, and she might die herself, and so I got to find them!"

The bartender looked hard at me, his beard and eyebrows both shading and setting off his piercing gaze. I gripped Thomas's watch and held the stare as best I could.

One of the other men called out, "What'd he say, Oscar? Cain't have secrets in an establishment like this, haw haw!"

The bartender kept looking at me but said, "Deal 'em out, Hawley, and watch your cards. That's your business!"

Everyone laughed.

Finally, he said to me, "Kansas City is a big place, son, and lots of folks are coming and going all the time. I an't heard of nobody like you're talking about."

"It's been about a month or more since we heard about the shooting."

The bartender shrugged his shoulders, then said, "Now you better go on, son." He nodded toward the door, and pretty soon I was out of it.

There was a similar establishment down the street and across, and after checking on Athens, I went there.

This place had two bartenders, one fat and one thin, two tables of gamblers, and some steady whiskey drinkers. It also had a woman, most likely a harlot, as my sisters would say, but respectably dressed. She came over to me with a smile and said, "Are you looking for someone, dear?"

Now, I have to say that this was the first time I had tried out my disguise on a woman, and it disconcerted me to do so. She looked me up and down quite frankly, but she hid what she was inspecting with her steady smile and receptive demeanor. I whispered, "I'm looking for my pa and some other relations."

"Pardon me, dear?"

I tried a bit harder, careful to deepen my croak as much as possible. I was unsure about that "dear." "I got some relations who—"

Her smile changed, became more amused. I was sure all at once that she knew I was a woman, and so began backing out of the saloon, saying, "Thanks." When I got through the door, I turned and walked very quickly down to the corner and around it. After a moment, I stopped, went back to the corner, and peered into the street that bar was in, but the woman had not come out. When I thought about it, I couldn't imagine what she might do even if she did recognize my sex. Proclaim it to the world? A man of the west, especially a Missourian, certainly would do so. In K.T., there had been regular stories of humiliations: a man wouldn't take a drink, and so the other men in the saloon bullied him until he either drank or pulled out his pistol and shot someone; a man on a steamboat wouldn't remove his hat, and another man ragged on him until he removed his hat, to reveal a knife in it. Men of the west liked to enforce social regularity with lots of yelling and insisting. Those who didn't participate liked to watch to see what might happen. But I didn't think that woman would have done anything, except maybe give me a sign. I was tempted to go back and find out—she'd had a warm smile, to tell the truth, and a longing for friendship suddenly smote me, but you couldn't have a letting down when you were in disguise. It made things too complicated.

There was another saloon in the side street where I was standing—no doubt every man in the state was guaranteed by law to a glass and a place at some bar or another—and so I went in there. This one was very dark. It was an old log structure, about twice the size of a claim cabin, with but two small windows, on either side of the door. It took some moments for my eyes to adjust to the dim light after I went in. The darkness gave me a spooky feeling. I could hear and sense others in there but couldn't tell, really, how many or what they were doing. The bartender greeted me and said, "Step to your right, sir. The bar's to your right."

I whispered, "You need some light in here."

"Well, sir, our patrons rather prefer this." He had an English accent. "It's a relief from the outer glare, you know."

"Oh."

"Whiskey?"

No doubt he couldn't see how young I was. Or maybe he didn't care.

"Sure," I said. "But mostly I'm looking for someone."

"A gentleman of the imbibing sort?"

"Pardon me?"

"Is your quarry a drinking man?"

"Oh. Yes."

"Name?"

"They changed their name. They killed an abolitionist over in K.T. back in June."

"Indeed! And what do you want with these brave
fellows?" The bartender's whisper had come to
match mine, which seemed appropriate in such a
spot.

"One of 'em's my pa, and the other two's my
uncle and my cousin. My ma wants 'em."

"Well, now," he said, and set a very small glass of
whiskey in front of me. I looked at it. He said, "Will
you be needing to chase that, then?"

"Pardon me?"

"Do you prefer to chase your shot of whiskey
with a drink of water?"

"Oh. No, thanks."

Another customer came up to the bar, and the
bartender walked off into the shadows. I glanced
around. No one seemed to be nearby, so I lifted the
shot glass to my mouth and touched the liquid in it
with my tongue. That or the fumes rising off the liquid sent me into a coughing fit. The bartender
returned.

"Unaccustomed to a fine malt, then?" he said.

I continued to cough, and he took away my shot
and poured it into a bucket under the bar. I shuddered
to think what would become of whatever was in that
bucket. Certainly, in Missouri, it would not go to
waste.

"Well, now. Tell me a bit more about these members of your family. Men of strong belief and ready action, then, like all the chivalry? Where are you from?"

"Palmyra, Missouri."

"Hmm."

"My cousin's the easiest to distinguish. He's about my height, got a pale moon face. Blue eyes, brown hair about down to his shoulders. My pa and my uncle look about alike. They got dark beards and long dark hair."

"That brings so many to mind, you know."

But I sensed that he did know something.

I said, mimicking pride, "An't everybody's shot a G—— d—— abolitionist, though! And my uncle an't a bashful sort. He would of talked about it."

"Many talk about it who haven't actually performed the deed, however."

I hadn't thought of that. The Englishman walked away again, and I adjusted my braces, which I had fixed up a bit better but which were still a nuisance. I was beginning to be able to distinguish things in the dim light, but clearly this was not a saloon where men did anything but drink quietly, their glasses at their fingertips. Any of the other customary Missouri pastimes—gambling, shooting, teasing, bragging, and even spitting—would be nearly impossible in here. The bartender and another man now approached me, and the bartender said, "Allow me to present Mr. Beaumont Pollifax, who prefers the appellation 'River Snake—' "

"I comes up quick and I comes up silent, and

sometimes I passes you by, and sometimes"—he leaned close to my face—"I bites!"

"Mr. Snake accords us the honor of his custom at our establishment every day, but we are not the only ones, because he maintains what you might call a route or a round that takes in something on the order of eight or ten establishments of all varieties and characters. Mr. Snake does seem to remember two men and a boy boasting of shooting a man in Kansas Territory who held sentiments that were repugnant to their own—"

"Now," said the River Snake, "it was toward dark, because I saw them as they was goin' in, and I was goin' in at the same time, and I noted that the sun was a-settin', because, you know, you got to get yourself right every day, or you can get all turned around. Once, I got to a point where I was so turned around thet I was awake when I couldn't get no whiskey, and I swore . . ." He trailed off, then looked at me, then said, "Well, if it was about dark, then I would of been goin' into the California—"

"Which is situated down by the river," said the bartender.

"And Joab, who's down there—"

"Employed in serving up refreshment for the patrons—"

"He been there a year or more, and you know, he never takes a drop, so he would remember everything them boys had to say. But they was pleased with themself, I'll say!"

I must have gasped, for I felt an inner constriction that was almost a swoon at the thought of their pleasure. The bartender turned a frankly inquisitive look upon me and said, "Plenty of the rougher sort down there, you know. Some of us hesitate to go amongst them."

"Them Kickapoo Rangers they had useta come down there," recollected the River Snake. "I stayed away from them boys while they was comin' in there. Almost decided to keep away from the California altogether, but it don't do to change your ways. That's how I got turned around that time."

I said, or croaked, "May I buy you a whiskey, Mr. Snake?"

"Well," he said, "anybody may buy me a whiskey. An't often anybody does, though, haw haw!"

The bartender poured out another of those little glasses, and the River Snake picked it up and seemed to throw it into his own face, except that his mouth was open to receive it. He then said, "Whew! Well, son, I'll walk ya down there, even though it's early in the day. I do believe I need a change."

I said, "Thank you, Mr. Snake."

The bartender watched us hard, his eyes following us out the door.

The sunshine of afternoon nearly knocked me over. The River Snake actually staggered, but he caught himself, then said, "Son, I don't know if I kin make it down there this time of day, but let me give it a try."

"I need to get my horse."

"That would be good. That'd be very good."

When I brought Athens over, the River Snake

leaned against him, and he half turned his face into the horse's shoulder as we walked slowly along. I would say that we made a strange picture, but that would imply that someone among the teeming busy throngs of Kansas City was looking at us.

At the California, the River Snake seemed to revive. At any rate, he woke up, told me to stay outside, opened the door, and returned a moment later with the bartender, who was all business. He certainly did remember that party of men, he said, as if he prided himself on his excellent memory and was pleased to show it off. Two bearded men and a beardless boy. "They was celebratin' a blow struck against the evil interloper," said the bartender.

"Was one of 'em named . . ." Nothing came to me, and then: "Abel?"

"Well, I don't know about that. One of 'em called another one 'Samson,' but I don't know if that was the given name or the last name, and they used the name Chaney, too, I think." That could be either, also, I realized.

But I was amazed at the success of my investigation. I had the wit to put a few coins in the bartender's hand, as a gesture toward the River Snake, and then to croak out my thanks, but after that, all I could do was get on Athens and give the old boy a kick. We trotted. Samson and Chaney! Samson and Chaney! Yes, of course! I could see them all the better now! I expected them to rise up in front of me on the street, their misdeeds written all over them, and recognition of me, the pale and screaming wife (Had I screamed? Had I not screamed? Perhaps only they knew), transforming their pleasure in themselves into fear and guilt. Ha! Or, as the Missourians said, haw haw!

Back at the newspaper office, I sat quietly at a desk and wrote my article. From time to time, I referred for stylistic models to the copies of old papers that were lying about in stacks. My article ran as follows:

As our friends are aware, our struggle against the thieves and murderers of the so-called Free State party takes many forms. Though most southern-rights sympathizers are good law-and-order men (however their patience is tried by the creeping slowness of the judiciary in Kansas), extreme elements do and must exist, for the sentiments of active and loyal southerners must have their outlet. Everyone knows that vigilance committees, who would seize the law and make righteousness their own, are frequently proposed by even the soberest men, whose patience has been sorely tried by the devilish antics of the so-called Free State party. Few should be surprised, then, that certain small groups of men, young men, have formed themselves around the territory and that they are only waiting for the opportunity of making a name for themselves.

Your correspondent, himself a young man, went out recently and beat the countryside in search of one of these elusive bands, in order to bring you news of their doings and of the sort of lives these young soldiers of the southern cause have been leading. We are not aware that any news of these young men has been printed in any other newspaper in the territory, and so all of their doings have the added interest of *mystery*.

I found five men, I will not say where, I will not say how, except to remark that their neighbors knew them, and were grateful for the protection their presence in the neighborhood afforded. I understood that a sixth was away from the camp on a provisioning expedition. Of the five present, Captain Joseph Mabee was clearly in command. Captain Mabee is a tall son of the deep south, Louisiana to be precise. Both circumstance and conviction brought him to our area—the circumstance being employment on a riverboat, the conviction being loyalty to honorable southern principles of freedom under the law. A fine horseman, Captain Mabee was especially grieved at the recent loss of his lovely mare to a ball from the gun of an abolitionist thief. He averred that he would most likely not be able to find or afford such a mount again, in spite of the excellent reputation of horseflesh in our area.

The other four members of the party shall remain nameless, in accordance with the demands of their chosen field of battle. Suffice it to say that of these men and boys (two were not above eighteen years old), two were native Missourians, one was a son of our sister state to the south, Arkansas, and one, a native Ohioan, came over to the pro-southern side because he was so disgusted with the deeds of the so-called Free State party. He said to me,

"They call themselves Americans, but I don't see it." None of these young soldiers could be said to be possessed of an education, but all have a rough eloquence as they discuss their adventures so far.

The group has been together since the Pottawatomie massacre in Kansas Territory, which all men know took place in May, shortly after the successful campaign of our forces against the abolitionist hellhole of Lawrence. These honorable young men were so outraged by those Pottawatomie murders that they felt they could not live without acting against the sort of criminals and madmen that were coming into the territory from the northern states. They therefore left their happy homes, much to the distress of each of their mothers, knowing that perhaps they would not soon see their families again but that the cause was a just one and that, at any rate, it had gotten their blood up so that they could sit by no longer. Three of the young men were friends, and two came in later.

As to their present style of life, it is, of course, rough and not without deprivation. From time to time, their neighbors offer them a good meal. Otherwise, they fall back upon their own cooking. They have been given shirts, boots, and even a pair of pants by grateful southerners, and the captain has been promised another mount to replace his much-lamented long-legged bay mare. In the meantime, the camp is full of the excellent fellowship that grows out of an active conscience satisfied by an active life. And the band is making plans to move against the enemy in the enemy's own territory, though how soon this will take place, your correspondent is not at liberty to reveal.

There are those among us who revile and deplore such groups as these, and it is true that they stand outside the law, but do they stand outside of moral righteousness? No one can deny that they answer a need felt in every breast for some stronger reply to the depredations of the so-called Free State party. We may wish the necessity for them gone, but in the meantime, we certainly wish them well!

Mr. Morton read this through, holding the paper close to his face and tapping his spectacles on the desk instead of positioning them on his nose, and afterward pronounced the writing "satisfactory but not bold enough. However, it will do for a first effort. Franklin can set it in type. He'll show you that part of the business one of these days." He patted me on the back. I smiled and nodded, and went outside.

I have to say that the composition of this piece put me into a welter of strong feelings. I had taken it up, still pleased with my discovery of "Samson" and "Chaney," in something of a playful humor. What you've got when you go in disguise are some feelings that belong to your original self and some feelings that belong to your new self and are feigned feelings in many ways, but some of these feelings overlap, and it's a job trying to keep them separate and identified. I thought my disguised self could go

ahead and write up those boys' story in the style of
Mr. Morton's paper and that it would remain outside
of me, like the hat or the boots I had stolen on the
boat. But what I found out was that my piece had a
way of talking back to me. Every lie I put down on
the paper made a claim, and every claim those lies
made, made me mad. But I couldn't seem to stop
them. They ran right down the pages, one after
another, each sentence that was a lie bringing forth
the next one, until I got to the end. The truth seemed
to protest, but it couldn't really get in there. There
wasn't a place for it, for one thing, and my project
couldn't afford it, for another. I had to grip Thomas's
watch pretty strongly while I was writing the second-
to-last paragraph, and pull it out and set it on the
desk, right under my gaze, while I was writing the
last paragraph. And then, to make it all the more
complicated and hard to take, when I reread the piece
I couldn't help being a little proud of it. It didn't tell
much of a story, but there were some nice turns of
phrase in it, and I was a bit insulted at Mr. Morton's
estimation of it. But then, after what you might call
the flood of writing had ebbed a bit, I was ashamed of
the sentiments it portrayed and also of how I thought
it would make people feel when they read it. But
then, after that, I was still a little proud of actually
having written something other than a letter, and
even of knowing that it was going to be set in type
and printed out. Ah, it was all a tangle, and it made
me want to run off to get away from it, but I couldn't
even do that, as I still had "Samson" and "Chaney" to
uncover before Mr. Morton asked me to write him

another piece and get myself into an even thicker tangle.

I felt very heavy and tired as I mounted the stairs to the newspaper office yet again, and thoughts of Thomas kept at bay by the perturbations of the day flooded over me. They were not good thoughts. What I saw was him turning away, him disappearing, him refusing to favor me with any conversation. It didn't matter that I had experienced such a thing only once, the evening of the horse race. Now I could not stop thinking of it.

It was late in the day, almost suppertime, and I was hungry, but there were quite a few men around the office and I wanted to mingle with them in spite of my low spirits. There was the chance someone might mention Samson and Chaney, but in addition to that, there was the news from K.T. I should say that I had my days in Kansas City right at the end of July, and so, while much was brewing that would boil over two or three weeks later, just at that time folks were more occupied with threats than they were with actual fighting. The threats always gave you the feeling that fighting could commence at any moment, so for a certain sort of fellow, there was always, in that humid air, the invigorating tingle that comes of anticipation. Men kept their weapons right beside them, loaded. They took their pistols into their hands, looked at them, cocked them, gave themselves up to the thought of shooting them off, or did shoot them—out the window, into the sky. I hadn't seen this sort of behavior in Lawrence, and I recognized how my old friends like Mrs. Bush would nod their heads knowingly: just the sort of thing she would expect of the Ruffians. The noise of these shots, which punctuated the otherwise noisy passage of the day like random strikings of a town clock, made everyone both irritable and exhilarated. "Haw, ya missed!" someone would shout, or "Save it for them abolitionists!" or just "Hey!" If the shot was close at hand, well, you had to recoil, but sometimes, if you were engrossed in something, you would just know that there had been a shot, but you wouldn't yourself have heard it. In short, we got habituated to it but were stirred up all the same. However, Mr. Morton didn't like anyone shooting off his pistols in the office, because it hindered the concentration of the typesetters and made them drop their forms.

All the talk in the office was of Jim Lane and his army. There had been much discussion of this army back in Lawrence, too, and we had known for sure that it was a significant force—four or five hundred men, well armed and well trained and all for the Free State cause. There were even said to be some regular West Point officers ("only one or two, but that can make a difference," Charles had said) attached to this army somehow ("not *exactly* in an official capacity"), and folks in Lawrence had felt particular reassurance in this, as if these men were going to take over the leadership of Lawrence now that Governor Robinson and nearly everyone else we had depended upon was gone or taken. I was so certain of these particulars that I still distinctly recollect the first rumor I heard in the offices of the *Freeman* that challenged them. I was sitting in my former seat by the cold stove, arranging myself in an attitude of manly repose, when behind me I heard a voice scoff, "Well, they an't much, that's what them boys said. Half of 'em are sick with a fever and half of 'em are women and young 'uns. Some army, haw!"

"There was a boy I knew back in Indiana who knew Lane. Haw! He was the same then! All talk! And his pa, too. The two of them, they could look at two scrawny heifers in a field and call 'em a herd of milk cows!"

I sat up.

"Anyway, some boys from Lawrence went out and rode up there and parleyed with Lane and said he couldn't bring his army—haw—into Kansas—"

"Too humiliatin'!"

"So—listen to this—he bawled!"

"Naw!"

"Yessir! He bawled like a baby and said that if the folks of K.T. didn't want him, then he would take his services elsewhere. What do you think of that?"

The two men couldn't stop laughing. Another man came over, chuckling, and said, "Yep. And now he's gone! Left his army—haw—in Nebraska and run off!" Now there was general laughter. I managed a big grin, just to keep in with them, but I found this news unaccountably alarming. The laughter grated on my sensibility so that I had to get up and walk about. The men in the newspaper office were great ones for spitting, and what with that and the litter and the ink and the mud of boots, the floor of the office was filthy. But now that I was a man, I didn't mind such things all that much anymore. I strolled around and contemplated this as a way of distracting myself from the bad news of home. The fact was, with Governor Robinson in prison, Lane had been the only one doing anything. Even folks with long-standing doubts of his competency, or his sanity, had come around to him over the summer, just because he was busy and we needed someone to be busy. But if these stories were true, then he showed himself to be a fool. And I knew they were true, because he had showed himself to be a fool before.

Someone noticed me, one of the other men who wrote for the paper. He was a wiry little man with a large head, on which he had pushed his hat far back. He said, "What's your name, son?"

I whispered, "Arquette. Lyman Arquette."

"That's right, you got some affliction with your voice box. Jack told me about it. Well, you done a good job on your piece, son. I read it. Now, some of us newspapermen, we take different names to write under, and Franklin wants to know what name you want on your piece, here." Franklin was the typesetter.

I croaked, "Different names?"

"Well, yeah. Now, I got three names I write under. One is my own, another is 'A Bona Fide Westerner,' and the third is 'Irascible.' That's for when I really get goin', you know, and my words are a little hot. Fact is, these three names got three different personalities, and I can get three articles into one paper if I have to, and nobody knows that I wrote 'em all. We all do. I may say that most of the time I can tell about the others, but most of the time they cain't tell about me. I could have four or five names if I wanted, but Jack don't like that. Anyway—"

"Lyman Arquette is fine."

"Now, boy, take it from me, you got to cover yourself a bit here. My suggestion is 'Young and Eager,' or some such thing. 'Young and Loyal to the Cause,' mebbe. Gives you a character, don't ya know, and makes it easier to write your piece, if you ask me." He tucked his thumbs in his braces and rocked back on his heels. "It's tempting to see your own name in print, but out here it's a little dangerous."

"How about Thomas Newton?" I don't know why I betrayed Thomas in this way, except that he was very much in my mind all the time, and it was a pleasure to say his name aloud.

"Now, that's downright dull, son. Say, though, what about 'Isaac Newton'? You heard of him, right? You put that on your piece, and folks'll pay attention to it, even if they don't know who he is or what he did. Most of 'em have heard that name and know he was something."

And so my piece was published under the name "Isaac Newton."

And Mr. Morton, joking, took to calling me "Sir."

I heard nothing of Chaney or Samson that evening, and by and by I was so hungry that I couldn't stay anymore but went off to find something to eat for my supper.

Back at the livery stable, I had hidden my case in what had appeared to be a disused trunk of some sort, in which there were dusty bits of harness and a blanket or two. I found it sure enough, but as I was pulling it out, thinking distractedly of Thomas, the Negro man who oversaw the place came up behind me and put his hand on my arm.

I started, set my case down, and turned around.

"Nah, young massa, ya cain't sleep heah na mah." This surprised me, since he hadn't said anything when I'd taken Athens away.

I shook my head, pretending to understand him less than I actually did.

"Got ta be off, massa. This is Massa Harry's livery. Ain' nabody 'lowed to sleep in da hay. You done it once, but I ain' gonna 'low it agin."

I croaked, "I'll help you with the horses."

"You sick, young massa?" He stepped back.

I put my hand to my throat—this was almost a reflex by now, and anyway, croaking was making my throat a little raw. "No, just hurt myself when I was a baby. I can help you throw out the hay to the animals and clean up. I don't want to get in a room with anybody."

"Well," said the man, "they's plenty o' drunks about."

I felt in my pocket and pulled out a dollar, but the man turned his head, then said, "Massa Harry don' like me to have no cash money. Ifn he was to find it on me, he'd think I was planning to run for sure." Then he eyed me closely and said, "You got a petticoat in your case, theah."

"I do?" I whispered.

"Well, you done lef' the case, so I spied into it."

"I don't mind." But I did, though only because I thought that he would know I was a woman. But he wasn't looking at me at all closely, as a few others had, and he said, "You got a use fo' dat petticoat?"

"No, not exactly."

"Well, my gal would love dat thing."

"How long can I stay, then?" I worked up a pretty loud croak.

"Long as you like, long as you keep out of Massa Harry's way. You kin spy him out easy enough, 'cause he weahs an eye patch and leans on a stick. He don' come around much, but he's mad when he do."

"Why's that?"

"Well, he's mad all the time. Missy says he done got hit on the haid sometime. I don' know."

"Shall I help you with the horses? I'm fond of horses."

"Nah. Dat petticoat's enough. I got mah ways heah, an' Massa Harry, he got a way o' knowin' ifn I'm workin' enough. He figures if I ain' workin' enough, then I'm plannin'."

"Don't be planning," I whispered suddenly.

"I ain' plannin'. Mah gal's up to Lexington. I ain' gonna run from dat gal!"

I didn't know who had urged the man not to plan, whether it was Lidie or Lyman. I said, "What's your name?"

"Nehemiah."

"Thank you, Nehemiah. I am L—Mr. Lyman." I caught myself, because although Thomas would have invited the man, clearly a slave, to call him Thomas, Lyman, of Palmyra, Missouri, would certainly have not. I opened my case and pulled out my petticoat. Nehemiah took it, looked it over, balled it up, and thrust it under his arm with a friendly smile. I smiled back at him, realizing that I understood him readily now; his way of talking just took a little getting used to. He said, "Nah I'se turnin' in fo de night. You bettah sleep back in da corner theah. Ain' nobody gonna see you back theah." And he went off.

Even though it had been a long day, I sat up in the hay for quite some time, marveling at my new situation and listening to the horses chewing and grunting nearby. In such an unpeaceful place, they made only peaceful sounds.

CHAPTER 21

Lyman Arquette Finds Success

It is a well known fact, that mental excitement tends to weaken the physical system, unless it is counter-balanced by a corresponding increase of exercise and fresh air.

—p. 43

THINGS WENT ON in this way for three more days. Each night, I came back to the livery rather late, after Nehemiah had made himself scarce, and in the morning I left with the first light. The angry Master Harry was a man I did not want to run into. Cane, eye patch: meeting such a fellow was not an alluring prospect. I continued to linger at the newspaper office, hoping for another chance to ride Athens, but Mr. Morton had enough articles for his next edition, what with all the news of Lane's army, and so he gave me to Franklin, who taught me to set type. I had the same trouble with setting type that I'd always had with sewing: my fingers were big and clumsy, and the fine work made me fidget and squirm. Franklin, of course, started me on headlines and advertisements, lots of white space and few words. It was tedious, but at least laying the words and letters into the forms backwards meant that I wasn't as aware of what the articles were saying. In fact, setting type was not unlike making tiny stitches—minute and repetitive but aiming for speed. And I had to concentrate, so that the passing conversation in the office escaped me, and I fell into contemplating any new life in a rather dreamlike fashion. I was not afraid. Something about the handiwork of it lulled my fears. I knew what they would be if I had them, though—not fears for my safey, nor even fears of discovery, but something more primitive and simple, like vertigo. I could not believe how I had rushed about for those first two days of my manhood: now that I was quiet, I intimidated myself. Existing inside of Lyman Arquette was much harder when all I had to do was grunt and pick type than ever it had been when I had to talk, and ride, and interview, and saunter about upon the street. This was when I almost gave it up—not when I had to exert myself, but when I didn't.

After three days, as July turned into August, I felt time pressing on me, and I resolved to come up with another plan if I was given nothing more to do besides setting type on the following Monday. It was now Friday evening. As I was walking to the livery stable a little earlier than usual, I saw a boy of about my age (as Lyman) with a case of peaches on the back of his wagon. He was selling them to passersby for a dime apiece, as much as a meal in some parts of town, but they looked about as bright and peachy as a peach could look, and I reflected that three of them would make supper enough for that night. I handed him my thirty cents, and he told me that for another nickel I could have a fourth, so I put one in my pocket for Nehemiah, should I see him.

I was thinking about Thomas when I turned the next corner, just before the livery, and almost saying to him that I couldn't go on with this, that it would be far better to go back to K.T. and find Frank, when I saw Master Harry, and Master Harry was angry indeed. He had a buggy pulled up by the Nehemiah horse pen, with a team of chestnuts hitched to it, and he was sitting on the seat with his wife beside him. Her head was turned down and away, and I could hear him shouting. Well, to tell you the truth, I couldn't resist. I was curious, and so I strolled by as though I had no business with the livery and didn't know Nehemiah at all.

"Boy, I told you them folks owed me for six weeks on them two mules!"

"They tole me they done paid, Massa Harry, an' they showed me a paper!"

"They didn't get no paper from me! Cain't you recognize my hand?"

"No, suh. Yes, suh. Well, it did look like yo' hand, suh. I reckon they tricked me, suh—"

Master Harry brandished his stick as if to strike Nehemiah, and his wife gasped, then said, "Harry, dear! For mercy's sake, not in the public street!"

He turned on her. "May I strike my property, ma'am, and discipline him?"

"Yes, Harry, but—"

"I said, '*May I discipline my own property, or are we living in Massachusetts now?*' "

"Yes, of course, Harry!"

"W*ell,* then." But he lowered the stick.

"Them Samsons done me out of twelve dollars! That's all your gal's food for a year, Nehemiah."

"No, suh! She a good gal! She work hard and

keep a bright face on, everybody say so, don't she, Missy Sarah?"

"Yes, Nehemiah, but—" The woman cast a fearful glance at the glowering countenance of her husband, which seemed to pulsate with anger and swell around the band that held the eye patch in place. She took a deep breath. "Nehemiah, of course Master Harry may do as he likes with Josie. You know that."

The look on Nehemiah's face was a complex one—sadness and fear and anger, too, though he was trying to conquer that, and over everything a veneer of respect. He dipped his head. I had slowed down, but now Master Harry was looking at me, so I sped up and walked around the corner into the next street, where I stopped and clutched that one word to my bosom. The Samsons! The Samsons had cheated Master Harry!

I waited in the shadow of one of the buildings there until I saw master and missy drive past, her with her bonnet pulled way forward and him whipping the chestnuts into a brisk trot. Then I ran back around the corner. Nehemiah was nowhere to be seen. I looked about, then called his name, and after a moment, he came from behind the shed. Without saying anything, I held out one of the peaches to him, and with only a brief hesitation, he took it and bit into it. There was a box there, turned on its side next to the corral, and I sat down on it. Nehemiah said nothing until he had finished his peach and sucked the last bits of juice off the pit. Then he said, "Missy won' let 'im hurt my gal. She loves my gal lak her own sissy."

"Is Josie your wife?" I whispered.

"Nah. She mah own gal. Her ma were Lil. She passed on yeahs ago."

I handed him another peach. After a bite of that, he said, "Dat waren't bad for Massa Harry. He been a lot worse den dat sometimes. He done shot his own brother, you know. Dem boys had a duel, and Massa Jacob got kilt. It 'bout kilt the old missy. She didn't last long after dat. She preferred Massa Jacob over Massa Harry, but dey waren't much daylight between de two of 'em, ifn you ask me. Dey was both hotheaded little boys. But Massa Jacob, he kiss her an' hug her, and Massa Harry, he push her away, so she saw it her way."

"What did they duel over?" I whispered.

"Somethang. Over bein' brothers, you ask me. Never did git along. Dey was lookin' fo' dat fight all dey lives."

He licked off the pit and put it in his pocket, and I handed him the third peach. They certainly did look delicious, I must say. I croaked, "Who are the Samsons?"

"Oh, *dem* boys!" He laughed.

"Well, they got you in trouble."

"Dey *is* trouble. Dey from over by Blue Sprang, theahabouts. Dem boys gonna be hung someday."

"Is there a boy named Chaney with them?"

"Don' know 'bout dat."

"When did they leave their mules here?"

"Well, dey come through with a bunch of animals a month or so ago. Couple mules, three or four horses, and dey put dem horses and mules up heah, and dey give me fi' dollars. Well, dat's enough fo' one week heah ifn yo is a stranger and Massa Harry don' know ya. He know dem, so he let dey old horse stay heah, four bits a week. Den dey rode off for a piece, den dey come back, and I say to dem dat dey owe fi' mo' dollars, and dey gi' me three, and dere wagon fo' what dey call security, and de wagon's settin' out heah, right wheah we sittin' nah. Well, one mornin', I gits heah an' dat wagon is long gone, and den about a week later, I see it comin' down the street, and I speak to de niggah who's drivin' it, and he say his massa done bought it faih and squaah, and dat massa, who war from Kentuck and new in town, he show Massa Harry de bill o' sale, an' a rifle an' a pistol and a long knife and a big evil grin, and so dat was dat for Massa Harry!" Nehemiah let out a big rolling laugh.

"Were there two men and a boy?"

"Nah, dey was three or four men. But dey was only two men who come by heah two day ago and git dem mules. They showed me a paper! Ha ha ha! I war a fool fo' dem! Ha ha ha!" The extortion of funds from Massa Harry cheered us both. I offered him the last peach, but he covered his mouth, gave a discreet eructation, and shook his head. I ate it myself. It was sublime, perhaps because I'd gotten some information, or perhaps because I found myself sublimely angry at Master Harry, the very type of a southern slavocrat villain, and exactly the sort of person Thomas thought peopled the south.

The thing, of course, was to go to Blue Springs. I knew that now. Even if these Samsons weren't the ones I was after, they might be cousins. Samson wasn't so common a name; it was less common than Newton, or Harkness. In all of Quincy, for example, we had been the only Harknesses. If someone had come looking for any of us, all of us would have known where to find the others. I briefly pondered persuading Mr. Morton that I needed to use Athens on newspaper business, as Blue Springs (I asked around) was twenty-five or thirty miles east, past Independence. But were I to find my Samsons, then there could be some difficulty in returning Athens to his owner. Additionally, I wasn't sure, either, that Athens would benefit by a thirty-mile trip or that I couldn't go faster, in the end, than he. Athens was an agreeable mount in his way, but I felt that I had fairly well plumbed his willingness to exert himself. And then another day of setting type confirmed my own reluctance to proceed any further in the newspaper business. Some other branch of letters, I thought, might be more to my taste. I mentioned this to Mr. Morton, by way of parting, and he laughed and handed me three dollars. "Typesetting always shakes 'em out," he remarked. I thanked him for giving me a try. As I walked down the long staircase to the street, I felt myself wake up.

When I returned to the livery stable that evening, a Saturday it was, I planned to probe Nehemiah a bit further about these Samsons, but he was nowhere to be found, and anyway, my conviction that they and Thomas's killers were the same men already approached certainty.

All the distractions of Kansas City and my new

life as a man did not at all deflect me from my sense that everything swirled around Thomas's killing and the justice to be exacted, as a ball on a rope swirls around the boy spinning in the center. Although I had never been a woman of much religious sentiment, I had faith in this—that every event and every step I might make must lead from Thomas to his killers, just as the engines and cars on rail tracks must lead from one station to the next. The distractions that beset, and even intrigued, both Lyman Arquette and Lidie Newton were entirely exterior to that. And so I got up early Sunday morning, pulled on my hat and boots, took up my case, and set out for Blue Springs. I had some biscuits that I saved from my supper the night before, and I ate them as I went along.

I also gazed around me, memorizing the seething activity of Kansas City. The day was a hot one, and business started early, then there would be a lull in the afternoon, when folks who wanted to would go to services. There was none of the Sunday quiet here that prevailed even in Quincy, not to mention in places like New England. Forgoing business one-seventh of the time couldn't be done where things were just building up. And anyway, there were few women around to present the claims of conscience.

It didn't take so long for me to get out of Kansas City. I was eager and strong, and it was easy to walk in trousers, as I had noticed before. Giving away my petticoat had lightened my case some, and I contemplated tossing the whole thing aside, but in the end I couldn't quite do that. It represented too much who I'd been. I was afraid to lose that entirely.

The difference between the look of the Missouri countryside and the look of K.T. countryside was striking. Missouri was regular land, the way you would see it in Illinois—hills and trees, fences and pasture, a regular amount of sky and a regular amount of privacy to everything. Houses and barns peeked out from groves and appeared around bends in the road. The hills and their canopy of trees ate up the vastness of the sky and broke up the wind— though there was a breeze, it eddied about rather than simply bearing down. And cultivation had made its mark. The area wasn't as settled as the area around Quincy—cabins as humble as ours in K.T. were visible here and there, some with hogs milling about them, revealing what they'd fallen to. Mostly these had given way to larger, more refined log houses, or even to clapboard dwellings, even to whitewashed ones. And I did pass big houses, set well back, glass windows elegantly ranged to either side of the front door. Not every field was being worked by slaves, not every wagon was being driven by a slave; I didn't see only slaves throwing out animal feed, or hanging out wash, or beating carpets, or weeding gardens. It varied from one farm to another: this one could be set in Illinois or Ohio, with its neat, small house and its diminutive yard; that other one could be set in Kentuck or Tennessee, with its columns and veranda, its wide approach, and its crew of dark laborers. Mostly I saw Negroes busy with hoes in fields of hemp. I knew Missouri was a great place for hemp, not so much for cotton, and I knew what a field of hemp looked like, but that was all I knew about it. White

men and boys were busy in fields, too, hoeing corn or
flax, say. Taken all in all, Missouri was a mixed-up
sort of place.

There was a great deal of traffic between Independence and Kansas City, even on a Sunday, and
many men on horseback, or driving wagons, went
by. Some of them offered me rides, and as the day got
hotter and my hat began to weigh upon my head and
my case to weigh upon my arm, I was tempted to
take one, but I had now been a man, a boy, for five or
six days, which put me in an odd situation. Any lady
could safely take a ride. No one would hurt, or even
challenge, a lady in those days, but then it was as
likely as black apples that a lady would be walking
along the side of the road, carrying her case. On the
other hand, no man, or boy, could safely take a ride,
because he was sure to be probed as to where he
came from, where he was going, what his business
was, who his friends were. This was the effect of the
goose question. And answers would have their
degree of rightness and their potential punishments.
Reflection gave me to believe that quizzes on the
goose question were ones I didn't necessarily know
the proper replies to. Tarring and feathering, whipping and throwing in the river, shooting and hanging,
had gotten to be things folks rather hankered to be
doing, as an outlet for their feelings. So I didn't
accept any rides. Pretty soon my feet began to hurt
inside my too large boots, but I took hold of
Thomas's watch in my pocket and went on. In the
middle of the day, I sat down under a large oak,

around on the side away from the road, and rested and dozed.

It was late in the day when I woke up, maybe an hour before sunset, and I didn't quite know how far I had gone or how far I had to go yet. I've got to say that I felt a moment of panic, or rather, I was once again intimidated by the largeness of my project. It seemed far beyond my strength and my wit. I had twenty-nine dollars now, with the three Mr. Morton had given me. Not much, but no doubt enough to get me to Blue Springs, to the Samsons there. After I was finished with them, I felt, I would have no need for money. I was hungry. I got up, smoothed down my clothes, took off my hat and put it on again, and resumed walking. In K.T., it was a regular thing that if someone was making his way in the countryside late in the day or at night, or if someone had no food, he might stop at any claim cabin he saw and ask for hospitality. Sometimes the places where he might stop had little enough to offer, but sharing was the rule, and in return the traveler might pay a bit of money, or do some work around the place. No doubt, even though Missouri was longer settled, it wasn't so surprising to farmers and householders by the side of the road when travelers did the same here. But of course, anything like this would expose me the same as taking a ride would. My hunger soon began to conflict with my prudence, though, and I wondered what to do. While it was August, and I knew there must be various things ripening by the side of the road, berries and whatnot, I didn't see any, and I was afraid to explore and to be caught stealing. I kept on walking, not so fast as before. The afternoon light reddened and grew shadowy, and not so many folks passed me, leading me to wonder if I had gotten off the road to Independence. I scrambled down to a little stream I passed and took some water. It was clear enough.

What could you eat? I hadn't ever thought much about this question before. In Quincy, I ate what was set before me—pork, sometimes chicken, bread, corn bread, butter. Cucumbers. Pickles. Steak. Greens. Apples. Peaches like the wonderful peaches I had shared with Nehemiah (peaches were ripe in Missouri; I looked around but saw no orchards). Watermelons, which grew in the sandy areas down by the river. Eggs. A lovely boiled egg. Cakes and especially pies. Alice had liked to make pies, had a definite way with a crust. Toast. Jam. Blackberry jam especially, seeds and all. I had picked and boiled down many a pail of blackberries myself. Hotcakes.

In K.T., we had prided ourselves on making do. Much was scarcer than in the States, though there were prairie chickens enough and turkeys. Bread flour was almost unknown, corn and cornmeal ubiquitous. Hot corncakes, stirred up with that limey water they had there, and a bit of salt. Well, there were many things worse and not many better. That was what I wanted right then—not anything fancier than that: just a dishful of fragrant yellow corncakes, with maybe a bit of honey on them.

These thoughts made me feel faint, I admit, but I didn't want to stop thinking them; that seemed like yet another deprivation, hunger beyond hunger. So I walked along, thinking of good food and feeling my stomach turn over and my mouth water. I'd heard that people could go without food for three days or more. Sometimes in the newspapers or other places, there were pieces about mountain men or parties of pioneers who went without food for weeks on end, and it wasn't as though we hadn't been a bit pinched from time to time the previous winter. In addition, I had eaten what most people would consider a good enough meal the previous evening. Nevertheless, a bit of hot sausage would be good, and some boiled potatoes with butter. Even a carrot, just a crisp raw carrot out of the ground. I cast my eye down each side of the road, but I didn't see any gardens. No doubt they were planted back near the houses. Each time I saw a house or a cabin, of whatever sort, I was tempted to turn toward it, but each time I saw a man or a woman in a field or in a yard, I knew I dared not. I kept on, Thomas's watch firmly clenched in my hand, but no doubt I wasn't making much progress. Soon enough, it was dark, and I went under some bushes, where, if I placed my case at my head, I could see a sliver of moon but was myself hidden from the sight of passersby. The ground was damp and soft with leaf mold. The sharp, earthy, woody smell helped to drive away thoughts of food, and I quickly fell asleep.

I woke up considerably bolder, and eager to vacate my night's bed, as small insects, or the ghosts of small insects, seemed to be crawling all over me—up my trouser legs and down the back of my neck. I scrambled out of the bushes and jumped up, throwing off my hat and running my hands through my hair, shaking my shoulders and stamping my feet. The sun was up, and I immediately heard the haw haw of Missouri laughter. I put my hat on and tried to summon some dignity. I coughed, then croaked, "Is there something funny, sir?"

"Haw haw haw haw!" shouted the man, who was sitting on his wagon seat, flicking his whip at the tips of his mule's ears. The mule stood there calmly, only shaking his ears as if at flies. "That was some little dance, boy, that was!"

I could still feel things running up and down under my clothes, so I snapped, "Thank you very much!" and reached under the greenery to retrieve my case.

"Now, boy, you been walking a long way, I ken tell by lookin' at ya! Where ya headed?"

"Independence. Blue Springs."

"Is that so? Haw haw haw. What's wrong with ya? Why are ya talkin' that way?"

It seemed tedious to tell, and even a bit dangerous to pursue further colloquy with this man, so I didn't answer but only adjusted my hat and coat and began down the road. After I had taken maybe five steps, he shouted, "That an't the way, boy! You got turned around!"

I stopped.

He laughed.

I glanced toward the wagon and saw that a Negro youngster of maybe ten or twelve had sat up in the back of the wagon and thrown off its covering. The child was now staring at me. I couldn't tell from either the cropped head or the shapeless garment whether it was a boy or a girl. The master saw me looking and turned around, shouting, "You lay down, now! You an't got to sit up and look around!" The child disappeared. Then he said to me, "Independence is that way," and pointed behind me. I tried to walk confidently forward, but after two steps I couldn't do it, and hesitated. The inevitable "Haw haw" rose from the wagon. In fact, the man was so excited that he laid the whip exuberantly across the mule's shoulders a couple of times and then stood up and slapped his thigh. The mule jumped forward, knocking the man off his feet. He fell back in the wagon.

Now it was my turn to laugh. And I could have sworn I heard a giggle from under the wagon canvas. The mule, however, came immediately to a halt, rather than running off, which would have been my preference. In the meantime, I got my bearings and saw that I was headed in the right direction, after all. The undergrowth that had provided me with shelter for the night had been to my right when I sought it and was still to my right; across the road was only rail fencing and pasture. Without glancing at the man or the wagon, I marched forward. Soon enough, the mule came up beside me, and then I felt a poke in the middle of my back—the whip, no doubt. I quickened my step. The mule quickened his step, and I felt another poke. All at once, I turned around and demanded, "Who are you?" in my most authoritative croak.

The man was grinning, showing clearly the effects of tobacco—his few teeth were brown as nuts—and behind him, a little dark head bobbed up, and a high voice said, "He Massa Philip!" then dropped down again. Master Philip spun around, his whip held high, but the child had disappeared. The shaft of the whip came down rather ineffectually on the canvas, then Master Philip spit into the road, raising a puff of dust. He turned around on the seat and faced me again. I had gotten a few yards off by now, maybe twenty, and I was walking fast, though every step was agony in my large, heavy boots. Over the night, my feet had swelled, and numerous tender spots from the day before now burned against the heavy leather as if I had no stockings on at all. But I hastened forward, looking for a break in the brush to slip through, out of the sight of a man who appeared to me possibly mad and certainly threatening. He whipped the mule into a trot and closed the distance between us. I stumbled and dropped my bag, which fell partly open, necessitating sufficient delay so that the mule came up beside me again. I looked at the man and began backing away. He said, "Now, boy, I notice about you that you an't got no manners. Here I am, your elder and better, no doubt, and I asked you a question, and you an't answered it but just croaked at me like a duck. Round these parts we know a thing or two about a thing or two, and I'm guessing you to be a stranger, and an unfriendly one at that. You some G—— d—— abolitionist, or something?"

I didn't say anything but turned and attempted to hurry away. A curve in the road now revealed a break in the fence across the way, and I thought if I ran I could get there and off into the field. I doubted whether Master Philip had enough interest in me to pursue me off the road. Nevertheless, he did whip up the mule to a steady trot, and they came on behind me. At the break in the fence, the mule was practically on top of me, Master Philip was haw-hawing to beat the band, and I was able to duck around in front of the animal, waving my arms and brandishing my bag in the mule's face, so that he threw up his head and came to a halt, toppling the man out of the wagon into the dirt. I slipped through the opening in the fence, hearing but not seeing Master Philip pick himself up with a torrent of curses. From the back of the wagon came high-pitched yelling: "Massa Ablishinist! Save me! Tak me 'long, Massa Ablishinist! Don' leave me wid Massa Philip! Tak me! Tak me!"

I ran across the field as far and as fast as I could, never looking back but hearing both the screaming and the cursing until they blended into one sound and then were lost in the other sounds of an August morning. When I stopped at last, out of breath and ready to drop, I couldn't be sure that I actually saw the wagon and the mule, nor did I care, as my pulse was pounding so hard in my ears that that itself made me afraid, and a kind of red cloud seemed to be closing over my sight from both sides. I staggered into the shade of a stand of hackberry trees and knelt down, resting the top of my head on the cool earth. I closed my eyes.

Perhaps I crouched in that position for ten minutes or a quarter of an hour, not unmindful of Master Philip but too overwhelmed by my own exertions to make much of him. Then I came more to myself and peered about. He was nowhere to be seen. I spied some deeper shade and crawled to it, and only then did I recall the pleas of the child.

At first they seemed only strange, as if, somehow, they were a performance that had nothing to do with me. Of course, they had nothing to do with Lyman Arquette, who was the boy walking along the side of the road, who was from Palmyra, Missouri, and for whom the institution of Negro servitude was a righteous and inevitable disposition of natural, and scripturally justifiable, inequality. A slave screaming to be saved was, to Lyman, a piece of disobedience that deserved punishment. If Lyman were a kindly fellow, then he would stay the master's hand from too severe a rain of blows and counsel Master Philip to attempt to win his servant's love and loyalty through gentler means. But all things considered, taking to his heels had been Lyman's wisest choice, given the unpredictable irascibility of Master Philip, who was certainly armed and might be happy to shoot a strange boy of no value to himself, while desiring only to whip his own property. It was surely not required of Lyman that he risk his life to preserve the child from but a few of the many, many blows he had received and was certain yet to receive.

And yet it was with Lydia Newton's ears that I heard the child's pleas. I knew perfectly well the difference between Lydia and Lyman, that Lyman was merely an outward appearance. Save me! There had been a full-throated note of pure desire and pure grief, mingled, in the child's plea. Tak me! Surely

Master Philip had heard the same desperation that I heard, the same hatred of himself, the same richly felt revulsion. Would he have then turned on the child and beaten it senseless, beaten it to death, beaten the hatred out of it? For I had noticed one thing in this far western territory, and it was that men, and southerners in particular, couldn't stand to be made to seem mean or dishonorable in their own eyes, that they would commit any aggression to efface that feeling. New Englanders, like Thomas, acted on what they called conscience, which made them seem self-righteous but also allowed them to turn away without a fight from those who disagreed with them. Southerners acted on what they called honor, which existed only in how they considered themselves to be regarded by others. Often, this made them friendly or sociable, but someone who thought ill of a southern man and made him see himself through disrespectful eyes had to be proven wrong, even if you had to kill him to do it.

Did I think I could have saved that child? No.

But his voice hurt me every time it came back to me, and I thought Thomas might have handled the whole incident more coolly and to better effect. Oh, Thomas! It seemed as if he pressed me hugely now, as hugely as ever he had alive.

A man and a boy who were coming out to hoe their field found me lying in the trees. When they had gotten to within a few paces, I sat up and put my hat on straight. As they were neither frowning with suspicion nor grinning with mischief, I suppressed the urge to run. The man came over to me, peered into my face, and poked me on the shoulder. He said, "You all right, boy? You're on our land, I reckon. An't got nothing fa ye. Best be gettin' on."

I got my feet under me and went to stand up, but I couldn't quite make it and fell back. The man pushed his hat to the rear of his head and gave himself a scratching, and the boy came over and stared down at me. He was a year or two younger than Lyman.

"Well, now," said the man. "Harley, run git yer ma." I closed my eyes. He raised his voice. "Tell her ta fix somethin' up fer this boy. He looks done in!"

And so it was that I came to spend the morning at the Elton farm, home of Burley, Harley, and Opah. Opah did bring me some mush with butter and milk in it, and she and Harley did take me back to their small house, but fortunately, I was so rank after over a week in the same clothes, with no bathing or washing facilities, that Opah refused to come near me and banished me to the barn with a towel and a lump of soap when I wouldn't let her take my hat or my jacket. A bit later, Harley appeared with a bucket of warm water, and then he ran off to help his father with the hoeing I had interrupted. I carried the bucket around to the side of the barn away from the house, and I washed my face and my short hair, took off my jacket and washed my neck and my arms, took off my shoes and stockings and washed my feet. Opah's cow and chickens watched me carefully, and a dog came, also, and sat at a distance, gazing sometimes at me and sometimes at something afar. I said as little as possible, croaking as low as possible, and they did what they were supposed to do, gave up intercourse with me as profitless. Toward noon, I turned the bucket upside down and set a dollar on the bottom, held down with a piece of a brick, then I set off across the fields again, toward the road. My feet were flaming. When I got there, Master Philip and his slave child were so gone that I could almost tell myself that they had never been there but had been figments of an early-morning dream.

Revived, I continued on my way toward Independence, and by late afternoon, the swelling of traffic unmistakably revealed that I was approaching that famous metropolis of the west. Independence is older than Kansas City or Lawrence by some twenty years, in fact looks to be of an age with Quincy, though differently built—no high bluff above the river and dark woods behind, but instead wide streets set in open, gentle hills, so that you feel the open spaces of the west are at hand, and all you need do is begin your journey. The streets were full of outfitting shops and emporia of every variety. Livery stables were everywhere, their yards full of horses and mules. I couldn't help letting some of the grays, especially, catch my eye, and it was easy to go from that to imagining that Jeremiah was only stolen, that he might turn up here of all places, but I kept walking. Lyman kept walking. Lydia gawked at everything—houses, low white fences, flower beds and blooming roses, ladies in buggies with their children beside them, the dark faces of slave women in kerchiefs, with yoked buckets over their shoulders, chatting at the town wells, folks of all ages and types, old and young, black and white, tall and short, rough and gentle, going in and out of buildings of all sorts, or idling at corners, chewing on their seegars or spitting into the street. Even after Kansas City, coming into Independence was like reentering the world. I could stop here, refresh myself, change into a dress or—

I turned in to a men's haberdashery, opening the door before I quite realized what I was doing. There, by pointing and croaking, I managed to purchase two shirts and a collar, as well as two pairs of stockings. Then, a ways down the street, I went into an eating establishment, and did just what I had done on the steamboat and in Kansas City: my dollar paid, I filled my plate as quickly as I could with everything close at hand (a piece of beefsteak, some beet pickles, corncakes and corn pudding, a piece of bread, some sliced cabbage, and a peach), and I wolfed it all down willy-nilly until I couldn't contain another morsel. This place wasn't so rough as some others; there were women here, but I ate like a man now, half through trying and half through habit—that is, I leaned over my plate, I wiped my mouth with my sleeve, I ate quickly and with a hearty appetite. I ate, in fact, as if no one were watching me (ladies always behaved as if someone were watching them, and more often than not, someone was, if only a sister or a friend), and when I was finished, I lolled in my chair and looked around, as if it were my prerogative to watch without being watched. Then I pushed my chair back with a scrape and sauntered outside. I did not, however, make use of the spittoon, as did most others; even for the sake of my masquerade, I could not enter so deeply into manly habits as *that*!

After supper, I made my way through Independence, turning south and traversing residential districts of considerable pretensions. It was well known in the west at that time that some Mormons made their home in Independence; not the same group that caused so much trouble back in Illinois and went to the great desert with handcarts, but Mormons nonetheless. I kept a curious eye open for some, but there was no telling. I'd heard that they didn't hold with slavery; perhaps some of the folks I saw passing in the streets unaccompanied by Negroes were Mormons. Well, it was a way to keep my eyes open and my feet moving. In my new stockings, both pairs, my boots were almost comfortable. I was well beyond Independence by midnight.

There is a rhythm to any long walk, I discovered, or rather, there is a rhythm, but there is also a movement. The rhythm is the beat of one's footsteps on the road, their steadiness denoting progress. When I was tired or discouraged, I took solace from that beat—my legs seemed to work of their own volition. There were times when I thought my feet couldn't take another step—my soles throbbed, or my boots rubbed my heels and toes raw, or the very bones ached—but somehow my legs walked me through those times: after a while, whatever had hurt no longer hurt but was deliciously quiet. Above this beat were the larger movements of the walk—morning, noon, nighttime, but also country and town, solitude and company, calm, boredom, fear, lively interest, discouragement. Sometimes I was thoroughly at home in my male costume, a boy marching along. Other times, my costume seemed to grate over me, or stand away from me, or interfere, and I was acutely aware of myself inside it, almost as if my person were trying to separate me from it. Yet other times, everything about me that I had been thinking of, including pain or discomfort, fell away. Here was something: there were times I was so fatigued that I didn't think I could walk five more steps, and then, a moment later, I would be suddenly afraid and find myself almost running. And after that, I would be less tired rather than more. Truly, there was so much to discover in such a walk that you could not discover it all the first time. I got well away from Independence before I settled down for the night by penetrating a large haystack in a field and pulling some of the hay down over me. I reckoned that I would make Blue Springs sometime the following day, as it was not so far from Independence to Blue Springs as it was from Kansas City to Independence.

Under the hay, I lay awake, even though only moments before I had been stumbling about half asleep, looking for a spot to sprawl. I yearned to remove my boots, which were heavy and constricting, even though I knew that I would pay tenfold in the agony of putting them on again in the morning for the relief of taking them off right then. If I took them off, my liberated appendages would swell overnight so that putting them on again would be a time-consuming agony. If I left them on, only the first twenty or thirty steps would be especially painful. I had decided ahead of time what I would do and how it would be, but now that I was lying under the hay, I seemed to be all feet, and all of me was crying out to be released.

Over all of that long day—all of those new scenes and new folks—lay the pleas of that slave child. The Eltons, who had no slaves, who had given me food, and water for washing, had seemed to bely that child's very existence, and after that there was Independence and more food, and all the miles between the early morning and this late night. My feet, of course, ached a constant assertion that there was no room in my thoughts for any idea other than boot removal. But nevertheless, in the quiet, fragrant, hidden darkness (I couldn't even see the moon through my covering of hay), the child's voice pierced me again, made me wonder what "could not" meant. I was certain that I could not have saved that child. On the other hand, I was carrying my pistol in my bag, and I knew how to use it. I had shot more than a few turkeys, which are much quicker and more suspicious than a man is. Had I kept a level head and not run off, had I reconnoitered instead of panicking, I might have gotten into some sheltered spot, loaded my pistol, and confronted Master Philip. In retrospect, I saw that Master Philip was a buffoon and a bully. A little courage on my part would have surprised and routed him, would it not? Lyman, of course, could not do such a thing, but so early in the morning, there had been no one around. With no one around, Lyman was in abeyance, wasn't he? Only Lydia was truly present, and she might have figured something out.

Well, I could only put my cowardice down to my femininity. There was the great shame of it. When all was said and done, it was Lydia who had panicked, Lydia who had run off, Lydia who hadn't the wit to do anything else but seek a hiding place. The west was full of men, and of the stories of men, who confronted bullies. That was practically the normal course of western acquaintance: man meets bully, man endures bully, man pulls a pistol out of his hat and subdues bully, man and bully become boon companions. How, indeed, did Lydia plan to confront Samson and Chaney, whoever they were, having so thoroughly caved in to Master Philip? Such questions eventually drove out all thoughts of my boots, but neither was there much hope of sleep. I saw that all I could do was grip Thomas's watch as tightly as I could and vow to do better, whatever that was.

Were I honest with myself, I would have to wonder why I had taken up the abolitionist cause. Thomas, of course, had made it attractive, so perhaps I had taken it up as a way of being courted. That afternoon with Frank in the creek at Roland's farm had changed forever my perception of Thomas, as there was such a mysteriously knowing verve in the way he'd passed that money to Frank and caused Frank to pass it to the man in the cave. I had found so much charm in that that I had never even spoken of it to Thomas but cherished my secret feelings like a talisman. Perhaps I hadn't wanted to hear a more mundane explanation of the incident. At any rate, we had so quickly set out for Lawrence, and so quickly taken up with our friends there, that I had gotten to be an abolitionist by reflex and, my sisters would have said, out of pure contrariness, as well ("just like Miriam"). Ah, well, my sister Miriam. When she was alive, I'd known of her abolitionism, of course, as it was the source of so much family dissension, but I hadn't cared all that much about it. Yet, after her death, I had let it come to be her defining feature for me, the thing that helped her, from all of them, love me. Possibly that was it. Such a plain young woman as myself could find love only among abolitionists. . . .

And then, in K.T., we abolitionists had been so hated, so stupidly, venally, cruelly, and ridiculously hated, that there was honor in being an abolitionist. For all their foibles, my friends there had been kindly, hardworking folks. I hated those who hated them, even hated the enemy more for my friends than they hated the enemy for themselves. But I couldn't, in all honesty, look upon that as a virtue. I had become a hater, the sort who wanted to hang, shoot, dismember, clear out, and otherwise dispose of those who wanted to hang, shoot, dismember, clear out, and otherwise dispose of me. That was what my abolitionism had amounted to in K.T.

But abolitionism was about slavery, after all, and the evidence of the Master Philip incident was that I hadn't many instinctive feelings about slavery. I had been slow to act because I had been slow to feel. Master Philip and the child had played out a little scene for me, and even in my fear, I had watched it as comic rather than as tragic. Only afterward did that child's voice come back to me as the voice of my conscience, you might say. I knew what I should have done only by surmising what Thomas would have done, and by then, of course, it was too late. It wasn't just having to hide among my enemies that made it hard to be an abolitionist in Missouri; it was also having no friends.

The sun was well up and my nest hot and dusty before I awoke the next day. There was little relief in the open, either, as it was a hot, thick day, with clouds piling in the west. By Thomas's watch it was past midmorning. I felt achy and vague, still full from my very heavy meal the night before, and also extremely thirsty. I had not picked a spot near water, and there were no streams nearby, so I made up my mind to approach the house I saw across the road. I must say that I was daunted, as it was one of those large places with columns, constructed of white-washed brick, that was set back on a lawn. As I trudged toward the veranda, a pain seemed to lift up through my neck into my head, lodging itself in two burning points at the back of my skull. I grew dizzy, paused, took my hat off, and put my head between my knees for a moment, got clear again, and resumed trudging. About ten yards from the house, I realized that I had left my case under the hay. I let out a groan and dropped to the grass. Going back to get it, and going on to the house without it, seemed equally impossible.

The green lawn stretched away on all sides. As I lay down within it, it grew as large as a prairie, seeming to run to the horizon, as a prairie did, and to end only in the same sort of threatening clouds that had so recently oppressed me with their torrential, fiery tempests. This lawn gave me such a lonely feeling, such a feeling of general abandonment, that I started to cry and therefore had to pull my hat over my face. The pain in my head, which had subsided somewhat, was now matched by pains elsewhere, the source of which was utterly mysterious to me, unless they were the evidence of some sort of general collapse of my soul and body under the pressures of grief and exhaustion. The darkness inside my hat gave me some relief, though, and as I lay there gripping Thomas's watch, I did feel myself swoon away.

"You be moanin' purty bad, ma'am," said a voice.

And in my own voice, Lydia's voice, I said, "Something is wrong with me." My voice came out high and light, as easy as water. I needed water. I said, "I'm thirsty," and I took the hat away from my eyes. A Negro woman was squatting beside me, perhaps thirty years of age, wearing a faded gown and a white kerchief around her head. She put her hand around the back of my neck; it was cool and firm, large and strong. She said, "You sit up, now, and I ken gi' you somethin' ta drink, 'cause I got milk right here from de springhouse."

I knelt forward and drank from a cup.

"What you be wearin' man's clothes for? Ain' you got no dress?"

"I want to kill someone."

The Negro woman laughed.

But after that her face closed over, and she said, "Missy Helen done seen you from de house, and she sent me down heah. I see her lookin' right now. You cain' lay out on de grass—"

And a voice called from the house, "Lorna! Who is that young man? See him off! I won't have any loiterers about with the master gone!"

Lorna stood up and went out of my sight. I closed my eyes. Sometime later, Lorna and her mistress were both kneeling above me. I opened my eyes and beheld their faces, framed in dark clouds, both looking seriously down at me, one black, one pale blond. The hand of the mistress, just a girl, smaller but no less cool than the hand of the slave, smoothed my hair away from my face. She said, "Lorna says you're a female."

I said nothing. She felt my cheeks and said, "I do believe you are a female. Well, mercy me! And you surely got a fever. Well, we'll take you in, I suppose, but it's a good thing for you you're a female, because Papa wouldn't like me to be taking in a man!"

I said, "I only need some water. I've got to get to Blue Springs."

They looked at me, then Lorna said, "You be walkin'? I ain' seen no horse nor buggy."

I nodded.

She said, "Ain' walkin' to no Blue Spring today. Big storm comin' up, for one thing. It gone rain any moment!"

And it was true. As they helped me sit up, I could feel it in the breeze.

In the kitchen, sitting on a bench beside a stove, a bowl of corn pudding in one hand and a spoon in the other, I was seized with the worst pain of all, and I swooned away right then and there.

CHAPTER 22

I Am Taken In

If domestics are found to be incompetent, unstable, and unconformed to their station, it is Perfect Wisdom which appoints these trials, to teach us patience, fortitude, and self-control; and, if the discipline is met, in a proper spirit, it will prove a blessing, rather than an evil.

—p. 205

I AWAKENED WITHOUT OPENING my eyes and lay in bed listening to the voices in the room. Through my eyelids I could tell that they had lit two candles. That, just that, was a divine luxury. And I lay between sheets, I could feel them, and I wore a nightgown, far too fine to be my own—where was my own?—and the voices were low and smooth.

"There, now," said the mistress, Helen. "That looks nice, I do think. Don't you, Lorna?"

"Very nice, missy."

"You didn't even look, Lorna! Take it in your hand and hold it up to the light. I mean that stem stitch. Look at those vines! Don't they look real?"

"Lak weeds, you mean? Dat mornin' glory vine is a weed, no mistake."

"Oh, Lorna. I think they look very pretty, and Minna will love them."

"Round de hem of her petticoat? Who gone see it?"

"She will simply know it's there. That's the best

joy of being well dressed, if you ask me. Whether or not anyone notices—"

"Massa James ain' gone notice, dat's for sure."

"Lorna, you shouldn't say that. Master James is going to be Minna's husband—"

"Then she de one who gone hafta love him, not me. I jes' got to keep my mouth shet."

"Yes, you do!"

"I know it!"

"I won't say another word."

They sat quietly for a few moments, then Helen said, "He's very handsome. He's a regular cavalier. And he's been to college in Virginia."

"So he say."

"Lorna!"

"Well, missy, ifn you don' want me to speak my mine, don' temp' me."

"I think he's a gentleman. He just has his own ways, is all."

"You nevah met no Virginny gentleman, Missy Helen."

"And you have?"

"Well, I have. Yes, I have."

"In Saint Louis?"

"Yes'm."

"And what do you know about them, pray tell?"

"I ain' sayin', 'cause den you'll say I talk too free."

"I won't."

There was a pause. Finally, Lorna said, "Well, missy, dem Virginny men, dey thinks awful highly of demself. Everythin' dey do say, 'I am bettah den you, and I know it and you know it, too,' but den dey treat everbody real nice, and dey always apologize when dey is forced to bring loaded guns and such into de house. And dey nevah nevah evah carry no knife in dey boottop. Dat's a fact."

By this time, Helen was laughing, and finally she said, "Goodness, Lorna, you do talk so free. I'm not saying too free; just free."

Now there was a long silence, and Lorna said in a low voice, "Well, sure 'nuf, she be awake, I reckon."

This was my cue. I stretched and yawned and opened my eyes. I was in a high-ceilinged white room with two tall black windows. Lorna sat near me, on the right side of the bed, sewing a shirt by the light of one candle, and Helen sat at the foot of the bed, beside the other candle. She had set aside her work and was leaning forward to look at me. I pushed myself with my hands and raised up out of the pillows.

"Oh!" exclaimed Helen. "How are you?"

I shook my head back and forth, then said, "I don't think I know."

"Do you have any pains?"

I reconnoitered. "A little. An ache, nothing much."

"Does your head hurt? You were holding your head and moaning in your sleep."

"I was?"

"Lorna gave you some drops, and you slept right through the storm."

"She did?"

"Deadly poison, I'm sure. Lorna is a deep one."

"My head feels like it did hurt, but doesn't hurt anymore. You know? It remembers hurting." I sounded silly.

"I'm dying to know who you are and why you were wearing men's clothes. I've so wanted to do that!" I saw Lorna look at her. "But Lorna says we have to let you rest absolutely for twenty-four hours, so you needn't tell me a single thing right now, but just think pleasant thoughts."

"Call me . . . Louisa," I said.

"Louisa?"

I nodded and closed my eyes. It was more pleasant to listen to them talk than to talk myself, which reminded my head to hurt again. There were steps out of the room, then back in again, and after a moment, I felt Lorna's cool hand under the back of my neck. When I sat up and opened my eyes, I saw that she had a basin beside her, and she was leaning over me. She said, "I got some broth here. Oxtail broth." She laid a napkin across my chest and then fed me in silence. From the end of the bed, Helen looked on eagerly. After a bit, she said, "I had a terrible fever one time. Papa thought sure I was going to die, and the doctor gave me up for lost, but Lorna just kept fixing that oxtail broth every day. It was a reason to live, I always said. Papa told me I was going to get up and see that all the cows had lost their tails!" She laughed merrily, and Lorna smiled a tiny smile.

"Now, missy," said Lorna, "you don' have to go tellin' everbody your life story."

I estimated that Helen was a year or two younger

than I, but she seemed even younger, still a girl, which I most assuredly was no longer.

After the broth, Lorna gave me a glass of cool well water to drink. It was clear all the way to the bottom, sweet and delicious. I drank it greedily, and she poured me another one. Then she said, "No wonder you thirsty."

I felt my forehead with my hand, and she said, "You ain' sick." She seemed to know what I was, if not sick. But I took her prohibition on Helen's asking me questions as permission to ask none of my own but simply to lie back in a state of comfortable ignorance, at least until the morning. I even felt Thomas's largeness slip away to a more comfortable distance, and as I turned over onto my side, I felt myself, maybe for the first time, turn away from my sense of his presence. In the morning, I thought, I would resume my journey to Blue Springs and my pursuit of the criminals Samson and Chaney. I sighed and nestled down into the pillows. The women continued with their sewing for a bit; just as I was sleepily wondering where the men, or man, might be, Helen said, "I suppose they'll be home sometime tomorrow. Maybe in the forenoon, if they get an early start."

"Your papa cain' ride as hard as he useta."

"Maybe by supper, then."

There was a pause, then they fell to whispering. I made out that I was the subject, and guessed that who I was and my reception by the men was the topic of discussion. They must have come to some conclusion, because soon enough the whispering died away, and I fell into a happy doze, in which everything pressing—where my bag was, where I was, where Samson and Chaney were, what was to become of me—seemed as remote as the czar of all the Russias. I was not asleep but instead floating in a dream of total comfort. It pleased me to wonder if I had ever been so comfortable in my life before. Certainly not in Kansas, or on the steamer, or in my recent peregrinations, but perhaps I had never been so comfortable even in Quincy, even in my own bed, where I had lain awake so many nights, dissatisfied, nursing complaints or, alternatively, cultivating fancies about my future.

The night went on. I drifted up and down in my dreams. One of the candles was quenched, but the other one burned steadily downward. Sometimes footsteps went in or out of the room, sometimes there were long periods of silence, sometimes there were even reassuring snores. I awoke for good shortly after dawn—the sun was bright and low in the window at the foot of my bed. It had only just risen above the horizon. I sat up.

The room looked different than it had the night before. No longer high-ceilinged and cavernous, it was now just a room, whitewashed and pleasant, but a bit on the small side. I lay in a four-poster, with bed curtains tied back on either side of the headboard. A green-and-white-checked oilcloth covered the floor, and a small wardrobe, two chairs, and two small tables formed the rest of the furniture. On one of the tables sat a basin and a pitcher. In one of the chairs sat Lorna, sleeping with her chin resting on her chest. Through the windows I could see the front lawn, whose vastness had defeated me the morning before. The view out the window made me remember my case, which was surely still under a haystack across the road, but when I threw my feet over the side of the bed and sat upright, I am sorry to say that all sense of well-being drained right out of me, and I thought I would swoon again. I must have made some sound, because Lorna woke up. She said, "Ah, me! Mornin' already." She adjusted the kerchief around her head, then eyed me. Finally, she shook her head. I pulled my feet back under the covers. She said, "Missy, you cain' get up. Least for a day or two yet. You done had you a baby!"

"What!"

"Well, it waren't no baby, but it mighta been, ifn you'd held on to it."

I gaped.

"You mean to tell me you didn't know you was in dat condition? I sweah ta mercy, you is a strange one. Did you think you is a man, really? I ain' nevah seen nobody lak you. You seem ta drop outta de sky, no horse nor mule nor bag nor nothin', dressed up lak a man on de lawn out theah, and den we got so much blood, and you was senseless to boot. Well, it war the bigges' thing to happen heahabouts in a considerable time!"

I said, "I knew, but I forgot about it."

"I ain' nevah heard of that befoah."

"Some men shot my husband." I thought that should be explanation enough. I lay down again. The small room was hardly so pleasant, the bed hardly so comfortable. I wasn't disconsolate just yet, only still wondering, only still taking it in, but I saw despair just ahead, and myself starting to drop toward it. I closed my eyes against the sunlight and heard Lorna leave the room.

Well, I had suspected my condition. I had just begun to wonder about it before Thomas was murdered, but hadn't yet mentioned it to him, and then it had seemed beyond my strength to utter a word about it even to Louisa. And then, after I got to Kansas City and became Lyman Arquette, my condition got to be that much more of a secret, even to myself. Lyman couldn't be said to be aware of it, and even Lydia was focused completely on Thomas's killers. Who was harboring the child-to-be? And it was also true in K.T. that women didn't put too much stock in a child, even a born baby, until it showed its powers of survival. That might not be until the child was one or even two years old. Louisa, with her knitting and naming and announcing, was uniquely sanguine compared to others I'd seen, almost all of whom had buried some. Most women, and I was among the majority, hardly dared let themselves hope for a joyful outcome, much less count on it as Louisa seemed to do.

Even so, I put a pillow over my face to block out the sun, which was filling both windows and blinding me. I was a blank.

Sometime later, Helen came in. By now I was lying quietly on my back, my arms at my sides. I was looking up at the ceiling. I felt closer to being dead than I ever had in my life. Helen looked far away, prettily dressed in a pink wrapper with roses stitched around the collar. She carried a tray with a plate of toast and a cup of tea on it. She looked at me expectantly but said only, "Good morning, Louisa! How did you sleep? It wasn't such a hot night, was it?"

Louisa! Oh, yes.

She set the tray beside me on the bed.

Sitting down in the chair closest to me, she looked at me kindly for a moment and then said, "Oh, my dear! Lorna told you what happened, didn't she? I knew she would. She always blurts everything out. You can't imagine the sort of trouble she gets into with Papa because of it. Last year he got so angry he sent her to my sister. Well! That went wrong, let me tell you. . . ." She paused, then her voice dropped. "Oh, mercy! I do think that if what happened to you were to happen to me, well, I would just die! When I get married, I want the little ones to come, just one after another. I love little ones. But Lorna says what happened to you happens all the time, and she thinks it's a blessing, really, but it's hard to see it for that, when . . ."

It was then that I realized I had lost everything. Something else might have happened: Samson and Chaney might have taken another road, and Thomas and I might have continued to our claim, put Jeremiah away for the night, gone to our little bed. I might have told him of my suspicions. It was August. Our crop would be ripening. Frank would certainly have turned up sometime, and by now I would have been sewing and knitting little clothes. Louisa would have taken a great interest in my condition, given me quantities of advice and assistance. We would have tormented ourselves with fears and worries—we had no money, war seemed perennially imminent, K.T. was hardly so hospitable as we had anticipated to either crops or men. I would have thought of Mrs. James, though perhaps never mentioned my thoughts. A midwinter birth in a rickety claim shack was something to be feared, was it not? What a treasure of fears these would have been! Now I feared nothing.

"Oh! I've made you cry!" said Helen. She took my hand. "I've said all the wrong things! I haven't talked about heaven at all, and heaven is our comfort! My mama could talk about heaven in the nicest way, as if it were a big lighted house and our whole life here was just a night journey, and at the end of it, after all the muddy roads and the rain and the cold wind and the hunger unto starvation, well, to see those lighted windows up ahead, and all the other travelers arriving at the door, and to hear the Host call out! She could make you welcome death—at least your own. I tried to welcome hers, I really did, but I was only a girl then, that was eight years ago now, it was hard. But she said, 'Ellie, love, I feel that I am entering the mansion, and I am expected there, don't grieve,' and so I didn't, so much, for her, but I surely did for myself. But there must be a special room in the mansion for those littlest souls—"

And then she, too, began to weep, putting her hands over her face and sobbing.

It astonished me that I had lost every single thing,

including, at the moment, my very name and history. Right beside me, practically right in the room with me, was the other life that I had not managed to live, a common mode of existence, the natural extension of my first twenty-one years, the very easiest thing to go on with, it must be said. And yet I had gotten onto a different track entirely, and I had followed it to this room, among these strangers. She hadn't said the wrong things, because nothing she might have said could have lessened my astonishment. I sat up and took a sip of the tea, and I was reminded how, when I got to Kansas City and woke up that first morning in the Humphry House, I had been so afraid, and it was a bite of something in my mouth that had gotten me over my fear. I took another sip. The tea was warm and bitter. I wondered what it would enable me to go on to. After drinking it, I took up the napkin and dried my tears.

"Oh, my goodness!" Helen sat up and took a deep breath. "Well, I am sorry for you, Louisa, and you may stay here as long as you care to, and you don't have to tell me a thing about yourself, though of course I am dying of curiosity. This toast is cold! Shall I have Delia make some more?"

"Who is Delia?"

"You haven't met her. She's the cook. I don't know what she was doing when you came yesterday. More than likely, she was down in the cellar, looking things over. She's a terrible one for hoarding, you know. She's always making more jam and more jam and telling Ike to plant more potatoes and turnips and such. She's scared to death we'll starve someday. Why, this winter—when it was so cold?—we were fairly bursting, she made us eat so much at every meal. She kept saying, 'You thin out, you gon' die, missy!' And she will never thin out herself! She doesn't say any of that to Lorna, though. No one tells Lorna what to do except Papa. When I was a girl, she had a husband come, you know, they had a ceremony and everything, even though Papa said no good would come of it, and he didn't hold with servants getting married. Her husband was Jake Taler, whose owner made rope in Independence, and Jake got around some. I saw him myself, two or three times, but Jake didn't tell her what to do, either. She told him what to do! I must say I am a bit afraid of Lorna myself."

"What happened to him?" I was much interested in the fates of husbands.

"Oh, I don't know. I was only a girl. It was before Mama died, even. It was Mama who persuaded Papa to let them have the ceremony. He got sold. Papa said he was worth too much money to stay around here. This country don't support a lot of niggers. That's what Papa says. Let me get you more toast."

She stood and picked up the tray, then walked out of the room.

Things went on like this for another day, as the men turned out to be delayed. Helen confided to me that she was very glad to see me, as she had had no one to talk to in weeks—her two friends who lived but a short ride away were gone to Saint Louis for the summer and wouldn't be back until the middle of September. Her sister Minna was up in Booneville at her aunt and uncle's farm, preparing for her October wedding to the mysterious Mr. Oates, said to be from Virginia. Mr. Oates had purchased a farm between Booneville and Lexington, and wanted to be married from there, and her older sister Bella had moved to Saint Louis two years before, after her own wedding. She, Helen, was the last one left unmarried, and though she had two local suitors, neither one interested her, but she supposed she was going to have to take one or the other in the end, unless the influx of real cavaliers, who were coming in to "deal with those abolitionists," should supply the area with superior possibilities.

From time to time, Lorna came in, and it was she who tended to me. She was utterly strict in her nursing. She gave me strengthening broths and teas, changed the bed linen, changed my nightdress, bathed me, especially my feet, which after two days out of my boots were considerably swollen and covered with blisters. She pricked each blister with a needle and squeezed out the water, then swabbed my feet with an infusion of witch hazel. After that she dusted them with fine cornmeal. The degree of refreshment afforded me by this procedure cannot be described. She and Helen washed my hair. I lay on my back across the bed (the sheets and the counterpane pulled back), with Lorna supporting me under the neck and Helen pouring warm water through my short hair, then rubbing my scalp with a fragrant soft soap, then more water to rinse. It had been maybe a year since I had bathed in warm water. Lorna carried it up, pitcher after pitcher, an endless supply. Then Helen brought in towels and gently, oh so gently, patted and kneaded the strands dry, commenting all the time on my hair's thickness and weight and color.

I said, "I suppose it came six or eight inches past my waist before I cut it off."

"I know it was splendid," exclaimed Helen. "I don't see how you brought yourself to give it up!"

"It was a great deal of trouble. I haven't missed it."

"But to do away with one's beauty like that!" She looked at me. "I mean . . ."

"When my husband was killed, that did away with my beauty, because he was the only man who ever found me beautiful." Saying this gave me a pang, but it was a delicious pang—I had been avoiding thoughts of Thomas since first awakening in this room.

"My goodness," said Helen. "That is the saddest thing I ever heard any woman say!"

"Is it?" I said. I thought "They shot my husband" was sadder.

And Helen said, "Lorna told me some men shot your husband." She was sitting behind me, lifting the short strands of hair off my neck and fluffing them. Then she ran her fingers from the back of my neck upward, lifting. Well, it was as sad to hear it as to say it. She said, "Was it . . . ? What was it . . . ?"

"It was as if they took everything inside me and gave it a cruel half twist and then left it that way. I just felt it from head to toe."

"Oh, my goodness!"

"My husband was a great reader. Often, he read aloud to me, and I loved his voice; it was so thoughtful and deep, and it filled our little place right up. But even more than that, I loved to watch him read silently. He was terribly absorbed. I never got over the pleasure of seeing him absorbed in something he loved to do." As I said these things, which I had never said before about Thomas, I realized how true they were. "Many things amused him. He had a little smile, which was almost not a smile but a very private look, that showed he was watching something or someone. I loved that look. He was a good man. And he aspired to be a good man, too."

"Oh, Louisa! What was his name?"

I almost said Charles, but that disguise seemed a betrayal, and what would it hurt to tell the truth? I said, "Thomas."

"Were you together for many years?"

"A few months. Ten months. This time last year, I hardly knew him."

"Was he from around here, then? We know everyone down to Blue Springs, but I've never seen you before. But if you're from over by Lexington, perhaps Papa knows your people."

She said this brightly, and I drew back, remembering where I was and who she was. I said, "He was from Kentuck. Round about Frankfort, I believe." Oh, Thomas! My sailmaking, oceangoing Bay State man! Perhaps it was I who would end up betraying you the most! I said, "I can't talk about it anymore. It hurts me to talk about it."

The day passed away, and Lorna allowed me to have a bit of supper—pieces of boiled chicken and some bread with blackberry jam on it, a sliced-up peach. She said, "You color is much bettah. You done got ovah dis thang pretty quick, I mus' say." She seemed suspicious.

"I doubt if I've hardly begun to get over it."

"If you a woman, you got to git ovah one thang aftah another, so you bettah start right quick."

"Helen said you had a husband."

"Still do, but I ain' seen 'im now fa seven yeah. He done got sold to Arkinsaw dese seven yeah ago." She spoke matter-of-factly. "He send me word from time to time." She smiled in spite of herself. "But you got your reasons 'at you ain' talkin', an' I got mine, and I ain' talkin', neider." She took up the tray and the dishes from my supper and left the room. She came back a bit later with a candle and her sewing and, while I dozed, sat beside me, turning the cuffs of someone's white shirt. Helen came in—I heard her light, sympathetic voice in my sleep—and then she went out. Sometime later, I woke up, woke up completely, and sat up in bed. I guess that it was fairly late, as Lorna had fallen asleep in her chair without blowing out the candle, which had burnt down almost to the holder. The shirt she was sewing lay in her lap, and she still held her needle in her fingers, though her thimble had fallen to the floor and was rolling about—most likely the noise had awakened me. I got up to blow out the candle—I had a horror of candles burning when everyone was sleeping and always had; there were too many stories of inadvertent tragedy—but I paused to gaze at Lorna, partly because when she was awake she seemed to repel your gaze or turn it away, as if you had no right to peruse her; and it was with some trepidation that I perused her now, fearful that she would wake up and punish me. She was of medium height, smaller than she seemed, broad-shouldered and large-busted. The white kerchief around her head set off her dark skin like a frame. She was not beautiful—perhaps she was too old for that, being past thirty, no doubt, but her face was utterly distinctive, with a high forehead and prominent cheekbones, a strong chin. Where Helen's visage reminded you of silk, Lorna's reminded you of stone, of something smooth and cool and impenetrable. Only her lashes, which were long where they lay against her cheeks, had a beauty to them. And her hands, too. Her hands were as lovely as they felt, slender and strong and, even in repose, full of their long history of getting things done. I blew out the candle and returned to my bed, where I lay for a long time wondering how soon I could get away from this farm and what I would do then. Soon enough, my present feeling of enforced leisure would give way to something else. It frightened me that for the first time in many months, I had no idea what that would be.

At any rate, they would not allow me to get up the next day, either, even though my strength was returning as impatience and irritability. For one thing, I knew my case was out there across the road, thrust under the hay. Without it, I hadn't even a dress to wear—my old brown dress that I had come to Kansas in was what I had left, since I had cut off the skirt of my cream-colored figured muslin—nor did I have Thomas's books that I had saved, nor did I have my pistol or my rounds of ammunition. Helen was tiny—her nightdress stopped just below my knees. My guess was that the papa was a small man, too, and so there would be no stealing of clothes. When Lorna came in with my breakfast, I said, "What did you do with my things I was wearing?"

"De girl done laundered dat shirt and dem stockin's. Dem boots waren't worth savin'; you done walked right through dey soles. Missy Helen kep' you watch fo' ya. I don' know what you gone do about a dress. You bigger dan everbody round heah."

"I've got a dress, but it's in my case that I put under the hay across the road. Can you get it for me?"

"We done had a terrible rain since den—"

She saw my face fall.

"But maybe de hay save it." She stared at me, then she shook her head and exclaimed, "I don' know wheah you come from, missy. You come outta some dream, seems to me."

"I came from Kansas." That I should not have said.

Lorna's mouth opened, then snapped shut. She lowered her voice. "Well, dat's a red-hot word round heah dat you don't want to be sayin' when Massa Richard come back. Massa Richard is death on Kansas. Ta heah him tell it, Kansas war stolen right away from him. Oh, he gits hot on de subjec' and starts runnin' his hands ovah his pistols lak he cain' wait to shoot someone. Dey all feel dat, so you bettah jes' not say de word. I say you is from Saint Louis or someplace lak dat."

"Palmyra?"

Now Lorna stared at me again, just for the smallest second, then she said, "Sure 'nuf. Palmyra is all right."

"When is Master Richard coming back?"

"I guess tonight. Delia, she makin' a good hot supper fo' him and dem others. Zak had to kill her four chickens, an' she makin' dumplin's."

My mouth began to water right then, so I sat up and ate my breakfast. I could see out the windows from there, so when, a few moments later, I discerned Lorna and Helen making their way across the lawn to the road, I could only smile. I got up and watched them. They came to the road, crossed it, and were hidden by trees. After that, they were gone for what seemed like a long time, but then they reappeared. Lorna was carrying my case, which even from this distance looked considerably the worse for wear, and Helen was talking to her. Halfway up the lawn, Helen, grinning, ran to the house with the news. I got back into my bed, and she burst into the room. "We found it! Oh, Louisa, I was so afraid for you! You never know who is walking along that road; it's a very well-traveled road. I was saying to Lorna that I despaired of finding it, and then what would you do? I couldn't have told you! But we did find it, and it isn't too wet, you'll see." She ran out of the room and called down the stairs, then came back in. "And it's heavy! I can't believe you carried it all this way from—from—well, from wherever!"

I couldn't remember where I had told Helen I was from, but then Lorna carried in my case, which was certainly battered and sodden. She set it on the floor, then she and Helen stepped back and looked at me expectantly. Obviously, I was to open it.

"Mercy!" said Helen. "I hope your things aren't ruined! Last year, Minna and I went to an outdoor party, and we got caught in a terrible storm and had to cross the muckiest field! Oh, my goodness, our dresses were just black halfway up the skirt, and worse! And our bonnets! We'd only worn them that once! We were so downcast, but Lorna and Delia managed . . ."

Reader, I opened it.

There, on the top, were Thomas's three books that I had saved—*Uncle Tom's Cabin,* the Emerson essays, and a book called *The Bigelow Papers,* by Mr. Lowell. With them was my own fat volume, Miss Beecher's housekeeping manual. I lifted them out and saw that Helen was looking at them, but I looked quickly away from her and didn't see her reaction to them, if she had one. Underneath them was my brown woolen dress, quite damp and ill-smelling. Its color had leached out onto the things below—my bloomer, my shoes, and such. No shawl. Ah, yes, in my haste to depart the *Missouri Rose,* I had left my shawl behind, with my hair wrapped inside it. There really wasn't much in my bag, and so we got very quickly to the pistol and the rounds of ammunition. Helen's eyes got wide, and I saw she was having a good look. Lorna picked up my woolen dress and said, "Dis is a heavy thang! Ain' you got no summer dress? You gone expire in dis thang, round heah."

"I cut the skirt off my dress to make a shirt out of it."

"You ain' got nothin' else beside dese thangs?"

"No."

"Well," said Helen, "I'm going to go over to The Poplars and talk to Mrs. Harris. I'm a pet of hers, and Maria and Dorothea have ever so many frocks that they didn't take with them to Saint Louis, and I know for sure they were planning to have ever so many more made when they got there. Dorothea is taller than you, Lorna."

"You ken try. Dey don' know what dey got in dat house, anyways. Dey don' open de cupboards from one yeah to de nex'. Ifn dey lose somethin', dey go get a new one, instead of jes' lookin' for de old."

"Lorna, that's such a slander!"

"It ain'! Dey servants talk! Dey servants is almost rich offa dem!"

"Well, then! That will give me something to do before Papa gets home!" And she marched out, full of purpose.

Lorna shook out my dress, and we both wrinkled our noses at the stink of mildew. I saw that the books were considerably damaged, too, with black spots on their covers and their pages all swollen. I touched them and gave out a sigh. Lorna said, "I seen dresses worse off den dis dat come back for yeahs' more good weahin'. I reckon Missy Helen gon' tek caeh of you. You her projec' now, so you get back into you bed and you'll see!" She gave one of her rare small smiles. The pistol had been with us the whole time, lying there at the bottom of my case. I could see Lorna not looking at it, and surely she could see me not looking at it. Now I bent down and closed the case, snapping the hasp with a sharp click. She said, "Dat case needs airin', too. It have quite a stink on its own." But she didn't reach for it, and presently she went out of the room, carrying the dress and the shoes. I got back into the bed. I was a bit tired, and anyway, until there was something decent for me to wear, I didn't have anywhere else to go.

I have to say that I was strangely calm, considering my situation. No doubt there was some lingering weakness owing to my collapse, a weakness of the soul as well as of the body. Perhaps that was the reason that I seemed to have changed utterly. Had I spent my girlhood exploring the forests and fields around Quincy? Had I swum the great river? Had I journeyed to Kansas, helped build a claim there, hunted prairie chickens and turkeys, ridden my horse all about? Had I walked up and down the streets of Lawrence, fled the *Missouri Rose,* gone about as a boy, and a restless one at that? Had I walked from Kansas City to Independence and from Independence to here? Had I endured the discomforts of bitter cold and blazing heat, high winds, pouring rain, jolting wagons, steamers run aground? Had I contin-

ued doing and doing and everlastingly doing? It
seemed that I had, but now I couldn't understand it.
Another person had done all of that. It exhausted and
oppressed me just to ponder it. The only good thing I
could think of was to give way entirely to the languor
I felt. I was hardly enterprising enough to get to the
windows of my room. Simply to lie upon the bed
was preferable, not even thinking any thoughts or
making any plans; plans implied future activity,
which seemed impossible, not to mention unappeal-
ing. What a luxury it was, knowing that Helen and
Lorna and the unknown Delia were seeing to everything and that all I needed to do was close my eyes!

I thought of Mrs. Bush, who had said more than
once that southerners in general and Missourians in
particular were simply shiftless and lazy. "Of course,
that's the greatest evil of all," she would say. "It robs
you of knowing the pleasure of activity. We who
came up in a cold climate must work to live! I can't
claim it as a virtue; if you sit still, you'll freeze to
death. If you ask me, that's the Lord's greatest gift to
every right-thinking person!" But she did claim it as
a virtue, they all did, though indeed, it was hardly so
simple as she thought. There was much to be said for
activity, and all the active ones actively said it. But I
saw now, or rather felt in my bones and sinews, that
there was much to be said for ease, as well. Look at
Helen! Whom did I know who was as appealing as
Helen? She was artless and charming and generous
and kind, as well as pretty and lively. Possibly she
had never done a lick of work in her life, besides

needlework, but then her needlework was exquisite. And the room I was in. I had never been in such a room, so well proportioned and fine, with these two windows. Windows were expensive, and you almost never saw two, especially two side by side, put there not because a room needed that much light or air but because the two looked pleasing. Someone, probably the papa, had said, not, "I need a window," but, "I want two windows, just here and here." Well, that was the essence of luxury, wasn't it? Wanting something that you didn't need, and then having it. I closed my eyes. It seemed that this was all the thinking I could manage for the morning.

In the afternoon, Helen, who was as good as her word, returned from The Poplars with two dresses that had been discarded by Dorothea the previous summer. One was a green lawn with a broad white collar, and the other was a light nankeen, almost buff-colored, with brown braid trim. They were very pretty, especially the nankeen, but both had to be let out in the waist and have their hems let down all the way and faced. "Isabelle can do that in no time," said Helen. "Old Mr. LaFrance had her sent down to New Orleans when she was ten, to be trained, and he sends her out to work now. She's a wonder. All the ladies and girls around fight to have Isabelle come and stay. You know, Lorna can't stand her. But I'll send Ike over on one of the mules to fetch her tonight, and she can walk over in the morning and get started. She's very quick! She earns Mr. LaFrance ever so much money. Papa always talks about it."

"Why can't Lorna stand her?"

"You'll have to ask her. Lorna is a deep one, I keep telling you. I go along for months, thinking Lorna is happy and content, and she never says a word, and then! Well, Papa said one more outburst and he wasn't going to be responsible for what would happen! So I beg Lorna to just let things go sometimes. I couldn't live without Lorna! When she went with Bella to Saint Louis, I was so envious! I had to pray every day to be a better person. Aren't these lovely dresses? I loved the nankeen last summer, but they have ever so much money at The Poplars, because Mrs. Harris's father had the sacking factory, and Mrs. Harris was his only child, she was Miss Darlington, and so when she married Mr. Harris, who has a very good farm there, they got it both coming and going, Papa says. So however much Dorothea or Maria likes a dress, well, they still only wear it half a dozen times, if that. . . ."

And so on. Helen was in and out all afternoon, prattling about this and that. She had on a very pretty dress herself, pale-blue sprigged muslin, very light and summery, but neatly made. She had a fine waist, a slender wrist, and a lovely neck. It made me happy to look at her.

Just before dark, there was a to-do on the lawn outside my windows, which I surmised was Papa returning from his journey. I was apprehensive about Papa. Surely he would be more suspicious of a strange woman masquerading as a boy and less moved by my condition than his daughter had been. My room was dark—Lorna had not yet brought a candle—so I moved to the window and looked out. There were seven horses out there, and three Negro boys holding them while the men dismounted. There was talking and laughter and shouting, and then the door below opened and the men disappeared from my sight, coming up the stairs and going underneath the porch roof. The three boys and two of the men, who must have been house slaves traveling with the party, led the horses off to the stables. Now I could hear the cheerful noises of the group rising up the stairwell. They tromped about in their boots, called to one another, laughed, smoked strong seegars. Helen's delighted voice wove itself among their deeper tones, and then everything grew muffled as, I suppose, they went in to their supper. Sometime later, when it was entirely dark, Lorna hastened in with a tray and a candle, but she only put the things down, then scurried out. I was happy enough at that; Delia had certainly done herself proud, for I had a dish of chicken stew with three feathery dumplings and plenty of carrots and peas from the garden, as well as a dish of new blackberries and cream. Everything was hot and utterly savory, and I relished each bite.

Nevertheless, with each passing moment, I grew more apprehensive. The big house rang with the sounds of men who, I suspected, had never restrained themselves. At any rate, I imagined five Roland Breretons below, fully armed, and their behavior circumscribed only by the slenderest thread of good manners. The west was full of men who flashed from raucous merriment to violent anger in a step, a moment, a breath. The signs of one—hilarity, loud talk, grins, knee and back slapping, jocular challenges—were always to be dreaded as signs of the other: anger, resentment, pugnacity. Should they pour up the stairs, knowing by instinct that an abolitionist, a Lawrenceite, a Bay Stater by marriage, was in the house, I thought, I could go out one of the windows and drop to the roof of the porch, and after that, well, there was no telling. I got out of bed and pulled my case closer to me and unclasped the hasps, so that my pistol was within easy reach. I got back under the coverlet.

On the other hand, I was Lyman Arquette no longer. I was a woman in a nightdress in a bed, more than defenseless, as entirely within a protected category as if I sat within a glass dome. Perhaps. It was a nice question—was an abolitionist lady still a lady? As far as I knew, this question remained untested, even in K.T.

It didn't take long for these musings to transform themselves into others. What if Samson and Chaney were down there? A pistol wasn't designed only for self-defense, wasn't designed primarily for self-defense, as everyone in K.T. knew but did not admit. A nightdress billowing about could easily hide a pistol. Men filing out of the dining room, seegars in hand, would hardly be bothered to glance up the staircase, which was half in darkness, anyway. I could scrutinize each one at my leisure as he crossed the hall (would they cross the hall?) from dining room to parlor. There was no knowing the layout, as I hadn't yet been in the lower story of the house. It gave me a hot chill to imagine such things, and once I had imagined them, I felt a breathless compulsion to act, and yet I did not move. I stayed still, quite rigid, in my bed, staring straight ahead out the window into the dark, with the candle flame curling about its wick at the edge of my gaze.

The noise from below continued, stamping and yelling sometimes, laughter other times, the clanking of crockery, steps from here to there. I would say now that it was the very mysteriousness of it all that kept me in my bed. The idea of Samson and Chaney carousing down below seemed to flash, in my mind, from reality to absurdity, back and forth. I hadn't the courage to find out, though. I made up my mind that there would be a more opportune moment. I made up my mind that it would be a poor return for Helen's hospitality to shoot her friends as they were getting up from their supper in her house. I made up my mind that revenge was more complicated than I had thought it would be, but then so was everything else one looks forward to with confidence. Lorna returned for my tray, saying only, "I sure 'nuf hope dat Massa Richard gets rid of dese cronies of his 'fore too late, 'cause I is ready for mah own bed tonight."

I shook off my rigidity. "Thank you for staying up with me these last two nights."

"Well, it waren't gone to be Missy Helen. Dat's for sure. But you is all right now. You got you color back. I reckon it didn't hurt you so much."

"I suppose I'll know that later."

"Spose so." And she went out.

Some time after that, Helen ran in. She had an evening frock on, of pale-yellow silk, and her hair was elaborately done up in a braided weave. She was smiling but agitated. She exclaimed, "Oh, Louisa, Papa is terrifically eager to meet you, so he sent Ike off right away, and now Ike's back, and Mr. LaFrance has promised to send Isabelle over in the wagon first thing! Isn't that splendid? But the other news is so frightening, I hardly dare tell you about it, in your condition, but I am bursting! Papa says not to worry, they won't get near us, he will hold them off, but—" She began gasping, then sat down on the bed, folded her hands in her lap, closed her eyes, and composed herself. "Papa says Lane's army in Nebraska, the one he ran away from, was just a ruse, and now he has a whole other one, three or four hundred or more, and he's been seen in Olathe! Mr. Perkins, who's down below, knew a man whose cousin saw him himself! You can't mistake Jim Lane—oh, he is a cruel-looking man, and they say his eyes are dead black until he decides to kill someone, and then they get a strange red light in them! And a man saw him and identified him positively and overheard him say that he was going to move on Missouri now! Oh, my!" She put her hands to her throat. "And Papa and Mr. Harris, he's down below as well, both say that that's been the plan all along, that the abolitionist criminals have all along meant to run us off our farms and steal our factories and bring in a lot of Irishmen to work in them for no wages at all, and you know, they never take care of their workers, but when they can't work, no matter how old they are, they just throw them out on the street to fend for themselves, and Chicago is full of those people, and Saint Louis, too. Bella told me about it in a letter—such a tragedy! But at the same time, it's so dangerous! And they'll do anything to a woman, they have no respect for women, beatings and everything unspeakable, and their best men don't care a pin for it but just step over the bodies in the street and walk right past crying children as if they weren't Christians at all!"

I dared not laugh at this torrent. I said, "I haven't heard such things myself. I—"

"But Papa says that we have him, and Ike and Jess and Malachi, and Mr. Harris has twenty or thirty, both at the factory and on the farm, and of course there's Morgan at home, though he's only sixteen, and Stephen up at the college, and he would certainly come home, if danger threatened. Mr. Harris's brothers were in the Texas war and are very bold fellows—but oh, I don't know how I shall go to sleep! Just imagine, you are sleeping ever so peacefully, and you suddenly awaken in the middle of the night, to find an abolitionist in your room, staring down at you, some Old John Brown sort of person, who isn't even human, really, but a terrible demon—oh, and you know he's going to hack you to pieces right there!"

"John Brown didn't hack any women to death."

But I said it sheepishly, the only way you would say something like that.

"And you know, they round up your people, and they make them go off, whether they want to or no, even the mammies and little ones, and they drive them north like cattle or sheep or something, and then, when they've got them so far from home that they can't ever return, no matter how much they want to, why, then they just let them go on their own. The skilled ones, like Mr. LaFrance's Isabelle, they might be all right, you know, but not everyone is skilled like that. Papa says it's even odds who takes care of whom. When the cholera came through here, my mama was out in the cabins washing and feeding and setting fires, and she wore herself out, so that Delia said to her that she wouldn't have been surprised if Mama'd ended up laying down her own life for her people, and that was why Delia would never leave her, no matter what. Even though they aren't all truly grateful like that, most are, and we're their family as much as anything else, and Jim Lane and John Brown and that awful Dr. Robinson just want to tear them away from us and drive them north into the snow! And you know they just can't tolerate the snow!" Here she burst into a fury of weeping.

I said, "I don't think you should be afraid of attack, Helen. I was just in Kansas City myself, and in Independence, too, and they weren't talking of that at all. They were talking of what a fool Jim Lane was and how he would never amount to anything." And, it is fair enough to add, I did believe this portion of what I was saying. "And Robinson is in prison."

"But that was days ago!"

"Yes, but a four-hundred-man army of real soldiers doesn't just turn up."

"But I'm sure it's the federals, who've turned their coats and made up their minds to break the laws and comfort the traitors. It's been months since John Brown and his sons hacked those men to death, and the federals haven't stirred a stump out of their camps, because they don't want to, no matter what the President tells them to do. Papa says it's just a scandal and they should all be court-martialed, but the New Englanders have all the money in the world, and they make sure things go their way! Oh, my goodness, who will protect us!" But even as she said this, she was already sighing and growing calmer. Finally, she said, "Papa said I must go off to bed, but I don't know how I'm going to sleep now! May I . . . May I . . ."

"Yes, you may sleep in here. I feel fine, and the bed is sufficiently large for the two of us, I think."

She was much relieved. I refrained from mentioning that should she awaken in the middle of the night, she would find an abolitionist right here in the room with her!

When she had gone to her own chamber and come back in her nightdress and wrapper, with her hair falling down her back and her candle in her hand, I said, ever so idly, "So tell me about your papa's guests," and she named Mr. Harris and Mr.

Perkins, and Mr. Smith and Mr. Chesbrough, but never Mr. Chaney or Mr. Samson. "They are all so old! Thirty-five, at least, and Mr. Chesbrough is fifty-six!" Her voice dropped to a whisper. "Truly I despair of ever finding a husband! Sometimes I almost wish for a war. Don't you think officers are very handsome-looking and serious? If they would all come and march around, and then declare a truce, it would certainly be splendid!"

CHAPTER 23

I Improve My Acquaintance with Papa

Nankeens look best, washed in suds, with a teacup of ley added for each pailful. Iron on the wrong side. Soak new nankeens in ley, for one night, and it sets the color perfectly.

—*pp. 288–89*

EVERYTHING HELEN HAD promised came quickly to pass. Isabelle arrived with the breakfast and inspected the two dresses while I was eating. As soon as Lorna took the tray away (the two women did avoid looking at one another), I stood up and was measured. Isabelle was not especially talkative, but she had a Louisiana lilt to her voice, "Lawsy, you be a big gal, missy. I don' know ifn we got enough goods in de skirt! Hmm. What we gone to face this with?" But then she set to work and made over the nankeen in no time. The green gown she elected to take home with her, as she had some stuff she could piece into it, and then, with a bit of trim . . . Helen was right: the woman was a genius.

I brushed my hair and put on the nankeen, which was flattering enough, perhaps as flattering a dress as I had ever had, and indeed I had never had a dress from Saint Louis, the reputed origin of this one. I felt it drape attractively about my figure. Mrs. Harris had also supplied an old petticoat, which, though rather too short, did the trick well enough.

It was thus that I was enabled to descend the stairs at suppertime and meet Papa.

I can hardly remember what I expected, perhaps some elegant long-haired sort, or, alternatively, a Ruffian so bearded that only his eyes were visible— as Mrs. Bush had said, Missourians all seemed to like to cultivate an abundance of hair—but Papa, Mr. Richard Aloysius Day, was small, almost tiny, and entirely bald. The top of his head rose only to my shoulder, and every chair that he habitually sat in had a high, hard cushion, upon which he perched like a bird, the better to stare at you, also like a bird. But he did not have a birdlike voice, but rather a lovely baritone, entirely the voice of another man, and in the parlor sat a large piano. In the course of my stay at Day's End Plantation, Papa himself sat down at the piano perhaps three or four times and sang. As Lorna later said to me, "It do stand your hair on end to hear dat big voice comin' out of dat little head, but he sing like some angel, sure 'nuf."

On my first night, however, I was as yet unaware of Papa's talents, only taken aback by the figure he made in the dining room at supper, sitting up in his chair with his napkin tucked into his collar and his fork lifted to dart at his food. By contrast, Helen, who was very attentive to him, looked like another animal entirely, a sleek filly, perhaps, all limbs and grace. What sort of animal did I look like to them, with my wisps of hair and my big hands and my plain face? Nothing local, I am sure.

We ate rabbit that Malachi had shot, cooked with a considerable quantity of mustard. Papa's fork popped little bits between his lips quickly, quickly, quickly, and his lips snapped shut over them. He cocked his shining head at me, ate a bit of bread, darted me a smile, let the wonderful baritone roll out. "Mrs. Bisket"—yes, I had taken Louisa's name— "my beloved daughter tells me that you are a wanderer in our country, without connections or resources."

"Yes, sir, she speaks truly."

"And yet you comport yourself in a ladylike manner and speak with educated tones. I am told you carry books in your case. I am a reading man. After we have supped, I will show you my library."

After a long moment of silence, I ventured, "I came west and discovered that conditions were not as they had been represented. I met with some misadventures."

"You and your husband came west with no company or connections? Very enterprising."

I pondered how much to divulge. The Massachusetts Emigrant Aid Company was, perhaps, the most famous "company" in the west or anywhere else. And Helen had mentioned the books to him, though I didn't know whether she'd named them. Finally, I thought the safest thing was to concede his assumptions. I said, "Yes. We had no company or connections out here."

"I offer my condolences on his death, my dear. The death of my own wife has been a permanent grief to me, and I have told my three daughters that I will never marry again."

This seemed as good a time as any to subside into

silence. Papa's manners and evident curiosity had a way of drawing me, so that it required positive resistance not to tell some story, either true or fabricated. But I was a little afraid that I would mix myself up if I spoke too voluminously, and there was this, as well—I didn't want Papa to get into the habit of expecting me to be forthcoming. For one thing, I was his guest, not his daughter, and for another, a trickle now could easily turn into a stream later, and then into a cataract. It was better that I should retain as much mystery as possible with Papa. My sisters would have asserted that such a course would be easy for me, as they had considered me backward and unsociable all my life, but it was far more difficult not to lay myself out to be agreeable in this house of strangers than it had been at home. Papa's every bright glance seemed to call up some response, some bit of intelligence. I ate industriously, as if I were famished, and soon I was exceedingly full.

"And so your husband had connections in the west?"

"Not really, no."

More rabbit.

"But surely he knew someone?"

"No; I would have to say no."

A forkful of greens.

"He didn't come from a large family, then?"

"No, not especially."

A bite of bread.

"And yourself? You've left many behind?"

"I have sisters."

More rabbit.

"They're all older."

A sip of well water.

"Much older."

"Your own father and mother?"

Another sip of water, to cool the heat of the mustard.

"They passed on."

As light and energetic as Papa was, I must say conversing with me was heavy work for him. Finally, Helen could stand it no longer, and she said, in an ever so low and respectful tone of voice, "Oh, Papa, I told you of Louisa's tragedy. She's disconsolate. We should . . ."

Papa ceased asking questions for now, but little looks, like little sparks of light, continued to flash across the table. After supper, I begged to be excused and went up to my room. I wasn't tired at all, but I saw that I was going to have to make the most of my ill health, so as to keep to my room and avoid Papa as much as possible.

This did not prove to be easy, as Papa was quite as cordial as Helen by nature, and there was the added spur of my mysteriousness that encouraged him to search me out and attempt to draw me. The very next morning, though I wasn't expected to take breakfast downstairs (Helen did not, either), Lorna brought me a note along with my tray, inviting me to take a look at Papa's library. Helen's door was still closed, as by Thomas's watch it was not much after seven, so there would be no protection from that quarter. Papa's handwriting was tall and narrow, but full of whorls and flourishes. It surprised me—perhaps I had expected it to be made up of a sort of pecking.

Papa was standing in a small room off the parlor, as sprucely fitted up as if he had been standing there like a diminutive statue all night long, only awaiting my coming to bring him to life. "Ah, my dear— Louisa, is it? Louisa Bisket. Unusual name, indeed. Never heard it before in these parts. But I know you aren't from these parts by your own testimony, don't I?"

I smiled and wished him good morning. He bowed over my hand.

"There was a Bisket at college with me, a class or two ahead. Tall fellow. Can't remember where his people were from, though."

I hazarded a question: where had Papa gone to college?

"That was a good time of life, wasn't it? College. Only spent a year there, in fact. Princeton College, it was. Not too many men from the west in those days at that college. They thought me an odd bird indeed!" He laughed. "Even though I had curls enough, and great mustaches, to boot!" He laughed again, and I laughed, too.

"However, the ministry was not the life for me. I was made to be a farmer, though a reading farmer. You'll see that I have a great many works on agriculture here in my library. I make it my practice to emulate the great Mr. Jefferson, who was a terrific improver and had sound ideas upon government and farming, and architecture, too! This house was designed according to Jeffersonian principles, though of course we have humbler materials to work with here in the west. Ah, well. The bank is an evil institution, and the rush of our civilization into the arms of money, as it were, is a great corruption!

"These are my books!" He turned and swept his little arm in an arc toward the two walls of books. I would guess that they numbered five hundred or so, indeed a sizable library for a Missouri farmer, and possibly a matter, had she known it, of significant surprise to Mrs. Bush, who always held that Missourians read only a few words of the Bible and wrote only their first names.

I did as I was expected, which was to step over to the shelves and admire. I couldn't resist saying, "My husband was a great reader." There was plenty to admire—Mr. Shakespeare's entire works, and those of Mr. Milton, and Dr. Johnson, and Mr. Joseph Addison. The poems of Mr. Pope were bound in red calf and decorated in gold, and of course there were some volumes of Mr. Jefferson's writings, as well. There was a whole shelf of volumes in French, and ten or a dozen titles in what appeared to be German. As I perused them, Papa stood back, his hands clasped behind him and a great smile on his face. *Ivanhoe, The Lady of the Lake, Rob Roy, Marmion, Quentin Durward.* I

touched one, and Papa said, "I am a lover of Scott.
He knows what freedom means to a man!" I put my
hand down at my side. Poe. I paused to look, and he
said, "I knew the poor fellow, can you imagine?
They drove him from pillar to post, but indeed, he
wasn't himself sinless by any means." I looked in
vain for Emerson, Hawthorne, Mr. Thoreau, Mrs.
Stowe, the books Thomas could not be without, but
in Papa's library, it was as if they had never lived.
The novelists and poets here were all English ones,
except for Madame Sand, who reposed, in French,
right beside Monsieur Hugo. I murmured, "I am
sorry I don't read French. But indeed, you have few
American writers here!"

Papa flared up at once. "Who is there? Only those
who spout treason and nonsense! Oh, my dear, you
will be sorry you said such a thing, because you will
find me unstoppable on the subject! Our nation is a
rosebud, blighted at its very opening by money and
industry and all of what I call the iron ways! Boilers!
Railroads! Steamboats! Armories! Coal dust, coal
smoke, coal stink! We are being hammered willy-
nilly into iron bonds! Where are you from?" His eyebrows shot upward, and without resisting, but quick
enough to lie, I said, "Palmyra."

"You are fortunate! Vow never to go to Chicago
or Cincinnati or New York's inferno! Such places
destroy your faith in the future!"

"I've never been to any of those cities. I've never
been to a city."

"And you are better for it, young lady! Come
with me!" Papa now grasped me by the elbow and

hurried me out of the library, first into the hall and then out a door that turned out to open onto a rear veranda that was at ground level. The kitchen wing of the house enclosed us to the right. To the left, there was a prospect of two fields divided by a rail fence, one a pasture with cows and horses in it and the other a field of hemp, tall, leafy, and ready to be harvested. Several oaks dotted the pasture, and the animals grazed peacefully in their shade. To the right, partially hidden by the kitchen wing, was the stables and, behind them, a barn. Both were built of brick, like the house, but they were not whitewashed, as the house was. It was a pleasant prospect, and I was thinking I would like to get a better look at the horses sometime, when Papa seemed to leap into the air with excitement. He shouted, "Look at this— is this not the most divine vision you've ever seen?" He raised both arms, threw back his head, and spun around. "The fit and proper stewardship of the land! The useful verdure consecrated to our improvement by the Lord Himself on one side and the devoted beasts on the other, whose very contentment and low intelligence recommend them to our service! Who made that pasture? I did! Who built that fence? I did! Who planted that crop? I did, yes! But it wasn't I! All I did was enter into a great preexistent circle and divide the plants from the beasts by a little fence, so that the beasts wouldn't trample the tender shoots. Everything is perfection here! The rain falls from the sky, and beasts partake of the fruits of the soil and then themselves create the soil! There is a great flowering, beauty announcing itself, and then God's messengers, the bees, go among the blossoms! All is given to us for our education and enjoyment, our nourishment and our contemplation! We hold out our hands, and what we need is placed in them!"

Papa took a few deep breaths, then came right up to me and looked up into my face. His bald head shone brightly in the morning sunlight. "To look at this, you wouldn't know that we live in a fallen world, would you?" I didn't have to respond, but I did think that his experience must have been considerably different from mine, if he supposed that I ever forgot that we lived in a fallen world. "Money!" he shouted. "Money, gold, cash, dollars! How does it get in everywhere, I ask you? How can it be that money has come between the land and its workers? Between a man and his dependents?" (Here one of the slaves happened to lead two horses, a mare and her half-grown colt, out of the stable area and toward the pasture.) "How can it be, this crime and this tragedy, that a man should have to pay money to purchase a fellowman to work his fields? That is the tragedy of our institution, not that we have these relationships of superiority and inferiority, as some wrongheaded northerners think, but that money has entered in and corrupted everything like a disease! You know why the slave is unhappy in his work? Not because he is a slave, but because he knows he represents a certain amount of money, a thousand dollars, say. He thinks that because he costs a thousand dollars, he *is* a thousand dollars, walking around. He feels himself rich! He's distracted from his God-given purpose on this earth, which is to serve, not the master and the mistress, but the beasts and the plants and the round of rain and drought and growth and harvest! The so-called master and mistress serve the selfsame thing! We are all servants! The land is the master!" I wondered what Thomas would say to this, whether he would maintain his composure.

The man leading the horses now opened the gate and led the pair through. Other horses in the field lifted their heads, and one of them whinnied. When the man had removed its halter, the colt frolicked away. A moment later, the mare trotted after him. One of the cows mooed. I said, "You have lovely horses here," but Papa could not be turned from his flow of eloquence.

"When you are in a city, young lady, the real master is hidden from you by paving stones and building blocks and iron rails, and you begin to think that the false master, money, is the real master. Did you know that when my father was a boy, before this present century, there was no objection to our institution? Of course not! The true master wasn't hidden from our sight then! Men lived on farms or in villages, they saw the green world every day, the right way of things was apparent to them. But now this misapprehension has gained sway in the north, in the land of cities, and here we are, fallen low and falling lower fast, and, my dear, they are so hostile to the right way of things that they've resolved to destroy

the last vestiges of it! That is money for you! There
can't be just a little of money, but everything has to
be money, money, money! Soon we'll be buying and
selling our own children, and some will say the problem is that there are children and parents, not that
money has come between them!"

I couldn't resist saying, "I've known one or two
northerners," but Papa was now red in the face and
red in the pate, and this last speech was accompanied
by considerable agitation. Had he been a large or
heavy man, I would have been in some uncertainty
for him, but he worked off his excitement by hopping
and jumping around on the grass below the veranda.
Soon enough a smile returned to his countenance,
and he said, "Well, my dear, if there are any volumes
you care to peruse, make yourself free! Bella was
something of a reader, but Minna and Helen don't
open a book from one year to the next."

I thanked him and requested a book I had
noticed, a novel called *Pride and Prejudice,* by Miss
Austen, which Thomas had mentioned but I had
never read.

"Ah!" said Papa with a delighted smile. "Miss
Austen! Few people know Miss Austen these days,
but she is quite a stylist for a woman, quite a splendid
stylist!" He took me back inside and placed the first
volume of the novel in my hand. He had hold of my
elbow, and he didn't let go until he had said one more
thing, which was, "Young lady, preserve yourself
from money!"

I nodded, reflecting that, at the moment, I was

almost entirely preserved from money and I hadn't before thought to be thankful for it.

It was lovely to have a book, such a treasure, all to myself, and I went out on the veranda, where I had seen some chairs. Morning shade still spread from this side of the house, which faced west. Soon I was deep into the story.

The weather was, of course, extremely hot, as this was Missouri and it was August. Perhaps, then, my lassitude in those days was heat-induced. Certainly, the custom of the house was for everyone, even the slaves, to retire in the middle of the day for a nap. Breakfast came early—at six. Supper came late—after eight. The two hours of napping in the afternoon produced in me a sense of helplessness; even after I had clothes to wear and could have departed, I looked to Helen to tell me what to do. Helen said, "Oh! Well, it's August! No one does much of anything in August. It's just so hot! I can't bear even to ride or to drive. The horses look so forlorn, all lathered up with the heat. It's better to leave the poor things alone!"

Papa did indeed have horses. One day, I explored the stables and saw that Papa was a real Missourian when it came to horseflesh, that is, an avid collector and a good judge. For the carriage, there was the matched pair of blacks, long-legged trotters with white stars and white hind fetlocks. For the farm-work there was a pair of heavy sorrel mares, in addition to four of their offspring, sorrel mules that Papa said were twice as tough as the mares and equally docile. Helen had a bay mare to ride and a gray pony to draw her in her cart, and Papa had several horses to choose from and to offer guests. All these were in addition to the breeding stock; along with music and literature, one of Papa's avocations was breeding racing horses. "Only in a small way," said Papa. "I can't claim to be able to afford the best stock, by any means. Racing is a rich man's sport. But we have some good Kentucky bloodlines here; yes, indeed." And I saw that he was one of those horsemen you frequently see, who pride themselves on their judgment rather than their pocketbook. In the early mornings before Helen came out of her room, I truly enjoyed strolling down to the stable area and watching the horses. And it wouldn't have been shameful, by any means, to see Jeremiah among these animals, switching his tail and making his way from clover patch to clover patch. The pony was Papa's only gray.

What to do for Thomas, what to do that he would not have disapproved of, how to honor him, even how to think of him, was a hot little nut of a question that I turned over and over, trying to crack, day after day. Often, of course, he was simply my husband, whom I missed as a wife must. There were countless things I wanted to say to him that could be said only to him, and not just observations or questions about great issues but, more often, little jokes or amusing sentences and, more often than that, smiles, glances. Had I realized when he was still alive how many times in a day Thomas and I would exchange a look, in the full confidence that each of us knew what the other was thinking? Could this have so quickly become a feature of our marriage without a real sense between us of loving friendship? And so, whatever our disagreements, there had been that, hadn't there? I entered these thoughts happily for a moment, even yearned for them, but they were their own punishment: the tie was broken and never to be renewed; my only ways of enjoying it were quiet reflection within myself or unsatisfactory communication to others of subtleties that they could neither understand nor appreciate. The very pleasures of such thoughts turned into an even larger loneliness than I had felt before I allowed myself to think them. But it was often the case that living with Papa and Lorna and Helen and Delia (a big woman but deceptively quick, who said little, and nothing to me— "She's very shy, especially of white folks," said Helen) and Malachi and Ike and all the others made me want to positively drag Thomas back from death and wring answers from him about who they were and what to think of them. Sometimes I felt myself in an argument with him, not because my views had changed but because this ease and these pleasures were so comfortable. Must I not be pleased by the graceful front of the house, which had surely been erected by slaves? Must my heart not lift at the sight of the horses—more and better horses than any Yankee would ever need or care to have? Must I not compliment Helen on the gowns that made her so pretty? Must I not eat with relish the game Malachi shot and Delia prepared? Must I not sink into the joys of a delightful novel during the day, when others were working? Must I not walk across the lawn, feeling its luxurious springiness in every step? Must I not smile in spite of myself when I opened my eyes every morning and saw the elegance of my chamber? Must I instead keep my eyes closed until I had marshaled my responses according to moral principle? Must I not look back upon our much humbler, our very unbeautiful, arrangements in K.T. with a sensation that was beginning to amount to revulsion? Thomas, perhaps, would not have felt this division at all. I yearned to ask him about it.

And how quickly did I need to flee?

For flight was certainly required. I knew and felt that I was in every way the wrong bird for this flock and that my every movement and remark revealed it. That Helen and Papa seemed to accept me was a testament more to their hospitality (or blindness) than anything else. Every morning, after I donned my gown and before I left my chamber, I made sure that my pistol and its ammunition were safe inside my case. Before my nap and at bedtime, I reassured myself that nothing had been touched or disturbed. These were not the actions of a proper guest.

Most important, I quizzed Thomas, how should I go on with pursuing his killers? How should I leave? What direction should I take? Where were money and transportation to come from? How should I disguise myself, now that Papa and all his connections knew of my existence, now that I was wearing costumes well known in the neighborhood, now that my men's clothes had been disposed of? What should I do after the deed was done, now that I was deep in enemy territory, settled territory, where the most desirable outcome, the deaths of Samson and Chaney, would certainly have ill consequences for me. In K.T., I had been planning revenge. In Missouri, I was most assuredly planning a crime for which I would be captured and punished, possibly killed (on balance, the easier consequence to ponder). I quizzed Thomas, but I got nothing from him. On this subject, he turned away from me. I had always been more bloody-minded than he, less judicious, more hasty and hot. And yet how could I let it go, and creep back to Quincy? It didn't seem possible. It didn't *feel* possible. And it didn't seem just. To turn and walk away from his killing, in fact, seemed to both represent and partake of the very absence of justice that was K.T. from top (President Pierce) to bottom (the unknowns who died from time to time without anyone's ever knowing who they were or how to get in touch with their loved ones). The hot days drifted by, and soon I had been with Helen and Papa for over a week.

It chanced, during this week, that Papa had few visitors and kept mostly to himself, though on most days he rode away to do business of some sort. His questioning of me and my refusal to answer became a more and more good-humored ritual (or, at any rate, good-humored on his side; on my side, fear gave my smiles and laughs a hollow quality). There

were no parties and little news. Perhaps out of disinclination to alarm Helen, Papa said little more about
Kansas than he had already. For several days after
her alarm, Helen tried to take things in hand and
make provision for a siege or something like it. She
and Lorna and Delia bustled here and there, especially down in the cellar below the house and out in
the root cellar cut into the hillside. They decided that
there was an abundance of provisions for two or
three months, anyway. But the sun shone and the
heat held, and the danger seemed to recede as life
kept on in its familiar way. To me, the idea of my
friends back in K.T. attacking Day's End Plantation
from either the road in front or the fields behind
seemed ludicrous. Papa had all the discernible
advantages.

On the evening of the thirteenth of August, however, two fellows came galloping over the lawn up to
the house just at suppertime, and Papa ran out to
meet them, while Helen, who had been telling us a
story of some biscuits she had been learning to make
that afternoon, sat staring at me, her mouth open, her
eyes wide, and her hand pressed to her throat. We
couldn't help it—we sat there still as rocks, listening
for the voices on the lawn to rise above a rumble.
They did not. Soon enough, the horsemen galloped
away and Papa returned to the table, a smile of reassurance so fixed on his face that it didn't reassure at
all. He was clearly alarmed and could hardly prevent
himself from hopping about. Nevertheless, he made
for his seat, sat down in it, and darted his fork at his

baked apple. But it was no use, and he threw down the utensil and stared at Helen for a second before saying, "Jim Lane has raised an army in Lawrence and attacked Fort Franklin. There was a great deal of shooting, and then they set the place afire! Our gallant men managed to defend themselves without a loss, but then the devil Lane rounded up the postmaster and threatened to hang him, until his wife begged for his life. I understand that it was only her great beauty and the devil Lane's susceptibility to the fair sex that preserved the man, if you'll pardon my referring to such things, my dear."

This had the ring of truth about it, but I said nothing, only stared at my plate. I thought all at once of Frank, who could easily have joined up with Lane, and was filled with dread.

Papa went on. "Only property has been lost, but the Kansas criminals have made a serious vow. I hesitate to mention it to you, my dear. We shall see."

"They're coming here!" cried Helen.

"Now, Helen—"

"They are! I can see it in your face!"

"Not right here, darling, not to Day's End—"

"What's to stop them?"

Jim Lane's foolishness, I thought, but of course I didn't open my mouth.

"It's seventy miles or more between here and there. We're back from the border a good ways. Senator Atchison won't allow it. The President—"

"Oh, they are demons! I wish they were dead. I—"

"Helen, my dear, calm yourself. Of course I am rattled a bit by the news, but I don't expect to be personally affected. Fort Franklin is right beside Lawrence, and Lawrence is days away. This is merely an example of the growing lawlessness of—"

"Oh, Papa! Oh, Papa!"

Now Papa's voice developed some steel, and he said, "Helen! I must insist that you calm yourself!" He leaned toward her and spoke almost in a whisper. "Don't you realize what a temptation this presents to the servants? If they were to think, however wrongly, that these abolitionist types are nearby, they would give in to temptation and try to get to them! They would think that they could leave us and find support and ease for the rest of their lives. They have childlike fantasies that will lead some of them astray. You, my dear, must fortify yourself and dissemble your fear, because they assume that you know something and that the more afraid you are, the closer the abolitionists are to the house. Helen! Do you understand me?"

"Yes, Papa." But her voice trembled.

"Now look at Louisa, here. She is far calmer and more realistic about this news. My dear, I wish you would strive to emulate Louisa. If you are going to have your own establishment, your husband will rely on you to always remain collected and even in your responses to daily trials. You cannot live otherwise!" In fact, I was far from composed but instead besieged with thoughts of Frank. I was stiff with anxiety.

Helen cast me a look, took some deep breaths, and made herself eat two bites of her baked apple. I smiled at Papa as best I could, more insensible than imperturbable, and attempted to keep on eating, too. But Papa was more agitated than he let on, and was soon galloping away on his horse to find out more. I spent the rest of the evening trying to avoid imagining Frank and Louisa and Charles and the others and trying to present Helen with an example of composure, reading, sewing, listening to her play the piano, until I finally took her into my bed once again and brushed her hair until we were, if not calm, then tired enough to sleep. After that, I lay awake myself, thinking of the pistol under the bed, until Papa and some of his friends rode up. I fell asleep to the drumming of their earnest voices. Helen thought I was her protector, but I knew that she was mine.

I held no affection for Franklin—Franklin was a wretched Ruffian town that Papa and Helen would deplore if ever they saw it—but the next day I said nothing at all as they mourned its (miserable) post office and its (crude) hotel, as well as its (regrettably unshot) citizenry. I even asked Papa where Franklin was and tried to maintain a demeanor of ignorant but well-meaning concern. What, I said, had Papa heard about this fellow Jim Lane?

He had begun, Papa said, as merely a scamp, but the influence of the abolitionists had transformed him into a bloodthirsty charlatan and brute.

Had Papa ever seen the fellow?

Certainly not—he was not curious about such

men—but others had seen him. He affected wild clothes, and his eyes blazed with iniquity, more so every day. The senators and congressmen who had seen him in Washington had told Atchison that if this was a fair type of "Free-Soiler," then by all means should the Union be preserved from them!

"Helen mentioned this man Robinson?"

"Ahh. Now, Robinson is a smooth one. Looks normal, respectable, even. Works carefully and slowly, said to be in thrall to his wife, who is even more calculating than he is himself." Papa shook his head. "These are the rumors, of course. I don't put much stock in rumor myself."

I nodded at the wisdom of this course.

The next day, there were even more alarms. It began in midmorning—the first cool morning we'd had. Helen had made up her mind that she was going to make an oilcloth for the back parlor, and Papa had brought her a sheet of canvas from town. This she had unrolled in the hallway, and she was laying lavender iris blossoms around the borders by means of a stencil. She had also made a stencil for the leaves, and she had a pot of green paint, too. She was just explaining to me how neat and colorful this oilcloth would make the back parlor look after she had impregnated it with enough coats of shellac, when a horse, once again, galloped up the front lawn to the porch. Papa nipped out of his library, where he had been working at some papers, scooted around us where we were kneeling over the canvas, and hurried out the front door, being careful to close it even in his rush. Helen sat up and looked out, then rose up and went over to the window, which was open, and listened. I began to admonish her about eavesdropping, but she suddenly exclaimed, "Oh, they're at it again!" and ran into the kitchen. Moments later, the messenger galloped away, and Papa entered, opening and closing the door with considerable care. He looked at me where I was kneeling between the two pots of paint, and he said, "Where's Helen?"

"She went into the kitchen."

"Good. She's not been raised in a manner that has prepared her for the sorts of perils we now have to fear. I regret that, but who was to know? Until last year, we lived in peace here, all of a like mind, expecting only to go on in perpetuity, like the yearly round of the seasons and the daily round of the sun." He sighed. "Ah, well. My dear Mrs. Bisket, I regret to inform you that there is another attack being per- petrated by the devil Lane even as we speak. Rather more in our direction, though still in Kansas."

"Mercy me! Where?" I exclaimed. I thought of Frank at once, with dread.

"They are marching. Or, they were marching as of last night. No one is quite sure to where, but we haven't the forces to turn them. They may sweep all before them! One thing is clear: Lane proposes to force a military solution to a political conflict, and we will have to answer him in kind."

We stared at one another, and then I slowly stood up, wiping my hands on a rag. Papa took my large hand between his two small ones and said in a dramatic voice, "Much might be asked of me, Mrs. Bisket. My older daughters are far away, and I have only my Helen, the most delicate flower of the three. I dare not commend her to servants, but I feel that I may commend her to you. Your coming here in this time of uncertainty has a fortuity to it that I cannot ignore, though I'm not a superstitious man. At the very least, I shall be away some of the time for the next period. Delia and Lorna know perfectly well how to run the house, and Malachi and Ike can take care of the farm. They love us and depend on us, and we upon them; that is the virtue of our institution. But to you I surrender my fairest and most precious possession, my Helen. I ask you to keep her safe and occupied! Should something untoward happen to me, then I ask you to take her into the custody of Bella, in Saint Louis, who has a fine establishment there. I feel that I may depend upon you!"

"Why?" I said, thinking distractedly of Frank still.

"Because you have a plain, honest look about you, which is more pleasing to a loving father than all the beauty in the world."

In short, I looked like a governess or a schoolmistress, and so could be relied upon to act like one.

Papa said, "Go to her, please!" And then he turned and went out.

I found Helen in the kitchen, crying by the stove, where Delia was brining some pickles, and not long after, Papa and one of the Negroes, whom I didn't recognize, galloped away. From time to time, Delia stroked Helen on her yellow hair, and then Lorna came in, carrying a large basket of white washing that she'd been doing over a fire in the yard. Her face was dark and steamy, and clearly her temper was short. She glanced at Helen and said, "De trouble of de world ain' touched you yet, so why you bawlin'?"

"I—" But remembering, I think, what her father had said to her two nights before, Helen simply wiped her tears away and sat up.

Now Delia spoke in a low voice. "Men is rushin' 'round wid guns and thangs. Nobody knows what gone happen, Lorna. You done got ta be a hard woman."

"Let's see what dey is to carry on about before we carries on, dat's what I say."

"You kin be a hard woman in good times, and you kin be a hard woman in bad times, and you always got a reason to be a hard woman, but it don' do you no good in the end. Dat's what *I* say," said Delia. Then she turned to Helen and said, "You eat some biscuit wid butter and honey on it, child, and you be better prepared fo' what's ta come." Then she made us places at the deal table where she had been working on the pickles and gave us each a plate. Lorna sniffed and went out.

Well, Jim Lane and his army got to Fort Saunders, sure enough, and they mounted an attack and went in shooting, but as everyone knows, they discovered rather soon (not right away, though) that the fort was undefended, unoccupied by a single soul.

They then left a skeleton force to maintain Free State control of the place, and then Lane took some of the men and went off to Nebraska. Thus he was not even present when an actual engagement happened to take place the next day. Of course, I heard nothing of Frank, but the intelligence seemed to be that there were no casualties. I took solace in that.

There was a man, Sam Walker, who had a claim right outside Lawrence, and also a ruffian named Titus, who was a great bully, much hated by the Free Staters, because he was always bragging and making threats. As I was able to piece the story together in the days to follow, from what I heard from Papa and some of his friends (who considered Titus a rough enough fellow, but right-thinking, and who spoke of Sam Walker as one of the criminal leaders whose traitorous perfidy to the Constitution put him outside the pale of civilization), Sam Walker and his men were heading north toward Topeka, looking for a fight, and Titus and his men were heading east, likewise looking for a fight, when they happened upon one another in the dark and skirmished in some woods. After the skirmish, in which no one was badly hurt, Sam Walker went to his claim, which wasn't far off. He woke up later in the morning to the sound of pounding on his cabin door, and when he opened it, a man he had never seen before declared that he had Titus's wife and two children with him on the Lecompton–Westport stage ("Oh, the cruelty of it," harangued Papa. "So typical of them!") and that if Sam Walker wanted Titus, he'd better do something about it now. So Walker and his men took over the prisoners and held them until a runner could get to Lawrence and summon the six-pound cannon they had there. Fifty horsemen then gathered near Titus's place (which Papa insisted upon calling "Fort Titus") and attacked at dawn on the morning of August 16. A Free-Soiler was killed, then the cannon leveled a wall of one of the buildings, and then Titus surrendered. When Walker went in, he saw a printed handbill hanging on the wall, advertising a five-hundred-dollar reward for his own head, to be paid by Titus! Then, according to Papa's reports, there was a great deal of fighting among the Free-Soilers about whether to kill the gallant Titus, but they hadn't the manhood to do it, and so he and some of his cronies ("gallant allies," said Papa) were carted off to Lawrence and imprisoned. A mob of Lawrenceites tried to get to him and hang him, but Walker or someone managed to preserve him, saying that war must be carried out by rule, and what we had here was a war. Papa agreed. All of Papa's friends agreed. What had been, on the one hand, a problem of governing and, on the other, a fight was now clearly rising up the scale and would soon be, if it wasn't already, an actual war. The hardest piece of all this intelligence, for me, was when Papa declared that the prisoners in Lecompton—that is, Governor Robinson and his associates—were to be summarily hung in retaliation for all of this. I will say that I felt my face go white and my body go cold when he said it, but I was so used to dissembling by now that I only smiled and said, "Surely that couldn't be according to the law," and then Papa said, "What law is there in Kansas?" and then it turned out not to be true. Those prisoners remained where they were, and other prisoners, taken in all of these skirmishes, were exchanged, and so hostilities, at least around Lawrence, ceased for the time being. Soon there were other rumors: Proslave households around Tecumseh were attacked and all their goods stolen and taken to Topeka, where the Free Staters divided them up and took them home. (Papa believed this one, but I didn't.) A man in Leavenworth made a bet that he could scalp an abolitionist before sundown, and won it. (I believed this, but Papa said he didn't think any southerner could do such a thing. I kept my beliefs to myself; Papa did not. Helen believed every bad thing she heard.) Many names came up, but Frank's wasn't among them, nor Charles's nor any other that I knew. That was my only comfort.

I summarize these events because at the time they were extraordinarily hard to understand, what with the comings and goings of Papa and his friends, the dislocations of the housekeeping and farming at Day's End Plantation, and my own confusions and frights, not to mention Helen's. I could not help worrying about Louisa and Charles and the Bushes and my other friends in Lawrence, especially as Louisa was approaching her time, and there was no telling what the Missourians were planning to do to Lawrence should Lane be unable to defend the town (and he was surely unable to defend the town). In Papa's normally neat and orderly house, the unfinished canvas lay on the hall floor for three days before Lorna and I rolled it up and set it off to the side. The pots of paint and brushes somehow got out onto the porch railing, where they were still sitting, untouched, when I left Day's End Plantation for good, some time later. For me, these things were the emblem of all the order that ended then and all the disorder that began.

One of these days, toward supper, Helen and I were up in her room, sorting through her gowns, as she had decided that she would make do with what she had for the winter and not ask Papa for anything luxurious until, should it happen, she was ready to put together her wedding clothes. Minna's wedding, to take place in October, had come in for much discussion, also, and Helen was trying to be sweet and judicious at the same time. "I don't think," she said, "that Minna really understands what we are having to put up with."

"Have you written to her?"

"Not in a week."

"Then how could she understand? The letter you read me about the linens was written two weeks ago or more."

"Is nothing going on in Lexington? They're right on the river. They must know more than we do, even."

"Has your papa written anything to her?"

"Papa is very indulgent of Minna, far more than

of me, if you must know the truth. It's because she's, well, plain. He feels sorry for her."

"Does he?"

"No one speaks of it, of course. But I guarantee you Minna is not planning to make do with all her old dresses."

"She is getting married."

"Yes, she is." She said this with decided sharpness, not at all the tone she had used about the subject before. I smiled and we were silent for a moment. Then she said, "I suppose Papa will bring all those men home tonight. It's terrible for Delia to have to make such a large supper, but I feel better when they're here, I must say. I always think, Go ahead, let them attack tonight, and they'll see what they get!"

"What men?"

"Oh, let's see. I guess Mr. Perkins and his nephew and Mr. Harris, of course, and Mr. Smith and Mr. Chesbrough. He has a brother, I think, but I don't know if he's coming. Possibly Mr. Long and a friend of his who lives over there whose wife died—what's his name? oh, Mr. Oleander Jackson; isn't that an amusing name? But he's ever so sad and serious. Mrs. Harris says he's looking for a new wife, and I surely hope he doesn't look in my direction! Some others have recently come into the neighborhood and are drilling with Papa. I surely hope he brings a few of them home; I surely do."

"Have you ever heard of any men named Mr. Samson and Mr. Chaney, from Blue Springs?" To tell the truth, my heart was suddenly pounding, though whether my fright came from anticipating how she might answer or simply from pronouncing the names of these devils aloud, I couldn't have said.

"No," said Helen, shaking out a particularly lovely pink silk gown and then inspecting some loose stitching at the waist. "I suppose Isabelle will have to look at this. It's always been one of my favorites, and I'm happy to keep wearing it, but I went to a dance in it, and don't you know, one of my partners stepped right on the skirt! Ugh! That's just the sort of suitor that's all around here. And then, of course, he was terribly sorry and went all red in the face. And his ears were nearly purple! That put me off even more than his clumsiness did, I swear!"

I had just about regained my composure when she said, "Oh, unless you mean Samson Perkins. His nephew is named Samson, too, though they call him Sam. And Chaney Smith is their friend. He's rather a rough character, and Papa doesn't really like him, but he's never *done* anything to require Papa denying him the house. We've heard things— What's the matter?"

By now I was lying back on the bed, as weak and faint as ever I'd felt in my life. The shock of knowing that Samson and Chaney were at hand, and had been in the house a few nights before, was more than I could stand. The fact is that ahead of time, you always think you are going to approach something gradually, with plenty of time and foresight to prepare yourself, but really everything is sudden, even those things you expect.

I saw that I might miss my chance if I didn't improve upon the evening's opportunity. To Helen, I said, "I think the heat must be affecting me. I didn't nap at all this afternoon."

"Oh, you must, then. Now that you have that green gown to wear, you'll be having supper with us, and it will be so lively! You certainly should rest beforehand. I had a lovely nap, and I feel so fresh! The heat isn't bothering me at all!"

Thus dismissed, I went to my room and closed the door. After sitting on my bed for a minute, I leaned down and dragged my case out and opened it. There wasn't much in it except the pistol, a tin of percussion caps, and some cartridges I had made weeks before and wrapped in a square of cloth. Here is what I did: I loaded the cartridges, six of them, into the cylinder. Then I loaded six percussion caps onto the cones. Then I laid the weapon on the neatly made bed and gazed at it for a long time. Everything about the black dragoon proclaimed something new, something entirely different from what had gone before. Thought had gone into its engineering, but no flourishes had gone into its decoration. It was not to be, as many guns I had seen over the years were, picked up and admired, even fondled. Men, I knew, named their rifles, cleaned and oiled them with pleasure, took as much pride in their workmanship as they might in a fine dog or a graceful picture. The black dragoon didn't invite that: it was so manufactured, so purely an object designed for a particular use— killing men—that it was impossible to feel affection for it. But with all that, here it was, and across the hall or across the best parlor, it was certainly capable of doing the required damage to Samson Perkins, his nephew Sam, and their friend Chaney Smith, especially if I took them by surprise, which I intended to do. How I imagined it was this: Their faces, the very ones I had seen on the Lawrence road, would turn and look at me just as they had that day, but this time I would raise my black dragoon and fire right into their laughter.

I turned my gaze from the gun on the bed and looked around the room. The windows looked outward; from where I was sitting, I could see only the tops of a few trees and the sky, which was hazy with heat. Even though I had made my own bed and hung up my clothes, Lorna had filled my pitcher, taken away the chamber pot, and pushed the net bed curtains back, not forgetting to arrange them in a graceful drape. The bureau was polished, and its small mirror shone. The pictures on the walls, of flowers and girls in white dresses standing in gardens, were pleasing enough, if a tad over-English and silly.

I looked at the gun again, dark against the white counterpane. The afternoon was drawing on, and soon enough I would hear the clatter of men and horses coming in. My plan was simple enough; if you were intending to commit what those around you considered a crime, but were not intending to get away with it, then that reduced the number of contingencies that you were required to foresee. I went around the bed to the little table where Thomas's watch lay, and picked it up. It was warm because the long rays of the sun had been shining on it, but the warmth seemed to come from somewhere else. I let myself think that it came from Thomas himself. I held it in my hand, stared out the window at the sky, and waited.

CHAPTER 24

I Am Doubly Surprised

*Those, only, who are free from care and anxiety,
and whose minds are mainly occupied by cheerful
emotions, are at full liberty to unveil their feelings.*
—*pp. 137–38*

I DIDN'T HAVE TO WAIT LONG, but as I was caught in a dreamlike state somewhere between panic and anticipation, it seemed both all too long and all too short. Only four of the men and their horses came up to the house; the rest went directly to the stables. While these four men stood with their animals and waited for Ike or someone else to come receive them, they blustered among themselves about their prowess and their intentions. Their voices were deep and carried through the open window, and all spoke in those half-belligerent, half-joking tones that Missourians seemed to specialize in.

"Them d—— black abolitionists an't seen nothin' till they try to get our niggers. We'll turn their heads around and show 'em their own backs, haw haw!"

"H——, back when I was in Ohio a year ago, if only I'd known they was coming our way! I woulda forestalled a few, I'll tell ya!"

"I hate goin' back there! They always look at ya like you're gonna eat with your knife and an't never seen a winder before! And then, when ya go to write

617

something, their d—— eyebrows go up with every word you write."

"I jes' stick my tongue between my lips like I ken barely form the letters, then I laugh!"

"Time for laughin' is past, boys! I say, let 'em come!"

I looked at the pistol on the bed and reflected upon the contrast between these men, among them Thomas's killers, and Thomas himself. That is the worst agony of a murder: that the worthy man has died and unworthy ones continue to live. The crude boasting and bragging of these four affected me like blows and left me breathless. Someone came and took away their horses, and then they came into the house. I could hear them laughing and stomping below, then I heard Helen's voice, and then I heard Papa's. I went over to the chest and picked up the towel Lorna had placed there for me and wiped my face with it, then I wrapped it around the pistol, leaving only the tip of the barrel showing and two inches or so of the stock. It was hard to keep in place, and I looked around the room for something to tie it, but there was nothing, unless I should elect to tear a strip off the bed curtains—but there was Helen's knock. I sat down on the bed and arranged my skirt over the wrapped gun. Helen entered with a smile. "Are you feeling any better? They're a little exuberant today. As Papa would say, they haven't gone without refreshment. But Delia made a lovely supper. Lots of cucumbers!"

I pulled the pistol close to myself and stood up as gracefully as possible. Actually, it wasn't heavy, and once I was standing, I had no trouble concealing it. I said, "Are they all here, then?"

"I think so. Lorna had to set another place for Mr. Lafayette. He's very old! I can't believe he's still drilling, but Papa says he won't give up! Oh, my, he hates the abolitionists. He came from Mississippi, you know. One of the best families in Tupelo, I'm told, but he's ever so old. Shh. He's right there!" We came down to the landing and looked over the banister at a tall, thin man with a hatchet face and a mane of white hair. A broadsword in a scabbard hung at his side, and he affected extremely large spurs. Another man joined him, clapped him on the back, and shouted in his ear: "That's quite a mount you've got, Lafayette. Want to sell 'im to someone who can actually ride 'im?"

"I'll shoot the beast first, Chesbrough! Do 'im a kindness that way!" They laughed. Others crowded in, jangling and clanking. Almost everyone, it appeared, was wearing a sword, and now I saw the rifles jumbled against the wall by the front door with their ramrods. Some of them looked seventy-five or a hundred years old, designed to go with knee britches and pigtails. I expected, of course, that the Samsons and Chaney would present themselves, perhaps that they would light up on their own, like paper lanterns with candles in them, but all the men were alike—equally strange to me, equally familiar with one another. The only one I recognized was Papa, who hopped among the others like a robin among crows, herding them with little pokes and prods toward the dining room. I felt the pistol through my dress and pulled back the hammer with my thumb. Then I said to Helen, "Where are Mr. Perkins and Mr. Smith?"

She whispered, "Mr. Smith is the one in the blue vest just coming out of the parlor, and Perkins is looking right at us. Hello, Mr. Perkins," she caroled. I looked at Perkins with a bright, deflective smile firmly fixed to my face. I looked at him straight, and I looked at him for a very long, careful moment. My finger eased around the trigger of the pistol. Samson Perkins saw Helen, then me, and smiled at us. I noticed that his teeth were white, and that he had all of them. I had never seen him before in my life.

Then I looked at Chaney Smith. For someone reputed to be a rough character, he looked benign enough—rather fat and soft, almost good-humored about the eyes. He wore a pince-nez, which he took off and polished while he waited for the other men to get through the doorway into the dining room.

The boy came closest. He had a round white face with a disgruntled look on it, and a shock of dirty blond hair. No mustaches or whiskers of any kind. Had I been pressed, I would have said that he looked rather like I had as a boy. He was not prepossessing in any way, but was he the boy who had shot Jeremiah in the neck and then laughed about it? In a hundred years, I could not have said for sure. I felt the pistol begin to slip out of my grasp and grabbed it, but my finger missed the trigger, and it did not go off. Helen gave me a startled look and said, "What on earth?" and I said, "I'll be right down," then spun on my heel and ran up the stairs to my room, where I closed the door, removed the cartridges from their chambers, and thrust the pistol under the bed. Then I ran out of the room and down the stairs.

I hardly remember this supper. I do not know how many men ate with us, or what we ate. I do know that Helen sat far away from me, at the other end of the table, which had been pulled out to its full length. Papa seemed in high spirits. There was a great deal of talk about what the abolitionists had done, would do, couldn't do, should be obliged to suffer, and would find out about. I don't remember any of it. There were many men at the table, perhaps a dozen. I scrutinized each of their faces with a rudeness allowed only to a woman. Maybe, I thought, if Chaney Smith and Samson Perkins weren't the culprits, I would recognize someone else. Stranger things had happened, had they not? And then there was this—the bartender in Kansas City had told me that "Chaney and Samson" were boasting about killing someone. If not Thomas, then whom? But in fact, I didn't care about that unknown whom. I cared about Thomas. Revenge was too frightening to be abstract; it had to be most particular and careful. I attempted to construe every face into one I had seen, but it was simply impossible, and of course, very soon, I lost the moment, as we ate our supper and each face became familiar. I thought of shooting them anyway, or some of them, those who talked in the most boasting, hateful way: "Oughta burn 'em out now!" "Shoulda done it months ago, when we had the chance!" "Some folks wouldn't hear of it, but they was dead wrong!" "I say, and I always did say, jest shoot the d—— black abolitionists as they come up the river. You kin tell who they are at a hundred yards, and pick 'em off at that distance, too, if you're any kind o' shot!" (Much laughter.) It went round and round as they worked themselves up to ever higher degrees of indignation, with Helen and me exchanging a glance every so often. The company got rowdier and rowdier, and finally Papa gave Helen the signal that she could escape, and we smiled and curtseyed our way out of the room.

"Now," she whispered at the bottom of the stairs, "we go up and lock ourselves in my room, as you never know what might happen, and although, of course, everyone respects Papa more than anyone, and listens to him, and he and Mr. Harris wouldn't let anything get out of hand, still, you never know. Papa and Mr. Harris aren't as young as some of the others, and maybe you've noticed that Papa is rather on the small side."

I thought of the pistol under my bed and said, "Get your work, and we'll go into my room. It isn't directly over either the dining room or the parlor. And bring your nightdress and wrapper, too."

We went up.

We went to bed.

Helen fell asleep, always sure in her heart that she was safe.

Papa got the men off in a clatter of hoofbeats and threats against the north.

Papa mounted the stairs and went into his own room.

I reflected upon the failure of my project.

It was easy now to follow the thread of failure

back through the last weeks and months, as easy as following a red thread through a blue weave. It was easy to see that all the circumstances that had seemed to point me here, to this house, tonight, to this fateful act of justice, had been nothing at all, just a jumble of chance encounters, wishful steps, ignorant certainties. It was easy to see that the world I saw bearing down on me and directing me had in fact issued out of me. I had been the light that, shining upward upon the random branches in the forest canopy, transformed them into a net. It was so easy to see this that I lay there lost in astonishment that I had been so foolish, but also lost in astonishment, fresh astonishment, that it had all happened, even that Thomas was dead, even that I had ever married, left Quincy, gone to Kansas. I had a sensation of waking up from everything in my life and finding it chimerical, the only reality being my fleshly person, my skin against my nightdress, my hand on my forehead. Where was I? What was I doing? The only answers I had were ones I couldn't believe: I was in Missouri, which was at war with Kansas; I, who had cared little about the slavery question, had become an abolitionist; the girl sleeping in bed beside me was someone I had not known the existence of a short time before; I had had a love, and he was dead; the dearest companion of my youth, my nephew Frank, had been lost, and I'd hardly even noticed. Such things had no existence within the realm of possibility. Only if Samson and Chaney had proved to be Samson and Chaney would it have all held together in a sensible fashion, but they had not and it had not.

Furthermore, I would not be shot or carried off to jail, but would have to find my own way out of this . . . whatever you might call it, into someplace more recognizable.

I lay awake all night, and at dawn was still awake when Helen stirred beside me, sat up, and said, "My goodness, I don't know which is worse, the attackers or the defenders. But you must never tell Papa I said such a thing! I expect he would think that I'm full of such rebellious thoughts! Well, perhaps I am."

She turned and looked at me. "You know," she said, "I'm not going to let you keep all your thoughts to yourself forever. I'm much too inquisitive for that. And as I get to like you more and more, it gets harder and harder not to know you!"

I said, "I'll tell you one thing right now, Helen. But only one. You may ask any question."

Now the look on her pretty, fresh face grew positively impish, and she took the tip of her blond braid in her fingers, bit it speculatively, then threw it over her shoulder. She said, "How did you meet your husband?"

I laughed out loud and said, "He was visiting a neighbor, and the neighbor came by to show him off to my brother-in-law, to try to start a fight, but my brother-in-law wasn't home, so they sat with my sister and me for a while. I thought he was plain-looking and a little gawky, but then I got to know him better."

"May I ask any more questions?"

"Not now."

"Tonight?"

I shook my head.

"Tomorrow?"

I nodded.

"First thing in the morning?"

"I suppose so."

"Lorna thinks she knows you."

"Why do you say that?"

"I heard her telling Delia."

"Has she ever been to Kansas"— I stumbled— "City?"

"Goodness, no."

Well, of course not. I had seen only one or two Negroes in K.T., had I not? "I must look like someone else she knows."

"I reckon. But I may ask another question tomorrow?"

"Yes."

"I have a whole day to think of one, then."

But her thoughts were still running on the same subject, because as we rose for the day and went about our morning ablutions, she broke out in a wail. "Louisa! Now you see my difficulty, don't you? Those men who were here last night, those are the best men we know! All of them have property, some of them have a great deal of property, and they truly think like we do about all the great issues. Not everyone does! There are quite a few around here who aren't strictly abolitionists, you know, or who don't care one way or another about the institution, but they can't afford slaves or don't have them. You should see how they live! The wives and children work right alongside the men, dawn to dusk every day. And they live all jumbled together in little houses or even cabins, and they don't have any nice dresses to wear, and no occasion to wear them, because they have no amusements! They just go to dirty little churches every Sunday, all day, and bring along dishes that they've made, and eat together sitting on a blanket, and how amusing is that? And they have ever so many children, because they need lots of people to work, and you know that when you keep having ever so many children, some of them die, and that's horrible, and then the mother dies from having so many, and then the father marries again, and it starts all over. Did you know that that devil John Brown has twenty-seven children? That's a very low way of doing things, like an animal! And then they try to tell us that God prefers that sort of life to this!" She swept her hand toward the windows and the front lawn. "How could He possibly prefer such a life for us, if He loves us?"

"But, Helen," I remonstrated, "when Adam and Eve were banished from the Garden, He condemned them to labor for their own bread."

"Don't you think that's a terribly hard religion? I know it comes from that, but Papa said none of our family were Puritans like that, that the Puritans were hateful people, and even the Dutch couldn't stand them, and so that's why they had to go to the New World, not because they were persecuted, but because they were hateful. And I don't think it's fair that they should come to New England and that our people should come to Virginia, an utterly different sort of place, and that in the end, they should put their hatefulness and hard religion over on the rest of us, after all! And you know what? It was those very people that started the slave trade, just to get rich. They treated those slaves much more horribly on those ships than ever Papa or Mr. Harris would treat even a dog, even a rat! Papa said they used to have more slaves in Newport, Rhode Island, than anywhere else in the United States, until the Irishmen came in, and it was cheaper to pay the poor benighted Irishmen, who don't know any better because of *their* religion, nothing and get rid of having to care for your slaves as a proper master does!"

"Helen . . ." But I paused, wanting to be careful of what I said. I dared not openly argue with her.

"So I can't go to one of those men who lives like that, with a wife and seventeen children. I don't want to be the first wife, who dies, and I don't want to be the second wife, who raises the first wife's brats, and I don't want my husband to be talking to me about my duty all the time! Isn't it better to have two or three children, like Bella and Minna and me, and teach us to sing and play the piano and sew and draw and write a fine hand and even make a pudding if we have to—but my goodness, what if I had to slaughter a hog and watch the blood run out, and chop the head off a chicken?"

I almost admitted that I, too, had found these activities distasteful and that I had avoided them whenever I could, so that my niece, Annie, had been forced to take my place. But I hadn't minded hunting, and dressing game, in K.T. I said, "When you are married, you'll find yourself doing what you have to do and not minding it so much. You'll love your husband, and you'll love your children even more."

"But I was not reared to work every day, all day, and to have my looks go by the time I'm twenty-five, and if I have to live that way, I will certainly die first!" She said it petulantly, almost as a childish threat, but in fact, it was probably true. I said, "Surely your papa will find you a husband to your taste."

"Where? You saw the gallery last night. And if I were to go off, like Bella or Minna, I would have to leave Papa all alone. Don't you love Papa? He's so lively and dear! How could I leave him and go to Georgia or South Carolina or somewhere?" She lowered her voice. "You know, Papa's always going on about land being good and money being evil, but if we were rich in money rather than in land, Papa and I could be together anywhere we chose. I think about this day and night, but I don't see a solution! I suppose it's better not to think about it at all, but just to let yourself be led about by the nose and to accept what happens to you, but my goodness, that seems an awfully spineless way to live!"

I finally laughed.

"Well, it is," said Helen.

There was a knock on the door, and I opened it. Outside it stood Lorna, with two trays. She said, "Well, at leas' I done foun' Missy. Two seconds later, and I woulda got worried. My land, you should see de dining room and de parlor. It look like dey had a war down dere! An' de girl and I, we got to clean dat up before Massa Richard come down!'"

I saw that she was annoyed with us for wasting her time. I said, "I'm sorry," and she said, "Ain' your fault, unless you been throwin' de dining room cha-iahs about. Done broke a winder! I sweah!" She set the trays down, one on the bed and one on the chest, and we ate our toast. Helen said, "I know Papa will give me Lorna for my wedding, at least. I couldn't stir a step without Lorna, and he knows that. She wouldn't leave me like she did Bella, either, because she likes me, and she never did like Bella."

"Did Lorna try to escape?"

She went over and closed the door, then lowered her voice. "It was Bella's fault. Bella has a miserable temper, you know. She can't help it. But she hit Lorna with a rolling pin, right over the head, and raised a terrible bruise, even though you never hit a house servant like that, but she was the same with me when we were children, she always hit me with anything that she had in her hand, and so Lorna got her mad, and she happened to have the rolling pin in her hand, and so she hit her and knocked her down! Oh, Papa was furious with Bella, and Ralph—that's Bella's husband—was, too. But then Lorna made it worse by running off, and they had to advertise, and the catchers caught her, and they beat her worse than Bella did. Papa says sometimes you can't control the catchers, because they are of a very low sort. Well, Bella was all set to sell her south, but Papa wouldn't let her and brought her back here and made her promise never to run off, because that's like stealing, you know, and so she has another chance, but it was such a to-do that if it happens again, Papa will surely just sell her south, because if the others see one run off and then go unpunished, well, it makes them restless."

We finished our breakfast and went out of the room. I felt well enough, in spite of my wakeful night, but everything about me had the quality of seeming magnified—larger, brighter, louder than usual—and I felt as though I were stretching myself to accommodate this, and that sometime the stretch might be too great, and I would snap.

Two days passed after the failure of my plan, and I told myself that I had to take things slowly and think carefully about what to do. I thought that I might write a letter to my sisters, asking them for money to get back to Quincy, but I had no way to post a letter, and secrecy was still such a habit with me that I couldn't quite bring myself to entrust my letter to Papa. But in addition to that, posting such a letter amounted to giving up on finding Thomas's killers, and I was so used to planning revenge that even without a plan, I couldn't give up the revenge. I thought it would be easier to come up with a plan than settle for nothing, so I solaced myself by carefully thinking the same thoughts over and over. And indeed, this was a time of great news and perturbation. Very soon, we all knew, the invisible boundary between fighting and war would be crossed, and so, many times every day, my carefully thought thoughts were scattered by some rumor or fear. The prevailing belief was that if Lane could not be stopped, he would be killed, and if he was killed, the northern newspapers would raise such a fuss that someplace like Leavenworth or Westport would be attacked by the federals, and then war would roll from there eastward, widening and inexorably speeding up, until the whole nation was drawn in. Papa said that in the days when it took weeks to get to the east by boat or coach, there might not have been such a danger, but now, with trains and telegraphs, there would be no stopping it. Or sometimes, instead of rolling east, it was said, the war would suck everything west, as if Leavenworth were an everwidening sinkhole that would soon enough engulf Boston, on the one hand, and Charleston, on the other. Under the influence of these thoughts, Papa wondered aloud what it might be like to go off to California, but really, he was too old for that, wasn't he? And so all of us in the house—Helen, Papa, myself, Lorna, I suppose, and even Delia, who counted her stores over and over—were in our separate ways disheartened and perturbed. I wondered about my sisters, whether they were going along in their usual fashion, all unaware of the world outside Quincy and likely to be ever so piqued should it impose itself upon them.

I had been at Day's End Plantation for about two weeks now, and every day had been hot, when suddenly there was a great summer storm, with thunder and lightning and hail, and the late-afternoon sky turned green, and we all had to go down into the cellar and wait it out, master, mistress, guest, and slaves. We had a couple of candles, and everyone was rather fearful, and so Papa said that we must sing songs, and began himself, by singing a song from an opera called *Figaro's Marriage,* by Mozart, who also wrote some pieces that some of the girls had played in school, when I was with Miss Beecher. Helen sang a Scottish song about getting up early one morning and seeing a fair maiden in the valley below. I then sang "Hard Times, Hard Times, Come Around No More." I sang this with feeling, in my plain voice, keeping the tune as well as I could. After that, each of the slaves sang a song, none of them songs I had ever heard before. Not everyone sang well—Lorna, for example, seemed unwilling to actually produce a melody, and instead almost talked her song. But Malachi liked to sing and had a wonderful clear voice, and he sang first a song about calling the water boy, and second a hymn called "Deep River." Papa said it was one of his favorite hymns, and he smiled broadly the whole time Malachi was singing it. After all of the singing, we came up out of the cellar and saw that the weather had cleared and that the storm had taken down only a few tree limbs. It wasn't even suppertime yet, but the air was cool and the haze had cleared off, and the fields that ran away from the house looked fresh and fruitful. Helen went up to her room, and I went into the day parlor, where I had the third volume of Miss Austen's novel to finish. Just before supper, Papa came into the parlor.

I was sitting on a sofa, and I have to say that I put down my book with some reluctance, as I was at the very interesting part where Elizabeth is caught visiting Mr. Darcy's estate in Derbyshire. I saw that Papa was dressed differently than he had been down in the cellar. He was now wearing crisp black trousers, a red brocade waistcoat, a fresh white cravat, and a neatly cut black jacket. He carried a stick with a silver knob, too. He reminded me by contrast of how trim and sober a figure Thomas had made in his black clothes when I first met him. I wondered where Papa was going and whether Helen and I would be alone for supper, in which case we might have a light, quick meal, and I could then get on with my reading.

"Are you alone, then, Mrs. Bisket?" said Papa.

"Helen is in her room, if you would like me to get her."

"Perhaps later."

Papa looked bright, with something of the air of a little spinning top, but I in no way associated this with myself, and anyway, my mind was still running on Thomas, so I was entirely unprepared to hear Papa exclaim, "My dear Mrs. Bisket, I feel that you are heaven-sent to us for some special purpose, and I cannot rest until I make known to you my fervent desire to bring you into our family as my bride!" During this speech, Papa had swooped down and perched beside me on the couch, and now he seized my hand in his two little ones and stared into my face. "Do let me go on! Everything here at Day's End Plantation is different since you came into the house. You are truly a presence! An angel, if I may say so, who brings us peace and a sense of well-being, even in these times of conflict and anxious dread. You make the two of us a family!"

"You haven't spoken to Helen about this!" That idea especially appalled me.

"Not yet, but I know she loves you like a sister. What a short step, then, to loving you like a mother?"

"I'm but two years older than Helen."

"But your demeanor is, if I may say so, a lifetime more womanly. I don't know your history, Mrs. Bisket, as yet. It's my fond hope that the intimate bonds of marriage will, might, encourage you to confide in me someday. . . ." He looked at me and hurried on. "But let's not get too far ahead. For the moment, I feel that you have been given to us to ease our troubles! We don't know what will happen. No one knows. Our nation is in great peril. I see no statesman, no Jefferson, nor even a Jackson, who can— d—— me, Mrs. Bisket, but this Kansas-Nebraska Act was a deal made in the devil's own kitchen, and the red men from whom the land was stolen have cursed it in perpetuity, that's my opinion. I've told Harris that for years: you throw off those Indians, and they leave their curses behind! Did you know that I spent a considerable time with the Indians myself in my early days? And I never held with selling up the Cherokees and driving them off, but they got richer than some of their neighbors, and their neighbors couldn't abide that! Excuse me!"

He got up and walked about the room, then sat down again. "On that subject, I will say only one thing: there has been enormous bungling from top to bottom; that's all I will say on the subject right now!" He took my hand again, but I removed it. He said, "Ah, please don't draw away. Let me believe that I have hope in my suit! Let me think that a few more days or weeks with us will persuade you to find us as necessary to your happiness as you are to mine, ours! Let me persuade myself that a longer sojourn at Day's End Plantation will convince you that we do have a little paradise here, all the more so should you confer upon it your angelic presence!"

I have to say that these speeches made me dizzy, as perhaps they were calculated to do. Watching Papa was like watching something small and sparkling that was moving very rapidly, and indeed, he was moving all the time, either around the room or beside me on the sofa. He made me feel vast and immobile, especially when he referred to me as a "presence." At first I didn't know what to say, as I was utterly surprised, but quickly I realized that Papa's intentions made my position, if possible, even more precarious than it had been. I was no longer a mysterious but essentially indifferent guest, who could move off of her own volition. Now I was someone from whom Papa wanted something, wanted it with impatience and even ardor. I had become, to Papa, something that had no relationship to who or what I actually was. There was certainly danger in that situation. I didn't think that I dared reject his suit right then and there, and I cast about for something to say. Finally, I managed, "Mr. Day, I don't believe that you and I are truly of one mind in all things."

"Ah! You see there! Your very want of openness—which in principle I don't disagree with, since I admire discretion in a lady—your very want of openness has prevented us from making the best use of our acquaintance here, but I truly feel that often, in these matters, it is better to act on instinct than on reason. My instinct is that we *are* of one mind!"

"But, sir, let's set this, just for argument: let's say that you and your daughter go to the Methodist church—"

"Which we do."

"—and that I have been in the habit of attending the Baptist church. Are we of one mind there? Could we be? I don't—"

"But my feeling is that these issues will fall away of themselves! I am a Romantic! Do you know what that is? Ah, they were marvelous boys! They saw more deeply into the heart than many an older man—"

"But what if I were an abolitionist, even?"

He threw back his head and laughed a great baritone laugh. He shouted, "Impossible! Ha ha ha ha!"

And it took all my forbearance to not respond to his amusement with a declaration. I sustained my smile and finally, when he was attending to me again, said, "I am, of course, flattered by your offer. You have been unfailingly kind to me, and I am grateful for that. You will have my reply on Monday morning, at breakfast time. That is three days from now. Until then, I feel that I need some seclusion—"

"To organize your thoughts! Yes, of course, my dear." He grinned. I could readily see that he felt assured of my positive response. I knew that he and Helen would be attending a long church service on Sunday, followed by an afternoon with the Harrises.

I had prepared the ground for begging off that, and it would be during those hours, between nine and six, that I would pack my bag and decamp. I thought that I might be able to sell Thomas's watch in Independence for steamboat fare back to Quincy, or, perhaps, for enough to live on until I could get a letter to Harriet and persuade her to send me some money.

I smiled sincerely at Papa and put my hand out to him. He took it and kissed it. I was sincerely grateful to him for goading me into coming up with a plan. He stood and bowed himself out of the room, nearly dancing with delight. At supper, half an hour later, Helen asked him why he seemed so happy, and he said, "Trust me, my dear; you shall know soon enough!" He was that certain of my reply.

CHAPTER 25

I Am Recognized

Carpet bags are very useful, to carry the articles to be used on a journey. The best ones have sides inserted, iron rims, and a lock and key.

—p. 316

THE FIRST THING I did was to finish my book, although I must say I did so with somewhat different feelings than I had had before Papa's offer. I no longer felt that living with Mr. Darcy at Pemberley was the be-all and end-all of existence, and I wondered how Elizabeth, who was so witty and lively that it was easy to feel a kinship with her, would assume authority over the invisible but necessary troop of servants. I wondered how she would transform herself from a girl into the representative of an institution so large and public that strangers could appear there and ask to be shown around. Papa's offer took away some of my gratification in the story, I must say.

The second thing I did was to ask Lorna what had become of my woolen dress. "Well," she said, "I don' think you need dat thing! It still smells to high heaven, an' it's been sitting out in de airin' shed fo' two weeks! I had de girl scrub it an' scrub it wi' de soda, until de nap is 'bout worn offn de flannel, but I'll bring it up ifn you want to have a look at it."

"I believe you. I suppose it's ruined, then."

"Pretty near, but I don' know. Maybe a few more days of dry weader will do de trick. Mos' of de last two weeks have been awful damp."

The third thing I did was clean and oil my pistol, then pack it with the percussion caps and the cartridges at the bottom of my bag. That, too, I could sell. I should mention here that Lorna had found the money sewn into my woolen dress and returned it to me. I counted that. There were seven dollars now. The bag (I looked at it critically) was worth very little. Perhaps, as well, I could sell one of the dresses Helen had gotten from the Harrises. The green had turned out quite pretty and unusual-looking, although, of course, any dress of mine was too long in the waist and the skirt to fit most women. But first I had to get someplace where I could sell things. That would be Independence. It had taken me a day to get from Independence to here, but actually, I didn't know how far a walk Independence was, because I didn't know how my strength had been affected by my condition, or by my run from that fellow Master Philip. In fact, most of the events after I'd eaten some supper in Independence (or was it dinner?) were exceedingly difficult to remember, rather like sifting through a bucket of sand to find small objects at the bottom.

I did all these things, and made my plans, only by stealing little bits of time and attention from other concerns. I felt that I dared not look as if I was about to bolt, not because I thought Papa would hurt me, or hold me his captive, but because I thought he would renew his suit in ever more pressing terms. Only if he thought he had said enough would he refrain from saying more.

In this time, it also happened that we heard that Governor Shannon of Kansas had resigned his position, telling President Pierce, according to Papa and his friends, that the devils in Kansas were harder to govern than the devils in H——. This sentiment was viewed in Missouri as a judicious observation by an unbiased observer, and it was widely expected that President Pierce would try to institute military law, enrolling all Missourians who cared to join in some sort of military policing arm that would have the privilege, the right, and the duty to destroy the G—— d—— abolitionists once and for all. Since it was an election year, the only discussion revolved around whether the outgoing President's party would have the stomach to support him in this most necessary course of action. As the executive arm of the government, he could do it on his own, but would he? There was talk around Papa's table of sending a delegation of the area's best men to advise the President on how to deal with the lily-livered members of his own party, who wouldn't do what had to be done even though it was plain as the nose on your face. Did anyone, north or south, want the abolitionists in power? No. Would they get there? As sure as ice melts in the spring. Could they be stopped? (Fists slam down on the table.) Got to be! There was some discussion about how the abolitionists had gotten to be so prominent all of a sudden. Every man at the table could remember a time when the criminals blackguards scoundrels traitors swine pardon my language ma'am were only laughed at. No one ever agreed with them five years ago, a year ago, six months ago. It was one of the great mysteries of history how they'd scrambled up from the bottom like that.

"Well, they got in all them Germans that come over here after that revolution they had there. Them German boys got ideas of their own, d—— 'em," said one.

"They hate the Germans. They hate the Irish, too. Only love niggers. You know why—it's twisted."

Looks, then pardoning in front of the ladies. Helen turning red. Me looking at my plate.

"The question is how they got in with the Washington men."

"There's a set of scoundrels to begin with. Lining their own pockets with both hands, don't care where it comes from."

"Money's at the bottom of it."

"Thayer's cellar is stacked with gold ingots. Where do you think he got 'em?"

"Pandering to others with a fondness for dark meat? Haw haw!"

"Sir!"

"Perhaps if the ladies are finished, they might excuse themselves, so that the gentlemen can speak freely."

We blushed our way out of the room, Helen giving me a significant look, half plea, half I-told-you-so. Each day, the talk got rougher, more violent, less softened by habitual good manners.

But mostly I kept to my room, trying to avoid Papa. On Saturday night, I went in to Helen and begged off the next day's scheme of church, followed by a party at the Harrises'. Helen smiled and gave me no protest, even though she'd been telling me for days how pleasant it was there, how delightful the victuals would be, how much I would enjoy Mrs. Harris and her sister. I knew right then that Papa had spoken to her of his offer, and I was tempted to let an intimation or two drop of my real intentions, only out of fondness for Helen, only so that she wouldn't feel that I had thought nothing of her and her kindness and good nature when I fled. But I dared not. I smiled back at her, as if we shared some knowledge and everything might easily turn out as she expected. After that, I went back to my own chamber and changed into my nightdress. I sat there for a minute, then got into bed and blew out my candle. I knew I had done so, because after blowing it out, I lay in the dark for quite a time. Even so, before I awakened, I sensed a candle in the room, a blur of light pressing on my heavy lids. But there was no sound. I came around ever so slowly, and as I opened my eyes, the candle went out, another mystery. I must have groaned, because a hand was instantly over my mouth, a dry, strong, firm hand. Lorna's hand. She whispered, "Hush now! I got somethin' to say to ya!"

I sat up. She took her hand away. She was leaning toward me in the dark, sitting in the same chair she had occupied when she was watching over me, wearing the same faded dress that seemed to float in the darkness, a white kerchief around her head.

"Missy Louisa! I knows you! I do! You don' think I do, but I do. I saw it all cleah las' week."

I looked at her, afraid to say a word.

"You done gi' me some money once."

"You must be mis—"

"No, I ain'! You didn' see me, but I saw ya. You was wadin' in a stream and you had a boy wid ya. You lef' four dollar on a rock fo' me."

I felt my jaw drop. I said, "Were you in a cave?"

"That war me, missy. Oh, I was cold dat day! I done swum the river and walked up de crick deah, and my draws was soakin' wet."

"Lorna!"

"Hush, now! Massa Richard is a light sleeper, and times he get up and walk around de house 'cause he's thinkin' on things."

I didn't know how not to believe her. I whispered, "It was a man in that cave!"

"No it waren't! It war me! Two days later, de catchers got me and beat me good and put me in de shackles and everythin', so don' say it waren't me, because I got de stripes to show for it! Now hush. I got somethin' to tell ya." She gave me a firm look, then said, "You is leavin' heah, ain' you?"

"How did Thomas know you were in that cave?"

"Dere was a man in dat town. He done come down from Wesconsin to do things fo' de Underground Railroad. He done bought a farm dere, by de river."

"Roger Howell!"

"Dat may be de name. I never seen de man." She shrugged that off. "I know you is leavin', because I looked under de bed and saw dat you packed you bag, an' I heared you beggin' off de outin' tomorra. Dey is gone be away all day and into de night, and dat's a good time fo' you to git off, ain' it?"

I didn't say anything.

"Well, you is takin' me wid ya."

I gasped.

"Yes, you is. Now make up you mine dat you is gone take me, because you is. You cain' gi' me four dollar one time and walk away from me de nex', dat's what I think!"

"I can barely get out of here myself!"

"You think I ain' got me a plan? I been plannin' this fo' a week, since I done seen who you is. I didn' know you at firs', 'cause you cut you haiah and had some men's clothes on and I didn' rightly believe it ware possible that it could be you, but you is a big gal. I ain' never seen another as big as you—tall, I mean, 'cause you ain' fat nohow—but however, I done worked it out."

"That wasn't my four dollars; that was my husband's!"

"De one dat was killed?"

"Yes."

"Den dis is somethin' you gone do fo' him. I done

made up my mine, missy, dat you came heah to git me, wheder you know it or not!"

"What's the plan, then?"

"I ain' gone tell you all de pieces right now. When I comes wid you breakfast in the mawnin', I'll tell you a little bit. But you jes' do what I tells you, and we is gone to be fine!"

She got up and seemed, in her light garments, to drift across the floor and out of the dark room. This gave the whole episode an even profounder appearance of ghostly unreality, and in fact, if it hadn't been for the feel of her hand on my face the first moment, I might have failed to believe any of this had happened. But it had; I must say that it woke me right up. My bag was packed, so I sat there and watched the light appear in my windows. Lorna! Lorna had claimed me! And added to that, Lorna had a plan she seemed confident about. I could put my own escape into her firm and capable hands. More important, I had a distinct sense of Thomas's approval. He seemed to move toward me, to be more lovingly present in my mind than he had been at any time since his death. Of course, Lorna was right. Aiding in her escape was the thing I had to do for Thomas that would somehow restore him to me.

And I wasn't afraid, not nearly as afraid as I'd been countless times before in the last year: not as afraid as when I'd escaped from the boat, not as afraid as when I'd gone into K.T., not as afraid as when I'd looked at Thomas and known for the first time that he would, indeed, be my husband. Even though aiding in the escape of a slave was, according to both Kansas law and Missouri law, a crime punishable by hanging, even though there was a war on, even though I hadn't the first notion of where we would go and how we would get there, I was not afraid. Lorna, after all, had a plan, and I had a purpose. That was enough for me.

In the morning, Helen came in before Lorna did. Still dressed in her wrapper, she looked fresh and pretty. I noticed that she had a way of arching her neck and turning the curve of her jaw that was utterly charming, a way of always smiling before she spoke, as if she could say only delightful things. She sat on my bed and took my hand in hers. She said, "Now, Louisa. You must know how I feel about you. I won't say a word about anything else, but you must know that."

"I know we've become friends and that I am very fond of you, Helen."

"Now, sometimes, Louisa, I just am dying of curiosity about who you are and where you came here from, but you've noticed that except for that one question, I never asked you about it?"

"I noticed that, my dear."

"There, you see. Mama always used to say that I worried things like a little terrier dog but that it was much more respectful to be patient and allow those you love—you see, there I've said it—to open themselves by themselves, so I've been very patient, and you know, that's been hard for me, but

I've made myself do it, because I see you are of a delicate sensibility and clearly some tragedy weighs upon your spirits that you don't wish to talk about—"

"I told you that my husband was killed—"

"But I know there's something more! Oh, my dear Louisa, you sang that song the other day about hard times, and I saw right into your immortal soul, and I said to Papa that you had been sent to us for a reason, and he took my meaning instantly!" She grasped my hands in hers. "However, I will say no more! Papa says I must be patient one more day, and so I will be. Oh, my dear!" And she threw her arms around me and embraced me ardently, and I thought how I had never heard such a group for declaring that Providence was sending them this person and that person for this reason and that reason. But I returned her embrace, for indeed, how could I not? I had never met anyone as artless and pretty and well disposed as Helen. She was, as my sisters would have said at once, spoiled to death, and yet kindness ruled her nature.

I said, "We'll see what happens," which was a kind of promise, and she went away happy and confident, saying, "Now, you stay up here; no need to see us off. You just dress at your leisure, and when we come in tonight, I'll tell you all about it. I am sure it will be such an amusing day, and my goodness, do we need something, with all this fighting!"

And so that was our farewell. An hour later, I

waved Helen and Papa off as they got into the carriage and Malachi got up on the box. Papa's favorite
"charger" was tethered to the back of the carriage, so
I saw that there was going to be drilling that afternoon. Moments later, the whole equipage trotted off,
and moments after that, I heard Lorna's foot on the
stairs, and then my door opened and she slid into the
room. She said, "I done tol' Delia dat you is keepin'
to you room today because you got you a bad head.
She down in de cellar fo' de hundred millionth time.
She jes' went down deah. So you tek you bag and
you go out de front doah and run down to de stable
deah and go round to de side away from de house,
and I will come."

Her manner, calm enough on the surface, all at
once communicated to me the enormity of what we
were doing, so that I took fright and stared at her. She
stared back at me, but only for a moment. Then she
went over and got my bag from under my bed and
thrust it into my hands, saying, "Ain' got time to git
sceahed. You git!" She held the door for me, and I
tiptoed out and looked down into the hallway. No
one. She whispered, "Git!" and I ran down the stairs
and out the door. Then there was the cushiony lawn
under my feet, then the brick wall of the stable, then I
was around on the other side, where Ike was standing, not looking at me. Ike wasn't very old, maybe
sixteen, and he worked away from the house. I knew
that he was trusted, along with Malachi, to ride off
from the farm carrying messages and doing errands.
I thought maybe he was Malachi's son, in fact, but I
didn't know; there was no apparent resemblance

between them. I didn't have any idea what he was doing here, or if he knew of our plan. I put down my bag and said nothing, only waited. Moments later, Lorna appeared, carrying some small things wrapped in a cloth over her arm. She was hugely calm. She smiled at Ike, and he pushed back a large door, revealing the gray pony, hitched to Helen's pony cart. Helen and I had taken it out twice in the last two weeks. Ike led the pony and the cart into the yard, and Lorna, with dignity, got up behind. Then they looked at me. I put my bag on the seat, got up myself, with a hand from Ike, and picked up the reins and the whip. No one said anything, and Ike stood there as I called "Get up!" to the pony and raised the whip. We trotted off. It was a very mysterious proceeding. At the road, I hesitated, and Lorna said, "You go lef'. We is takin' de pony to Independence to pick up a present fo' Massa Richard dat Missy Helen lef' deah."

"What's the present?"

"Mah goodness, I don' know. Deah ain' no present!"

The pony went along at a crisp trot, sometimes tossing his little head, but tireless and quick in his bright pony way. I glanced back at Lorna. She said, "Don' look at me! Now, I kin tell you ain' had no slaves befoah, so you got to be ceahful, 'cause you don' know how to be wid a slave! You cain' be lookin' at me all de time! You be lookin' wheah you wants to go, and I be lookin' at you."

"You don't treat Helen that way."

"Dat's in de house. Out amongst folks, I is

respectful, 'cause I'm tellin' you, de way things are around heah dese days, you nevah know when someone is gone to tek it on hisself to teach some gal a lesson, and dey got all de weapons in de worl' to teach it wid."

"Lorna, I'm sc—"

"Now, I ain' gone let you go on about dat, 'cause I is sceahed myself, an' I ain' gone let you get me worked up, and me get you worked up an' all. We is jus' gone go 'long one bit at a time."

"All right," I said. A man passed us on a horse and tipped his hat. I was too scared to do anything, and as soon as he passed, Lorna took me up short. "Now," she said, "you got to show good mannahs to dese mens and ladies dat we pass, 'cause Lawd, do dey notice dat. You got to gi' dem a big smile and nod you haid. You is havin' a good time, heah! You is dressed up fine and got you bonnet on and gone out for a ride wid you gal, and you is proud to be seen! Dis is a fine pony cart indeed!" I had to laugh, and when the next man passed, I gave him such a look and flourished the whip in such a way that the pony tossed his head and began to canter, until I brought him back to a trot. I said to Lorna, "Tell me more of the plan."

But she shook her head.

I guess we must have left Day's End Plantation about seven-thirty or eight, and we bowled along at a good pace. I can't say that I recognized the way we went—that's how far gone I had been on my walk. I had to take Lorna's word for it that this was indeed the road to Independence. I said, "Lorna, I only have seven dollars!"

"I got me a bit o' change."

"I thought slaves weren't allowed to have money."

"What you is allowed to do and what you do ain' always de same thang. I got me a husband, don' I, an' he goes out ta work at his trade of hoss breakin', don' he? An' his massa done told him he could buy hisself free, so he been savin' all he could, but he ain' been keepin' it all for hisself."

This seemed very simple. I said, "How does he get it to you?"

"Massa Richard don' open any lettahs I gits— Missy Helen don' let 'im—so deah I is. She give me de money and reads me ifn he write anything, but mostly he jes' sends money. He ain' good at writin' nohow. Jes' his mark, and a heart shape fo' me. He a good worker, and he'll git on any hoss deah is. He knows how ta gentle 'em right down. I been savin' fo' some five yeahs. Why you askin' all dese questions?"

"Because I could be hanged for aiding in your escape, and I would like to know what the likelihood of that is."

That put an end to our conversation for the time. I wondered how much money she had, and let myself imagine a hundred dollars. The sun got high, and I estimated we were heading on to about noon. I had let the pony alternate walking and trotting, trying to conserve him as much as possible, but now he was drooping, and I started looking around for a place for him to drink. There was nothing but a stream that ran through a little field some distance from the road. I said, "I've got to water the pony. It's hot." I halted him, got down from the seat, and began to unhitch him. Lorna said, "You cain' do dat."

"Why not?"

" 'Cause I's sittin' heah."

"Well, get down, then."

"I don' know 'bout ponies and hosses. I's afraid of 'em."

"I'm not. I'll do it."

"I cain' watch you work. Someone maht come 'long an' see you workin' and me sittin'."

"The pony's got to drink. What would Helen do?"

"Helen wouldn' think of de pony."

"Well, the pony's lathered up, and there isn't a breeze, so whatever happens, the pony's got to drink."

Lorna looked all around and, seeing no one, lay down in the grass beside the road, half under a bush. We exchanged a glance, then she said, "You tek de pony down to de stream. Ifn any mans comes 'long, I'll be groanin' and moanin', and den you bring me back some watah, too. I'll pull my legs up like I done been took bad wid de cramp."

And sure enough, when I was down at the stream, letting the pony drink his fill, a cart went along, and Lorna moaned and groaned, and the man got out of the cart and tried to stir her up, and so she moaned and groaned all the louder, until I led the pony up from the stream and he saw me, waved, and got back into his cart and drove away. When he was gone and I had hitched the pony back up, she said, "I didn' know him. I never seen him. I reckon he's new in dese parts. But dat war a close call. Everbody 'round heah knows I is Massa Richard's gal." Her confidence seemed total. I thought she must have learned from her previous attempt, and I imagined her working things out very carefully in her mind and just waiting for someone like me, an opportunity, to happen along.

As we got back into the pony cart, I was a little chastened by all the things I didn't know.

Now I allowed the pony to walk for the rest of the afternoon, and pretty soon the traffic thickened and I began to see houses closer together. We had gotten to the outskirts of Independence. I tried not to glance at Lorna but to look straight ahead as if I knew my destination. I smiled and waved to anyone who seemed interested in me, and Lorna kept her head down, afraid of meeting anyone who had seen her at Day's End Plantation. All the same, I saw her glancing covertly here and there, perhaps at the seething business that was Independence, Missouri, in those days, even on Sunday. For one thing, there was the old business of outfitting settlers for the west. But now, in addition, there was the new business of war. The business of war was, first and foremost, a business of men gathering in doorways and on street corners. Every space seemed to be filled

with men, who were either talking among themselves or listening to others talk. I say talk, but I
mean shout and yell and argue. Not every man was
gathered like this; plenty were riding through, driving through, pushing themselves through, getting
wagons loaded or unloaded, but these men were on
the alert for what the other men were doing. The
gatherings drew men into them. Most of these men
drifted off, but they couldn't stay away for long—
there was too much to be said, shouted, yelled. And
there were no women anywhere. I figured they were
staying indoors unless the war forced them out. That
was the way it had been in Lawrence in the winter.
There was also that customary Missouri sound, the
regular bang and pop, always startling, of guns being
shot off as an expression of feeling or opinion. I was
careful to refrain from looking at Lorna so that we
were well into town before I noticed the expression
on her face. She looked terrified. I was so amazed
that I stared at her and, finally, whispered, "What's
the matter?"

She said, "I ain' nevah seen it lak dis."

"How often have you been here?"

"Three times in all."

My heart sank.

I halted the pony in front of a hotel.

Lorna muttered, "What you doin'?"

"We need to get inside somewhere."

She looked up at the building and said, "What do
dat word say?"

"It says 'hotel.' "

"We got to pay out some money?"

"Maybe a little."

"Ain' got much."

I tried to speak brightly in spite of my growing dread. "You can sell things in Independence. I've got some things to sell." Did this include the pony and the cart? I wasn't sure my thieving could go quite that far. Mindful of Lorna's instructions, I got myself out of the cart and went into the hotel as if I were alone, trying with all my might not to look as panicky as I felt. I hadn't actually gotten Lorna to reveal her plan, had I? She followed me closely and kept her head down. On the scale of luxury, this establishment fell somewhere closer to the Humphry House, where Thomas and I had spent the night in Kansas City the year before, than to the Free State Hotel, in Lawrence, which was burned up during the sacking, but the staircase was complete, no looking through the risers to the cellar three or four floors below, and it did look as though it had private rooms. There was a man standing in a doorway across the room, and as we entered, he came forward. Lorna was close behind me, my bag in one of her hands and her bundle in the other. I saw that things were up to me, at least for now. I threw back my shoulders and looked around critically. I said, "What would I pay for a room for the night? A private room, one night?"

The man pulled off his hat. "Four dollars, ma'am."

"Oh, my goodness, that's much—"

"And the gal is four bits. We got quarters out back."

I could hear Lorna counting in her head as well as if she were doing it out loud. I drew myself up and looked around. She hadn't made a sound, had she? I thought, Here's one for you, Frank, and said, "I will give you three dollars, sir, and my gal has to stay with me. She's deaf, you know, deaf as the doorpost, and she can't be with others because she can't make out what folks are telling her to do. I got to have her with me."

Lorna neither moved nor made a sound, but only stood with her head lowered.

I went on. "She's a good gal, but I just don't know what to do with her. Can't sell her, because she's useless to anyone else. But I swear!"

The man looked at me.

I went on, leaning toward him, but speaking loudly enough for Lorna to hear. "My paw shot her. You can't see the scars because she's got her kerchief on. He didn't mean to, he was drunk, and he wasn't even a mean drunk in those days, but it was late at night, and she was just a girl, and she was getting up to get him a candle, and he had his rifle with him, and he was coming in, and he just shot her!" I put my hand on Lorna's arm and brought her forward, as if there were something to see, and the man looked at her with eager curiosity, as if he were seeing it, and then he nodded. He said, "Well, ma'am, we are busy with this war—"

"My goodness me! I am so frightened, I feel that I must throw myself on your mercy for this one night!" I opened my reticule and pulled out three dollars. "We are trying to get out of this country and back to Saint Louis." I leaned forward again and lowered my voice. "I have been disappointed in love, sir!"

The man stepped back. I stepped forward.

"A certain captain of the militia, whose name I shall not reveal, brought us out here by steamboat and then, when we got here, produced a wife and four children! I fled, but my hopes were far different than this, and I am low on funds." I let him look into my reticule just for a second. "Sir! I needn't tell you about the state of my feelings! I can see by the look on your face that you are in sympathy with me—" I turned away as if to hide my face, and caught a glimpse of Lorna. Her face was as sober and impenetrable as wood. I turned to the man again. "My gal doesn't understand. I've had a hard time communicating these betrayals to her—"

At last, he was overwhelmed. He said, "You ken have the room, ma'am."

"The Lord himself looks down upon you with approval, and you shall be rewarded, I am sure."

"I hope so, ma'am."

I handed him the three dollars, and we went up the stairs. Three or four doors were open, and I peeked into the rooms. They were dirty, but they had beds and floors and solid walls. I chose the corner one, so that if we talked, it was less likely that anyone would hear us. We went in; I closed the door; Lorna set down our things. There was nothing for it now, and we both knew it. I felt so disheartened that I couldn't even speak. We looked hard at each other, and I saw that I had done it again, that is, taken a stranger for a companion and set out on a journey whose destination I had no notion of. I hadn't any idea what Lorna was thinking. I sat on the bed and Lorna sat on the chair, and we were quiet for a long time.

CHAPTER 26

I Sully My Character

Reverses of fortune, in this land, are so frequent and unexpected, and the habits of the people are so migratory, that there are very many in every part of the Country, who, having seen all their temporal plans and hopes crushed, are now pining among strangers, bereft of wonted comforts, without friends, and without the sympathy and society, so needful to wounded spirits.

—p. 257

I COULD NOT OVERCOME the conviction that Lorna would be recognized in Independence by someone who had seen her at the plantation, and so I left her in the room, sitting in the chair, wedged against the door, while I went out to dispose of the pony and sell my belongings. The hotel was around the corner from a livery stable, so I put the pony and the cart there for a while—fifty cents. Not far from there was an outfitter's store; they were everywhere about and selling every item, new and old, from wheels and wagons down to fine linen handkerchiefs and lengths of French lace. There were even picture frames that still contained painted miniatures and daguerreo-types of their owners, a gallery of portraits of those who themselves had gone on to unknown fates but here awaited some sort of final disposition of their images. There was far more than I had ever seen in Horace's store in Quincy, and that was a measure, perhaps, of all the things that men and women thought they couldn't do without when they left their homes in the east and then decided that they must do without before they headed onto the prairie, then the desert and the mountains beyond. I wondered if the backtrackers heading east against the flow ever came through again, looking for their old things, trying to remake, if only in part, the life they'd thought to leave behind but now hoped to take up afresh.

The proprietor stood behind his counter, smiling. When he saw I had goods rather than money, his face fell. Ah. My goods. There were few enough of them. I pulled out the dress. He looked at it impassively and set it aside. I laid the four books on the table, three of Thomas's and my Miss Beecher. He opened them and saw that the pages were stiff and discolored. He noted that Miss Beecher herself had written me a note in the flyleaf of her treatise: "To my student, with all best wishes," and he was unimpressed. He set the book aside. From my pocket, I pulled Thomas's watch. It was warm, as I had been holding it. I set it on the counter, and he picked it up, opened the case, looked at it, shook it, noted the time, and compared it with his own watch, which he took out of his watch pocket. All he said was, "Right time," then he set it aside, and I had the sense of it apart from me, cooling. All the same, I didn't grieve for it then. It was heavy with too many memories and inner pangs. I felt almost relieved to give it up.

And I was relieved to give up the pistol, the cartridges I had made, and the percussion caps. I pulled them out of the bag and laid them gently on the counter, and for the first time the proprietor looked pleased. He was a western man, after all, and he ran his hand over the barrel and the stock, then he touched the hammer and the trigger with his forefinger. He said, "Don't git too many of these in. Most folks are wanting to keep theirs."

"It's a black dragoon."

"I know that. Had two of 'em in. Handy thing."

"Yes, folks say so."

"An't everything it's cracked up to be, though."

"Nothing is."

"That's the truth, too."

He looked over the goods again, calculating. He picked up Thomas's watch, set it down, ran his hand over the pistol, looked into Mrs. Beecher. Finally, he said, "These guns is twelve dollars new."

"You can see that I've kept it very clean. I never let it get fouled."

"It's your own weapon, ma'am?"

"It's my own weapon."

"How often you got to change the time on this watch?"

"Once every two weeks, by about five minutes."

"Is that so?"

"Yes, sir."

He looked at the watch again, weighed it in his hand. Then he looked over the array and said, "I got forty dollars for ya, and that's only because it looks to me like you're all by yourself out here and these are your things."

"They are."

"This is what you do, ma'am. You take my forty dollars, and then you get yourself by stage to Lexington, away from the war here. That should cost you about two dollars or so. Then you get on the steamboat there, and you go on down the river and get away from this place, because I'm telling you right now that all of K.T. and western Missouri is going to be burning in a month, and if I didn't have me so many goods here, and such a big establishment, I'd be leaving myself, but I sent away my wife and daughter, back to Illinois. This an't no place for you, ma'am." He handed me the forty dollars.

I said, "I will certainly take your advice."

"Remember, I told you. Everything them hotheads say they want, they're going to make sure they git it."

"Yes, sir." I turned my back on everything I owned and walked out of the store.

Although it was Sunday, as I've said, it was widely known all over the west that the Lord approved of business going forward when there was a great deal of business to be done, and so I was perfectly able to go into another store and purchase some provisions—early apples and pears, some potatoes and carrots and hard biscuits. I also bought us each a cup. These things came to two dollars and eighty-two cents.

Now I went back to the hotel. As I entered the door and mounted the stairs, I did feel a panic rise in my throat, as if, upon going to my room, I might see something horrible, but all was quiet. Lorna was sitting where I had left her, and when I pushed on the door, she peered out with one eye, then let me in. I showed her the money and food, then sat down upon the bed. I thought we might eat, but I wasn't hungry, probably from fear, and Lorna didn't take anything. In my absence, she had put the room to rights as best she could, but it would still take a deal of scrubbing to make it appealing. For a while, we didn't talk but sat there listening to the conversation and the noises that came through the walls, the door, the windows to the outside. At last, it became apparent that we might talk softly, if we went to the outer corner of the room, between the two small, dirty windows that looked out on the street, one of which had a broken pane of glass. We had to get a couple of things out of the way, and first things first, I whispered, "I can't bring myself to steal the pony and the cart."

"We ain' stealin' 'em. We gone fine a boy to brang 'em. Dere's boys dat come to de house from time to time, carrying a message or a parcel. We gone fine a boy like dat and give 'im a dollar. I reckoned dat in."

"It's going to take me a while to find one."

"Dey's boys all 'round. We cain' leave heah till afta dark, nohow."

Then I said, "Lorna, where are we going?"

"Kansas."

The very idea filled me with horror.

She said, "Dat's free soil."

"But it isn't. The law is officially just like Missouri law, or worse."

"Massa Richard say all de abolishinists have de run of the place and have de say-so dere. He and dem others yell about it all de time."

"It's not true, and there's a war on there, too."

She stared at me, resistant.

"I was just there. I came from there. Remember? I told you that one day."

"You did, but den you say you come from over by de river, wheah I seen you before."

"I went out to Kansas with my husband, who gave you that money. We lived in Lawrence."

Now Lorna gave a big grin and whispered, "Massa Richard say dat's de devil's own town!"

"Well, folks in Lawrence say that Missouri is the devil's own country."

"An' it is, for me. As soon as Massa Richard and his cronies got so heat up about Lawrence, well, me and Jake, we thought dat war de place for us!"

"But it's been burned once, and my husband was shot there! You can't escape into a war that's getting fiercer and fiercer. There are all sorts of bands of men roaming about, looking for a chance to kill someone."

"Dat's de closest place."

"Maybe, but you have to listen to me. The men who shot my husband didn't stop to find out anything about him, or us. They rode up to us, took a look at us, and shot him. They shot our horse, too, for no reason. Kansas is different, even from Missouri. Nothing stops anyone there. Whatever builds up here in the east, in Kansas folks let it out. If you and I go into Kansas, a white woman and a black woman, someone on some side will stop us, because there's three types of people there—the ones who want slavery, the ones who don't want slavery, and the ones who don't want slavery or any Negroes in the state. All of them will wonder about us. All of them will think they can stop us and torment us and take us up for some reason or another. Lorna, you never see a black woman and a white woman together in Kansas."

"I cain' stay in Missouri. I'm in slavery in Missouri. I cain' do it." She went over to the chair by the door and put her face in her hands. I lay down on the dirty bed and stared at the floorboards of the room above and the rickety joists holding them up. I fell into an uneasy sleep, so exhausted that I couldn't wake, though repeatedly disturbed by half-heard sounds of boots in the hallway outside the room, boots above us, yelling and shots outside. In my dreams, I missed the peace of Day's End Plantation, because surely that quiet, whatever it boded, was better than this disquiet. Then I woke up, and I saw that Lorna, in her chair, had fallen into a doze, too. My spirits were low, and I felt a good deal of fear, but I didn't long for Day's End Plantation. That was something. I lay there, and shortly Lorna woke up. She looked over, saw that I was awake, and sat up. She took her time adjusting her clothes and the kerchief on her head, standing and even trying to use the tiny looking glass that was hanging on one wall. When she was entirely straight and neat, she went over to the corner where we had talked earlier, and so I got up and joined her there. She no longer looked fearful but appeared settled and ready. She whispered, "I see what we got to do, Missy Louisa. We got to go on de boat as missy and gal. We got to sink into de wallpaper, like, an' stay wheah we look like we belong."

"Lots of women and children and servants are moving east. We'll fit right in."

"But we got to leave dis town. We done slep' now. We got to leave as soon as de darkness come."

I nodded.

"Wheah are de pony and de cart?"

"I put them in a livery stable."

And that was the last we spoke of them. We both knew that in spite of our best intentions and greatest care, to return to the pony and the cart was to put ourselves in danger, especially as the cart was a gaily painted one, green with red striping. If we had escaped detection so far (and there was no telling if we had), we would risk it unnecessarily by drawing attention to the pony cart. And so, here was another thing I thought I wouldn't do that I did when the time came. I realized then that there was no telling what you might do if it looked like you had to do it. That was the lesson of K.T., wasn't it?

I had no bag now, so Lorna wrapped the provisions in her bundle, which itself was none too large, and she stationed herself against the door while I went out to look for the stage to Lexington. I was soon disappointed. The stage company was overburdened with business—they were sending folks east in all sorts of vehicles, behind all sorts of draft animals. "Do you know the Missouri roads, ma'am?" said the clerk in a friendly way.

"I haven't been on them."

"Ah. Well, ma'am, they have quite a reputation, and it an't a good one. I myself feel that when we send these folks off, we are sending them into the wilderness. And I can't speak for the drivers, either. Most of them carry their kegs of highly rectified whiskey with them, within easy reach." He leaned over the desk to me. "Good deal of fighting along the way, ma'am. That's what we hear. Of course, you can go west."

"West!"

"Yes, ma'am. There's plenty of room going west to Kansas City, and you can get passage there. You'd think the steamboats would stay away, but they are drawn to it! And the passage is very high now. Twenty dollars or more."

"Twenty dollars! It was twelve, and before that it was eight."

"War is surely a good opportunity, ma'am."

"How much is the stage to Kansas City?"

"Ten dollars, ma'am."

"I have a gal."

"She can ride on top for eight, walk alongside and get up from time to time for four."

"She can walk alongside the stage for four dollars?"

"Yes, ma'am. The driver will allow her to get up four times for ten minutes a time, by his pocket watch."

"That's—"

"That's what the market will bear, ma'am." He gave me a cheerful smile and stuck his pencil behind his ear, probably pondering the cascade of money pouring through Independence now that would surely at least trickle in his direction.

Lorna, I have to say, was less than astonished by my report. All she said was, "Den we have to walk. You know de way out o' dis town?"

Well, I did.

Though we never spoke of it, in the back of both our minds was the knowledge that Papa would soon be looking for us, and the course of action we had chosen, to stay during daylight in Independence and then make off after dark, could easily be the wrong choice. If it had taken us half a day to get from the plantation by pony cart, it would take much less than that for Papa and his friends to gallop there on fresh horses. It all depended upon when they returned from the Harris plantation and how quickly it was revealed that I was gone, Lorna was gone with me, and the pony cart was gone with the both of us. Perhaps because we never spoke of it, it was all too easy to imagine the smoothest and quickest possible pursuit on their part, all too easy to envision that moment of looking up and seeing them, him, Papa, right before you, his little arm raised and something in his hand. A whip? A gun? All too easy to wonder what would happen then, upon discovery. And wondering that seemed to stop me in my tracks, make it impossible to move or act. But perhaps speaking about it would add fancy upon fancy, hers upon mine, mine upon hers. We didn't dare.

We were impatient for full darkness. When it came, we fixed our hair and got ourselves together and passed out of the now crowded hotel without looking either left or right, me in front, Lorna a step or two behind, me with my head high, Lorna with hers low. I went down the stairs, my hand skimming the banister. I strode through the lower room and looked at no one who was looking at me. I went outside and down the outer steps, which numbered four. I turned left, west, and marched along. I saw that walking to Kansas City was going to be considerably harder in a skirt and light shoes than it had been in trousers and boots, but there was no help for that. We passed men on horseback, men in wagons, men afoot. We passed groups of men, men in twos and threes, solitary men. It seemed that all of them looked first at me and second at Lorna, and all speculated about us, but no one stopped us. We walked on, and soon enough the town gave way to countryside. Just about then, when we were alone, Lorna said, "What time do ya make it?"

I said, "I don't know. I sold the watch."

That was all we said.

I thought of how, the last time I passed this way, I had crawled under bushes or haystacks to sleep at night and had confidently, more or less, gone my way during the day. I remembered how intent I had been upon finding Samson and Chaney. My resolve had given me the confidence to be a boy, hadn't it? To march along in broad daylight, booted, trousered, braced, behatted, full of purpose and showing it, like a man. Now we paused in the darkness and listened to noises, looked about us, caught each other's glance and looked away, dreading the very dread we might see. When others passed us, we drew ourselves into ourselves, aiming to pass unnoticed, trying not to look as if we were ready to flee. Ladylike dignity was the key to safe passage, as boyish self-confidence had been before. And I got tired. Lorna didn't. She said, "What's de mattah wid ya? Ya slowin' down!"

"I'm tired. It's the middle of the night."

"No, it ain'. My guess, it ain' pas' ten. We got to go quick as we ken till daylight. We ken res' den, though I ain' goin' to one o' dem hotels again! I sweah, dat place was filthy! Missy Helen couldn' have slep' a wink deah!"

"I can hardly keep awake."

"I'm jes' glad I is out in de country walkin', 'stead o' sewin' on Massa Richard's shirts by candlelight!"

"Is Master Richard a cruel master?"

"No."

"Did he ever beat you?"

"Not so's you'd notice much. He aim for me wid his razor strap one time. He only yell a lot. He don' evah beat de boys, 'cause he ain' big enough. He buy dem off wid presents."

I laughed.

"Why you laughin'?"

"Because that's not the way the northerners think slaves live."

"Slaves live all differnt. But dey all slaves. Dey all got to do what dey is tol' to do."

"I didn't see anyone tell you what to do much at Day's End Plantation."

"Now you soun' like Massa Richard. When I

come back deah a year ago, he say, 'This place is heaven, Lorna! We all have our work to do and we do it, and then we receive our nourishment and our rest, and we rise to do our work again. It's all the same for master and servant, Lorna. The world you want to get to is a far darker place than Day's End Plantation!' " Her mimicry of Papa's intonation and way of expressing himself was perfect, and so I laughed again, but then I sobered up and said, "And so it is, Lorna. A woman I know and both of her little boys starved to death not far from me this past winter. I might have, too, but for a friend. What will you do, all alone?"

"I ain' gone be all alone. My man is buyin' hisself free."

"Couldn't he buy you free?"

"Tek 'im twelve yeah to buy hisself! In twelve yeah, I ain' gone be fit to have babies. Anyway, Massa Richard already done tol' me dat he don' want to sell me, 'cause I is de best trained and he cain' get no one like me no more, wid de ablishinists and all. He say, 'We have to draw upon our own resources, Lorna. Not like former times!' "

"You sound just like him."

"Well, I been heahin' 'im talk since I war a youngun. Hush, now."

We quieted, and I could hear horses, more than one, trotting along. Without even thinking about it, I stepped over behind a tree, and Lorna stepped in beside me. We pressed against the tree and looked at each other, making no sound. The horses trotted by, two of them. One of the riders was saying, ". . .

shoulda shot 'im a long time ago, but Halloran
wouldn't let me, haw haw!" It was a regret I had
heard often enough—Missouri and Kansas were
filled with folks who, in the opinion of other folks,
would have been shot long before this if better judgment had prevailed. The horses trotted away, and
when we could no longer hear them, we stepped out
from behind the tree and resumed walking. I was no
longer sleepy. I said, "Why shouldn't you be a slave,
Lorna? What if all those preachers are right, and the
Lord says that Negroes are best in slavery?"

" 'Cause I don' want to be, an' I know my own
mine bettah dan dose preachahs know de Lawd's
mine, I think."

"Does my question insult you?"

"You is ignorant and you ain' got good mannahs,
but I don' caeh. I is ignorant myself. I cain' read and I
cain' write nothin' but 'Lorna.' An' I ain' got good
mannahs, neider, 'cause I ain' got de patience for
'em. Delia, she got good mannahs, an' look wheah
she got."

"Where did she get?"

"She got her baby took from 'er an' sold. Dat's
one thing."

I didn't know what to say, even though I'd read
Mrs. Stowe's book. Lorna was in the mood for talking, though. She seemed a much less crusty person
than she'd been at the plantation. She said, "I reckon
Massa Richard don' talk about dat much, and maybe
he nevah tol' Missy Helen dat at all. You know, dey
make ol' missy out to be a saint in heaven, but when
it come right down to it, she waren't dat at all. She

nevah barked, but she didn' mine bitin'. An' she could sell a niggah quick as you please. Missy Bella is a lot like 'er, but dey nevah says dat, 'cause Missy Bella, she jes' cain' control herself. She git mad and she hit out. But ol' missy, she git jes' as mad, but den she lay in wait for ya, when you thought she ware ovah it. Dat's what happen wid Delia. She had a year-old boy wid her man, who daid now, boy name Mosie. Well, one day she done somethin' dat missy didn' like—I nevah hear what it was. Missy say, 'Delia, you have seriously displeased me today!' an' den Delia thought she forgot about it. 'Bout two months latah, missy had her a baby dat war Helen, an' she say she ain' got no milk for de new baby, cain' get none, none would come. So she tol' Massa Richard he got to sell Mosie so Delia would nuss baby Helen, and Massa Richard, he go 'bout wid a long face for a day or so, but in de end, ol' missy got her way, like she always did, from smilin' and makin' up to 'im, and dey done sold dat chile, dey say he war weaned, it wouldn' hurt him to go off, jes' like he war a horse or suchlike, and right den I tol' myself I ain' havin' no babies on dat place, no mattah what my man say. Well, Delia, she cry and moan about dat boy for yeahs, but when ol' missy died, she wep' for her, too, and she love Missy Helen and all, but I didn' shed no tears for ol' missy, and I always held it against Missy Helen, wheder it her fault or no. I do hold a grudge, dat's for sure."

I don't know why I found this story so shocking, as I had heard stories like this many times, but to hear it in Lorna's own voice, and to know Helen and Papa and Delia and to imagine the scenes in the very rooms of Day's End Plantation that I knew so well made it hard for me to take in. I exclaimed, "I believe you!" and Lorna looked at me and said, "Well, why shouldn' you? I is tellin' de truth. I war ten or eleven den, I guess, still a girl, but I knowed by dat time what it would be to be a woman on dat place, an' when my man come 'round, I tol' 'im dat we ain' makin' no babies for ol' missy to sell away, and anyway, he done went off to buy hisself real quick after we done got married."

"I know such things happen."

"We don' know all dat happen in slavery, an' I always thought we don' want to know. Ifn my days is good enough, an' I hate 'em, den I cain' think about de days of de others, dat is terrible bad, down Louisiana way an' dem other places."

"You are quite a philosopher, Lorna."

"Is dat so?" She sounded both skeptical and resentful, and I saw that talking about these things had made her angry. I said, "I'm sorry to be so inquisitive."

She harrumphed, and we walked on in silence.

Twice more, horses came by, once a group of three, once a group of four, and both times we found places to hide while they passed. The men were all drunk, and not especially observant, or they might have seen our light-colored dresses or heard us rustle the leaves. It is impossible for a woman in a long skirt and a petticoat to be absolutely, or even relatively, silent. I knew we would be better off the road. But this was the only way I knew to Kansas City, and

I was afraid of getting lost in the darkness. Nor did we want to appear furtive. Not escapees, but a woman and her girl, a little bit short of funds owing to high prices and romantic betrayal. That's who we were, if only we could remember to be that. We made good progress, though I had pains up my legs from the lightness of my shoes, which seemed to give way to every little stone or pebble.

After a while, I said, "Tell me more. Tell me about the last time you ran away."

"Missy Bella sent me off wid some money for de shoppin'. I war sposed to pick up some gown she done ordered. I didn' have my own money wid me deah. So she give me about fifty dollar, and she say, 'Now, don' you run off, gal,' and so I did. A nigger I knew who worked on a steamboat, he got me upriver pretty far, almost neah to your place, but den I had to git out in de night when de boat went close to the bank, and den I stuck by de river for some three, four days, till I got to dat cave deah. You cain' trust anybody in Illinois. Dat's what all de niggers along deah say. You got to git to Wesconsin. But dat man you knew, he knew some niggers 'long deah. Dey done said he was big in de Underground Railroad. I thought I war gone make it, but some catchers spied me when I was sleepin' and come back later wid de dogs, and dat war dat. But I don' want to talk about slavery no more. I is done wid it."

"I need to talk about something, or I'll fall asleep."

"Den you tell me."

"What?"

"Tell me about Wesconsin."

"That's north of Illinois. It's a long way."

"Is dey all ablishinists up deah?"

"They voted not to carry out the Fugitive Slave Act."

"When I tol' Massa Richard I war headed dat way, after dey caught me, he say it too d——— cold for a niggah up deah, and all dey got is Indians, who don' caeh about de cold."

"It is wild country."

"I don' mine de cold. I done fine las' winter. Delia and Ike say dey was dying, and Massa Richard, he done lay in 'is bed for four days wid three quilts ovah 'im, but I didn' mine. Delia had de stove goin' in de kitchen all day and all night, and she made us eat like hogs."

"But not many white people even want to go to Wisconsin. I hear it's good in Ohio. That's where my sister had a school before she died. A school for Negro children."

"I'll go deah, den."

"But she died. The school is disbanded for now."

"But dey let her have it. I ain' nevah heard of a place wheah dey let some lady have a school for nig-gah children before."

"You can get there by steamboat, if I take you."

"Oh, I 'spect you is takin' me, den."

I said, "All right."

"Ifn you took me to Kansas, maybe you could get rid of me sooner."

"Yes, by us being shot. I could get rid of both of us pretty quick, I'll bet. I won't go back there."

"Kin I learn to read deah?"

"You can learn to read anywhere there's something to read."

"Well, den, as Massa Richard would say, '*may* I learn to read deah?' Because I *may not* learn to read heah."

"Yes, you may learn to read there." Then I thought of something. "How does your husband know you're escaping?"

"He don'! My Lawd, Missy Louisa, sometime you sound so smart, and den you say somethin' so thick, like you haid's made o' wood!"

That put me in my place.

Though surely it was now the middle of the night, I felt less exhausted than I had earlier and ready to eat, but Lorna had the provisions, and I was hesitant to say anything, until at last she sighed and remarked, "I spose we oughta eat somethin', but I hates to stop."

"We can walk and eat."

"Cain' do dat. Dat's bad for you insides. Give you de cramp. Dey's some hackberry bushes ovah deah. We kin set undah 'em."

I was grateful for that.

Now Lorna opened her bundle and laid out our apples and pears. What had looked appetizing when I purchased it looked paltry and cold in the darkness, and I sighed. Then Lorna unwrapped a cloth of her own, and I saw that she had a stack of corncakes. I said, "Where did you get those?"

"Delia made 'em for Malachi, she thought." She laughed. "She always tol' me, 'Lorna, ifn I see you rummagin' 'round de kitchen or de cellar, I kin read you mine!' But she didn'."

The corncakes were light, delicious, and sweet, perfect with the apples, which were not quite ripe and very tart. I saw what else was in her bundle, too—the cup I'd bought, some squares of cloth, an apron, a pair of stockings, and a pair of shoes with wooden soles. That was all. She saw me looking but said nothing, and I turned away. After all, there was no telling how many times she had looked into my bag. After a bit, she said, "You man war a ablishinist."

"Yes, he was. He was from Massachusetts."

"Is dey all ablishinists deah, too?"

"Seems like it."

"You evah bin deah?"

"No. I've only ever been here, in Kansas, and in Illinois."

"My man war reared up in Georgia, den his massa bring 'im to Kentuck, wheah he larn to ride a hoss, den dey come heah, den he gone to Arkinsaw, and de las' time I heah from him, he war in Tennessee. An' in between deah, he done gone to Texas for some little time! An' all I done is sit deah on Massa Richard's place, goin' from de quartahs to de house and back to de quartahs! I done wasted my time!"

"You went to Saint Louis."

"Well, now, dat was a sight! Missy Bella send me out every day to do de shoppin', and de stores deah is somethin'. And ain' jes' niggahs doin' de shoppin' nohow! Deah war plenty to see, I tell ya, but dat war a pestilential place, too! When de summer come on, it git so hot, like deah was fiahs burnin', and den folks start comin' down wid de fevah and all kind o' sickness! You couldn' git a breeze nohow, sometime fo' days! Ain' no place to live, even wid all dem stores!"

"My husband was a sailor for a long time, on the ocean. He went to the Indies. His father has a sail-making factory."

"How long war you married?"

"About ten months."

"Dey comes and dey goes, don't dey?"

"I didn't get to know him very well." I longed to tell her all about him, or maybe just to talk about him freely, but I didn't know how to start, so I held my tongue.

She spoke ruefully. "I knows Ike and Malachi bettah dan I knows my man. An' I knows Massa Richard bettah dan I knows any of 'em, since I been watchin' him ever since I war a chile. Too bad fo' dat!"

We threw our apple cores under the bush, then Lorna wrapped the remainder of the food in her bundle again. She said, "Why you askin' all dese questions? I ain' nevah knowed a white woman who asked me so many questions." But she didn't sound resentful this time, so I said, "My husband was an abolitionist, and I knew a lot of abolitionists in Kansas, but in spite of their sentiments against slavery, most of them hadn't met too many slaves. I suppose I just want to learn something."

"Well, you know what? I ain' a talker. Massa

Richard always complainin' dat you cain' get a word out of me, and Delia thinks I is hard as a nut, and she say to me, 'Lorna, you ain' got no heart dat I kin see.' She say dat to me time and time again, 'cause whatever happen, I don' say nothin' 'bout it. But tonight my mouth is jes' runnin'!" She smiled one of her rare smiles, and we got up and went out to the road.

Just after that, we had our biggest scare of the night, when we heard some dogs in the distance, both barking and howling. At this, Lorna stood stock-still and grabbed my arm. She whispered, "Missy! Farm dogs bark, but catchers' dogs, dey howl! He done foun' us!" I didn't think he had—the dogs were far away and didn't sound like they were getting any closer; but my thoughts didn't matter. A cold, painful fright seized my flesh right then, so that I couldn't move and I couldn't breathe and I started to shiver. I felt that Lorna was shivering, too, right beside me. The only thing that kept me from moaning aloud was the fear of making a sound, as if the dogs in the distance were evidence of enemies all around us, close enough to touch us. I grabbed Lorna around the shoulders and pulled her to me, and then, after half a second, she grabbed me around the waist, and we stood like that, holding each other up, waiting for the inevitable, it seemed, shock of capture.

But it didn't come. The barking and howling dogs faded away, the night sounds of rustling leaves and owls reasserted themselves, and Lorna and I stepped apart and marched on, still shaken, and also, I think, a little embarrassed that we had been so suddenly and utterly turned into cowards. After that, we didn't talk for some time, maybe an hour or two. In fact, I rather forgot about her, as I grew dizzier and dizzier with fatigue, and more and more intent upon simply putting one foot in front of the other. Just before dawn, when we could see the beginning of a heavy, overcast day, I must have been staggering around, because Lorna pointed out a haystack and said we could sleep on the protected side, but only for a little while. It was the most dangerous thing we did, but we had good luck and slept undisturbed until well after sunup, perhaps even until eight o'clock or so. When we woke, we were much disheveled, and one thing I will always remember about that fateful day was that Lorna stood me up and brushed me down, picked the hay out of my hair and straightened my bonnet, and then carefully did the same to herself. She said, "Now, you cain' be lookin' like a runaway. You got to be lookin' like a walker from dis place to dat place." She gave me a pear, and we walked on.

Well, I liked it. I liked the deception of it. When the day was well begun, there were folks all over the place, on horseback, in wagons, even in buggies. As we got farther from Independence, we got braver about who might or might not know Lorna, and certainly no one would know me. I walked with my head high, a woman with her gal. That militia fellow shouldn't have betrayed my virtue like that! He had certainly done me a great wrong! I had believed him implicitly, because he was of good family, well spoken, and educated at, let's say, Princeton, just like Papa. A girl such as myself, who had lost her parents, was surely unprotected in this world from the designs of scheming cads such as my erstwhile lover, and didn't his wife and children look a sight! She was careworn, and they were bedraggled, two boys and two girls, all little ones, the children of a natural betrayer, who would betray them in the end, as well. . . .

I smiled at my own story and raised my chin just a degree, for I had almost but not quite fallen. I had preserved myself in the end, had I not, for something better, and should I die before getting back to my relations in the east, well, I would know that I had lost nothing of real value—

"Whisht!" said Lorna, just behind my ear. I looked around, but only for a second, because Lorna said, "Don' look!" I did glimpse a man and a woman approaching, coming down from their house on foot, and two slaves, a man and a half-grown girl, weren't far behind them. Lorna whispered, "Turn 'round and slap me good, and do it now!"

I raised my hand and whipped around, and made such contact that Lorna's head snapped back and her hand went straight to her cheek. Her eyes closed, but she said, "Dat war good."

I screamed, "You lost my shoes? You stupid girl! You left my shoes behind! That's the last straw; I'm going to beat you for that! Ah!" I pretended to be surprised by the interruption, as the man and woman came up to us. I turned on them. "Can you believe this? Here we are in the middle of this godforsaken war, betrayed and abandoned, and she's lost my other pair of shoes! How stupid can one gal be!" I took a deep breath and said, "You must tell me, are we in Kansas or in Missouri? I do believe I am lost, and I'm dreadfully afraid that if I get into Kansas by mistake, they'll steal my girl and kill me!" I turned on Lorna. "Though don't think that would be a loss! You are worse than useless!"

"Now, ma'am," said the man. "I kin see that your patience has been much tried here, but an't no call for—"

"Yes," said the woman. They looked at me approvingly in spite of their remonstrations, and then the woman put her arm through mine. She said, "I saw you and your gal walking down the road here, and I said, 'I do wonder about them,' because you know, we see just about everything around here, including niggah-stealing—"

I exclaimed, "Lord have mercy, we are in Kansas!"

"No, no, no," said the woman. "Kansas is five mile or more. You're safe in Missouri now." And she turned me and walked me toward the house, which was no Day's End Plantation but more of a western farmhouse. She said, "We've only got Delilah and Job here. He's so old, we just take care of him, and she's training. But back in Mississippi, before we came out here, we had ten in the field and five in the house! Our neighbor, Mr. Lazarus Jennison, he had five hundred! He was a very fine man, from an old, old family with roots in Virginia. We were close friends before we came out here. Ah, well, I miss those days. May I offer you some refreshment?"

"Thank you very much. My name is Miss Jane

Horn, and this is my girl, Ila, and I really don't want
to let her out of my sight, I must say, because there's
no telling what mess she'll get into!"

"Delilah can take her into the kitchen and find
her a bite—"

"Please, ma'am! I've lost everything now, and I
do fear—" I summoned a tear or two.

"My dear! Very well, we can sit in the kitchen
with them! But how can we help you? What in the
world has happened?"

And so we sat together in the kitchen, myself,
Lorna, Delilah, and Mrs. May Thornton, drinking
milk and eating biscuits from their breakfast, and I
spun out my abandonment story, then nobly refused
all aid but said we only wanted to be on our way to
Kansas City, so that we could make our boat, the
Kansas Star, which we knew was leaving at evening.
From time to time, Lorna put her hand to her cheek
and rubbed it and gave me a petulant glance, but she
kept quiet. Mr. Thornton came in and went out, only
saying, "Now, May, the horses are working on the
farm today; don't ask me!"

Profuse thanks managed to get us away just after
noon. When we were well out into the road, I apolo-
gized to Lorna for hitting her so hard. She said,
"Missies always hit hard. Massas don' hit so hard." I
took that as approval.

We were more careful now and didn't chat at all.
Lorna stayed two or three paces behind me and, as
always, kept her head down. But she was tremendously strong, and the sound of her steps on the road
behind me were firm and even, always pushing me

onward, always reminding me that it was a long way between here and Ohio, and it wouldn't be easy to get there. It was tempting for me to think of this escape as an adventure—no one had truly been hanged in Kansas or Missouri for slave stealing that I knew of, though getting shot was certainly a possibility, but as a woman, and an unarmed one at that, I might not get shot in the end. But we had been gone more than twenty-four hours from Day's End Plantation, and so far, our escape seemed more like a success than a failure.

We came into Kansas City late in the afternoon. It was now almost three weeks since I had left the town, and once again it was entirely different, and different, as well, from Independence, for Kansas City was in a full state of war, with troops of men in all varieties of uniform gathered together, marching, drilling, riding madly to and fro. The sound of weapons firing, always a feature of Kansas City life, was now almost constant. I saw that we had to get to the river as quickly as possible, get on a boat, and hide out there. A year earlier, this wouldn't have been difficult at all, as all there was to Kansas City was the levee and the bluff above it. Now the town spread out in all directions, and I couldn't tell where the river was. Lorna and I couldn't help being daunted by the activity and the noise. As much as we knew we had to move deliberately forward, appearing confident and even at ease with our situation, it was nearly impossible not to stop and gape, not to startle, not to glance furtively around. Any number of shouts could be directed at us, could they not? And any of those

could be just a warning to get out of the way (everyone on foot was in the way), but any of them could
likewise be the Recognition. Lorna had lived at
Papa's all her life, some thirty years, as I guessed.
There was no telling how many guests had passed
through there, gotten to know her, knew now of her
escape. Nevertheless, here in Kansas City, the balance of my fears had shifted, and I was now more
afraid of getting caught up in an all-out war than I
was of capture. Indeed, the newspapers pasted up
here and there, on fences and walls, as well as those
tossed in the street, all declared, "WAR! WAR!" in
giant letters. Shannon had fled, and others were fleeing. I began to wonder whether we could get on a
boat, and if so, when, and what it would cost. Twenty
dollars for each of us suddenly seemed cheap, if that
was our only chance. Thirty would stretch us, and
forty break us. Forty seemed impossible, but you
could see at a glance that in Kansas City right then,
all bets were off. We came to a street corner, and I
turned imperiously to Lorna and barked, "The boats
may be full, Ila! We need to come up with another
plan in case they are!"

"Yes, missy," said Lorna, submissively.

We marched on. I brought myself to ask directions to the levee, but the man I asked said, "Ma'am,
I jes' got here myself! I don't know up from down
here! An't it excitin'?" And he spit at my feet and
rushed off, pistols thumping at his sides. We walked
on. Talking itself seemed so dangerous that I could
summon the courage to do it only once. After a few

more minutes, Lorna muttered, "We is gone de wrong way!"

"I don't think so."

"I does!"

She smiled as she spoke to me, trying to please me for the eyes of any and all onlookers, but her voice carried grit. She muttered, "Ask agin! It gettin' dark."

I thought darkness would be some respite myself, but I didn't dare argue with her. Even so, I could hardly bring myself to speak. Every man around seemed the incarnation of danger. Finally, I spotted a boy. A boy of the sort I recognized perfectly, a lounging boy with a seegar in his mouth, thirteen or fourteen, white-blond of hair and brown of face. I approached him, and he said, "Hey, ma'am."

"I need to get to the river, where the steamboats are."

"I need four bits for my supper."

I opened my reticule. The boy looked into it, idly, shamelessly. I handed him fifty cents, and he took the money in his hand and tossed it into the air. Only after catching it and depositing it in his pocket did he look at me again. "Everbody knows the river's down that way, but I bet you an't goin' to find no boat unless you booked your passage last month, 'cause ever boat is d—— full!"

"We can try."

"You go down that street . . . Nah, I'll show ya." He spun around in front of us, whipped off his hat and stuck it on his head again, then trotted off. Lorna and I trotted after him. After a moment, he looked back at me and paused. When I had caught up to him, he said, "That your gal?"

"Yes."

"She looks mad."

"She just looks that way."

"I wish I had a gal."

"You do?"

"Nah, not for me, but you kin get eight hunderd dollars for a gal in these parts. Lots of 'em have run off, that's why."

"Where to?"

"What's the matter with you—an't you got no sense? The ablishinists get 'em all together and run 'em off to Ioway. They do that ever night! Last night alone, they got twenty-three gals and ten boys! Probably the catchers'll only get half of 'em back."

"Who told you that?"

"Everbody knows that." He plucked the seegar out of the corner of his mouth, spit in the dust, and put the seegar back. I said, "Is the area well supplied with catchers?"

"Yeah, but they an't good ones. I could be a catcher. They git twenty percent around here. That's good money! If your gal run off, and I caught her, you'd have to give me a hunderd and sixty dollars to git her back!"

"What if I didn't have that money?"

"Then I could keep her."

"I don't believe that's true."

"Well, it is. Man told me. His brother was a catcher, and he was goin' to git into the business his-

self! There's the river. You got another two bits?" I
saw that he was looking carefully at Lorna, so I
handed him some more money, and he tipped his hat,
then ran off. We made our way down to the boats.
The shafts of late-afternoon light had blued now, and
I thought soon we would be doubly safe, in the darkness, on some boat. Of boats there were not too
many, but the levee was seething with activity, much
more than it had been three weeks earlier, when I'd
fled the *Missouri Rose*. That was the first boat I
searched for, fearful that the captain would know me,
but it wasn't there. We had four choices—the *Herald,*
the *Jack Smith,* the *Missourian,* and the *Southern
Joy*. Of these, the *Southern Joy* looked the biggest, so
I began with it. Lorna stuck close behind me. We
strolled up the plank to the Texas deck, and I took a
moment to gaze around, arranging myself a bit and
trying to spy out the captain. The *Southern Joy*
wasn't quite as new as it looked from a distance—the
white and gold paint on the railings was dingy and
cracked, and the decking had buckled in many
places. My thoughts strayed to the boiler, but I pulled
them back. A door to the saloon opened, and the captain, an extremely tall man in a dusty blue uniform,
emerged. When he saw me, he smiled, but it was a
closed-over sort of smile that didn't give me much
hope, and in fact, he said at once, "Now, ma'am,
don't be askin' me about passage down to Saint
Louis, because I cannot do a thing for you! I got me a
boatload o' women and children already, fit to sink
where we sit, and them sandbars between here and
there is goin' to be a trial, so don't ask me, unless you

got you some little ones, because I am makin' provision for mothers with little ones."

"How can you do that?"

"Well, I turn back the others who an't got no little ones, don't I? I hope I never see such a time of tribulation as this again! I did not learn this river in order that I might choose one over another, and once this time is over, I will again leave that privilege to the Lord in His heaven!"

I had seen so few women and children in Kansas City that I thought he must have all of them on board his boat. I said, "Thank you, anyway."

"Don't thank me, ma'am, because I an't worthy of thanks!" He walked on past me, shaking his head. Lorna whispered, "Offer 'im mo' money!" but I shook my head. I led the way down the plank, and we went on to the *Herald.*

The *Herald* made no pretense at all of being luxurious, and I doubted the boiler even more profoundly, but it was right beside the *Southern Joy.* It did not bode well that there were only two men aboard, Negroes, one sweeping and the other doing some carpentry work. I said, "May I find your captain?"

"Nah, ma'am," said the carpenter. The sweeper didn't even look up. "He done disappeared."

"Is the boat planning to go downriver?"

"Nah, ma'am. She ain'."

"Why not?"

Now the sweeper and the carpenter looked at one another and shrugged, then the carpenter said, "Don' know, ma'am." Lorna took in a breath, and they both looked at her curiously, but I put my hand on her arm. The two men went back to work, and we made our way down the plank. Lorna was breathing heavily. I said, "There are two more!" But I, too, was more disheartened than I let on. Our endeavor had now taken on a feeling of futility.

The *Jack Smith* was a trim little craft, as neat and clean in reality as the owners of the *Southern Joy* would have liked their boat to be. I could see that she had a shallow draft, good for the Missouri, and that the windows of the saloon were shining and newly washed. Men and a few women passed up and down the plank, and the captain stood by the deck railing. I looked up at him from the levee below, immobile, until Lorna gave me a poke in the back. The captain watched us every step up the plank, then tipped his hat, but he didn't say a word. Lorna dared not poke me again, but I felt her inner impatience. Finally, I said, "We're looking for passage downriver."

"Are ya now?"

"To Saint Louis."

"Well, well, well."

"When are you leaving?"

"Could be anytime." He continued to inspect us, first me, then Lorna, at his leisure. His scrutiny gave me a heavy feeling of dread, but I smiled and kept my head up.

"I need passage for myself and my gal. We've been aban . . ." But I let my voice trail off, unable to find the energy for that good lie. I coughed. "I have been abandoned here in this—"

"Have you now?"

There was something entirely sinister about his manner, and Lorna reacted to it, too, taking a small step back. This was his signal for removing his gaze once again from me to her. Folks passed us. I felt pinned to the spot, until finally I managed to say, "No doubt you are besieged with passengers."

"I got room. Gal got to go below, and you got to take another lady in with ya."

"I—"

"Gal kin do your business all day and go to ya after seven in the mornin', but she got to sleep with them others. Always have done it that way, always will. But I didn't make ladies go together till now."

"What's the fare?"

"Twenty-two for you and eighteen for yer gal, here."

I allowed myself a little smile.

"And you have room?"

"Got two rooms left, two passengers to each room. Cain't tell who you're gonna be with, though."

"That's fine. When do you leave?" With so little room left, I fully expected him to say tonight, or tomorrow morning, but he said, "Two, three days."

"Oh! Why so long?"

"Waitin' for a repair to the wheel. Can't get a workman here to save your life! They all got their guns and are headed for Lawrence. Fool's errand, if you ask me." My spirits, which had lifted, dropped into my shoes. He said, "You want the room?"

"Maybe."

"Pay me now, then."

"But we need to leave sooner than that. I want to try the last boat."

"Can't hold it for you. Last two."

"Can't I just try the last boat? Maybe she's going down sooner!"

He shrugged. "Maybe. You got five, ten dollars?"

I neither nodded nor shook my head.

"I kin hold it for you for that."

"That would seriously compromise my funds. . . ." I looked around, not daring to consult Lorna but not receiving any sense of what she wanted to do, terrified of being stuck in Kansas City for three days, but more terrified of being stuck there even longer. The sense of desperation I felt was new even for me and perhaps partly owing to my fear of this man. I shrank from putting us into his hands, and I tried to discern what it was about him that roused my suspicions so. It was impossible to tell—he was a plain-looking man. I looked at him, then looked down toward the levee, undecided. There below, staring up at me, was David B. Graves, the original David B. Graves. He looked at me, looked at Lorna, who was right beside me, then tipped his hat to me and walked away. I nearly fell down and, in fact, sank against Lorna, who bore me up with a look of surprise on her face. The captain of the *Jack Smith* said, "Are you ill, ma'am?"

"We've walked a considerable distance."

After a long, heavy moment, he said, "You and your gal kin go into the lounge for ten minutes. That's all, though, jes' ten minutes. It's over there."

Down on the levee, David B. Graves was making his way through the crowd, and he wasn't strolling or ambling, he was striding. I said to the captain, "Thank you for your kindness, sir. Perhaps if I sit down, I can gather my thoughts." I let Lorna bear me up just a bit. When the door closed behind us, we hurried to a corner and sat down with our heads together. I whispered, "Lorna! You have to walk away from me as soon as we leave here!"

"Why's dat?"

"A man recognized me who knows me."

"You done said you don' know nobody round heah."

"I don't, but this man turned up. He keeps turning up, and he's been good to me, but he's terrifically sound on the goose question, and I took some money from him. It's too involved a story to—"

"I cain' go apart from you! Dey'll stop me fo' sure!"

"Make out to be shopping for me or something, or looking for a doctor. I can be taken with something, a fit or a bad head. But you have to get away. He can't see us together, because he knows me well enough to know I would never have a gal! We have to get away from the river and try to find a place to hide." Now the *Jack Smith*'s departure three days thence presented itself in a different light. I would pay our passage, then we would secrete ourselves somewhere—with Nehemiah at the livery stable, perhaps? or out in the country?—and then make our way back at the last moment. I wasn't thinking very clearly, but I felt a rush of desperate strength that made me think we could try anything and possibly succeed. Lorna looked hesitant and even afraid, and I remembered my first sight of her face on the front lawn of Day's End Plantation, and how I could tell by looking at her that she would know what to do with me. And she had known. I took her hands in mine and squeezed them. I whispered, "We'll pay our money to the captain, then you help me down the plank and across the levee. I'll wave good-bye to you and sit down somewhere, and you go off with your bundle, and if anyone asks you, you say your missy is Jane Horn and you are looking for a doctor, but then, if they direct you to a doctor, wander around without finding him, and soon it will be dark! Don't get too far away, and when it's dark, I'll find you. I think I know a place to hide." I hoped I could talk Nehemiah into something.

Lorna nodded, and we stood up. She helped me out the door of the lounge. I saw at once that right there, at the top of the plank, the captain was having an altercation with three men. One of them was David B. Graves, and he saw me before I could step back into the saloon. Lorna was holding me up, and he and she exchanged a glance, too. He said, in a hard voice, "There they are. Harmon, you grab the niggah!"

"This is my boat!" thundered the captain.

"You an' gonna be a party to nigger-stealin', are ya?" shouted one of the men, and Lorna and I stepped back into the saloon and slammed the door.

"I ain' nevah seen dose men!" exclaimed Lorna. "How dey know?"

"It's me! It's me, Lorna!"

And she gave me one anguished look, only one. In the next moment, I saw her inure herself, draw away, begin to take this in. I grabbed her hand and ran across the room to the largest window. As the men entered the door, I kicked at the window and pounded at it until, as they rushed over to us, it broke. I stepped through and tried to pull Lorna with me, but the pieces of glass still in the frame slowed us, and the men grabbed us. Mr. Graves was the one who grabbed me, and when he did, I slapped him. And when I slapped him, I covered his face with my blood. The other two men grabbed Lorna by the shoulders and the feet, and while the captain held the door, the three of them dragged us out onto the deck and threw us down. Perhaps we had fought them hard. They were breathing heavily. I don't know. All I remember is how frenzied it made me to know that it was through me that Lorna had been betrayed.

There was quite a crowd of men on the deck, and a few women, too, and all their mouths hung open. Mr. Graves, his face and shirt red and glistening, exclaimed, "Gentlemen! We have foiled a nigger-stealing right in our midst! Night has fallen! Some of us are bloodied! But you may all rest assured that a man's property will be restored to him! And that the thief, a young lady though she is, shall be *punished*!" The assembled Missourians gave out a clamorous cheer, and the two men who had hold of Lorna dragged her off. She was quiet, neither protesting nor crying. It was me that was screaming "No! No! *No!*"

until I could no longer see her and no longer manage to utter a word.

The crowd dispersed. The captain said, "Git 'er off my boat!" and Mr. Graves gripped me by the arm and half pushed, half pulled me down the plank. When we got to the bottom, he said, "Mrs. Newton, I regret any elegiac sentiments I might have expressed toward you on an earlier occasion. I will say no more."

CHAPTER 27

I Backtrack

> *. . . it must be borne in mind, that the estimate of evils and privations depends, not so much on their positive nature, as on the character and habits of the person who meets them.*
>
> —*p. 39*

IT TOOK THE CATCHERS, I later learned, about two days to find Papa and match up his runaway with Lorna. That boy had been right: there were catchers everywhere, and every one of the lot was busy scaring up trade. For his part, Papa had wasted no time putting together an advertisement in Independence in which both Lorna and I were described. My height was against me; I was said to be "a plain tall woman in a nankeen dress and green bonnet with short hair and large hands"—unmistakable. Lorna was described as "a serviceable slave-girl, solidly built, of a discontented disposition, with a vertical scar on the left side of her neck, just under the ear, an inch and a half long." I, her friend, hadn't noticed the scar. Papa, her enemy, had.

Mr. Graves took me to the jailhouse for safekeeping, but the sheriff and his wife didn't make me stay in the jail; they put me upstairs in one of the rooms, with the door locked. The sheriff himself didn't seem to want to have much to do with me, and his wife, Mrs. Hopewell, said, "We an't never had a lady in the jail before. I told my Frederick that I just can't do that, at least till they decide what to do with you."

"Are they going to hang me?"

"They hate nigger-stealin'. No tellin' what they will do. My Frederick says he don't know what it will be like, findin' a judge and a jury in these days. He says they should of shot you at the time and been done with it, instead of involving the law. I know that sounds hard, but he an't really a hard man, for a sheriff. I reckon it will depend upon Mr. Day and his views in the matter. I don't expect they will tar and feather you, though. That's what they gener- ally like to do, but I don't suppose they'll do it to a lady."

She gave me a Bible to read, with the remark, "They had slaves in Bible days, didn't they, now?"

"What did they do with Lorna?"

"Oh, the catchers do something, I expect. I don't like to think about it myself." She shook her head violently, as if shaking off the whole subject.

She washed my hands and bound the cuts. They throbbed for a day or two. Since I couldn't write, she had me dictate a letter to my sisters. What I dictated was a few dry sentences. What she wrote was the fol- lowing. It read:

To my dear sisters in the east—
I am sure you will be surprised and dis- mayed to learn that I am put in jail in Kansas City for niggah-stealing, which I did even though the man I stole the niggah from was good

to me and gave me the hospitality of his house for two or three weeks before I run off with the gal. There is no telling what they are going to do with me, they might hang me but they haven't hanged a female in Missouri, at least around these parts, for a long time, as long as the sheriff can remember. Maybe I will be lucky and not be hanged. If I am hanged, then this is my last words to you. I am heartily sorry for what I have done, and for the shame I have brought upon my dear family. I trust in the Lord to do what he thinks best with me after I have passed into his loving hands. If I am not hung, then you need to send me some money so that I can leave this place and come back home to you, as the sheriff and his wife can do nothing for me, even though they are God-fearing and charitable people, and the state makes no provision for Niggah-stealers. If you do not send me means, then surely I will get into trouble again. Forty dollars will be enough.

> Your dear sister,
> LYDIA HARKNESS NEWTON

Mrs. Hopewell had her heart set upon sending this letter, as she was very proud of it, and so I let her. She told me that it would probably take two weeks for the money to arrive, and that if they didn't hang me, she would charge me ten dollars for two weeks' room and board, "And let me tell you, you can't get it no cheaper in Kansas City in these days!"

Now I came into a state of being talked to and done to. While the sheriff was too embarrassed to come in, Mr. Graves, who had an interview with me the day this letter was written, seemed entirely in his confidence. He entered the room, had the door locked behind him, and started booming at once. I was sitting in a chair by the window, looking out, but I hadn't seen him coming down the street. He exclaimed, "Mrs. Newton! Was I staggered when I saw you and that gal up there on that boat deck? Indeed I was! Staggered, and then, very shortly afterwards, in a matter of an eye blink, I was dismayed. Ma'am, I was hurt for you! You have got no business with this nigger-stealing, which is a very low thing to do, and now look where you have landed! The sheriff of this town, I don't mind telling you, is a man of rigorous moral views, and he said to me, 'David B. Graves, I find myself in a dilemma. This isn't a plain killin' or one man cheating another or even a horse-thievin', which we've got plenty of in these parts and is always clear-cut. This is all bound up in other things. You may say that this is a clear-cut crime, but as a sheriff, I say that this crime is defiled by opinion! A sheriff hates to see that.' Mrs. Newton, if you had just gotten on the *Missouri Rose* the way you pretended to do, well, ma'am, you wouldn't have fallen so low as this! That's what I deplore, myself. This whole matter just sullies my esteem for you, and, indeed, for your late husband—"

"What happened to Lorna?"

"I am not going to get into personalities here. Maybe that is your difficulty, ma'am, but I won't do it! I look at the principle involved, and I see a transgression, and I look no farther!"

"You knew we were abolitionists the first time you met us. You were kind to us."

"Now, ma'am, we've got some sophistry here. Everybody in the world knows that views are different from acts. I do verily believe that as citizens of this great republic, we may proclaim our views far and wide, from the highest mountain, if need be, and let no man stop us, and I do believe a woman may do so, as well, and in that I am what you might call progressive, but I do believe it! That is why we have made our home on this continent and away from the sinks of Europe, if I may so term them. Should the day come that the institution of servitude and bondage that we have in this state pass on, then I say, so be it, that is the will of God and His people, and David B. Graves says, so be it. But I see all around me far less judicious men than myself, who descend from views to acts, and what has come of it but sorrow, horror, and conflict, as you yourself can testify, Mrs. Newton? What do these acts do but inflame others? What is their result but war? I, I am a commercial man! Do I wish to put my commerce at the service of one side or the other? I do not! My principle is to serve both sides, to have no sides, indeed, but to serve all! What will become of me? What will become of us all?"

"But she wanted to be free!"

"If I wanted to be a horse or a bird of the air or a fine lady in Richmond, Virginia, should I then have my wish? We are born who we are, and we get nowhere pinin' to be otherwise."

He had on his most orotund manner, and he was

so smoothly certain of himself that it was impossible to argue further.

We fell silent for a few moments, then he said, "I find that in spite of all, Mrs. Newton, I still feel a protective spirit in your behalf, and I do promise right here and now to do all I can to prevent your rashness from resulting in yet another tragic outcome!"

"But you put me here!"

"Ma'am, I confess. I am fatally divided on this subject. I see the act, I see the principle, I see the person. This brings into my intentions a strange flux." He rose.

I couldn't thank him. I only sighed. He bowed and left. It occurred to me afterward that he had been talking in his inflated style. He was a strange man, I thought, a real chameleon, and it seemed somehow fitting that it was he who betrayed me.

The next day, shortly after my breakfast, the key turned in the door, and Mrs. Hopewell's oval face peeped in and announced Papa. Then he was there. He was exceptionally well dressed, even for him, in fine white trousers, shining black boots, a light-blue waistcoat, and a buff frock coat. He carried cane, gloves, and hat in his hand. His little bald head shone as if from vigorous buffing, but his face was sober, even drawn. He entered, perched on the chair beside the door, and regarded me with birdy sadness. I admit that this made me more ill at ease than I had expected to be (I had all along suspected that Papa would be unable to resist seeing me). Rather than meeting his disconsolate gaze with righteous anger on Lorna's behalf, I met it with some mortification.

At long last, he said, in his roundest, richest tones, "Helen is extremely distressed."

"I suspected that. I—"

"Perhaps you don't know how thoroughly you have smashed all of her affections. She had a sincere fondness, even love, for you yourself, and you not only left without a word after leading her to believe that the outcome of my offer would be a happy one, you stole away the other dearest person in her circle. Though your plot has not succeeded, thanks to the quick thinking and true principle of Mr. Graves, from Helen's point of view it might as well have, as Lorna is as thoroughly ripped from her as if you had succeeded."

"What have you done with Lorna?"

"Did you think of that before you hatched your plot? Did you wonder how Lorna might suffer if your plot failed?—and many more of them do fail than succeed. The catchers are not a merciful or deliberate class of men. They do necessary work, and they have the necessary temperament for it."

"Where is Lorna?"

"Don't adopt so high a tone with me, miss! What has become of Lorna is not your business, and I won't allow you to think so by divulging her whereabouts. In fact, Lorna was never your business, though you claimed her as such. But I understand your late husband was an abolitionist, and I know that we expect ladies to be guided by their husbands, no matter what misguided views they themselves hold."

I supposed that if I told Papa that Lorna had

claimed ME, it might be worse for her, wherever she was. I put my head down and bit my lip. Papa took this gesture as a submissive one. He continued, "I know, Mrs. Newton—for I know your true name now—that you have too fine a spirit to persist in folly and recklessness. I forgive you much in the name of your grief. The Lord himself knows that I was beside myself with grief for two years after my late wife passed on. Although you seem composed, of course much feeling runs deep. That's the sort of woman you are. I can feel that. This foolishness of stealing my servant surely grows out of the mental instability produced by your experiences in this country at so young an age." He sighed.

"Lorna wanted to escape." But I whispered it.

"Ah, Lorna! No one could ever say that Lorna was ill-treated or uncared for. Lorna herself couldn't say it and didn't say it. In fact, she often expressed a wordless thanks to me for according her the privileges she exercised in my service. No one can ever convince me that Lorna doesn't love us and doesn't know the virtues of the position she held in our family until now. Delia said to me just yesterday, 'Massa Richard, dat Lorna don' know nothin', if she done dis thing! I tol' her and tol' her all dese yeahs to thank de Lawd for her blessin's and fergit de res', and I thought she done listened to me, but I see she ain'.' Mrs. Newton, I have made a study of Lorna over these years, and I know her inside and out. Once in a while, once in every few years, even, something would seize Lorna and force her to act foolishly, to act against herself. My late wife felt it should have been beaten out of her at a young age, but I erred and could not take so strong a hand. Now I regret that. But Harris is always telling me that if you don't beat them sooner you will beat them later, and you do them good to give them a taste of the lash—"

"Please!" I exclaimed. "I can't bear this! You are wrong in every way! Down to the roots you are wrong!"

We stared at each other. His gaze went from my face to my bandaged hands and back to my face. His countenance was not hard but, instead, sympathetic, sentimental, without the least doubt of what he was saying and thinking. He sighed. He said, "You are so obdurate for such a young lady! I fear for you, I honestly do. Life itself will teach you what well-disposed elders cannot."

It was useless to talk to him, useless to talk to them all, but I tried a different tack, one last time. "Oh, sir, please do me that last kindness of telling me what has been done with Lorna! Please, I beseech you!"

First he shook his head, then a look of some pain crossed his face. Then, at last, he said, "I could only do what her actions demanded. I had to sell her south. She knew that would happen if she listened to your blandishments, and it did. She has only herself to blame. But I am weak enough to feel it. And it has broken Helen's heart."

Mine, too, I thought.

Before leaving, Papa took my hand and kissed the bandage. His last words to me were, "This is a tragedy."

I continued to sit at the window, looking out and listening to the muffled clanging of cell doors below. As befitted a person in a state of being talked to and done to rather than talking and doing, I didn't have many thoughts, but I did wonder about the tragedy of it. No doubt Papa was right that this was a tragedy, though certainly we would differ on what parts of it were tragic. And I wasn't as sophisticated about tragedy as Papa was, with his fine library and his college education. But a tragedy did seem to me to be something that took place on one spot—at home, perhaps, where all the characters were gathered together and all knew each other and the actions of each destroyed the others. I myself didn't feel like a character in a tragedy. For one thing, I didn't really fear they would have the gumption to hang me. Everyone in Kansas City was too distracted for that. And if I wasn't hanged, then I probably wouldn't be shot. Shooting was something folks seemed to do on impulse, and when the impulse passed, they couldn't bring themselves to do it, only to say that they should have done it. Mostly, I suspected, I would be talked to and talked about: opinion was the real currency of the west. Somehow, I would get back to Quincy, where my sisters surely would not care to know about what had happened to me, and where they would insist in all sorts of ways that we just forget it and get on with finding something useful for me to do. This did not smack of tragedy, but of what, I didn't know enough to say.

Time passed more slowly in the jailroom than ever it had before in either K.T. or Missouri, where time had a way of fleeing. Now there was plenty of time to sense each pain sprout, grow, blossom, and give way to another. Although I didn't sleep, I did wake up, and each awakening was a shock. Thomas was dead. Yes, dead. The journey was over, and he wasn't at the end of it, as somehow I'd hoped, expected, imagined he was, without even knowing I was doing so. It is wrong to say that you can watch someone closed in his coffin, put in the ground, and covered over, and not expect him to be there when you turn around. It is wrong to say that you can visit his grave, even kneel upon it and place prairie flowers upon it and have all your associates speak of it as if they know it as his grave, and believe that he is in it. I hadn't believed that he was in it, or perhaps I wouldn't have left him there, so far away. Had I had ten years with him, or thirty years, perhaps I would have come to the end of him and let him die, but in only ten months, I had hardly gotten through the beginning of him: the kindness, the air of amusement, the love of myself that never seemed to falter no matter how unwifely, unwomanly, I acted. And then there was his desire to act on principle. All of these things about him I had hardly begun to contemplate. And it is wrong to think, as I sensed others thinking, that a ten-month marriage is only a glancing blow in a woman's life. With each painful moment there in that jailroom, I felt how much I wouldn't be getting past that ten months.

I had no child. I supposed that most women I knew would say, considering my circumstances, that this was fortunate. Lorna would have said so; my sisters would have said so. And in the pantheon of dead children, mine was one of the unknowns—his or her face only a speculation, his or her name only a fancy. My child hadn't had even the tenuous hold on life that Mrs. James's baby had had. My mother had once told me to think of all my dead brothers and sisters as crystal spirits. The Lord poured His wine into them for a time, and that helped us to see their features, and then, for His own reasons, He poured it out again and took their transparent selves back to Him. I don't know where she got this idea; possibly from our minister. I hadn't thought of this image in years, but now, in the jailroom, it haunted me. My child, our child, hadn't gotten even that far, could have held no wine. Nothing about him or her was revealed. I mourned this mystery as if it were his or her very self. Mrs. Hopewell heard me weeping and came in from time to time to give me cups of tea, apparently gratified by my remorse and my show of womanly feeling.

And Frank was no doubt dead, too, and it was such a grievous thought that thinking it through was beyond my strength.

And what about Lorna? What in the world had made me think I had anything in the way of strength or quick wits to offer Lorna? Our escape had been a fool's errand from beginning to end. She had looked to me for aid, and I had let her do so, all the time that it was actually me counting on her. It seemed, looking back, that I couldn't have fled without her, that the luxury and languor of Papa's plantation would have inexorably gummed me up, immobilized me, and when Lorna claimed me and insisted I help her, she invested me with the power to move. Everyone felt Lorna's concentrated force—Helen couldn't do without her, Bella had had to fight her, Papa had to summon all his faculties to assert himself over her, and after acquaintance of only a week or two, I had accepted her as my reviver, felt the cool, firm sensation of her hand on my neck as a promise. It was hard to see Lorna simply, as another desperate woman powerless against the institution of servitude, against Missouri and Kansas and guns and horses and catchers and dogs and distance and lack of funds and chance, but that's what she was in the end, wasn't she? And the ways she would have to pay for her mistake in trusting me I would never get to know and always be tempted and terrified to imagine.

It was all very different from the bills we had pored over in Horace's store, with their pictures of wide streets, square blocks, libraries, mills, stores, and ladies' improvement societies everywhere. Now, even though I had been to K.T. and seen the chicanery there firsthand, I still didn't know if those bills were simply wishes or if they were pure frauds, and if the latter, whether someone else had defrauded us or if we had simply defrauded ourselves.

What K.T. and Missouri really were was talk. People in the west made a big house of words for themselves and then lived inside it, in a small room of deeds. And now that I was silent, that didn't mean the talk didn't still surge and storm around me. From the other rooms in the jail, from outside, through my window, open or closed, I heard constant shouting,

calling, talking (and shooting), day and night. Everyone loved to talk, to boast, to threaten, to claim, to
damn, to preen, to narrate, to lie, to pile word upon
word, expression upon expression. That's how Jim
Lane got so big in K.T.—he was the best talker. But
after you talked for a while, it seemed, you ended up
talking yourself into acting. Didn't matter what side
you were on or what your principles were; if you
talked about them long enough, well, you had to act
on them. Now that I was in jail, I didn't know what I
thought about principles anymore. It seemed as
though the main result of having any was disloca-
tion, injury, pain, and death. But of course, that left
out Lorna.

Mrs. Hopewell asked me if I was praying enough
and should she get the minister over? She knew a
good one, who could make the hardest criminal pray
like a child. More talk, I thought. I told her I was
praying all I could.

Papa elected to drop charges and to pay my way
back to Quincy. When the sheriff came to tell me this
himself, relief was evident in his face and his manner. He said, "Ma'am, I booked you passage on this
boat the *Jack Smith.*

"You mean it hasn't left yet?" This gave me a little smile.

"Leaves tonight. But there wasn't any ladies who
wanted to be in a room with ya, so I had to pay double. That was forty-four dollars. Mr. Day, he paid for
it. You got yerself any money to git from St. Louis to
Quincy?"

"You took the money in my reticule."

"That shall be returned to you in due time, ma'am."

"Well, how much is there?"

" 'Bout thirty-six dollars, ma'am."

"Well, then."

"Well, then, I guess you are fixed up. One little word from me, miss."

"What's that?"

"Don't be comin' back this way, now. You have used up the goodwill of this office here."

"I won't," I said. And I meant that.

I will pass over the details of my return down the Missouri River. The boat was filled with women and children, mostly Missourians, who were fleeing the Kansas-Missouri war. At any other time, we might have been startled by the various groundings, alarms, stoppages, and rumors of boiler troubles that punctuated our five days aboard, but in fact these mundane incidents were reassuring in a way. To be delayed, to have to get off the boat in the middle of the night, even to contemplate one's death by boiler explosion, gave one the reassurance of normality when compared to war, the war all of us were leaving our friends to fight. Although I didn't converse with many others, I did overhear what they had to say, about Atchison's army and Lane's army and other armies here and there, all of them, according to rumor, plentifully supplied with weapons, rage, and drink. Under the pressure of these reports, I dreamed so often of Lawrence burning to the ground that I came to wonder if it really had burned, if Louisa was sending me some sign. It was true that after Governor Shannon departed the territory, his second in command, the temporary governor, Woodson, a proslave fellow much admired by the Missourians, immediately declared Kansas Territory in a state of insurrection, which gave license to every Missourian to burn, hang, dismember, clear out, scalp, shoot, tar and feather, and do away with, or at least plan to, anyone not thoroughly sound on the goose question. There was much fear on the boat, some weeping, continuous prayers, and many long faces. Groundings and stoppages and alarms gave us something to do.

All was different in Saint Louis. We arrived early in the morning, and I went straight across the levee and asked after the *Mary Ida* or the *Ida Marie*. The *Ida Marie* was going upriver that very day, and so I paid my ticket and walked about for an hour before going on board. I was unescorted and sunburned, my short hair stuck out from under my Kansas-style bonnet, my nankeen dress showed considerable wear and tear. Even so, it took me a while to realize that I was being stared at, and to recognize that I looked a strange being among the citizens of Saint Louis. For their part, they looked strange to me as well, neat, buttoned up, careful. Suspicious. Quiet. Mannerly. Men carried newspapers that talked about the war, but the business of the town showed no knowledge of it. Business, even the always booming business of the levee, went on at a deliberate, unfrenzied pace. And there was a singular absence of gunshots, of anyone even flourishing a weapon. When I asked a question, where I might find a bite to eat, it was my voice that was too loud, my manner that was too insistent, my request that seemed outlandish. Perhaps it was embarrassing, but, in fact, I was beyond embarrassment now. I suspected that I would never feel truly embarrassed again.

After Papa, Lorna, Mr. Graves, Helen, after Louisa and Charles and Frank and Thomas, after Mrs. Bush and the Jenkinses and the Jameses and all the rest of them, it was calming to travel in what seemed to be a cell of anonymity. I sat in my stateroom or in the lounge. I even strolled on the deck, first of the *Jack Smith* and then of the *Ida Marie*. I read no books, having none, and did no needlework, having none of that, either, but kept my healing hands in my lap and looked out at the river, first the Missouri, then the Mississippi. I listened to the other women gossiping and talking to their children, shushing their infants and confiding in one another, ordering their slaves about, if they had them, or deploring those who ordered their slaves about, if they did not. I thought I would never really join that world again, that I could not, nor did I want to. I was a different animal now, a horse among cows, a duck among geese.

My sisters had no knowledge of my homecoming, and so there was no one to greet me when the *Ida Marie* tied up at dawn on September 1 and I walked down the plank and onto the soil of Illinois. Quincy's high bluff put the levee and, indeed, at this time of the day, most of the river into deep shadow. I felt the darkness. Had I gone so far, with such a struggle, and circled back to where I came from, with nothing at all to show for it? Less than nothing? I had indeed. On the other hand, that steep climb up Maine Street from the river was easy for me now.

It was surely only six-thirty or so, and I stood outside Beatrice's familiar green door for a few minutes before knocking. In former days, I would have walked in. But I knew that this time I might appear as a ghost and give everyone a fright—they needed a knock to know that it was a person outside. I waited and knocked again, then suddenly the door opened, and there, a joy absolute and unexpected in his very person, was my nephew Frank. He had a yellow shirt on, brown trousers, and a green cap pushed back on his head. He had an apple in his hand. He stared at me. I stared at him. We stood like that until Beatrice's voice from the back of the house called out, "Is there someone at the door? Did someone answer the door? Frank? Where are you?" Then she said, "Well, land o' mercy! I just yesterday sent that woman in the jail money for you! How did you get here? Lydia, I swear, I am displeased with you—you are nothing but trouble in two states and one territory!" And then she threw her arms around me and burst into tears.

Well, how simple it came to seem once we put it all together! Frank's story was this: Exactly one day after I left Lawrence with Mr. Graves and Mr. Graves and the fair songstress Davida, a letter arrived for me from Harriet, insisting that Frank return to Quincy, as they had just heard of the sack of Lawrence. This letter was dated at the end of May but had been delayed in a bundle of confiscated mail in Leavenworth for over a month. The day after that, Frank himself turned up in Louisa's shop, shoeless, hatless, seegar-less, horseless, and hungry, looking for me and Thomas; and two days after that, brother Roland himself turned up, with a team of horses, three rifles, two pistols, a knife, two kegs of cornmeal, one of flour, and one of highly rectified whiskey, all of which he had purchased in Weston as a way of financing his search for Frank: upon receiving no reply to Harriet's letter, he had resolved to take a look for himself. He now sold these in Lawrence for a tidy profit, and returned to Westport with Frank in tow. At this point, everyone felt confident that I was on my way to Quincy. Meanwhile, what had happened to Frank was strange enough, even by K.T. standards. He had gotten in with a fellow named George Lambert, who had two brothers with him. With Frank and several other boys, they made up a band of some eight young men, George at twenty-five or so the eldest. The Lamberts said at first that they were Emigrant Aid Company folks and that they knew Old Brown and meant to find him down in Osawatomie and join his army. While they rode around for six weeks, they never met up with Brown (a good thing, because Brown got into a few deadly battles). After a while, it turned out that Lambert and his brothers were really Mormons and had spent the previous winter out in Utah Territory but had been kicked out for some reason, Frank thought for stealing some money. Guerrilla conditions were of the most basic sort—none of the boys knew how to hunt except Frank, and then the horses got into some sort of poisonous plant and three of them died, including Frank's mount. Of his companions, Frank only said, "They didn't seem to know what to do with themselves. They never even looked around for anything to pick up to trade and sell. I don't know. I was pretty disgusted, myself. When I had to walk back to Lawrence, I ate better than when we rode around takin' stuff." He promised faithfully to attend school when he got back to Quincy. This was why he was presently with Beatrice, in town. Horace walked him to school and delivered him right into the hands of the schoolmaster every day and received him from those same hands every afternoon. Otherwise, Frank employed himself under Horace's direction at his store. They did not talk about Kansas.

The question of my whereabouts had come up in mid-August, some three weeks after I'd left the *Missouri Rose,* because it took until then for the captain of that boat to see Mr. Graves and tell him of my disappearance, for Mr. Graves to happen to run into Charles, for Charles to tell Louisa, for Louisa to write Harriet, and for Harriet to receive the letter. And then, even as they were wondering what had become of me, they received Mrs. Hopewell's letter about my imminent hanging. Beatrice exclaimed, "And to tell you the truth, Lydia, I wasn't a bit surprised."

As it happened, there wasn't a war in Kansas after all. The President sent in as governor a fellow named Geary, who'd already seen everything out in San Francisco in terms of big talk, big greed, and the consequences of that, and this Geary, whom Louisa wrote me about with such enthusiasm that she decided to throw out all her former notions and name her daughter Mildred Gearina Bisket, "faced down the bullies and brought them to heel, and now we only depend upon the election for our real apotheosis into a law-abiding state rather than a *territory of human beasts.*" Other news was that Charles had bought another pair of mules and was planning to build a warehouse on Vermont Street. "Let them burn it down and us out; our little Mildred Gearina shows that we *multiply and increase!*"

But of course, the presidential election did not then go the abolitionist way, and after that there was what some folks called peace for a little space, even in K.T. And after the election, in Illinois—never a slave state, but also never an anti-slave state—those two men Senator Douglas and Mr. Lincoln got very famous, more famous than anyone else in the whole country, which was a source of pride to many and a source of shame to others, since, as my sister Harriet said, "Why don't folks realize that this trash just isn't worth talking about? It ruins everything, but the strangest people start bringing it up, and then you've got to say something, so of course, you've got to make up your mind! I can't abide that!"

I thought that I might have someone to talk to in Frank, but at first there was never the occasion—he was kept mighty busy at school and at the store. Roland didn't have to work as hard as he had to oversee Frank's daredevil proclivities—the guerrilla business, especially the starvation and boredom, had dinned that sort of thing out of the boy for good and all, it seemed. Now he had his sights on a commercial future. There was this, too: Frank was no longer a chatty boy. His voice had deepened, and he walked like a man. He was taller, his hands were bigger, and he had assumed a man's taciturnity. We seemed thoroughly divided by sex and experience from our old friendship. Perhaps he accepted the family view, subscribed to but rarely stated, that I had lost and abandoned him in K.T., owing to some sort of abolitionist brain fever. My irresponsibility concerning Frank as a helpless child adrift upon the prairie was so thoroughly disapproved of that my sisters were nearly speechless with it. It was only owing to Providential intercession that Frank had been restored to the family circle. As a result, Alice and Harriet became substantially more religious after our return.

I did take the cars to Boston and met Thomas's father and mother and brothers, as well as friends of theirs who shared their abolitionist views and on balance felt that events in Kansas would issue in a much-needed cleansing of the national soul with regard to that single blot on our pristine character, Negro servitude. Remarks were made to the effect that Geary had actually done every right-thinking citizen a disservice in averting all-out war. Many expressed that same view we used to have in Kansas, that conflict there would serve as a national sinkhole, going so deep and growing so vast that the whole nation would fall into it, from California to Boston, but with this distinction: whereas in Kansas we thought of this as the natural end of what we saw all around us, but all the same something sane men should avert, in Boston there was a great deal of talk about the necessity of it—of getting something done with at last, of expelling the pus of the infection (or cutting off the limb to save the life), or of revealing the wrath of the Lord once and for all to the southern sinner.

Myself, I kept quiet after a few days of this. In my presence, these sorts of things were all they could talk about. Someone would ask me a question, and I would begin my answer, and at my second or third hesitant word, my interlocutor would exclaim, "Yes! Just as I thought!" and then go on and on about how he or she (many of the most ardent abolitionists were shes) deeply felt that his or her own views were fully borne out by my experiences and everything that I was saying, and then I would hear a full discourse on every aspect of the issue, more aspects of the issue than I'd ever thought existed. These men and women went away shaking their heads, of course, but also smiling. They made large, agreeable groups, and their opinions were much bolstered by one another. I got to be something of a celebrity for attempting to aid the escape of a slave, and they loved to have me talk about Lorna. Some even wept openly at her story, and one day, someone "very close to Mr. Thayer himself" asked me to give a series of lectures, or perhaps one lecture only, about her. Something, anything. How good this would be as a way of raising money for the cause of abolition in Kansas could not be expressed.

I was disinclined to do this, and I pondered my disinclination at length. Did I owe it to Lorna to tell her story to the world? Was that my last gesture for her, to use her and what we had done together to raise money to buy guns and cannon to be sent to Kansas? Mr. Thayer's friend candidly admitted one thing—Lorna herself would never benefit from my telling her story. There was no telling what had happened to her; she'd gotten sold south, just like someone out of Mrs. Stowe's book, and if she was as obdurate as I made her out to be, well, not all masters were as forgiving as this Mr. Day seemed to be. There could be no hope for Lorna individually, but her cause could be helped through helping the cause of all of those in bondage, and money, money, money, that was the key. Every man who'd been to Washington, D.C., knew that as well as he knew his own mother's name. Thomas's mother herself appealed to me to give this lecture. She was a very old woman, bedridden most of the day. Thomas had indeed been her favorite of all the boys, and it was clear that his death was not supportable for her. She was very kind and loving to me, and she made up her mind that I must do this lecture for Thomas and his beliefs and what he died for. I couldn't explain that I found myself increasingly unable to speak about any of these issues—that the very certainty of everyone around me drove all certainty out of me. She pleaded with me, and I agreed.

The hall was the same size as, or larger than, Danake Hall in Quincy, the only other place of the sort that I'd ever entered. Even the stage was nearly the same size as the stage whereon I'd viewed those scenes from *Macbeth* and *Dombey and Son* more than a year before. And it was crowded. The title of my lecture, given it by Mr. Thayer's friend, was "Latest News from the War in Kansas, with a FIRST-HAND ACCOUNT of a foiled SLAVE ESCAPE in Missouri." Mr. Thayer himself was expected to attend but got delayed out of town, and I never met him.

Standing on the stage, looking out at the audience, was daunting and horrifying, especially after the lights that lit them up were doused and I couldn't see past the torches at my feet, which dazzled my eyes. I could hear them, though, shuffling and wheezing and coughing and sneezing and moving about, and even though I knew they were New Englanders and didn't tote guns and shoot them off routinely, as westerners did, guns seemed to be out there, as we all knew what the funds would be going for. I began to speak, and a voice or two shouted, "Louder!" and so I pressed more volume out of my lungs and voice box. It wasn't easy, and the lecture, advertised for only an hour, seemed like a path up a very steep hill and I had to carry myself up on breath alone, which seemed akin to, and as impossible as, flying. I had no energy for it; perhaps that was what made every word about Lorna seem like a betrayal of her, every word about Papa and Helen a betrayal of myself. I mixed up my story, got a few things backwards, tried to straighten them out. It was confusing to me, and so I suppose it was many times more confusing to the audience. My lecture was not a success.

But that made no difference. The audience acclaimed me. Here I was. There I had been. Giving testimony was more important than the testimony given. They clapped and applauded and shouted and passed the hat, until I was numbed by the whole experience and had to be led off the stage, a smile fixed to my face. Afterward, there was a reception with refreshments and much conversation. They were excited by everything I had to say, fortified for the conflict ahead, bright and eager, men, women, young, old. My lecture *was* a success.

I asked Thomas's mother not to require any more lectures of me, and she agreed, remarking that perhaps everything was just too fresh, and of course there was my grief for Thomas.

There was, but that wasn't it, though I allowed her to believe that it was. What it was was a revisitation, but far more strange and disturbing, to those feelings I had had that morning in Saint Louis, of being too big, too loud, too strange, of bringing tidings that were too unwelcome. No one could describe what was true in Kansas and Missouri. Hardly any Kansan or any Missourian, I thought, could describe what was true there to another Kansan or Missourian, even one supposedly on his or her side. To say what was true, you had to look into the eyes of your interlocutor and see something there that you recognized. I didn't think you could do that about Kansas or Missouri. And when I looked into the eyes of my new friends in Boston, I didn't see anything I recognized there, either. The more they embraced me and drew me in, the less I felt like one of them, like a woman, even like a human being. I felt like a new thing, hardly formed, wearing a corset and a dress and a shawl and a bonnet and a pair of ladies' boots, carrying a parasol in my gloved hand, but inside that costume something else, which didn't fit, something I felt myself to be but couldn't name. By Christmas, I couldn't tolerate Medford any longer, and I went back to Quincy for a while. At least there I was accustomed to feeling out of place.

And that, I suppose, is the end of my Kansas story. Everyone knows the end of *the* story, about the war and all of that. And most people know about the Lawrence Massacre, in August of '63. The fellow Quantrill, who led it, was said to be about Frank's age. No one had heard of him during my time in K.T., but he must have been as mad with rage as any of them, because he oversaw the killing of some two hundred men or so, all of them civilians, many of them in front of their wives and children. And as always, they burned what houses they could burn. I heard later from Louisa that Charles was safe—off in Leavenworth—and Governor Robinson hid in a gulch, while Jim Lane ran off across a field in his drawers. But Mr. Stearns, who had the store, was shot, and old Mr. Smithson was, too, and many, many others. Louisa wrote: "I never thought I would thank the Lord that the Bushes both passed on with that fever last winter, but I do, for no one who saw what those devils did will ever forget or forgive. The Lord Himself isn't powerful enough to make you do it."

One thing is left to tell. After I returned from subsequent travels, and Frank returned from fighting in the war, with General Grant at Vicksburg for a while, then in Virginia, he was twenty-three years old and looked forty. It was only then that we ever spoke of K.T., and then it was only to agree that whatever anyone else thought, after K.T., nothing, not Bull Run nor Gettysburg, certainly not the raid at Harpers Ferry that some thought started it all, not the Emancipation nor the burning of Atlanta, not the killing of the President, nothing ever surprised either of us ever again.

LARGE PRINT EDITIONS

Look for these and other Random House Large Print books at your local bookstore

American Heart Association, *American Heart Association Cookbook, 5th Edition Abridged*
Berendt, John, *Midnight in the Garden of Good and Evil*
Brinkley, David, *David Brinkley*
Brinkley, David, *Everyone Is Entitled to My Opinion*
Byatt, A. S., *Babel Tower*
Carter, Jimmy, *Living Faith*
Chopra, Deepak, *The Path to Love*
Ciaro, Joe, editor, *The Random House Large Print Book of Jokes and Anecdotes*
Crichton, Michael, *Airframe*
Crichton, Michael, *The Lost World*
Cronkite, Walter, *A Reporter's Life*
Cruz Smith, Martin, *Rose*
Daley, Rosie, *In the Kitchen with Rosie*
Dexter, Colin, *Death Is Now My Neighbor*
Flagg, Fannie, *Daisy Fay and the Miracle Man*
Flagg, Fannie, *Fried Green Tomatoes at the Whistle Stop Cafe*
Fulghum, Robert, *Maybe (Maybe Not): Second Thoughts from a Secret Life*
García Márquez, Gabriel, *Of Love and Other Demons*
Gilman, Dorothy, *Mrs. Pollifax, Innocent Tourist*
Guest, Judith, *Errands*
Hailey, Arthur, *Detective*
Hepburn, Katharine, *Me*
Koontz, Dean, *Intensity*
Koontz, Dean, *Sole Survivor*

(continued)

Koontz, Dean, *Ticktock*
Krantz, Judith, *Spring Collection*
Landers, Ann, *Wake Up and Smell the Coffee!*
le Carré, John, *The Tailor of Panama*
Lindbergh, Anne Morrow, *Gift from the Sea*
Mayle, Peter, *Anything Considered*
Mayle, Peter, *Chasing Cezanne*
McCarthy, Cormac, *The Crossing*
Michael, Judith, *Acts of Love*
Michener, James A., *Mexico*
Mother Teresa, *A Simple Path*
Patterson, Richard North, *The Final Judgment*
Patterson, Richard North, *Silent Witness*
Peck, M. Scott., M.D., *Denial of the Soul*
Phillips, Louis, editor, *The Random House Large Print Treasury of Best-Loved Poems*
Pope John Paul II, *Crossing the Threshold of Hope*
Pope John Paul II, *The Gospel of Life*
Powell, Colin with Joseph E. Persico, *My American Journey*
Rampersad, Arnold, *Jackie Robinson*
Rendell, Ruth, *The Keys to the Street*
Rice, Anne, *Servant of the Bones*
Shaara, Jeff, *Gods and Generals*
Snead, Sam with Fran Pirozzolo, *The Game I Love*
Truman, Margaret, *Murder at the National Gallery*
Truman, Margaret, *Murder on the Potomac*
Truman, Margaret, *Murder in the House*
Tyler, Anne, *Ladder of Years*
Updike, John, *Golf Dreams*
Whitney, Phyllis A., *Amethyst Dreams*